BEA BUZZ BOOKS

EXCERPTS FROM OVER 30 TOP FALL 2012 TITLES

FROM
PUBLISHERS
LUNCH

www.ingramcontent.com

CONTENTS

THE EXCERPTS

INTRODUCTION

As the publishing business gathers for another Book Expo America, promoting the discovery of new titles and authors is increasingly the primary focus of publishers and retailers alike as ever more books from traditional houses, digital start-ups and expanding self-publishing platforms compete for readers', (and convention-goers'), attention. BEA itself has moved from a bookselling show to an industry gathering place and a launch pad for fall books, and this year the convention begins the long-debated transition into welcoming passionate readers and fans into what has always been a trade-only event.

At the heart of it all is the work itself, from the established bestsellers that drive store traffic to the brand-new voices that will enliven the fall literary scene and the breakout authors whose audiences are expanding. With digital reading now a staple in many readers lives, we are excited to harness the medium to share some of the showcase books and authors of BEA, along with a broad selection of highly-touted debuts and a great sampling of prominent new books in the fast-growing field of young adult literature.

For the first time, trade professionals in unlimited numbers can start reading the books we'll all be hearing about and talking about at BEA. Start Junot Díaz's *This is How You Lose Her*, Barbara Kingsolver's *Flight Behavior*, and J.R. Moehringer's *Sutton* before hearing them read at the marquee breakfast events; sample Neil Young's memoir before his lunchtime convention interview; or start National Book Foundation 5 Under 35 honoree Shani Boianjiu's *The People of Forever Are Not Afraid* before hearing the pitch at the Buzz Book panel. But we also have more debuts, great YA, and samples from established bestsellers than fits on any single stage (or can be crammed into any giveaway tote bag).

Each title is accompanied by rights information, publicity contacts, marketing plans and more for actionable follow-up. If the author is appearing at BEA or the full galley is available there, we let you know. Titles are presented in rough order of planned publication, running from early August through January 2013, and additional lists organize the excerpts by debuts and breakouts, literary titles, nonfiction and YA. While we present samples from 33 fall titles, Sarah Weinman's extensive overview that follows this introduction curates many dozens more of notable fall books you will find featured at BEA and promoted and covered in the months ahead.

In addition to this "trade edition" ebook, we are publishing a slightly revised version (which omits the trade-focused information and click-throughs) for readers everywhere, also provided as a free download. *Buzz Books 2012* (ISBN: 978-0-9854910-1-7) is available now through all major ebookstores, distributed for us by Ingram. It's the first time we know of that general readers have had access to so many great books well ahead of actual publication, with click-throughs to pre-order when the stores allow. Please share the excitement with your customers, your readers, your mailing and media lists as we work together as a community to develop new ways of bringing deserving authors' words to the attention of new audiences.

For over a decade, Publishers Lunch has focused on using electronic media to connect trade publishing professionals to each other to do business more efficiently. We focus on "solving information problems and presenting information opportunities," trying to constantly innovate and experiment on behalf of our community. It is a true honor to be able to present so much exciting forthcoming material in a single package, and we thank the publishers, authors, agents and other participants for their enthusiastic participation.

Michael Cader

May 2012

THE BIG FALL BOOKS PREVIEW

While this book features substantial excerpts from 33 eagerly-anticipated fall titles, they are just a snapshot of what will be published between September and January. The early part of the fall season is a lot more crowded than the back half, for which you can thank the election cycle. Publishers don't want to compete with politics, the truism goes, since the electorate—and the media—won't be focusing much on books until after the presidential votes have been cast. This year the hole seems to be even wider, though gaps are made to be filled, and there's some counter-programming in place as well.

Perennial bestselling authors such as John Grisham, James Patterson, Lee Child, and Michael Connelly have new instant hits coming soon, while JK Rowling's first novel for adults has extraordinary expectations to match. On the literary front, Michael Chabon, Ian McEwan, Tom Wolfe, and Zadie Smith will release new novels after several quiet years, while novelists Salman Rushdie, Chinua Achebe, and Richard Russo switch gears into memoir. Expect tons of media attention for books from such celebrities as Arnold Schwarzenegger, Dennis Leary, Kirstie Alley, and Stephen Colbert. Jon Meacham, David Nasaw, and the late William Manchester (with help from Paul Reid) seem poised for further critical acclaim for their forthcoming biographies of Thomas Jefferson, Joseph P. Kennedy, and Winston Churchill, respectively. As for younger readers, Scholastic's *39 Clues* starts over again with a new series, with installments by James Dashner (*The Maze Runner*) and Carrie Ryan (*The Forest of Hands and Teeth*), while Jeff Kinney's *Diary of a Wimpy Kid #7, Dog Days*, will bow with a record first printing in the millions on October 13. And Amazon Publishing launches its first full list (after soft-launching with a single title in March), including books by celebrities Billy Ray Cyrus and Penny Marshall, self-help author Tim Ferriss, and literary-minded novelists and memoirists.

To help sift through the many thousands of fall titles, we've selected what we think are among the most noteworthy literary, commercial, and breakout titles for adults and children, broken down into key categories.

LITERARY FICTION

The season in litfic kicks off with two novels that ranked high in the informal "what are you most anticipating" survey we sent to a variety of booksellers, industry types and literary critics: *Telegraph Avenue* by Michael Chabon and *NW* by Zadie Smith, each releasing on September 11. Both authors are featured at BEA's author breakfast on June 6; both are publishing after a long hiatus from novels: Chabon's last was his 2007 *The Yiddish Policeman's Union*, and Smith's was *On Beauty* from 2005. Both *NW* and *Telegraph Avenue* overlap in the basic premise, exploring a small but diverse group of people living in a specific neighborhood (Chabon's current Berkeley, CA hometown, Smith's Northwest London, where she grew up).

Tom Wolfe will also have a novel out this fall, his first in eight years, with *Back to Blood* (Little, Brown, October 23). He's switched publishers after 43 years with FSG and switches locales, to Miami, to examine contemporary America post-meltdown as filtered through the city's sweltering heat and strange politics. Most hope it will be on the level of *Bonfire of the Vanities* or *A Man in Full* instead of *I Am Charlotte Simmons*. Mark Helprin's *In Sunlight and in Shadow* (HMH, October), his first novel since 2005, is already tipped to rank alongside his best work, the classic *A Winter's Tale* (1983) and *A Soldier of the Great War* (1991). Following on his Pulitzer-winning novel from 2007, *The Brief Wondrous Life of Oscar Wao*, Junot Díaz is already stoking high expectations with a new short story collection, *This is How You Lose Her* (Riverhead, September), while author of the bestselling memoir *The Tender Bar* J.R. Moehringer makes his fiction debut with *Sutton* (Hyperion, September). Ian McEwan is changing gears yet again after his previous novel *Solar* disappointed many, with *Sweet Tooth* (Nan A. Talese/Doubleday, November 13), an early 1970s spy thriller featuring a beautiful MI5 agent set loose in, of all things, the literary world.

A number of literary stalwarts return with new works, such as Barbara Kingsolver's *Flight Behavior* (Harper, November 6) and T.C. Boyle's *San Miguel* (Viking, September). Booker Prize winner Howard Jacobson's *Zoo Time* (Bloomsbury, October), is already being billed as his funniest novel ever. Martin Amis channels his younger, acid satire with *Lionel Asbo: State of England* (Knopf, August 21), and Alice Munro's new short story collection, *Dear Life*, in November, proves all talk of her retirement really was greatly exaggerated. Eighty-year-old James Salter, recently feted by the *Paris Review* at their annual revel, breaks his decade-long silence with *All That Is* (Knopf, October 16), and in January, George Saunders finally returns to short stories with *The Tenth of December*, and a new publisher, Random House. A.M. Homes moves back to fiction (following a critically acclaimed memoir, *The Mistress's Daughter*, in 2007) with *May We Be Forgiven* (Viking, October) while Mark Danielewski's *The Fifty-Year Sword* (Pantheon, October) will be available to a wider readership after a limited edition published only in Europe last year.

What of the breakouts, books by authors positioned as on the verge of expanding their readership to wider audiences? There are at least a few of those you can expect to hear about. Already booksellers are full of effusive praise for Jami Attenberg's fourth novel *The Middlesteins* (Grand Central, October), a saga of a very fractured family that could well be dubbed "The Corrections in Chicago" – stoked further by a blurb from Jonathan Franzen. He also endorses Amity Gaige's third novel *Schroder* (Twelve, February), which tracks an East German immigrant's decision to Americanize his name, Clark Rockefeller-style, and how that identity choice reverberates into his adult life, dissolving marriage, and the relationship with his child. The buzz is just as loud for Brooklyn bookseller Emma Straub's *Laura Lamont's Life in Pictures* (Riverhead, September), a loosely fictionalized account of 1940s starlet Jennifer Jones, tracking her rise and fall against a changing Hollywood at its most glamorous. Look out, too, for BEA Buzz Panel pick Antoine Wilson's *Panorama City* (HMH, September), in which a 28-year-old man ponders impending fatherhood, masculinity, and his own struggling self.

FICTION - DEBUT

No preview of literary fiction would be complete without looking at debut novels, books that come flush with expectation without any existing sales record. Last year's BEA was a launchpad for such first novels as Chad Harbach's *The Art of Fielding*, Erin Morgenstern's *The Night Circus* and Justin Torres's *We the Animals*. Among the debuts we excerpt are Shani Boianjiu's collection of stories about Israeli Defense Force trainees *The People of Forever Are Not Afraid* (Hogarth Press, September)—picked last fall by Nicole Krauss as one of the National Book Foundation's 5 under 35 writers to watch, M.L. Stedman's *The Light Between Oceans* (Scribner, August 7), Peter Heller's post-apocalyptic tale of a man's solo flight voyage, *The Dog Stars* (Knopf, August 7), Amanda Coplin's sensitive portrayal of young women seeking refuge with a recluse in *The Orchardist* (Harper, September) and Hanna Pylväinen's Scandinavian family saga *We Sinners* (Holt, August). The BEA Buzz picks feature a number of big debut titles, too, such as Vaddey Ratner's harrowing tale of a young girl surviving the Khmer Rouge regime *In The Shadow of the Banyan* (S&S, August) and Rachel Joyce's charming *The Unlikely Pilgrimage of Harold Fry* (Doubleday, July).

We're looking forward to a number of other works running the gamut: Michael Ennis's *The Malice of Fortune* (Doubleday, September), a thriller featuring the improbable crime-solving duo of Leonard da Vinci and Niccolo Machiavelli; Kathleen Alcott's *The Dangers of Proximal Alphabets* (Other Press, September), about a woman and two men who form a makeshift family unit that breaks apart when two members fall for each other; Ayana Mathis's *The Twelve Tribes of Hattie* (Knopf, January) a robust look at race and impossible love in the 1930s; Robin Sloan's previously self-published *Mr. Penumbra's Twenty-Four Hour Bookstore* (FSG, September); and David Gillham's *City of Women* (Amy Einhorn Books/Putnam, September), tipped as the latest discovery by the editor who published Kathryn Stockett's *The Help* and Sarah Blake's *The Postmistress*.

COMMERCIAL FICTION

As always, the fall season brings a number of titles by authors who can dependably book a place on bestseller lists. James Patterson should garner much attention in particular with *Zoo* (Little, Brown, September 3), cowritten with Michael Ledwidge, since its premise – coordinated animal attacks against humans around the world that can only be solved by a single idealistic young biologist – is epic in scale. John Grisham, fresh off his spring baseball-themed chart-topper *Calico Joe*, will almost certainly repeat the trick with *The Racketeer* (Doubleday, October 23), as will Lee Child's latest Jack Reacher novel *A Wanted Man* (Delacorte, September 25). Michael Connelly's new Harry Bosch crime novel, *The Black Box* (Little, Brown, November 25) is something more special, marking the twentieth anniversary of the character's debut and the author's twenty-fifth book. Dennis Lehane, after reviving his Kenzie/Gennaro detective series, now returns to his historical Boston trilogy with *Live By Night* (William Morrow, October). The previous title in the trilogy was *The Given Day*.

Both Ken Follett and Justin Cronin will issue the middle installments of their respective trilogies: *Winter of the World* (Dutton, September) revisits the same cast of characters caught up in the tumult of major 20th century events featured in 2010's *Fall of Giants*, and *The Twelve* (Ballantine, October 12) returns to the post-apocalyptic zombie territory Cronin debuted in *The Passage*. Author of *The Alienist* Caleb Carr will try his hand at a historical thriller set in medieval Germany with *The Legend of Broken* (Random House, November), his first novel since 2005, while Dustin Thomason – on his own, without his *Rule of Four* partner Ian Caldwell – goes into techno-thriller territory with *12/21* (Random House, August 21.)

In crime fiction, Louise Penny continues her French-Canadian Inspector Gamache series with *The Beautiful Mystery* (Minotaur Books, August 28), finding more ingenious ways to murder people in the small Quebec town of Three Pines. The Scandinavian boom persists with Jo Nesbo's *Phantom* (Knopf, September) and Lene Kaaberbol and Agnete Friis' *Invisible*

Murder (Soho Press, October) leading that pack. After several supernatural outings, Michael Koryta moves back to straight crime fiction with *The Prophet* (Little, Brown, September), centered around the murder of a high school girl and how it affects the town and its local football team. Writing as Chase Novak, Scott Spencer eschews his usual literary voice entirely to take on the haunted house story with *Breed* (Mulholland, September.) Michael Sears draws on personal experience at Paine Webber and Jefferies & Co for his Wall Street thriller *Black Fridays* (Putnam, September) while, in January, former CIA agent Valerie Plame teams up with Sarah Lovett on *Blowback*, the first in a new crime series starring a Plame-like protagonist. And we'd be remiss if we didn't mention *The Cocktail Waitress* by James M. Cain (Hard Case Crime, September) the long-lost final novel by the noir master that, after years of searching, was finally unearthed – and is supposed to be quite a lot better than the last books Cain published before his death, at 85, in 1977.

But really, the fall fiction schedule all revolves around Rowling. After shuffling release dates because of the presidential election, publishers must also reckon with the September 27 arrival of *The Casual Vacancy*. Little, Brown will see if readers respond as enthusiastically to a blackly comic tale of small town wars among the locals as they did to the Potterverse. If they do, everybody wins. If they don't, the nail-biting begins.

NON-FICTION – CONVERSATION STARTERS

In this category we lumped together books that are designed to generate media, debate, and reader conversation – including notable political titles as well as journalistic, concept-driven releases. Since their last book, *Killing Lincoln*, was among the top-selling non-fiction books of 2011, Bill O'Reilly and Martin Dugard repeat the same conceit for *Killing Kennedy* (Holt, October), their theory of how JFK was assassinated. Stephen Colbert offers a sequel of sorts to his comedic political book *I Am America (and So Can You)* with *America Again* (Grand Central, October). Jeffrey Toobin expands his *New Yorker* essays on the Supreme Court with *The Oath* (Doubleday, September), looking closely at how the highest-ranking judicial branch has fared during the Obama administration. Hanna Rosin turns her controversial *Atlantic* cover story into *The End of Men* (Riverhead, October). It's about the growing economic and cultural power of women, and what it means for their opposite gender. Feministing's Jessica Valenti considers the "mommy wars," and asks the question few dare to consider: *Why Have Kids?* (Amazon Publishing, November). Fivethirtyeight.com statistical wunderkind Nate Silver examines the subject of prediction in *The Signal and the Noise* (Penguin Press, September) just in time to come up with new polls for the presidential election. *Wired* editor-in-chief Chris Anderson follows up on *The Long Tail* with *Free with Makers* (Crown, October) on DIY culture and "the new industrial revolution." Many years in the making is Pulitzer Prize winner Hedrick Smith's *Who Stole the American Dream? And Can We Get It Back?* (Random House, September) a comprehensive look at how that mythmaking concept has been gutted over the last forty years, and how it might be possible to bring back some of that magic.

NON-FICTION – HISTORY AND BIOGRAPHY

In the nearly four years since David Foster Wallace died, he's turned into a generational icon. Posthumous writing published by Little, Brown, like the Pulitzer finalist novel *The Pale King* and forthcoming essay collection *Both Flesh and Not*, add to the mythos. Wallace's reputation surely will be cemented with D.T. Max's biography *Every History Is A Ghost* (Viking, October 30), an expansion of Max's 2009 *New Yorker* essay. In a truly posthumous biography, William Manchester could not complete the third and final volume of his acclaimed account of Winston Churchill when he died in 2004, but Paul Reid has stepped up to do so, working from Manchester's notes. The result is *The Last Lion: Defender of the Realm, 1940 – 1965* (Little, Brown, October), recounting the British Prime Minister's final years in power during WWII and afterwards. The previous two books in the series are not yet issued as ebooks, but the new installment—listed as weighing 1.6 pounds in print—will be available digitally as well. Historian David Nasaw follows up his biography of Andrew Carnegie with a look at a different American mogul, Joseph P. Kennedy, in *The Patriarch* (Penguin Press, November). After winning the Pulitzer for his biography of Andrew Jackson, Jon Meacham takes on another American president in November with *Thomas Jefferson: The Art of Power*, published by his employer, Random House, where Meacham is an editor-at-large.

MEMOIR

This fall a number of major novelists are turning to memoir to expound upon stories that helped form their essence or are an integral part of their biography but remained elusive to the public. Perhaps the most anticipated memoir is from Salman Rushdie with *Joseph Anton* (Random House, September). The 600-page volume describes the years he spent in hiding after a fatwa was issued against him by Iranian clerics for his 1989 novel *The Satanic Verses*. The memoir's title is from his security code name—the first names of two favorite writers, Conrad and Chekhov. Then there is Chinua Achebe's *There Was a Country* (Penguin Press, October), in which the 81-year-old writer, still best known for *Things Fall Apart*, offers a personal history of the late 1960s Biafran War that tore apart his native Nigeria. In Richard Russo's *Elsewhere* (Knopf, November), the Pulitzer Prize-winning novelist looks at his upstate New York upbringing, the backbone of all his fiction, and the complex relationship with his late mother.

Celebrities and important cultural figures, as always, have plenty to say about themselves in book format. Once again, the question is whether they will reveal more of what readers want to know about them than what they want readers to know. Former action star and California governor Arnold Schwarzenegger may claim *Total Recall* (Simon & Schuster, October) about his life and work, co-written with Peter Petre, but how candid will he be about his marriage to Maria Shriver or the rockier aspects of his personal and political life? Singer Tony Bennett, in his untitled memoir (Harper, December) has nearly nine decades of music-making memories to draw on, a concoction likely to favor entertaining anecdotes over big reveals. Anticipation is already off the charts for Neil Young's *Waging Heavy Peace* (Blue Rider Press, October 2), who will sit for a live interview at BEA on June 6. And when Penny Marshall's memoir *My Mother Is Nuts* is published in October, will the book be strong enough to match the vote of confidence as Amazon Publishing's first big deal?

In addition, former Oakland A's and St. Louis Cardinals manager Tony La Russa will draw on the highs and lows of a storied baseball career in *One Last Strike* (William Morrow, September). On the public affairs stage, former United Nations secretary general Kofi Annan writes on *Interventions: A Life in War and Peace* (Penguin Press, September). BEA Buzz pick *Brain On Fire* (Free Press, December) is Susannah Calahan's account of viral meningitis that lands her in hospital and forces her to reckon with everything, including her journalism. The most harrowing true story of the fall will likely emerge from Damien Echols, one of the "West Memphis 3" imprisoned for a trio of horrible child murders they did not commit. Blue Rider will publish the untitled book on September 3.

The memoir aimed most directly at book-lovers, though, is Will Schwalbe's *The End of Your Life Book Club* (Knopf, October), in which the former editor-in-chief of Hyperion turned co-founder of Cookstr.com and his dying mother form a two-person book club, reading favorites and new discoveries alike.

YOUNG ADULT AND CHILDREN'S BOOKS

Even as Suzanne Collins' *The Hunger Games* trilogy may continue to rank high on children's bestseller lists, a number of other brand-name authors and series will vie for attention. Dav Pilkey's *Captain Underpants* saga returns with *The Revolting Revenge of the Radioactive Robo-Boxers* (Scholastic, January 15). The same multimedia concept that was the basis for Scholastic's *39 Clues* series now reasserts itself with *The Infinity Ring*, which starts with James Dashner's *A Mutiny In Time* on August 28 and continues with the next book by Carrie Ryan. Author of the bestselling *A Series of Unfortunate Events* books Lemony Snicket comes back with a new series, *Who Could That Be At This Hour?* (Little, Brown, October), the first in the four-volume *All The Wrong Questions* series featuring illustrations by Canadian artist Seth. Ally Condie concludes her dystopian *Matched* trilogy with *Reached* (Dutton, November 13) and Maggie Stiefvater starts a paranormal series with *The Raven Boys* (Scholastic, September 18).

Co-star of the Fox series *Glee* (and BEA children's breakfast host) Chris Colfer makes his children's debut with the fairy tale-inflected *The Land of Stories: The Wishing Spell* (Little, Brown Young Readers, July 17), while *Sesame Street* star Sonia Manzano examines the life of a girl growing up in Spanish Harlem in *The Revolution of Evelyn Serrano* (Scholastic, September 1). Kadir Nelson offers an illustrated picture book edition of Martin Luther King's famous speech *I Have a Dream* (Schwartz & Wade, October), and Lois Lowry continues her Newbery-award winning *Giver* series with *Son* (Houghton Mifflin Harcourt Children's, October.) Finally, Jeff Kinney's new *Wimpy Kid* title (Amulet, November 13) teases readers with the slogan "love is in the air."

The middle–grade BEA Buzz picks also offer a host of intriguing titles, such as W.H. Beck's *Malcolm At Midnight* (Houghton Mifflin Harcourt Children's, September), 17-year-old Stefan Bachmann's *The Peculiar* (Greenwillow, September), Charles Gilman's humorous series starter *Tales From Lovecraft Middle School #1* (Quirk Books, September), Marissa Moss's *With Love From Paris: Mira's Sketchbook* (Sourcebooks Jabberwocky, September) and Grace Lin's *Starry River of the Sky* (Little, Brown Young Readers, October).

For teens, the BEA Buzz panel features a wide range of titles, including speculative dystopian fiction like Gennifer Albin's *Crewel* (FSG Young Readers, October) and Meagan Spooner's *Skylark* (Carolrhoda Books, October); Donna Cooner's tale of a girl grappling with gastric bypass surgery, *Skinny* (Point/Scholastic, October); Ashley Edward Miller and Zack Stentz's *Colin Fischer* (Razorbill, November), featuring an Encyclopedia Brown-like character with Asperger's syndrome; and Kat Zhang's science fiction story of hybrid humans *What's Left of Me* (HarperCollins Children's, September). Expect to hear quite a lot about Jessica Khoury's new dystopian series, which kicks off with *Origin* (Razorbill, September 4), among the great YA titles excerpted here. We also feature the first in a trilogy that is a collaboration between YA authors Jenny Han and Siobhan Vivian, *Burn for Burn* (Simon & Schuster Children's, September), as well as the latest books from Ned Vizzini, *The Other Normals* (HarperTeen, September) and Scholastic editor-in-chief David Levithan's *Every Day* (Knopf Children's, September).

It's an exciting season of new books ahead. Readers will find their way to many of the books previewed here and others yet to be discovered. In the meantime, enjoy this chance to sample dozens of anticipated titles before they hit the market.

BUZZ AUTHORS APPEARING AT BEA

Libba Bray

Junot Díaz

Jenny Han/Siobhan Vivian

Jessica Khoury

Dennis Lehane

Sarah J. Maas

James Meek

Lawrence Norfolk

Kevin Powers

Hanna Pylväinen

Teresa Rhyne

Bill Roorbach

Neil Young

THE DOG STARS

a novel

PETER HELLER

SUMMARY

A riveting, powerful debut novel from an award-winning adventure writer: the story of a pilot surviving in a world filled with loss—and of what he is willing to risk to rediscover, against all odds, connection, love, and grace.

Hig survived the flu that killed everyone he knows. His wife is gone, his friends are dead, he lives in the hangar of a small abandoned airport with his dog, his only neighbor a gun-toting misanthrope. In his 1956 Cessna, Hig flies the perimeter of the airfield or sneaks off to the mountains to fish and pretend that things are the way they used to be. But when a random transmission somehow beams through his radio, the voice ignites a hope deep inside him that a better life—something like his old life—exists beyond the airport. Risking everything, he flies past his point of no return—not enough fuel to get him home—following the trail of the static-broken voice on the radio. But what he encounters and what he must face—in the people he meets, and in himself—is both better and worse than anything he could have hoped for.

EXCERPT

i

I keep the Beast running, I keep the 100 low lead on tap, I foresee attacks. I am young enough, I am old enough. I used to love to fish for trout more than almost anything.

My name is Hig, one name. Big Hig if you need another.

If I ever woke up crying in the middle of a dream, and I'm not saying I did, it's because the trout are gone every one. Brookies, rainbows, browns, cutthroats, cutbows, every one.

The tiger left, the elephant, the apes, the baboon, the cheetah. The titmouse, the frigate bird, the pelican (gray), the whale (gray), the collared dove. Sad but. Didn't cry until the last trout swam upriver looking for maybe cooler water.

Melissa, my wife, was an old hippy. Not that old. She looked good. In this story she might have been Eve, but I'm not Adam. I am more like Cain. They didn't have a brother like me.

Did you ever read the Bible? I mean sit down and read it like it was a book? Check out Lamentations. That's where we're at, pretty much. Pretty much lamenting. Pretty much pouring our hearts out like water.

They said at the end it would get colder after it gets warmer. Way colder. Still waiting. She's a surprise this old earth, one big surprise after another since before she separated from the moon who circles and circles like the mate of a shot goose.

No more geese. A few. Last October I heard the old bleating after dusk and saw them, five against the cold bloodwashed blue over the ridge. Five all fall, I think, next April none.

I hand pump the 100 low lead aviation gas out of the old airport tank when the sun is not shining, and I have the truck too that was making the fuel delivery. More fuel than the Beast can burn in my lifetime if I keep my sorties local, which I plan to, I have to. She's a small plane, a 1956 Cessna 182, really a beaut. Cream and blue. I'm figuring I'm dead before the Beast gives up the final ghost. I will buy the farm. Eighty acres of bottomland hay and corn in a country where there is still a cold stream coming out of the purple mountains full of brookies and cuts.

Before that I will make my roundtrips. Out and back.

*

I have a neighbor. One. Just us at a small country airport a few miles from the mountains. A training field where they built a bunch of houses for people who couldn't sleep without their little planes, the way golfers live on a golf course. Bangley is the name on the registration of his old truck, which doesn't run anymore. Bruce Bangley. I fished it out of the glove box looking for a tire pressure gauge I could take with me in the Beast. A Wheat Ridge address. I don't call him that, though, what's the point, there's only two of us. Only us for at least a radius of eight miles, which is the distance of open prairie to the first juniper woods on the skirt of the mountain. I just say, Hey. Above the juniper is oak brush then black timber. Well, brown. Beetle killed and droughted. A lot of it standing dead now, just swaying like a thousand skeletons, sighing like a thousand ghosts, but not all. There are patches of green woods, and I am their biggest fan. I root for them out here on the plain. Go Go Go Grow Grow Grow! That's our fight song. I yell it out the window as I fly low over. The green patches are spreading year by year. Life is tenacious if you give it one little bit of encouragement. I could swear they hear me. They wave back, wave their feathery arms back and forth down low by their sides, they remind me of women in kimonos. Tiny steps or no steps, wave wave hands at your sides.

I go up there on foot when I can. To the greener woods. Funny to say that: not like I have to clear my calendar. I go up to breathe. The different air. It's dangerous, it's an adrenalin rush I could do without. I have seen elk sign. Not so old. If there are still elk. Bangley says no way. Way, but. Never seen one. Seen plenty deer. I bring the .308 and I shoot a doe and I drag her back in the hull of a kayak which I sawed the deck off so it's a sled. My green sled. The deer just stayed on with the rabbits and the rats. The cheat grass stayed on, I guess that's enough.

Before I go up there I fly it twice. One day, one night with the goggles. The goggles are pretty good at seeing down through trees if the trees aren't too heavy. People make pulsing green shadows, even asleep. Better than not checking. Then I make a loop south and east, come back in from the north. Thirty miles out, at least a day for a traveler. That's all open, all plains, sage and grass and rabbit brush and the old farms. The brown circles of fields like the footprint of a crutch fading into the prairie. Hedgerows and windbreaks, half the trees broken, blown over, a few still green by a seep or along a creek. Then I tell Bangley.

I cover the eight miles dragging the empty sled in two hours, then I am in cover. I can still move. It's a long way back with a deer, though. Over open country. Bangley covers me from halfway out. We still have the handsets and they still recharge with the panels. Japanese built, good thing. Bangley has a .408 CheyTac sniper rifle set up on a platform he built. A rangefinder. My luck. A gun nut. A really mean gun nut. He says he can pot a man from a mile off. He has done. I've seen it more than once. Last summer he shot a girl who was chasing me across the open plain. A young girl, a scarecrow. I heard the shot, stopped, left the sled, went back. She was thrown back over a rock, a hole where her waist should have been, just about torn in half. Her chest was heaving, panting, her head twisted to the side, one black eye shiny and looking up at me, not fear, just like a question, burning, like of all things witnessed this one couldn't be believed. Like that. Like fucking why?

That's what I asked Bangley, fucking why.

She would have caught you.

So what? I had a gun, she had a little knife. To like protect her from me. She maybe wanted food.

Maybe. Maybe she'd slit your throat in the middle of the night.

I stared at him, his mind going that far, to the middle of the night, me and her. Jesus. My only neighbor. What can I say to Bangley? He has saved my bacon more times. Saving my bacon is his job. I have the plane, I am the eyes, he has the guns, he is the muscle. He knows I know he knows: he can't fly, I don't have the stomach for killing. Any other way probably just be one of us. Or none.

I also have Jasper, son of Daisy, which is the best last line of alarm.

So when we get sick of rabbits and sunfish from the pond, I get a deer. Mostly I just want to go up there. It feels like church, hallow and cool. The dead forest swaying and whispering, the green forest full of sighs. The musk smell of deer beds. The creeks where I always pray to see a trout. One fingerling. One big old survivor, his green shadow idling against the green shadows of the stones.

Eight miles of open ground to the mountain front, the first trees. That is our perimeter. Our safety zone. That is my job.

He can concentrate his firepower to the west that way. That's how Bangley talks. Because it's thirty miles out, high plains all other directions, more than a day's walk, but just a couple of hours west to the first trees. The families are south ten miles but they don't bother us. That's what I call them. They are something like thirty Mennonites with a blood disease that hit after the flu. Like a plague but slow burning. Something like AIDS I think, maybe more contagious. The kids were born with it and it makes them all sick and weak and every year some die.

We have the perimeter. But if someone hid. In the old farmsteads. In the sage. The willows along a creek. Arroyos, too, with undercut banks. He asked me that once: how do I know. How do I know someone is not inside our perimeter, in all that empty country, hiding, waiting to attack us? But thing is I can see a lot. Not like the back of the hand, too simple, but like a book I have read and reread too many times to count, maybe like the Bible for some folks of old. I would know. A sentence out of place. A gap. Two periods where there should be one. I know.

I know, I think: if I am going to die—no If—it will be on one of these trips to the mountains. Crossing open ground with the full sled. Shot in the back with an arrow.

Bangley a long time ago gave me bulletproof, one of the vests in his arsenal. He has all kinds of shit. He said it'll stop any handgun, an arrow, but with a rifle it depends, I better be lucky. I thought about that. We're supposed to be the only two living souls but the families in at least hundreds of square miles, the only survivors, I better be lucky. So I wear the vest because it's warm, but if it's summer I mostly don't. When I wear it, I feel like I'm waiting for something. Would I stand on a train platform and wait for a train that hasn't come for months? Maybe. Sometimes this whole thing feels just like that.

Twitter: Want to discuss or share what you just read? Use the hashtag #beaSTARS to connect with others.

ABOUT THE AUTHOR

Peter Heller holds an MFA from the Iowa Writers' Workshop in both fiction and poetry. An award-winning adventure writer and longtime contributor to NPR, Heller is a contributing editor at *Outside* magazine, *Men's Journal*, and *National Geographic Adventure*, and a regular contributor to *Bloomberg Businessweek*. His previous books include *Kook*; *The Whale Warriors*; and *Hell or High Water: Surviving Tibet's Tsangpo Gorge*.

Imprint: Knopf
BEA Booth #: 3940
Print ISBN: 978-0-307-95994-2
Print price: $24.95
eBook ISBN: 978-0-307-96093-1
eBook price: $9.99
Publication date: 8/7/2012
Publicity contact: Lena Khidritskaya LKhidritskaya@randomhouse.com
Editor: Jennifer E. Jackson
Agent: David Halpern

memoirs

of an

imaginary

friend

matthew dicks

SUMMARY

Imaginary friend Budo narrates the irresistibly original story of his friendship with eight-year-old Max, whom he rescues from the perils of a misguided teacher, in this enchanting novel in the vein of *The Curious Incident of the Dog in the Night Time*. Jodi Picoult raves, "A novel as creative, brave, and pitch-perfect as its narrator, an imaginary friend named Budo, who reminds us that bravery comes in the most unlikely forms. It has been a long time since I read a book that has captured me so completely, and has wowed me with its unique vision. You've never read a book like this before. As Budo himself might say: Believe me."

EXCERPT

Chapter 1

Here is what I know:

My name is Budo.

I have been alive for five years.

Five years is a very long time for someone like me to be alive. Max gave me my name.

Max is the only human person who can see me.

Max's parents call me an imaginary friend.

I love Max's teacher, Mrs. Gosk.

I do not like Max's other teacher, Mrs. Patterson.

I am not imaginary.

Chapter 2

I am lucky as imaginary friends go. I have been alive for a lot longer than most. I once knew an imaginary friend named Philippe. He was the imaginary friend of one of Max's classmates in preschool. He lasted less than a week. One day he popped into the world, looking pretty human except for his lack of ears (lots of imaginary friends lack ears), and then a few days later, he was gone.

I'm also lucky that Max has a great imagination. I once knew an imaginary friend named Chomp who was just a spot on the wall. Just a fuzzy, black blob without any real shape at all. Chomp could talk and sort of slide up and down the wall, but he was two-dimensional like a piece of paper, so he could never pry himself off. He didn't have arms and legs like me. He didn't even have a face.

Imaginary friends get their appearance from their human friend's imagination. Max is a very creative boy, and so I have two arms, two legs, and a face. I'm not missing a single body part and that makes me a rarity in the world of imaginary friends. Most imaginary friends are missing something or other and some don't even look human at all. Like Chomp.

Too much imagination can be bad, though. I once met an imaginary friend named Pterodactyl whose eyes were stuck on the ends of these two gangly, green antennas. His human friend probably thought they looked cool, but poor Pterodactyl couldn't focus on anything to save his life. He told me that he constantly felt sick to his stomach and was always tripping over his own feet, which were just fuzzy shadows attached to his legs. His human friend was so obsessed with Pterodactyl's head and those eyes that he had never bothered to think about anything below Pterodactyl's waist.

This is not unusual.

I'm also lucky because I'm mobile. Lots of imaginary friends are stuck to their human friends. Some have leashes around their necks. Some are three inches tall and get stuffed into coat pockets. And some are nothing more than a spot on the wall, like Chomp. But thanks to Max, I can get around on my own. I can even leave Max behind if I want.

But doing so too often might be hazardous to my health.

As long as Max believes in me, I exist. People like Max's mother and my friend Graham say that this is what makes me imaginary. But it's not true. I might need Max's imagination to exist, but I have my own thoughts, my own ideas, and my own life outside of him. I am tied to Max the same way that an astronaut is tied to his spaceship by hoses and wires. If the spaceship blows up and the astronaut dies, that doesn't mean that the astronaut was imaginary. It just means that his life support was cut off.

Same for me and Max.

I need Max in order to survive, but I'm still my own person. I can say and do as I please. Sometimes Max and I even get into arguments, but nothing ever serious. Just stuff about which TV show to watch or which game to play. But it *behooves* me (that's a word that Mrs. Gosk taught the class last week) to stick around Max whenever possible, because I need Max to keep thinking about me. Keep believing in me. I don't want to end up *out of sight, out of mind*, which is something Max's mom sometimes says when Max's dad forgets to call home when he is going to be late. If I am gone too long, Max might stop believing in me, and if that happens, then *poof.*

Chapter 3

Max's first-grade teacher once said that houseflies live for about three days. I wonder what the life span of an imaginary friend is? Probably not much longer. I guess that makes me practically ancient.

Max imagined me when he was four years old, and just like that, I popped into existence. When I was born, I only knew what Max knew. I knew my colors and some of my numbers and the names for lots of things like tables and microwave ovens and aircraft carriers. My head was filled with the things that a four-year-old boy would know. But Max also imagined me much older than him. Probably a teenager. Maybe even a little older. Or maybe I was just a boy with a grown-up's brain. It's hard to tell. I'm not much taller than Max, but I'm definitely different. I was more together than Max when I was born. I could make sense of things that still confused him. I could see the answers to problems that Max could not. Maybe this is how all imaginary friends are born. I don't know.

Max doesn't remember the day that I was born, so he can't remember what he was thinking at the time. But since he imagined me as older and more together, I have been able to learn much faster than Max. I was able to concentrate and focus better on the day I was born than Max is able to even today. On that first day I remember Max's mother was trying to teach him to count by even numbers, and he just couldn't get it. But I learned it right away. It made sense to me because my brain was ready to learn even numbers. Max's brain wasn't.

At least that's what I think.

Also, I don't sleep, because Max didn't imagine that I needed sleep. So I have more time to learn. And I don't spend all my time with Max, so I've learned lots of things that Max has never seen or heard before. After he goes to bed, I sit in the living room or the kitchen with Max's parents. We watch television or I just listen to them talk. Sometimes I go places. I go to the gas station that never closes, because my favorite people in the world except for Max and his parents and Mrs. Gosk are there. Or I go to Doogies hot-dog restaurant a little ways down the road or to the police station or to the hospital (except I don't go to the hospital anymore because Oswald is there and he scares me). And when we are in school, I sometimes go to the teacher's lounge or another classroom, and sometimes I even go to the principal's office, just to listen to what's going on. I am not smarter than Max, but I know a lot more than him just because I am awake more and go places that Max can't. This is good. Sometimes I can help Max when he doesn't understand something so well.

Like last week Max couldn't open a jar of jelly to make a peanut butter and jelly sandwich. "Budo!" he said. "I can't open it."

"Sure you can," I said. "Turn it the other way. Lefty loosy. Righty tighty." That is something I hear Max's mom say to herself sometimes before she opens a jar. It worked. Max opened the jar. But he was so excited that he dropped it on the tile floor, smashing it into a million pieces.

The world can be so complicated for Max. Even when he gets something right, it can still go wrong.

I live in a strange place in the world. I live in the space in between people. I spend most of my time in the kid world with Max, but I also spend a lot of time with adults like Max's parents and teachers and my friends at the gas station, except they can't see me. Max's mom would call this *straddling the fence*. She says this to Max when he can't make up his mind about something, which happens a lot.

"Do you want the blue Popsicle or the yellow Popsicle?" she asks, and Max just freezes. Freezes like a Popsicle. There are just too many things for Max to think about when choosing.

Is red better than yellow?

Is green better than blue?

Which one is colder?

Which one will melt fastest?

What does green taste like?

What does red taste like?

Do different colors taste different?

I wish that Max's mom would just make the choice for Max. She knows how hard it is for him. But when she makes him choose and he can't, I sometimes choose for him. I whisper, "Pick blue," and then he says, "I'll take blue." Then it's done. No more straddling the fence.

That's kind of how I live. I straddle the fence. I live in the yellow and the blue world. I live with kids and I live with adults. I'm not exactly a kid, but I'm not exactly an adult, either.

I'm yellow *and* blue.

I'm green.

I know my color combinations, too.

Chapter 4

Max's teacher is Mrs. Gosk. I like Mrs. Gosk a lot. Mrs. Gosk walks around with a meter stick that she calls her meter-beater and threatens students in a fake British accent, but the kids know she's just trying to make them laugh. Mrs. Gosk is very strict and insists that her students work hard, but she would never hit a student. Still, she is a tough lady. She makes them sit up straight and work on their assignments in silence, and when a child misbehaves, she says, "Shame! Shame! Let all the boys and girls know your name!" or "You will get away with that nonsense when pigs fly, young man!" The other teachers say Mrs. Gosk is old-fashioned, but the kids know that she is tough because she loves them.

Max doesn't like many people, but he likes Mrs. Gosk.

Last year, Max's teacher was Mrs. Silbor. She was strict, too. She made the kids work hard like Mrs. Gosk does. But you could tell that she didn't love the kids like Mrs. Gosk does, so no one in the class worked as hard as they do this year. It's strange how teachers can go off to college for all those years to learn to become teachers, but some of them never learn the easy stuff. Like making kids laugh. And making sure they know that you love them.

I do not like Mrs. Patterson. She's not a real teacher. She's a para-professional. This is someone who helps Mrs. Gosk take care of Max. Max is different than other kids so he doesn't spend the whole day with Mrs. Gosk. Sometimes he works with Mrs. McGinn in the Learning Center, and sometimes he works on his speech with Mrs. Riner, and sometimes he plays games with other kids in Mrs. Hume's office. And sometimes he reads and does homework with Mrs. Patterson.

As far as I can tell, no one knows why Max is different from the rest of the kids. Max's father says that Max is just a late bloomer, but when he says that, Max's mom gets so angry that she stops talking to him for at least a day.

I don't know why everyone thinks Max is so complicated. Max just doesn't like people in the same way other kids do. He likes people, but it's a different kind of liking. He likes people from far away. The farther you stay away from Max, the more he will like you.

And Max doesn't like to be touched. When someone touches Max, the whole world gets bright and shivery. That's how he described it to me once.

I can't touch Max, and Max can't touch me. Maybe that's why we get along so well.

Also, Max doesn't understand when people say one thing but mean another. Like last week, Max was reading a book at recess and a fourth grader came over and said, "Look at the little genius." Max didn't say anything to the boy because he knew if he said something, the fourth grader would stay there longer and keep bothering him. But I know that Max was confused, because it sounded like the boy was saying that Max was smart even though the boy was actually being mean. He was being sarcastic, but Max doesn't understand sarcasm. Max knew the boy was being mean, but only because that boy is always mean to Max. But he couldn't understand why the boy would call him a genius, since being called a genius is usually a good thing.

People are confusing to Max, so it's hard for him to be around them. That's why Max has to play games in Mrs. Hume's office with kids from the other classes. He thinks it's a big waste of time. He hates having to sit on the floor around the Monopoly board, because sitting on the floor is not as comfortable as sitting in a chair. But Mrs. Hume is trying to teach Max to play with other kids, to understand what they mean when they sarcasm or joke around. Max just doesn't understand. When Max's mom and dad are fighting, Max's mom says that his dad can't see the forest for the trees. That's like Max except it's with the whole world. He can't see the big things because of all the little things that get in his way.

Today Mrs. Patterson is absent. When a teacher is absent, it usually means that the teacher is sick or her child is sick or someone in her family has died. Mrs. Patterson had someone in her family die once. I know this because sometimes the other teachers will say nice things to her like, "How are you holding up, dear?" and sometimes they whisper to each other after she has left the room. But that was a long time ago. When Mrs. Patterson is absent, it usually means that it is Friday.

There's no substitute for Mrs. Patterson today so Max and I get to stay with Mrs. Gosk all day which makes me happy. I don't like Mrs. Patterson. Max doesn't like her, either, but he doesn't like her in the same way he doesn't like most of his teachers. He doesn't see what I see because he's too busy looking at the trees. But Mrs. Patterson is different from Mrs. Gosk and Mrs. Riner and Mrs. McGinn. She never smiles for real. She's always thinking something different in her head than what is on her face. I don't think she likes Max, but she pretends that she does, which is even scarier than just not liking him.

"Hello, Max, my boy!" Mrs. Gosk says as we walk into the classroom. Max doesn't like when Mrs. Gosk calls him "my boy" because he is not *her boy*. He has a mother already. But he won't ask Mrs. Gosk to stop calling him "my boy" because asking her to stop would be harder than listening to Mrs. Gosk say "my boy" every day.

Max would rather say nothing to everyone than something to one person.

But even though Max doesn't understand why Mrs. Gosk calls him "my boy" he knows that she loves him. He knows that Mrs. Gosk is not being mean. Just confusing.

I wish I could tell Mrs. Gosk not to call Max "my boy," but Mrs. Gosk can't see or hear me and there's nothing I can do to make her see or hear me. Imaginary friends can't touch or move things in the human world. So I can't open a jelly jar or pick up a pencil or type on a keyboard. Otherwise I would write a note asking Mrs. Gosk not to call Max "my boy."

I can bump up against the real world, but I can't actually touch it.

Even so, I am lucky because when Max first imagined me, he imagined that I could pass through things like doors and windows even when they are closed. I think it's because he was afraid that if his parents closed his bedroom door at night I might get stuck outside the room, and Max doesn't like to fall sleep unless I'm sitting in the chair next to his bed. This means that I can go anywhere by walking through the doors and windows, but never through walls or floors. I can't pass through walls and floors because Max didn't imagine me that way. That would've been too strange for even Max to think about.

There are other imaginary friends who can walk through doors and windows like me, and some who can even walk through walls, but most can't walk through anything and get stuck in places for a long time. That's what happened to Puppy, a talking dog who got stuck in the janitor's closet overnight a couple of weeks ago. It was a scary night for his human friend, a kindergartener named Piper, because she had no idea where Puppy was.

But it was even scarier for Puppy, because getting locked in a closet is how imaginary friends sometimes disappear forever. A boy or girl accidentally (or sometimes, *accidentally on purpose*) locks an imaginary friend in a closet or a cabinet or basement and then *poof*! Out of sight, out of mind. The end of the imaginary friend.

Being able to pass through doors can be a lifesaver.

Today I want to stay put in the classroom because Mrs. Gosk is reading

Charlie and the Chocolate Factory aloud to the class, and I love it when Mrs. Gosk reads. She has a whispery, thin voice, so all the kids must lean in and be absolutely silent in order to hear, which is great for Max. Noises distract him. If Joey Miller is banging his pencil on his desk or Danielle Ganner is tapping her feet on the floor like she does all the time, then Max can't hear anything but the pencil or the feet. He can't ignore sounds like the other kids can, but when Mrs. Gosk reads, everyone must be perfectly quiet.

Mrs. Gosk always chooses the best books and tells the best stories from her own life that somehow relate to the book. Charlie Bucket does something crazy and then Mrs. Gosk tells us about a time when her son, Michael, did something crazy, and we all laugh our heads off. Even Max sometimes.

Max doesn't like to laugh. Some people think it's because he doesn't think things are funny, but that is not true. Max doesn't understand all funny things. Puns and knock-knock jokes make no sense to him, because they say one thing but mean another. When a word can mean a bunch of different things, he has a hard time understanding which meaning to choose. He doesn't even understand why words have to mean different things depending on when you use them, and I don't blame him. I don't like it much, either.

But Max finds other things hilarious. Like when Mrs. Gosk told us how Michael once sent twenty cheese pizzas and the bill to a school-yard bully as a joke. When the police officer came to their house to scare Michael, Mrs. Gosk told the police officer to "take him away" to teach her son a lesson. Everyone laughed at that story. Even Max. Because it made sense. It had a beginning, a middle, and an end.

Mrs. Gosk is also teaching us about World War II today, which she says is not in the curriculum but should be. The kids love it, and Max especially loves it because he thinks about wars and battles and tanks and airplanes all the time. Sometimes it is the only thing that he thinks about for days. If school was only about war and battles and not math and writing, then Max would be the best student in the whole wide world.

Today Mrs. Gosk is teaching us about Pearl Harbor. The Japanese bombed Pearl Harbor on December 7, 1941. Mrs. Gosk said that the Americans were not ready for the sneak attack because they couldn't imagine the Japanese attacking us from so far away.

"America lacked imagination," she said.

If Max had been alive in 1941, things might have been different because he has an excellent imagination. I bet that Max would have imagined Admiral Yamamoto's plan perfectly, with the midget submarines and the torpedoes with the wooden rudders and everything else. He could have warned the American soldiers about the plan because that is what Max is good at. Imagining things. He has a lot going on inside of him all the time so he doesn't worry so much about what is going on outside him. That's what people don't understand.

That's why it's good for me to stick around Max whenever I can. Sometimes he doesn't pay enough attention to the things around him. Last week he was about to get on the bus when a big gust of wind blew his report card right out of his hands and between bus 8 and bus 53. He ran out of line to get it, but he didn't look both ways, so I yelled, "Max Delaney! Stop!"

I use Max's last name when I want to get his attention. I learned that from Mrs. Gosk. It worked. Max stopped, which was good, because a car was passing by the school buses at that moment, which is illegal.

Graham said that I saved Max's life. Graham is the third imaginary friend at the school right now, as far as I know, and she saw the whole thing. Graham is a girl but she has a boy's name. She looks almost as human as I do, except her hair stands up like someone on the moon is pulling on each individual strand. It doesn't move. It's as solid as a rock. Graham heard me yell at Max and tell him to stop, and then after Max was back in line, she walked over to me and said, "Budo! You just saved Max's life! He would've been squished by that car!"

But I told Graham that I saved my own life, because if Max ever died, I think I would die, too.

Right?

I think so. I've never known an imaginary friend whose human friend died before he disappeared. So I'm not sure.

But I think I would. Die, I mean. If Max died.

Twitter: Want to discuss or share what you just read? Use the hashtag #beaFRIEND to connect with others.

ABOUT THE AUTHOR

Matthew Dicks is a writer and elementary school teacher. His articles have been published in the *Hartford Courant* and he has been a featured author at the Books on the Nightstand retreat. He is the author of two previous novels, *Something Missing* and *Unexpectedly Milo*. Dicks lives in

Newington, Connecticut, with his wife, Elysha, and their daughter, Clara. His websites are MatthewDicks.com and matthewdicks.typepad.com.

Imprint: St. Martin's Press
BEA Booth #: 3358
Printed galley at BEA: yes
Contact for printed galley: Jeanne-Marie.Hudson@stmartins.com
Print ISBN: 978-1-250-00621-9
Print price: $24.99/$28.99 Can
eBook ISBN: 978-1-250-02400-8
eBook price: $11.99/$12.99 Can
Publication date: 8/21/2012
Publicity contact: Dori Weintraub
Dori.Weintraub@stmartins.com
Rights contact:
Serial: Chris.Scheina@stmartins.com
International: Taryn Fagerness
Editor: Brenda Copeland
Agent: Taryn Fagerness
Agency: Taryn Fagerness
Promotional Information:
- National Print Publicity
- Featured Title at BEA
- National Print Advertising
- Online Advertising Campaign
- PrePub Advertising
- Advance Reader's Editions
- Indiebound Whitebox Campaign
- Blog, Email, and Social Media Campaign
- Read-it-First.com Selection
- Reading Group Guide & Promotion on ReadingGroupGold.com
- Library Marketing Campaign

WE SINNERS

a novel

HANNA PYLVÄINEN

SUMMARY

Stunning debut novel drawn from the author's own life experience tells the moving story of a family of eleven in the American Midwest, bound together and torn apart by their faith.

EXCERPT

Pox

She should have told him already about the church but she hadn't. The warnings were all there—he could name all of her siblings, and he looked at her too deliberately, and when he hugged her she was caught too long against his chest. Every morning she decided she would tell him, but every afternoon it was too tempting to go one more day, one more minute where he found a way to hold her fingers as she passed him a note. But now she knew he was going to ruin it all and ask her to the dance, she could feel it— she avoided him carefully but fussed with her hair, nearly sick with the twin terrors of him asking her or not asking her, not sure to which end she should assign her hope.

But he found her—he knew her schedule, and he found her lagging behind after class, talking to the teacher. In the hall he pushed at her shoulder with his shoulder and they seemed alone, despite the swarm of people.

"So," he said, "are you going to the dance?" She kept walking because it was a thing to do. "With me, I mean." She found this to be charming, and against her will she was flattered through and through. She looked at him. Her ears hurt with heat. She saw it was stupid to have ever pretended, even to herself, that she could go. "Well," she said, but the word caught.

"You're coming," he said.

Her smile was more mischievous than she felt.

"Please come," he said. He nearly whispered it in her ear. She looked at him. She detected sweat where his hair began to curl. It moved her, that someone like Jude could feel nervous talking to her.

"Well," she said. She thought of the many available lies—she had to babysit, the baby was sick. There was always something, there was nothing like six younger siblings for providing an excuse. But in her mind a minister warned that she should always confess her faith, and it occurred to her, Jude watching her, that confession was what it was. And she confessed. She said things about the church, her voice shaking out of time with her knee. She listed, idly, some things she couldn't do—nail polish and movies and music with a beat.

"So you can't go to a dance?" he said. "Someone's going to what? Punish you?"

"No, I mean—if you are tempted to do something, you know, maybe it's better to just not do it. So maybe there are good movies out there but I mean there are so many bad ones, so just don't watch them."

"Just don't dance, because dancing is—"

She blushed.

"Man." She saw on his face that she should not have told him.

"Sorry," she said softly. She wanted him to hold her, she wanted to sit in his big arms, like stupid girls did. She would cry. Hey, he would say, it's okay. Instead he walked away without waiting to see what she would do. She watched him go, watched him walk his easy lope.

Before her last class she thought she saw him down the hall, or maybe it was someone else, tall and heavy with dark hair. She pushed into the bathroom, where girls staggered themselves around the mirror. They put on mascara, only on their top lashes, two coats, one under, one over. "Hey," someone said, "is it true you can't even go to the movies?"

"Oh, that," Brita said. "Why?"

"Someone said."

"Oh," Brita said, "well, it's not that big of a deal." But she crept into a stall—she saw his name on the wall—and she thought about praying but it felt too vain to pray for something so small, and she didn't. She pretended to take a long time and she fished through her bag for nothing, but there was a line and she could hear the annoyance in the shuffle of feet.

She told Tiina what had happened. They were tuning their violins before orchestra. "Does everyone know?" Tiina said, a peg spinning free. "Do my friends know?" She nearly teared.

"Jeez," Brita said, "it's not that big of a deal," but she knew she was talking to herself. Still, she steeled herself, and she made it through the day, without seeing Jude again, without seeing his friends, without seeing her friends. She was almost out of the building when she heard their last name. "It's true," someone was saying, someone she didn't even know. "They're brainwashed. The whole family. They don't even have a TV."

Brita sat on the bus and pinched her thigh. She said the word to herself again and again, so it would mean less and less, and then nothing. The Rovaniemis were brainwashed. She was brainwashed. She thought about the people she thought were brainwashed, people who believed the world was ending on a specific date, people who saw aliens, people who believed meditating could make you lift off the ground. The Amish, with their claptrap horses and carts and orange reflectors to keep away motorized traffic. She felt better, thinking about people who were actually brainwashed, and she shook the word from herself, listening to the song piped through the bus, something she wasn't supposed to listen to, and she watched Tiina do her homework across the aisle, her pencil skidding across the worksheet, the answers easy and known. Tiina didn't look brainwashed—Tiina looked almost unremarkable, her hair softly brunette, to the shoulders, everything average except her eyes, hooded, heavy, hinting at Finns who had moved to America and married more Finns, and more Finns again. But otherwise she—they—looked normal, their jeans the same cut as everyone else's, only cheaper, their shirts bold and basic colors, rising to modest places, but normal. This isn't what brainwashed looks like, she told herself, and she took out her own reading.

When they got home, adding their backpacks to the pile at the door, her mother was abrasively cheerful, pinching everyone. "We found a house," her mom said. She did a jig. She said they were having pizza delivered. They never had pizza delivered.

"How many bedrooms?" Brita asked. She felt suspicious.

"Three, but, well, we can convert the basement into another. So four, maybe five."

Her mom took Tiina's hands and they jigged together.

"Four," Brita repeated. She went upstairs. She looked around the room she shared with her sisters, her dresser drawer askew again, her underwear hanging over the edge. She sat on the bottom bunk. She thought about the dance. She imagined what it was like to accidentally step on Jude Palmer's polished shoe, to smell his father's cologne in a darkened gym. Probably stupid, she decided, probably it was better she wasn't going anyway. It was okay, she was different. They were different. They were in the world, but not of the world. And now they were moving, to someplace where people didn't know yet that they were different. She thought of her new teachers, their faces when they would meet her parents at conferences. Seven kids? Laughs politely stopped when they realized it wasn't a joke.

#

The school year mercifully ended. She did not see Jude, and he did not try to see her. She took all his notes and walked them out to the re-cycling bin at the end of the driveway late at night, stuffing them care-fully between pages of newspaper. She said goodbye to her friends, pretending sadness but feeling relief, sensing already the inevitability of growing apart. Her friends would switch from one practice boy-friend to the next and fight for midnight curfews, and she would spend her Saturday nights at some church family's house, singing the same church hymns, eating cheese and crackers, always unable to get her volleyball serve over the net. She was seeing already that everyone was right, that believing friends were better, if only because you suf-fered together.

When true summer came, she threw herself into helping them move—of course her family hadn't hired a real estate agent, or movers, and they collected cardboard boxes from the dumpsters behind grocery stores. And of course in the midst of this, Julia—only five, but somber in her suffering—kept getting ear infections and needed tubes put in her ears, and their van broke down again, and again her dad would come home silent, bitter about needing to buy a new van at the same time they were trying to buy a house, snapping when no one brought their dishes to the sink. "You want me to put them away, huh, me?" he said through his teeth. Worse, their new home wouldn't be ready before they moved, and they needed somewhere to live for the inter-vening month. Instead of going to a motel, like normal people, her mom had decided they would move into her cousin's apartment since she was gone for the summer, trying to get engaged in Finland.

When they had finally packed a storage unit with cribs and bikes and bunk beds, everything in multiples, they drove out to their cousin's apartment complex, her parents quiet, a church CD on, the windows down. They piled out of the van, hauling sleeping bags and garbage bags stuffed with clothes. A woman in heavy makeup and dyed red hair was wagging her finger, trying to count them as they marched up the back stairs. "Seven," her mom said to the woman, sharply. "No divorces. No twins." Brita slung the baby on her hip, lightly.

In the apartment she stood in the living room, which was also the din-ing room, and looked around herself at the miniature stove, at the couch, which did not pull out into a bed. The confines of the room packed and amplified the heat. On the kitchen table there was a note from her cousin. Eat the food, it said. Avoid the landlord, white hair, big dog—he didn't know they were there. She missed them. Love and God's Peace—these final words in Finnish.

At night the heat did not rest. Brita put her pillowcase in the freez-er, but the relief was so temporary it was hardly worth the wait. One month, Brita thought, but when she woke she discovered she itched. She touched her face, the back of her neck. She looked at her arms. She looked around herself, at the waking kids and her mother, in the kitchen making puuroa, as if anyone wanted to eat something hot in this weather. She looked at Tiina, who was trying to ignore the baby climbing on her back and pulling at her hair. She saw the spots on the baby first, then on Tiina. She checked the little kids. "Mom," she said, "Mom, come look," and when her mom began to laugh, Brita could not.

"It's the chicken pox saga," her mom said as they ate a lunch of bologna- and- cheese sandwiches on the living room floor, because now the folding table was covered in calamine lotion and the diapers, and newspapers with ads for new vans circled in crayon. "Maybe we should get a hotel," her dad said. Her mom laughed and laughed. The little kids laughed because she was laughing. Her mouth was open and Brita could see her fillings.

#

A week of oatmeal baths passed. The little kids rotated in and out of the tub, and by the time it was Brita's turn the water was not even lukewarm, the residual oatmeal still on her feet when she stepped out, the towel damp from the other kids, the knob turning and jostling as someone tried to come in. All day she itched, but she would not scratch. She had a vision of appearing at her new school with scars, and every day she counted the number of pockmarks on her face. There was one particular mark that, in its close proximity to the somehow sexual organ of her mouth, she desperately needed to fade away. She borrowed winter gloves from her cousin's closet, so she couldn't scratch, but at night she would wake to find the gloves strewn and her scabs bleeding.

When it grew dark her parents let her and Tiina go outside. They sat on the back stairs and sniffed at the cigarette butts. "How do I look," Tiina said, posing with a stub hanging between her lips.

"Stupid," Brita said, but she thought Tiina looked cool.

"Do you miss him?"

Brita rolled her eyes.

Otherwise they never left the apartment. "I'm being held hostage," Tiina would scream from time to time, without prompting. She taped strips of paper to the windows to look like bars.

Her parents took them out a few times, to places with air conditioning—outdoor-equipment stores, the mall—but people stared. They looked like the walking plague.

"Look, Mom," a little kid said, "it's the chicken pox family."

#

At last her parents left them home alone. "Kids in charge," her mother said. They said they needed to run out for more calamine, but really they probably needed a break. Brita and Tiina went into the bedroom and began to go through her cousin's dresser. They examined a collection of sporty thongs. They searched for love letters, makeup, and finally found a single stick of concealer.

The boys banged on the door. Julia had run out of the apartment, they yelled. Brita left Tiina with the little kids and made her way outside, along the balcony. She was nervous because she had seen the landlord just that morning, out in the courtyard with a graying dog. She hurried down the back stairs to the lower balcony, hissing in Finnish, rounding the corner to find Julia talking shyly to a youngish guy with a thick scar, wide as a finger, that cut across his brow. The scar ruined his good looks, making him approachable. "Dad ran over the cat," Julia was saying. "The other week, before we moved. He was so mad he broke the garage door." Julia wasn't contagious anymore—none of them were—but she looked contagious, with her picked skin and her tired eyes, and her starkly blond hair caught by sweat to her neck.

"How many of you are there, anyway? I keep hearing all these feet." He was holding plastic grocery bags full of frozen lasagnas and frozen pizzas and frozen french fries.

"Seven," Julia said, before Brita could stop her.

"Your parents must be pretty busy," he said. He laughed to himself. He shifted the bags from one hand to the other.

"What's your name?" Julia asked.

"Steve," he said, smiling patiently.

"Hi," Brita interrupted apologetically. She took Julia's sweaty hand, talking in Finnish, reciting the Lord's Prayer because it was the only Finnish she could speak in full sentences. She tossed her hair over her shoulder and did not look back.

#

Brita looked for Steve, but she never saw him. People went outside only to walk to their cars, or to let their dogs out, and so she watched the dogs play with each other in the courtyard like children, happy to be among their own. When the landlord appeared with his army buzz cut and giant hound, the others called their dogs in, leaving the landlord's dog to nose the doorsills alone.

Things were looking up, Brita thought. She hardly ever thought about Jude. The air was cooling. By the time evening fell, half the people in the complex were out on their balconies in folding chairs, sipping iced drinks. Her mom let them take turns sitting out on the balcony. The rest sat on the couch, reading books they had already read. In the kitchen her dad made roast beef sandwiches. The baby crawled into the kitchen and her dad pointed a finger at her and crouched down and said in a pretend growl, "Who's you, who's the chunkiest chunkerton I've ever seen? It's you, champer-damper, it's you," and scooped her up. It was the same voice he had used with the cat before the cat had died. He was good, people said, with animals and children, and when Brita saw him like this she wished he would still do that with her, but she was too old now to be teased, and too young to be talked to seriously. Sometimes he said things to her about work, or even money, but not in a confiding way. "What do you think I make?" he asked once, at a store, when she said she needed socks and then appeared at the register with new packs for everyone.

Above her father's singsong came the cry of a woman outside. There was a general launch to the door, except from her parents, who looked up tiredly from the lists of vehicle sales. "What is it?" her mom said. Out the window Brita saw the landlord making his way across the grass stiffly but steadily. She saw the red-haired woman with her hand over her mouth.

"Something with a dog," Tiina said from out on the balcony. Brita looked out the door—Steve was running along the balcony toward them.

"The landlord's dog bit your little girl," he said. Her mother rose sharply.

Brita stared at the sight of him at their door. She looked at their apartment, the sleeping bags everywhere. She bet the apartment smelled of them, of too many people. She saw him notice where cereal had been sprinkled and ground into the carpet.

Julia appeared with one hand over her back, the landlord behind her like an abashed parent. "She scared him pretty bad," he said. "She just came up behind him, and he's blind in one eye, he doesn't like that. Max never bit anyone before," he said. Julia turned around and Brita saw that Julia's T-shirt was stained with small pools of blood, like spilled juice, and her mom lifted the shirt to reveal a series of puncture wounds. More people appeared at the door, the red-haired lady with her little dog, the old Chinese man who smoked on the back stairs as if he were hiding it from his wife. They all stood at the entrance to the apartment and Brita tried to think of a way to get them outside and gone and not staring, but there was nothing to be done. The ambulance had to be called and a towel had to be pressed to Julia's back and everyone had to fawn over Julia and stare around the apartment.

"She didn't even tear up," the red-haired lady said, "not one drop. Steve saw the bite."

"Brutal," Steve confirmed. He eyed Julia's bite marks warily and made noises of sympathy. Brita couldn't stop herself from toying with her hair, but soon the ambulance came and took Julia and her mom away, and the apartment emptied—she thought Steve made eye contact with her before he left—and the landlord apologized half-heartedly, stiffly, clearly at a loss as to what to do about his dog, or this gigantic family camping out in one of his own apartments.

#

The landlord came by the next weekend to apologize again. "Anything I can do, let me know," he said. He spoke slowly, each syllable costing something. "Maybe this fan," he said, pointing to the noisy tumbling above them. Her mom said the drain was slowed from the oatmeal baths, and he kneeled in their bathroom with no shirt on, jamming a plunger with surprising force. His body shook and he made noises that were awkward to hear, and he swore sometimes, and her mother pushed them away from the bathroom door.

Their neighbors sympathized with them. They told stories about Max nipping other kids, even his own granddaughter. Someone brought over cookies. Someone left a box of used markers and crayons at their door.

Brita wondered what Steve thought of them now, if he felt bad for them. She shaved her legs with her cousin's razor and used her cousin's concealer stick on her pockmarks, and she borrowed the red-haired lady's folding chair and sat on the balcony with her feet up on the railing. She made ice water and wore sunglasses and imagined the sun was tanning instead of searing her.

She had chilled her legs twice with the melting ice cubes when Steve came out, walking through the courtyard, not toward his car but toward the landlord's door, at the corner of the complex. She watched him walk, hands in his pockets. He had a more hangdog air than Jude—more guarded, she decided. He knocked, stepped back, knocked again.

"Yes?" she heard the landlord say, not quite friendly. Brita sat up in her chair and leaned against the railing to watch. Steve had a broad back, a swimmer's shoulders.

"I was just coming," Steve said, "because—I'm on the lower floor." He said something else, and then she heard, "—the baby's always crying."

Brita burned. Everything burned, her face, her ears. She tried to get up slowly, but her sweaty skin stuck to the chair and the chair clanged against the cement. She moved to the edge of the wall and tried to pull the chair quietly shut.

"Are you okay?" she heard Steve say. Brita turned back and saw Steve leaning over the fallen form of the landlord. Max was keening, licking his face with perverse exuberance. "Hey," Steve said, looking up, noticing her, "you guys have a phone, right? Can you call and get help?"

She ran inside and got her mom to call and rushed back downstairs, the little kids following. She'd gotten as close to Steve as she dared, when she saw that the landlord had, all over his face and hands, the familiar scabs of their chicken pox, only heavier, not like a childhood sickness but like a disease. Along one cheek the pox was so thick she couldn't see the space of skin in between. Other neighbors showed up. The red-haired lady leaned over the landlord and put her hand to his forehead uselessly.

"What's going on? Is he okay?" her mom said, appearing on the lawn. She chatted anxiously with Steve. Brita saw that her feet were bare, like they always were in summer, and she wished her mom would wear shoes. She saw her mother suddenly as Steve must see her, her face pleasant and round like Finnish faces could be, but devoid of makeup, giving her a harried look, especially with her hair hanging limply in the heat, curling some from an old perm. She looked, Brita realized, tired. She looked her age—she looked like someone with too many kids, someone too busy to wear anything but a black cotton dress.

"We can take him," her mom said, pointing at Max.

"Are you sure?" Steve said. "Really, it's okay."

"Julia just scared him before—it'll be fine," she said. "And it's only fair," she added, with an ironic smile. Steve shrugged and handed her the leash. "Kids, come," she said, "up," and they went, Max slow going up the flight of stairs. From inside the apartment they stood and watched the ambulance arrive, with its lonely whine and beating lights. They watched the paramedics wheel the landlord away, and then Steve make his way back to his apartment.

Julia cried and said she thought Max was going to bite her again.

"You have to get back on the horse," her mom said firmly.

"When I was little, I was maybe Brita's age, I fell off Big Red and he bit my arm, and even while my arm was bleeding my dad put me back on the horse." Tiina and Brita looked at each other and rolled their eyes. She always told this story.

Max roamed unhappily around the apartment. They put out a bowl of water for him, but he wouldn't touch it. "No one try to pet him," her mom said. She kept the baby strapped into the car seat on the counter. The baby cried and Brita tried to amuse her by hanging things in front of her face, keys, measuring spoons, her hair, but she was too old for that now. Finally Brita lifted her and walked her around the apartment, trying not to think of Steve and what he had said about them, trying to keep the baby from crying.

Her dad came back from looking at vans. "No seat belts in the back bench," he said, sighing. He saw the dog. "Why do we have this?" he asked.

"The landlord has the chicken pox," Brita told him, "from us."

"From who?" he said, as if he hadn't heard. Her mom made them clean. Brita was sure this was because she was worried someone would come to pick up the dog, and she wanted the place to seem neat. Brita wiped the counter and rolled up the sleeping bags. Tiina found the vacuum cleaner and went at the carpet. The little kids threw all the toys in a cardboard box and tried to stack the books but they kept falling, and they gave up.

But no one came. Finally they unrolled the sleeping bags and turned out the lights. Her dad put Max in the bathroom with a towel on the floor and a bowl of cut-up hot dogs from the fridge. For a few minutes Max whimpered, and then he was quiet.

All the next day no one came. No one called. All day Brita stayed inside. She did not want to see Steve. She did not want to think of Steve. She hated that she had gone so quickly from trying to not think about Jude to trying to not think about Steve. The little kids held races around the balcony and she yelled at them to run more quietly.

"Nels is cheating," Simon whined. "He keeps pulling my shirt."

"Cheat more quietly," Brita said.

Her mom sent Brita down to try the landlord's door and Brita moved hurriedly, in case of Steve, but she didn't see him, or his car in the parking lot. She knocked hard, trying to peek through the plastic slats of curtains, but the apartment was dark and silent.

Her mom called the hospital, but they wouldn't put her through. "Can you put his family on?" she said, tense, annoyed.

His family wasn't there, the nurse said.

The little kids crabbed and her mom snapped and yelled at them and then broke down, crying. Her dad came home and saw her crying and yelled, and the little kids ran into the bathroom to hide from him.

"Let's just leave," her mom said, her face and voice taut with tears.

"You think I want to be here?" her dad said. "You think I think this is fun?" he yelled, and then he turned around and left, and they all went quiet but he wasn't there to hear it. They all made their own sandwiches and poured their own milk and sat and read quietly, and the boys didn't even fight about wanting to read the same comic, and they spread it out on the floor and dripped jelly onto its pages together. They were in this tableau, the mood mild, almost serene, when her dad came in, carrying milk shakes and fries, cheerful as a form of penitence. "Serve it up," her mom sang, "nice and hot, maybe things aren't as bad as you thought." Fries fell to the floor and Max sniffed them but didn't eat them.

One more week, Brita thought, one more week.

Twitter: Want to discuss or share what you just read? Use the hashtag #beaSINNERS to connect with others.

ABOUT THE AUTHOR

Hanna Pylväinen graduated from Mount Holyoke College and received her MFA from the University of Michigan, where she was also a postgraduate Zell Fellow. She is the recipient of a MacDowell Colony residency and a fellowship at the Fine Arts Work Center in Provincetown, Massachusetts. She is from suburban Detroit.

Imprint: Henry Holt
BEA Booth #: 3358
Author Appearance: Galley Giveaway Wednesday June 6th, 9am
Printed galley at BEA: yes
Contact to request printed galley: Christine.Choe@hholt.com
Print ISBN: 9780805095333
Print price: $23.00
eBook ISBN: 9780805095340
eBook price: $10.99
Publication date: 8/21/2012

Publicity contact: Patricia Eisemann Patricia.Eisemann@hholt.com
Rights contact(s): Devon Mazzone Devon.Mazzone@fsgbooks.com
Editor: Gillian Blake
Agent: Amy Williams
Agency: McCormick & Williams
Promotional Information:
- Author Tour
- First serial *Harper's Magazine*
- BEA Galley Giveaway

The

LIGHT

—

BETWEEN

—

OCEANS

a novel

M. L. STEDMAN

SUMMARY

After four harrowing years on the Western Front, Tom Sherbourne returns to Australia and takes a job as the lighthouse keeper on Janus Rock, nearly half a day's journey from the Western coast. To this isolated island, where the supply boat comes once a season and shore leaves are granted every other year at best, Tom brings a young, bold and loving wife, Isabel. Years later, after two miscarriages and one still birth, the grieving Isabel hears a baby's cries on the wind. A boat has washed up on shore carrying a dead man and a living baby. Tom, whose records as a lighthouse keeper are meticulous and whose moral principles have withstood a horrific war, wants to report the man and infant immediately. But Isabel has taken the tiny baby to her breast. Against Tom's judgment, they claim her as their own and name her Lucy. When she is two, Tom and Isabel return to the mainland and are reminded that there are other people in the world. Their choice has devastated one of them. M. L. Stedman's mesmerizing, beautifully-written novel seduces us into accommodating Isabel's decision to keep this "gift from God." And we are swept into a story about extraordinarily compelling characters seeking to find their north star in a world where there is no right answer.

"An extraordinary and heart-rending book about good people, tragic decisions and the beauty found in each of them."

—Markus Zusak, author of *The Book Thief*

EXCERPT

27th April 1926

On the day of the miracle, Isabel was kneeling at the cliff's edge, tending the small, newly made driftwood cross. A single fat cloud snailed across the late-April sky, which stretched above the island in a mirror of the ocean below. Isabel sprinkled more water and patted down the soil around the rosemary bush she had just planted.

". . . and lead us not into temptation, but deliver us from evil," she whispered.

For just a moment, her mind tricked her into hearing an infant's cry. She dismissed the illusion, her eye drawn instead by a pod of whales weaving their way up the coast to calve in the warmer waters, emerging now and again with a fluke of their tails like needles through tapestry. She heard the cry again, louder this time on the early-morning breeze. Impossible.

From this side of the island, there was only vastness, all the way to Africa. Here, the Indian Ocean washed into the Great Southern Ocean and together they stretched like an edgeless carpet below the cliffs. On days like this it seemed so solid she had the impression she could walk to Madagascar in a journey of blue upon blue. The other side of the island looked back, fretful, toward the Australian mainland nearly a hundred miles away, not quite belonging to the land, yet not quite free of it, the highest of a string of under-sea mountains that rose from the ocean floor like teeth along a jagged jaw bone, waiting to devour any innocent ships in their final dash for harbor.

As if to make amends, the island – Janus Rock – offered a lighthouse, its beam providing a mantle of safety for thirty miles. Each night the air sang with the steady hum of the lantern as it turned, turned, turned; even-handed, not blaming the rocks, not fearing the waves: there for salvation if wanted.

The crying persisted. The door of the lighthouse clanged in the distance, and Tom's tall frame appeared on the gallery as he scanned the island with binoculars. "Izzy," he yelled, "a boat!" and pointed to the cove. "On the beach – a boat!"

He vanished and re-emerged a moment later at ground level. "Looks like there's someone in it," he shouted. Isabel hurried as best she could to meet him, and he held her arm as they navigated the steep, well-worn path to the little beach.

"It's a boat all right," Tom declared. "And – oh cripes! There's a bloke, but—"

The figure was motionless, flopped over the seat, yet the cries still rang out. Tom rushed to the dinghy, and tried to rouse the man before searching the space in the bow from where the sound came. He hoisted out a woolen bundle: a woman's soft lavender cardigan wrapped around a tiny, screaming infant.

"Bloody hell!" he exclaimed. "Bloody hell, Izzy. It's—"

"A baby! Oh my Lord above! Oh Tom! Tom! Here – give it to me!"

He handed her the bundle, and tried again to revive the stranger: no pulse. He turned to Isabel, who was examining the diminutive creature. "He's gone, Izz. The baby?"

"It's all right, by the looks. No cuts or bruises. It's so tiny!" she said, then, turning to the child as she cuddled it, "There, there. You're safe now, little one. You're safe, you beautiful thing."

Tom stood still, considering the man's body, clenching his eyes tight shut and opening them again to check he wasn't dreaming. The baby had stopped crying and was taking gulps of breath in Isabel's arms.

"Can't see any marks on the fellow, and he doesn't look diseased. He can't have been adrift long . . . You wouldn't credit it," He paused. "You take the baby up to the house, Izz, and I'll get something to cover the body."

"But, Tom—"

"It'll be a hell of a job to get him up the path. Better leave him here until help comes. Don't want the birds or the flies getting at him though – there's some canvas up in the shed should do." He spoke calmly enough, but his hands and face felt cold, as old shadows blotted out the bright autumn sunshine.

*

Janus Rock was a square mile of green, with enough grass to feed the few sheep and goats and the handful of chickens, and enough topsoil to sustain the rudimentary vegetable patch. The only trees were two towering Norfolk Pines planted by the crews from Point Partageuse who had built the light station over thirty years before, in 1889. A cluster of old graves remembered a shipwreck long before that, when the *Pride of Birmingham* foundered on the greedy rocks in daylight. In such a ship the light itself had later been brought from England, proudly bearing the name Chance Brothers, a guarantee of the most advanced technology of its day, capable of assembly anywhere, no matter how inhospitable or hard to reach.

The currents hauled in all manner of things; flotsam and jetsam swirled as if between twin propellers: bits of wreckage, tea chests, whalebones. Things turned up in their own time, in their own way. The light station sat solidly in the middle of the island, the keeper's cottage and outbuildings hunkered down beside the lighthouse, cowed from decades of lashing winds.

In the kitchen, Isabel sat at the old table, the baby in her arms, wrapped in a downy yellow blanket. Tom scraped his boots slowly on the mat as he entered, and rested a callused hand on her shoulder. "I've covered the poor soul. How's the little one?"

"It's a girl," said Isabel with a smile. "I gave her a bath. She seems healthy enough."

The baby turned to him with wide eyes, drinking in his glance. "What on earth must she make of it all?" he wondered aloud.

"Given her some milk too, haven't I, sweet thing?" Isabel cooed, turning it into a question for the baby. "Oh, she's so, so perfect, Tom," she said, and kissed the child. "Lord knows what she's been through."

Tom took a bottle of brandy from the pine cupboard and poured himself a small measure, downing it in one. He sat beside his wife, watching the light play on her face as she contemplated the treasure in her arms. The baby followed every movement of her eyes, as though Isabel might escape if she did not hold her with her gaze.

"Oh, little one," Isabel crooned, "poor, poor little one," as the baby nuzzled her face in toward her breast. Tom could hear tears in her voice, and the memory of an invisible presence hung in the air between them.

"She likes you," he said. Then, almost to himself, "Makes me think of how things might have been." He added quickly, "I mean . . . I didn't mean . . . You look like you were born to it, that's all." He stroked her cheek.

Isabel glanced up at him. "I know, love. I know what you mean. I feel the same."

He put his arms around his wife and the child. Isabel could smell the brandy on his breath. She murmured, "Oh Tom, thank God we found her in time."

Tom kissed her, then put his lips to the baby's forehead. The three of them stayed like that for a long moment, until the child began to wriggle, thrusting a fist out from under the blanket.

"Well," Tom gave a stretch as he stood up, "I'll go and send a signal, report the dinghy; get them to send a boat for the body. And for Miss Muffet here."

"Not yet!" Isabel said, as she touched the baby's fingers. "I mean, there's no rush to do it right this minute. The poor man's not going to get any worse now. And this little chicken's had quite enough of boats for the moment, I'd say. Leave it a while. Give her a chance to catch her breath."

"It'll take hours for them to get here. She'll be all right. You've already quietened her down, poor little thing."

"Let's just wait. After all, it can't make much difference."

"It's all got to go in the log, pet. You know I've got to report everything straightaway," Tom said, for his duties included noting every significant event at or near the light station, from passing ships and weather, to problems with the apparatus.

"Do it in the morning, eh?"

"But what if the boat's from a ship?"

"It's a dinghy, not a lifeboat," she said.

"Then the baby's probably got a mother waiting for it somewhere on shore, tearing her hair out. How would you feel if it was yours?"

"You saw the cardigan. The mother must have fallen out of the boat and drowned."

"Sweetheart, we don't have any idea about the mother. Or about who the man was."

"It's the most likely explanation, isn't it? Infants don't just wander off from their parents."

"Izzy, anything's possible. We just don't know."

"When did you ever hear of a tiny baby setting off in a boat without its mother?" She held the child a fraction closer.

"This is serious. The man's dead, Izz."

"And the baby's alive. Have a heart, Tom."

Something in her tone struck him, and instead of simply contradicting her, he paused and considered her plea. Perhaps she needed a bit of time with a baby. Perhaps he owed her that. There was a silence, and Isabel turned to him in wordless appeal. "I suppose, at a pinch . . ." he conceded, the words coming with great difficulty, "I could – leave the signal until the morning. First thing, though. As soon as the light's out."

Isabel kissed him, and squeezed his arm.

"Better get back to the lantern room. I was in the middle of replacing the vapor tube," he said.

As he walked down the path, he heard the sweet notes of Isabel's voice as she sang, "Blow the wind southerly, southerly, southerly, blow the wind south o'er the bonnie blue sea." Though the music was tuneful, it failed to comfort him as he climbed the stairs of the light, fending off a strange uneasiness at the concession he had made.

CHAPTER 1

16th December 1918

"Yes, I realize that," Tom Sherbourne said. He was sitting in a spartan room, barely cooler than the sultry day outside. The Sydney summer rain pelted the window, and sent the people on the pavement scurrying for shelter.

"I mean very tough." The man across the desk leaned forward for emphasis. "It's no picnic. Not that Byron Bay's the worst posting on the Lights, but I want to make sure you know what you're in for." He tamped down the tobacco with his thumb and lit his pipe. Tom's letter of application had told the same story as many a fellow's around that time: born 28 September 1893; war spent in the Army; experience with the International Code and Morse; physically fit and well; honorable discharge. The rules stipulated that preference should be given to ex-servicemen.

"It can't—" Tom stopped, and began again. "All due respect, Mr. Coughlan, it's not likely to be tougher than the Western Front."

The man looked again at the details on the discharge papers, then at Tom, searching for something in his eyes, in his face. "No, son. You're probably right on that score." He rattled off some rules: "You pay your own passage to every posting. You're relief, so you don't get holidays. Permanent staff get a month's leave at the end of each three-year contract." He took up his fat pen and signed the form in front of him. As he rolled the stamp back and forth across the inkpad he said, "Welcome"—he thumped it down in three places on the paper—"to the Commonwealth Lighthouse Service." On the form, "16th December 1918" glistened in wet ink.

*

The six months' relief posting at Byron Bay, up on the New South Wales coast, with two other keepers and their families, taught Tom the basics of life on the Lights. He followed that with a stint down on Maatsuyker, the wild island south of Tasmania where it rained most days of the year and the chickens blew into the sea during storms.

On the Lights, Tom Sherbourne has plenty of time to think about the war. About the faces, the voices of the blokes who had stood beside him, who saved his life one way or another; the ones whose dying words he heard, and those whose muttered jumbles he couldn't make out, but who he nodded to anyway.

Tom isn't one of the men whose legs trailed by a hank of sinews, or whose guts cascaded from their casing like slithering eels. Nor were his lungs turned to glue or his brains to stodge by the gas. But he's scarred all the same, having to live in the same skin as the man who did the things that needed to be done back then. He carries that other shadow, which is cast inward.

He tries not to dwell on it: he's seen plenty of men turned worse than useless that way. So he gets on with life around the edges of this thing he's got no name for. When he dreams about those years, the Tom who is experiencing them, the Tom who is there with blood on his hands, is a boy of eight or so. It's this small boy who's up against blokes with guns and bayonets, and he's worried because his school socks have slipped down and he can't hitch them up because he'll have to drop his gun to do it, and he's barely big enough even to hold that. And he can't find his mother anywhere.

Then he wakes and he's in a place where there's just wind and waves and light, and the intricate machinery that keeps the flame burning and the lantern turning. Always turning, always looking over its shoulder.

If he can only get far enough away – from people, from memory – time will do its job.

*

Thousands of miles away on the west coast, Janus Rock was the furthest place on the continent from Tom's childhood home in Sydney. But Janus Light was the last sign of Australia he had seen as his troopship steamed for Egypt in 1915. The smell of the eucalyptus had wafted for miles offshore from Albany, and when the scent faded away he was suddenly sick at the loss of something he didn't know he could miss. Then, hours later, true and steady, the light, with its five-second flash, came into view – his homeland's furthest reach – and its memory stayed with him through the years of hell that followed, like a farewell kiss. When, in June 1920, he got news of an urgent vacancy going on Janus, it was as though the light there were calling to him.

Teetering on the edge of the continental shelf, Janus was not a popular posting. Though its Grade One hardship rating meant a slightly higher salary, the old hands said it wasn't worth the money, which was meager all the same. The keeper Tom replaced on Janus was Trimble Docherty, who had caused a stir by reporting that his wife was signaling to passing ships by stringing up messages in the colored flags of the International Code. This was unsatisfactory to the authorities for two reasons: first, because the Deputy Director of Lighthouses had some years previously forbidden signaling by flags on Janus, as vessels put themselves at risk by sailing close enough to decipher them; and secondly, because the wife in question was recently deceased.

Considerable correspondence on the subject was generated in triplicate between Fremantle and Melbourne, with the Deputy Director in Fremantle putting the case for Docherty and his years of excellent service, to a Head Office concerned strictly with efficiency and cost and obeying the rules. A compromise was reached by which a temporary keeper would be engaged while Docherty was given six months' medical leave.

"We wouldn't normally send a single man to Janus – it's pretty remote and a wife and family can be a great practical help, not just a comfort," the District Officer had said to Tom. "But seeing it's only temporary . . . You'll leave for Partageuse in two days," he said, and signed him up for six months.

There wasn't much to organize. No one to farewell. Two days later, Tom walked up the gangplank of the boat, armed with a kitbag and not much else. The SS *Prometheus* worked its way along the southern shores of Australia, stopping at various ports on its run between Sydney and Perth. The few cabins reserved for first-class passengers were on the upper deck, toward the bow. In third class, Tom shared a cabin with an elderly sailor. "Been making this trip for fifty years – they wouldn't have the cheek to ask me to pay. Bad luck, you know," the man had said cheerfully, then returned his attention to the large bottle of over-proof rum that kept him occupied. To escape the alcohol fumes, Tom took to walking the deck during the day. Of an evening there'd usually be a card game belowdecks.

You could still tell at a glance who'd been over there and who'd sat the war out at home. You could smell it on a man. Each tended to keep to his own kind. Being in the bowels of the vessel brought back memories of the troop ships that took them first to the Middle East, and later to France. Within moments of arriving on board, they'd deduced, almost by an animal sense, who was an officer, who was lower ranks; where they'd been.

Just like on the troop ships, the focus was on finding a bit of sport to liven up the journey. The game settled on was familiar enough: first one to score a souvenir off a first-class passenger was the winner. Not just any souvenir, though. The designated article was a pair of ladies' drawers. "Prize money's doubled if she's wearing them at the time."

The ringleader, a man by the name of McGowan, with a mustache, and fingers yellowed from his Woodbines, said he'd been chatting to one of the stewards about the passenger list: the choice was limited. There were ten cabins in all. A lawyer and his wife – best give them a wide berth; some elderly couples, a pair of old spinsters (promising), but best of all, some toff's daughter traveling on her own.

"I reckon we can climb up the side and in through her window," he announced. "Who's with me?"

The danger of the enterprise didn't surprise Tom. He'd heard dozens of such tales since he got back. Men who'd taken to risking their lives on a whim – treating the boom gates at level crossings as a gallop jump; swimming into rips to see if they could get out. So many men who had dodged death over there now seemed addicted to its lure. Still, this lot were free agents now. Probably just full of talk.

The following night, when the nightmares were worse than usual, Tom decided to escape them by walking the decks. It was two a.m. He was free to wander wherever he wanted at that hour, so he paced methodically, watching the moonlight leave its wake on the water. He climbed to the upper deck, gripping the stair rail to counter the gentle rolling, and stood a moment at the top, taking in the freshness of the breeze and the steadiness of the stars that showered the night.

Out of the corner of his eye, he saw a glimmer come on in one of the cabins. Even first-class passengers had trouble sleeping sometimes, he mused. Then, some sixth sense awoke in him – that familiar, indefinable instinct for trouble. He moved silently toward the cabin, and looked in through the window.

In the dim light, he saw a woman flat against the wall, pinned there even though the man before her wasn't touching her. He was an inch away from her face, with a leer Tom had seen too often. He recognized the man from belowdecks, and remembered the prize. Bloody idiots. He tried the door, and it opened.

"Leave her alone," he said as he stepped into the cabin. He spoke calmly, but left no room for debate.

The man spun around to see who it was, and grinned when he recognized Tom. "Christ! Thought you were a steward! You can give me a hand, I was just—"

"I said leave her alone! Clear out. Now."

"But I haven't finished. I was just going to make her day." He reeked of drink and stale tobacco.

Tom put a hand on his shoulder, with a grip so hard that the man cried out. He was a good six inches shorter than Tom, but tried to take a swing at him all the same. Tom seized his wrist and twisted it. "Name and rank!"

"McKenzie. Private. 3277." The unrequested serial number followed like a reflex.

"Private, you'll apologize to this young lady and you'll get back to your bunk and you won't show your face on deck until we berth, you understand me?"

"Yes, sir!" He turned to the woman. "Beg your pardon, Miss. Didn't mean any harm."

Still terrified, the woman gave the slightest nod.

"Now, out!" Tom said, and the man, deflated by sudden sobriety, shuffled from the cabin.

"You all right?" Tom asked the woman.

"I – I think so."

"Did he hurt you?"

"He didn't . . ." – she was saying it to herself as much as to him – "he didn't actually touch me."

He took in the woman's face – her gray eyes seemed calmer now. Her dark hair was loose, in waves down to her arms, and her fists still gathered her nightgown to her neck. Tom reached for her dressing gown from a hook on the wall and draped it over her shoulders.

"Thank you," she said.

"Must have got an awful fright. I'm afraid some of us aren't used to civilized company these days."

She didn't speak.

"You won't get any more trouble from him." He righted a chair that had been overturned in the encounter. "Up to you whether you report him, Miss. I'd say he's not the full quid now."

Her eyes asked a question.

"Being over there changes a man. Right and wrong don't look so different any more to some." He turned to go, but put his head back through the doorway. "You've got every right to have him up on charges if you want. But I reckon he's probably got enough troubles. Like I said. Up to you," and he disappeared through the door.

Twitter: Want to discuss or share what you just read? Use the hashtag #beaOCEANS to connect with others.

ABOUT THE AUTHOR

M.L. Stedman was born and raised in Western Australia, and now lives in London. *The Light Between Oceans* is her first novel.

Imprint: Scribner
BEA Booth #: 3657
Printed galley at BEA: Yes
Contact for printed galley: Katie Monaghan (media requests), Wendy Sheanin (bookseller requests)
Print ISBN: 9781451681734
Print price: $25.00
eBook ISBN: 9781451681765
eBook price: $11.99
Publication date: 7/31/2012
Publicity contact: Katie Monaghan katherine.monaghan@simonandschuster.com
Rights contact: Paul O'Halloran paul.ohalloran@simonandschuster.com
Editor: Nan Graham
Agent: Susan Armstrong
Agency: Conville & Walsh
Territories sold:
    UK: Transworld
    US: Scribner/Simon & Schuster
    Canada: Scribner/Simon & Schuster
    Australia: Random House of Australia
    Brazil: Rocco
    China: under offer
    Czech Republic: Albatros Media
    Denmark: Forlaget Turbulenz
    Finland: Karisto
    France: Editions Stock
    Germany: Blanvalet
    Greece: Patakis
    Israel: Keter
    Italy: Garzanti Libri
    Korea: Munhakdongne
    Netherlands: De Boekerij
    Norway: Schibsted Forlag
    Poland: Albatros
    Portugal: Presenca
    Russia: AST
    Serbia: Laguna
    Slovakia: Ikar
    Spain: Salamandra
    Spain/Catalan: Edicions 62 (Grup62)

Taiwan: Crown
Turkey: Pegasus
Promotional Information:
- National author tour
- National print advertising in *The New Yorker*
- National radio advertising-NPR
- National print and radio publicity campaign
- Author video online
- Reading group guide online
- SimonandSchuster.com features

BOOKSELLER BLURBS:

"Brilliant storytelling. Profound, shockingly sure-footed for a debut writer. The world does stop as you are swept into Tom and Izzy's world. It is truly one of the most exquisite novels I have ever read. I cannot wait to share this gift with our readers. What a thrill."
—Roxanne Coady, RJ Julia Booksellers, Madison, CT

"Page-turner; characters you love; characters that perplex you; phenomenal story imagination; an ending you didn't expect; different from anything you've read; M.L. Stedman's *The Light Between Oceans* has all that and so much more. This is a magnificent read!
—Jake Reiss, The Alabama Booksmith Birmingham, AL

"You know when the plane is dark and you are reading with your light on, one of few, and you start crying and really would like to hide that fact but you can't turn off the light because you really really want to finish this book? I am still thinking about this book and asking what was the right thing to do?"
—Annie Philbrick, Bank Square Books, Mystic, CT

"Loved it!!!!! I was pulled into the story from the start and got emotionally involved with the characters. I had tears running down my face as I read the last few chapters. Stedman is an incredible writer."
—Susan Barthold, Barnes & Noble, Jenkintown, PA

"This is a tender and touching love story. Told with beauty and longing, *The Light Between Oceans* left me deeply moved."
—Sheryl Cotleur, Book Passage, Corte Madera, CA

"This book is just stunning. I thought I knew what was going to happen but I didn't. I loved that it was a love story and then it wasn't and then it was. I loved the scenes on the island. I loved that it was a moral story. So far this year it's number one and a very, very hard act to follow."
—Sue Boucher, Lake Forest Book Store, Lake Forest, IL

"I loved the book. An ENTHRALLING tale - Stedman has a magical way with words. She writes like a painter, creating a picture that lingers well after you've moved on to the next page."
—Liz Murphy, The Learned Owl Book Shop, Hudson, OH

"I love the way the story unfolds without giving you a glimpse of where it's going. The author manages to have you empathize with all the various people whose lives are interconnected through Lucy-Grace, even though they want diametrically opposite outcomes."
—Nicola Rooney, Nicola's Books, Ann Arbor, MI

"Stolen baby or adopted child? So much depends on perspective in this riptide of a novel that sweeps characters and readers alike into cross-currents of sympathy and sorrow. Stedman is an outrageously good story teller."
—Emily Crowe, The Odyssey Bookshop, South Hadley, MA

"What a read, hard to believe this is a first time author, such grace, such striking images."
—Jane Dawson, Porter Square Books, Cambridge, MA

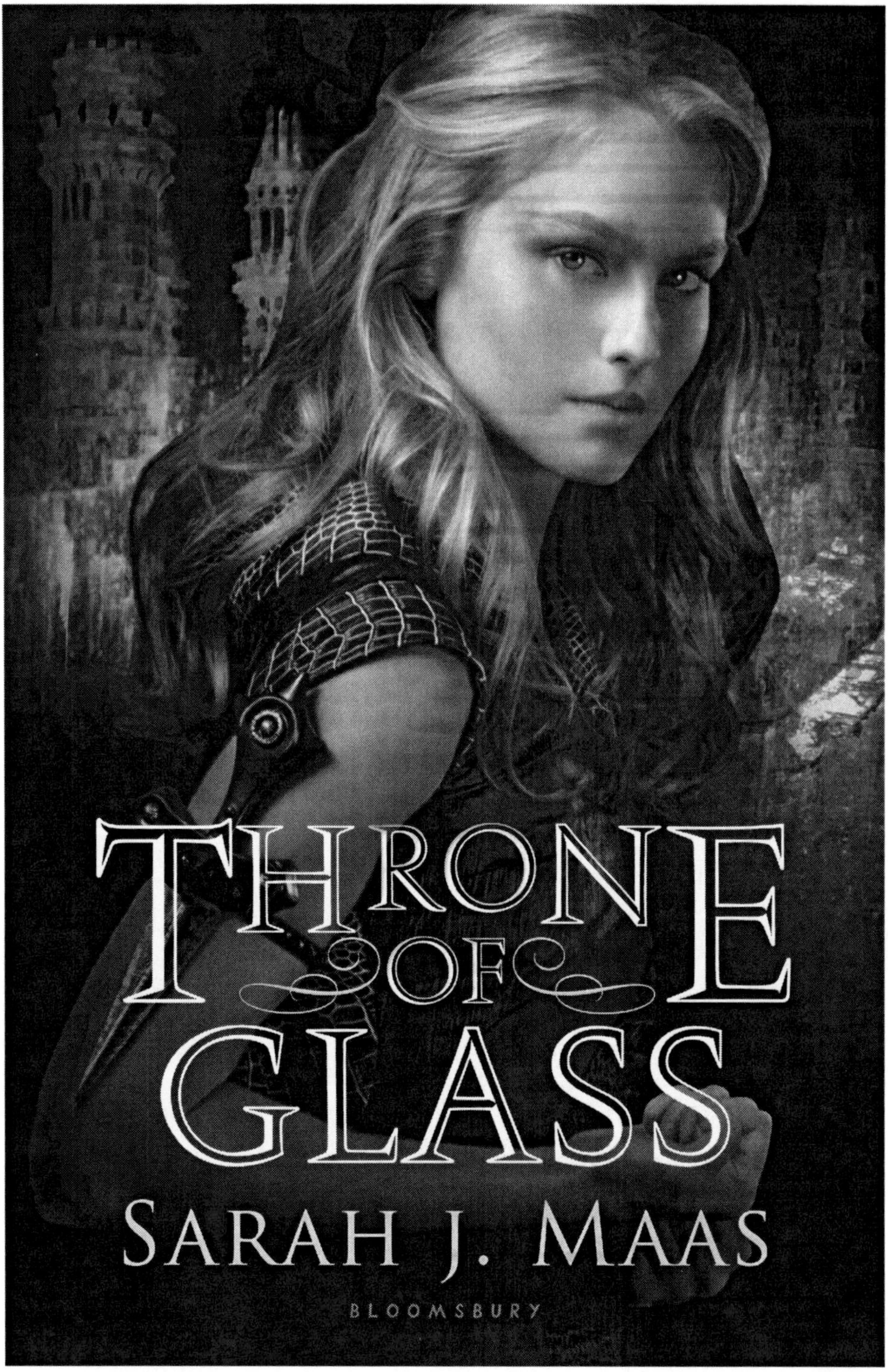
THRONE
OF
GLASS
SARAH J. MAAS
BLOOMSBURY

SUMMARY

In a land without magic, an assassin has been summoned. Her name is Celaena Sardothien. Celaena comes not to kill the king but to win her freedom. If she defeats twenty-three killers, thieves, and warriors in a competition, she is released from prison to serve as the king's champion. But when her competitors start dying one by one, Celaena's fight for freedom becomes a fight for survival, and a desperate quest to root out the evil before it destroys her world.

EXCERPT

Chapter 1

After a year of slavery in the Salt Mines of Endovier, Celaena Sardothien was accustomed to being escorted everywhere in shackles and at sword-point. Most of the thousands of slaves in Endovier received similar treatment—though an extra half-dozen guards always walked Celaena to and from the mines. That was expected by Adarlan's most notorious assassin. What she did not usually expect, however, was a hooded man in black at her side—as there was now.

He gripped her arm as he led her through the shining building in which most of Endovier's officials and overseers were housed. They strode down corridors, up flights of stairs, and around and around until she hadn't the slightest chance of finding her way out again.

At least, that was her escort's intention, because she hadn't failed to notice when they went up and down the same staircase within a matter of minutes. Nor had she missed when they zigzagged between levels, even though the building was a standard grid of hallways and stairwells. As if she'd lose her bearings that easily. She might have been insulted, if he wasn't trying so hard.

They entered a particularly long hallway, silent save for their footsteps. Though the man grasping her arm was tall and fit, she could see nothing of the features concealed beneath his hood. Another tactic meant to confuse and intimidate her. The black clothes were probably a part of it, too. His head shifted in her direction, and Celaena flashed him a grin. He looked forward again, his iron grip tightening.

It was flattering, she supposed, even if she didn't know what was happening, or why he'd been waiting for her outside of the mine shaft. After a day of cleaving rock salt from the innards of the mountain, finding him standing there with six guards hadn't improved her mood.

But her ears had pricked when he'd introduced himself to her overseer as Chaol Westfall, Captain of the Royal Guard, and suddenly, the sky loomed, the mountains pushed from behind, and even the earth swelled toward her knees. She hadn't tasted fear in a while—hadn't let herself taste fear. When she awoke every morning, she repeated the same words: I will not be afraid. For a year, those words had meant the difference between breaking and bending; they had kept her from shattering in the darkness of the mines. Not that she'd let the captain know any of that.

Celaena examined the gloved hand holding her arm. The dark leather almost matched the dirt on her skin.

She adjusted her torn and filthy tunic with her free hand and held in her sigh. Entering the mines before sunrise and departing after dusk, she rarely glimpsed the sun. She was frightfully pale beneath the dirt. It was true that she had been attractive once, beautiful even, but—Well, it didn't matter now, did it?

They turned down another hallway, and she studied the stranger's finely-crafted sword. Its shimmering pommel was shaped like an eagle mid-flight. Noticing her stare, his gloved hand descended to rest upon its golden head. Another smile tugged on the corners of her lips.

"You're a long way from Rifthold, Captain," she said, clearing her throat. "Did you come with the army I heard thumping around earlier?" She peered into the darkness beneath his hood, but saw nothing. Still, she felt his eyes upon her face, judging, weighing, testing. She stared right back. The Captain of the Royal Guard would be an interesting opponent. Maybe even worthy of some effort on her part.

Finally, the man raised his sword-hand, and the folds of his cloak fell to conceal the blade. As his cloak shifted, she spied the gold wyvern embroidered on his tunic. The royal seal.

"What do you care for the armies of Adarlan?" he replied. How lovely it was to hear a voice like her own—cool and articulate—even if he was a nasty brute!

"Nothing," she said, shrugging. He let out a low growl of annoyance.

Oh, it'd be nice to see his blood spill across the marble. She'd lost her temper once before—once, when her first overseer chose the wrong day to push her too hard. She still remembered the feeling of embedding the pickaxe into his gut, and the stickiness of his blood on her hands and face. She could disarm two of these guards in a heartbeat. Would the captain fare better than her late overseer? Contemplating the potential outcomes, she grinned at him again.

"Don't you look at me like that," he warned, and his hand drifted back toward his sword. Celaena hid her smirk this time. They passed a series of wooden doors that she'd seen a few minutes ago. If she wanted to escape, she simply had to turn left at the next hallway and take the stairs down three flights. The only thing all the intended disorientation had accomplished was to familiarize her with the building. Idiots.

"Where are we going again?" she said sweetly, brushing a strand of her matted hair from her face. When he didn't reply, she clenched her jaw.

The halls echoed too loudly for her to attack him without alerting the whole building. She hadn't seen where he'd put the key to her irons, and the six guards that trailed them would be nuisances. Not to mention the shackles.

They entered a hallway hung with iron chandeliers. Outside the windows lining the wall, night had fallen and lanterns kindled, so bright they offered few shadows to hide in.

From the courtyard, she could hear the other slaves shuffling toward the wooden building where they slept. The moans of agony amongst the clank of chains made a chorus as familiar as the dreary work songs they sang all day. The occasional solo of the whip added to the symphony of brutality Adarlan had created for its greatest criminals, poorest citizens, and latest conquests.

While some of the prisoners were people accused of attempting to practice magic—not that they could, given that magic had vanished from the kingdom—these days, more and more rebels arrived at Endovier. Most were from Eyllwe, one of the last countries still fighting Adarlan's rule. But when she pestered them for news, many just stared at her with empty eyes. Already broken. She shuddered to consider what they'd endured at the hands of Adarlan's forces. Some days, she wondered if they would have been better off dying on the butchering blocks instead. And if she might have been better off dying that night she'd been betrayed and captured, too.

But she had other things to think about as they continued their walk. Was she finally to be hanged? Sickness coiled in her stomach. She was important enough to warrant an execution from the Captain of the Royal Guard himself. But why bring her inside this building first?

At last, they stopped before a set of red and gold glass doors so thick that she couldn't see through them. Captain Westfall jerked his chin at the two guards standing on either side of the doors, and they stomped their spears in greeting.

The captain's grip tightened until it hurt. He yanked Celaena closer, but her feet seemed made of lead and she pulled against him. "You'd rather stay in the mines?" he asked, sounding faintly amused.

"Perhaps if I were told what this was all about, I wouldn't feel so inclined to resist."

"You'll find out soon enough." Her palms became sweaty. Yes, she was going to die. It had come at last.

The doors groaned open to reveal a throne-room. A glass chandelier shaped like a grapevine occupied most of the ceiling, spitting seeds of diamond fire onto the windows along the far side of the room. Compared to the bleakness outside of those windows, the opulence felt like a slap to the face. A reminder of just how much they profited from her labor.

"In here," the Captain of the Guard growled, and shoved her with his free hand, finally releasing her. Celaena stumbled, her callused feet slipping on the smooth floor as she straightened herself. She looked back to see another six guards appear.

Fourteen guards, plus the captain. The gold royal emblem embroidered on the breast of black uniforms. These were members of the Royal Family's personal guard: ruthless, lightning-swift soldiers trained from birth to protect and kill. She swallowed tightly.

Lightheaded and immensely heavy all at once, Celaena faced the room. On an ornate redwood throne sat a handsome young man. Her heart stopped as everyone bowed.

She was standing in front of the Crown Prince of Adarlan.

Chapter 2

"Your Highness," said the Captain of the Guard. He straightened from a low bow and removed his hood, revealing close-cropped chestnut hair. The hood had definitely been meant to intimidate her into submission during their walk. As if that sort of trick could work on her. Despite her irritation, she blinked at the sight of his face. He was so young!

Captain Westfall was not excessively handsome, but she couldn't help finding the ruggedness of his face and the clarity of his golden brown eyes rather appealing. She cocked her head, now keenly aware of her wretched dirtiness.

"This is she?" the Crown Prince of Adarlan asked, and Celaena's head whipped around as the captain nodded. Both of them stared at her, waiting for her to bow. When she remained upright, Chaol shifted on his feet, and the prince glanced at his captain before lifting his chin a bit higher.

Bow to him indeed! If she were bound for the gallows, she would most certainly not spend the last moments of her life in groveling submission.

Thundering steps issued from behind her, and someone grabbed her by the neck. Celaena only glimpsed crimson cheeks and a sandy mustache before being thrown to the icy marble floor. Pain slammed through her face, light splintering her vision. Her arms ached as her bound hands kept her joints from properly aligning. Though she tried to stop them, tears of pain welled.

"That is the proper way to greet your future king," a red-faced man snapped at Celaena.

The assassin hissed, baring her teeth as she twisted her head to look at the kneeling brute. He was almost as large as her overseer, clothed in reds and oranges that matched his thinning hair. His obsidian eyes glittered as his grip tightened on her neck. If she could move her right arm just a few inches, she could throw him off balance and grab his sword...The shackles dug into her stomach, and fizzing, boiling rage turned her face scarlet.

After a too-long moment, the Crown Prince spoke. "I don't quite comprehend why you'd force someone to bow when the purpose of the gesture is to display allegiance and respect." His words were coated with glorious boredom.

Celaena tried to pivot a free eye to the prince, but could only see a pair of black leather boots against the white floor.

"It's clear that you respect me, Duke Perrington, but it's a bit unnecessary to put such effort into forcing Celaena Sardothien to have the same opinion. You and I know very well she has no love for my family. So perhaps your intent is to humiliate her." He paused, and she could have sworn his eyes fell on her face. "But I think she's had enough of that." He stopped for another moment, then asked: "Don't you have a meeting with Endovier's Treasurer? I wouldn't want you to be late, especially when you came all this way just to meet with him."

Understanding the dismissal, her tormentor grunted and released her. Celaena peeled her cheek from the marble, but lay on the floor until he stood and left. If she managed to escape, perhaps she'd hunt down this Duke Perrington fellow and return the warmth of his greeting.

As she rose, she frowned at the imprint of grit she left behind on the otherwise spotless floor, and at the clank of her shackles echoing through the silent room. But she'd been trained to be an assassin since the age of eight, since the day the King of the Assassins found her half-dead on the banks of a frozen river and brought her to his keep. She wouldn't be humiliated by anything, least of all being dirty. Gathering her pride, she tossed her long braid behind a shoulder and lifted her head. Her eyes met with those of the prince.

Dorian Havilliard smiled at her. It was a polished smile, and reeked of court-trained charm. Sprawled across the throne, he had his chin propped by a hand, his golden crown glinting in the soft light. On his black doublet, an emblazoned gold rendering of the royal wyvern occupied the entirety of the chest. His red cloak fell gracefully around him and his throne.

Yet there was something in his eyes, strikingly blue—the color of the waters of the southern countries—and the way they contrasted with his raven-black hair that made her pause. He was achingly handsome, and couldn't have been older than twenty.

Princes are not supposed to be handsome! They're sniveling, stupid, repulsive creatures! This one…this…How unfair of him to be royal and beautiful.

She shifted on her feet as he frowned, surveying her in turn. "I thought I asked you to clean her," he said to Captain Westfall, who stepped forward. She'd forgotten there was anyone else in the room. She looked at her rags and stained skin, and, for the first time in a long while, the three long, white scars on her back stung with a phantom pain. Though she'd sworn not to think about it, she couldn't suppress the twinge of shame. What a miserable state for a girl of former beauty!

At a passing glance, one might think her eyes blue or gray, perhaps even green depending on the color of her clothing. Up close, though, these warring hues were offset by the brilliant ring of gold around her pupils. But it was her golden hair that caught the attention of most, hair that still maintained a glimmer of its glory. In short, Celaena Sardothien was blessed with a handful of attractive features that compensated for the majority of average ones; and, by early adolescence, she'd discovered that with the help of cosmetics, these average features could easily match the extraordinary assets.

But now! Standing before Dorian Havilliard as little more than a gutter rat! Her face warmed as Captain Westfall spoke. "I didn't want to keep you waiting."

The Crown Prince shook his head when Chaol reached for her. "Don't bother with the bath just yet. I can see her potential." The prince straightened, keeping his attention on Celaena. "I don't believe that we've ever had the pleasure of an introduction. But, as you probably know, I'm Dorian Havilliard, Crown Prince of Adarlan, perhaps now Crown Prince of most of Erilea."

She ignored the surge and crash of bitter emotions that awoke with the name.

"And, you're Celaena Sardothien, Adarlan's greatest assassin. Perhaps the greatest assassin in all of Erilea." He studied her tensed body before he raised his dark, well-groomed brows. "You seem a little young." He rested his elbows on his thighs. "I've heard some rather fascinating stories about you. How do you find Endovier after living in such excess in Rifthold?"

Arrogant ass.

"I couldn't be happier," she crooned as her jagged nails cut into her palms.

"After a year, you seem to be more or less alive. I wonder how that's possible when the average life expectancy in these mines is a month."

"Quite a mystery, I'm sure." She batted her eyelashes and readjusted her shackles as if they were lace gloves.

The Crown Prince turned to his captain. "She has somewhat of a tongue, doesn't she? And she doesn't sound like a member of the rabble."

"I should hope not!" Celaena interjected.

"Your Highness," Chaol Westfall snapped at her.

"What?" Celaena asked.

"You will address him as 'Your Highness.'"

Celaena gave him a mocking smile, and then returned her attention to the prince.

Dorian Havilliard, to her surprise, laughed. "You do know that you're now a slave, don't you? Has your sentence taught you nothing?"

Had her arms been unshackled, she would have crossed them. "I don't see how working in a mine can teach anything beyond how to use a pickaxe."

"And you never tried to escape?"

A slow, wicked smile spread across her lips. "Once."

The prince's brows rose, and he turned to Captain Westfall. "I wasn't told that."

Celaena glanced over her shoulder at Chaol, who gave his prince an apologetic look. "The Chief Overseer informed me this afternoon that there was one incident. Three months—"

"Four months," she interrupted.

"Four months," Chaol said, "after Sardothien arrived, she attempted to flee."

She waited for the rest of the story, but he was clearly finished. "That's not even the best part!"

"There's a 'best part?'" the Crown Prince said, face caught between a wince and a smile.

Chaol glared at her before speaking. "There's no hope of escaping from Endovier. Your father made sure that each of Endovier's sentries could shoot a squirrel from two hundred paces away. To attempt to flee is suicide."

"But you're alive," the prince said to her.

Celaena's smile faded as the memory struck her. "Yes."

"What happened?" Dorian asked.

Her eyes turned cold and hard. "I snapped."

"That's all you have to offer as an explanation for what you did?" Captain Westfall demanded. "She killed her overseer and twenty-three sentries before they caught her—almost at the wall. A finger's tip from the wall before the guards knocked her unconscious."

"So?" Dorian said.

Celaena seethed. "So? Do you know how far the wall is from the mines?" He gave her a blank look. She closed her eyes and sighed dramatically. "From my shaft, it was three-hundred-sixty-three feet. I had someone measure."

"So?" Dorian repeated.

"Captain Westfall, how far do slaves make it from the mines when they try to escape?"

"Three feet," he muttered. "Endovier sentries usually shoot a man down before he's moved three feet."

The Crown Prince's silence was not her desired effect. "You knew it was suicide," he said at last, the amusement gone.

Perhaps it had been a bad idea for her to bring up the wall. "Yes," she said.

"But they didn't kill you."

"Your father ordered that I was to be kept alive for as long as possible—to endure the misery that Endovier gives in abundance." A chill that had nothing to do with the temperature went through her. "I never intended to escape." The pity in his eyes made her want to hit him.

"Do you bear many scars?" asked the prince. She shrugged and he smiled, forcing the mood to lift as he stepped from the dais. "Turn around, and let me view your back." Celaena frowned, but obeyed as he walked to her, Chaol stepping closer. "I can't make them out clearly through all this dirt," the prince said, inspecting what skin showed through the scraps of her shirt. She scowled, and scowled even more when he said: "And what a terrible stench, too!"

"When one doesn't have access to a bath and perfume, I suppose one cannot smell as finely as you, Your Highness."

The Crown Prince clicked his tongue and circled her slowly. Chaol—and all the guards—watched them with hands on their swords. As they should. In less than a second, she could get her arms over the prince's head and have her shackles crushing his windpipe. It might be worth it just to see the expression on Chaol's face. But the prince went on, oblivious to how dangerously close he stood to her. Perhaps she should be insulted. "From what I can see," he said, "there are three large scars—and perhaps some smaller ones. Not as awful as I expected, but…well, the dresses can cover it, I suppose."

"Dresses?" He was standing so near that she could see the fine thread detail on his jacket, and smelled not perfume, but horses and iron.

Dorian grinned. "What remarkable eyes you have! And how angry you are!"

Coming within strangling distance of the Crown Prince of Adarlan, son of the man who sentenced her to a slow, miserable death, her self-control balanced on a fragile edge—dancing along a cliff.

"I demand to know," she began, but the Captain of the Guard pulled her back from the prince with spine-snapping force. "I wasn't going to kill him, you buffoon."

"Watch your mouth before I throw you back in the mines," the brown-eyed captain said.

"Oh, I don't think you'd do that."

"And why is that?" Chaol replied. Dorian strode to his throne and sat down, his sapphire eyes bright.

She looked from one man to another and squared her shoulders. "Because there's something you want from me, something you want badly enough to come here yourselves. I'm not an idiot, though I was foolish enough to be captured, and I can see that this is some sort of secret business. Why else would you leave the capital and venture this far? You've been testing me all this time to see if I am physically and mentally sound. Well, I know that I'm still sane, and that I'm not broken, despite what the incident at the wall might suggest. So I demand to be told why you're here, and what services you wish of me, if I'm not destined for the gallows."

The men exchanged glances. Dorian steepled his fingers. "I have a proposition for you."

Her chest tightened. Never, not in her most fanciful dreams, had she imagined that the opportunity to speak with Dorian Havilliard would arise. She could kill him so easily, tear that grin from his face…She could destroy the king as he had destroyed her…

But perhaps his proposition could lead to escape. If she got beyond the wall, she could make it. Run and run and disappear into the mountains and live in solitude amongst the dark green of the wild, with a pine-needle carpet and a blanket of stars overhead. She could do it. She just needed to clear the wall. She had come so close before…

"I'm listening," was all she said.

Twitter: Want to discuss or share what you just read? Use the hashtag #beaTHRONE to connect with others.

ABOUT THE AUTHOR

Sarah J. Maas is a New York native who currently lives in the California desert. This is her first novel, though she has a large on-line fanbase who eagerly support her writing.

Imprint: Bloomsbury
BEA Booth #: 3458
Author appearances: Signing in the autographing area, Wednesday, June 6th
Printed galley at BEA: yes
Contact for printed galley: Katy Herschberger
Print ISBN: 9781599906959
Print price: $17.99
eBook ISBN: 9781599909394
eBook price: $14.99

Publication date: 8/7/2012
Publicity contact: Katy Herschberger katy.herschberger@bloomsbury.com
Rights contact: Beth Eller beth.eller@bloomsbury.com
Editor: Michelle Nagler
Agent: Tamar Rydzinski
Agency: Laura Dail Literary Agency, Inc.
Territories sold:
    Bloomsbury- UK and Australia
    Dogan Kitap- Turkey
    Santillana- Spain
    Dtv junior- Germany
    Record- Brazil
Promotional Information:
- Aggressive social media campaign pre-publication
- Dedicated Facebook page at THRONEOFGLASS
- Twitter promotion @BWKids and @SJMaas
- Strong pre-publication digital push with the release of four e-only novellas
- Extensive national consumer advertising at publication and through the Fall
- Targeted national publicity campaign

every day

david levithan

Every day a different body.
Every day a different life.
Every day in love with the same girl.

SUMMARY

A has no friends. No parents. No family. No possessions. No home, even. Because every day, A wakes up in the body of a different person. Every morning, a different bed. A different room. A different house. A different life. A is able to access each person's memory, enough to be able to get through the day without parents, friends, and teachers realizing this is not their child, not their friend, not their student. Because it isn't. It's A. Inhabiting each person's body. Seeing the world through their eyes. Thinking with their brain. Speaking with their voice.

It's a lonely existence—until, one day, it isn't. A meets a girl named Rhiannon. And, in an instant, A falls for her, after a perfect day together. But when night falls, it's over. Because A can never be the same person twice. But yet, A can't stop thinking about her. She becomes A's reason for existing. So each day, in different bodies—of all shapes, sizes, backgrounds, walks of life—A tries to get back to her. And convince her of their love. But can their love transcend such an obstacle?

EXCERPT

Day 5994

I wake up.

Immediately, I have to figure out who I am. It's not just the body—opening my eyes and discovering whether the skin on my arm is light or dark, whether my hair is long or short, whether I'm fat or thin, boy or girl, scarred or smooth. The body is the easiest thing to adjust to, if you're used to waking up in a new one each morning. It's the life, the context of the body, that can be hard to grasp.

Every day I am someone else. I am myself—I know I am myself—but I am also someone else.

It has always been like this.

The information is there. I wake up, open my eyes, understand that it is a new morning, a new place. The biography kicks in, a welcome gift from the not-me part of the mind. Today I am Justin. Somehow I know this—my name is Justin—and at the same time I know that I'm not really Justin, I'm only borrowing his life for a day. I look around and know that this is his room. This is his home. The alarm will go off in seven minutes.

I'm never the same person twice, but I've certainly been this type before. Clothes everywhere. Far more video games than books. Sleeps in his boxers. From the taste of his mouth, a smoker. But not so addicted that he needs one as soon as he wakes up.

"Good morning, Justin," I say. Checking out his voice. Low. The voice in my head is always different.

Justin doesn't take care of himself. His scalp itches. His eyes don't want to open. He hasn't gotten much sleep.

Already I know I'm not going to like today.

It's hard being in the body of someone you don't like, because you still have to respect it. I've harmed people's lives in the past, and I've found that every time I slip up, it haunts me. So I try to be careful.

From what I can tell, every person I inhabit is the same age as me. I don't hop from being sixteen to being sixty. Right now, it's only sixteen. I don't know how this works. Or why. I stopped trying to figure it out a long time ago. I'm never going to figure it out, any more than a normal person will figure out his or her own existence. After a while, you have to be at peace with the fact that you simply are. There is no way to know why. You can have theories, but there will never be proof.

I can access facts, not feelings. I know this is Justin's room, but I have no idea if he likes it or not. Does he want to kill his parents in the next room? Or would he be lost without his mother coming in to make sure he's awake? It's impossible to tell. It's as if that part of me replaces the same part of whatever person I'm in. And while I'm glad to be thinking like myself, a hint every now and then of how the other person thinks would be helpful. We all contain mysteries, especially when seen from the inside.

The alarm goes off. I reach for a shirt and some jeans, but something lets me see that it's the same shirt he wore yesterday. I pick a different shirt. I take the clothes with me to the bathroom, dress after showering. His parents are in the kitchen now. They have no idea that anything is different.

Sixteen years is a lot of time to practice. I don't usually make mistakes. Not anymore.

I read his parents easily: Justin doesn't talk to them much in the morning, so I don't have to talk to them. I have grown accustomed to sensing expectation in others, or the lack of it. I shovel down some cereal, leave the bowl in the sink without washing it, grab Justin's keys and go.

Yesterday I was a girl in a town I'd guess to be two hours away. The day before, I was a boy in a town three hours farther than that. I am already forgetting their details. I have to, or else I will never remember who I really am.

Justin listens to loud and obnoxious music on a loud and obnoxious station where loud and obnoxious DJs make loud and obnoxious jokes as a way of getting through the morning. This is all I need to know about Justin, really. I access his memory to show me the way to school, which parking space to take, which locker to go to. The combination. The names of the people he knows in the halls.

Sometimes I can't go through these motions. I can't bring myself to go to school, maneuver through the day. I'll say I'm sick, stay in bed and read a few books. But even that gets tiresome after a while, and I find myself up for the challenge of a new school, new friends. For a day.

As I take Justin's books out of his locker, I can feel someone hovering on the periphery. I turn, and the girl standing there is transparent in her emotions—tentative and expectant, nervous and adoring. I don't have to access Justin to know that this is his girlfriend. No one else would have this reaction to him, so unsteady in his presence. She's pretty, but she doesn't see it. She's hiding behind her hair, happy to see me and unhappy to see me at the same time.

Her name is Rhiannon. And for a moment—just the slightest beat—I think that, yes, this is the right name for her. I don't know why. I don't know her. But it feels right.

This is not Justin's thought. It's mine. I try to ignore it. I'm not the person she wants to talk to.

"Hey," I say, casual to a fault.

"Hey," she murmurs back.

She's looking at the floor, at her inked-in Converse. She's drawn cities there, skylines around the soles. Something's happened between her and Justin, and I don't know what it is. It's probably not something that Justin even recognized at the time.

"Are you okay?" I ask.

I see the surprise on her face, even as she tries to cover it. This is not something that Justin normally asks.

And the strange thing is: I want to know the answer. The fact that he wouldn't care makes me want it more.

"Sure," she says, not sounding sure at all.

I find it hard to look at her. I know from experience that beneath every peripheral girl is a central truth. She's hiding hers away, but at the same time she wants me to see it. That is, she wants Justin to see it. And it's there, just out of my reach. A sound waiting to be a word.

She is so lost in her sadness that she has no idea how visible it is. I think I understand her—for a moment, I presume to understand her—but then, from within this sadness, she surprises me with a brief flash of determination. Bravery, even.

Shifting her gaze away from the floor, her eyes matching mine, she asks, "Are you mad at me?"

I can't think of any reason to be mad at her. If anything, I am mad at Justin, for making her feel so diminished. It's there in her body language. When she is around him, she makes herself small.

"No," I say. "I'm not mad at you at all."

I tell her what she wants to hear, but she doesn't trust it. I feed her the right words, but she suspects they're threaded with hooks.

This is not my problem; I know that. I am here for one day. I cannot solve anyone's boyfriend problems. I should not change anyone's life.

I turn away from her, get my books out, close the locker. She stays in the same spot, anchored by the profound, desperate loneliness of a bad relationship.

"Do you still want to get lunch today?" she asks.

The easy thing would be to say no. I often do this: sense the other person's life drawing me in, and run in the other direction.

But there's something about her—the cities on her shoes, the flash of bravery, the unnecessary sadness—that makes me want to know what the word will be when it stops being a sound. I have spent years meeting people without ever knowing them, and on this morning, in this place, with this girl, I feel the faintest pull of wanting to know. And in a moment of either weakness or bravery on my part, I decide to follow it. I decide to find out more.

"Absolutely," I say. "Lunch would be great."

Again, I read her: What I've said is too enthusiastic. Justin is never enthusiastic.

"It'll be cool," I add.

She's relieved. Or, at least, as relieved as she'll allow herself to be, which is a very guarded form of relief. By accessing, I know she and Justin have been together for over a year. That's as specific as it gets. Justin doesn't remember the exact date.

She reaches out and takes my hand. I am surprised by how good this feels.

"I'm glad you're not mad at me," she says. "I just want everything to be okay."

I nod. If there's one thing I've learned, it's this: We all want everything to be okay. We don't even wish so much for fantastic or marvelous or outstanding. We will happily settle for okay, because most of the time, okay is enough.

The first bell rings.

"I'll see you later," I say.

Such a basic promise. But to Rhiannon, it means the world.

At first it was hard to go through each day without making any lasting connections, leaving any life-changing effects. When I was younger, I craved friendship and closeness. I would make bonds without acknowledging how quickly and permanently they would break. I took other people's lives personally; I felt their friends could be my friends, their parents could be my parents. But after a while, I had to stop. It was too heartbreaking to live with so many separations.

I am a drifter, and as lonely as that can be, it is also remarkably freeing. I will never define myself in terms of anyone else. I will never feel the pressure of peers or the burden of parental expectation. I can view everyone as pieces of a whole, and focus on the whole, not the pieces. I have learned how to observe, far better than most people observe. I am not blinded by the past or motivated by the future. I focus on the present, because that is where I am destined to live.

I learn. Sometimes I am taught something I have already been taught in dozens of other classrooms. Sometimes I am taught something completely new. I have to access the body, access the mind and see what information it's retained. And when I do, I learn. Knowledge is the only thing I take with me when I go.

I know so many things that Justin doesn't know, that he will never know. I sit there in his math class, open his notebook, and write down phrases he has never heard. Shakespeare and Kerouac and Dickinson. Tomorrow, or some day after tomorrow, or never, he will see these words in his own handwriting, and he won't have any idea where they came from, or even what they are.

That is as much interference as I allow myself.

Everything else must be done cleanly.

Rhiannon stays with me. Her details. Flickers from Justin's memories.

Small things, like the way her hair falls, the way she bites her fingernails, the determination and resignation in her voice. Random things. I see her dancing with Justin's grandfather, because he's said he wants a dance with a pretty girl. I see her covering her eyes in a scary movie, peering between her fingers, enjoying her fright. These are the good memories. I don't look at any others.

I only see her once in the morning, a brief passing in the halls between first and second period. I find myself smiling when she comes near, and she smiles back. It's as simple as that. Simple and complicated, as most true things are. I find myself looking for her after second period, and then again after third and fourth. I don't even feel in control of this. I want to see her. Simple. Complicated.

By the time we get to lunch, I am exhausted. Justin's body is worn down from too little sleep and I, inside of it, am worn down from restlessness and too much thought.

I wait for her at Justin's locker. The first bell rings. The second bell rings. No Rhiannon. Maybe I was supposed to meet her somewhere else. Maybe Justin's forgotten where they always meet.

If that's the case, she's used to Justin forgetting. She finds me right when I'm about to give up. The halls are nearly empty, the cattle call has passed. She comes closer than she did before.

"Hey," I say.

"Hey," she says.

She is looking to me. Justin is the one who makes the first move. Justin is the one who figures things out. Justin is the one who says what they're going to do.

It depresses me.

I have seen this too many times before. The unwarranted devotion. Putting up with the fear of being with the wrong person because you can't deal with the fear of being alone. The hope tinged with doubt, and the doubt tinged with hope. Every time I see these feelings in someone else's face, it weighs me down. And there's something in Rhiannon's face that's more than just the disappointments. There is a gentleness there. A gentleness that Justin will never, ever appreciate. I see it right away, but nobody else does.

I take all my books and put them in the locker. I walk over to her and put my hand lightly on her arm.

I have no idea what I'm doing. I only know that I'm doing it.

"Let's go somewhere," I say. "Where do you want to go?"

I am close enough now to see that her eyes are blue. I am close enough now to see that nobody ever gets close enough to see how blue her eyes are.

"I don't know," she replies.

I take her hand.

"Come on," I tell her.

This is no longer restlessness—it's recklessness. At first we're walking hand in hand. Then we're running hand in hand. That giddy rush of keeping up with one another, of zooming through the school, reducing everything that's not us into an inconsequential blur. We are laughing, we are playful. We leave her books in her locker and move out of the building, into the air, the real air, the sunshine and the trees and the less burdensome world. I am breaking the rules as I leave the school. I am breaking the rules as we get into Justin's car. I am breaking the rules as I turn the key in the ignition.

"Where do you want to go?" I ask again. "Tell me, truly, where you'd love to go."

I don't initially realize how much hinges on her answer. If she says, *Let's go to the mall,* I will disconnect. If she says, *Take me back to your house,* I will disconnect. If she says, *Actually, I don't want to miss sixth period,* I will disconnect. And I should disconnect. I should not be doing this.

But she says, "I want to go to the ocean. I want you to take me to the ocean."

And I feel myself connecting.

It takes us an hour to get there. It's late September in Maryland. The leaves haven't begun to change, but you can tell they're starting to think about it. The greens are muted, faded. Color is right around the corner.

I give Rhiannon control of the radio. She's surprised by this, but I don't care. I've had enough of the loud and the obnoxious, and I sense that she's had enough of it, too. She brings melody to the car. A song comes on that I know, and I sing along.

And if I only could, I'd make a deal with God . . .

Now Rhiannon goes from surprised to suspicious. Justin never sings along.

"What's gotten into you?" she asks.

"Music," I tell her.

"Ha."

"No, really."

She looks at me for a long time. Then smiles.

"In that case," she says, flipping the dial to find the next song.

Soon we are singing at the top of our lungs. A pop song that's as substantial as a balloon, but lifts us in the same way when we sing it.

It's as if time itself relaxes around us. She stops thinking about how unusual it is. She lets herself be a part of it.

I want to give her a good day. Just one good day. I have wandered for so long without any sense of purpose, and now this ephemeral purpose has been given to me—it feels like it has been given to me. I only have a day to give—so why can't it be a good one? Why can't it be a shared one? Why can't I take the music of the moment and see how long it can last? The rules are erasable. I can take this. I can give this.

When the song is over, she rolls down her window and trails her hand in the air, introducing a new music into the car. I roll down all the other windows and drive faster, so the wind takes over, blows our hair all around, makes it seem like the car has disappeared and we are the velocity, we are the speed. Then another good song comes on and I enclose us again, this time taking her hand. I drive like that for miles, and ask her questions. Like how her parents are doing. What it's like now that her sister's off at college. If she thinks school is different at all this year.

It's hard for her. Every single answer starts with the phrase *I don't know.* But most of the time she does know, if I give her the time and the space in which to answer. Her mother means well; her father less so. Her sister isn't calling home, but Rhiannon can understand that. School is school—she wants it to be over, but she's afraid of it being over, because then she'll have to figure out what comes next.

She asks me what I think, and I tell her, "Honestly, I'm just trying to live day to day."

It isn't enough, but it's something. We watch the trees, the sky, the signs, the road. We sense each other. The world, right now, is only us. We continue to sing along. And we sing with the same abandon, not worrying too much if our voices hit the notes or the right words. We look at each other while we're singing; these aren't two solos, this is a duet that isn't taking itself at all seriously. It is its own form of conversation—you can learn a lot about people from the stories they tell, but you can also know them from the way they sing along, whether they like the windows up or down, if they live by the map or by the world, if they feel the pull of the ocean.

She tells me where to drive. Off the highway. The empty back roads. This isn't summer; this isn't a weekend. It's the middle of a Monday, and nobody but us is going to the beach.

"I should be in English class," Rhiannon says.

"I should be in bio," I say, accessing Justin's schedule.

We keep going. When I first saw her, she seemed to be balancing on edges and points. Now the ground is more even, welcoming.

I know this is dangerous. Justin is not good to her. I recognize that. If I access the bad memories, I see tears, fights, and remnants of passable togetherness. She is always there for him, and he must like that. His friends like her, and he must like that, too. But that's not the same as love. She has been hanging on to the hope of him for so long that she doesn't realize there isn't anything left to hope for. They don't have silences together; they have noise. Mostly his. If I tried, I could go deep into their arguments. I could track down whatever shards he's collected from all the times he's destroyed her. If I were really Justin, I would find something wrong with her. Right now. Tell her. Yell. Bring her down. Put her in her place.

But I can't. I'm not Justin. Even if she doesn't know it.

"Let's just enjoy ourselves," I say.

"Okay," she replies. "I like that. I spend so much time thinking about running away—it's nice to actually do it. For a day. Instead of staring outside the window, it's good to be on the other side of the window. I don't do this enough."

There are so many things inside of her that I want to know. And at the same time, with every word we speak, I feel there may be something inside of her that I already know. When I get there, we will recognize each other. We will have that.

ABOUT THE AUTHOR

David Levithan is a children's book editor in New York City, and the author of several books for young adults, including *Boy Meets Boy*, *Love Is the Higher Law*, and *Every You, Every Me*. He co-authored *Will Grayson* with John Green and, *Nick & Norah's Infinite Playlist*, *Naomi and Ely's No Kiss List*, and *Dash & Lily's Book of Dares* with Rachel Cohn. He lives in Hoboken, New Jersey.

Imprint: Random House Children's Books; Alfred A. Knopf BFYR
BEA Booth #: 3940
Print ISBN: 978-0-307-93188-7
Print price: $16.99
eBook ISBN: 978-0-307-97563-8
eBook price: $10.99
Publication date: 8/28/2012
Publicity contact: Judith Haut jhaut@randomhouse.com
Editor: Nancy Hinkel
Agent: Bill Clegg
Agency: William Morris Agency

THIS IS HOW YOU LOSE HER

JUNOT DÍAZ

SUMMARY

The Pulitzer Prize winner and bestselling author writes about the heart-break and radiance that is love.

EXCERPT

The Sun, the Moon, the Stars

I'm not a bad guy. I know how that sounds—defensive, unscrupulous—but it's true. I'm like everybody else: weak, full of mistakes, but basically good. Magdalena disagrees. She considers me a typical Dominican man: a sucio, an asshole. See, many months ago, when Magda was still my girl, when I didn't have to be careful about almost everything, I cheated on her with this chick who had tons of eighties freestyle hair. Didn't tell Magda about it, either. You know how it is. A smelly bone like that, better off buried in the backyard of your life. Magda only found out because homegirl wrote her a fucking *letter.* And the letter had *details.* Shit you wouldn't even tell your boys drunk.

The thing is, that particular bit of stupidity had been over for months. Me and Magda were on an upswing. We weren't as distant as we'd been the winter I was cheating. The freeze was over. She was coming over to my place and instead of us hanging with my knucklehead boys—me smoking, her bored out of her skull—we were seeing movies. Driving out to different places to eat. Even caught a play at the Crossroads and I took her picture with some bigwig black playwrights, pictures where she's smiling so much you'd think her wide-ass mouth was going to unhinge. We were a couple again. Visiting each other's family on the weekends. Eating breakfast at diners hours before anybody else was up, rummaging through the New Brunswick library together, the one Carnegie built with his guilt money. A nice rhythm we had going. But then the Letter hits like a *Star Trek* grenade and detonates everything, past, present, future. Suddenly her folks want to kill me. It don't matter that I helped them with their taxes two years running or that I mow their lawn. Her father, who used to treat me like his hijo, calls me an asshole on the phone, sounds like he's strangling himself with the cord. You no deserve I speak to you in Spanish, he says. I see one of Magda's girlfriends at the Woodbridge mall—Claribel, the ecuatoriana with the biology degree and the chinita eyes—and she treats me like I ate somebody's favorite kid.

You don't even want to hear how it went down with Magda. Like a five-train collision. She threw Cassandra's letter at me—it missed and landed under a Volvo—and then she sat down on the curb and started hyperventilating. Oh, God, she wailed. Oh, my God.

This is when my boys claim they would have pulled a Total Fucking Denial. Cassandra who? I was too sick to my stomach even to try. I sat down next to her, grabbed her flailing arms, and said some dumb shit like You have to listen to me, Magda. Or you won't understand.

Let me tell you something about Magda. She's a Bergenline original: short with a big mouth and big hips and dark curly hair you could lose a hand in. Her father's a baker, her mother sells kids' clothes door to door. She might be nobody's pendeja but she's also a forgiving soul. A Catholic. Dragged me into church every Sunday for Spanish Mass, and when one of her relatives is sick, especially the ones in Cuba, she writes letters to some nuns in Pennsylvania, asks the sisters to pray for her family. She's the nerd every librarian in town knows, a teacher whose students love her. Always cutting shit out for me from the newspapers, Dominican shit. I see her like, what, every week, and she still sends me corny little notes in the mail: So you won't forget me. You couldn't think of anybody worse to screw than Magda.

Anyway I won't bore you with what happens after she finds out. The begging, the crawling over glass, the crying. Let's just say that after two weeks of this, of my driving out to her house, sending her letters, and calling her at all hours of the night, we put it back together. Didn't mean I ever ate with her family again or that her girlfriends were celebrating. Those cabronas, they were like, No, jamás, never. Even Magda wasn't too hot on the rapprochement at first, but I had the momentum of the past on my side. When she asked me, Why don't you leave me alone? I told her the truth: It's because I love you, mami. I know this sounds like a load of doo-doo, but it's true: Magda's my heart. I didn't want her to leave me; I wasn't about to start looking for a girlfriend because I'd fucked up one lousy time.

Don't think it was a cakewalk, because it wasn't. Magda's stubborn; back when we first started dating, she said she wouldn't sleep with me until we'd been together at least a month, and homegirl stuck to it, no matter how hard I tried to get into her knickknacks. She's sensitive, too. Takes to hurt the way water takes to paper. You can't imagine how many times she asked (especially after we finished fucking), Were you ever going to tell me? This and Why? were her favorite questions. My favorite answers were Yes and It was a stupid mistake. I wasn't thinking.

We even had some conversation about Cassandra—usually in the dark, when we couldn't see each other. Magda asked me if I'd loved Cassandra and I told her, No, I didn't. Do you still think about her? Nope. Did you like fucking her? To be honest, baby, it was lousy. That one is never very believable but you got to say it anyway no matter how stupid and unreal it sounds: say it.

And for a while after we got back together everything was as fine as it could be.

But only for a little while. Slowly, almost imperceptibly my Magda started turning into another Magda. Who didn't want to sleep over as much or scratch my back when I asked her to. Amazing what you notice. Like how she never used to ask me to call back when she was on the line with somebody else. I always had priority. Not anymore. So of course I blamed all that shit on her girls, who I knew for a fact were still feeding her a bad line about me.

She wasn't the only one with counsel. My boys were like, Fuck her, don't sweat that bitch, but every time I tried I couldn't pull it off. I was into Magda for real. I started working overtime on her again, but nothing seemed to pan out. Every movie we went to, every night drive we took, every time she did sleep over seemed to confirm something negative about me. I felt like I was dying by degrees, but when I brought it up she told me that I was being paranoid.

About a month later, she started making the sort of changes that would have alarmed a paranoid nigger. Cuts her hair, buys better makeup, rocks new clothes, goes out dancing on Friday nights with her friends. When I ask her if we can chill, I'm no longer sure it's a done deal. A lot of the time she Bartlebys me, says, No, I'd rather not. I ask her what the hell she thinks this is and she says, That's what I'm trying to figure out.

I know what she's doing. Making me aware of my precarious position in her life. Like I'm not aware.

Then it was June. Hot white clouds stranded in the sky, cars being washed down with hoses, music allowed outside. Everybody getting ready for summer, even us. We'd planned a trip to Santo Domingo early in the year, an anniversary present, and had to decide whether we were still going or not. It had been on the horizon awhile, but I figured it was something that would resolve itself. When it didn't, I brought the tickets out and asked her, How do you feel about it?

Like it's too much of a commitment.

Could be worse. It's a vacation, for Christ's sake.

I see it as pressure.

Doesn't have to be pressure.

I don't know why I get stuck on it the way I do. Bringing it up every day, trying to get her to commit. Maybe I was getting tired of the situation we were in. Wanted to flex, wanted something to change. Or maybe I'd gotten this idea in my head that if she said, Yes, we're going, then shit would be fine between us. If she said, No, it's not for me, then at least I'd know that it was over.

Her girls, the sorest losers on the planet, advised her to take the trip and then never speak to me again. She, of course, told me this shit, because she couldn't stop herself from telling me everything she's thinking. How do you feel about that suggestion? I asked her.

She shrugged. It's an idea.

Even my boys were like, Nigger, sounds like you're wasting a whole lot of loot on some bullshit, but I really thought it would be good for us. Deep down, where my boys don't know me, I'm an optimist. I thought, Me and her on the Island. What couldn't this cure?

Let me confess: I love Santo Domingo. I love coming home to the guys in blazers trying to push little cups of Brugal into my hands. Love the plane landing, everybody clapping when the wheels kiss the runway. Love the fact that I'm the only nigger on board without a Cuban link or a flapjack of makeup on my face. Love the redhead woman on her way to meet the daughter she hasn't seen in eleven years. The gifts she holds on her lap, like the bones of a saint. M'ija has tetas now, the woman whispers to her neighbor. Last time I saw her, she could barely speak in sentences. Now she's a woman. Imagínate. I love the bags my mother packs, shit for relatives and something for Magda, a gift. You give this to her no matter what happens.

If this was another kind of story, I'd tell you about the sea. What it looks like after it's been forced into the sky through a blowhole. How when I'm driving in from the airport and see it like this, like shredded silver, I know I'm back for real. I'd tell you how many poor motherfuckers there are. More albinos, more cross-eyed niggers, more tígueres than you'll ever see. And I'd tell you about the traffic: the entire history of late-twentieth-century automobiles swarming across every flat stretch of ground, a cosmology of battered cars, battered motorcycles, battered trucks, and battered buses, and an equal number of repair shops, run by any fool with a wrench. I'd tell you about the shanties and our no-running-water faucets and the sambos on the billboards and the fact that my family house comes equipped with an ever-reliable latrine. I'd tell you about my abuelo and his campo hands, how unhappy he is that I'm not sticking around, and I'd tell you about the street where I was born, Calle XXI, how it hasn't decided yet if it wants to be a slum or not and how it's been in this state of indecision for years.

But that would make it another kind of story, and I'm having enough trouble as it is with this one. You'll have to take my word for it. Santo Domingo is Santo Domingo. Let's pretend we all know what goes on there.

I must have been smoking dust, because I thought we were fine those first couple of days. Sure, staying locked up at my abuelo's house bored Magda to tears, she even said so—I'm bored, Yunior—but I'd warned her about the obligatory Visit with Abuelo. I thought she wouldn't mind; she's normally mad cool with the viejitos. But she didn't say much to him. Just fidgeted in the heat and drank fifteen bottles of water. Point is, we were out of the capital and on a guagua to the interior before the second day had even begun. The landscapes were superfly—even though there was a drought on and the whole campo, even the houses, was covered in that red dust. There I was. Pointing out all the shit that had changed since the year before. The new Domino's and the little plastic bags of water the tigueritos were selling. Even kicked the historicals. This is where Trujillo and his Marine pals slaughtered the gavilleros, here's where the Jefe used to take his girls, here's where Balaguer sold his soul to the Devil. And Magda seemed to be enjoying herself. Nodded her head. Talked back a little. What can I tell you? I thought we were on a positive vibe.

I guess when I look back there were signs. First off, Magda's not quiet. She's a talker, a fucking boca, and we used to have this thing where I would lift my hand and say, Time out, and she would have to be quiet for at least two minutes, just so I could process some of the information she'd been spouting. She'd be embarrassed and chastened, but not so embarrassed and chastened that when I said, OK, time's up, she didn't launch right into it again.

Maybe it was my good mood. It was like the first time in weeks that I felt relaxed, that I wasn't acting like something was about to give at any moment. It bothered me that she insisted on reporting to her girls every night—like they were expecting me to kill her or something—but, fuck it, I still thought we were doing better than anytime before.

We were in this crazy budget hotel near Pucamaima. I was standing on the balcony staring at the Septentrionales and the blacked-out city when I heard her crying. I thought it was something serious, found the flashlight, and fanned the light over her heat-swollen face. Are you OK, mami?

She shook her head. I don't want to be here.

What do you mean?

What don't you understand? I. Don't. Want. To. Be. Here.

This was not the Magda I knew. The Magda I knew was super courteous. Knocked on a door before she opened it.

I almost shouted, What is your fucking problem! But I didn't. I ended up hugging and babying her and asking her what was wrong. She cried for a long time and then after a silence started talking. By then the lights had flickered back on. Turned out she didn't want to travel around like a hobo. I thought we'd be on a beach, she said.

We're going to be on a beach. The day after tomorrow.

Can't we go now?

What could I do? She was in her underwear, waiting for me to say something. So what jumped out of my mouth? Baby, we'll do whatever you want. I called the hotel in La Romana, asked if we could come early, and the next morning I put us on an express guagua to the capital and then a second one to La Romana. I didn't say a fucking word to her and she didn't say nothing to me. She seemed tired and watched the world outside like maybe she was expecting it to speak to her.

By the middle of Day 3 of our All-Quisqueya Redemption Tour we were in an air-conditioned bungalow watching HBO. Exactly where I want to be when I'm in Santo Domingo. In a fucking resort. Magda was reading a book by a Trappist, in a better mood, I guess, and I was sitting on the edge of the bed, fingering my useless map.

I was thinking, For this I deserve something nice. Something physical. Me and Magda were pretty damn casual about sex, but since the breakup shit has gotten weird. First of all, it ain't regular like before. I'm lucky to score some once a week. I have to nudge her, start things up, or we won't fuck at all. And she plays like she doesn't want it, and sometimes she doesn't and then I have to cool it, but other times she does want it and I have to touch her pussy, which is my way of initiating things, of saying, So, how about we kick it, mami? And she'll turn her head, which is her way of saying, I'm too proud to acquiesce openly to your animal desires, but if you continue to put your finger in me I won't stop you.

Today we started no problem, but then halfway through she said, Wait, we shouldn't.

I wanted to know why.

She closed her eyes like she was embarrassed at herself. Forget about it, she said, moving her hips under me. Just forget about it.

I don't even want to tell you where we're at. We're in Casa de Campo. The Resort That Shame Forgot. The average asshole would love this place. It's the largest, wealthiest resort on the Island, which means it's a goddamn fortress, walled away from everybody else. Guachimanes and peacocks and ambitious topiaries everywhere. Advertises itself in the States as its own country, and it might as well be. Has its own airport, thirty-six holes of golf, beaches so white they ache to be trampled, and the only Island Dominicans you're guaranteed to see are either caked up or changing your sheets. Let's just say my abuelo has never been here, and neither has yours. This is where the Garcías and the Colóns come to relax after a long month of oppressing the masses, where the tutumpotes can trade tips with their colleagues from abroad. Chill here too long and you'll be sure to have your ghetto pass revoked, no questions asked.

We wake up bright and early for the buffet, get served by cheerful women in Aunt Jemima costumes. I shit you not: these sisters even have to wear hankies on their heads. Magda is scratching out a couple of cards to her family. I want to talk about the day before, but when I bring it up she puts down her pen. Jams on her shades.

I feel like you're pressuring me.

How am I pressuring you? I ask.

I just want some space to myself every now and then. Every time I'm with you I have this sense that you want something from me.

Time to yourself, I say. What does that mean?

Like maybe once a day, you do one thing, I do another.

Like when? Now?

It doesn't have to be now. She looks exasperated. Why don't we just go down to the beach?

As we walk over to the courtesy golf cart, I say, I feel like you rejected my whole country, Magda.

Don't be ridiculous. She drops one hand in my lap. I just wanted to relax. What's wrong with that?

The sun is blazing and the blue of the ocean is an overload on the brain. Casa de Campo has got beaches the way the rest of the island has got problems. These, though, have no merengue, no little kids, nobody trying to sell you chicharrones, and there's a massive melanin deficit in evidence. Every fifty feet there's at least one Eurofuck beached out on a towel like some scary pale monster that the sea's vomited up. They look like philosophy professors, like budget Foucaults, and too many of them are in the company of a dark-assed Dominican girl. I mean it, these girls can't be no more than sixteen, look puro ingenio to me. You can tell by their inability to communicate that these two didn't meet back in their Left Bank days.

Magda's rocking a dope Ochun-colored bikini that her girls helped her pick out so she could torture me, and I'm in these old ruined trunks that say "Sandy Hook Forever!" I'll admit it, with Magda half naked in public I'm feeling vulnerable and uneasy. I put my hand on her knee. I just wish you'd say you love me.

Yunior, please.

Can you say you like me a lot?

Can you leave me alone? You're such a pestilence.

I let the sun stake me out to the sand. It's disheartening, me and Magda together. We don't look like a couple. When she smiles niggers ask her for her hand in marriage; when I smile folks check their wallets. Magda's been a star the whole time we've been here. You know how it is when you're on the Island and your girl's an octoroon. Brothers go apeshit. On buses, the machos were like, Tu sí eres bella, muchacha. Every time I dip into the water for a swim, some Mediterranean Messenger of Love starts rapping to her. Of course, I'm not polite. Why don't you beat it, pancho? We're on our honeymoon here. There's this one squid who's mad persistent, even sits down near us so he can impress her with the hair around his nipples, and instead of ignoring him she starts a conversation and it turns out he's Dominican, too, from Quisqueya Heights, an assistant DA who loves his people. Better I'm their prosecutor, he says. At least I understand them. I'm thinking he sounds like the sort of nigger who in the old days used to lead bwana to the rest of us. After three minutes of him, I can't take it no more, and say, Magda, stop talking to that asshole.

The assistant DA startles. I know you ain't talking to me, he says.

Actually, I say, I am.

This is unbelievable. Magda gets to her feet and walks stiff-legged toward the water. She's got a half-moon of sand stuck to her butt. A total fucking heartbreak.

Homeboy's saying something else to me, but I'm not listening. I already know what she'll say when she sits back down. Time for you to do your thing and me to do mine.

That night I loiter around the pool and the local bar, Club Cacique, Magda nowhere to be found. I meet a dominicana from West New York. Fly, of course. Trigueña, with the most outrageous perm this side of Dyckman. Lucy is her name. She's hanging out with three of her teenage girl cousins. When she removes her robe to dive into the pool, I see a spiderweb of scars across her stomach.

I also meet these two rich older dudes drinking cognac at the bar. Introduce themselves as the Vice-President and Bárbaro, his bodyguard. I must have the footprint of fresh disaster on my face. They listen to my troubles like they're a couple of capos and I'm talking murder. They commiserate. It's a thousand degrees out and the mosquitoes hum like they're about to inherit the earth, but both these cats are wearing expensive suits, and Bárbaro is even sporting a purple ascot. Once a soldier tried to saw open his neck and now he covers the scar. I'm a modest man, he says.

I go off to phone the room. No Magda. I check with reception. No messages. I return to the bar and smile.

The Vice-President is a young brother, in his late thirties, and pretty cool for a chupabarrio. He advises me to find another woman. Make her bella and negra. I think, Cassandra.

The Vice-President waves his hand and shots of Barceló appear so fast you'd think it's science fiction.

Jealousy is the best way to jump-start a relationship, the Vice-President says. I learned that when I was a student at Syracuse. Dance with another woman, dance merengue with her, and see if your jeva's not roused to action.

You mean roused to violence.

She hit you?

When I first told her. She smacked me right across the chops.

Pero, hermano, why'd you tell her? Bárbaro wants to know. Why didn't you just deny it?

Compadre, she received a letter. It had evidence.

The Vice-President smiles fantastically and I can see why he's a vice-president. Later, when I get home, I'll tell my mother about this whole mess, and she'll tell me what this brother was the vice-president of.

They only hit you, he says, when they care.

Amen, Bárbaro murmurs. Amen.

All of Magda's friends say I cheated because I was Dominican, that all us Dominican men are dogs and can't be trusted. I doubt that I can speak for all Dominican men but I doubt they can either. From my perspective it wasn't genetics; there were reasons. Causalities.

The truth is there ain't no relationship in the world that doesn't hit turbulence. Mine and Magda's certainly did.

I was living in Brooklyn and she was with her folks in Jersey. We talked every day on the phone and on weekends we saw each other. Usually I went in. We were real Jersey, too: malls, the parents, movies, a lot of TV. After a year of us together, this was where we were at. Our relationship wasn't the sun, the moon, and the stars, but it wasn't bullshit, either. Especially not on Saturday mornings, over at my apartment, when she made us coffee campo-style, straining it through the sock thing. Told her parents the night before she was staying over at Claribel's; they must have known where she was, but they never said shit. I'd sleep late and she'd read, scratching my back in slow arcs, and when I was ready to get up I would start kissing her until she would say, God, Yunior, you're making me wet.

I wasn't unhappy and wasn't actively pursuing ass like some niggers. Sure, I checked out other females, even danced with them when I went out, but I wasn't keeping numbers or nothing.

Still, it's not like seeing somebody once a week doesn't cool shit out, because it does. Nothing you'd really notice until some new chick arrives at your job with a big butt and a smart mouth and she's like on you almost immediately, touching your pectorals, moaning about some moreno she's dating who's always treating her like shit, saying, Black guys don't understand Spanish girls.

Cassandra. She organized the football pool and did crossword puzzles while she talked on the phone, and had a thing for denim skirts. We got into a habit of going to lunch and having the same conversation. I advised her to drop the moreno, she advised me to find a girlfriend who could fuck. First week of knowing her, I made the mistake of telling her that sex with Magda had never been top-notch.

God, I feel sorry for you, Cassandra said. At least Rupert gives me some Grade A dick.

The first night we did it—and it was good, too, she wasn't false advertising—I felt so lousy that I couldn't sleep, even though she was one of those sisters whose body fits next to you perfect. I was like, She knows, so I called Magda right from the bed and asked her if she was OK.

You sound strange, she said.

I remember Cassandra pressing the hot cleft of her pussy against my leg and me saying, I just miss you.

Another perfect sunny Caribbean day, and the only thing Magda has said is Give me the lotion. Tonight the resort is throwing a party. All guests are invited. Attire's semiformal, but I don't have the clothes or the energy to dress up. Magda, though, has both. She pulls on these super-tight gold lamé pants and a matching halter that shows off her belly ring. Her hair is shiny and as dark as night and I can remember the first time I kissed those curls, asking her, Where are the stars? And she said, They're a little lower, papi.

We both end up in front of the mirror. I'm in slacks and a wrinkled chacabana. She's applying her lipstick; I've always believed that the universe invented the color red solely for Latinas.

We look good, she says.

It's true. My optimism is starting to come back. I'm thinking, This is the night for reconciliation. I put my arms around her, but she drops her bomb without blinking a fucking eye: tonight, she says, she needs space.

My arms drop.

I knew you'd be pissed, she says.

You're a real bitch, you know that.

I didn't want to come here. You made me.

If you didn't want to come, why didn't you have the fucking guts to say so?

And on and on and on, until finally I just say, Fuck this, and head out. I feel unmoored and don't have a clue of what comes next. This is the endgame, and instead of pulling out all the stops, instead of pongándome más chivo que un chivo, I'm feeling sorry for myself, como un parigüayo sin suerte. I'm thinking over and over, I'm not a bad guy, I'm not a bad guy.

Club Cacique is jammed. I'm looking for that girl Lucy. I find the Vice-President and Bárbaro instead. At the quiet end of the bar, they're drinking cognac and arguing about whether there are fifty-six Dominicans in the major leagues or fifty-seven. They clear out a space for me and clap me on the shoulder.

This place is killing me, I say.

How dramatic. The Vice-President reaches into his suit for his keys. He's wearing those Italian leather shoes that look like braided slippers. Are you inclined to ride with us?

Sure, I say. Why the fuck not?

I wish to show you the birthplace of our nation.

Before we leave I check out the crowd. Lucy has arrived. She's alone at the edge of the bar in a fly black dress. Smiles excitedly, lifts her arm, and I can see the dark stubbled spot in her armpit. She's got sweat patches over her outfit and mosquito bites on her beautiful arms. I think, I should stay, but my legs carry me right out of the club.

We pile in a diplomat's black BMW. I'm in the backseat with Bárbaro; the Vice-President's up front driving. We leave Casa de Campo behind and the frenzy of La Romana, and soon everything starts smelling of processed cane. The roads are dark I'm talking no fucking lights and in our beams the bugs swarm like a Biblical plague. We're passing the cognac around. I'm with a vice-president, I figure what the fuck.

He's talking about his time in upstate New York but so is Bárbaro. The bodyguard's suit's rumpled and his hand shakes as he smokes his cigarettes. Some fucking bodyguard. He's telling me about his childhood in San Juan, near the border of Haiti. Liborio's country. I wanted to be an engineer, he tells me. I wanted to build schools and hospitals for the pueblo. I'm not really listening to him; I'm thinking about Magda, how I'll probably never taste her chocha again.

And then we're out of the car, stumbling up a slope, through bushes and guineo and bamboo, and the mosquitoes are chewing us up like We're the special of the day. Bárbaro's got a huge flashlight, a darkness obliterator. The Vice-President's cursing, trampling through the underbrush, saying, It's around here somewhere. This is what I get for being in office so long. It's only then I notice that Bárbaro's holding a huge fucking machine gun and his hand ain't shaking no more. He isn't watching me or the Vice-President he's listening. I'm not scared, but this is getting a little too freaky for me.

What kind of gun is that? I ask, by way of conversation.

A P-90.

What the fuck is that?

Something old made new.

Great, I'm thinking, a philosopher.

It's here, the Vice-President calls out.

I creep over and see that he's standing over a hole in the ground. The earth is red. Bauxite. And the hole is blacker than any of us.

This is the Cave of the Jagua, the Vice-President announces in a deep, respectful voice. The birthplace of the Taínos.

I raise my eyebrow. I thought they were South American.

We're speaking mythically here.

Bárbaro points the light down the hole but that doesn't improve anything.

Would you like to see inside? the Vice-President asks me.

I must have said yes, because Bárbaro gives me the flashlight and the two of them grab me by my ankles and lower me into the hole. All my coins fly out of my pockets. Bendiciones. I don't see much, just some odd colors on the eroded walls, and the Vice-President's calling down, Isn't it beautiful?

This is the perfect place for insight, for a person to become somebody better. The Vice-President probably saw his future self hanging in this darkness, bulldozing the poor out of their shanties, and Bárbaro, too buying a concrete house for his mother, showing her how to work the air-conditioner but, me, all I can manage is a memory of the first time me and Magda talked. Back at Rutgers. We were waiting for an E bus together on George Street and she was wearing purple. All sorts of purple.

And that's when I know it's over. As soon as you start thinking about the beginning, it's the end.

I cry, and when they pull me up the Vice-President says, indignantly, God, you don't have to be a pussy about it.

That must have been some serious Island voodoo: the ending I saw in the cave came true. The next day we went back to the United States. Five months later I got a letter from my ex-baby. I was dating someone new, but Magda's handwriting still blasted every molecule of air out of my lungs.

It turned out she was also going out with somebody else. A very nice guy she'd met. Dominican, like me. Except he loves me, she wrote.

But I'm getting ahead of myself. I need to finish by showing you what kind of fool I was.

When I returned to the bungalow that night, Magda was waiting up for me. Was packed, looked like she'd been bawling.

I'm going home tomorrow, she said.

I sat down next to her. Took her hand. This can work, I said. All we have to do is try.

Twitter: Want to discuss or share what you just read? Use the hashtag #beaLOSE to connect with others.

ABOUT THE AUTHOR

Junot Díaz is the author of *Drown* and *The Brief Wondrous Life of Oscar Wao,* which won the National Book Critics Circle Award and the Pulitzer Prize and was named *Time*'s # 1 Fiction Book of 2007. He is the recipient of the PEN / Malamud Award and the Dayton Literary Peace Prize. Born in Santo Domingo, Díaz is a professor at MIT.

Imprint: Riverhead Books
BEA Booth #: 3922
Author appearances: Adult Book & Author breakfast, Tuesday, June 5th.
Print ISBN: 9781594487361
Print price: $26.95
eBook ISBN: 9781101596951
eBook price: $12.99
Publication date: 9/11/2012
Publicity contact: Mih-Ho Cha Mih-Ho.Cha@us.penguingroup.com
Rights contact: Nicole Aragi nicole@aragi.net
Editor: Rebecca Saletan
Agent: Nicole Aragi
Agency: Aragi Inc
Promotional Information:
• National marketing and publicity campaign
• Author tour
• National print reviews and features
• NPR interviews
• National print, radio and online advertising and social media

THE PEOPLE OF FOREVER ARE NOT AFRAID

A NOVEL

SHANI BOIANJIU

SUMMARY

The searing, riveting debut novel about young women coming of age in the military, from one of the National Book Foundation's 5 under 35. Yael, Avishag, and Lea grow up together in a tiny, dusty Israeli village, attending a high school made up of caravan classrooms, passing notes to each other to alleviate the universal boredom of teenage life. When they are conscripted into the army, their lives change in unpredictable ways, influencing the women they become and the friendship that they struggle to sustain. Yael trains marksmen and flirts with boys. Avishag stands guard, watching refugees throw themselves at barbed-wire fences. Lea, posted at a checkpoint, imagines the stories behind the familiar faces that pass by her day after day. They gossip about boys and whisper of an ever more violent world just beyond view. They drill, constantly, for a moment that may never come. They live inside that single, intense second just before danger erupts.

In a relentlessly energetic voice marked by caustic humor and fierce intelligence, Shani Boianjiu creates a heightened reality that recalls our most celebrated chroniclers of war and the military, while capturing that unique time in a young woman's life when a single moment can change everything.

EXCERPT

The Sound Of All Girls Screaming

We, the boot camp girls, stand in a perfect square that lacks one of its four sides. Our commander stands in front of us, facing the noon sun. She squints. She screams.

"Raise your hand if you are wearing contact lenses."

Two girls raise their hands. The commander folds her arm to look at her watch. The two girls do the same.

"In two minutes and thirty seconds, I want to see you back here from the tents. Without your contact lenses, understood?" the commander shouts.

"Yes, commander," the girls shout, and their watches beep. They run. Dusts of sand trail the quick steps of their boots.

"Raise your hand if you are asthmatic," the boot camp commander shouts.

None of the girls raise their hands.

"Are you asthmatic?" the boot camp commander shouts.

"No, commander," all the girls shout.

I don't shout. I didn't get it that I was supposed to; I already didn't raise my hand.

"Are you asthmatic, Avishag?" the commander yells, looking at me.

"No, commander," I shout.

"Then answer next time," the commander says. "Speak up so I can hear you, just like everyone else."

In my IDF boot camp, the only combat-infantry boot camp for females, we can't tell what will become of us next based on what questions we raise our arms for. I know the least because I was the first of the girls in my class to be drafted, so I didn't have any friends to get info from, and my brother Dan never told me anything about the army even when he was alive. I got so annoyed when people asked me if I was still planning to go into the army after he died, I decided to volunteer for combat just to make people stop assuming. I wanted to do something that will make people never assume ever.

One can never assume in my boot camp. A week ago, we were asked to raise our hands if we weighed below fifty kilos. Then we were asked to raise our hands if we had ever shared needles or had unprotected sex shortly before we were drafted. It was hard to know what to assume from that. The army wanted our blood. Two liters, but you got strawberry Kool-Aid and white bread while the needle was inside you. The self-proclaimed sluts and druggies served it to the girls who were pumping their fists, trying to make the blood gush out quicker.

"Faster," the commander screamed.

"My hand feels like there is ice on it," one of the other soldiers said. "It feels frozen." She was lying on the field bed across from mine. I wanted to reach over and grab her hand, so that she would be less cold, so that I would be less alone. I couldn't. Because of the needle in my arm, because it would have been a mistake. Mom said that if I want to get a good posting after boot camp, I have to learn how to control my mouth. Mom was once an officer, and now she is a history teacher, and all. She left for Jerusalem a few weeks after Dan died, but in the end she had to come back and help me get ready for the army. Single moms have to come back always.

The girl on the field bed next to mine freaked out. She extended the arm with the needle away from her body, like it was cursed. Her face turned red. "I think it is taking too much blood. Can someone check? Can someone see if it is taking too much blood?"

I knew I should not say anything.

"I want to go home," she said. "I don't like this."

She looked very young. And eventually I spoke. "It's fine," was what I said.

That's when the commander intervened. "No one said you could talk," she shouted.

I was the only one who was punished. During shower hour, I had to dig a hole in the sand large enough to bury a boulder the size of five heads. The commander said the boulder represented my "shame." She smiled when she explained that. None of the girls helped. They just stood on the sand, waiting in line for the showers, and watched.

Now, the army wants us to know what it is like to be suffocated. That's why they asked about contact lenses and asthma. It is ABC day. Atomic, Biological, Chemical. Every soldier has to go through that, not just girls in combat, they said. But it is especially important for us, because we will have to maintain functionality in the event of an unconventional attack.

We stand in two lines on top of a sandy hill. We help each other put the gas masks on.

"You are doing it all wrong Avishag," the commander yells at me. "All wrong."

She stretches one of the black elastic bands tighter, and my hair is pulled so tightly it is as if someone had taken a handful of my hair and tried to pull it off my scalp. Except that someone doesn't let go. The mask is on my face to stay.

With our masks on, we all look like the bodies of soldiers with the heads of robotic dogs. The big gray filter stretches like a snout. The sun heats the black plastic of the mask, and the heat radiates inwards. The sheer plastic above my eyes is stained, and wherever I turn the world looks framed and distant, a dirty cheap painting of sand, then sand from another angle.

The commander goes down the line, breaking plastic miniatures of bananas. "Each one of your ABC kits has a few of these little bananas. If you break it and you still smell bananas, your mask is not sealed right."

I can feel the veins at the back of my head choking. When the commander passes by me, waving the tiny banana, I can smell it. Bananas. Bananas and sand.

"I can smell bananas and—" I say. My voice vibrates inside of the mask. My words, they fail me. I want to talk. All the time. About Dan. About things Yael said I still don't understand. The banana fields by our village when they burn. Everything. I am an idiot. Like it matters what I am thinking.

"No one said you could speak," my commander shouts. "Just get one of your friends to fix it," she says. They call the other soldiers, "Your friends." I hate that. They are other soldiers. They are not my friends. Even Mom said, you don't go into the army to make friends. Don't be fooled. Just look at what happened to Dan.

The commander lets us into the tent two at a time. My partner is a tall girl called Gali. We watch one of the girls who had entered before us lift the cover of the tent and run back outside as if she is on fire, her mouth dripping with saliva, her eyes closed and wet, her nose running in green and yellow. She runs with her mouth open, her arms stretched to the sides. She runs far, her small green body becoming a speck on the empty horizon.

Gali laughs, and I do too. I did hear from Sarit, Lea's older sister, that the tear gas tent is the first place commanders can get personal with their boot camp soldiers. They ask them the same four questions:

Do you love the army?

Do you love the country?

Who do you love more, your mother or father?

Are you afraid to die?

The commanders get a kick out of this because first they ask these questions when the soldier has her mask on, but then they get to ask them when the soldier is in the tear gas tent without the mask, and watch her panic. That is the goal of the exercise. To train you not to panic in the event of an atomic, biological or chemical attack. I fail to see the point of this. I told that to Sarit, I told her, in that case, why don't they just shoot us so we know what that feels like, but she said, don't get smart. We get to run out of the tent when we feel we are choking. Sarit said they expect you to stay as long as you can. I asked what's as long as you can, and she asked, how long can you breathe underwater?

It is our turn.

Gali and I bend below the tent's folds and enter it. It is dark inside, and so warm I feel as though the buttons of my uniform are burning my wrists. I can feel it. I can see it. The tent is full of poison. I know it, but the mask doesn't let it harm me. I feel like a cheater.

The commander, strangely, is just as identifiable with the mask on. The way she stands, with her arms behind her back, holding the handle of her gun. Her chin is raised high. She starts with Gali. Gali stands even taller, perking up her chin.

"How are you feeling with the mask, soldier?"

"Good."

"Do you love the army?"

"Yes. It is hard but it is a rewarding experience and I learn a lot."

"Do you love your country?"

"Yes."

"Who do you love more, your mother or your father?"

"I can't really answer that. I think I love them both the same amount, but in different ways."

"Are you afraid to die?"

"No."

"Take off your mask. You can run out when you feel you have to."

I watch Gali fumble to untie the elastic of her mask and then remove it. Immediately, her face crumbles inwards like she is sucking on a punctured straw.

"Do you love the army?"

Gali opens her mouth to speak, and then closes it quickly. She is drooling already. She opens her mouth again, smaller this time, and grunts out a sound. "Yeah."

"Do you love your country?"

Gali is flapping her arms near her throat, like a fish.

"Ahhh," she mumbles, and the mucous from her nose falls to her mouth. She runs out like a stork.

Now it is me.

"Do you love the army?" my commander asks.

"Yes and no, I mean I definitely believe that it is important in a country like ours to serve in the army, but I hope for peace and on a personal level of course boot camp presents its own hardships and also—"

"Enough. Are you afraid to die?" she asks. She skips two questions. She knows I am trouble, although I have barely caused any yet. Maybe trouble isn't something you do, it is something you are. I think Dan told me that once, but what do I know about what he said, or meant.

"No, I am not afraid to *die*," I say. Short and concise. What she wants to hear, and, also, the truth.

"Take off your mask. You can run out when you feel you have to," my commander says. She sounds different than when she said it to Gali. More content.

I take off my mask and at first I feel nothing but the pain in my scalp. Then I feel the fire, the burn. I cannot open my eyes. I stop taking air in through my nose. But I open my mouth, I do.

And I talk. I have been waiting for so long. This is my chance. As long as I am choking, I am allowed. Yael and Lea are not here to drown my words with their chatter. No one in my family is around to ignore me. My talking serves a purpose. My talking, my tears, are a matter of national security. A part of our training. I will be prepared for an attack by unconventional weapons. I could save the whole country, that's how prepared I'll be. My entire head is burning but my mouth rolls off words; they taste like bananas, and they go on and on and on.

My commander runs out of the original four questions. She has to make up a new one.

"What is your earliest memory?" she asks. It is a question they used to ask before someone was brilliant enough to come up with the Mom and Dad question.

I don't leave on my own. She tells me to.

I talk and I talk and I talk.

I think I stayed inside the tear gas tent longer than any soldier has ever before.

Outside is when I cannot breathe. I cannot open my eyes and, although I do not want them to, my feet start running on their own, faster and faster. I can taste blood in my mouth coming from my nose, and my throat burns as though it is stuffed with boiling oil. The skin of my face is rubbed with sandpaper. I run and I run, until arms catch me, midair, and hold me for a very long time. When I can finally see again, through the water in my eyes, I see where I was heading: the cliff. It is my commander's arms that grabbed me. She held me, before I fell. My commander, this was her job.

They are sure I cheated, although they cannot for the life of them imagine how I did it. I am told I stayed in a tent full of tear gas for over two and a half minutes, and they say that is just not possible, that there must have been some funny business going on. It felt like I was talking longer. It felt like in that time I got to tell everything, almost.

After I change my uniform, I have to see the commander of the base. I enter the room, salute with my gun, and stare at him.

For a second, I think he is reaching for his gun. That the commander of the base is going to kill me. Sometimes I think things I know are not true. But he is just reaching for his cigarettes. His nostrils flare when he drags in the smoke. He gestures for me to sit across from him, and when I drop onto the office chair I can see that the hairs inside his nose are gray, like life lines of spiders. He crushes his cigarette in an ashtray made of a green grenade shell, and then reaches for another one.

It seems he is only interested in killing himself, and slowly. He doesn't care about killing me. It makes me sad that he cares about himself more than about me. Say I am just not being realistic, but it still makes me sad when people are like that. Most people are like that. Dan was like that, in the end. Only interested in killing himself.

The commander of the base says I need to get my act together. That don't I know? People are dying. He hopes I will take some time to think of ways I can become a better soldier.

"And just a general point. Your commander says you keep on speaking when you are not spoken to. Why do you do that?" he asks.

"I don't know. I guess I have all these thoughts," I say.

"One day soon you need to wake up and realize that your thoughts are interrupting everyone else."

My punishment is to sleep that night with my gas mask on. Creative and humiliating all at once. I am sort of impressed.

I wish I were a better soldier. At night, I think about everything except how to become a better soldier, no matter how hard I try. Dan, Mom, Yael. People who are not me, and not soldiers. Even my dad; thoughts from when I was little and not a soldier.

All night long, I stare at the ceiling of the tent through the sheer plastic; it frames the thick green cloth, all this green, like an impressionist painting. The knobs at the back of the mask pierce into my scalp.

If I cry, it is not because I hope that one of the girls in the tent will hear me and wake up. We only get five hours of sleep each night. And we are not friends.

I cannot sleep, so I imagine one of two things could happen.

I could wake up after a night with my gas mask on and find out that Iran had bombed Israel, and that I am the last living person in the whole country, that the mask had saved me. The other girls in the tent would be dead and blue-faced, and I would march out of the gates of the base and into the Negev desert, where dehydration could kill me, or chemicals poisoning the skin of my body could kill me, but those things don't kill me. What kills me is that I have no one to talk to.

Another thing that could happen is that Iran doesn't bomb Israel, at least not on that day, and that I reach the place Yael says is the end of the world. I finish boot camp. I finish the army. I go to Panama and Guatemala and Argentina. There are Israelis, of course, swarms of them everywhere. But finally, they all leave, and I am the last Israeli tourist left in Ushuaia, Argentina, the closest city to Antarctica, the end of the world. The bookstores are all in Spanish. The lakes are too cold for a swim. At the bars, all the clients are middle-aged Frenchmen, and I am alone.

My earliest memory. I open my eyes and see the small room through plastic. My father is wearing his mask, and my baby sister is on the carpet inside a gas protective incubator, because she is too small for a mask of her own. Dan keeps on taking his mask off, and Dad slaps him. Dad takes off his own mask to take sips from his Araq bottle. It is 1991 and missiles are falling from Iraq. On the radio they say not to go into the underground shelters. They say to seal one room of the house with duct tape, wear the masks, drink a lot of water, and hope for the best. On the radio they say missiles are falling in region M, our region. We live in some town other than the village then. I don't know where. My parents are arguing. "Duct tape?" my mother asks. "This is silly."

I do not know all the details of this – I hear about it later, and it becomes my memory. That night, I do not yet have enough words to make a sentence. All I remember is my mother, her dark face bare, collecting me in her arms, and running up the wooden steps onto the roof. Rain falls on the palm trees below, but my mother removes my mask and pulls my chin up, high up in the air. A ball of light rips through the night sky in pink and ember and blaze. My mother drowns her chin in my hair. We watch, and if I am alone I do not yet know it.

I stare at the ceiling of the tent through the sheer plastic into the night. The knobs at the back of the mask pierce into my scalp. I am crying, and not because I hope that one of the girls in the tent will wake up.

But then one does wake up. The blood one, the one who thought too much of her blood was being taken. She is awake, but she does not realize that I am a person, her fellow soldier, and in my field bed and crying inside a gas mask. My suffocated whines sound to her like the words of an animal.

"Is that a cat?" she whispers, a sound as spiky as a blade that pierces through the air and tent and ears. "Girls! There is a cat in the tent."

"A cat?" Gali asks. She does not bother whispering.

"Help me. I am allergic. I may die." The blood girl waits for the words of another person.

The mask protects me. They cannot see my face. They cannot see my mouth. They do not know that it was me who made the sound. If I scream, if I scream right now, a deafening and smashing and muted scream, there is a chance, there is always a small chance that no one will ever know it was me. It will be the sound of all girls screaming.

And so.

I scream. I scream as if this is the last time in my life I'll ever speak my voice, and maybe it is. It is as if no one hears me, hears me right now.

I scream the fear of blood, and ember, and blaze. I scream the terror of the beeping watches and boots treading the sand, and the panic brought upon by a reek that thinks it is bananas. The sound of the words I scream is the groan of my shame, my shame that is not a boulder, my shame that I never agreed to bury.

If you really want to, I will tell you the words I scream, I will tell you all the sounds and words and letters. But first you have to, you have to swear that you really want to hear it from me.

Twitter: Want to discuss or share what you just read? Use the hashtag #beaAFRAID to connect with others.

ABOUT THE AUTHOR

Shani Boianjiu was born in 1987 in a small town on the Israel/Lebanon border, and she served in the Israeli Defense Forces for two years. Her fiction has been published in *Vice* magazine and *Zoetrope: All Story*. Shani is the youngest recipient ever of the National Book Foundation's 5 under 35 Award, for which she was chosen by Nicole Krauss. She lives in Israel.

Imprint: Crown Trade Group; Hogarth
BEA Booth #: 3940
Print ISBN: 978-0-307-95595-1
Print price: $24.00
eBook ISBN: 978-0-307-95596-8
eBook price: $11.99
Publication date: 9/11/2012
Publicity contact: ddrake@randomhouse.com
Editor: Alexis Washam
Agent: Jin Auh
Agency: The Wylie Agency

AMANDA COPLIN

The

ORCHARDIST

A NOVEL

SUMMARY

At the turn of the 20th century in a rural stretch of the Pacific Northwest, a reclusive orchardist, Talmadge, tends to apples and apricots as if they were loved ones. A gentle man, he's found solace in the sweetness of the fruit he grows and the quiet, beating heart of the land he cultivates. One day, two teenage girls appear and steal his fruit from the market and later return to the outskirts of his orchard to see the man who gave them no chase. Feral, scared, and very pregnant, the girls take up residence on Talmadge's land and indulge in his deep reservoir of compassion. Just as the girls begin to trust him, men arrive in the orchard with guns, and the shattering tragedy that follows will set Talmadge on an irrevocable course not only to save and protect but to reconcile the ghosts of his own troubled past.

EXCERPT

His face was lined and pitted as the moon. He was tall, though not extraordinarily so, broad of shoulder and thick without being stocky, though one could see how he would pass into stockiness; he had already taken on the barrel-chested sturdiness of an old man. His ears were elephantine, a feature most commented on when he was younger, when the ears stuck out from his head; but now they had darkened like the rest of his sun-exposed flesh and lay against his skull more than at any other time in his life, and were tough, the flesh granular like the rind of some fruit. He was clean-shaven, large-pored; his skin was oily. In some lights his flesh was gray; others tallow; others, red. His lips were the same color as his face, had given way to the overall visage, had begun to disappear. His nose was large, bulbous. His eyes were cornflower blue. His eyelashes nothing to speak of now but when he was young they were thick-black—and his cheeks bloomed, and his lips were as pure and sculpted as a cherub's—and these things together made the women compulsively kiss him, lean down on their way to do other chores, collapse him to their breast. All his mother's sisters he could no longer remember, from Arkansas, who were but shadows of shadows now in his consciousness. Oh my lovely, they would say— oh my sweet lamb.

His arms were sun-darkened and flecked with old scars. He combed his hair over his head, a dark wing kept in place with pine-scented pomade.

He regarded the world—objects right in front of his face—as if from a great distance. For when he moved on the earth he also moved in other realms—in the knowledge of his past which he thought of directly no more, besides a few times, in certain seasons, in certain shades, when memories alighted on him like sharp-taloned birds: his complicity in certain grand failures, having mostly to do with his sister. And there were other, constant, preoccupations he likewise half-acknowledged, in which his attention was nevertheless steeped in at all times: present and past projects in the orchard; desires he had had as a young man, worries, fears of which he remembered only the husks; trees he had hoped to plant; experiments with grafting and irrigation; jam recipes; cellar temperatures; chemical combinations for poisoning or at least discouraging a range of pests—deer and rabbits and rodents and grubs, a universe of insects; how to draw bees. Important was the weather, and patterns of certain years, the likelihood of repetition meteorologically speaking, what that would mean for the landscape; the wisdom of the almanacs, the words of other men, other orchardists, the unimportant but mostly the important words. He thought of where he would go hunting next fall. Considered constantly the state of his land, his property, his buildings, his animal. And mostly he thought of the weather that week, the temperature, and existence of, or potential for, rainfall; recent calamities and how he was responding to them; the position of the season; his position in the rigid scaffolding of chores—what he would have to do that day, that afternoon and evening, how he would prepare for the next morning's work; when were the men coming, and would he be ready for them?—but he would be ready for them, he always was, he was anything if not prepared. He considered those times in life when he had uttered words to a person—Caroline Middey or Clee, or his sister, his mother, or a stranger who had long forgotten him—he wished he had never uttered, or had uttered differently—or he thought of the times he remained silent when he should have spoken as little as a single word. And, at the farthest edges of this all, he considered his own death, and if there was a God, and—if there was, or if there was not—what it all meant.

Now, at his back, the shrouded bushels of apples and apricots rustled in the wagonbed, the wagon creaking forward beneath the weight; the old, old familiar rhythm in accordance with these leagues of thought. Dazzled and suspended by the sun. The mountains cold at his back. It was June; the road was already dusty. His frame slightly hunkered down, the floppy calfskin hat shielding his brow under which was a scowl holding no animosity. The large hands, swollen knuckles, loosely holding the reins.

He entered town, drew down the main street. Hitched up outside the feed and supply store, watered the mule. While he was setting up the fruit stand—tugging forward each burlap-covered bushel in the back of the wagon and unveiling them and beginning to unload them—

a woman rounded the corner and gained the platform, approached him. Half her face was mottled and pink, as if burned, her mouth an angry pucker. She held defensively to her breast a burlap sack, and bent over and inspected the up-tilted bushel of Arkansas Blacks. She reached for an apple but did not touch it; glanced dubiously at a bushel of paler apples he presently uncovered. What're those?

He glanced down. Greenings. Rhode Island Greenings.

When he spoke his voice was low and sounded unused—he cleared his throat. The woman waited, pretended not to notice. All of these unspeaking men. She considered the apples beneath his gaze. All right. I'll take a few of those. From the folds of her skirt she brought out a dull green change purse. How much?

He told her. She pinched out the correct change and handed it to him.

As he filled the sack with fruit, the woman turned and gazed behind her. After a moment she said:

Look what the cat drug in. Those two looking over here like that, you aren't careful, they'll come rob you. Hooligan-looking. She sniffed.

After a moment he looked where she nodded. Down the street, under the awning of the hardware store, two girls—raggedy, smudge-faced—stood conspiratorially, half turned towards each other. When they saw Talmadge and the woman observing them, they turned their backs to them. He handed the burlap sack to the woman, the bottom heavy and misshapen with fruit.

You be here next week?

He nodded, and the woman nodded as well, and then after a moment, after gazing at the apples again, she turned and stepped off the platform, moved off down the street.

From the wagon he retrieved his wooden folding chair and sat down next to the bushels. Wind gusted and threw sand onto the platform, and then it was quiet. Rain was coming; maybe that evening, or early the next day. Movement caught his eye; the girls stood with their shoulders pressed together, looking into the window of the dry goods store now. A gust of wind blew their dresses flat against their calves but they remained motionless. He pulled his cap low. What did two girls mean to him? He dozed. Woke to someone addressing him:

That you, Talmadge? Those girls just robbed you.

He righted his cap. A slack-mouthed boy stood gaping at him.

I saw them do it, said the boy. I watched them do it. You give me a nickel, I'll run them down and get your apples back for you.

The girls had gotten farther than Talmadge would have expected. They made a grunting sound between them, in their effort at speed. Apples dropped from their swooped-up dresses and they crouched or bent awkwardly to retrieve them. The awkwardness was due, he saw, to their grotesquely swollen bellies. He had not realized before that they were pregnant. The nearer one—smaller, pouting, her hair tangled in a great hive around her face—looked over her shoulder and cried out, let go the hem of her dress and lurched forward through the heavy thud of apples. The other girl swung her head around. She was taller, had black eyes, the hard startle of a hawk. Her hair coiled in a thick braid over her shoulder. She grabbed the other girl's wrist and yanked her along and they went down the empty road like that, panting, one crying, at a hobble-trot. He stopped and watched them go. The boy, at his side, looked wildly back and forth between Talmadge and the ragged duo. I can get them, I can catch them, Talmadge, he said. Wildly back and forth.

Talmadge, the boy repeated.

Talmadge watched the girls retreat.

He and his mother and sister came into the high valley in the summer of eighteen fifty-seven, when he was nine years old. They had come from the north-central portion of the Oregon Territory, where his father had worked the mines. When the mines collapsed, their mother did not even wait for the body of their father to be dredged up with the rest, but set off with Talmadge and his sister. They traveled north and then west, west and then north.

They walked, mostly, and rode in wagons when they came along. They crossed the Wallowas and the Blue Mountains, and then came across great baked plains, what looked to be a desert. And then when they reached the Columbia they took a steam boat upriver until its confluence with another river, where the steamboat did not go farther. They would have to walk, said the steamboat operator, uncertain; if they were thinking of going across the mountain pass, they would have to find someone—a trapper, an Indian—to guide them. And still Talmadge's mother was undaunted. From the confluence of the river they walked four days toward the mountains. The elevation climbed; the Cascades rose before them like gods. It was May; it snowed. Talmadge's sister was cold; she was hungry. Talmadge rubbed her hands in his own and told her stories of the food they would eat, when they set up house: cornbread and bacon gravy, turnip greens, stewed apples. Their mother said nothing to these stories. What was the voice she heard, why did she walk north and then west, west and then north, as if drawing toward a destination already envisioned?

They had heard that many, many miles away, but not so many as before they started, on the other side of the mountains, was the ocean. Constant rain. Greenness. Maybe that's where they were going, thought Talmadge. Sometimes—but how could this be? how could a child think this of his mother?—he thought she was leading them to their deaths. Their mother was considered odd by the other women at the mining camp; he knew this, he knew how they talked about her. But there was nothing really wrong with her, he thought (forgetting the judgment of a moment before): it was just that she wanted different things than those women. That was what set them and his mother apart. Where some women wanted mere privacy, she yearned for complete solitude that verged on the violent; solitude that forced you constantly back upon yourself, even when you did not want it anymore. But she wanted it nonetheless. From the time she was a small girl she wanted to be alone. The sound of other peoples' voices grated on her: to travel to town, to interact with others who were not Talmadge or Talmadge's father or sister, was torture to her: it subtracted days from her life. And so they walked: to find a place that would absorb and annihilate her: a place to be her home, and the home for her children. A place to show her children: and you belong to the earth, and the earth is hard.

They climbed through cold-embittered forest and sought respite in bright meadows thick with wildflowers and insect thrumming. Maybe, thought Talmadge, they had already died, and this was heaven. It was easy, at moments, to believe. They came to a mining camp where five men sat inside an open hut, shivering, malnourished, warming their hands around a fire. It was lightly raining outside. When Talmadge and his mother and sister came and stood before them, the men looked at them as if they were ghosts. Their mother asked the men if they had any food to spare. The men just stared at her. They stared at the children. Where are you going? said one of the men finally. You shouldn't be here. The men had some beans that they shared with them, ate them straight out of the can. And then—Talmadge would always remember this—a man took out a banjo and began to play, and eventually, to sing. His teeth were crooked and stained, as was his mustache and his beard. His eyes were light blue and watery. He sang songs about a place that sounded familiar to Talmadge: Tennessee. It was where his own father was from. Talmadge thought later that the man was crying. But why was he crying? He missed his home, said Talmadge's mother.

The men told them that there was a post ten miles up the creek where they could trade for supplies. It was a good time to travel, since it was summer, but in the winter it would be impassable. Talmadge and his mother and sister set off from the miners and reached the trading post later that day. And then they kept walking. What are you doing, the people said. Turn around. You have two young children. There were two days of rain, and cold. His sister developed a hacking cough. And then they came through dense forest, and stood on the rim of a valley lit up as if it was the end or the beginning of the world. A valley of bright yellow grass. Quiet, still. His sister caught her breath beside him. He could feel his mother's silent, reluctant satisfaction.

On a sunny plateau above a creek, beside a filthy miner's shack, stood two diseased Gravenstein apple trees. Beyond the creek the outlying field was bordered by forest. To the east was a dark maw that was the opening of a canyon. Three weeks later they discovered a cabin a mile away into the canyon and through the forest, along a portion of the upper creek. And here, as well as down below, was a miner's sluice box situated along a shallow portion of the creek. One of the first chores Talmadge's mother assigned herself was to dismantle the sluice box and take this, as well as other tools she found pertaining to that trade, and bury them in the forest. I've had enough of mining for one lifetime, she said.

• • •

For a year he and his mother and sister tended the ailing trees and also planted vegetables from seeds his mother had sewn into the linings of their winter clothes. The summer of the next year they sold fruit to the miners at Peshastin Creek, and traded for supplies at the post in Icicle.

Late that first summer and then again in the spring, a band of native men came out of the forest with a head of over two hundred horses. The men did not try to speak to Talmadge or his mother or sister; and neither did Talmadge or his mother or sister attempt to speak to the men. They remained in the field for three days.

When the men arrived again the following summer, Talmadge's mother went down to the field where they camped and offered them fruit and vegetables, loaves of potato bread. The men accepted her gifts; and when they returned, four weeks later, they offered her a deer they had killed, strapped to the back of a horse.

They were horse wranglers—mostly Nez Perce at that time, but later, there were also men from other tribes: Palouse, Yakama, Cayuse, Walla Walla, Umatilla. They hunted horses in the ranges to the southeast—the Blue Mountains, the Wallowas, the Steens, the Sawtooths—and trained them and sold them at auctions abroad. They had been stopping over in the valley for the last decade or so to feed and rest the horses, and to avoid the lawmen who scouted the countryside searching for rogue bands such as theirs.

On their trips south, after selling the horses at auction—when the men came into the orchard with their herd largely diminished, and many of them sporting handsome leather vests and saddlebags—they brought gifts for Talmadge and his sister: candy, or bits of milk glass in the shapes of animals. They let Talmadge and his sister explore their packs, and took them on easy rides around the field, the children sitting before the men in the saddles.

These trips south the men would stay just overnight, and would be gone by the time Talmadge woke in the morning. The ash of their firepits not yet cold and the general odor of horses and tobacco hung in the air for hours afterward, provoking in the young Talmadge a particular melancholy, and emptiness.

Their mother died of a respiratory disease in the spring of eighteen sixty. Two years later he and his sister harvested two acres of apples and one acre of apricots, and with the money they earned from selling the fruit they razed the miner's shack and built a two-room cabin. He was fifteen years old and his sister was fourteen. The next spring they planted three plum trees around the side of the cabin, and the first apples trees inside the canyon mouth.

In the fall of eighteen sixty-four he contracted smallpox and nearly died. The sickness left him badly scarred, and partially deaf in his right ear. In the spring of the next year the canyon flooded, and they lost many apple trees. That summer, in eighteen sixty-five, his sister went into the forest beyond the field, to collect herbs, and did not return. He enlisted the help of the miners at the Peshastin camp, and when they did not find her, he asked the native men who came through with the horses if they would help him search. One of them found her bonnet, and another, her picking basket. That was all they ever found.

The one who found her bonnet was a boy named Clee. He was the nephew of the leader of the men and was several years younger than Talmadge. They had been acquainted before—Clee often played with Talmadge and his sister in the outlying field and forest, games that would have made little sense to the adults, if they had observed them. Sometimes the men brought other other boy children along, but Clee was always among them. He was related to many of the men by blood, but he did not have any immediate family. His mother had died of disease; his father and two of his brothers had died in wars in the fifties. Other brothers had simply disappeared. When he found Talmadge's sister's bonnet, his own family had been gone—his mother and father, his brothers, his sisters—and how many sisters had he had?—some for only a matter of months. He did not let Talmadge's sister pass with silence, with quiet acceptance, like the other men did, who were not very surprised. She had run away, or the forest had claimed her, they thought. It was not so very uncommon. But Clee was the one who told Talmadge, with certain quiet resolve uncommon for someone his age: We will look for her. And he did. He tried, with his skills, to track her, but she could not be tracked. Maybe, at one time she could have been, but no longer. He circled and re-circled where he had found the article of clothing. When the men set up camp, far away from where she had disappeared, he nevertheless toured a wide perimeter, watching out. The other men regarded him warily but did not interrupt him, did not mock him. For awhile he shared Talmadge's grief. And though he never stopped looking for the sister—not really—he forgot what she looked like. He would know her when he saw her, he thought.

Out of this brief obsession their friendship solidified. When the men passed through with the horses, Talmadge and Clee sat out on the porch in the evening, looking out over the land and with a view of the field below where the other men camped, their fires like distant stars. Clee and Talmadge smoked tobacco, and did not speak much. Sometimes one or both of them would come away from the evening—and who was the first to move? Had they slept?—with the impression that leagues had been discussed between them, where in fact maybe they had said nothing to each other all night. Talmadge knew little of Clee's past—and Clee had forgotten Talmadge's sister's name, her face—but the young men appeared regularly in each other's dreams, where it was as if their chests were unstoppered, and they walked together and sometimes turned and faced each other directly, and spoke volumes.

By the time Talmadge was forty the orchards had grown to almost twenty-five acres. On the hill above the creek was the cabin and three acres of apricot trees, and around the side of the cabin, surrounding the shed, a half-acre of plum trees. In the field across the creek, before the canyon mouth, nearly a quarter-mile away, were nine acres of apples; and inside were twelve acres.

The men helped him groom and harvest the orchards in season, and he in turn lied to authorities who infrequently came through asking about the men and their business. Also, when the bulk of the fruit became too much for Talmadge to manage at harvest time, he sent a portion with the men, who sold it at auctions and fairs, and he split the profit with them.

The claim was officially one hundred and sixty acres under the Homestead Act of eighteen sixty-two; he purchased the land as soon as he was able, on his eighteenth birthday. Over the years he bought the lots around it as well so that he owned over four hundred acres of land. He left this other land uncultivated, was satisfied to keep it as forest. A bachelor's whim, said the townspeople, who knew little about him.

• • •

Three days after he saw the girls in town, he was braced aloft in an apricot tree and saw them come out of the upper forest. He quit the shears and watched them. It was morning. They paused at the treeline and then came down through the far pasture, their dark hair like flags riding the grass. At the edge of the yard they hesitated, discussing between themselves—what?—glancing repeatedly at the cabin, at the outlying land.

He climbed out of the tree, the shears clamped in his armpit. When he walked out of the orchard, the taller, long-haired girl with the braid over her shoulder turned to him, and froze. The other girl—her hair also dark and long, but fuzzy, tangled, unkempt—had been chattering to the other, but, when she saw him, ceased. Both stood watching him, their eyes swarming the shears. He stopped twenty yards from them.

You all lost? he called. They looked away at the trees. The shorter one—younger one, he decided—held her mouth open and panted slightly. Their faces were filthy. Even from where he stood, he saw their arms discolored with dirt.

He crossed the yard and went into the cabin. He laid the shears on the table and took his time stoking the ashes in the woodstove. When he went outside again, they had come closer, but feinted back when he came out onto the porch. He gathered the buckets from the nails near the door, went down to the creek and filled the buckets with water; returned to the cabin. As he mounted the rise in the orchard, he saw the lawn was empty. Then he saw them; he tried not to fix them directly, where they lay now in the border between the lawn and the outer grass, peering out, thinking themselves hidden.

In the cabin he rebuilt the fire, and made thick cakes out of meal and creek water, and fried them over the stove. Lost himself in the task. When he came to, he thought: Why was he making so many? And then he had to remind himself: the girls, the girls had come to eat with him. He set the cakes on the table along with an uncapped jar of milk. He hesitated. Finally he left the cabin, shears in hand, and walked to the apple orchard, a deeper section up the creek, leaving them to themselves.

Late afternoon, when he returned to the cabin, there was no sign of them. The food had been eaten. The plates were clean. They had even eaten the crud on the griddletop, the charred remains of the mealcakes. The bowl on the table was empty of fruit. He stood for a moment, then checked the cold pantry. They had taken his eggs and milk. Backing out, he checked the cupboard by the stove. They had taken his cornmeal, and salt. He waited a moment, then went out onto the porch and looked across the lawn, at the trees. They were not there any longer, he thought; they had gone. He looked at the trees. Dusk settled within the branches, touched the ground.

Inside, he took off his boots, and slept.

Twitter: Want to discuss or share what you just read? Use the hashtag #beaORCHARD to connect with others.

ABOUT THE AUTHOR

Amanda Coplin was born in Wenatchee, Washington in 1981. She received her BA from the University of Oregon, and MFA from the University of Minnesota. A recipient of residencies from the Fine Arts Work Center in Provincetown, Massachusetts and the Ledig House International Writers Residency Program in Ghent, New York, she currently resides in Minneapolis, Minnesota.

Imprint: HarperCollins
BEA Booth #: 3339
Printed galley at BEA: yes
Print ISBN: 9780062188502
Print price: $26.99
eBook ISBN: 9780062188526
eBook price: $21.99
Publication date: 9/1/2012
Editor: Terry Karten
Agent: Bill Clegg
Agency: William Morris Endeavor
Promotional Information:
- Online publicity campaign targeting major national sites and blogs
- Author appearances in Portland, San Francisco, Seattle, and the Pacific Northwest region
- National media, radio, and print reviews and features
- Robust marketing campaign, coordinated blog tour
- Major book club outreach
- Social media campaign on Goodreads
- Outreach to academic and library markets

JASPER FFORDE

New York Times Best-Selling Author

THE

LAST

DRAGONSLAYER

JACKET NOT FINAL

SUMMARY

In the good old days, magic was indispensable—it could both save a kingdom and clear a clogged drain. But now magic is fading: Drain cleaner is cheaper than a spell, and magic carpets are used for pizza delivery. Fifteen-year-old foundling Jennifer Strange runs Kazam, an employment agency for magicians—but it's hard to stay in business when magic is drying up. And then the visions start, predicting the death of the world's last dragon at the hands of an unnamed Dragonslayer. If the visions are true, everything will change for Kazam—and for Jennifer. Because something is coming. Something known as...Big Magic.

EXCERPT

Once, I was famous. My face appeared on T-shirts, badges, commemorative mugs, and posters. I made front-page news, appeared on TV, and was even a special guest on *The Yogi Baird Daytime TV Show. The Daily Clam* called me "the year's most influential teenager," and I was the Mollusc on Sunday's *Woman of the Year.* Two people tried to kill me, I was threatened with jail, had fifty-eight offers of marriage, and was outlawed by King Snodd IV. All that and more besides, and in less than a week.

My name is Jennifer Strange.

Chapter 1 Practical Magic

It looked set to become even hotter by the afternoon, just when the job was becoming more fiddly and needed extra concentration. But the fair weather brought at least one advantage: dry air makes magic work better and fly farther. Moisture has a moderating effect on the mystical arts. No sorcerer worth their sparkle ever did productive work in the rain—which probably accounts for why getting showers to *start* was once considered easy, but getting them to *stop* was nearly impossible.

We hadn't been able to afford a company car for years, so the three sorcerers, the beast, and I were packed into my rust-and-orange-but-mostly-rust Volkswagen for the short journey from Hereford to Dinmore. Lady Mawgon had insisted on sitting in the passenger seat because "that's how it will be," which meant that Wizard Moobin and the well-proportioned Full Price were in the back seat, with the Quark-beast sitting between the two of them and panting in the heat. I was driving, which might have been unusual anywhere but here in the Kingdom of Hereford, which was unique in the Ununited Kingdoms for having driving tests based on maturity, not age. That explained why I'd had a license since I was thirteen, while some were still failing to make the grade at forty. It was lucky I could. Sorcerers are easily distracted, and letting them drive is about as safe as waving around a chain saw at full throttle in a crowded nightclub.

We had lots to talk about—the job we were driving to, the weather, experimental spells, King Snodd's sometimes eccentric ways. But we didn't. Price, Moobin, and Mawgon, despite being our best sorcerers, didn't really get along. It wasn't anything personal; sorcerers are just like that—temperamental, and apt to break out into petulant posturing that takes time and energy to smooth over. My job of running Kazam Mystical Arts Management was less about spells and enchantments, diplomacy and bureaucracy, then about babysitting. Working with those versed in the Mystical Arts was sometimes like trying to knit with wet spaghetti: just when you thought you'd gotten somewhere, it all came to pieces in your hands. But truth to tell, I didn't really mind. Were they frustrating? Frequently. Were they boring? Never.

"I do wish you wouldn't do that," said Lady Mawgon in an aggrieved tone as she shot a disapproving glance at Full Price. He was changing from a human to a walrus and then back again in slow, measured transformations. The Quarkbeast was staring at him strangely, and with each transformation there wafted an unpleasant smell of fish around the small car. It was good the windows were open. To Lady Mawgon, who in better days had once been sorceress to royalty, transforming within potential view of the public was the mark of the hopelessly ill-bred.

"Groof, groof," said Full Price, trying to speak while a walrus, which is never satisfactory. "I'm just tuning up," he added in an indignant fashion, once de-walrussed or re-humaned, depending on which way you looked at it. "Don't tell me you don't need to."

Wizard Moobin and I looked at Lady Mawgon, eager to know how she was tuning up. Moobin had prepared for the job by tinkering with the print of the *Hereford Daily Eyestrain*. He had filled in the crossword in the twenty minutes since we'd left Kazam. Not unusual in itself, since the *Eyestrain's* crossword is seldom hard, except that he had used printed letters from elsewhere on the page and *dragged* them across using the power of his mind alone. The crossword was now complete and more or less correct—but it left an article on Queen Mimosa's patronage of the Troll War Widows Fund looking a little disjointed.

"I am not required to answer your question," replied Lady Mawgon haughtily, "and what's more, I detest the term *tuning up*. It's *quazafucating* and always has been."

"Using the old language makes us sound archaic and out of touch," replied Price.

"It makes us sound as we are meant to be," replied Lady Mawgon, "of a noble calling."

Of a once *noble calling*, thought Moobin, inadvertently broadcasting his subconscious on an alpha so low, even I could sense it.

Lady Mawgon swiveled in her seat to glare at him. "Keep your thoughts to yourself, young man."

Moobin thought something to her but in high alpha, so only she could hear it. I don't know what he thought, but Lady Mawgon said, "Well!" and stared out the side window in an aggrieved fashion.

I sighed. This was my life.

Of the forty-five sorcerers, movers, soothsayers, shifters, weather-mongers, carpeteers, and other assorted mystical artisans at Kazam, most were fully retired due to infirmity, insanity, or damage to the vital index fingers, either through accident or rheumatoid arthritis. Of these forty-five, thirteen were potentially capable of working, but only nine had current licenses—two carpeteers, a pair of pre-cogs, and most important, five sorcerers legally empowered to carry out Acts of Enchantment. Lady Mawgon was certainly the crabbiest, and probably the most skilled. As with everyone else at Kazam, her powers had faded dramatically over the past three decades or so, but unlike everyone else, she'd not really come to terms with it. In her defense, she'd had farther to fall than the rest of them, but this wasn't really an excuse. The Sisters Karamazov could also claim once-royal patronage, and they were nice as apricot pie. Mad as a knapsack of onions, but pleasant nonetheless.

I might have felt sorrier for Mawgon if she weren't so difficult all the time. Her intimidating manner made me feel small and ill at ease, and she rarely if ever missed an opportunity to put me in my place. Since Mr. Zambini's disappearance, she'd gotten worse, not better.

"Quark," said the Quarkbeast.

"Did we have to bring the beast?" Full Price asked me.

"It jumped in the car when I opened the door."

The Quarkbeast yawned, revealing several rows of razor-sharp fangs. Despite his placid nature, the beast's ferocious appearance almost guaranteed that no one ever completely shrugged off the possibility that he might try to take a chunk out of them when they weren't looking. If the Quarkbeast was aware of this, it didn't show. Indeed, he might have been so unaware that he wondered why people always ran away screaming.

"I would be failing in my duty as acting manager of Kazam," I said, in an attempt to direct the sorcerers away from grumpiness and more in the direction of teamwork, "if I didn't mention how important this job is. Mr. Zambini always said that Kazam needed to adapt to survive, and if we get this right, we could possibly tap a lucrative market that we badly need."

"Humph!" said Lady Mawgon.

"We all need to be in *tune* and ready to hit the ground running," I added. "I told Mr. Digby we'd all be finished by six this evening."

They didn't argue. I think they knew the score well enough. In silent answer, Lady Mawgon snapped her fingers and the Volkswagen's gearbox, which up until that moment had been making an expensive-sounding rumbling noise, suddenly fell silent. If Mawgon could replace gearbox bushings while the engine was running, she was tuned enough for all of them.

I knocked on the door of a red-brick house at the edge of the village, and a middle-aged man with a ruddy face answered.

"Mr. Digby? My name is Jennifer Strange of Kazam, acting manager for Mr. Zambini. We spoke on the phone."

He looked me up and down. "You seem a bit young to be running an agency." "I'm sixteen," I said in a friendly manner.

"Sixteen?"

"In two weeks I'll be sixteen, yes."

"Then you're actually fifteen?"

I thought for a moment. "I'm in my sixteenth *year*."

Mr. Digby narrowed his eyes. "Then shouldn't you be in school or something?"

"Indentured servitude," I answered as brightly as I could, trying to sidestep the contempt that most free citizens have for people like me. As a foundling, I had been brought up by the Sisterhood, who'd sold me to Kazam four years before. I still had two years of unpaid work before I could even *think* of applying for the first level that would one day lead me, fourteen tiers of paperwork and bureaucracy later, to freedom.

"Indentured or not," replied Mr. Digby, "where's Mr. Zambini?"

"He's indisposed at present," I replied, attempting to sound as mature as I could. "I have temporarily assumed his responsibilities."

"'Temporarily assumed his responsibilities'?" Mr. Digby repeated. He looked at the three sorcerers, who stood waiting at the car. "Why her and not one of you?"

"Bureaucracy is for little people," retorted Lady Mawgon in an imperious tone.

"I am too busy, and paperwork exacerbates my receding hair issues," said Full Price.

"We have complete confidence in Jennifer," added Wizard Moobin, who appreciated what I did perhaps more than most. "Foundlings mature quickly. May we get started?"

"Very well," replied Mr. Digby, after a long pause in which he looked at us all in turn with a *should I cancel?* sort of look. But he didn't, and eventually went and fetched his hat and coat. "But we agreed you'd be finished by six, yes?"

I said that this was so, and he handed me his house keys. After taking a wide berth to avoid the Quarkbeast, he climbed into his car and drove away. It's not a good idea to have civilians around when sorcery is afoot. Even the stoutest incantations carry redundant strands of spell that can cause havoc if allowed to settle on the general public.

Nothing serious ever happened; it was mostly rapid nose hair growth, oinking like a pig, blue pee, that sort of stuff. It soon wore off, but it was bad for business.

"Right," I said to the sorcerers. "Over to you."

They looked at each other, then at the ordinary suburban house.

"I used to conjure up storms," said Lady Mawgon with a sigh.

"So could we all," replied Wizard Moobin.

"Quark," said the Quarkbeast.

None of the sorcerers had rewired a house by spell before, but by reconfiguring the root directory on the core spell language of ARAMAIC, it could be done and with relative ease—as long as the three of them pooled their resources. It had been Mr. Zambini's idea to move Kazam into the home improvement market. Charming moles out of gardens, resizing stuff for the self-storage industry, and finding lost things was easy work, but it didn't pay well. Using magic to rewire a house, however, was quite different. Unlike electricians, we didn't need to touch the house in order to do it. No mess, no problems, and all finished in under a day.

I stood by my Volkswagen to be near the car radiophone, the most reliable form of mobile communication we had these days. Any calls to the Kazam office would ring here. I wasn't just Kazam's manager; I was also the receptionist, booking clerk, and accountant. I had to look after the forty-five sorcerers, deal with the shabby building that housed us all, and fill out the numerous forms that the Magical Powers (amended 1966) Act required when even the *tiniest* spell was undertaken. I did all this because (1) the Great Zambini couldn't because he was missing, (2) I'd been part of Kazam since I was twelve and knew the Mystical Arts Management business inside out, and (3) no one else wanted to.

I looked across to where Wizard Moobin, Lady Mawgon, and Full Price were still sizing up the house. Sorcery wasn't about mumbling a spell and letting fly—it was more a case of appraising the problem, planning the various incantations to greatest effect, *then* letting fly. The three of them were still in the appraising stage, which generally meant a good deal of staring, tea, discussion, argument, more discussion, tea, and more staring.

The phone bleeped.

"Jenny? It's Perkins."

The Youthful Perkins was one of the only young sorcerers at Kazam and was serving a loose apprenticeship. His particular field of interest was Remote Suggestion, although he wasn't very good at it. He'd once attempted to get us to like him more by sending out a broad *Am I cool or what?!* suggestion on the wide subalpha, but he mixed it up with the suggestion that he often cheated at Scrabble, and then wondered why everyone stared at him and shook their heads sadly. It had been very amusing until it wore off, but not to Perkins. Because we were close to the same age, we got along fairly well and I kind of liked him. But since this might have been a *suggestion* generated by him, I had no way of knowing if I truly liked him or not.

"Hey, Perkins," I said. "Did you get Patrick off to work in time?"

"Just about. But I think he's back on the marzipan again."

This was worrying. Patrick of Ludlow was a Mover. Although not possessed of the sharpest mind, he was kind and gentle and exceptionally gifted at levitation and earned a regular wage for Kazam by removing illegally parked cars for the city. It took a lot of effort—he would sleep fourteen hours of twenty-four—and the marzipan echoed back to a darker time in his life that he didn't care to speak of.

"So what's up?"

"The Sisterhood sent round your replacement. What do you want me to do with him?"

I'd been wondering when this would happen. The Sisterhood traditionally supplied Kazam with a foundling every four years, as it took a long time to train someone in the somewhat unique set of skills and mildly elastic regard for reality required for Mystical Arts Management, and the dropout rate was high. Sharon Zoiks had been the fourth, I had been the sixth, and this new one would be the seventh. We didn't talk about the fifth.

"Pop him in a taxi and send him up. No, cancel that. It'll be too expensive. Ask Nasil to carpet him up. Usual precautions. Cardboard box?"

"Absolutely. By the way, I've got two tickets to see Sir Matt Grifflon live in concert. Do you want to go?"

"Who with?"

"With? *Me*, of course."

"I'll think about it."

"Right," he said, then mumbled something about how he knew at least twelve people who would literally kill to see singing sensation Sir Matt, and hung up.

In truth, I would very much like to see Sir Matt Grifflon in concert. Aside from being one of King Snodd's favorites, he was a recording star and quite handsome in a lantern-jaw-and-flowing-mane kind of way. But I decided I should pass, despite my curiosity about finding out what going on a date was like. Even if Perkins *was* using some beguiling spell, it was a bad idea to get involved with anyone in the Mystical Arts. There is a very good reason why they are all single. Love and magic are like oil and water—they just don't mix.

I stood and watched the three sorcerers stare at the house from every direction, apparently doing nothing. I knew better than to ask them what was going on or how they were doing. A moment's distraction could unravel a spell in a twinkling. Moobin and Price were dressed casually and without any metal, for fear of burns, but Lady Mawgon was in traditional garb. She wore long black crinolines that rustled like leaves when she walked and often sparkled in the darkness. During the kingdom's frequent power cuts, I could always tell when it was she gliding down one of Zambini Towers' endless corridors. Once, in a daring moment, someone had pinned stars and a moon cut from silver foil to her black dress, which made her incandescent with rage. She ranted to Mr. Zambini for almost twenty minutes about how no one was taking their calling seriously, and how could she be expected to work with such infantile nincompoops? Zambini spoke to everyone in turn, but he probably found it as funny as the rest of us. We never discovered who did it, but I reckoned it was Full Price.

With little else to do except keep an eye on the three sorcerers, I sat down on a handy garden bench and read Wizard Moobin's newspaper. The text that he had moved around the paper was still out of place, and I frowned. Tuning spells like these were usually temporary, and I would have expected the text to drift back to its original position. Sorcery was like running a marathon—you needed to pace yourself. Sprint too early, and you could find yourself in trouble near the finish line. Moobin must have been feeling confident to tie off the end of the spell so the effect would be permanent. I looked under the car and noted that the gearbox was shiny like new and didn't have a leak. It looked like Lady Mawgon was having a good day too.

"Quark."

"Where?"

The Quarkbeast pointed one of his razor-sharp claws toward the east as Prince Nasil streaked past much faster than he should have. He banked steeply, circled the house twice, and came in for a perfect landing right next to us. He liked to carpet standing up like a surfer, much to the disdain of Owen of Rhayder, who sat on his carpet in the more traditional cross-legged position at the rear. Nasil wore baggy shorts and a Hawaiian shirt, too, which didn't go down well with Lady Mawgon.

"Hi, Jenny," said Nasil with a grin. "Delivery for you." He handed me a flight log to sign as the Quarkbeast wandered off.

At the front of the carpet was a large Yummy Flakes cereal box, which opened to reveal a tall and gangly lad with curly sandy-colored hair and freckles that danced around a snub nose. He was wearing what were very obviously hand-me-down clothes. He stared at me with the air of someone recently displaced and still confused over how they should feel about it.

Twitter: Want to discuss or share what you just read? Use the hashtag #beaDRAGON to connect with others.

ABOUT THE AUTHOR

Jasper Fforde, the author of the best-selling *Thursday Next* books and the *Nursery Crime* mysteries, has a devoted worldwide fan base. He lives with his family in Wales. Visit his website at www.jasperfforde.com.

Imprint: Harcourt Books
BEA Booth #: 3447, 3448
Printed galley at BEA: yes
Contact for printed galley: jennifer.groves@hmhpub.com
Print ISBN: 978-0-547-73847-5
Print price: $16.99
eBook ISBN: 978-0-547-93542-3
eBook price: $9.99
Publication date: 9/4/2012
Publicity contact: Jennifer Groves jennifer.groves@hmhpub.com
Rights contact: Candace Finn candace.finn@hmhpub.com
Editor: Jeannette Larson
Agent: Claire Conrad
Agency: Janklow & Nesbit
Promotional Information:
• National media campaign
• Author tour
• Bookseller sweepstakes
• Advance bound manuscripts for limited distribution
• Extensive special effect ARC distribution
• Educator guide/reader discussion guide
• Video trailer
• Series website
• Print and online consumer advertising and promotion

The jungle hides a girl who cannot die.

ORIGIN

JESSICA KHOURY

SUMMARY

An electrifying action-romance that's as thoughtful as it is tragic. Pia has grown up in a secret laboratory hidden deep in the Amazon rain forest. She was raised by a team of scientists who have created her to be the start of a new immortal race. But on the night of her seventeenth birthday, Pia discovers a hole in the electric fence that surrounds her sterile home—and sneaks outside the compound for the first time in her life. Free in the jungle, Pia meets Eio, a boy from a nearby village. Together, they embark on a race against time to discover the truth about Pia's origin—a truth with deadly consequences that will change their lives forever. *Origin* is a beautifully told, shocking new way to look at an age-old desire: to live forever, no matter the cost. This is a supremely compelling debut novel that blends the awakening romance of *Matched* with the mystery and jungle conspiracy of *Lost*.

EXCERPT

"Pia." His hand runs up my arm to my elbow, leaving goose bumps in its wake. "You shouldn't have to sneak in and out like this, hiding under their cars." He shakes his head, angry crinkles at the corners of his eyes. "You live in fear of these people. Why won't you admit it? It's a cage, Pia. You must see that. You must feel it every time you look over your shoulder. Look, you're doing it now!"

I *am* looking over my shoulder, but it's not because of what he's saying. It's because the spot where my ride home should be—is empty.

The sound of rumbling engines comes from the direction of the river, and I crouch in the ferns with Eio and watch as a Jeep drives past. It's driven by the guard who was supposed to be returning from his shift, and he's carrying two passengers. Strangers: a brunette woman and white-haired man.

"Oh, no," I moan. There's no doubt in my mind as to who they are.

Corpus.

"They're early," I breathe.

"Who is that?" Eio kneels beside me, his hand still on mine.

"They're from the outside. They've come to see me." And when they arrive in Little Cam and ask for me, the truth will be known. Everything—and everyone—will be compromised. Me, Aunt Harriet, Eio.

No. Not Eio. I can't let him get caught up in this. I remember what I told him the morning I sneaked back into Little Cam: "*If they found out you knew too much about me, they might . . .*" I'm still not sure what they would do, but I know I don't want to find out.

More rumbling. Another Jeep is coming. This one, also driven by a guard, is carrying the Corpus representatives' luggage.

"I have to get on one of those Jeeps," I whisper. "Eio, I absolutely must get back into Little Cam without anyone noticing."

He looks like he wants to argue with me about it, but he sighs and nods. "I will help."

"How—"

But he's already gone, ghosting through the jungle after the Jeeps. The second one drives past me just as Eio disappears from view. Then I hear a screech, a shout, and muffled yelling. Following Eio's footsteps, I make my way toward the commotion, then press myself against a Brazil nut tree, out of sight of the Jeeps. By peering around the trunk, I can see everything.

Eio is standing in the middle of the road, arms folded across his chest, blocking the last Jeep. The driver is standing up, yelling, and waving for him to move. This truck has no passengers, just the piled luggage in the back. The other vehicle has gone on; I can see its taillights through the trees. They probably didn't notice what happened.

Eio's eyes flicker to me. He starts shouting back to the driver in Ai'oan. The driver clearly doesn't understand a word, but I've picked up enough of the language to catch most of it.

"Get in, Pia bird, before he runs me over!" he shouts. "You want to go back to that place? Now is your chance. Go, before this idiot does something stupid and I'm forced to put arrows in him!"

Trusting him to keep the driver's attention, I run to the Jeep and vault over its side, landing in a pile of suitcases. I curl up on the dirty mat on the floor and pull a polka-dotted valise over myself. The shouting, mostly consisting of the driver's curses about the stupidity of natives, goes on for a minute more, then finally the Jeep jerks, sputters, and starts rumbling down the road. I poke up my head just enough to peer back. Eio stands on the side of the road, hands at his sides, watching me.

I give him a small wave and a smile, which he doesn't return. Instead, he pulls a passionflower from the quiver on his shoulder and holds it aloft. The message is clear. *Come back soon.*

"I hope so," I whisper. Then the road bends like Eio's bow, and the boy with the flower is lost to the tangled greenery of the jungle.

CHAPTER 20

From under the luggage, I can hear the groan of the gates as we pass into Little Cam, followed by shouts as everyone gathers to greet the visitors. I imagine the smiling faces of the scientists masking their nervousness and the curious eyes of the maintenance workers peering from the back of the crowd. I was supposed to be there. Supposed to be in front, with Uncle Paolo, the first one Corpus saw as they entered the gates of our little compound. I feel like pressing my face into the polka dots of the valise and screaming with frustration. Why are they here two days early? No one whispered a word of this to me this morning. My only conclusion is that no one else knew either.

Perhaps these Corpus people *meant* to surprise us. Catch us off guard. Like the trick questions Uncle Antonio sometimes throws at me in my studies, designed to make me stumble and backtrack, to reevaluate my hypotheses and even discard them altogether. I hate those questions; they're the only ones that throw me offbeat and mar my otherwise spotless record.

I realize that instead of anticipating the Corpus visitors with excitement, as I have been, maybe I ought to have had more dread. I regarded Uncle Paolo's nervousness with amusement. Perhaps I should have taken it as a warning.

The engines of the Jeeps shut off.

I'm trapped. If I jump out now, everyone will see. If I stay here, they'll find me when they unload the suitcases. That is, if Uncle Paolo hasn't already noticed me missing. What will I say? That this was my first time sneaking out? That I didn't go far? *Ai'oans? What Ai'oans? Never heard of them.* I imagine myself shifting from foot to foot as I say the words, my eyes darting anywhere but to Uncle Paolo's face. Not for the first time, I curse my lousy lying skills.

Just when I resign myself to my doom, I hear a loud, whooping laugh that can only be Aunt Harriet's. It comes from nearby and gets louder; she's walking toward my Jeep.

"I'll help with the luggage!" she says. "No, no, I've got it! I'm sturdier than I look!"

Suddenly the valise is lifted from my face, and there she is. Her expression barely flickers at the sight of me packed under the suitcases. "I'll distract them," she whispers. "You better be quick."

She hauls the valise over the side of the Jeep, chattering on about the humidity and the mosquitoes and the other trials of the jungle, and then I hear a thump. Aunt Harriet swears, and I hear the pounding of feet running to her. Drawing a deep breath, as if I could suck courage into my lungs, I peek over the luggage to scope the scene.

The valise is lying open at Aunt Harriet's feet, its contents—consisting of women's clothes—spread across the dirt. The brunette woman from Corpus, wearing a white pantsuit totally unsuited to the jungle, is glaring at Aunt Harriet as her colleague tries not to notice the frilly underwear scattered around Aunt Harriet's feet. Taking advantage of the moment and using every ounce of my speed, I roll over the other side of the Jeep and land in a crouch. Everyone on this side of the caravan is too focused on Aunt Harriet and the woman to notice the blur of a girl breezing around the corner of the garage.

Once I'm well out of sight, I sink against the side of the garage and suck down air, hoping to drown my nerves in oxygen. My clothes are a ruin, my hair is in knots, and there's river mud coating my arms and legs and neck. There's no way I can face Corpus like this.

The B Dorms are eighty yards away, and the path to the building is lined with tall shrubs. If I stay low and move quickly, I can make it there in a matter of seconds. I sidle around the garage, then crouch low, draw a breath, and break into a sprint.

I can still hear the sounds of the crowd, which now include the shouts of Uncle Paolo as he tries to calm everyone down. Without missing a step, I slip through the door of B Labs and race down the hall to the pool. In less than a minute I strip and dive into the water. I swim to the other side, leaving a trail of mud swirling behind me, but by the time I climb out, the dirt is sinking to the bottom. I take only a second to slide past the mirror in the locker room to check for any residual mud, then I'm wrapping a towel around me and heading for the door.

By the time I reach the crowd out front, only two and a half minutes have passed. It's almost as if I never left the Jeep. Soaked, mostly naked, and barefoot, I have no choice but to face everyone.

"*There* you are," a voice growls, and Uncle Antonio grabs my wrist. "Swimming, Pia? Honestly? I've been searching for half an hour! Paolo said you'd be with Harriet. Harriet said you never showed up. I almost thought you'd climbed the fence and run off into the jungle!"

"Ha!" I bleat. "That—that's crazy, Uncle Antonio! I was . . . swimming. See?" I yank a lock of my dripping hair, then decide it's a perfect time to change the subject. "What's going on?"

He bites. "They radioed us forty minutes ago, said they were standing on the banks of the Little Mississip, waiting for a ride." He shakes his head. "Threw the whole place into chaos. Paolo's been yelling non-stop, I'm pretty sure Haruto had a minor stroke, and now Harriet's gone and dumped their underwear in the mud." Uncle Antonio leads me through the crowd, still muttering. "Damn Corpus *would* pull this kind of stunt."

We emerge between Uncle Paolo and Uncle Sergei, who are apologizing profusely to the scowling woman for Aunt Harriet's clumsiness. But when Uncle Antonio clears his throat and everyone turns to stare at us, they all fall silent.

Feeling extremely self-conscious and clinging to my flimsy towel as if it could somehow rewind this day to its innocent beginnings, I smile my brightest.

"Sir and madam," Uncle Paolo says, a vein in his eyelid pulsing so strongly his whole temple twitches, "here she is. Our Pia."

I know he meant to give me an entire speech to recite at this moment, in order to win Corpus over from the start, but the surprise arrival has thrown pretty much all of Uncle Paolo's planning out the window. So I'm left to my own wits, which are still frayed and raw from the encounter with the anaconda this morning.

Was it only this morning? Resisting the urge to sigh and run straight to my bed, I nod to the visitors. "Hello. Welcome to Little Cam."

I try not to wince at the way their eyes roam my body. Neither says hello back to me or offers their name. Despite the fact their eyes are glued to me, I have a feeling that neither of them sees me. They look at me the way Uncle Paolo looks at the lab rats; you can almost see the calculations running across their eyeballs. Summing, subtracting, weighing, and comparing. They don't see a seventeen-year-old girl. They see the result of a particularly long and expensive experiment. And from the intensity and silence of their stares, I can't even tell if they like what they see.

"I'm sure you're hungry and tired," Uncle Paolo says at last. They nod and keep staring as they follow Uncle Paolo and me to the B Dorms, where they'll be put for the duration of their stay. Which is still, as far as I know, undetermined.

Once we're in the dorm and Uncle Antonio helps sort out their luggage, I whisper to Uncle Paolo that I'm going to go change for dinner. He nods distractedly, the tic in his eye still going at full blast. I slip away, glad to be forgotten.

Well, not quite forgotten. The two visitors watch me as I walk down the hall and through the door, as if their eyes were leashed to my heels.

Even as I cross Little Cam, my towel drawn as securely as it can go around me, I feel the weight of those two gazes like chains hung around my neck.

*****

Their names are Victoria Strauss and Gunter Laszlo, I learn during dinner, and together they run the monster of a company that is Corpus. I learn all of this from Aunt Harriet, who sits beside me. The Corpus duo sits with Uncle Paolo and the rest of the Immortis team at their own table. Every five seconds, at least one of them glances over their shoulder at me. I consider sticking my tongue out or picking my nose, but then I remember what Uncle Sergei said about them shutting us down, and I keep my rude gestures to myself.

"They have operations in over twenty countries," Aunt Harriet whispers as she attacks her spaghetti. "Most of them are top secret. There's not a government in the world that can touch these guys. They've got fingers in everything—weapons development, banking, space exploration. But their main focus is biotech research and, more specifically, genetic engineering. In other words," she chops her noodles so they'll fit on her fork, "*you.*"

"How do you know so much about them?"

"They're the ones who recruited me. It was Strauss who approached me first. The woman's psychotic." The fork stabbing turns vicious.

"Why?" I ask. "Is it a personality disorder? Schizophrenia? I can't imagine that someone who's bipolar or delusional would be given a job as important—"

"She's not *literally* psychotic, Pia. Good heavens. I meant it figuratively. She's nuts. Don't you think for a minute I didn't spill *her* suitcase by accident. Oh, no." A meatball suffers a gruesome death beneath Aunt Harriet's knife. "That woman deserves more than just muddy underwear."

"Why?"

"I hear they plan on staying several days. I'm sure you'll figure it out by then."

After dinner, Uncle Paolo suggests the guests retire for the night, but Strauss and Laszlo shake their heads and point toward me. Inwardly, I cringe. After Aunt Harriet's description, I have no idea what to expect from them.

We gather in my lab, which feels tiny once eight people—me, the Immortis team, and the Corpus representatives—are crammed inside of it. I sit on the examination table and hope with every cell in my body that they don't ask me to strip down. They don't, thankfully, but they do comb over every page in my files, which are extensive. Hours go by as Strauss and Laszlo interrogate Uncle Paolo and the rest of the team. What kinds of leukocytes does my body produce against diseases? What are the differences between my chromosomes and those of a normal human? What is my normal level of telomerase? All questions I could answer in my sleep. But no one asks *me*. Strauss and Laszlo have been here for hours, and not once has either of them spoken a word to me. I have a feeling that if I *did* say something, they might startle and stare as if an amoeba had suddenly asked them if they enjoyed their breakfast.

After the questions, they want to see demonstrations of my unique properties, starting with my unbreakable skin. Uncle Paolo picks up a scalpel and hands it to Strauss.

I almost refuse, but Mother, without even looking me in the eye, takes my hand and rolls up my sleeve before I can speak. Strauss seems to relish the blade as it presses against my skin, and I think I see a little of the woman Aunt Harriet seems to loathe so deeply.

"Remarkable," Strauss breathes as she hands the scalpel to Laszlo. "Not a scratch on her."

I'm forced to lie back and not grimace as Laszlo runs the blade over my arm and even my cheek. *It doesn't cut, but it still hurts!* I want to scream, but I can't. Uncle Paolo's eyes are on me at every moment, compelling me to comply. So I close my eyes and think about the future. About the first immortal I'll create. *It'll have to be a male. Maybe I'll get to name him. Maybe . . .* Slowly, as if swimming up through water, Eio's face slips into my mind. *Maybe I'll name him George. . . .* Eio, his body arcing into a perfect dive as he leaps from the top of the waterfall. *Or Peter or Jack . . .* Eio's eyes full of stars as we sit by the river. *Klaus or Sven or Heinrich. Good names. They were all scientists here at one time or another. . . .* Eio leading me through the jungle, holding his hand out, urging me to take it . . .

"Open your eyes, Pia," Mother says.

For a moment, I'm disoriented. There are strange faces looming over me, shining lights in my eyes, watching my pupils shrink and retreat. *Fire*, I think. *You really want to see something? Use firelight.* I stare up at Strauss and Laszlo, willing myself not to blink as they pry at my eyelids.

It's two in the morning when they finally run out of questions to ask. Uncle Jakob yawns into the back of his hand, and Uncle Haruto's eyes are bloodshot.

"Well," Uncle Paolo says, his fingers drumming the exam table by my knee. "What do you think?"

Strauss and Laszlo exchange looks, then glance at me.

"We should speak privately, Dr. Alvez," Laszlo says. His voice never seems louder than a whisper, so everyone has to crane to hear him.

Uncle Paolo nods. "All right, everyone. That's it for tonight."

Apparently "privately" means just Uncle Paolo and the two Corpus representatives, but at this hour, no one seems to mind. They shuffle out, yawning and rubbing their eyes.

I trail behind, but when we reach the stairwell, I stop to tie my shoelace.

No one notices that I'm wearing slip-ons.

Once I hear the door shut behind the others, I lightly slip back down the hall. I don't have to go far. My sense of hearing is well above average.

"Yes, yes, there's no denying she's a marvel," Laszlo is saying, his voice severe. "Subject 77 is perfect. Everything we could have hoped for and more. Which is exactly why we're wondering what the delay is, Alvez. We need *more* of them. She's no good to us on her own."

Subject 77 . . . I have a number?

"We need her if we're to speed up the process," Uncle Paolo replies. I can hear his fingers still drumming the table. "Pia's mind is more advanced than ours could ever be. You've been after a shortcut to immortality for years, haven't you? Well, she's the only one who will discover it, if it even exists. And she's not ready."

I'm ready! I almost yell it out. *I'm ready, oh, am I ready!*

"What exactly are you waiting for?" That's Strauss.

"I've been giving her the Wickham tests right on schedule, but her scores aren't yet at the level necessary for full induction onto the Immortis team."

"The board is growing anxious," Strauss replies. "They want results."

"Pia *is* a result. The greatest result humanity's ever seen. The board will just have to be patient. Anyway, don't *you* control the board? If I remember correctly, whatever you say goes. No questions. No complaints."

"Fine. You want to play it straight? *We* want results. Unlike you, not all of us are inspired by terms like 'the good of mankind' or 'building a better future.' We don't want a race of immortals in five generations. We want solutions *now*. Sato's experiments proved that immortality couldn't be attained by someone born mortal. Fine. We've accepted that. But there are those of us who will have children and grandchildren in the coming years."

"But—"

"*Yes*, we control the board," Strauss continues as if Uncle Paolo had never spoken. "But without more results, without more forward momentum, we'll lose that control. And Paolo. You don't want us to lose control. There are those at Corpus who strongly feel that this operation should be stationed in the States—under a different team."

No, no, no . . . don't shut us down.

"So take Pia to them. Hell, let them all take scalpels to her if they want. Once they see her, they'll shut up about results."

My knees weaken, and I sink against the wall. My hands run up and down my arms as I imagine a hundreds scalpels digging into my skin.

"You know we can't do that," Laszlo replies. "Word would get out. Genisect would start World War III just to get their hands on her. They suspect, you know. They've suspected for years. Why do you think we only risk coming down here once every few decades? They're watching us. Pia is the holy grail of modern science, Alvez; we can't parade her around like a prize pig!"

"All right, point taken. But I'm telling you, she's not ready! We should focus on Dr. Fields's cloning research. It's our best angle."

Silence. Then Strauss: "Dr. Fields isn't going to be cooperating much longer."

"What do you mean?"

Yes, what do you mean?

"The sister. She's dead."

"What?"

"Fields doesn't know. She *can't* know, for as long as possible. The minute she finds out, she'll be gone. We need her research, Alvez. She's the best in her, well, *field*."

What's going on?! I clap a hand over my mouth to prevent myself from shouting aloud.

"It comes down to Pia," Strauss continues. "When is the next Wickham test scheduled?"

"Three months. And it's not the last one. There are three more—"

"It *is* the last one, and it's happening tomorrow."

"I—Victoria, that's impossible. It's too soon. She's not ready."

"But she will be. After tomorrow."

"Victoria, really, I—"

"*Tomorrow*." Her voice lowers. I have to strain to hear. "I will speak plainly, Alvez, because we both know what Corpus is capable of. Remember Geneva?"

Complete silence.

Then Strauss continues. "There are at least twenty scientists I can think of who would *kill* for the chance to have your job. Your job and the jobs of your entire team. Don't make it come to that. I swear, Alvez, if you resist us on this—"

A strangled murmur from Uncle Paolo.

"What was that?" Strauss asks.

"It won't come to that. As you say. Tomorrow."

I hear a rustling of papers and shoes and sense that the conversation is wrapping up.

Heart hammering and skin the temperature of liquid nitrogen, I flee the building.

Twitter: Want to discuss or share what you just read? Use the hashtag #beaORIGIN to connect with others.

ABOUT THE AUTHOR

Jessica Khoury was born and raised in Georgia. She attended public school followed by homeschooling, and earned her bachelor's degree in English from Toccoa Falls College. *Origin* is her first novel. She lives with her husband, Benjamin, in Toccoa, Georgia.

Imprint: Razorbill
BEA Booth #: 3922
Author appearances: The author will sign at BEA.
Printed galley at BEA: yes
Contact for printed galley: yrpublicity@us.penguingroup.com

Print ISBN: 9781595145956
Print price: $17.99
eBook ISBN: 9781101590720
eBook price: $10.99
Publication date: 9/4/2012
Publicity contact: Shanta Newlin shanta.newlin@us.penguingroup.com
Rights contact: Kim Ryan kim.ryan@us.penguingroup.com
Editor: Laura Arnold
Agent: Lucy Carson
Agency: Friedrich Agency
Territories sold:
    Germany, the Netherlands
Promotional Information:
- 250,000 copy announced first print run
- National media campaign
- Extensive ARC distribution, book trailer, author video
- Massive blogger outreach five months leading up to publication
- Author blog tour
- Major consumer advertising campaign including TV, print and online
- Extensive online and social media promotion
- High-impact 9-copy floor display with riser
- Anchor Penguin's Big Five Breathless Reads campaign Fall 2012
- Major promotion and ARC distribution at all national school and library conferences

the

Yellow

Birds

a novel

Kevin

Powers

SUMMARY

"The war tried to kill us in the spring," begins this breathtaking account of friendship and loss. In Al Tafar, Iraq, twenty-one-year old Private Bartle and eighteen-year-old Private Murphy cling to life as their platoon launches a bloody battle for the city. In the endless days that follow, the two young soldiers do everything to protect each other from the forces that press in on every side: the insurgents, physical fatigue, and the mental stress that comes from constant danger.

Bound together since basic training when their tough-as-nails Sergeant ordered Bart to watch over Murph, the two have been dropped into a war neither is prepared for. As reality begins to blur into a hazy nightmare, Murph becomes increasingly unmoored from the world around him and Bartle takes impossible actions.

With profound emotional insight, especially into the effects of a hidden war on mothers and families at home, *The Yellow Birds* is a groundbreaking novel about the costs of war that is destined to become a classic.

EXCERPT

Chapter 1

September 2004

Al Tafar, Nineveh Province, Iraq

The war tried to kill us in the spring. As grass greened the plains of Nineveh and the weather warmed, we patrolled the low-slung hills beyond the cities and towns. We moved over them and through the tall grass on faith, kneading paths into the windswept growth like pioneers. While we slept, the war rubbed its thousand ribs against the ground in prayer. When we pressed onward through exhaustion, its eyes were white and open in the dark. While we ate, the war fasted, fed by its own deprivation. It made love and gave birth and spread through fire.

Then, in summer, the war tried to kill us as the heat blanched all color from the plains. The sun pressed into our skin, and the war sent its citizens rustling into the shade of white buildings. It cast a white shade on everything, like a veil over our eyes. It tried to kill us every day, but it had not succeeded. Not that our safety was preordained. We were not destined to survive. The fact is, we were not destined at all. The war would take what it could get. It was patient. It didn't care about objectives, or boundaries, whether you were loved by many or not at all. While I slept that summer, the war came to me in my dreams and showed me its sole purpose: to go on, only to go on. And I knew the war would have its way.

The war had killed thousands by September. Their bodies lined the pocked avenues at irregular intervals. They were hidden in alleys, were found in bloating piles in the troughs of the hills outside the cities, the faces puffed and green, allergic now to life. The war had tried its best to kill us all: man, woman, child. But it had killed fewer than a thousand soldiers like me and Murph. Those numbers still meant something to us as what passed for fall began. Murph and I had agreed. We didn't want to be the thousandth killed. If we died later, then we died. But let that number be someone else's milestone.

We hardly noticed a change when September came. But I know now that everything that will ever matter in my life began then. Perhaps light came a little more slowly to the city of Al Tafar, falling the way it did beyond thin shapes of rooflines and angled promenades in the dark. It fell over buildings in the city, white and tan, made of clay bricks roofed with corrugated metal or concrete. The sky was vast and catacombed with clouds. A cool wind blew down from the distant hillsides we'd been patrolling all year. It passed over the minarets that rose above the citadel, flowed down through alleys with their flapping green awnings, out over the bare fields that ringed the city, and finally broke up against the scattered dwellings from which our rifles bristled. Our platoon moved around our rooftop position, grey streaks against the predawn light. It was still late summer then, a Sunday, I think. We waited.

For four days we had crawled along the rooftop grit. We slipped and slid on a carpeting of loose brass casings left over from the previous days' fighting. We curled ourselves into absurd shapes and huddled below the whitewashed walls of our position. We stayed awake on amphetamines and fear.

I pushed my chest off the rooftop and crested the low wall, trying to scan the few acres of the world for which we were responsible. The squat buildings beyond the field undulated through the tinny green of my scope. Bodies were scattered about from the past four days of fighting in the open space between our positions and the rest of Al Tafar. They lay in the dust, broken and shattered and bent, their white shifts gone dark with blood. A few smoldered among the junipers and spare tufts of grass, and there was a heady mix of carbon and bolt oil and their bodies burning in the newly crisp air of morning.

I turned around, ducked back below the wall and lit a cigarette, shielding the cherry in my curled palm. I pulled long drags off it and blew the smoke against the top of the roof, where it spread out, then rose and disappeared. The ash grew long and hung there and a very long time seemed to pass before it fell to the ground.

The rest of the platoon on the roof started to move and jostle with the flickering half-light of dawn. Sterling perched with his rifle over the wall, sleeping and starting throughout our waiting. He jerked his head back occasionally and swiveled to see if anyone had caught him. He showed me a broad disheveled grin in the receding dark, held up his trigger finger and daubed Tabasco sauce into his eyes to stay awake. He turned back toward our sector, and his muscles visibly bucked and tensed beneath his gear.

Murph's breath was a steady comfort to my right. I had grown accustomed to it, the way he'd punctuate its rhythm with a well-practiced spit into an acrid pool of dark liquid that always seemed to be growing between us. He smiled up at me. "Want a rub, Bart?" I nodded. He passed me a can of care-package Kodiak, and I jammed it into the cup of my bottom lip, snubbing out my cigarette. The wet tobacco bit and made my eyes water. I spat into the pool between us. I was awake. Out of the grey early morning the city became whole. White flags hung in a few scattered windows in the buildings beyond the bodies in the field. They formed an odd crochet where the window's dark recesses were framed by jagged glass. The windows themselves were set into whitewashed buildings that became ever brighter in the sun. A thin fog off the Tigris dissipated, revealing what hints of life remained, and in the soft breeze from the hills to the north the white rags of truce fluttered above those same green awnings.

Sterling tapped at the face of his watch. We knew the muezzin's song would soon warble its eerie fabric of minor notes out from the minarets, calling the faithful to prayer. It was a sign and we knew what it meant, that hours had passed, that we had drawn nearer to our purpose, which was as vague and foreign as the indistinguishable dawns and dusks with which it came.

"On your toes, guys!" the LT called in a forceful whisper.

Murph sat up and calmly worked a small dot of lubricant into the action of his rifle. He chambered a round and rested the barrel against the low wall. He stared off into the gray angles where the streets and alleys opened onto the field to our front. I could see into his blue eyes, the whites spiderwebbed with red. They had fallen farther into his sockets during the past few months. There were times when I looked at him and could only see two small shadows, two empty holes. I let the bolt push a round into the chamber of my rifle and nodded at him. "Here we go again," I said. He smiled from the corner of his mouth. "Same old shit again," he answered.

We'd come to that building as the moon flagged to a sliver in the first hours of the battle. There were no lights on. We crashed our vehicle through a flimsy metal gate that had once been painted dark red but had since rusted over, so that it was hard to tell what part had been painted red and what part was rust. When the ramp dropped from our vehicle we rushed to the door. A few soldiers from first squad rushed to the back, and the rest of the platoon stacked up at the front. We kicked in both doors at the same time and ran in. The building was empty. As we went through each room, the lights affixed to the front of our rifles cut narrow cylinders through the dark interior, but they were not bright enough to see by. The lights showed the dust we'd kicked up. Chairs had been turned over in some of the rooms, and colorfully woven rugs hung over the windowsills where the glass had been shot out. There were no people. In some of the rooms we thought we saw people and we yelled out sharply for the people who were not there to get on the floor. We went through each room like that until we got to the roof. When we got to the roof, we looked out over the field. The field was flat and made of dust and the city was dark behind it.

At daybreak on the first day our interpreter, Malik, came out onto the flat concrete roof and sat next to me where I leaned against the wall. It was not yet light, but it almost appeared to be because the sky was white the way the sky is when it's heavy with snow. We heard fighting across the city, but it had not reached us yet. Only the noise of rockets and machine guns and helicopters swooping down near vertical in the distance told us we were in a war.

"This is my old neighborhood," he told me.

His English was exceptional. There was a glottal sound in his voice, but it was not harsh. I'd often asked him to help me with my sparse Arabic, trying to get my pronunciation of this or that word right. "Shukran." "Afwan." "Qumbula." *Thank you. You're welcome. Bomb.* He'd help, but he always ended our exchanges by saying, "My friend, I need to speak English. For the practice." He'd been a student at the university before the war, studying literature. When the university closed, he came to us. He wore a hood over his face, worn khaki slacks and a faded dress shirt that appeared to be ironed freshly every day. He never took his mask off. The one time Murph and I had asked him about it, he took his index finger and traced the fringe of the hood that hung around his neck. "They'll kill me for helping you. They'll kill my whole family."

Murph hunched low and trotted over from the other side of the roof where he had been helping the LT and Sterling set up the machine gun after we'd arrived. Watching him move, I got the impression that the flatness of the desert made him nervous. That somehow the low ridgelines in the distance made the dried brown grasses of the flood-plain even more unbearable.

"Hey, Murph," I said. "This is Malik's old stomping grounds."

Murph ducked quickly and sat next to the wall. "Whereabouts?" he asked.

Malik stood up and pointed to a strip of buildings that seemed to grow organically in odd, not quite ninety-degree sections. The build-ings stood beyond the field at the beginning of our sector. A little far-ther past the outskirts of Al Tafar, there was an orchard. Fires burned from steel drums and trash heaps and sprung up seemingly without cause around the edges of the city. Murph and I did not stand up, but we saw where Malik pointed.

"Mrs. Al-Sharifi used to plant her hyacinth in this field." He spread his hands out wide and moved his arms in a sweeping motion that reminded me of convocation.

Murph reached for the cuff of Malik's pressed shirt. "Careful, big guy. You're gonna get silhouetted."

"She was this crazy old widow." He had his hands on his hips. His eyes were glazed over with exhaustion. "The women in the neighborhood were so jealous of those flowers." Malik laughed. "They accused her of using magic to make them grow the way they did." He'd paused then, and put his hands on the dried mud wall we'd been leaning against. "They were burned up in the battle last fall. She did not try to replant them this year," he finished brusquely.

I tried to imagine living there but could not, even though we had pa-trolled the same streets Malik was talking about and drank tea in the small clay hovels and I'd had my hands wrapped in the thinly veined hands of the old men and women who lived in them. "All right, bud-dy," I said. "You're gonna get your ass shot off if you don't get down."

"It is a shame you didn't see those hyacinths," he said.

And then it started. It seemed as if the movement of one moment to the next had its own trajectory, a thing both finite and expansive, like the endless divisibility of numbers strung out on a line. The tracers reached out from all the dark spaces in the buildings across the field, and there were many more bullets than streaks of phosphorescence. We heard them tear at the air around our ears and smack into the clay brick and concrete. We did not see Malik get killed, but Murph and I had his blood on both of our uniforms. When we got the order to cease fire we looked over the low wall and he was lying in the dust and there was a lot of blood around him.

"Doesn't count, does it?" Murph asked.

"No. I don't think so."

"What're we at?"

"Nine sixty-eight? Nine seventy? We'll have to check the paper when we get back."

I was not surprised by the cruelty of my ambivalence then. Nothing seemed more natural than someone getting killed. And now, as I reflect on how I felt and behaved as a boy of twenty-one from my position of safety in a warm cabin above a clear stream in the Blue Ridge, I can only tell myself that it was necessary. I needed to continue. And to continue, I had to see the world with clear eyes, to focus on the essential. We pay attention only to rare things, and death was not rare. Rare was the bullet with your name on it, the IED buried just for you. Those were the things we watched for.

I didn't think about Malik much after that. He was an incidental figure who only seemed to exist in his relation to my continuing life. I couldn't have articulated it then, but I'd been trained to think war was the great unifier, that it brought people closer together than any other activity on earth. Bullshit. War is the great maker of solipsists: how are you going to save my life today? Dying would be one way. If you die, it becomes more likely that I will not. You're nothing, that's the secret: a uniform in a sea of numbers, a number in a sea of dust. And we somehow thought those numbers were a sign of our own insignificance. We thought that if we remained ordinary, we would not die. We confused correlation for cause and saw a special significance in the portraits of the dead, arranged neatly next to the number corresponding to their place on the growing list of casualties we read in the newspapers, as indications of an ordered war. We had a sense, something we felt only in the brief flash of synapse to synapse, that these names had been on the list long before the dead had come to Iraq. That the names were there as soon as those portraits had been taken, a number given, a place assigned. And that they'd been dead from that moment forward. When we saw the name Sgt. Ezekiel Vasquez, twenty-one, Laredo, Texas, #748, killed by small-arms fire in Baqubah, Iraq, we were sure that he'd walked as a ghost for years through South Texas. We thought he was already dead on the flight over, that if he was scared when the C-141 bringing him to Iraq had pitched and yawed through the sky above Baghdad there had been no need. He had nothing to fear. He'd been invincible, absolutely, until the day he was not. The same, too, for Spc. Miriam Jackson, nineteen, Trenton, New Jersey, #914, dead as a result of wounds sustained in a mortar attack in Samarra, at Landsthul Regional Medical Center. We were glad. Not that she was killed, only that we were not. We hoped that she'd been happy, that she took advantage of her special status before she inevitably arrived under that falling mortar, having gone out to hang her freshly washed uniform on a line behind her connex.

Of course, we were wrong. Our biggest error was thinking that it mattered what we thought. It seems absurd now that we saw each death as an affirmation of our lives. That each one of those deaths belonged to a time and that therefore that time was not ours. We didn't know the list was limitless. We didn't think beyond a thousand. We never considered that we could be among the walking dead as well. I used to think that maybe living under that contradiction had guided my actions and that one decision made or unmade in adherence to this philosophy could have put me on or kept me off the list of the dead.

I know it isn't like that now. There were no bullets with my name on them, or with Murph's, for that matter. There were no bombs made just for us. Any of them would have killed us just as well as they'd killed the owners of those names. We didn't have a time laid out for us, or a place. I have stopped wondering about those inches to the left and right of my head, the three-miles-an-hour difference that would have put us directly over an IED. It never happened. I didn't die. Murph did. And though I wasn't there when it happened, I believe unswervingly that when Murph was killed, the dirty knives that stabbed him were addressed "To whom it may concern." Nothing made us special. Not living. Not dying. Not even being ordinary. Still, I like to think there was a ghost of compassion in me then, and that if I'd had a chance to see those hyacinths I would have noticed them.

Malik's body, crumpled and broken at the foot of the building, didn't shock me. Murph passed me a smoke and we lay down beneath the wall again. But I could not stop thinking about a woman Malik's conversation had reminded me of, who'd served us tea in small, finely blemished cups. The memory seemed impossibly distant, buried in the dust, waiting for some brush to uncover it. I remembered how she'd blushed and smiled, and how impossible it was for her to not be beautiful, despite her age, a paunch, a few teeth gone brown and her skin appearing like the cracked, dry clay of summer.

Perhaps that is how it was: a field full of hyacinth. It was not like that when we stormed the building, not like that four days after Malik died. The green grasses that waved in the breeze were burned by fire and the summer sun. The festival of people on the market street with their long white shifts and loud voices were gone. Some of them were lying dead in the courtyards of the city or in its lace of alleys. The rest walked or rode in sluggish caravans, on foot or in orange and white jalopies, in mule-drawn carts or in huddled groups of twos and threes, women and men, the old and young, the whole and wounded. All that was the life of Al Tafar left in a drab parade out of the city. They walked past our gates, past Jersey walls and gun emplacements, out into the dry September hills. They did not raise their eyes in the curfewed hours. They were a speckled line of color in the dark and they were leaving.

A radio crackled in the rooms beneath us. The lieutenant quietly gave our situation report to our command. "Yes, sir," he said, "roger, sir," and it passed, at each level more removed from us, until I am sure somewhere someone was told, in a room that was warm and dry and safe, that eighteen soldiers had watched the alleys and streets of Al Tafar through the night and that X number of enemies were lying dead in a dusty field.

The day had almost broken over the city and the ridges in the desert when the low, electric noise of the radio was replaced by the sound of the lieutenant's boots padding up the staircase to the roof. Mere outlines took shape, and the city, vague and notional at night, became a contoured and substantial thing before us. I looked west. Tans and greens emerged in the light. The gray of mud walls, of buildings and courtyards arranged in squat honeycombs, receded with the rising sun. A few fires burned in the grove of thin and ordered fruit trees a little to the south. The smoke rose through a gently tattered canopy of leaves only slightly taller than a man and leaned obediently to the wind coming across the valley.

The lieutenant came up to the roof and lowered himself into a slouch, his upper body parallel to the earth, his legs chugging, until he reached the wall. He sat with his back against the wall and gestured for us to gather around him.

"All right, guys. This is the deal."

Murph and I leaned against each other until the weight of our bodies found their balance. Sterling inched closer to the lieutenant and fixed his eyes in a hard glare that traversed the rest of us on the roof. I looked at the lieutenant as he spoke. His eyes were dim. Before he continued he let out a short, bright sigh and rubbed a rash the color of washed-out raspberries with two fingers. It covered a small oval from his sharp brow line down onto his left cheek and seemed to follow the rounded path of his eye socket

The LT was a distant person by nature. I don't even remember where he was from. There was something restrained about him, something more than simple adherence to nonfraternization. It was not elitism. He seemed to be unknowable, or slightly adrift. He sighed often. "We're here until midday or so," he said. "Third platoon is going to push through the alleys to our northwest and try to flush them to our front. Hopefully they'll be too scared to do much shooting at us before we…" He paused and brought his hand down from his face, reached into the pockets on his chest beneath his body armor and fished for a cigarette. I handed him one. "Thanks, Bartle," he said. He turned to look at the orchard burning to the south. "How long have those fires been going?"

"Probably started last night," said Murph.

"OK, you and Bartle keep an eye on that."

The column of smoke that bent beneath the wind had straightened. It cut a black runny line across the sky.

"What was I saying before that?" The lieutenant looked absently over his shoulder and inched his eyes up over the wall. "Fuck me," he muttered.

A specialist from second squad said, "Hey, no sweat, LT, we got it."

Sterling cut him off. "Shut the fuck up. LT's done when he says he's fucking done."

I didn't realize it then, but Sterling seemed to know exactly how hard to push the LT so that discipline remained. He didn't care if we hated him. He knew what was necessary. He smiled at me and his straight, white teeth reflected the early morning sun. "You were saying, sir, that hopefully they'll be too scared to shoot before…" The LT opened his mouth to finish his thought, but Sterling continued, "Before we fucking kill the hajji fucks."

The lieutenant nodded his head and slouched over and trotted downstairs. We crawled back to our positions to wait. A fire had begun to burn in the town, its source obscured by walls and alleys. Thick black smoke seemed to join from a hundred fires all over Al Tafar, becoming one long curl up toward heaven.

The sun gathered itself behind us, rising in the east, warming the collar of my blouse, baking in the salt that clotted in hard lines and snaked around our necks and arms. I turned my head and looked right into it. I had to close my eyes, but I could still see its shape, a white hole in the darkness, before I turned west again and opened them.

Two minarets rose, like arms, up from the dusty buildings, slightly obscured now and then by smoke. They were dormant. No sound had come from them that morning. No adhan had been called. The long line of refugees that snaked its way out of the city for the past four days had slowed. Only a few old men bent over worn canes of cedar shuffled between the field of dead and the grove of trees. Two gaunt dogs bounced around them, nipped their heels, retreated when struck, and then started in on them again.

And it began once more. The orchestral whine of falling mortars arrived from all around us. Even after so many months beneath them, there was a blank confusion on the faces of the platoon. We stared at one another with mouths agape, fingers strangling the grips of our rifles. It was a clear dawn in September in Al Tafar, and the war seemed narrowly focused, as if it occurred only in this place, and I remember feeling like I had jumped into a cold river on the first warm day of spring, wet and scared and breathing hard, with nothing to do but swim.

"Incoming!"

We moved by rote, our bodies made prostrate, our fingers interlaced behind our heads, our mouths open to keep the pressure balanced.

And then the sound of the impacts echoed off into the morning. I didn't raise my head until the last reverberation faded.

I looked over the wall slowly, and a din of voices shouted, "All clear!" and "I'm up!"

"Bartle?" Murph huffed.

"I'm up, I'm up," I said quietly, and I was breathing very hard and I looked out over the field and there were wounds in the earth and in the already dead and battered bodies and a few small juniper trees were turned up and on their sides where the mortars fell. Sterling ran to the opening in the floor and yelled down to the LT, "Up, sir." He moved to each one of us on the roof, smacking the back of our helmets, "Get ready, motherfuckers," he said.

I hated him. I hated the way he excelled in death and brutality and domination. But more than that, I hated the way he was necessary, how I needed him to jar me into action even when they were trying to kill me, how I felt like a coward until he screamed into my ear, "Shoot these hajji fucks!" I hated the way I loved him when I inched up out of the terror and returned fire, seeing him shooting too, smiling the whole time, screaming, the whole rage and hate of these few acres, alive and spreading, in and through him.

And they did come, shadowed in windows. They came out from behind woven prayer rugs and fired off bursts and the bullets whipped past and we'd duck and listen as they smacked against the concrete and mud-brick and little pieces flew in every direction. They ran through trash-strewn alleys, past burning drums and plastic blowing like clumps of thistle over the ancient cobblestones.

Sterling yelled a long time that day before I squeezed the trigger. My ears had already rung out from the noise and the first bullet I released into the field seemed to leave my rifle with a dull pop. It kicked up a little cloud of dust when it hit and it was surrounded by many other little clouds of dust just like it.

Rounds by the hundreds shook dust off the ground, the trees and buildings. An old car crumpled and collapsed beneath the dust. Once in a while, someone ran between the buildings, behind the orange and white cars, over the rooftops, and they'd surround themselves with little clouds of dust.

A man ran behind a low wall in a courtyard and looked around, astonished to be alive, his weapon cradled in his arms. My first instinct was to yell out to him, "You made it, buddy, keep going," but I remembered how odd it would be to say a thing like that. It was not long before the others saw him too.

He looked left, then right, and the dust popped around him, and I wanted to tell everyone to stop shooting at him, to ask, "What kind of men are we?" An odd sensation came over me, as if I had been saved, for I was not a man, but a boy, and that he may have been frightened, but I didn't mind that so much, because I was frightened too, and I realized with a great shock that I was shooting at him and that I wouldn't stop until I was sure that he was dead, and I felt better knowing we were killing him together and that it was just as well not to be sure you are the one who did it.

But I knew. I shot him and he slumped over behind the wall. He was shot again by someone else and the bullet went through his chest and ricocheted, breaking a potted plant hanging from a window above the courtyard. Then he was shot again and he fell at a strange angle— backward over his bent legs—and most of the side of his face was gone and there was a lot of blood and it pooled around him in the dust.

A car drove toward us along the road between the orchard and the field of dead. Two large white sheets billowed from its rear windows. Sterling ran to the other side of the building, where the machine gun was set up. I looked through my scope and saw an old man behind the wheel and an elderly woman in the back passenger seat.

Sterling laughed. "Come on, motherfuckers."

He couldn't see them. I'll yell, I thought. I'll tell him they are old, let them pass.

But bullets bit at the crumbling road around the car. They punched into the sheet metal.

I said nothing. I followed the car with my scope. The old woman ran her fingers along a string of pale beads. Her eyes were closed.

I couldn't breathe.

The car stopped in the middle of the road, but Sterling did not stop the shooting. The bullets ripped through the car and out the other side. The holes in the car funneled light, and the smoke and dust hung in the light. The door opened and she fell from the old car. She tried to drag herself to the side of the road. She crawled. Her old blood mixed with the ash and dust. She stopped moving.

"Holy shit, that bitch got murdered," Murph said. There was no grief, or anguish, or joy, or pity in that statement. There was no judgment made. He was just surprised, like he was waking from a long afternoon nap, disoriented, realizing that the world has continued uninterrupted in spite of the strange things that may have happened while you slept. He could have said that it was Sunday, as we did not know what day it was. And it would have been a sudden thing to notice that it was Sunday at a time like that. But he spoke the truth either way, and it wouldn't have mattered much if it had been Sunday, and since none of us had slept in a long time, none of it really seemed to matter much at all.

Sterling sat down behind the wall next to the machine gun. He waved us to him and took a piece of pound cake from the cargo pocket on his trousers as we listened to the final bursts of nervous firing peter out. He broke the dry cake into three pieces. "Take this," he said. "Eat."

The smoke rose and began to disappear. I watched the old woman bleed on the side of the road. The dust blew in languid waves and began to swirl slightly. We heard shots again. Beyond a building a small girl with auburn curls and a tattered sundress stepped out toward the old woman. Errant bullets from other positions kicked up the dust around her in dry blooms.

We looked to Sterling. He waved us off. "Someone get on the net and tell those fuckers it's just a kid," he said.

The girl ducked behind the building, then emerged again, this time shuffling toward the old woman very slowly. She tried dragging the body, and her face contorted with effort as she pulled the old woman by her one complete arm. The girl described circles into the fine dust as she paced around the body. The path they made was marked in blood: from the car smoking and ablaze, through a courtyard ringed by hyacinths, to the place where the woman lay dead, attended by the small child, who rocked and moved her lips, perhaps singing some desert elegy that I couldn't hear.

The ash from the burning of clay bricks and the fat of lean men and women covered everything. The pale minarets dominated the smoke, and the sky was still pale like snow. The city seemed to reach upward out of the settling dust. Our part was over, for a while at least. It was September and though there were few trees from which leaves could fall, some did. They shook off the scarred and slender branches, buffeted by the wind and light descending from the hills to the north. I tried to count the leaves as they fell, removed from their moorings by the impact of mortars and bombs. They shook. A thin sheaf of dust floated off each one.

I looked at Murph and Sterling and the rest of the platoon on the roof. The LT walked to each of us and put his hand on our arms, speaking softly, trying to soothe us with the sound of his voice, the way one would with frightened horses. Perhaps our eyes were wet and black, perhaps we bared our teeth. "Good job," and "You're OK," and "We're gonna be OK," he said. It was a hard to believe that we'd be OK and that we'd fought well. But I remember being told that the truth does not depend on being believed.

The radio came on again. Before long the LT would give us another mission. We would be tired when the mission came, but we would go, for we had no alternative. Perhaps we'd had them once: alternatives, other paths to take. But our course was certain then, if unknown. It was going to be dark before we knew it. We had lived, Murph and me.

I try so hard now to remember if I saw any hint of what was coming, if there was some shadow over him, some way I could have known he was so close to being killed. In my memory of those days on the rooftop, he is half a ghost. But I didn't see it then, and couldn't. No one can see that. I guess I'm glad I didn't know, because we were happy that morning in Al Tafar, in September. Our relief was coming. The day was full of light and warm. We slept.

Twitter: Want to discuss or share what you just read? Use the hashtag #beaBIRDS to connect with others.

ABOUT THE AUTHOR

Kevin Powers joined the army at the age of 17, later serving a year as a machine gunner in Mosul and Tal Afar, Iraq in 2004 and 2005. After his honorable discharge, he muddled through a series of jobs, but eventually quit the last of them and enrolled in Virginia Commonwealth University, where he graduated in 2008 with a Bachelor's degree in English. He is currently a Michener Fellow in Poetry at the University of Texas at Austin, where he will receive his MFA in 2012.

Imprint: Little, Brown and Company
BEA Booth #: 3627
Author appearances: Wednesday, June 6, Lunch (by invitation only) and signing in the corral, 3:00pm.
Printed galley at BEA: yes
Print ISBN: 9780316219365
Print price: $24.99
eBook ISBN: 9780316219358
eBook price: $12.99
Publication date: 9/11/2012
Publicity contact: Nicole Dewey nicole.dewey@hbgusa.com
Editor: Michael Pietsch
Agent: Peter Straus
Agency: RCW Literary Agency

John

Saturnall's

A NOVEL

Feast

Lawrence Norfolk

SUMMARY

Twelve years in the writing, *John Saturnall's Feast* is a masterpiece from one of England's greatest living historical novelists. Set in rural England in the early seventeenth century, *John Saturnall's Feast* is the story of a young orphan who begins working in the kitchens of Buckland Manor House, and grows to become one of the greatest cooks of his generation. John's elaborate creations, great jellied desserts with glazed baubles, and rich forcemeats and stews, are unrivaled in their creativity and execution—and he cooks for aristocratic guests visiting the Manor including King Charles I and his wife. When the young daughter of the Lord of the Manor, Lady Lucretia, vows to fast until her father calls off her engagement to her insipid husband-to-be, it falls to John to try to cook her delicious foods that might tempt her to eat. As John serves meals to Lucretia, an illicit attraction grows between them, but fate is conspiring against the pair—Lucretia's marriage cannot be undone, and the English Civil War is about to break out. Reminiscent of *Wolf Hall, Jonathan Strange & Mr Norrell,* and works by David Mitchell and Peter Carey, *John Saturnall's Feast* is a fantastically rich novel of food, forbidden love, turbulent history, and ancient myths. Beautifully produced with illustrations and recipes, and printed in two colors of ink, it is a delight for all the senses.

EXCERPT

From The Book of John Saturnall: A Broth of Lampreys and All the Fishes that swam in the Days before Eden.

Kings raise their Statues and Churchmen build Cathedrals. A Cook leaves no Monument save Crumbs. His rarest Creations are scraped by Scullions. His greatest Dishes are destined for the Dung-heap. And as those Dishes care naught for their Origin, so None now, I aver, could name the Rivers that watered Saturnus's Gardens, nor number the Fishes that swam in those Quanats and Jubs. But swim they did, those Salmons, Sturgeons, Carps and Trouts, and Eels called Lampreys did nourish themselves upon those Fishes, which Beasts I learned to dress from an Heretical Friend.

Heat water in a Kettle so that you may endure to dip your Hand in but not to let it stay. Put in your Lampreys fresh from the River for the Time it takes to say an Ave Maria, quoth he. Hold the Head in a Napkin lest it slip. With the Back of a Knife scrape off the Mud which rises in great Ruffs and Frills all along the Fish until the Skin will look clean and shining and blue. Open the Belly. Loosen the String found under the Gall (cast that out and the Entrails) and pull it away. It will retch much. Pick out the black Substance under the String, cutting towards the Back as much as is needful. Dry the Fish in Napkins. Now the Lamprey is dressed.

For the cooking, throw the Eels boldly in a great Pan foaming with Butter or slip them at your Ease in a simmering Kettle for no longer (as my Acquaintance put it) than a hurried Miserere. Add a Bay Leaf. Let your Fishes swim till the Waters be cold.

For the Broth take Mace, crushed Cumin, Coriander seeds, Marjoram and Rue, and at last (if you may find it) add that Root, famous in Antiquity for its healing Properties and its peculiar Scent, being at once bituminous and having the sweetness of flowers . . .

* * *

The kitchen was not as large as John had imagined. A line of tables ran along one wall. At the end, three pots stood over a flickering fire tended by a ginger-haired boy. From a doorway opposite came the sound of water splashing and the banging of pots and pans. A man so expressionless he might have been any age looked out from that room.

'That's Mister Stone,' said Philip. 'Head of the Scullery. And that boy over there's Alf.'

'It's not so big,' John ventured. 'The kitchen,' he added when Philip looked puzzled. How could all the men in red livery work in here?

Philip grinned. 'Kitchen's not big enough,' he said to Alf who looked puzzled too for a moment. Then he too smiled.

Philip led John across the flagstone floor and pulled aside a thick leather curtain. A deep hum reached John's ears. A short passage led to some steps and a set of heavy double doors. As he followed Philip, the din got louder. Then the boy heaved on a handle and the door swung open.

'This is the kitchen.'

A wave of noise broke over John, voices shouting, pots banging, pans clanging, knives and cleavers thudding on blocks. But he hardly heard the din. A great flood of aromas swamped the noise, thick as soup and foaming with flavours: powdery sugars and crystallised fruit, dank slabs of beef and boiling cabbage, sweating onions and steaming beets. Fronts of fresh-baked bread rolled forward then sweeter cakes. Behind the whiffs of roasting capons and braising bacon came the great smoke-blackened hams which hung in the hearth. Fish was poaching somewhere in a savoury liquor at once sweet and tart, its aromas braided in twirling spirals . . . The silphium, thought John.

A moment later it was lost in the tangle of scents that rose from the other pots, pans and great steaming urns. The rich stew of smells and tastes reaching into his memory to haul up dishes and platters. For a moment he was back in the wood. His mother's voice was reciting the dishes and the spiced wine was settling like a balm in his stomach, banishing his cold and hunger, even his anger. He closed his eyes and breathed in the scents, drawing them deeper and deeper . . .

'Are you all right?'

'What?' John opened his eyes with a start. Philip Elsterstreet was peering anxiously at his face.

'You not going to be sick, are you?'

John managed a shake of his head.

'Good.' Philip pointed to a dark wooden board nailed above the door. 'Being sick's against the rules.'

Thick pillars supported a vaulted ceiling. Half-moon windows were set high in one wall. Heavy tables filled the middle of the kitchen where men wearing aprons and head scarves chopped, hacked, jointed and tied. Boys lurched between them, staggering under trays and pans towards the wide arches and passage on the far side. At a table near the centre, a circle of men whirled white cloth bundles about their heads as if performing a strange dance.

'Kitchen's older'n the house, Master Scovell says,' Philip went on. 'The fire's even older. If it goes out.' The boy drew a finger across his throat. 'That's it.'

At that moment the men whirling cloths all flung them down at once. Out tumbled a heap of bright green leaves.

'Sallet board,' Philip explained. 'Nothing but leaves allowed on that.'

Behind the sallet board, a cook was hauling down trays the size of small cartwheels from a heavy rack mounted beside a tall dresser. As John watched, he began rolling them over the floor with a call of 'Mind yer backs!'. Men and boys swayed aside as the rumbling discs teetered across the room to topple into a pair of waiting hands. A stack of pewter bowls clattered onto each tray which was carried to the far side of the kitchen. There an enormous hearth stretched the full width of the room. At one end, a long-moustached man drew slow figure-of-eights with a stirring lathe in a pot while his stockier companion wielded a ladle. Fist-sized gobbets of steaming grey porridge slopped stickily into the bowls.

'End of breakfast service,' said Philip. 'For us, I mean. Them up there are still stuffing their faces.'

He gestured up at the ceiling with a dismissive look.

'Up there?'

'The Household. We don't have much to do with them down here. Except feeding them, of course.'

All around the kitchen, the cooks barked orders: 'Water here!' or 'Sharpener!' or 'Dressed and in!' Then an under-cook or a boy would run over to deliver something, or take it away, or lend a hand in another of the kitchen's inscrutable operations.

Beyond the tall dresser John glimpsed a passageway and the foot of a staircase. Across the kitchen, flanked by stacks of firewood, a great chimney breast rose above a gaping hearth. Then a new scent wafted past John's nostrils: sharp but rich. Nestled in straw in a wooden crate on the nearest bench lay a dozen or more fruits, bright yellow with waxy, finely mottled skins. He had seen them in the book, but now he stared.

'Ain't you never seen a lemon before?' Philip Elsterstreet asked.

'Course I have,' John muttered. 'I just didn't know.'

'Know what?'

John hesitated. 'I didn't know they were yellow.'

Philip gave him another odd look. At the far end of the hearth near the arches and the passage, a great cloud of steam billowed up. The smell of fish soup wafted across the kitchen. John saw four men dressed in tunics and aprons step back from the scalding steam. One turned and caught sight of the boys.

'You two!' called the short bald man across the kitchen. 'Come here!'

'That's Master Henry,' whispered Philip. 'Josh's brother.'

'I know,' said John, trying to remember how exactly he was meant to address the man. Look at their faces, he thought. Or not look.

'The other three are the Heads of the Kitchen. Mind your tongue. Especially around Vanian.'

'Who's Vanian?'

'In the middle. Looks like a rat.'

The hearth yawned wider as they approached. John stared up at the wheels and chains of an enormous spit. Above a low fire, an array of simmering pots rose in size to a cauldron large enough to boil a pig.

'That's Master Scovell's copper,' Philip told him in an undertone. An under-cook was applying gentle blasts from a bellows to the glowing embers beneath. John caught the strange smell again. Lilies and pitch, thinner than he remembered.

'Where's Joshua?' Henry Palewick demanded as they approached. 'And that other fellow. Face like a horse.'

'Ben Martin,' said John. After a long pause he remembered to add, 'Master Henry.'

Henry Palewick began questioning Philip on what they were doing in the kitchen where, as Philip and everyone else knew, no one but kitchen staff were permitted unless by invitation. Not even Mister Pouncey could enter unbidden, as Philip well knew. Not even Sir William himself . . .

The rat like Vanian flicked shrewd black eyes over John then returned to his discussion with the other two, which centred on a kettle suspended in the cauldron. The whiff of Ben's parcel hovered under the delicious aroma of fish. Suddenly John felt hungry. The men, he saw, were sipping from a ladle which they passed between them. The tallest of the three slurped and smiled.

'Whether or not Miss Lucretia consumes it, the kitchen has discharged its duty,' he declared cheerfully. He towered a whole head over the others. 'A simple broth is most apt for a young stomach, especially a stomach which chooses privation over nourishment. Lampreys. Crab shells ground fine. Stockfish and. . .' He sniffed then frowned.

'Simple, Mister Underley?' jibed Vanian in a nasal voice. 'If it is simple, then how is it spiced?'

'Came in a parcel this morning,' Henry Palewick offered. 'Down from Soughton. Master Scovell had it out in a moment. Smelled like flowers to me. Whatever it was.'

'Which flowers?' demanded the fourth man of the quartet, in a foreign accent. He pointed a large-nostrilled nose at Henry. 'Saffron, agrimony and comfrey bound the cool-humoured plants; meadowsweet, celandine and wormwood the hot. Which did this smell resemble?'

'That's Master Roos,' whispered Philip to John. 'Spices and sauces.'

'What does it matter, Melichert?' answered Henry with a weary sigh. 'It is a broth of fish and lampreys.'

'Hardly a full description,' Vanian snapped disdainfully. 'One might as well ask a laundry maid how to weave a sheet. One may as well ask this boy!' he concluded contemptuously.

Heads turned. The other cooks peered down. John realised belatedly that Vanian was indicating himself. Before he could retreat, the rat-faced man had beckoned John forward and lifted the lid of the pot.

'Approach, boy,' he ordered, then turned to the others. 'Let us discover how well the untrained palate performs.' Vanian smirked. 'Or fails to perform.'

Beads of yellow oil trembled on the surface. A deep orange liquid shimmered beneath. A puff of pungent steam wafted up, carrying a rich salty smell. Lilies hung behind it, and the pitch. But they were blanched, or blended somehow. John sniffed and the aroma began to uncurl, the flavours separating on his palate, a strange sensation rasping the back of his throat. For the first time since Buckland, John's demon brought out his spoon.

'Observe,' began Vanian in a lofty tone, 'how the broth subsumes its parts into a single liquor, each one transformed. Let us begin with the spices.' He looked expectantly at John for a theatrical moment. 'No? Then allow me . . . '

'Mace,' said John.

Underley's head turned. Roos raised his eyebrows. Henry Palewick stared.

'Crushed cumin,' John continued. 'Coriander seeds, marjoram, rue. Vinegar. Some honey and . . .' His voice trailed off. All four Head Cooks were staring at him. Vanian's black eyes narrowed.

'And?'

He could smell the plant from the wood. But something in Vanian's look made him hold his tongue. Before the cook could ask again, a commotion sounded across the kitchen.

From the door, Mister Fanshawe and Mister Wichett approached like complementary red and green islands, surrounded by their clerks. At the rear, trailed a stony-faced Josh Palewick. At the front, leading the little mob, was the black-haired kitchen boy. Coake's gleeful face found John.

'There he is!' the boy shouted.

'Hold him!' called Fanshawe. 'Take that boy!'

But none of the kitchen staff moved at the Household man's order. As Fanshawe's green-liveried clerks strode forward, John thrust his way between a startled Henry Palewick and Melichert Roos and ran.

The flight of steps rose before him. He passed it and fled down the passageway that led into the depths of the kitchen, the shouts of the clerks pursuing him as he wove his way between porters and cooks who toted baskets or trays, searching a hiding place but finding only more kitchens where fires burned and aproned men worked at tables or store rooms or larders from which a great jumble of tastes and smells gusted down the passage: hanging game, cheeses, yeast, warm bread . . .

He turned a corner, then another. Heart thudding, feet pounding, John ran. Ran as if every soul in Buckland were after him again. Behind him, angry voices called to each other. The kitchens seemed endless but at last the passage began to empty. At a final junction, John ran left and found himself in a dead end. A cobweb-shrouded doorway pierced the wall. He forced the rusted handle down and the heavy door swung back.

A cellar.

John gazed around the cavernous space. Light entered through a grate. A hearth broke the far wall, quite as great as the one in the kitchen. He edged along the wall, searching for a hiding place. Suddenly something knocked his elbow. A moment later a deafening clang sounded in his ears. A pan had fallen to the floor.

As John's eyes adjusted to the light, he saw benches and shelves stacked with pots, glass jars, kettles and pans. He was standing in a kitchen, he realised. But one abandoned with all its equipment. He looked around at the strange place. Then the clerks' shouts sounded, echoing down the passage outside.

He would be caught here, he thought. Then he would be thrown out. Why had he allowed himself to believe that he might find a place at Buckland Manor? What use had Sir William Fremantle, Lord of the Vale of Buckland, for the son of Susan Sandall? Fanshawe's clerks would find him and haul him out. He would be put in the Poor house in Carrboro. Or sent back to the parish.

The shouts drew nearer. But now the din from the kitchen rose too as if someone had opened a connecting door or this neglected place had come back to life. And through the faint clatter and roar he heard a different sound. A voice.

John cast about, his eyes probing the gloom. It came from inside the hearth, he realised. From an opening in the side-wall. A girl's voice.

Peering in, John saw a narrow staircase rise into darkness. The voice drifted down. Somewhere outside, he heard his pursuers draw closer. Quickly, John began to climb.

Spider webs brushed his face. Dust clogged his nostrils. He stifled a sneeze and felt his way up, the voice growing louder with every steep step. The girl seemed to be scolding someone. Rounding the last turn, he saw a crack of light. The outline of a door and a latch.

'Now sit up straight, Lady Pimpernel,' came the voice. 'A Lady of the Queen's closet should never slouch before Her Majesty, should she, Mama? No. Only the Lady of the Footstool may sit before Her Majesty. I beg your pardon, Mama. Did you speak?'

Mama made no answer. So the girl's voice continued.

'There now. Are we all in our places? You too, Lady Whitelegs? Good. Now listen.'

After a short pause, she began to recite in a sing-song voice.

'Come live with me, and be my love, And we will all the pleasures prove, That valleys, groves, hills and fields, Woods, or steepy mountain yields . . . '

At the girl's recital, a strange hilarity gripped John. The shepherd would make his lover a bed of roses, she declared. He would clothe her in a cap of flowers, a mantle embroidered with leaves and a gown of lambswool. She was all but singing now.

'A belt of straw and ivy buds,
With coral clasps and amber studs:
And if these pleasures may thee move
Come live with me and be my love.'

Then the voice dropped. John leaned closer, straining after the next words. Suddenly, he lost his balance. Grabbing at the door frame he caught the latch. The door swung open and he pitched forward, sprawling full-length on the floor. Behind him, he heard the door swing back. The latch clicked shut.

He was lying on the floor of a long high-ceilinged gallery. Sunlight flooded in through a row of tall windows. As his dazzled eyes adjusted to the brightness, he saw a girl of about his own age perched in a window seat and holding a small black book. She pointed a sharp nose at John.

'Those stairs go to the kitchens,' she declared. 'But you are not dressed like a kitchen boy. You are dressed more in the manner of a rogue. Or a thief.'

The girl wore a dark green dress with a bright red hem. A fine silver chain looped about her neck disappeared into her bodice. Her hair was plaited in elaborate coils but her feet were stockinged, dangling above the dusty floor. A pair of black boots with silver-tipped laces lay beside her. 'Which are you?' she demanded.

John looked around the gallery. 'I'm not a thief,' he said. 'Or a rogue.'

She smelt faintly of rose water. A smile hovered behind her features as if wary of showing itself. Her dark eyes examined him.

'You should kneel, you know,' the girl said. 'Or stand in my presence and avert your eyes. You do not recognise me, do you?'

Josh's instructions had not included what to do if faced with a girl. John got to his feet.

'I am Lady Lucretia Fremantle, daughter of Sir William and Lady Anne of the Vale of Buckland,' the girl announced. When John said nothing, she added, 'I have other titles as well.'

He stood before her in his blue damp-smelling coat, his stained shirt and mud-streaked breeches. Itchy tufts of hair stuck out of his scalp.

'Do you have a name?' she asked.

'John Saturnall.'

'John Saturnall, your ladyship,' the girl corrected him. 'What brings you here, Master Saturnall?'

'I came to join the Household.'

'But now you have run away.'

'They won't have me.'

She regarded him pertly from the window seat. He shifted from one foot to the other. In the alcove behind the girl, he saw a cloak laid out like a blanket. Some clothes had been rolled up to form a pillow. Four dolls watched him from the makeshift bed. Lady Pimpernel, he thought. Lady Whitelegs. Mama. He remembered the maids' chatter in the servants' yard.

'You've run away too,' he said.

'That is hardly possible, John Saturnall,' the girl said archly. 'I live here. What brings you here?'

She glanced about the dusty gallery. One of her plaits had come loose at the back, he noticed. And her hands were grimy.

'I heard you singing.'

'Singing? I think not.'

'Yes, you were.' John cleared his throat then attempted an imitation of the girl's sing-song voice. 'Come live with me, and be my love . . . '

'There was more, about steep valleys and clothes.' But he trailed off as Lucretia gave an unamused shake of her head.

'What place did you hope for?' she asked.

John thought of the great vaulted room below, the flood of tastes and smells that washed through it. 'In the kitchen,' he said.

'Cooking?' She spoke as if the notion repelled her.

'Can't eat otherwise,' John said. 'Your ladyship.'

'Eat?' She wrinkled her nose. 'I do not glut myself like some.'

Her face looked like fine white china, he thought. Cold and perfect like one of her dolls. She regarded him in silence across the corridor. But then the silence was broken.

A gurgle sounded in the long gallery, a low liquid rumble that reverberated off the bare boards and rolled around the walls. The stertorous groan brought a frown of surprise to John's brow, a frown that soon turned to a grin. For a blush reddened the cheek of Lucretia Fremantle. The rumbling emanated from her stomach.

'Sounds like you ought to,' John told her, still grinning. But the girl did not smile.

'Be quiet!' she hissed.

'Isn't me making a racket.'

'How dare you!'

He saw her whole face redden. Her eyes narrowed. She glared at him furiously. He stared back, puzzled.

'It's only your belly,' he said to mollify her. 'Calling for dinner.'

'How dare you!' she spat. Her loose plait swung as she got to her feet. 'Keep your thoughts to yourself!'

Before John could utter another word, voices sounded outside. He saw his own alarm mirrored in the girl's face. For an instant they stared at each other, united in the fear of discovery. Then Lucretia's eyes narrowed. Her mouth opened.

'Here!' she shouted down the gallery. 'He's in here!'

They dragged him down to the kitchens. Mister Fanshawe was waiting.

'Send word to the Constable,' the Clerk of the Household instructed two of his clerks. 'Then take him to the gate.'

'One moment, Mister Fanshawe, begging your pardon,' John heard Josh say. 'Let me explain it to him first . . .' Josh's face appeared in front of John. 'See, Sir William hasn't got a place here after all. You'll be going back Carrboro way . . .'

'To the Poor house,' clarified Coake. His flat face carried a broad smile.

'It's not so bad as I let on,' mumbled Josh.

'Not if you like picking rags,' Coake scoffed.

'That's enough, Coake,' Mister Fanshawe said. 'Take him out.'

John felt the hand on his neck force him forward. But he had not taken three steps when a deeper voice sounded.

'Let him up.'

John felt himself released. He straightened slowly. A tall grey-haired man with a close-cropped beard and grey-blue eyes stood beside the hearth. He wore the kitchen's red livery and a long white apron. A copper ladle swung from the cord tied about his waist. Mister Fanshawe, looking uncomfortable, offered a full bow.

'Master Scovell,' the Clerk of the Household addressed the man.

'Welcome stranger,' Scovell replied and the red-liveried men smiled among themselves. 'Has the Household resolved to pay the Kitchen a visit?'

Fanshaw shifted uneasily. 'Your boy Coake led us here, Master Scovell. We were in pursuit.' The man sounded flustered.

'He was troubling Lady Lucretia,' Coake added.

'This boy's petition has been refused. Here it is.' Fanshaw opened his ledger and handed over the grimy pages. Scovell took them, glanced at the words then peered down. 'John Sandall?'

John hesitated.

'He says he's called John Saturnall,' Josh offered.

At that the Master Cook raised his eyebrows. As he peered over the priest's creased letter, John felt the man's gaze burrow under his skin. What had Josh said about looking people in the eye?

'Your mother is mentioned here,' the Master Cook said.

'Yes, Master Scovell.'

'She does not accompany you?'

'She . . . she died, Master Scovell.'

He had not said the words before. He saw the Master Cook's gaze slide away. For a moment he seemed lost in some private contemplation. Then he eyed John again.

'You wish to join the Kitchen, John Saturnall?'

'Master Scovell!' remonstrated Mister Fanshawe.

'Yes?'

'Mister Pouncey has given his answer! This boy is not of a character to join the Household. See here? His mother was accused of witchcraft.'

'Not by any here,' answered Scovell. 'Unless she was of your acquaintance, Mister Fanshawe?'

The men of the kitchen hid their smiles. The clerks with Fanshawe looked about uncomfortably.

'The boy absconded, Master Scovell!' Mister Fanshawe protested. 'He was found in the Solar Gallery . . . '

'Ah yes, those who stray where they should not.' Scovell turned on the man. 'Your own presence here, Mister Fanshawe, might be mistaken for trespass by uncharitable opinion. Unbidden strangers in the kitchen . . . But of course it is mere unfamiliarity. Wilful boys will run amok. We have our own penalties down here for such miscreant spirits. And those,' Scovell directed a stern look at Philip Elsterstreet, 'who admit such miscreants among us.'

The Master Cook turned again to John. Now his grey-blue eyes danced lightly.

'Do you wish to serve among us, John Saturnall?'

He stared back, silenced by this reversal in his fortunes. At last, he found his tongue.

'Yes,' he managed. 'Yes, Master Scovell.'

Scovell raised his ladle and swung and for one instant John thought the Master Cook intended to dash out his brains. But the heavy implement whistled over his head to strike the side of the cauldron. The deep clang drew a startled look from Fanshawe and his clerks, a scowl from Coake and a broad smile from Philip Elsterstreet. Josh nodded his satisfaction while Ben Martin looked almost pleased. All around the great room, every cook, under-cook and kitchen boy turned his gaze to John. Scovell held up his ladle for silence.

'John Saturnall, the Master Cook announced, 'Welcome to the kitchens.'

Twitter: Want to discuss or share what you just read? Use the hashtag #beaFEAST to connect with others.

ABOUT THE AUTHOR

Lawrence Norfolk is the author of the critically acclaimed novels *Lemprière's Dictionary*, *The Pope's Rhinoceros*, and *In the Shape of a Boar*. *Lemprière's Dictionary* was named a *New York Times* Notable Book of the Year and won the Somerset Maugham Prize, and Norfolk's works have been shortlisted for many international prizes, including the IMPAC Prize and the James Tait Black Memorial Award. He lives in London.

Imprint: Grove Press
BEA Booth #: 4139
Author appearance at BEA: signing from 11:00 – 12:00 Tuesday, June 5.
Printed galley at BEA: yes
Contact for printed galley: Deb Seager dseager@groveatlantic.com
Print ISBN: 9780802120519
Print price: $25.00
eBook ISBN: 9780802193957
eBook price: $25.00
Publication date: 9/4/2012
Publicity contact: Deb Seager dseager@groveatlantic.com
Rights contact: Amy Hundley ahundley@groveatlantic.com
Editor: Morgan Entrekin
Agent: Carole Blake
Agency: Blake Friedmann
Territories Sold
    Grove/Atlantic - USA
    Bloomsbury – UK
    Knaus – Germany
    Grasset – France
    De Bezige Bij – Netherlands
    Frassinelli – Italy
    Rosinante – Denmark
    Libri – Hungary
    Argo – Czech Republic
    Nemira – Romania
    Gourmet – Bulgaria
Promotional Information:
- Prepublication reading copies available
- 6-city tour (Boston, New York, Washington, D.C., San Francisco, Portland, Seattle)
- Major review coverage

- Promotion at regional trade shows
- Giveaways on Shelf Awareness, Goodreads, Amazon Vine, and EarlyWord
- IndieBound bookseller outreach campaign and newsletter cooperative advertising available

WILDERNESS

A NOVEL

LANCE WELLER

SUMMARY

Charles Frazier's *Cold Mountain* meets David Guterson's *East of the Mountains* in this sweeping historical novel of a Civil War veteran's last journey on the Pacific Coast. Thirty years after the Civil War's Battle of the Wilderness left him maimed, Abel Truman has found his way to the rugged, majestic coast of Washington State, where he lives alone in a driftwood shack with his beloved dog. *Wilderness* is the story of Abel, now an old and ailing man, and his heroic final journey over the snowbound Olympic Mountains. As Abel makes his way into the foothills he his haunted by his memories of the horrors of the war and the savagery he took part in and witnessed. And yet, Abel has somehow managed to hold on to his humanity, finding weigh stations of kindness along his path. In its contrasts of light and dark, wild and tame, brutal and tender, and its attempts to reconcile a horrific war with the great evil it ended, Wilderness not only tells the moving tale of an unforgettable character, but a story about who we are as human beings, a people, and a nation.

EXCERPT

One

Call These Men Back

1899

In the fall of that year, an old man walked deeper into the forest and higher into the hills than he had since he was young and his life was still a red thing, filled with violence. He walked longer and farther than he had since he was a soldier, campaigning with the Army of Northern Virginia in the Great War of the Rebellion when the world was not yet changed and his body was not yet shattered.

He began his journey late in the year, when the sky seemed a mirror of the ocean: flat and gray and stretching out to a horizon where darkness presided. The old man did not know he was going until he rose one morning and gathered his things—the old Winchester that had served him so well these long years of exile, his walking stick, his blanket roll and haversack—and set off southward down the dark, wet, cold, and windswept beach.

He lived beside the sea in the far northwest corner of these United States, and in the nights before he left he sat before his tiny shack watching the ocean under the nightblue sky. Seagrass sawed and rustled in a cool, salty wind. A few drops of rain fell upon his face, wetting his beard and softly sizzling in the fire. This light rain but the after-rain of the last night's storm, or perhaps the harbinger of harder rains yet to come. The shack creaked softly with the wind while the tide hissed all along the dark and rocky shore. The moon glowed full from amidst the rain clouds, casting a hard light that slid like grease atop the water. The old man watched ivory curlers far to sea rise and subside noiselessly. Within the bounds of his little cove stood sea stacks weirdly canted from the wind and waves. Tide gnawed remnants of antediluvian islands and eroded coastal headlands, the tall stones stood monolithic and forbidding, hoarding the shadows and softly shining purple, ghostblue in the moon- and ocean- colored gloom. Grass and wind-twisted scrub pine stood from the stacks, and on the smaller, flatter, seaward stones lay seals like earthen daubs of paint upon the night's darker canvas. From that wet dark across the bay came the occasional slap of a flipper upon the water that echoed into the round bowl of the cove, and the dog, as it always did, raised its scarred and shapeless ears.

Their shack stood at the edge of the dark forest just above the high-tide line and beside a slow, tannic river. The door, only an opening in one wall covered by an old piece of faded blanket, looked out upon the gray ocean. The old man's tiny house was but one room with a packed earth floor and walls of wind-dried driftwood of various shapes and thickness. It was bone white and silvery in its coloring and ill suited in every way for providing home or shelter. The leaking roof was fashioned partially from scrap board he had scavenged from the mill outside Forks—he'd towed the boards north up the coast behind his boat back when his boat was sound and had painted his roof red with river mud that had long since faded to a general rust color. The door, when there had been a door, had been nothing more than long pieces of driftwood and chunks of tree bark held together with a craze of baling wire.

Off to one side there had once been a lean-to built from the same lumber, but the old man had fallen through it one night before the dog came, when he was out of his mind with drink and sorrow. He'd knocked the whole shelter over with his weight, chopped it apart in anger, and his carpentry skills were not such that he could later fathom how to set it all right again. The salvaged wood now lay pieced together tilewise on the riverbank, serving as a sort of dock for the old man to clean fish upon and stand free of mud when he washed.

The rocker in which he sat was a found item, having washed ashore one fine spring day five years ago and needing but minor repairs to its caning. The old man sat every evening to face the watery horizon and watch the sun fall, when he could see it for the rain, and to listen to the way the forest behind him hushed as light bled slowly from it.

All along the shore, behind the cabin and down the banks of the river, stood the dark wilderness, tumbling in a jade wave to the shore. Numberless green centuries of storm and tide had stranded massive logs of driftwood against the standing trunks so they lay in long heaps and mounds. Strange quiet citadels of wood, sand, and stone. Natural reliquaries encasing the dried bones of birds and fish, raccoons and seals, and the sad remains of drowned seamen carried by current and tide from as far away as Asia. Seasons of sun over long, weary years had turned the great logs silver, then white. The endless ranks of wood provided the old man's home with a natural windbreak in storm seasons, and he spent many nights awake, listening to the mournful sound of the wind at play in the tangle.

A fire burned from the little stone-lined pit before the cabin the night before he left. Yellow flames danced up into the dark, and the burning wood shivered and popped upon bright embers that shone like tiny, pulsing hearts lit bright. As he sat rocking and watching the flames at their work, the old man did not yet know that he was going, and yet, hunched before his fire, he could feel something within him shift. Beside him, the dog sensed his despair and knew what the old man did not and knew that he would soon try a thing and fail at it and that they would soon be traveling. The dog also knew they would not return. It knew these things the same way a dog knows well the heart of the man it loves and understands it in better ways than the man could ever hope. The old man patted the dog's head absently, and the dog looked up at him a moment before settling its chin upon its forepaws and closing its eyes.

The old man sat and rocked and tried not to remember his younger days when he was a married man and soldiering was the furthest thing from his mind. He tried hard not to see his wife, his infant daughter. After a while, the breath that escaped his bearded lips was hot, and he covered his eyes with his right palm and left it there until it was over.

Far to the west, where the night was fast upon the ocean's rim, the clouds had blown back and the old man could see stars where they dazzled the water. He breathed and rocked before the fire. His thoughts, beyond his control, went from painful recollections of women and family to worse remembrances of war because it had been his experience that one often led to the other—stoking its fires until there was not a man who could resist and, upon yielding, survive as a man still whole.

The old man began to tremble, though the wind was still mild and the rain still warm. He could not help but see, once again, war's sights and hear war's sounds and know, once more, war's hard gifts that are so difficult to live with after war. And then the old man closed his damp eyes again and thought of the blue door he had found on the northward beach that morning.

* * *

He'd risen midmorning, after a late night spent waiting out the storm, and went downstream to wash. Checking his lines at the river mouth where it fanned darkly into the ocean, he found a single butterfish struggling weakly on his handmade hook. He watched it from the sandy, crumbling bank—a bright little teardrop shape hung quivering in bark-colored water. The old man hauled it in and cleaned it, fried and ate it all, without much thought and with no joy whatsoever. He threw the dog the innards and what he could not himself finish and watched it eat, after which it wandered off into the forest to scare up whatever else it could. The old man carefully washed his plate in the river, dried it on an old rag he kept for that purpose, and replaced it neatly on the table near his cot.

His breakfast finished, he set to doing chores about his home. He used a hand axe to split shingles from likely shaped chunks of driftwood and used these to mend his roof. He worked slowly, carefully, favoring his crippled left arm that would never straighten from the angle in which it had healed while he lay wounded in the Wilderness of Spotsylvania after battle there in May of 1864. The previous night's storm, though mild, had set the shack to trembling and blown rain sideways through the walls. He patched the walls with mud and handfuls of thick moss, and after finishing the job, the old man took up his rifle and set off north along the beach. The dog appeared out of the forest and ran ahead through the surf where it was shallow and fast and cold, then cut back toward the forest to stand atop a high dune, shaking head-to-tail so water flew from it in sprays of silver. It was part Labrador and part something else, and it stood waiting for the old man—a patch of black and gold and red against the dark forest behind.

Without realizing it, the old man walked soldierwise with his rifle at right shoulder shift, his tough palm cradling the butt plate and his steps measured and even as though to conserve strength for a day's hard marching. He walked a beach lit bright by sudden sunlight escaping the close-packed clouds and felt the hard wind sweeping in off the water. He tasted salt, could feel the wind scouring his flesh and crackling in his beard. He drew his lips back as though such wind, such salt and raw fierceness, might bleach clean his river-stained teeth and kindle heat in the hollow, cold places within him.

With the tide rising, the old man was forced up amidst the tide-stacked driftwood and he picked his way carefully, mindful of the waves and his balance. The great silvery logs lay crosswise and askelter like huge breastworks against the battle line of the ocean, the onrushing attack of the tide. Climbing over and around them got the old man to thinking of battles despite himself. How they'd rush screaming and hollering through some field, some forest or farmer's woodlot, where musket smoke hung from the branches in pale tatters like strange moss. How they'd go down on their knees in fallen leaves or dew-slick grass, firing blindly and fast. No skill to it. No time for aiming. Driving powder and shot down the barrel and pulling free the rammer and fitting the firing caps and raising the pieces to their cramped, bruising shoulders. Kneeling there, sobbing and loading and screaming and firing and loading again, hearing the shouts and cries and sobs of those everywhere around. The great, rolling, throaty percussion of cannon and the sharp crackle of riflefire swelling up and up like an orchestra in the throes of some grand flourish. And that sound rolled together into a single noise, a solitary booming wail of a sound that had no correlation to any other sound the world makes or that a man makes upon it.

Until the Wilderness, he had hardly been touched by battle, and he had seen his share. The old man, who was then a young soldier named Abel Truman, had only been scratched and bruised, had never gotten sick, and was thought by many to be a lucky man. Men took bets on how Abel would fare that day. They shifted their places about to march near him, as though his good luck might shield them. In the end it rarely did. And while other men died everywhere all around him at Malvern Hill, while other men fell rudely shocked into their deaths in the green cornfields at the base of Cedar Mountain and in the cool, piney shade of the West Wood beyond Sharpsburg, Abel Truman was not touched until the Battle of the Wilderness, and then it had been very bad.

The old man sat resting on a silvery log. The tide was falling in the early afternoon and the ocean lay gray and foam-cluttered, touched on the horizon by steel clouds shot through with shafts of pale sunlight that stood like great, clean columns on the heaving swells. In the shallows were otters at their play. The dog padded about, sniffing after the strewn purple dung of raccoons and chasing those gulls that landed nearby. After a time, the old man took out a little sack and from that a brown twist of dried venison. He sat eating in the sun, letting it warm him through. He sat eating and trying to empty his mind to the moment, but once started, he could not turn himself from memories of his war.

Too many times to count he'd felt hot metal go buzzing past. The little winds that followed, sharp and cool. He'd felt them come plucking hard at his sleeves and pants legs as though to gently steer him from his path. Holes blown through his canteen and four good hats lost as though borne back by strong wind. Abel had even seen bullets mid-flight—small and dark and fat as horseflies. He remembered one in particular: how he whipped his head around in time to follow its path into the wide, sunburned forehead of Huntley Foster just behind him. A man who had found his way through Second Manassas and Antietam and Chancellorsville and who had wagered good writing paper on Abel's luck. The moment of Huntley's death in front of Culp's Hill: a sharp, flat crack and a look of bottomless surprise on Huntley's face. His mouth fell open in mute astonishment as though he recognized the moment for what it was, and a silent question formed in his liquid eyes, as though he'd ask of Abel something and would have his answer. Huntley had fallen back with the ball mixed in with the contents of his skull, a wide tongue of blood laid across the bridge of his nose. When Abel made his way back later, he found Huntley in a bank of fallen leaves. The boy's eyes were open, now questioning someone else, and his pockets were all turned out, his shoes and writing paper gone.

Abel had seen many men die just so and worse. Scores of men. Men whose bodies were dashed apart like waves against stone. He thought of Gully Coleman. He thought of David Abernathy and tried hard not to think of poor Ned.

Now, an old man sitting in the sun taking his lunch, Abel thought that if he concentrated hard enough, he could call them all back to memory. Each man who died in his sight and whose face he knew. Recall them and let them live again, even if only for a moment and only in his mind. Abel breathed, feeling the steady work of the cool air within him. He sat thinking that if he could call these men back, he would ask of them many, many things.

Abel Truman sat with his right hand open on his thigh, his left arm cocked tight against his ribcage, and the sun on his face. His crippled arm throbbed, as it often did. He wondered why he was left behind. Why, after his daughter's death and his wife's and all those good men and boys he marched with. Not to become an old man on a beach where no one ever came. Not just to live steeping in pain and memories of pain, he reckoned. Not unless God were even crueler than he'd proved himself to be.

And, because it was a day for such things, Abel conjured an unwanted vision of his daughter, who was when she died still too young for them to have settled on a name for and so went unnamed to her tiny grave. He had risen early that morning and lifted her from the cradle he'd built for her. It was well before the war and he was still whole and he held her in his strong left hand while with his right hand he reached to move the blanket from her face. It was a blue paler than the swaddling. A darker blue around her lips and darker still about her eyes, and she was so cold. Behind him, Elizabeth called his name. He turned, and in so turning dropped the child to the floor.

Even now, sitting in the sun on this dark beach, the gorge rose up Abel's throat to remember the look on his wife's face. The shock of realization and, finally, the pale, outraged blame that darkened like a bruise until it rotted her with hate.

Abel felt the sun against his eyelids, saw heat pounding redly through the thin panes of flesh that separated his eyes from the air and closed him from all the rest of the world. For no reason at all, he suddenly remembered Elizabeth's voice when it still loved him—deep and throaty, not what you'd expect from her small frame—and how she'd sing quietly small, sad songs of her own composition that he sometimes thought might break his heart. He remembered her white skin and her strong fingers and her square face. The brown, sun-dazed hair that stuck to the back of her neck when she sweated, and the way that she stood when she stood close to him.

The old man opened his eyes. Such remembering was hard on him. He blinked wetly, sighed, and looked over at the dog. It sat looking from the venison in Abel's hand to his face and back again. Slowly, deliberately, Abel put the twist into his mouth. The dog cocked its head and popped its jaws. Abel chewed and gave the dog a look and the dog sighed. Drool dripped from its under jaw. After a while, Abel stood. He looked down at the dog. "You are pitiful," he told it. He looked to sea, then reached into the bag and tossed the dog a piece of meat before continuing up the beach.

He walked a long time with the tide falling and the sound of rattling pebbles and the pungent iodine stink of the waves. Bits of fishing net, broken boards, jade-colored glass floats drifted over the ocean from Japan, and a stove-in cooking pot that Abel knelt to examine before tossing away again. At one point, he thought he saw two figures on the beach far to the north. He waved, but if they saw him, they did not show it, and when he looked again they were gone.

By and by, the old man came upon a pale blue door lying abandoned in the sand. It had a rusted knob and a rusted knocker and it lay athwart the high-tide line as though to shut something away beneath the cold black sand. Abel walked around the door while the dog sniffed at it, barked once, and scrambled off to chase gulls.

He squatted beside the door and touched its weathered surface. Flies rose from the wet weeds and went exploring the air around his head. For all the sweet reek of tide and rot, the door, baking in the sudden afternoon sun, put Abel in mind of pitch pine, maple leaves, green trailers. Tree bark.

How the mind works, by what strange paths it pursues memory. The old man smiled, remembering how it had been in his soldiering days to boil any dark liquid and call it coffee. Roasted corn and apple cores and peanut shells. Withered potatoes and crushed acorns. Tree bark. The only requirements were that the drink be dark-unto-black, scalding hot, and ungodly strong. Abel could taste the brew suddenly, so sharp was his memory of it, and he remembered the little pouch of coffee he'd found in the haversack of a dead Union boy in the Wilderness. He remembered how rich and pure and good that real coffee had smelled, and how, on smelling it and then finding amongst the other possibles a wondrous handful of real white sugar, he'd ignored the pain in his newly ruined arm and broken down to cry like a child.

How the mind works when presented, without warning, with sights and sounds and smells and doors.

The old man frowned, staring at the door lying on the sand. He did not see it but saw, instead and for just a moment, the blue front door of the home his wife and he had once made—framed by two little windows lit softly from within by lamplight. And then he was gone from there and stood instead in the dark, cool shadows of the Wilderness watching a tow-haired boy with both eyes shot away destroy his left arm with a lucky pistol shot. He stood instead on that old, red ground they'd fought and refought for. Ribcage curves stood from the grass like strange plantings while gray skulls grinned eyeless and mute from brown leaves like stones.

Parts of the Wilderness had been afire that night, and the air was thick with the stink of burning sweet woods, scorched hair, and stale powdersmoke. Burning horseflesh raised a pall of greasy black smoke against the starlight. Other flesh burned there too that night to raise a stench more shocking still. And the dark that night was hot and orange.

Abel Truman wandered far behind the army's lines, stumbling through the dark with the soft, mournful cries of the whippoorwill dogging his bloody heels. There was a bullet fast in his upper thigh that had not touched the bone, and another somewhere in the soft part of his trunk—a wound he was afraid to look at in case he was killed without knowing it.

The Union boy, when Abel found him, lay alone in back of the Confederate lines where their afternoon charge had reached its terminus in smoke and leafy green confusion. He lay alone in the deep woods with both eyes shot away and one knee blown redly open so a white, round knob of bone came poking through his trousers. Abel heard the soft, sick creak of the joint when the boy tried to sit up, and as his sack coat fell open, Abel saw a hole in the boy's chest that he couldn't have plugged with his thumb.

On hearing Abel enter the glade where he lay, the boy lifted a pistol from somewhere about his person and fired from his darkness at the greater dark beyond. Abel felt his arm destroyed. He fell, and when he reared back up the boy was dead, and Abel went pawing through his haversack after the smell of coffee.

Two days later, Abel stood before a tiny shack in the Wilderness fronted by another blue door, and this time, he was taken in. The reek of human fear and human hurt, the warm sweetness of mother's milk at the back of his throat—kindnesses he did not deserve.

A wind had risen on the coast. It blew sea foam along the beach and froze the gulls mid-flight, static and quiet, as though hung by threads from the dark clouds. The old man knelt in the wind beside the old door with his hard palm covering his mouth and his rifle crosswise on his lap. Nearby, the dog sat watching. When the old man sat unmoving for a long time, the dog came up, tilted its head to one side, and turned three tight circles before settling onto the sand.

Abel uncovered his face. He took a great, deep breath. The dog stood quickly. The wind set the old man's clothes to snapping and stood the dog's thick fur at strange angles. The old man's crippled arm ached, as it often did in cold wind. He took a long last look at the blue door, then silently gathered his things and set off for home with the dog running off ahead and the wind at his back, making the walking much easier.

Now, Abel Truman sat before his fire in the night with the dog lightly sleeping at his feet. Flames jumped orange and yellow from the shallow pit. He sat watching the water, remembering times gone by. When he reached down to stroke the dog behind its ears, it woke and looked at him, then sighed and settled its head between its paws to lie staring with contentment at the fire.

After a time, the old man stood and went into the dark shack. He held a small, burning stick plucked from the fire and with it lit two candle scraps standing palely from waxy puddles on a rough table. Tossing the stick back out the door onto the fire, Abel stood looking at his cot and, stacked beside it, the few volumes he read from each night before sleep. A dog-eared King James Bible with a worn calfskin cover. An old *Farmer's Almanac* borrowed from Glenn Makers the year before last. Abel had read bits from the Bible and nearly all the almanac—if for nothing else than to try and anchor himself in the world by staying aware of planting seasons and predicted weathers, now passed. He touched with two fingers the covers of these and some few other books of his keeping, then turned to a shelf on the back wall where sat a small pine box.

The old man sniffed deeply and rubbed his cocked left arm. Through his shirt, he felt a thick map of scar tissue—the gristle grown through and around shattered bones that had knit themselves back all wrong. He imagined shriveled tendons embedded with old, cold, corroded flakes of metal that frayed the nerves yet still allowed him some little use of the hand. He thought of Hypatia and the taste of her milk. He thought of the blue door of the cabin she'd occupied in the dark of the Wilderness of Spotsylvania and of another blue door closed upon a home and family long lost. Abel took a breath and set the box on the table in the flickering candlelight.

The first thing he took from it was the Union bullet she had cut from his arm. Its tip was splayed and flattened, and by certain lights you could still see a fine craze where the fibers of his shattered capitulum had engraved the metal while it was still fast and hot. Abel sniffed again and put it in his pocket, then took from the box a little crucifix fashioned from a piece of bone or something like bone. Abel never knew exactly what it was. There was an old bloodstain on the transom, faded now to the color of tree bark that took the shape of a bird wing mid-flight. David Abernathy had died holding the crucifix aloft that day in the Wilderness. How dark the mouth of the cannon. Abel shuddered.

He took a deep breath. Let it out. He held the cross in his palm as though to judge its value, weighing it in the manner of a prospector with a gold-flecked stone who wonders if this be true gold or something false and therefore foolish. The cross hung from a salt-wearied leather thong, and Abel, having reached a careful decision, slipped it around his neck and turned back to the box.

He lifted from it a brass picture frame no bigger than his palm with a hinged brass cover set with a steel Maltese cross. It was, on the whole, as beaten and weather-scoured and tired-looking as the old man's face, his hands, his heart. He opened it carefully and looked upon the tintype within. The frame joints had gone green with age; the thin glass cracked from side to side and turned a smoky yellow, glooming the image behind. But it was all right; the old man did not need to see their faces anymore for he knew them well by his heart's own photogravure.

There hung behind them, mother and child, a painted canvas lush with green valleys and white waterfalls, blue rivers, high clouds. In the far distance, snowy mountains purple under the sun. All this detail reduced to a general, brown fogginess that obscured even their faces and clothes where they sat posed upon an ornate, highbacked settee placed before the backdrop. Their dressfronts starched and their skirts arranged just so about their crossed and folded legs. The mother held the daughter's hand, and their free hands were composed precisely on the armrests. Their faces serious as befitting a moment of high gravity—neither smiled but for their eyes, and the girl was the softened echo of her mother and her mother so very beautiful. In all, a proper keepsake for a soldier gone to war to help him dream of home and hearth, and indeed the Union boy who'd shot Abel wore it on a chain near his heart when Abel found it. And there were long times and many afterward that Abel stared upon the tintype and fancied there his own wife's face, his own daughter's, had they lived and posed thusly for him.

As it often did these past months, the old man's heart fell to beating all wrong. A scrim of sweat broke upon his forehead and his breath whistled in his chest. He shut the frame carefully and reached to grip his knee with his right hand as he leaned to better breathe. He began to cough, hot and harsh and sick and foul tasting, and he coughed a long time. When it was done, Abel spat out the door into the dark so he would not see its color. After he felt right again, and before he could reconsider, he opened the frame once more, pried out the glass, then stepped toward the fire and turned the tintype out into the flames. He watched the bleary image blacken and after a while tossed the frame itself upon the coals. The dog watched him, and he lifted his chin. "It was a poor thing to thieve a thing like that," he said softly.

Abel stood beside the fire and watched the ocean move constantly, restlessly, in the outer dark. He looked at the stars that glistened hard and cold through gaps in the clouds and at the hazy moon behind. He looked at the dog where it lay sleeping by the snapping fire. Older now, it tired easily and slept hard, its long legs moving restlessly as it gave soft little puppy-barks from its dreams. Abel watched it for a time, then shed his clothes and stood naked, pale and ghostly in the shadows.

He started across the wrecked driftwood toward the sand, picking his way along carefully. The tide seethed and rattled along the shore. It sprayed and echoed on the stones in the deeper waters and slapped against itself still farther out, under the moon as it moved beyond the clouds, where men could not dwell nor prosper. Beds of kelp, like inky stains upon the general darkness, bobbed on the swells while mounds of it, beached days past, lay quietly afester with night-becalmed sand fleas near the driftwood bulwarks. Glancing to the little river that cut sharply and dark through the sand, Abel saw the largest wolf he'd ever seen, standing in the current watching him.

The old man stood stock-still. The wolf stared and did not move. Silver, moon-struck water fell from its underjaw and its hackles were raised in a dark ridge somehow reminiscent of other predators, saurian and long-extinct. They were silent together in their separate places on the shore—the old man and the wolf—and when it finally stepped from the river and turned to lope back into the forest, Abel saw the moonlight glint hard and fast off a crude, handmade collar round its neck and wondered how much dog was in it.

"I'll be damned," he said softly, thinking maybe he was or would be. "I'll be goddamned." Then he turned back toward the ocean and walked out into it.

Abel caught his breath as the cold, cold water closed around his bare thighs. He looked down the lean, pale line of his body and felt the ache throb freshly in his ruined elbow and down his forearm to the center of his palm as though the old, violent metal had spread corrosion to those places. The dark water swallowed whole his lower half while moonlight reflected his torso back, pinning and twinning him upon the water as though he faced there some pale, wavering alternate self. A doppelgänger with a history, perhaps, separate from his own but that had been fetched, after all, to the very same place, the very same ending. With all the same hurts and sorrows and ill-healed wounds. And this is what you get, said Abel, panting and struggling with the cold. This is what you get.

He breathed deeply, shudderingly. The sharp stones beneath his naked feet made him wish he had worn his boots. The old bits of metal still within him cooled further still in the cold water and set ice points of pain through the meat of his muscles, along the curved piping of his bones. Setting his lips together, he started forward once more with purpose and determination as though he had become, one last time, the soldier of his youth. But no bands played and no banners waved and no comrades marched beside him, for all had died long ago. The only thing to urge him onward was, perhaps, a wolf watching from the deep of the forest behind him. Abel walked until he was a head upon the waves and the waves broke over him. He spat salt and his eyes stung and streamed but he did not weep.

And then he floated. His feet no longer touched stone or sand and his head was no longer exposed to the moon and the night. The old soldier closed his eyes and floated between earth and air with the cold water touching every part of him. He shut his eyes, tasted the sharp flavor of ocean salt and imagined it seeping into him, claiming him back—his poor, ragged flesh—to leave behind bleached and knuckled bones, bits of rusted metal, forever knocking along the floor of the sea.

Beside the fire, the dog raised its head. It stood slowly, stretching and yawning and twisting about to bite after its own haunches where the fur was matted and tangled. Wandering down to the water, it climbed stiffly over the driftwood to sniff the old man's tracks in the sand. And then it smelled another thing—a wild dog-shaped scent beside the river—and whined and paced and turned about a moment with indecision before continuing down toward the sea. And when it came upon the old man where he lay, the dog whined again and licked his face. A wave surged up around them and pushed the old man's body through the sand and the dog danced up out of the cold water, then came sniffing back after it had receded. It nuzzled the old man's neck and licked his ear and the old man began to cough. He sputtered and coughed and sat up with his eyes red and his nose running. After a moment, he leaned to vomit. The saltwater left the back of his throat raw and he sneezed a thick clot of bloody snot into his palm that he wiped off on the sand.

Abel Truman sat staring at the water, trying to will warmth back into his limbs while the dog licked salt from his crooked arm. He looked at it, and then stood. "You just shut up," he said. "Bet if you was to try it, it'd throw you back too." Then he turned to make his slow way back to the shack, where the fire still burned up out of its little stone ring while, for its part, the dog paused beside the little river to stare across it at a dark patch of disturbed sand and the tracks that led from it into the forest. It bristled and growled softly until Abel called to it from beside the fire, "Get over here, you old cuss," he said. "Don't you know there's a wolf about?" The dog huffed its indignation twice, then turned to join the old man in his shack.

That night the old man dreamed a dream terrifying and strange. Buried without a coffin, he clawed the suffocating earth and broke to air with his mouth full of dirt. Around him, campfires burned on a vast and featureless plain. The feminine curve of hills in dark silhouette marked the horizon and there were fires there too, and stars in the sky. The very air was dark as though the dark had become a part of it and it was cold. White flames that shed no heat flapped on twisted black braids of wood.

And there were men that he knew gathered in that place with their hands stretched flameward. Taylor there. And old Hoke who lost his leg to the hip at the base of Culp's Hill and who died in the ambulance two days later. David Abernathy and old Joe and Gully Coleman and Scripture Lewis. Ned was there, breaking Abel's heart forever. And countless others known to him and not. Dark crowds gathered around tiny fires. Their breath smoked palely and all were utterly silent, standing like sentinels or crouching apelike in the glassy cold.

Abel called but no one turned. He stood apart from them and when he stumbled forward he woke with his face wet and his thin blanket bunched up around his neck. He breathed into the dark. After a while he flung an arm out from the cot and called the dog to him and it rose stiffly and came.

The next morning, the old man left the shack while the dog stood beside the firepit with its head raised to sniff the morning breezes. It pawed the ground, turned three tight circles, and settled down in its usual place near where the warmth of the fire should have been.

The old man's steps were loud upon the upriver trail, and the dog's ears stood half cocked with listening. It waited a long time, twice longer than it knew it should take the old man to make his toilet and return. In the distance, it could hear him walking on the forest paths and swearing and coughing up great quantities of phlegm, as was his morning custom. After a time, the dog realized the old man had crossed over the river into the shade of the trees beyond. It stood quickly, shook itself, and sniffed the air once more before it bent its nose to the soil to find the old man's scent upon the earth and follow.

Twitter: Want to discuss or share what you just read? Use the hashtag #beaWILD to connect with others.

ABOUT THE AUTHOR

Lance Weller has published short fiction in several literary journals. He won Glimmer Train's Short Story Award for New Writers and was nominated for a Pushcart Prize. A Washington native, he has hiked and camped extensively in the landscape he describes. He lives in Gig Harbor, WA, with his wife and several dogs.

Imprint: Bloomsbury
BEA Booth #: 3458
Printed galley at BEA: yes
Contact for printed galley: marketingusa@bloomsbury.com

Print ISBN: 9781608199372
Print price: $25.00
eBook ISBN: 9781620400616
eBook price: $19.99
Publication date: 9/4/2012
Publicity contact: Sara Mercurio sara.mercurio@bloomsbury.com
Rights contact: Joanna Everard Joanna.everard@bloomsbury.com
Editor: Anton Mueller
Agent: Jim Trupin
Agency: JET Literary
Promotional Information:

- Early previews to bloggers and booksellers on NetGalley, IndieBound Early Access, and Amazon Vine
- Bookseller dinners in Portland and Seattle with author
- Author to attend PNBA and SIBA
- Social media campaign on Bloomsbury's accounts will share original essays from the author and a video on the book
- Major national advertising campaign will include *The New York Times Book Review*, print and online advertising in the *Portland Oregonian*, the *Seattle Times* and the *San Francisco Chronicle*
- Major push to reading groups via GoodReads, LibraryThing, and The Reading Room
- Events and signings throughout the Pacific NW

BOOKSELLER BLURBS:

"Weller has crafted a novel of stories within stories, all interwoven in prose so exquisite and descriptive that you will want to read *Wilderness* more than one time, and all in one sitting to capture this novel in its salvific beauty. Put aside your day, open up *Wilderness* and take a dive into this fabulous work of fiction."
—Annie Philbrick, Bank Square Books, Mystic, CT

"This is a brave, bold, singular book."
—Rick Simonson, Elliott Bay Book Company, Seattle, WA

Dear Bookseller,

I owe so much to bookstores. My first job in high school was at a little bookstore in Scottsdale, Arizona. The few dollars I earned as a clerk helped keep me and my mother afloat, and the two eccentric gents who ran the store gave me prophetic advice, a lifetime reading plan, and badly needed tough love, all of which I describe at length in my memoir, The Tender Bar.

Above all I owe the success of that memoir to countless booksellers, who embraced it and championed it—and continue to do so, thank goodness. On book tour I got to meet many of those booksellers, and to spend many enchanted evenings at some of America's finest bookstores, one of the great experiences of my writing life.

Now, it's with both gratitude and hopefulness that I send booksellers my first work of fiction, a historical novel about the legendary bank robber Willie Sutton.

I chose Sutton as a subject for several reasons. First, it felt like the perfect moment, historically and culturally, to tell the story of a man who became a folk hero by waging war on banks. Also, I've been fascinated for years by the legend of Sutton, who was consummately New York, quintessentially Irish, thoroughly noir. My grandfather spoke often about Willie the Actor, as did the men at my Uncle Charlie's saloon.

But it gives me particular pleasure to tell my friends in the community of booksellers that I was drawn to Sutton because he might have been the most literate criminal in American history. While in prison, while escaping prison, while hiding from police, he was never without books. (He favored classics.) He even wrote two books of his own, which he called autobiographies, though they were fiction through and through.

I can't wait to talk with you in the months to come about Sutton, about books, about all things book-related—and to thank you again for all you've done for The Tender Bar.

Best,

J.R. Moehringer

SUTTON

the new novel from J.R. Moehringer, author of the
New York Times bestselling *The Tender Bar*

SUMMARY

Willie Sutton was driven by two things—a lost love and a fierce vendetta against banks. Among the most notorious criminals in American history, he spent half his life in prison, the other half on the run. Then came Christmas Eve, 1969. Sutton's surprise parole from Attica sparked a media frenzy. Every journalist and talk show host wanted an interview. Sutton, however, granted only one. Sixty-eight years old, in failing health, he spent all that Christmas with a newspaper reporter and photographer, driving around New York City, visiting the scenes of his many heists, betrayals, heartbreaks and escapes. The result was a strangely cursory front-page article, filled with half-truths and platitudes. Notably missing was any mention of Sutton's first accomplice, the girl who led him into a life of crime, then broke his heart. *Sutton,* a historical novel based on extensive research, is a comic, moving, gritty imagining of that mysterious Christmas, and the remarkable life that preceded it, a life defined by thrills, follies, unseen bravery and treachery, and the long shadow of a doomed, unforgettable romance.

EXCERPT

He's writing when they come for him.

He's sitting at his metal desk, bent over a yellow legal pad, talking to himself, and to her—as always, to her. So he doesn't notice them standing at his door. Until they run their batons along the bars.

He looks up, adjusts his large scuffed eyeglasses, the bridge mended many times with Scotch tape. Two guards—one fat and soft and pale, as if made from Crisco, the other tall and scrawny and with a birthmark like a penny on his right cheek. You can almost make out Abraham Lincoln.

Crisco hitches up his belt. On your feet, Sutton. Admin wants you. Sutton stands.

Birthmark points his baton. What the? You crying, Sutton?

No sir.

Don't you lie to me, Sutton. I can see you been crying.

Sutton touches his cheek. His fingers come away wet. I didn't know I was crying sir.

Crisco waves his baton at the legal pad. What's that?

Nothing sir.

He asked you what is it, Birthmark says.

Sutton feels his bum leg starting to buckle. He grits his teeth at the pain. My novel sir.

They look around his book-filled cell. He follows their eyes. It's never good when the guards look around your cell. They can always find something if they have a mind to. They scowl at the books along the floor, the books along the metal cabinet, the books along the cold-water basin. Sutton's is the only cell at Attica filled with copies of Dante, Plato, Shakespeare, Freud. No, they confiscated his Freud. Prisoners aren't allowed to have psychology books. The warden thinks they'll try to hypnotize each other.

Crisco smirks. He gives Birthmark a nudge—get ready. Novel, eh? What's it about?

Just—you know. Life sir.

What the hell does an old jailbird know about life?

Sutton shrugs. That's true sir. But what does anyone know?

Word is leaking out. A dozen print reporters have already arrived and they're huddled at the front entrance, stomping their feet, blowing on their hands. One of them says he just heard—snow on the way. Lots of it. Nine inches at least.

They all groan.

Too cold to snow, says the veteran in the group, an old wire service warhorse in suspenders and black orthopedic shoes. He's been with UPI since the Scopes trial. He blows a gob of spit onto the frozen ground and scowls up at the clouds, then at the main guard tower, which looks unnervingly like Sleeping Beauty's Castle in Disneyland.

Too cold to stand out here, says the reporter from the *New York Post*. He mumbles something disparaging about the warden, who's refused three times to let the media inside the prison. The reporters could be drinking hot coffee right now. They could be using the phones, making last-minute plans for Christmas. Instead the warden is trying to prove some kind of point. Why, they all ask, why?

Because the warden's a prick, says the reporter from *Time*, that's why.

The reporter from *Look* holds his thumb and forefinger an inch apart. Give a bureaucrat this much power, he says, and watch out. Stand back.

Not just bureaucrats, says the reporter from the *New York Times*. All bosses eventually become fascists. Human nature.

The reporters trade horror stories about their bosses, their editors, the miserable jerk-offs who gave them this god-awful assignment.

There's a brand-new journalistic term, appropriated from war in Asia, frequently applied to assignments like this, assignments where you wait with the herd, usually outdoors, exposed to the elements, knowing full well you're not going to get anything good, certainly not anything the rest of the herd won't get. The term is clusterfuck. Every reporter gets caught in a clusterfuck now and then, it's part of the job, but a clusterfuck on Christmas Eve? Outside Attica Correctional Facility? Not cool, says the reporter from the *Village Voice*. Not cool.

The reporters feel especially hostile toward that boss of all bosses, Governor Nelson Rockefeller. He of the Buddy Holly glasses and the chronic indecision. Governor Hamlet, says the reporter from UPI, scowling at the walls. Is he going to do this thing or not?

He yells at Sleeping Beauty's Castle: Shit or get off the pot! Defecate or abdicate!

The reporters nod, grumble, nod. Like the prisoners on the other side of this thirty-foot wall, they grow restless. The prisoners want out, the reporters want in, and both groups blame The Man. Cold, tired, angry, ostracized by society, both groups are close to rioting. Both fail to notice the beautiful moon slowly rising above the prison.

It's full.

The guards lead Sutton from his cell in D Block through a barred door, down a tunnel and into Attica's central command center—what prisoners call Times Square—which leads to all cell blocks and offices. From Times Square the guards take Sutton down to the deputy warden's office. It's the second time this month that Sutton has been called before the dep. Last week it was to learn that his parole request was denied—a devastating blow. Sutton and his lawyers had been confident. They'd won support from prominent judges, discovered loopholes in his convictions, collected letters from doctors vouching that Sutton was close to death. But the three-man parole board simply said no.

The dep is seated at his desk. He doesn't bother looking up. Hello, Willie. Hello sir.

Looks like we're a go for liftoff.

Sutton blinks, massages his leg. Sir?

The dep waves a hand over the papers strewn across his desk. These are your walking papers. You're being let out.

Let—out? By who sir?

The dep looks up, sighs. Head of corrections. Or Rockefeller. Or both. Albany hasn't decided how they want to sell this. The governor, being an ex-banker, isn't sure he wants to put his name on it. But the head of corrections doesn't want to overrule the parole board. Either way it looks like they're letting you walk.

Walk sir? Why sir?

Fuck if I know. Fuck if I care.

When sir?

Tonight. If the phone will stop ringing and reporters will stop hounding me. If I can get these goddamn forms filled out.

Sutton stares at the dep. Then at the guards. Are they joking? They look serious.

The dep turns back to his papers. Godspeed, Willie.

The guards walk Sutton down to the prison tailor. Every man released from a New York State prison gets a release suit, a tradition that goes back at least a century. The last time Sutton got measured for a release suit, Calvin Coolidge was president.

Sutton stands before the tailor's three-way mirror. A shock. He hasn't stood before many mirrors in recent years and he can't believe what he sees. That's his round face, that's his slicked gray hair, that's his hated nose—too big, too broad, with different-size nostrils—and that's the same large red bump on his eyelid, mentioned in every police report and FBI flyer since shortly after World War I. But that's not him—it can't be. Sutton has always prided himself on projecting a certain swagger, even in handcuffs. He's always managed to look suave, dapper, even in prison grays. Now, sixty-eight years old, he sees in the tailor's mirror that all the swagger, all the dapper and suave are gone. He's a baggy-eyed stick figure. He looks like Felix the Cat. Even the pencil-thin mustache, once a source of pride, looks like the cartoon cat's whiskers.

The tailor stands beside Sutton, wearing a green tape measure around his neck. An old Italian from the Bronx, with two front teeth the size of thimbles, he shakes a handful of buttons and coins in his pocket as he talks.

So they're letting you out, Willie. Looks like.

How long you been here? Seventeen years.

How long since you had a new suit of clothes?

Oh. Twenty years. In the old days, when I was flush, I'd get all my suits custom-made. Silk shirts too. D'Andrea Brothers.

He still remembers the address: 587 Fifth Avenue. And the phone number. Murray Hill 5-332. He still remembers lots of things, though he's particular about what—and when.

Sure, Tailor says, D'Andrea, they did beautiful work. I still got one of their tuxes. Step up on the block.

Sutton steps up, grunts. A suit, he says. Jesus, I thought the next thing I'd be measured for would be a shroud.

I don't do shrouds, Tailor says. No one gets to see your work.

Sutton looks down at the three reflected Tailors. It's not enough to do nice work? People have to see it?

Tailor spreads his tape measure across Sutton's shoulders, down his arm. Show me an artist, he says, who doesn't want praise.

Sutton nods. I used to feel that way about my bank jobs.

Tailor looks at the triptych of reflected Suttons, winks at the middle one. He stretches the tape measure down Sutton's bum leg. Inseam thirty-two, he announces. Jacket thirty-eight short.

I was a forty reg when I came in this joint. I ought to sue.

Tailor laughs softly, coughs. What color you want, Willie?

Anything but gray.

Black then. I'm glad they're letting you out, Willie. You've paid your debt. Forgive us our debts, Willie says, as we forgive our debtors.

Tailor crosses himself.

That from your novel? Crisco asks.

Sutton and Tailor look at each other.

Tailor points a finger gun at Sutton. Merry Christmas, Willie.

Same to you, friend.

Sutton points a finger gun at Tailor, cocks the thumb hammer. Bang.

The reporters talk about sex and money and current events. Altamont, that freaky concert where those four drugged-out hippies died— who's to blame? Mick Jagger? The Hells Angels? Then they gossip about their more successful colleagues, starting with Norman Mailer. Not only is Mailer running for mayor of New York, but he just got one million dollars to write a book about the moon landing. Mailer—the guy writes history as fiction, fiction as history, inserts himself into ev- erything. He plays by his own rules while his rule-bound colleagues

get sent to Attica to freeze their balls off. Fuck Mailer, they all agree.
And fuck the moon.

They blow on their hands, pull up their collars, make bets about whether or not the warden will ever be publicly exposed as a cross-dresser. Also, they bet on which will happen first—Sutton walks or Sutton croaks. The reporter from the *New York Post* says he hears Sutton's not just knocking at death's door, he's ringing the bell, wiping his feet on the welcome mat. The reporter from *Newsday* says the artery in Sutton's leg is clogged beyond repair—a doctor who plays racquetball with the reporter's brother-in-law told him so. The reporter from *Look* says he heard from a cop friend in the Bronx that Sutton still has loot stashed all over the city. Prison officials are going to free Sutton and then the cops are going to follow him to the money.

That's one way to solve the budget crisis, says the reporter from the *Albany Times Union*.

The reporters share what they know about Sutton, pass around facts and stories like cold provisions that will have to get them through the night. What they haven't read, or seen on TV, they've heard from their parents and grandparents—and great-grandparents. Sutton is the first multigeneration criminal in history, the first bank robber ever to build a lengthy career—it spans five decades. In his heyday Sutton was the face of American crime, one of a handful of men to make the leap from public enemy to folk hero. Smarter than Machine Gun Kelly, saner than Pretty Boy Floyd, more likable than Legs Diamond, more peaceable than Dutch Schultz, more romantic than Bonnie and Clyde, Sutton saw bank robbery as high art and went about it with an artist's single-minded zeal. He believed in study, planning, hard work. And yet he was also creative, an innovator, and in the end he proved to be a tenacious survivor. He escaped three maximum-security prisons, eluded cops and FBI agents for years. He was Henry Ford by way of John Dillinger—with dashes of Houdini and Rasputin. The reporters know all about Sutton's stylish clothes, his impish smile, his love of books, the glint of devilment in his bright blue eyes, so blue that the FBI once described them in bulletins as azure. It's the rare bank robber who moves the FBI to such lyricism.

What the reporters don't know, what they and most Americans have always wanted to know, is whether or not Sutton, who was always known for being nonviolent, had anything to do with the brutal gangland murder of Arnold Schuster. A fresh-faced twenty-four-year-old from Brooklyn, a baseball-loving Coast Guard veteran, Schuster caught the wrong subway one afternoon and found himself face to face with the legend. Caught up in Sutton's web, he was dead three weeks later, and his unsolved murder might be the most tantalizing cold case in New York City history.

The guards march Sutton back to Admin. A clerk cuts him two checks. One for $169, salary for seventeen years at various prison jobs, minus taxes. Another for $40, the cost of a bus ticket to Manhattan. Every released prisoner gets bus fare to Manhattan. Sutton takes the checks—this is really happening. His heart begins to throb. His leg too. They're throbbing at each other, like the male and female leads in an Italian opera.

The guards march him back to his cell. You got fifteen minutes, they tell him.

He stands in the middle of his cell, his eight-by-six home for the last seventeen years. Is it possible that he won't sleep here tonight? That he'll sleep in a soft bed with clean sheets and a real pillow and no demented souls above and below him howling and cursing and pleading with impotence and rage and fury? The sound of men in cages—nothing can compare with it. He sets the shopping bag on the desk and carefully packs the manuscript of his novel. Then the spiral notebooks from his creative writing classes. Then his copies of Dante, Shakespeare, Plato. Then Kerouac. Prison is where you give yourself permission to live. A line that saved Sutton on many long nights. Then the dictionary of quotations, which includes the most famous line by America's most famous bank robber, Willie Sutton, a.k.a. Slick Willie, a.k.a. Willie the Actor.

Carefully, tenderly, he packs the Ezra Pound. Now you will come out of a confusion of people. And the Tennyson. Come into the garden, Maud, I am here at the gate alone. He says the lines under his breath. His eyes mist. They always do. Finally he packs the yellow legal pad, the one on which he was writing when the guards came for him. Not his novel, which he recently finished, but a suicide note, the one he began composing an hour after the parole board's rejection. So often, he thinks, that's how it happens. Death stands at your door, hitches up its pants, points its baton at you—then hands you a pardon.

At five o'clock the dep lets Sutton make a few phone calls. First he dials his lawyer, Katherine. She's incoherent with joy.

We did it, Willie. We did it!

How did we do it, Katherine?

They got tired of fighting us. It's Christmas, Willie, and they were just tired.

It was easier to give up.

I know how they felt, Katherine.

And the newspapers certainly helped, Willie. The newspapers were on your side.

Which is why Katherine's cut a deal with one of the biggest newspapers. She mentions which one, but Sutton's mind is racing, the name doesn't register. The newspaper is going to whisk Sutton on its private plane to Manhattan, put him up at a hotel, and in exchange he'll give them his exclusive story. It's the only way to get him down to New York City tonight.

Unfortunately, Katherine adds, that means you'll have to spend Christmas Day with a reporter instead of family. Is that okay?

Sutton thinks of his family. He hasn't spoken to them in years. He thinks of reporters—he hasn't spoken to them ever. He doesn't like reporters. They only care about facts. Still, this is no time to make waves.

That'll be fine, Katherine.

Now, do you know anyone who can pick you up outside the prison and drive you to the airport?

I'll find someone.

He hangs up, dials Donald, who answers on the tenth ring.

Donald? It's Willie. What are you doing?

Who's this?

Willie.

Oh. Hey. Drinkin a beer, watching *The Flying Nun.*

Listen. It seems like they might be letting me out tonight.

They're letting you out, or you're letting yourself out?

It's legit, Donald. They're opening the door.

Hell freezing over?

I don't know. But the devil's definitely wearing a sweater. Can you pick me up at the front gate?

Near the Sleeping Beauty thing? Yeah.

Of course.

Sutton asks Donald if he can bring him a few items. Anything, Donald says. Name it.

A TV van from Buffalo roars up to the gate. A TV reporter jumps out, fusses with his microphone. He's wearing a two-hundred-dollar suit, a camel-hair topcoat, gray leather gloves, silver cuff links. The print reporters elbow each other. Cuff links—have you ever?

The TV reporter strolls up to the print reporters and wishes everyone a Merry Christmas. Same to you, they mumble. Then silence.

Silent Night, the TV reporter says.

No one laughs.

The reporter from *Newsweek* asks the TV reporter if he read Pete Hamill in this morning's *Post*. Hamill's eloquent apologia for Sutton, his plea for Sutton's release, addressed as a letter to the governor, might be the reason they're all here. Hamill urged Rockefeller to be fair. If Willie Sutton had been a GE board member or a former water commissioner, instead of the son of an Irish blacksmith, he would be on the street now.

The TV reporter stiffens. He knows the print guys think he doesn't read— can't read. Yeah, he says, I thought Hamill nailed it. Especially his line about banks. There are some of us today, looking at the mortgage interest rates, who feel that it is the banks that are sticking us up. Also, I got a lump in my throat at that bit about Sutton reuniting with a lost love. Willie Sutton should be able to sit and watch the ducks in Prospect Park one more time, or go to Nathan's for a hot dog, or call up some old girl for a drink.

This sets off a debate. Does Sutton actually deserve to be free? He's a thug, says the *Newsday* reporter—why all the adulation?

Because, says the *Post* reporter, he's a god in parts of Brooklyn. Just look at this huge crowd gathering outside the prison.

There are now more than two dozen reporters and another two dozen civilians—crime buffs, police radio monitors, curiosity seekers. Freaks. Ghouls.

But again, says the *Newsday* reporter, I ask you—why?

Because Sutton robbed banks, the TV reporter says, and who the hell has a kind word to say for banks? They should not only let him out, they should give him the key to the city.

What I don't get, says the *Life* reporter, is why Rockefeller, a former banker, would let out a bank robber.

Rockefeller needs the Irish vote, says the *Times Union* reporter. You can't get reelected in New York without the Irish vote and Sutton's like Jimmy Walker and Michael Collins and a couple Kennedys in one big Mulligan stew.

He's a fuckin thug, says the *Newsday* reporter, who may be drunk.

The TV reporter scoffs. Under his arm he's carrying last week's *Life* magazine, with Charles Manson on the cover. He holds up the magazine: Manson glares at them, at no one, at everyone.

Compared to Manson, the TV reporter says, and the Hells Angels, and the soldiers who slaughtered all those innocents at My Lai—Willie Sutton is a pussycat.

Yeah, says the *Newsday* reporter, he's a real pacifist. He's the Gandhi of Gangsters.

All those banks, the TV reporter says, all those prisons, and the guy never fired a single shot. He never hurt a fly.

The *Newsday* reporter gets in the TV reporter's face. What about Arnold Schuster?, he says.

Aw, the TV reporter says, Sutton had nothing to do with Schuster. Says who?

Says me.

And who the fuck are you?

I'll tell you who I'm not—I'm not some burned out hack.

The *Times* reporter jumps between them. You two cannot get in a fistfight about whether or not someone is nonviolent—on Christmas Eve.

Why not?

Because if you do I'll have to write about it.

The talk swings back to the warden. Does the man realize that the temperature is now close to zero? Oh you bet he realizes. He's loving this. He's on some kind of power trip. Everybody these days is on a power trip. Mailer, Nixon, Manson, the Zodiac Killer, the cops—it's 1969, man, Year of the Power Trip. The warden's probably watching them right now on his closed-circuit TV, sipping a brandy and laughing his fat ass off. It's not enough that they have to be drawn into this massive clusterfuck, but they also have to be the dupes and patsies of some crypto fascist macho dick?

You're all welcome to sit in my truck, the TV reporter says. It's warm. We've got TV. *Flying Nun* is on.

Groans.

Sutton lies on his bunk, waiting. At seven o'clock Crisco appears at the door.

Sorry, Sutton. It's not happening.

Sir?

Birthmark appears behind Crisco. New orders just came down from the dep, he says—no go.

Why what?

Why sir?

Crisco shrugs. Some kind of beef between Rockefeller and the parole department. They can't agree who's going to take responsibility, or how the press release should be worded.

So I'm not—?

No.

Sutton looks at the walls, the bars. His wrists. The purple veins, bubbled and wormy. He should've done it when he had the chance.

Crisco starts laughing. Birthmark giggles. Just kidding, Sutton. On your feet.

They unlock the door, lead him down to the tailor. He strips out of his prison grays, puts on a crisp new white shirt, a new blue tie, a new black suit with a two- button front. He pulls on the new black socks, slips on the new black wingtips. He turns to the mirror. Now he can see the old swagger.

He turns to Tailor. How do I look?

Tailor jiggles his coins and buttons, gives a thumbs-up.

Sutton turns to the guards. Nothing.

Crisco alone leads Sutton through Times Square, then through the yard between Admin and the front entrance. God it's cold. Sutton cradles his bag of belongings and ignores the cramping and burning and searing pain shooting down his leg. A plastic tube is holding open the artery and he can feel it getting ready to collapse like a paper straw.

You need an operation, the doctor said after the insertion of the tube six months ago.

If I wait on the operation, will I lose the leg, Doc?

No, Willie, you won't lose the leg—you'll die.

But Sutton waited. He didn't want some prison doctor opening him up. He wouldn't trust a prison doctor to open a checking account. Now it seems he made the right call. He might be able to have an operation at a real hospital, and pay for it with the proceeds of his novel. Provided there's still time. Provided he lives through this night, this moment. Tomorrow.

They reach the front. They walk around the metal detector, around the signin table, and come to a black metal door. Crisco unlocks it. Sutton steps forward. He looks back at Crisco, who's belittled and beaten him for the last seventeen years. Crisco has censored Sutton's letters, confiscated his books, denied his requests for soap and pens and toilet paper—slapped him when he forgot to put a sir at the end of a sentence. Crisco braces himself—this is the moment prisoners like to get things off their chests. But Sutton smiles as if something inside him is opening like a flower. Merry Christmas kid.

Crisco's head snaps back. He waits a beat. Yeah. Merry Christmas, Willie. Good luck to you.

It's six o'clock.

Crisco pushes open the door and Willie Sutton walks out.

A photographer from *Life* shouts, Here he is! Three dozen reporters converge. The freaks and ghouls push in. TV cameras veer toward Sutton's face. Lights, brighter than prison searchlights, hit his eyes.

How's it feel to be free, Willie?

Do you think you'll ever rob another bank, Willie?

What do you have to say to Arnold Schuster's family?

Sutton points to the full moon. Look, he says.

Three dozen reporters and two dozen civilians and one archcriminal look up at the night sky. It's the first time Sutton has seen the moon, face to face, in seventeen years and it takes his breath.

Look, he says again. Look at this beautiful clear night God has made for Willie.

In the distance Sutton sees a man with pumpkin-colored hair and stubborn orange freckles leaning against a red 1967 Pontiac GTO. Sutton waves, Donald hurries over. They shake hands. Donald shoves aside several reporters, leads Sutton to the GTO. When Sutton is settled into the passenger seat, Donald slams the door and shoves another reporter, just for fun. He runs around the car, jumps behind the wheel, mashes the gas pedal. Away they go, sending up a wave of wet mud and snow and salt.

It sprays the reporter from *Newsday*. His face, his chest, his shirt, his overcoat. He looks down at his clothes, then up at his colleagues: Like I said—a thug.

Sutton doesn't speak. Donald lets him not speak. Donald knows. Donald walked out of Attica nine months ago. They both stare at the icy road and the frozen woods and Sutton tries to organize his thoughts. After a few miles he asks if Donald was able to get that thing they discussed on the phone.

Yes, Willie.

Is she alive?

Don't know. But I found her last known address.

Donald hands over a white envelope. Sutton holds it like a chalice. His mind starts to go. Back to Brooklyn. Back to Coney Island. Back to 1919. Not yet, he tells himself, not yet. He shuts off his mind, something he's been good at all his life. Too good, one prison shrink told him.

He slides the envelope into the breast pocket of his new suit. Twenty years since he's had a breast pocket. It was always his favorite pocket, the one where he kept the good stuff. Engagement rings, enameled cigarette cases, leather billfolds from Abercrombie. Guns.

Donald asks who she is and why Sutton needs her address. I shouldn't tell you, Donald.

We got no secrets between us, Willie.

We've got nothing but secrets between us, Donald.

Yeah. That's true, Willie.

Sutton looks at Donald and remembers why Donald was in the joint. A month after Donald lost his job on a fishing boat, two weeks after Donald's wife left him, a man in a bar told Donald he looked beat. Donald, thinking the man was insulting him, threw a punch, and the man made the mistake of returning fire. Donald, a former college wrestler, put the man in a choke hold, broke his neck.

Sutton turns on the radio. He looks for news, can't find any. He leaves it on a music station. The music is moody, sprightly—different.

What is this, Donald?

The Beatles.

So this is the Beatles.

They say nothing for miles. They listen to Lennon. The lyrics remind Sutton of Ezra Pound.

Donald downshifts the GTO, turns to Willie. Does the name in the envelope have anything at all to do with—you know who?

Sutton looks at Donald. Who?

You know. Schuster?

No. Of course not. Jesus, Donald, what makes you ask that?

I don't know. Just a feeling.

No, Donald. No.

Sutton puts a hand in his breast pocket. He thinks. Well, he says, I guess maybe it does—in a roundabout way. All roads eventually lead to Schuster, right, Donald?

Donald nods. Drives. You look good, Willie Boy.

They say I'm dying.

Bullshit. You'll never fuckin die.

Yeah. Right.

You couldn't die if you wanted to.

Hm. You have no idea how true that is.

Donald lights two cigarettes, hands one to Sutton. How about a drink?

What an interesting idea. A ball of Jameson, as my Daddo used to say, would really hit the spot.

Donald pulls off the highway and parks outside a low-down roadhouse.

Sprigs of holly and Christmas lights strung over the bar. Sutton hasn't seen Christmas lights since his beloved Dodgers were in Brooklyn. He hasn't seen any lights other than the prison's eye-scalding fluorescents and the bare sixty-watt bulb in his cell.

Lights, Donald. Lights. You know you've been in hell when a string of tiny bulbs over a crummy bar looks more beautiful than Luna Park.

Donald jerks his head toward the bartender, a young blond girl wearing a tight paisley blouse and a miniskirt. Speaking of beautiful, Donald says.

Sutton stares. They didn't have miniskirts when I went away, he says quietly, respectfully.

You've come back to a different world, Willie.

Donald orders a Schlitz. Sutton asks for Jameson. The first sip is bliss. The second is better than sex. The third is a right cross. Sutton swallows the rest in one searing gulp and laughs and slaps the bar and asks Miniskirt for another.

The TV above the bar is showing the news.

Our top story tonight. Willie the Actor Sutton, the most prolific and elusive bank robber in American history, has been released from Attica Correctional Facility. In a surprise move by Governor Nelson Rockefeller . . .

Sutton stares into the grain of the bar top, thinking: Nelson Rockefeller. Grandson of John D. Rockefeller Sr., close friend of— Not yet, he tells himself. Not yet.

He reaches into his breast pocket, touches the envelope.

Now Sutton's face appears on the screen. His former face. An old mug shot. No one along the bar recognizes him. Sutton gives Donald a sly smile. They don't know me, Sutton says out of the corner of his mouth. I can't remember, Donald, the last time I was in a room full of people who don't know me. Feels nice.

Donald orders another round. Then another.

I hope you have money, Sutton says. I only have two checks from Governor Rockefeller.

Which will probably fuckin bounce, Donald says, slurring.

Say, Donald—want to see a trick?

Always.

Sutton limps down the bar. He limps back. Ta da.

Donald blinks. I don't think I get it.

I walked from here to there without a hack hassling me. Without a con messing with me. Ten feet—two more feet than the length of my fuckin cell, Donald. And I didn't have to call anyone sir before or after. Have you ever seen anything so amazing?

Donald laughs.

Ah, Donald—to be free. Actually free. There's no way to describe it to someone who hasn't been in the joint.

Everyone should have to do time, Donald says, smothering a belch, so they could know.

Time. Willie looks at the clock over the bar. Shit, Donald, we better go.

Donald, legally drunk, drives them along icy back roads. Twice they go skidding onto the shoulder. A third time they almost hit a snowbank.

You okay to drive, Donald?

Fuck no, Willie, what gave you that idea?

Sutton grips the dashboard. He stares in the distance at the lights of Buffalo.

He recalls that speedboats used to run booze down here from Canada.

This whole town, Sutton says, was run by Polish gangs back in the twenties. Donald snorts. Polish gangsters—what'd they do, stick people up and hand over their wallets?

They'd have cut the tongue out of your head for saying that. The Poles made us Micks look like choirboys. And the Polish cops were the cruelest of all. Shocking, Donald says with heavy sarcasm.

Did you know President Grover Cleveland was the executioner up here?

Is that so?

It was Cleveland's job to knot the noose around the guy's neck, drop him through the gallows floor.

A job's a job, Donald says.

They called him the Hangman of Buffalo. Then his face wound up on the thousand-dollar bill.

Still reading your American history, I see, Willie.

They arrive at the private airfield. They're met by a young man with a square head and a deep dimple in his square chin. The reporter. He shakes Sutton's hand and says his name, but Sutton is drunker than Donald and doesn't catch it.

Pleasure to meet you kid.

Same here, Mr. Sutton.

Reporter has thick brown hair, deep black eyes and a gleaming Pepsodent smile. Beneath each smooth cheek a pat of red glows like an ember, maybe from the cold, more likely from good health. Even more enviable is Reporter's nose. Thin and straight as a shiv.

It's a very short flight, he tells Sutton. Are you all set?

Sutton looks at the low clouds, the plane. He looks at Reporter. Then Donald. Mr. Sutton?

Well kid. You see. This is actually my first time on an airplane.

Oh. Oh. Well. It's perfectly safe. But if you'd rather leave in the morning.

Nah. The sooner I get to New York the better.

The plane has four seats. Two in the front, two in the back. Reporter straps Sutton into one of the backseats, then sits up front next to the pilot. A few snowflakes fall as they taxi down the runway. They come to a full stop and the pilot talks into the radio and the radio crackles back with numbers and codes and Sutton suddenly remembers the first time he rode in a car. Which was stolen. Well, bought with stolen money. Which Sutton stole. He was almost eighteen and steering that new car down the road felt like flying. Now, fifty years later, he's going to fly through the air. He feels a painful pressure building below his heart. This is not safe. He reads every day in the paper about another plane scattered in pieces on some mountaintop, some field, some lake. Gravity is no joke. Gravity is one of the few laws he's never broken. He'd rather be in Donald's GTO right now, fishtailing on icy back roads. Maybe he can pay Donald to drive him to New York. Maybe he'll take the bus. Fuck, he'll walk. But first he needs to get out of this plane. He claws at his seat belt.

The engine gives a high piercing whine and the plane rears back like a horse and goes screaming down the runway. Sutton thinks of the astronauts. He thinks of Lindbergh. He thinks of the bald man in the red long johns who used to get shot from a cannon at Coney Island. He closes his eyes and says a prayer and clutches the bag full of belongings on his lap. When he opens his eyes again the full moon is Jackie Gleasoning him through his window.

Within thirty minutes they make out the lights of Manhattan. Then the Statue of Liberty glowing green and gold out in the harbor. Sutton presses his face against the window. The plane tilts sideways and swoops toward La Guardia. The landing is smooth. As they slow and taxi down the runway Reporter turns to check on Sutton. You okay, Mr. Sutton?

Let's go again kid.

Reporter smiles.

They walk side by side across the wet, foggy tarmac to a waiting car. Sutton thinks of Bogart and Claude Raines. He's been told he looks a little like Bogart. Reporter is talking. Mr. Sutton? Did you hear? I assume your lawyer told you all about tomorrow? Yeah kid.

Reporter checks his watch. Actually, I should say today. It's one in the morning.

Is it, Sutton says. Time has lost all meaning. Not that it ever had any.

You know that your lawyer has agreed to give us exclusive rights to your story. And you know that we're hoping to visit your old stomping grounds, the scenes of your, um. Crimes.

Where are we staying tonight?

The Plaza.

Wake up in Attica, go to bed at the Plaza. Fuckin America.

But, Mr. Sutton, after we check in, I need to ask you, please, order room service, anything you like, but do not leave the hotel.

Sutton looks Reporter over. Fur-collared trench coat, dark brown suit, cashmere scarf, cap-toed brown lace-ups. The kid's not yet twenty-five, Sutton guesses, but he's dressed like an old codger. He's dressed, Sutton thinks, like a damn banker.

My editors, Mr. Sutton. They're determined that we have you to ourselves the first day. We can't let anyone know where you are, and we can't have anyone shooting your picture.

In other words, kid, I'm your prisoner.

Reporter gives a nervous laugh. Oh, ho, I wouldn't say that.

I'm in your protective custody.

Just for one day, Mr. Sutton.

Twitter: Want to discuss or share what you just read? Use the hashtag #beaSUTTON to connect with others.

ABOUT THE AUTHOR

J.R. Moehringer, winner of the Pulitzer Prize for feature writing in 2000, is a former national correspondent for *The Los Angeles Times* and a former Nieman Fellow at Harvard University. Moehringer is the author of *The New York Times* bestselling *The Tender Bar* and co-author of *Open* by Andre Agassi.

Imprint: Hyperion
Printed galley at BEA: yes
Contact for printed galley: Christine Ragasa christine.ragasa@abc.com
Print ISBN: 9781401323141
Print price: $27.99
eBook ISBN: 9781401304775

eBook price: $14.99
Publication date: 9/25/2012
Publicity contact: Christine Ragasa christine.ragasa@abc.com
Rights contact: Jill Sansone jill.sansone@abc.com
Editor: Elisabeth Dyssagaard
Agent: Mort Janklow
Agency: Janklow and Nesbitt

DENNIS LEHANE

LIVE BY NIGHT

A Novel

SUMMARY

Combining edgy suspense and the vivid period detail that made *The Given Day* a smashing success, award-winning, bestselling author Dennis Lehane delivers a masterful epic of Prohibition-era America told through the story of a charismatic young gangster on his rise through the glitz and the violence of the Roaring '20s.

EXCERPT

Chapter 2 The Lack In Her

Joe lived on the top floor of a boarding house in the West End, just a short walk from the riot of Scollay Square. The boarding house was owned and operated by the Tim Hickey Mob, which had long had a presence in the city but had flourished in the six years since the 18th Amendment took effect.

The first floor was usually occupied by Paddys right off the boat with woolen brogues and bodies of gristle. One of Joe's jobs was to meet them at the docks and lead them to Hickey- owned soup kitchens, give them brown bread and white chowder and gray potatoes. He brought them back to the boarding house where they were packed three to a room on firm, clean mattresses while their clothes were laundered in the basement by the older whores. After a week or so, once they'd gotten some strength back and freed their hair of nits and their mouths of poisoned teeth, they'd sign voter registration cards and pledge bottomless support to Hickey candidates in next year's elections. Then they were set loose with the names and addresses of other immigrants from the same villages or counties back home who might be counted on to find them jobs straight away.

On the second floor of the boarding house, accessible only by a separate entrance, was the casino. The third was the whore floor. Joe lived on the fourth, in a room at the end of the hall. There was a nice bathroom on the floor that he shared with whichever high rollers were in town at the moment and Penny Palumbo, the star whore of Tim Hickey's stable. Penny was twenty-five but looked seventeen and her hair was the color bottled honey got when the sun moved through it. A man had jumped off a roof over Penny Palumbo; another had stepped off a boat; a third, instead of killing himself, killed another guy. Joe liked her well enough; she was nice and wonderful to look at. But if her face looked seventeen, he'd bet her brain looked ten. It was solely occupied, as far as Joe could tell, by three songs and some vague wishes about becoming a dress maker.

Some mornings, depending on who got down to the casino first, one brought the other coffee. This morning, she brought it to him and they sat by the window in his room looking out at Scollay Square with its striped awnings and tall billboards as the first milk trucks puttered along Tremont Row. Penny told him that last night a fortune teller had assured her she was destined to either die young or become a Trinitarian Pentecostal in Kansas. When Joe asked her if she was worried about dying, she said sure, but not half as much as moving to Kansas.

When she left, he heard her talking to someone in the hall, and then Tim Hickey was standing in his doorway. Tim wore a dark pinstripe vest, unbuttoned, matching trousers and a white shirt with the collar unbuttoned and no tie. Tim was a trim man with a fine head of white hair and the sad, helpless eyes of a death row chaplain.

"Mr. Hickey, sir."

"Morning, Joe." He drank coffee from an old-fashion glass that caught the morning light rising off the sills. "That bank in Pittsfield?"

"Yeah?" Joe said.

"The guy you want to see comes in here Thursdays, but you'll find him at the Upham's Corner place most other nights. He'll keep a Homberg on the bar to the right of his drink. He'll give you the lay of the building and the out route too."

"Thanks, Mr. Hickey."

Hickey acknowledged that with a tip of his glass. "Another thing 'member that dealer we discussed last month?"

"Carl," Joe said, "yeah."

"He's up to it again."

Carl Laubner, one of their black jack dealers, had come from a joint that ran dirty games and they couldn't convince him to run a clean game here, not if any of the players in question looked less than a hundred percent white. So if an Italian or a Greek sat down at the table, forget it. Carl magically pulled 10s and aces for hole cards all night, or at least until the swarthier gents left the table.

"Fire him," Hickey said. "Soon as he comes in."

"Yes, sir."

"We don't run that horseshit here. Agreed?"

"Absolutely, Mr. Hickey. Absolutely."

"And fix the twelve slot, will you? It's running loose. We might run a straight house, but we're not a fucking charity, are we, Joe?"

Joe wrote himself a note. "No, sir, we are not."

Tim Hickey ran one of the few clean casinos in Boston, which made it one of the most popular casinos in town, particularly for the high class play. Tim had taught Joe that rigged games fleeced a chump maybe two, three times at the most before he got wise and stopped playing. Tim didn't want to fleece someone a couple of times; he wanted to drain them for the rest of their lives. Keep 'em playing, keep 'em drinking, he told Joe, and they will fork over all their green and thank you for relieving them of the weight.

"The people we service?" Tim said more than once. "They visit the night. But we live in it. They rent what we own. That means when they come to play in our sandbox, we make a profit off every grain."

Tim Hickey was one of the smarter men Joe had ever known. At the start of Prohibition, when the mobs in the city were split down ethnic lines—Italians mixing only with Italians, Jews mixing only with Jews, Irish mixing only with Irish—Hickey mixed with everyone. He aligned himself with Giancarlo Calabrese who ran the Pescatore Mob while old man Pescatore was in prison, and together they started dealing in Caribbean rum when everyone else was dealing in whiskey. By the time the Detroit and New York gangs had leveraged their power to turn everyone else into subcontractors in the whiskey trade, the Hickey and Pescatore mobs had cornered the market on sugar and molasses. The product came out of Cuba mostly, crossed the Florida Straits, got turned into rum on US soil, and took midnight runs up the Eastern Seaboard to be sold at an eighty percent mark-up.

As soon as Tim had returned from his most recent trip to Tampa, he'd discussed the botched job at the Southie furniture warehouse with Joe. He commended Joe on being smart enough not to go for the house take in the counting room ("That avoided a war right there," Tim said), and told him when he got to the bottom of why they'd been given such a dangerously bad tip, someone was going to hang from rafters as high as the Custom House spire.

Joe wanted to believe him because the alternative was to believe Tim had sent them to that warehouse because he'd *wanted* to start a war with Albert White. It wouldn't be beyond Tim to sacrifice men he'd mentored since they were boys with the aim of cornering the rum market for good. In fact nothing was beyond Tim. Absolutely nothing. That's what it took to stay on top in the rackets—everyone had to know you'd long ago amputated your conscience.

In Joe's room now, Tim added a spot of rum from his flask to his coffee and took a sip. He offered the flask to Joe but Joe shook his head. Tim returned the flask to his pocket. "Where you been lately?"

"I been here."

Hickey held his gaze. "You've been out every night this week and the week before. You got a girl?"

Joe thought about lying but couldn't see the point. "I do, yeah."

"She a nice girl?"

"She's lively. She's. . . " Joe couldn't think of the precise word, ". . . something."

Hickey came off the doorjamb. "You got yourself a blood sticker, huh?" He mimed a needle plunging into his arm. "I can see it." He came over and clamped a hand on the back of Joe's neck. "You don't get many shots at the good ones. Not in our line. She cook?"

"She does." Truth was, Joe had no idea.

"That's important. Not if they're good or bad, just that they're willing to do it." Hickey let go of his neck and walked back to the doorway. "Talk to that fellah about the Pittsfield thing."

"I will, sir."

"Good man," Tim said and headed downstairs to the office he kept behind the casino cashier.

***

Carl Laubner ended up working two more nights before Joe remembered to fire him. Joe had forgotten a few things lately, including two appointments with Hymie Drago to move the merch' from the Karshman Furs job. He had remembered to get to the slot machine and tighten the wheels good but by the time Laubner came in on his shift that night, Joe was off with Emma Gould again.

Since that night at the basement speakeasy in Charlestown, he and Emma had seen each other most nights. Most, not every. The other nights she was with Albert White, a situation Joe had thus far managed to characterize as annoying, though it was fast approaching the intolerable.

When Joe wasn't with Emma, all he could think about was when he would be. And then when they did meet, keeping their hands off each other went from an unlikely proposition to an impossible one. When her uncle's speakeasy was closed, they had sex in it. When her parents and siblings were out of the apartment she shared with them, they had sex in it. They had sex in Joe's car and sex in his room after he'd snuck her up the back stairs. They had sex on a cold hill, in a stand of bare trees overlooking the Mystic River, and on a cold November beach overlooking Savin Hill Cove in Dorchester. Standing, sitting, lying down—it didn't make much difference to them. Inside, outside—same thing. When they had the luxury of an hour together, they filled it with as many new tricks and new positions as they could dream up. But when they only had a few minutes, then a few minutes would do.

What they rarely did was talk. At least not about anything outside the borders of their seemingly bottomless addiction for one another.

Behind Emma's pale eyes and pale skin lay something coiled and caged. And not caged in a way that it wanted to come out. Caged in a way that demanded nothing come in. The cage opened when she took him inside her and for as long as they could sustain their lovemaking. In those moments, her eyes were open and searching and he could see her soul back there and the red light of her heart and whatever dreams she may have clung to as a child, temporarily untethered and freed of their cellar and its dark walls and padlocked door.

Once he'd pulled out of her, though, and her breathing slowed to normal, he would watch those things recede like the tide.

Didn't matter, though. He was starting to suspect he was in love with her. In those rare moments when the cage opened and he was invited in, he found a person desperate to trust, desperate to love, hell, desperate to live. She just needed to see he was worthy of risking that trust, that love, that life.

And he would be.

He turned twenty years old that winter and he knew what he wanted to do with the rest of his life. He wanted to become the one man Emma Gould put all her faith in.

***

As the winter wore on, they risked appearing in public together a few times. Only on the nights when she had it on good authority that Albert White and his key men were out of town and only at establishments that were owned by Tim Hickey or his partners.

One of Tim's partners was Phil Cregger, who owned the Venetian Garden restaurant on the first floor of the Bromfield Hotel. Joe and Emma went there on a frigid night that smelled of snow even though the sky was clear. They'd just checked their coats and hats when a group exited the private room behind the kitchen and Joe knew them for what they were by their cigar smoke and the practiced bonhomie in their voices before he ever saw their faces—pols.

Aldermen and selectmen and city councilors and fire captains and police captains and prosecutors—the shiny, smiling, grubby battery that kept the city's lights on, barely. Kept the trains running and the traffic signals working, barely. Kept the populace ever aware that that those services and a thousand more, big and small, could end—*would* end—were it not for their constant vigilance.

He saw his father at the same moment his father noticed him. It was, as it usually was if they hadn't seen each other in a while, unsettling if for no other reason than how completely they mirrored one another. Joe's father was sixty. He'd sired Joe late after producing two sons at a more respectably youthful age. But whereas Connor and Danny carried the genetic strains of both parents in their faces and bodies and certainly their height, (which came from the Fennessy side of the family, where the men grew tall), Joe had come out the spitting image of his old man. Same height, same build, same hard jawline, same nose and sharp cheekbones and eyes sunk back in their sockets just a little further than normal, which made it all the harder for people to read what he was thinking. The only difference between Joe and his father was one of color. Joe's eyes were blue whereas his father's were green; Joe's hair was the color of wheat, his father's the color of flax. Otherwise, Joe's father looked at him and saw his own youth mocking him. Joe looked at his father and saw liver spots and loose flesh, Death standing at the end of his bed at three AM, tapping an impatient foot.

After a few farewell handshakes and backslaps, his father broke from the crowd as the men lined up for their coats. He stood before his son. He thrust out his hand. "How are you?"

Joe shook his hand. "Not bad, sir. You?"

"Tip top. I was promoted last month."

"Deputy Superintendent of the BPD," Joe said. "I heard."

"And you? Where are you working these days?"

You'd have to have known Thomas Coughlin a long time to spot the effects of alcohol on him. It was never to be found in his speech, which remained smooth and firm and of consistent volume even after half a bottle of good Irish. It wasn't to be found in any glassiness of the eyes. But if you knew where to look for it, you could find something predatory and mischievous in the glow of his handsome face, something that sized you up, found your weaknesses, and debated whether to dine on them.

"Dad," Joe said, "this is Emma Gould."

Thomas Coughlin took her hand and kissed the knuckles. "A pleasure, Miss Gould." He tilted his head to the maître d'. "The corner table, Gerard, please." He smiled at Joe and Emma. "Do you mind if I join you? I'm famished."

***

They got through the salads pleasantly enough.

Thomas told stories of Joe's childhood, the point of which was invariably what a scamp Joe had been, how irrepressible and full of beans. In his father's retelling, they were whimsical stories fit for the Hal Roach shorts at a Saturday matinee. His father left out how the stories had usually ended—with a slap or the strap.

Emma smiled and chuckled at all the right places but Joe could see she was pretending. They were all pretending. Joe and Thomas pretended to be bound by the love between a father and son and Emma pretended not to notice that they weren't.

After the story about six-year-old Joe in his father's garden—a story told so many times over the years Joe could predict to a breath his father's pauses—Thomas asked Emma where her family hailed from.

"Charlestown," she said and Joe worried he heard a hint of defiance in her voice.

"No, I mean before they came here. You're clearly Irish. Do you know where your ancestors were born?"

The waiter cleared the salad plates as Emma said, "My mother's father was from Kerry and my father's mother was from Cork."

"I'm from just outside Cork," Thomas said with uncommon delight.

Emma sipped her water but didn't say anything, a part of her missing suddenly. Joe had seen this before—she had a way of disconnecting from a situation if it wasn't to her liking. Her body remained, like something left behind in the chair during her escape, but the essence of her, whatever made Emma *Emma*, was gone.

"What was her maiden name, your grandmother?"

"I don't know," she said.

"You don't *know?*"

Emma shrugged. "She's dead."

"But it's your heritage." Thomas was flummoxed.

Emma gave that another shrug. She lit a cigarette. Thomas showed no reaction but Joe knew he was aghast. Flappers appalled him on countless levels—women smoking, flashing thigh, lowering necklines, appearing drunk in public without shame or fear of civic scorn.

"How long have you known my son?" Thomas smiled.

"Few months."

"Are you two—?"

"Dad."

"Joseph?"

"We don't know what we are."

Secretly he'd hoped Emma would take the opportunity to clarify what, in fact, they were, but instead she shot him a quick look that asked how much longer they had to sit here and went back to smoking, her eyes drifting, anchorless, around the grand room.

The entrees reached the table and they passed the next twenty minutes talking about the quality of the steaks and the Bearnaise sauce and the window treatments Cregger had recently installed.

During dessert, Thomas lit his own cigarette. "So what is it you do, dear?"

"I work at Papadikis Furniture."

"Which department?"

"Secretarial."

"Did my son pilfer a couch? Is that how you met?"

"Dad," Joe said.

"I'm just wondering how you met," his father said.

Emma lit a cigarette and looked out at the room. "This is a real swank place."

"It's just that I'm well aware how my son earns a living. I can only assume that if you've come into contact with him, it was either during a crime or in an establishment populated by rough characters."

"Dad," Joe said, "I was hoping we'd have a nice dinner." "I thought we just did. Miss Gould?"

Emma looked over at him.

"Have my questions this evening made you uncomfortable?"

Emma locked him in that cool gaze of hers, the one that could freeze a fresh coat of roofing tar. "I don't know what you're on about. And I don't particularly care."

Thomas leaned back in his chair and sipped his coffee. "I'm on about you being the type of lass who consorts with criminals, which may not be the best thing for your reputation. The fact that the criminal in question happens to be my son isn't the issue. It's that my son, criminal or no, is still my son and I have paternal feelings for him, feelings which cause me to question the wisdom of his consorting with the type of woman who knowingly consorts with criminals." Thomas placed his coffee cup back on the saucer and smiled at her. "Did you follow all that?"

Joe stood. "Okay, we're going."

But Emma didn't move. She dropped her chin to the heel of her hand and considered Thomas for some time, the cigarette smoldering next to her ear. "My uncle mentioned a copper he has on his payroll, name of Coughlin. That you?" She gave him a tight smile to match his own and took a drag off her cigarette.

"This uncle would be your Uncle Robert, the one everyone calls Bobo?"

She flicked her eyelids in the affirmative.

"The police officer to whom you refer is named Elmore Conklin, Miss Gould. He's stationed in Charlestown and is known to collect shakedown payments from illegal establishments like Bobo's. I rarely get over to Charlestown, myself. But as Deputy Superintendent, I'd be happy to take a more focused interest in your uncle's establishment." Thomas stubbed out his cigarette. "Would that please you, dear?"

Emma held out her hand to Joe. "I need to powder."

Joe gave her tip money for the ladies room attendant and they watched her cross the restaurant. Joe wondered if she'd return to the table or grab her coat and just keep walking.

His father removed his pocket watch from his vest and flicked it open. Snapped it closed just as quickly and returned it to its pocket. The watch was the old man's most prized possession, an eighteen karat Patek Phillippe given to him over two decades ago by a grateful bank president.

Joe asked him, "Was any of that necessary?"

"I didn't start the fight, Joseph, so don't criticize how I finished it." His father sat back in his chair and crossed one leg over the other. Some men wore their power as if it were a coat they couldn't get to fit or to stop itching. Thomas Coughlin wore his like it had been tailored for him in London. He surveyed the room and nodded at a few people he knew before looking back at his son. "If I thought you were just making your way in the world on an unconventional path, do you think I'd take issue with it?"

"Yes," Joe said, "I do."

His father gave that a soft smile and a softer shrug. "I've been a police officer for thirty-seven years and I've learned one thing above all else."

"That crime never pays," Joe said, "unless you do it at an institutional level."

Another soft smile and a small tip of the head. "No, Joseph. No. What I've learned is that violence procreates. And the children your violence produces will return to you as savage, mindless things. You won't recognize them as yours, but they'll recognize you. They'll mark you as deserving of their punishment."

Joe had heard variations of this speech over the years. What his father failed to recognize—besides the fact that he was repeating himself—was that general theories need not apply to particular people. Not if the people—or person—in question was determined enough to make his own rules and smart enough to get everyone else to play by them.

Joe was only twenty, but he already knew he was that type of person.

But to humor the old man, if for no other reason, he asked, "And what exactly are these violent offspring punishing me for again?"

"The carelessness of their reproduction." His father leaned forward, elbows on the table, palms pressed together. "Joseph."

"Joe."

"Joseph, violence breeds violence. It's an absolute." He unclasped his hands and looked at his son. "What you put out into the world will always come back for you."

"Yeah, Dad, I read my catechism."

His father tipped his head in recognition as Emma came out of the powder room and crossed to the coat check room. His eyes tracking her, he said to Joe, "But it never comes back in a way you can predict."

"I'm sure it doesn't."

"You're not sure of anything except your own certainty. Confidence you haven't earned always has the brightest glow." Thomas watched Emma hand her ticket to the coat check girl. "She's quite easy on the eyes."

Joe said nothing.

"Outside of that, though," his father said, "I fail to grasp what you see in her."

"Because she's from Charlestown?"

"Well, that doesn't help," his father said. "Her father was a pimp back in the old days and her uncle has killed at least two men that we know of. But, I could overlook all that, Joseph, if she weren't so. . ."

"What?"

"Dead inside." His father consulted his watch again and barely suppressed the shudder of a yawn. "It's late."

"She's not dead inside," Joe said. "Something in her is just sleeping."

"That something?" his father said as Emma returned with their coats. "It never wakes up again, son."

***

On the street, walking to his car, Joe said, "You couldn't have been a little more. . .?"

"What?"

"Engaged in the conversation? Social?"

"All the time we been together," she said, "all you ever talk about is how much you hate that man."

"Is it *all* the time?"

"Pretty much."

Joe shook his head. "And I've never said I hate my father."

"Then what have you said?"

"That we don't get along. We've never gotten along."

"And why's that?"

"Because we're too fucking alike."

"Or because you hate him."

"I don't hate him," Joe said, knowing it, above all things, to be true.

"Then maybe you should climb under his covers tonight."

"What?"

"He sits there and looks at me like I'm trash? Asks about my family like he knows we're no good all the way back to the Old Country? Calls me fucking *dear?*"

She stood on the sidewalk shaking as the first snowflakes appeared from the black above them. The tears in her voice began to fall from her eyes. "We're not people. We're not respectable. We're just the Goulds from Union Street. Charlestown trash. We tat the lace for *your* fucking curtains."

Joe held up his hands. "Where is this coming from?" He reached for her and she took a step back.

"Don't touch me."

"Okay."

"It comes from a lifetime, okay, of getting the high hat and the icy mitt from people like your father. People who, who, who. . .who confuse being lucky with being better. We're not less than you. We're not shit."

"I didn't say you were."

"He did."

"No."

"I'm not shit," she whispered, her mouth half open to the night, the snow mingling with the tears streaming down her face.

He put his arms out and stepped in close. "May I?"

She stepped into his embrace but kept her own arms by her side. He held her to him and she wept into his chest and he told her repeatedly that she was not shit, she was not less than anyone, and he loved her, he loved her.

***

Later, they lay in his bed while thick, wet snowflakes flung themselves at the window like moths. "That was weak," she said.

"What?"

"On the street. I was weak."

"You weren't weak. You were honest."

"I don't cry in front of people."

"Well, you can with me."

"You said you loved me."

"Yeah."

"Do you?"

He looked in her pale, pale eyes. "Yes."

After a minute she said, "I can't say it back."

He told himself that wasn't the same as saying she didn't feel it.

"Okay."

"Is it really okay? Because some guys need to hear it back."

Some guys? How many guys had told her they loved her before he came along?

"I'm tougher than them," he said and wished it were true.

The window rattled in the dark February gusts and a foghorn bayed and down in Scollay Square several horns beeped in anger.

"What do you want?" he asked her.

She shrugged and bit a hangnail and stared across his body out the window.

"For a lot of things to never have happened to me."

"What things?"

She shook her head, drifting away from him now.

"And sun," she mumbled after awhile, her lips sleep swollen. "Lots and lots of sun."

Twitter: Want to discuss or share what you just read? Use the hashtag #beaNIGHT to connect with others.

ABOUT THE AUTHOR

Dennis Lehane is the author of nine novels—including *The New York Times* bestsellers *Moonlight Mile*; *Gone, Baby, Gone*; *Mystic River*; *Shutter Island*; and *The Given Day*—as well as *Coronado*, a collection of short stories and a play. He and his wife, Angie, divide their time between Boston and the Gulf Coast of Florida.

Imprint: William Morrow
BEA Booth #: 3339, 3340
Author appearances: Ticketed Signing Tuesday, June 5, 3:00 pm - 4:00 pm, Table #: 5
Printed galley at BEA: yes
Contact for printed galley: Kimberly Chocolaad Kimberly.Chocolaad@ harpercollins.com
Print ISBN: 9780060004873

Print price: $27.99
eBook ISBN: 9780062200297
eBook price: $14.99
Publication date: 10/2/2012
Publicity contact: Shelby Meizlik Shelby.Meizlik@harpercollins.com
Rights contact: Michelle Corallo (Domestic only) Michelle.Corallo@ harpercollins.com
Penn Whaling Penn@rittlit.com (Foreign only)
Editor: Claire Wachtel
Agent: Ann Rittenberg
Agency: Ann Rittenberg Literary Agency, Inc.
Promotional Information:
- National advertising campaign
- National online advertising, including Facebook
- 15-City television satellite tour
- 25-City radio satellite tour
- Author appearances in Boston, New York, Tampa
- National radio promotions
- Major digital marketing and publicity campaign
- Month-by-month teaser campaign feature in the Hot@Harper news-letter
- Library marketing, including galley mailings
- Pre-publication online buzz campaign, including early consumer reads and viral video
- Blogger campaign, including e-cards
- Reading group guide available online at HarperCollins.Com/readers

TAP OUT

BY ERIC DEVINE

SUMMARY

In Pleasant Meadows, seventeen-year-old Tony Antioch has learned that survival comes down to one simple formula; keep your head down and your mouth shut. But with a mother who serves as a punching bag for her boyfriends and a meth-dealing biker gang that is hungry for recruits, Tony finds himself in deep without knowing exactly how he got there. Mixed Martial Arts classes provide an escape but may not be all that he needs to break a seemingly endless and hopeless cycle. Tony has the blood and guts, but is it enough to give him the glory of living his own life freely?

Tap Out is at once gritty, powerful, and unapologetic, and offers an honest look into one teen's struggle to break the cycle and carve a path of his own choosing.

EXCERPT

Chapter 1

I am a pussy. I know this, and not much else.

A wet smack sounds in the next room. My mother cries in pain. "Please, Cameron, I didn't mean anything." He hits her again, twice, dense flesh on flesh.

"The fuck you didn't," Cameron, my mother's boyfriend, slurs. She must have made some joke that he was too drunk to understand. Again.

So he's kicking the shit out of her. Again.

I'm sitting on the corner of my bed, listening, but not doing anything, even though I want to. My muscles are all coiled, tight, like I'm ready to roll, but I won't. Cameron is wiry, works construction, and could toss me across the fucking room. At least that's what I tell myself about him, *this* boyfriend. I've had excuses for all the others as well, and an entire list of reasons for my father.

He hits her again, a dull thud, the sound of his fist hitting her head. "You gonna apologize or what?"

"I'm sorry. I'm sorry. I didn't mean anything."

Another blow, and she hits the wall. The house vibrates. "Damn straight, you dumb bitch." The door squeals as he pounds down the hall and the fridge opens. He's grabbing a beer, or two. The can clicks and pops, followed by the sound of him falling into the recliner. The volume on the TV goes up: lots of screaming and yelling.

Fuck, maybe it's over. I grab the back of my head and bury my face into the crooks of my elbows. I want to block out the sound of him and forget what I just heard, but my mom's crying seeps through the paper-thin walls. I hate the noise, but more, I hate how common it is. How many times has she been like this? It's impossible to keep track, there's been so many.

Her cry lifts and then is muffled. She must be using her pillow. I hope so, because if he hears her . . . Hopefully she'll be able to calm herself and then sit, red-faced and swollen, and wait for Cam to get a sleepy buzz. Then, like always, she can ice or shower, depending on how bad it is. Once it started, it only took them three months to find this pattern. Not a record, but pretty fast.

Wonder how long it took for her and my dad?

He's the reason I'm such a little bitch now, hiding out instead of stepping up. As a kid I never once went after him, just daydreamed about taking him out. In the end I didn't have to; he just left. As have all the rest. But Cameron's still hanging around, and this time I see myself stepping into her bedroom when he's wailing on her. I grab his arm midswing and twist him around. He sees me and his eyes go wide, but then he gets that sneer like he always does. But before he can do anything, I head-butt him. He collapses to his knees, grabbing his face as the blood pumps out. I ignore it and put my fist into his jaw. No, through it. My mom screams, but I ignore her and enjoy his pain. He goes to speak but realizes that his jaw is shattered and I laugh, because I know in that moment I could kill him. I may not be big, but you don't get beat your entire life without hardening.

I *could* take him out. I have the capacity, and that is enough for me, because I don't want to actually do it and be like him, or the others. In my fantasy I help my mother up and walk her out of the room, away from the oozing mass in the corner. We step into a cleaner version of our life, where we're not confined to our prison of a trailer and no one sees us as white trash.

It's never gonna happen though, so there's no point in wishing for it. I stand up and walk to the bathroom and the trailer wobbles. Or it could be I'm still amped and it feels that way. Or the fucking thing may really be falling apart. Why wouldn't it? Everything else is.

I piss and brush my teeth. The TV blares and I listen: an announcer's voice. Fuck. I peer down the hall. He's watching a cage match. Two guys hop around a mat. One is all tatted up and has blood leaking out of his nose. The other is so thin that his abs look like individual plates. I don't know how they can even be in the same weight class, but they throw jabs back and forth and then the tatted one kicks. The skinny one catches it, and the tatted guy's eyes go wide. He knows what's coming, and sure as shit the skinny dude latches on to the tatted guy's leg like a monkey to a tree and takes him to the mat. The skinny guy squeezes on the tatted guy's leg and arches his own back, every muscle popping. The ref hovers over them, wearing the same black latex gloves we wear at Vo-Tec, and the tatted guy screams as the blood pumps faster. He looks up, grinds his teeth, and then taps the mat. Fight's over.

"Fucking leg bar." Cameron tosses an empty can to the floor and then pops open another.

I head back to my room and have to shake away the fantasy rising again. I'll stay awake all night if I don't put it out of my mind. I sit on my bed and can hear my mom still crying. I lie back and pull a pillow over my head, but it doesn't help. Her tears still seep through, and the sound of another fight beginning on the TV punches in.

Chapter 2

I'm standing out by the Pleasant Meadows park sign, waiting for the bus. There's not one thing pleasant about this place and no meadow that I've ever seen. Feet scuffle down the lane, and the girls giggle, while Rob's laugh echoes.

"There's my little bitch." Rob wraps an arm around my neck and squeezes. My head throbs as he pulls me down. "You ready to suck it? Huh?" His crotch is inches from my face, and I go limp, just hang as dead weight in his arms. "Man." He lets go. "No fucking fun if you don't fight back."

"Leave Tony alone. His house was on fire last night." Amy kicks Rob in the ass. I stand and tuck my hands into my pockets, happy to be out of the hold, but not if I have to talk about this. "Cameron?" She takes a drag off her cigarette and closes an eye when she exhales.

"Yeah." There's no point in denying it. Everyone knows everybody's business around here, and sadly, mine is real fucking common. I kick the loose stone at our feet.

"Fucking temper. But hot as a motherfucker. I'd do him." Amy licks her lips.

"You'd do your fucking dog, you whore." Charity lights a cigarette and juts her chin.

"If his dick were big enough. Holla!"

The girls laugh, and Rob shakes his head.

"For real, man. You need to get ready for when he turns on you. I'll show you some moves." Rob pops into stance, like the fighters on TV from last night, and paws at the back of my neck. He's wearing his MMA gym's hoodie today. Like every day. But he's got a point about Cameron, just like I was thinking last night. Sooner or later they all turn on me: all her boyfriends, and my dad, too. But Cameron just doesn't seem to be going anywhere. He doesn't have the ability to be disgusted with us, or himself. But fuck Rob and his karate-ass shit. There's no ring at my house.

"Yeah. I wanna grapple with you. So we can get *real close* to each other."

Rob's eyes draw together. "Yo, it's not like that."

"Really? You just wanted me to suck your dick."

The girls laugh.

"Fuck you, Tone. I'll kick your ass right here. No grappling." He pops his stance again and weaves around me. I used to be able to take him back in middle school, and even freshman year. But now? Maybe. He is bigger, but that doesn't always matter.

Brakes hiss behind us, and the bus door wrenches open. "Put them cigarettes out!" Hack-Face, the bus driver, leans over her seat. She looks like someone once went over her with a cleaver. Every inch of her skin is wrinkled and red.

The girls take long drags, and then step on the butts and mount the stairs. They exhale as they pass Hack-Face. Rob's still in his stance and I shake my head and turn my back on him.

I sit alone because I don't feel like talking to Rob. He'll just want to go on and on about fighting and the gym, and with last night still swirling in my head, it's about the last topic I want to deal with. He's been trying to get me to join ever since he started last year, but it's not like I've got the money. All the guys who go there wear the same hoodie with the gym's logo on front—two figures, one standing, the other lying on the mat—and some quote on the back. Either that or it's those ugly fucking tapout shirts or the ones with images of fighters on them. It's like they're in fifth grade again, busting a nut over some A-Rod or McGwire jersey. No, I really don't want to be one of them, either.

***

I spin the dial on my locker and then check the schedule taped inside. It's Thursday, but I don't have a clue what day in the rotation it is. A girl nearby closes her locker. "Hey, what's today?"

She looks at me, squints, and her mouth forms a wiggly line, like she wants to say something, but can't find the words. It's always like this. Kids know I'm trash from who I hang with, but not from the way I look. I keep myself clean, ironing board in the bedroom and everything pressed. I do my own laundry and make damn sure my kicks stay spotless, so if I'm on my own, they have to guess. "Thursday." She presses her books close to her chest.

I shake my head. "No. What day?" I point at my schedule.

"Oh." She straightens. "C-Day."

"Thanks." She's got her back to me before I speak, but at least she spoke. Shit, C-day blows. Bio, then PE, then English. Afternoons are always Vo-Tec, but it doesn't make up for the three long hours I'm here. The bell rings and kids look around, waiting for the first person to take off. Eventually, we all do.

I don't even know why I gotta take bio. Not like I'm gonna be a fucking doctor or some shit. Mr. Bransfield starts writing notes on the board, and kids get out their binders or notebooks. I don't have a notebook or a pen. Not even a book bag. I look at the extra textbook he makes me use and listen. Period. If it sticks, it sticks. He's written something up there about the three layers of the skin. Who gives a shit? Skin's so thin, might as well all be one.

I skim the section we're supposed to read and catch words like "ruptured capillaries" and "trapped blood" and "trauma," but I know all this shit. A fucking bruise happens when something hits you. A hand, a belt, a shoe. Who gives a fuck what occurs beneath the surface?

***

Mrs. Myers gives us a quiz on the first chapter of this book, *Lord of the Flies*, I didn't read. Don't ever read. At least not since I was a kid. So I guess at the answers and probably fail. Mrs. Myers asks us to pass up the paper and then read Chapter Two for the rest of the class. I don't have a copy, and she doesn't hand out loaners like Bransfield, so I put my head on my desk and pop my hoodie over. Lights out.

The bell rings. I pull myself together, rub my face, and head to the main entrance. I could go to lunch, but none of the other Vo-Tec fucks do. It's the hassle of getting the shit for free. We all do, but have to give the ugly, old, hair-netted bitch who runs the register this special card. That's if we remember to bring it. Which is never. So the old hag has to yell to some other old hag to look up a "Free lunch." Asks our last name and yells that, too. That's a mistake I've only made once.

Somebody opens a bag of chips and passes it around. Rob, Amy, and Charity chow down. The girls all go to become hairdressers or some nail salon shit. We go and work on cars. I grab a handful and think to take more. This is the first I've eaten today.

***

"Afternoon boys." Mr. Greyson wipes his hands on a rag, but they're still black when he finishes. I breathe in the greased air and love it. "As you can see, we've got a project for today." He throws a thumb at the pickup, a 250, new, black, and beautiful. "Just an oil change. But we'll do the filter and check the fluids and brakes too."

Greyson's a hard ass, but he's the only one who can get away with it because he's the only one who actually teaches us something useful. He smacks the clipboard he pulls from his shop table. "Looks like Rob and Tony have the honors."

My stomach drops, but Rob pumps his fist. "Sweet!"

"Good, get to it. Remember the pan." Greyson whips the air with his hand. "The rest of you, follow me." The group walks to the pair of junkers that we learn from, these piece of shit cars, stripped down, like dead, open bodies for doctors. Rob and I grab the tools we need. We weren't allowed to touch anything our freshman year, just watch and memorize. Sophomore year, we could hand off tools. Junior year, we could touch. Now I know almost every tool and how to change oil, tires, and bulbs. I can monitor electrical systems, brake rotors, and on and on. It isn't a great living, but I could be a mechanic anywhere, and get the fuck out of here.

I check that the bay is clear and that the truck is secure, and then hit the switch on the lift and the truck rises. Rob moves under, pan in hand, already wearing latex gloves. I love that we're given the chance to keep our hands clean.

"You should at least come to one class." Rob unscrews the nut, and the oil drips.

"How many times do I need to tell you? I'm not into it."

"Till you change your mind." Rob turns his back to me. "Read this."

"Douche, I don't give a shit about your fucking sweatshirt."

Rob spins and puts a thumb into my collarbone. I go to my knees; the pain is so sudden.

"Everything all right over there?" Greyson calls.

"Yup." Rob waves with his free hand.

So do I. "All right. Fucking quit."

Rob releases and turns his back, again. I wipe my neck with a clean rag, but nothing comes away. Still, I think about kicking out his legs and watching him fall into the pan of oil, but I just read his sweatshirt for the hundredth fucking time, because if I don't he'll keep asking: *The cage will reveal your true self. Whether you like it or not.* I shove him. "All right. Happy?"

"Not until you find out, fucker."

I stand and move to the lift control. "Well, that isn't happening today." I shrug. "Screw that shit in before I crush you."

Rob stares at me for a moment, his typical bad-ass stance. They must teach this shit, and I feel like flipping him off, but that's not the point. I know what he's thinking, that he could take me out right here. Fuck, maybe he thinks he's so fast he could get to me before I hit the lift button? I don't like it, but his cockiness reminds me of Cameron, and I'm glad that he turns and does his job.

We finish and Greyson checks on us, gives a grunt, and says, "Nice work." After that we clean up and then hit up the bus for home. As soon as we're off Amy and Char light up.

"Tonight, Tone." Amy blows a ring. "You need to run and hide, come on over."

Everyone laughs, but Amy looks at me with her fuck-me eyes. She means it, but there's no way I'm putting my dick in her. She's been used so much, I bet the shit's like a baseball glove. I open my mouth to make the joke, but don't bother. I just don't have the energy. "Whatever." I wave them off, and Rob walks with me. He slaps my shoulder.

"You change your mind, I'll be rolling past round six." I shake my head, just because I don't feel like speaking, and am glad that he just lets it go. "All right, catch you tomorrow." He takes off, and I turn toward my house. I heard someone once say that all of us in the park live in sardine cans, and I guess that's true. My house is small, metal, and looks like it should be thrown away. The smell is pretty rancid as well. But I don't have anything else, so I head in.

Mom's not home and the place is a fucking mess. Cameron's cans are spilling out of the garbage, or lying next to the chair. Dishes and food containers from my mom's work spill across the counter. It looks like spaghetti, but I turn away from it. I'm not *that* hungry, and I'm not cleaning up their shit, even though I'll get bitched at later. Whenever she fucking gets home from the diner. Fuck her. She had time to clean.

I go to my room and close the accordion door. Unlike the rest of this heap, my room's clean. Everything has a place and is put there. I take off my shoes and line them alongside my other pair, beneath my bed. It squeaks when I hop on it, but is damn comfortable. I lie back and stare at the ceiling. Brown water stains dot the corner. The last time it rained heavy I woke up wet. Cameron said he'll fix it, but I think he's just grunt labor, doesn't know how to do a damn thing for himself. My stomach growls so I roll to my side and pull my knees up to my chest. Hope my mom brings home leftovers or I may have to eat that spaghetti. I grab the blanket from the foot of my bed and pull it over me. Cover everything. The only thing to do is sleep and wait for whatever's next.

***

"Whad'ya mean I can't come in?"

I sit up. It's dark and Cam's voice is worming in from outside. She must be holding the door open. I get into position to roll.

"Not tonight. I'm not in the mood."

"You're always in the mood, baby. Can't resist this." Cameron laughs. It's throaty, sounding like he's working up a hawker, and I'd like to strangle that noise inside him, not out of him. I want him to hear the way he sounds to me.

"Cam, fuck off! I ain't having this shit tonight. It's been a long fucking . . ." The slap sounds as if he's hit her flush in the cheek, wet and fleshy. She doesn't finish.

"I don't give a fuck! Boo fucking hoo. You had to work. I did, too. Now let me in."

I roll my legs over the side of the bed and slide my feet into my sneakers. I don't know why. I'm not going anywhere, especially not outside. I'd only *like* to strangle him, not actually do it.

"Go away."

"What, you got someone else in there?"

I stand and push back my door. It's like I'm in someone else's body, because this is not me. Ever since the first time I can remember my dad going after her, pulling her hair down to the floor, where she became eye-level with me, I've frozen. Then, I just couldn't understand why he'd want her in that position. Now, after seven years with him and a dozen or so of her boyfriends, I understand all too well.

"No, no one else is in here. Just Tony, and he's sleeping."

"Sleepin'? That little bitch is taking a nap. Let me wake his ass up."

My insides tighten, and I grab the doorframe. What the fuck am I doing? I look into the hall. My mom's standing in the doorway, and her face is drawn, eyes puffy. She's spent. This fucker needs to leave because she doesn't have anything left to fight with. But between her and my pussy ass, what can we do? She holds up her hands. "Cameron, go home. Enough."

"Yeah, yeah. Same ol' shit, 'Yer nuthin' but a drunk.' Save it. Cuz you'll be callin', crying to me about how sorry you are."

I step into the hall and lock my jaw, grinding my teeth. He's right, that's exactly what she does, but it doesn't mean she has to, again.

"Just go." Her voice is a whisper.

"All right." His feet crunch outside, and I relax. Fuck, maybe he's got more sense than I thought. Or is just too loaded to continue. I lean against the wall, and the sound of him hitting her, like someone slapping down beer cans, brings me back to standing. His hands fly through the open door, and my mom grabs the frame to keep from falling. He catches her square in the eye with a fist, and she goes down on her side. I'm down the hall in five steps. She's trying to stand, and he's on the steps grabbing her legs.

"No!" I can't stop myself. Here I am, out of my room, not fantasizing, but about to enter the mix.

Both of them freeze and look at me, my mother's eyes wide, her mouth bleeding and hanging open. Cameron's forehead knots, but then he smiles. That fucking smirk pulls across his face. "Woo hoo. Big man steppin' up. All right!"

I look at my mother, her bloody face, spit and snot dribbling out her mouth and nose. I've seen this image so many times that it's left me numb. I know it's wrong, but she looks pathetic to me, lying on the ground again, helpless. Cameron laughs, and I look up, into his eyes. They're sinister, like something from a nightmare, and I feel again. First fear and then panic. My mother's not helpless, he's just fucking evil, and now that I'm standing up to him, for her, I can't go down as easily.

I rush to the door, and he slips, trying to react. I pull my mother's legs inside and then slam the door in place. I lock it just as he grabs the handle, but the door is secure, so he pounds on the thin metal.

"You fucking pussy. Get yer ass out here. I'll fuck you up real good. Then I'll fuck yer mother." He laughs again and pounds some more.

Again, I want to strangle his words in his throat. I help my mother up and move her to the couch. Cameron's still pounding and screaming. This is nothing like my fantasy. My head spins, but I go to the bathroom and wet a washcloth. I bring it back and hand it to my mom.

"Thank you." Her voice is low, and she does not look at me. I sit next to her, and she cleans her face, and we both seem to tune out whatever the fuck he's screaming out there, something about his dick. "I thought he was different, honey. Really."

I open my mouth to speak because I can't imagine what she saw in him that was any different from the others. He's a fucking loser with a dead-end job, who drinks until he passes out, and when he feels like it, beats the shit out of her. But I keep my comments to myself. She's still wearing her work uniform. He must have followed her or have been waiting. Maybe it's not her fault—this time.

She looks at me out of the corner of her eye. "At least I know who you are."

I nod but not because I'm agreeing. I don't know what else to do because I don't know that who I am is as solid as she thinks. Up until five minutes ago, I never once stood up to any of the men in her life. It's not as if she has ever asked me to, but with what she just said, it makes me feel as if she's been waiting. Unreal. Even my own mother thought I was a pussy. But maybe, just maybe, I'm not.

Twitter: Want to discuss or share what you just read? Use the hashtag #beaTAP to connect with others.

ABOUT THE AUTHOR

Eric Devine is currently a writer, high school English teacher, educational consultant, and CrossFit coach. He is also the author of *This Side of Normal*. He lives in Waterford, New York, with his family, and can be found online at ericdevine.org.

Imprint: Running Press
BEA Booth #: 3604
Printed galley at BEA: yes
Contact for printed galley: Seta.Zink@Perseusbooks.com
Print ISBN: 9780762445691
Print price: $9.95
eBook ISBN: 9780762447008
eBook price: $9.95

Publication date: 9/11/2012
Publicity contact: Seta.Zink@Perseusbooks.com
Rights contact: Jennifer Schaper Jennifer.Schaper@PerseusBooks.com
Editor: Lisa Cheng
Agent: Kate McKean
Agency: Howard Morhaim Literary Agency, Inc.
Promotional Information:
• Feature title at BEA and ALA
• Trade and targeted consumer advertising
• National print and online reviews
• Regional appearances
• Extensive social marketing campaign targeting teen readers

NEW YORK TIMES BESTSELLING AUTHOR

JENNY HAN &
SIOBHAN VIVIAN

BURN
FOR
BURN

SUMMARY

Jenny Han, the author of *The New York Times* bestselling *The Summer I Turned Pretty* series and Siobhan Vivian, the acclaimed author of *The List*, team up for *Burn for Burn*, the first book in a captivating trilogy. Set on postcard-perfect Jar Island, *Burn for Burn* introduces three very different girls who want the same thing: sweet, sweet revenge. LILLIA used to trust boys, but not anymore. Not after what happened this summer. And she'll be damned if she lets the same thing happen to her little sister. KAT is through with being called a freak. She's over the rumors, the insults, the cruel jokes made at her expense. It all goes back to one person—her ex-best friend—and Kat's ready to make her pay. Six years ago, MARY left Jar Island because of a boy. But she's not the same girl anymore. Now that she's back, he's gonna be in trouble... cause she's coming after him. These three girls learn that sometimes, the only way to make things right is to do something wrong....

EXCERPT

MARY

The morning fog has painted everything white. It's exactly like one of my rabbit-hole dreams, where I get trapped, suspended in a cloud, and I can't seem to wake myself up.

Then the foghorn blares, the mist breaks into lace, and I see Jar Island, spread out along the horizon just like in one of Aunt Bette's paintings.

That's when I know for sure that I've done it. I've actually come back.

One of the workers ties the ferry to the dock with a thick white rope. Another lowers the bridge. The captain's voice comes over the loudspeaker. "Good morning, passengers. Welcome to Jar Island. Please make your way down to the bridge, and enjoy this beautiful summer day."

I'd almost forgotten how beautiful it is here. The sun has lifted above the water, and it lights everything up yellow and bright. A hint of my reflection in the window stares back at me—pale eyes, lips parted, windblown blond hair. I'm not the same person I was when I left here, in seventh grade. I'm older, obviously, but it's not just that. I've changed. When I see myself now, I see someone strong. Maybe even pretty.

Will he recognize me, I wonder? Part of me hopes he doesn't. But the other part, the part that left my family to come back, hopes he does. He has to. Otherwise, what's the point?

I hear the rumble of cars parked on the freight deck as they get ready to drive off. There's a bunch more on shore, in a long line that reaches the entrance to the parking lot, waiting to pull aboard for the return trip back to the mainland. One more week of summer vacation left. I step away from the window, smooth my seersucker sundress, and go back to my seat to get my things. The seat next to mine is empty. I stick my hand underneath, feeling around for what I know is there. His initials. RT. I remember the day he carved them with his Swiss Army knife, just because he felt like it.

I wonder if things have changed on the island. Does Milky Morning still have the best blueberry muffins? Will the Main Street movie theater have the same lumpy green velvet seats? How big has the lilac bush in our yard grown?

It's strange to feel like a tourist, because the Zanes have lived on Jar Island practically forever. My great-great-great-grandfather designed and built the library. One of my mom's aunts was the very first woman to be elected alderman of Middlebury. Our family plot is right in the center of the old cemetery in the middle of the island, and some of the headstones are so old and moss covered, you can't even see who's buried there.

Jar Island is made up of four small towns. Thomastown, Middlebury, which is where I'm from, White Haven, and Canobie Bluffs. Each town has its own middle school, and they all feed into Jar Island High. During the summer the population swells to several thousand vacationers. But only about a thousand or so people live here year round.

My mom always says Jar Island never changes. It's its own little universe. There's something about Jar Island that lets people pretend the world has stopped spinning. I think that's part of the charm, why people want to spend summers here. Or why the diehards put up with the hassles that come with living here year round, the way my family used to.

People appreciate that there isn't a single chain store, shopping mall, or fast-food restaurant on Jar Island. Dad says there's something like two hundred separate laws and ordinances that make building them illegal. Instead people buy their groceries at local markets, get prescriptions filled at soda-shop pharmacies, pick out beach reads at independent bookstores.

Another thing that makes Jar Island special is that it's a *true* island. There are no bridges or tunnels connecting it to the mainland. Aside from the one-strip airfield that only rich people with private planes use, everyone and everything comes in and goes out on this ferry.

I pick up my suitcases and follow the rest of the passengers off. The dock runs straight into the welcome center. An old 1940s school bus painted with the words "JAR ISLAND TOURS" is parked in front and getting washed. A block behind that is Main Street—a quaint strip of souvenir shops and lunch counters. Above it rises Middlebury's big hill. It takes a second for me to find it, and I have to shade my eyes from the sun, but I pick out the pitched red roof of my old house at the tippy top.

My mom grew up in that house, along with Aunt Bette. My bedroom used to be Aunt Bette's bedroom, and it looks out at the sea. I wonder if that's where Aunt Bette's sleeping now, or if she kept it for me.

I'm Aunt Bette's only niece; she doesn't have any children of her own. She never knew how to act around kids, so she treated me like an adult. I liked it, getting to feel grown-up. When she'd ask me questions about her paintings, what I felt about them, she actually listened to what I had to say. But she was never the kind of aunt who'd get on the floor and help me do a puzzle, or who'd want to bake cookies together. I didn't need her to be. I already had a mom and dad who'd do those things.

I think it'll be great, living with Aunt Bette now that I'm older. My parents both baby me. Perfect example—my curfew is still ten o'clock, even though I'm seventeen. I guess after everything that happened, it makes sense that they're extra protective.

The walk home takes longer than I remember, maybe because my suitcases are slowing me down. A few times I stick out my thumb to the cars chugging up the hill. Some of the locals hitchhike on Jar Island. It's an accepted thing, a way to help out your neighbors. I was never allowed to, but for the first time I don't have my mom or dad looking over my shoulder. No one picks me up, which is a bummer, but there's always tomorrow or the next day. I have all the time in the world to hitchhike or do whatever I want.

I walk right past my driveway without realizing it and have to double back. The bushes have grown big and bristly, and they hide the house from the road. I'm not surprised. Gardening was Mom's thing, not Aunt Bette's.

I drag my bags the last few feet and stare at the house. It's a three-story colonial covered in gray cedar shingles, white shutters bolted to each of the windows, and with a cobblestone wall edging the yard. Aunt Bette's old tan Volvo is parked in the driveway, and it's covered in a blanket of tiny purple flowers.

The lilac bush. It's grown taller than I thought possible. And even though plenty of flowers have fallen, the branches still sag with the weight of millions more. I take as deep a breath as I can.

It's good to be home.

LILLIA

It's that time of year again, the end of August, only one more week till school starts. The beach is crowded, but not July Fourth–crowded. I'm lying on a big blanket with Rennie and Alex. Reeve and PJ are throwing a Frisbee around, and Ashlin and Derek are swimming in the ocean. This is our crew. It's been this way this since the ninth grade. It's hard to believe we're finally seniors.

The sun is so bright, I can feel my tan getting even more golden. I wriggle my body deeper into the sand. I love the sun. Next to me Alex is putting more sunscreen on his shoulders.

"God, Alex," Rennie says, looking up from her magazine. "You need to bring your own sunscreen. You used up half my bottle. Next time, I'm just going to let you get cancer."

"Are you kidding me?" Alex says. "You stole this out of my cabana. Back me up, Lil."

I push myself up on to my elbows and sit up. "You missed a spot on your shoulder. Here, turn around."

I squat behind him and rub a dollop of sunscreen onto his shoulder. Alex turns around and asks, "Lillia, what kind of perfume do you wear?"

I laugh. "Why? Do you want to borrow it?" I love to tease Alex Lind. He's so easy.

He laughs too. "No. I'm just curious."

"It's a secret," I say, patting him on the back.

It's so important for a girl to have a signature scent. A scent every-one knows you by, so that when you walk down the hallway at school, people turn and look, like a Pavlovian response or something. Every time they smell that perfume, they'll think of you. Burnt sugar and bluebell, that's the Lillia scent.

I lie back down on the blanket and flip onto my stomach. "I'm thirsty," I announce. "Will you pass me my Coke, Lindy?"

Alex leans over and rummages through the cooler. "All that's left is water and beer."

I frown, and look over at Reeve. He's got a Frisbee in one hand, my

Coke in the other. "Ree-ve!" I yell out. "That was mine!"

"Sorry," he calls back, not sounding sorry at all. He throws the Frisbee in a perfect arc, and it lands over by some cute girls sitting in beach chairs. Exactly where he wanted it to land, I'm sure.

I look over at Rennie, whose eyes are narrow.

Alex stands up and brushes sand off his shorts. "I'll get you another soda."

"You don't have to," I say. But of course I don't mean it. I really am thirsty.

"You're going to miss me when I'm not here to get your drinks," he says, grinning at me. Alex, Reeve, and PJ are going on a deep-sea fishing trip tomorrow. They'll be gone for a whole week. The boys are always around; we see them nearly every day. It will be strange to finish out the summer without them.

I stick my tongue out at him. "I won't miss you one bit!"

Alex jogs over to Reeve, and then they head off to the hot dog stand down the beach.

"Thanks, Lindy!" I call out, feeling sentimental all of a sudden. He is so good to me.

I look back over at Rennie, who's smirking. "That boy would do anything for you, Lil."

"Stop it."

"Yes or no. Do you think Lindy's cute? Be honest."

I don't even have to think about it. "Yeah, he's obviously cute. Just not to me." Rennie has gotten it into her head that Alex and I should become a couple, and then she and Reeve can become a couple, and we can go on double dates and weekend trips together. As if my parents would ever let me go away with guys! Rennie can go ahead and get an S.T.D. from Reeve if she wants, but Alex and I are not happening. I don't see him that way, and he doesn't see me that way. We're friends. That's it. Rennie gives me a look, but thankfully she doesn't push it any further. Holding up her magazine, she asks, "What do you think about me doing my hair like this for homecoming?" It's a picture of a girl in a sparkly silver dress, her blond hair flowing behind her like a cape.

Laughing, I say, "Ren, homecoming is in October!"

"Exactly! Only a month and a half away." She waves the magazine at me. "So what do you think?"

I guess she's right. We probably should start thinking about dresses. There's no way I'm buying mine from one of the boutiques on the island, not when there's a 90% chance some other girl will show up wearing it too. I take a closer look at the picture. "It's cute! But I doubt there'll be a wind machine."

Rennie snaps her fingers. "Yes! A wind machine. Amazing idea, Lil."

I laugh. If that's what she wants, that's what she'll get. Nobody ever says no to Rennie Holtz.

We're discussing possible homecoming looks when two guys come over by our blanket. One is tall with a crew cut and the other is stockier, with thick biceps. They're both cute, although the shorter one is cuter. They're definitely older than us, definitely not in high school.

Suddenly I'm glad I'm wearing my new black bikini and not my pink and white polka-dot one.

"Do you girls have a bottle opener?" the tall one asks.

I shake my head. "You can probably borrow one from the concessions stand, though."

"How old are you girls?" the built one asks me.

I can tell Rennie is into him, the way she tosses her hair over to one side and says, "Why do you want to know?"

"I want to make sure it's okay to talk to you," he says, grinning. He's looking at her now. "Legally."

She giggles, but in a way that makes her sound older, not like a kid. "We're legal. Barely. How old are you guys?"

"Twenty-one," the taller one says, looking down at me. "We're seniors at UMass, here for the week."

I adjust my bikini top so it doesn't show so much. Rennie just turned eighteen, but I'm still seventeen.

"We're having a party tonight at our house down Shore Road in Canobie Bluffs. You should come." The built one sits down next to Rennie. "Give me your number."

"Ask nicely," Rennie says, all sugar and spice. "And then maybe I'll think about it."

The tall guy sits down next to me, at the edge of the blanket. "I'm Mike."

"Lillia," I say. Over his shoulder I see the boys coming back. Alex has a Coke in his hand for me. They're looking at us, probably wondering who these guys are. Our guy friends can be superprotective when it comes to non-islanders.

Alex frowns and says something to Reeve. Rennie sees them too; she starts giggling extra loud and tossing her hair around again.

The tall guy, Mike, asks me, "Are those guys your boyfriends?"

"No," I say. He's looking at me so intently, I blush.

"Good," he says, and smiles at me. He has really nice teeth.

I smile back.

KAT

It's the beginning of a perfect summer night, the kind where all the stars are out and you don't need a sweatshirt, even down by the water. Which is a good thing, because I left mine at home. I passed out after I got home from work, slept right though dinner. When I woke up, I had, like, five seconds to catch the last ferry to the mainland, so I threw whatever clothes were on my floor into my bag, high-fived my dad good-bye, and ran the whole way from T-Town to the Middlebury harbor. I know I forgot something, but Kim will let me pick through her closet, so whatever.

Main Street is packed. Hardly any of the stores are open at this hour, but it doesn't matter. Tourists just aimlessly mosey along, stopping at the windows to peer inside at the crappy Jar Island–branded sweat-shirts and visors.

I hate August.

I groan as I push past them and make my way to Java Jones. If I want to be awake for the Puppy Ciao encore set, I'm going to need caffeine.

Puppy Ciao is playing at the music store where Kim works, a place called Paul's Boutique on the mainland. Paul's Boutique has an at-tached garage space where they have shows, and if it's a band I want to see, Kim lets me stay the night at her apartment. She lives right above the store. The bands usually crash there too, which is cool. The singer in Puppy Ciao looked pretty hot on their album cover. Not as hot as the drummer, but Kim says that drummers are always trouble.

I take the stairs up to Java Jones two at a time. But as I'm about to push the door open, one of the workers twists the lock.

I knock on the glass. "I know you're closing, but could you hook me up with a quick triple shot to go?"

Ignoring me, the worker unties his apron and unplugs the neon sign. The front window goes dark. I realize that I probably sound like one of the rich a-hole Jar Island tourists who think store hours don't apply to them, the kinds of entitled snobs I'm forced to deal with all day at the marina. So I flick my half-smoked cigarette to the curb, push my hands deep into my pockets so my cutoffs sink low on my hips, and throw in a desperate, "Please! I'm local!"

He turns and stares at me like I'm a huge pain in the ass, but then his face softens. "Kat DeBrassio?"

"Yeah?" I squint at him. He looks familiar, but I can't place him.

The guy unlocks the door and opens it. "I used to race dirt bikes with your brother. " He holds the door open for me. "Careful. Floor's wet. And tell Pat I say 'what up.'"

I nod and walk on tiptoes in my motorcycle boots past another employee pushing a knotted mop back and forth. Then I heave my bag up onto the counter while the guy makes my drink. That's when I notice that Java Jones isn't completely empty. There's one last customer left.

Alex Lind is sitting alone at one of the back tables, hunched over a small notebook. I think it's his diary or something. I've caught him secretly scribbling things down in it a couple of times, when he thought he was being stealth. He's never showed it to me before. Probably because he thinks I'd make fun of whatever is inside it.

The truth is, I probably would. It's not like hanging out for a few weeks makes us *actual* friends.

I'm not going to interrupt him. I'll just get my drink and go. We already said our good-byes this afternoon. But then his pencil grinds to a halt in the middle of a page. Alex bites down on his lower lip, closes his eyes, and thinks for a second. He looks like a little kid concentrating on his nightly prayers, vulnerable and sweet.

I'm going to miss the dude.

I quick rake my fingers through my bangs and call out, "Yo, Lind."

He opens his eyes, startled. Alex quickly slides his notebook into his back pocket and shuffles over so he's next to me. "Hey, Kat. What are you up to?"

I roll my eyes. "I'm going to Kim's to see a band. Remember?" I told him not five freaking hours ago, when he stopped by the marina on my lunch hour. That's how we started hanging out. We met at the yacht club in June. I knew who Alex was before then, obviously. It's not like our high school is huge. We'd never actually talked to each other. Maybe once or twice in art last year.

Alex came by one day with a new speedboat. As he tried to drive away, he stalled out.

I threw him out of the driver's seat and gave him a quick lesson. Alex was impressed with how I handled his boat. A few times, when I really gunned it, I saw him grip the sides, white-knuckled. It was kind of cute.

I was kind of hoping he'd hang out with me today for the rest of my shift so work would be less boring. And because I knew he was heading out tomorrow for his fishing trip. But Alex left me to meet his friends at the beach. His real friends.

"Yeah," Alex says, nodding. "That's right." Then he leans forward and rests his elbows on the counter. "Hey, tell Kim I said thanks again for letting me stay over, okay?"

I took Alex to see Army of None play at the record store in July. He'd never heard of them before we started hanging out, but now they're his favorite band. I was kind of embarrassed, because Alex wore a Jar Island country club polo shirt, cargo shorts, and flip-flops to the show. Kim gave me a look as soon as we walked in, because he was dressed so corny. Alex bought one of the band T-shirts and put it on right away. People who wear the shirt of the band they are going to see play are lame, but it was better than his polo shirt for sure. Once the show started, Alex blended in just fine, bobbing his head along to the music in time with everyone else. And he was super polite at Kim's apartment. Before he got into his sleeping bag, he grabbed the empty beer bottles and put them out in the alley for recycling.

"Do you want to come with me? The show's sold out, but I can get you in."

"I can't," he says with a heavy sigh. "Uncle Tim wants to set sail at dawn." Alex's uncle Tim is a balding perma-bachelor. He doesn't have a family or any real responsibilities, so his money goes to toys—like the new yacht he and Alex and his friends are taking out on a bros only deep-sea fishing trip.

I shrug. "Well, then, I guess this is good-bye for real." I salute him like a navy officer. "Have a good trip," I say, sarcastic, because I don't mean it. I wish he wasn't going. Without Alex coming to visit me at work, this week is going to completely suck.

He straightens up. "I can give you a ride to the ferry."

"Don't worry about it."

I start to walk away, but he grabs the strap of my bag and pulls it off my shoulder. "I want to, Kat."

"Fine. Whatever."

As he drives down toward the ferry landing, Alex keeps staring at me out of the corner of his eye. I don't know why it makes me feel weird, but it does. I turn and look out the window, so he can't see me, and I say, "What's with you?"

He lets out a big sigh. "I can't believe summer's already over. I don't know. I feel like I wasted it."

Before I can stop myself, I say, "You wasted it with your loser friends, maybe. Not hanging out with me." And I hate myself for sounding like I care.

Usually, Alex defends his friends when I make fun of them, but this time, he doesn't say anything.

For the rest of the ride, I think about what's going to happen when school starts, if Alex and I will still be friends. Sure, we've hung out a bunch this summer, but I don't know if I want to associate with the kid at school. In public.

Alex and I . . . we work best like this. When it's just us.

Alex pulls into the ferry parking lot. Before he has a chance to park, I make a split-second decision and say, "I can bail on the show, if you want to hang out tonight." It's not like I'm some Puppy Ciao groupie. Plus, they'll probably come around again. But me and Alex? This might be it for us. Our last night. And I think, on some level, we both know it.

Alex grins. "Seriously? You'll stay with me?"

I open my window and light up a cigarette to hide the fact that I'm smiling too. "Yeah, why not? I want to see this Richie Rich yacht for myself."

So that's where Alex takes us. We pull up to his uncle Tim's mansion, where the thing is docked. As we walk toward it, I immediately start making fun of how gaudy it is, but what I'm thinking is, *Holy crap. This yacht is way nicer than my freaking house.* It's definitely the nicest boat I've ever seen. Better than any of the other yachts in the marina.

Alex climbs aboard first, and I'm right behind him. He gives me a quick tour, and it's even more posh on the inside. Italian marble and about a hundred flat-screen televisions, and a wine cellar filled with bottles from Italy, France, South Africa.

I think of Rennie. She'd die over this place.

Just as quick, I push her out of my head. It hardly happens anymore, but I hate that it happens at all.

I'm trying to figure out the stereo when Alex comes up beside me. Really close beside me. He pushes my hair off to one side. "Kat?"

I freeze. Alex's lips brush against my neck. He grabs my hips and pulls me toward him.

He's not my type. Not even close

That's why it's so crazy. Because as soon as I turn my head, we're kissing. And I suddenly feel like I've been waiting the whole summer for it to happen.

Twitter: Want to discuss or share what you just read? Use the hashtag #beaBURN to connect with others.

ABOUT THE AUTHORS

Jenny Han and Siobhan Vivian met in graduate school in New York City and have been inseparable ever since. They share books, pretty dresses, and a love of Buffy the Vampire Slayer. The idea for *Burn For Burn* began over cupcakes, as the best ones usually do.

Jenny Han is *The New York Times* bestselling author of *The Summer I Turned Pretty*, *It's Not Summer Without You*, and *We'll Always Have Summer*. Visit her at www.dearjennyhan.com.

Siobhan Vivian is the author of *The List*, *Not That Kind Of Girl*, *Same Difference*, and *A Little Friendly Advice*. Visit her at www.siobhanvivian.com.

Imprint: S&S Books for Young Readers
BEA Booth #: 3658
Author appearances: Both authors in attendance at all events:
June 4th: Book Blogger Con breakfast
June 5th: YA Panel 1-2 pm — Uptown Stage
June 6th: CBC Tea: 3:30-4:45, Room 1E12/13
June 7th: ARC signing Table 12 Autographing Area
Printed galley at BEA: yes
Contact for printed galley: Paul Crichton Paul.Crichton@simonandschuster.com

Print ISBN: 9781442440753
Print price: $17.99
eBook ISBN: 9781442440777
eBook price: $9.99
Publication date: 9/12/2012
Publicity contact: Paul.Crichton paul.crichton@simonandschuster.com
Rights contact: Stephanie Voros Stephanie.voros@simonandschuster.com
Editor: Zareen Jaffery
Agent: Emily Van Beek
Agency: Folio Literary
Territories sold:
    Novo Conceito in Brazil
    Hanser in Germany
Promotional Information:
- Author Tour
- National online advertising
- Extensive blogger outreach
- Dedicated Facebook page
- Sunblock promotional item
- Chapter sampler distribution

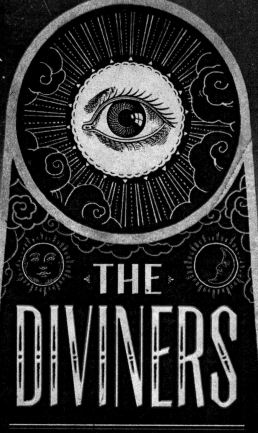

THE DIVINERS

NEW YORK TIMES BESTSELLING AUTHOR

Libba Bray

SUMMARY

Evie O'Neill has been exiled from her boring old hometown and shipped off to the bustling streets of New York City — and she is pos-i-toot-ly thrilled. New York is the city of speakeasies, shopping, and movie palaces! Soon enough, Evie is running with glamorous Ziegfield girls and rakish pickpockets. The only catch is Evie has to live with her Uncle Will, curator of The Museum of American Folklore, Superstition and the Occult—also known as "The Museum of the Creepy Crawlies." When a rash of occult-based murders comes to light, Evie and her uncle are right in the thick of the investigation. And through it all, Evie has a secret: a mysterious power that could help catch the killer—if he doesn't catch her first.

EXCERPT

A Late-Summer Evening

In the town house at a fashionable address on Manhattan's Upper East Side, every lamp blazes. There's a party going on—the last of the summer. Out on the terrace overlooking Manhattan's incandescent skyline, the orchestra takes a much-needed break. It's ten thirty. The party has been on since eight o'clock, and already the guests are bored. Fashionable debutantes in pastel chiffon party dresses wilt into leather club chairs like frosted petits fours melting under the July sun. A cocky Princeton sophomore wants his friends to head down to Greenwich Village with him, to a speakeasy he heard about from a friend of a friend.

The hostess, a pretty and spoiled young thing, notes her guests' restlessness with a sense of alarm. It is her eighteenth birthday, and if she doesn't do something to raise this party from the dead, it will be the talk for days to come that her gathering was as dull as a church social.

Raising from the dead.

The weekend before, she'd been forced to go antiquing upstate with her mother—an absolutely hideous chore, until they came upon an old Ouija board. Ouija boards are all the rage; psychics have claimed to receive messages and warnings from the other side using Mr. Fuld's "talking board." The antiques dealer fed her mother a line about how it had come to him under mysterious circumstances.

"They say it's still haunted by restless spirits. But perhaps you and your sister could tame it?" he'd said with over-the-top flattery; naturally, her mother lapped it up, which resulted in her paying too much for the thing. Well, she'd make her mother's mistake pay off for her now.

The hostess races for the hall closet and signals to the maid. "Do be a darling and get that down for me."

The maid retrieves the board with a shake of her head. "You oughtn't to be messing with this board, Miss."

"Don't be silly. That's primitive."

With a zippy twirl worthy of Clara Bow, the hostess bursts into the formal living room holding the Ouija board. "Who wants to commune with the spirits?" She giggles to show that she doesn't take it seriously in the least. After all, she's a thoroughly modern girl—a flapper, through and through.

The wilted girls spring up from their club chairs. "What've you got there? Is that a wee-gee board?" one of them asks.

"Isn't it darling? Mother bought it for me. It's supposed to be haunted," the hostess says and laughs. "Well, I don't believe that, naturally." The hostess places the heart-shaped planchette in the middle of the board. "Let's conjure up some fun, shall we?"

Everyone gathers 'round. George angles himself into the spot beside her. He's a Yale man and a junior. Many nights, she's lain awake in her bedroom, imagining her future with him. "Who wants to start?" she asks, positioning her fingers close to his.

"I will," a boy in a ridiculous fez announces. She can't remember his name, but she's heard he has a habit of inviting girls into his rumble seat for a petting party. He closes his eyes and places his fingers on the scryer. "A question for the ages: Is the lady to my right madly in love with me?"

The girls squeal and the boys laugh as the planchette slowly spells out Y-E-S.

"Liar!" the lady in question scolds the heart-shaped scrying piece with its clear glass oracle.

"Don't fight it, darling. I could be yours on the cheap," the boy says.

Now spirits are high; the questions grow bolder. They're drunk on gin and good times and the silly distraction of the fortune-telling. *Every mornin', every evenin', ain't we got fun?*

"Say, let's summon a real spirit," George challenges.

A knot of excitement and unease twists in the hostess's gut. The antiques dealer had cautioned against doing just this. He warned that spirits called forth must also be put back to rest by breaking the connection, saying good-bye. But he was out to make a buck with a story, and besides, it's 1926—who believes in haunts and hobgoblins when there are motorcars and aeroplanes and the Cotton Club and men like Jake Marlowe making America first through industry?

"Don't tell me you're scared?" George smirks. He has a cruel mouth. It makes him all the more desirable.

"Scared of what?"

"That we'll run out of gin!" the boy in the fez jokes, and everyone laughs.

George whispers low in her ear, "I'll keep you safe." His hand is on her back.

Oh, surely this is the most glorious night in existence!

"We summon now the spirit of this board to heed our call and tell us our fortunes true!" the hostess says with great intonation broken by giggles. "You must obey, spirit!"

There is a moment's pause, and then the planchette begins its slow migration across the scarred board's gothic black alphabet, spelling out a word.

H-E-L-L-O

"That's the spirit," someone quips.

"What is your name, o great spirit?" the hostess insists.

The planchette moves quickly.

N-A-U-G-H-T-Y J-O-H-N

George raises an eyebrow mischievously. "Say, I like the sound of that. What makes you so naughty, old sport?"

Y-O-U-L-L S-E-E

"See what? What are you up to, o naughty one?"

Stillness.

"I want to dance! Let's go uptown to the Moonglow," one of the girls, a pouty drunk, slurs. "When's the band comin' back, anyway?"

"In a minute. Don't have kittens," the hostess says with a smile and a laugh, but there's warning in both. "Let's try another question. Do you have any prophecy for us, Naughty John? Any fortune-telling?" She casts a sly glance at George.

The scryer remains still.

"Do tell us something else, won't you?"

Finally, there is movement on the board. "I...will...teach...

you . . . fear," the hostess reads aloud.

"Sounds like the headmaster at Choate," the boy in the fez teases. "How will you do that, old sport?"

I-S-T-A-N-D-A-T-T-H-E-D-O-O-R-A-N-D-K-N-O-C-K

I-A-M-T-H-E-B-E-A-S-T

T-H-E-D-R-A-G-O-N-O-F-O-L-D

"What does that mean?" the drunken girl whispers. She backs away slightly.

"It doesn't mean anything. It's gibberish." The hostess scolds her guest, but she feels afraid. She turns on the boy with the reputation for trouble. "You're making it say that!"

"I didn't. I swear!" he says, crossing his heart with his index finger.

"Why are you here, old sport?" George asks the board.

The planchette moves so quickly they can barely keep up.

I-H-O-L-D-T-H-E-K-E-Y-S-O-F-H-E-L-L-A-N-D-D-E-A-T-H

W-R-A-T-H-I-S-C-O-M-E-A-R-M-A-G-E-D-D-O-N-B-A-B-Y-L-O-N-W-H-O-R-E

"Stop it this instant!" the hostess shouts.

WHORE-WHORE-WHORE the piece repeats. The bright young things remove their fingers, but the piece continues to move.

"Make it stop, make it stop!" one girl screeches, and even the jaded boys pale and move back.

"Stop, spirit! I said stop!" the hostess shouts.

The planchette falls still. The party guests glance at one another with wild eyes. In the other room, the band members return to their instruments and strike up a hot dance number.

"Oh, hallelujah! Come on, baby. I'll teach you to dance the Black Bottom." The drunken girl struggles to her feet and pulls the boy in the fez after her.

"Wait! We have to spell out good-bye on the board! That's the proper ritual!" the hostess pleads as her guests desert her.

George slips his arm around her waist. "Don't tell me you're afraid of Naughty John."

"Well, I . . ."

"You know it was the old boy," he says, his breath tickling her ear sweetly. "He has his tricks. You know how that sort is."

She does know how that sort is. It was probably that wretched boy all along, playing them for fools. Well, she is nobody's fool. She is eighteen now. Life will be an endless swirl of parties and dances. *Night or daytime, it's all playtime. Ain't we got fun?* Her earlier fears have been put to bed. Her party looks like it will rage into the night. The carpets have been rolled up, and her guests dance full out. Long strands of pearls bounce against drop-waist dresses. Spats strike defiantly at the wood floors. Arms thrust out, pushing against the air—all of it like some feverish Dadaist painting come to life.

The hostess stashes the board in the cupboard, where it will soon be forgotten, and races toward the parlor with its bright electric lights—Mr. Edison's modern marvel—and joins the last party of the summer without a care.

Outside, the wind lingers for a moment at those lighted windows; then, with a gusty burst of energy, it takes its leave and scuttles down the sidewalks. It twines itself briefly around the cloche hats of two fashionable young ladies gossiping about the tragic death of Rudolph Valentino as they walk a poodle along the East River. It moves on, down neon-drenched canyons, over the elevated train as it rattles above Second Avenue, shaking the windows of the poor souls trying to sleep before morning comes—morning with its taxi horns, trolley cars, and trains; the bootblacks buffing the wingtips of businessmen in Union Square; the newsies hawking the day's headlines in Times Square; the telephone operators gazing longingly at the new shawl-collar coats tempting them from store windows; the majestic skyscrapers rising over it all like gleaming steel, brick, and glass gods.

The wind idles briefly before a jazz club, listening to this new music punctuating the night. It thrills to the bleat of horns, the percussive piano strides born of blues and ragtime, the syncopated rhythms that echo the jagged excitement of the city's skyline.

On the Bowery, in the ornate carcass of a formerly grand vaudeville theater, a dance marathon limps along. The contestants, young girls and their fellas, hold one another up, determined to make their mark, to bite back at the dreams sold to them in newspaper advertisements and on the radio. They have sores on their feet but stars in their eyes. Farther uptown, the Great White Way, named for the blinding incandescence of its theater lights, empties of its patrons. Some stage-door Johnnies wait in the alleys, hoping for a glimpse of the glamorous chorus girls or for a chance at an autograph from one of Broadway's many stars. It is a time of celebrity, of fame and fortune and grasping, and the young burn with secret ambition.

The wind takes it all in with indifference. It is only the wind. It will not become a radio star or a captain of industry. It will not run for office or fall in love with Douglas Fairbanks or sing the songs of Tin Pan Alley, songs of longing and regret and good times (*ain't we got fun?*). And so it travels on, past the slaughterhouses on Fourteenth Street, past the unfortunates selling themselves in darkened alleys. Nearby, Lady Liberty hoists her torch in the harbor, a beacon to all who come to these shores to escape persecution or famine or hopelessness. For this is the land of dreams.

The wind swoops over the tenements on Orchard Street, where some of those starry-eyed dreams have died and yet other dreams are being born into squalor and poverty, an uphill climb. It gives a slap to the laundry stretched on lines between tenements, over dirty, broken streets where, even at this hour, hungry children scour the bins for food. The wind has existed forever. It has seen much in this country of dreams and soap ads, old horrors and bloodshed. It has played mute witness to its burning witches, and has walked along a Trail of Tears; it has seen the slave ships release their human cargo, blinking and afraid, into the ports, their only possession a grief they can never lose. The wind was there when President Lincoln fell to an assassin's bullet. It smelled of gunpowder at Antietam. It ran with the buffalo and touched tentative fingers to the tall black hats of Puritans. It has carried shouts of love, and it has dried tears to salt tracks on more faces than it can number.

The wind skitters down the Bowery and swoops up the west side, home of Irish gangs like the Dummy Boys, who ride horseback along Ninth Avenue to warn the bootleggers. It swoops along the mighty Hudson River, past the vibrant nightlife of Harlem with its great thinkers, writers, and musicians, until it comes to rest outside the ruin of an old mansion. Moldering boards cover the broken windows. Rubbish clogs the gutter out front. Once upon a time, the house was home to an unspeakable evil. Now it is a relic of a bygone era, forgotten in the shadow of the city's growth and prosperity.

The door creaks on its hinges. The wind enters cautiously. It creeps down narrow hallways that twist and turn in dizzying fashion. Diseased rooms, rotted with neglect, branch off left and right. Doors open onto brick walls. A trapdoor gives way to a chute that empties into a vast subterranean chamber of horrors and an even more terrifying room. It stinks still: of blood, urine, evil, and a fear so dark it has become as much a part of the house as the wood and nails and rot.

Something stirs in the deep shadows, something terrible, and the wind, which knows evil well, shrinks from this place. It flees toward the safety of those magnificent tall buildings that promise the blue skies, *nothing but blue skies*, of the future, of industry and prosperity; the future, which does not believe in the evil of the past. If the wind were a sentinel, it would send up the alarm. It would cry out a warning of terrors to come. But it is only the wind, and it knows well that no one listens to its cries.

Deep in the cellar of the dilapidated house, a furnace comes to life with a death rattle like the last bitter cough of a dying man laughing contemptuously at his fate. A faint glow emanates from that dark, foul-smelling earthen tomb. Yes, something moves again in the shadows. A harbinger of much greater evil to come. Naughty John has come home. And he has work to do.

Evie O'Neill, Zenith, Ohio

Evie O'Neill pressed the sagging ice bag to her throbbing forehead and cursed the hour. It was noon, but it might as well be six in the morning for the pounding in her skull. For the past twenty minutes, her father had been beating his gums at her about last night's party at the Zenith Hotel. Her drinking had been mentioned several times, along with the unfortunate frolic in the town fountain. And the trouble that came between of course. It was gonna be a real beast of a day, and how. Her head beat out requirements: *Water. Aspirin. Please stop talking.*

"Your mother and I do not approve of drinking. Have you not heard of the Eighteenth Amendment?"

"Prohibition? I drink to its health whenever I can."

"Evangeline Mary O'Neill!" her mother snapped.

"Your mother is secretary of the Zenith Women's Temperance Society. Did you think about that? Did you think about how it might look if her daughter were found carousing drunk in the streets?"

Evie slid her bruised eyeballs in her mother's direction. Her mother sat stiff-backed and thin-lipped, her long hair coiled at the nape of her neck. A pair of spectacles—"cheaters," the flappers called them—sat at the end of her nose. The Fitzgerald women were all petite, blue-eyed, blond, and hopelessly nearsighted.

"Well?" her father thundered. "Do you have something to say?"

"Gee, I hope I won't need cheaters someday," Evie muttered.

Evie's mother responded with a weary sigh. She'd grown smaller and more worn since James's death, as if that long-ago telegram from the war office had stolen her soul the moment she had opened it.

"You young people seem to treat everything like a joke, don't you?" Her father was off and running—*responsibility, civic duty, acting your age, thinking beyond tomorrow.* She knew the refrain well. What Evie needed was a little hair of the dog, but her parents had confiscated her hip flask. It was a swell flask, too—silver, with the initials of Charles Warren etched into it. Good old Charlie, the dear. She'd promised to be his girl. That lasted a week. Charlie was a darling, but also a thudding bore. His idea of petting was to place a hand stiffly on a girl's chest like a starched doily on some maiden aunt's side table while pecking, birdlike, at her mouth. *Quel tragique.*

"Evie, are you listening to me?" Her father's face was grim.

She managed a smile. "Always, Daddy."

"Why did you say those terrible things about Harold Brodie?"

For the first time, Evie frowned. "He had it coming."

"You accused him of...of..." Her father's face colored as he stammered.

"Of knocking up that poor girl?"

"Evangeline!" Her mother gasped.

"Pardon me. 'Of taking advantage of her and leaving her in the family way.'"

"Why couldn't you be more like..." her mother trailed off, but Evie could finish the sentence: Why couldn't you be more like James?

"You mean, dead?" she shot back.

Her mother's face crumpled, and in that moment, Evie hated herself a little.

"That's enough, Evangeline," her father warned.

Evie bowed her throbbing head. "I'm sorry."

"I think you should know that unless you offer a public apology, the Brodies have threatened to sue for slander."

"What? I will not apologize!" She stood so quickly that her head doubled its pounding and she had to sit again. "I told the truth."

"You were playing a game—"

"It wasn't a game!"

"A game that has gotten you into trouble—"

"Harold Brodie is a louse and a lothario who cheats at cards and has a different girl in his rumble seat every week. That coupe of his is pos-i-tute-ly a petting palace. *And* he's a terrible kisser to boot."

Evie's parents stared in stunned silence.

"Or so I've heard."

"Can you prove your accusations?" her father pressed.

She couldn't. Not without telling them her secret, and she couldn't risk that. "I will not apologize."

Evie's mother cleared her throat. "There is another option."

Evie glanced from her mother to her father and back. "I won't breeze to military school, either."

"No military school would have you," her father muttered. "How would you like to go to New York for a bit, to stay with your Uncle Will?"

"I...ah...as in, Manhattan?"

"We assumed you'd say no to the apology," her mother said, getting in her last dig. "I spoke to my brother this morning. He would take you."

He would take you. A burden lifted. An act of charity. Uncle Will must have been defenseless against her mother's guilt-ladling.

"Just for a few months," her father continued. "Until this whole situation has sorted itself out."

New York City. Speakeasies and shopping. Broadway plays and movie palaces. At night, she'd dance at the Cotton Club. Days she'd spend with Mabel Rose, dear old Mabesie, who lived in her uncle Will's building. She and Evie had met when they were nine and Evie and her mother had gone to New York for a few days. Ever since, the girls had been pen pals. In the last year, Evie's correspondence had dwindled to a note here and there, though Mabel continued to send letters consistently, mostly about Uncle Will's handsome assistant, Jericho, who was alternately "painted by the brushstrokes of angels" and "a distant shore upon which I hope to land." Yes, Mabel needed her. And Evie needed New York. In New York, she could reinvent herself. She could be somebody.

She was tempted to blurt out a hasty yes, but she knew her mother well. If Evie didn't make it seem like a punishment to be endured, like she had "learned her lesson well," she'd be stuck in Zenith, apologizing to Harold Brodie after all.

She sighed and worked up just the right amount of tears—too much and they might relent. "I suppose that *would* be a sensible course. Though I don't know *what* I'll do in Manhattan with an old bachelor uncle as chaperone and all my dear friends back here in Zenith."

"You should have thought of that before," her mother said, her mouth set in a gloating smile of moral triumph.

Evie suppressed a grin. *Like shooting fish in a barrel*, she thought.

Her father checked his watch. "There's a train at five o'clock. I expect you'd better start packing."

Evie and her father rode to the station in silence. Normally, riding in her father's Lincoln Boattail Roadster was a point of pride. It was the only convertible in Zenith, the pick of the lot at her father's motorcar dealership. But today she didn't want to be seen. She wished she were as inconsequential as the ghosts in her dreams. Sometimes, after drinking, she felt this way—the shame over her latest stunt twining with the clamped-down anger at the way these petty, small-town people always made her feel: "Oh, Evie, you're just too much," they'd say with a polite smile. It was not a compliment.

She *was* too much—for Zenith, Ohio. She'd tried at times to make herself smaller, to fit neatly into the ordered lines of expectation. But somehow, she always managed to say or do something outrageous— she'd accept a dare to climb a flagpole, or make a slightly risqué joke, or go riding in cars with boys—and suddenly she was "that awful O'Neill girl" all over again.

Instinctively, her fingers wandered to the coin around her neck. It was a half-dollar her brother had sent from "over there" during the war, a gift for her ninth birthday, the day he'd died. She remembered the telegram from the war department, delivered by poor Mr. Smith from the telegram office, who mumbled an apology as he handed it over. She remembered her mother uttering the smallest strangled cry as she sank to the floor, still clutching the yellowed paper with the heartless black type. She remembered her father sitting in his study in the dark long after he should have been in bed, a forbidden bottle of Scotch open on his desk. Evie had read the telegram later: REGRET TO INFORM YOU...PRIVATE JAMES XAVIER O'NEILL . . . KILLED IN ACTION IN GERMANY . . . SUDDEN ATTACK AT DAWN . . . GAVE HIS LIFE IN SERVICE TO OUR COUNTRY . . . SECRETARY OF WAR ASKS THAT I CONVEY HIS DEEPEST SYMPATHIES ON THE LOSS OF YOUR SON....

They passed a horse and buggy on its way to one of the farms just outside town. It seemed quaint and out of place. Or maybe she was the thing that was out of place here.

"Evie," her father said in his soft voice. "What happened at the party, pet?"

The party. It had been swell at first. She and Louise and Dottie in their finery. Dottie had lent Evie her rhinestone headache band, and it looked so spiffy resting across Evie's soft curls. They'd enjoyed a spirited but meaningless debate about the trial of Mr. Scopes in Tennessee the year before and the whole idea that the lot of humanity was descended from apes. "I don't find it hard to believe in the slightest," Evie had said, cutting her eyes flirtatiously at the college boys who'd just sung a rousing twelfth round of "The Sweetheart of Sigma Chi." Everyone was drunk and happy. And Harold came around with his flattery.

"*Five-foot-two, eyes of blue, has anybody seen my Eeee-vieee?*" he sang and bowed at her feet.

Harry was handsome and terribly charming and, despite what she'd said earlier, a swell kisser. If Harry liked a girl, that girl got noticed. Evie liked being noticed, especially when she was drinking. Harry was engaged-to-be-engaged to Norma Wallingford. He wasn't in love with Norma—Evie knew that—but he was in love with her bank account, and everyone knew they'd marry when he graduated from college. Still, he wasn't married yet.

"Did I tell you that I have special powers?" Evie had asked after her third drink.

Harry smiled. "I can see that."

"I am quite serious," she slurred, too tipsy not to take his dare. "I can tell your secrets simply by holding an object dear to you and concentrating on it." There were polite chuckles among the party-goers. Evie fixed them with a defiant stare, her blue eyes glittering under heavily kohled lashes. "I am pos-i-*tute*-ly serious."

"You're pos-i-lute-ly lit, is what you are, Evie O'Neill," Dottie shouted.

"I'll prove it. Norma, give me something—scarf, hat pin, glove."

"I'm not giving you anything. I might not get it back." Norma laughed.

Evie narrowed her eyes. "Yes, how smart you are, Norma. I am starting a collection of only right-hand gloves. It's ever so bourgeois to have two."

"Well, you certainly wouldn't want to do anything *ordinary*, would you, Evie?" Norma said, showing her teeth. Everyone laughed, and Evie's cheeks went hot.

"No, I leave that to you, Norma." Evie brushed her hair away from her face, but it sprang back into her eyes. "Come to think of it, your secrets would probably put us to sleep."

"Fine," Harold had said before things could get really heated. "Here's my class ring. Tell me my deep, dark secrets, Madame O'Neill."

"Brave man, giving a girl like Evie your ring-ski," someone shouted.

"Quiet, *s'il vous plait*-ski!" Evie commanded with a dramatic flair to her voice. She concentrated, waiting for the object to warm in her hands. Sometimes it happened and sometimes it did not, and she hoped on the soul of Rudolph Valentino that this would be one of those times it took. Later, she'd have a headache from the effort—that was the downside to her little gift—but that's what gin was for. She'd numbed herself a bit already, anyway. Evie opened one eye a slit. They were all watching her. They were watching, and nothing was happening.

Chuckling, Harry reached for his ring. "All right, old girl. You've had your fun. Time for a little sobering up."

She wrenched her hands away. "I *will* uncover your secrets— just you wait and see!" There were few things worse than being ordinary, in Evie's opinion. Ordinary was for suckers. Evie wanted to be special. A bright star. She didn't care if she got the most awful headache in the history of skull-bangers. Shutting her eyes tightly, she pressed the ring against her palms. It grew much warmer, unlocking its secrets for her. Her smile spread. She opened her eyes.

"Harry, you naughty boy . . ."

Everyone pressed closer, interested.

Harold laughed uncomfortably. "What do you mean?"

"Room twenty-two at the hotel. That pretty chambermaid . . .

L...El...Ella! Ella! You gave her a big wad of kale and told her to take care of it."

Norma moved closer. "What's this about, Harry?"

Harry's mouth was tight. "I'm sure I don't know what you're talking about, Evangeline. Show's over. I'll have my ring back now."

If Evie had been sober, she might have stopped. But the gin made her foolishly brave. She tsk-tsked him with her fingers. "You knocked her up, you bad boy."

"Harold, is that true?"

Harold Brodie's face was red. "That's enough, Evie! This isn't funny any longer."

"Harold?" Norma Wallingford.

"She's lying, sweetheart." Harold, reassuring.

Evie stood and did a little Charleston on the table. "That's not what your ring says, pal."

Harold grabbed for Evie and she squeaked out of reach, grabbing a tumbler from someone's hand. "Holy moly! It's a raid! A Harold Brodie raid! Run for your lives!"

Dottie had grabbed the ring and given it back to Harry. Then she and Louise had practically dragged Evie outside. "Sister, you are blotto. Let's go."

"I remain unflapper-able in the face of advuss...adverse... trouble. Oh, we're moving. Wheee! Where are we going?"

"To sober you up," Dottie said, tossing Evie into the freezing fountain.

Later, after several cups of coffee, Evie lay shivering in her wet party dress under a blanket in a darkened corner of the ladies' lounge. Dottie and Louise had gone to find her some aspirin, and, alone and hidden, she eavesdropped as two girls stood before the gilt-framed mirrors gossiping about the row Harold and Norma had gotten into.

"It's all that awful Evie O'Neill's fault. You know how she is."

"She never knows when to let well enough alone."

"Well, she's really done it this time. She's finished in this town. Norma will see to that."

Evie waited till she heard them leave, then moved to the mirror. Her mascara had left big black splotches under her eyes, and her damp curls drooped. Her wretched headache was really kicking up its heels in earnest. She looked as messy as she felt. She wished she could cry, but crying wouldn't help anything.

Harold burst in, closing the door behind him and holding it shut. "How did you find out?" he growled, grabbing her arm.

"I t-told you. I g-got it from your—"

His hand tightened around her arm. "Stop fooling around and tell me how you know! Norma's threatening to leave me thanks to your little party trick. I demand a public apology to clear my name."

She felt woozy and sick, the aftereffects of her object reading. It was like a mean drunk followed by the worst hangover you could imagine. Harold Brodie wasn't a charming, good-time playboy, she now realized. He was a cad and a coward. The last thing she was going to do was apologize to somebody like that.

"G-go chase yourself, Harry."

Dottie and Louise pounded on the door from the other side. "Evie? Evie! Open up!"

Harold let go of her arm. Evie could feel a bruise starting. "This isn't over, Evangeline. Your father owes his business to my father. You might want to reconsider that apology."

Evie threw up all over Harold Brodie.

"Evie?" her father prompted now, bringing her back to the moment.

She rubbed her aching head. "It was nothing, Pop. I'm sorry you caught hell for it."

He didn't take her to task for saying *hell.*

At the station, her father left the engine idling long enough to see her to the platform. He tipped the porter to take her trunks, and made sure they would be delivered to her uncle's apartment in New York. Evie carried only her small plaid valise and a beaded handbag.

"Well," her father said, glancing down at the idling convertible. He passed her a ten-spot, which Evie tucked into the ribbon of her gray felt cloche. "Just a little pin money."

"Thanks, Pop."

"I'm no good with good-byes. You know that."

Evie forced a devil-may-care smile. "Sure. It's jake, Pop. I'm seventeen, not seven. I'll be just fine." "Well."

They stood awkwardly on the wooden platform.

"Better not let the breezer leave without you," she said, nodding toward the convertible.

Her father kissed her lightly on the forehead and, with a final admonishment to the porter, drove away. As the Lincoln shrank to a point down the road, Evie felt a pang of sadness, and something else. Dread. That was the word. Some unknowable, unnameable fear. She'd been feeling it for months, ever since the dreams began.

"*Man, I got those heebies/Got those heebies, the heebie jeebie blues. . . .*" Evie sang softly and shivered.

A pair of Blue Noses on the next bench glared their disapproval at Evie's knee-length dress. Evie decided to give them a real show. She hiked her skirt and, humming jauntily, rolled down her stockings, exposing her legs. It had the desired effect on the Blue Noses, who moved down the platform, clucking about the "disgrace of the young." She would not miss this place.

A cream coupe swerved dangerously up the road and came to a stop below, just narrowly missing the platform. Two smartly dressed girls stepped out. Evie grinned and waved wildly. "Dottie! Louise!"

"We heard you were leaving and wanted to come see you off," Louise said, climbing over the railing.

"Good news travels fast."

"In this town? Like lightning."

"It's swell. I'm too big for Zenith, Ohio, anyway. In New York, they'll understand me. I'm going to be written up in all the papers and get invited to the Fitzgeralds' flat for cocktails. After all, my mother's a Fitzgerald. We must be related *somewhere.*"

"Speaking of cocktails..." Grinning, Dottie retrieved what looked like an innocent aspirin bottle from her pocketbook. It was half-filled with clear liquid. "Here. Just a little giggle water to see you through. Sorry it couldn't be more, but my father marks the bottles now."

"Oh, and a copy of *Photoplay* from the beauty parlor. Aunt Mildred won't miss it," Louise added.

Evie's eyes pricked with tears. "You don't mind being seen with the town pariah?"

Louise and Dottie managed weak smiles—confirmation that Evie was the town pariah, but still, they'd come.

"You are absolute angels of the first order. If I were Pope, I'd canonize you."

"The Pope would probably love to turn a cannon on you!"

"New York City!" Louise twirled her long rope of beads. "Norma Wallingford will eat herself to bits with envy. She's sore as hell about your little stunt." Dottie giggled. "Spill: How'd you really find out about Harold and the chambermaid?"

Evie's smile faltered for a moment. "Just a lucky guess."

"But—"

"Oh, look! Here comes the train," Evie said, cutting off any further inquiry. She hugged them tightly, grateful for this last kindness. "Next time you see me, I'll be famous! And I'll drive you all over Zenith in my chauffeured sedan."

"Next time we see you, you'll be on trial for some ingenious crime!" Dottie said with a laugh.

Evie grinned. "Just as long as they know my name."

A blue-uniformed porter hurried people aboard. Evie settled into her compartment. It was stuffy, and she stood on the seat in her green silk-satin Mary Janes to open the window.

"Help you with that, Miss?" another porter, a younger man, offered.

Evie looked up at him through lashes she had tinted with cake mascara that morning and offered him the full power of her Coty-red smile. "Oh, would you, honey? That'd be swell."

"You heading to New York, Miss?"

"Mm-hmm, that's right. I won a Miss Bathing Beauty contest, and now I'm going to New York to be photographed for *Vanity Fair*."

"Isn't that something?"

"Isn't it, just?" Evie fluttered her eyelashes. "The window?"

The young man released the latches and slid the window down easily. "There you are!"

"Why, thank you," Evie purred. She was on her way. In New York, she could be anyone she chose to be. It was a big city—just the place for big dreamers who needed to shine brightly.

Evie angled her head out the train window and waved to Louise and Dottie. Her bobbed curls blew about her face as the sleepy town slowly moved behind her. For a second, she wished she could run back to the safety of her parents' house. But that was like the fog of her dreams. It was a dead house—had been for years. No. She wouldn't be sad. She would be grand and glittering. A real star. A bright light of New York. "See you soon-ski!" she yelled.

"You bet-ski!"

Her friends were shrinking to small dots of color in the smoke-hazed distance. Evie blew kisses and tried not to cry. She waved slowly to the passing rooftops of Zenith, Ohio, where people liked to feel safe and snug and smug, where they handled objects every day in the most ordinary of ways and never once caught glimpses into other people's secrets that should not be known or had terrible nightmares of dead brothers. She envied them just a bit.

"You gonna stay up there the whole ride, Miss?" the porter asked.

"Just wanna say a proper good-bye," Evie answered. She turned her hand in a last benediction, waving to the houses like a queen. "So long, suckers! You're all wet!"

Twitter: Want to discuss or share what you just read? Use the hashtag #beaDIVINE to connect with others.

ABOUT THE AUTHOR

Libba Bray is the author of *The New York Times* bestseller *Beauty Queens*, the 2010 Printz Award-winning *Going Bovine*, and the acclaimed *Gemma Doyle* trilogy. She lives in Brooklyn, New York.

Imprint: Little, Brown Books for Young Readers

BEA Booth #: 3632
Author appearances:
Wednesday, June 6th
12:15 pm: ABA Speed Dating Lunch With Children's Authors (Room 1E14/15)
3:00 pm: *The Diviners* galley signing at the Little, Brown Books for Young Readers booth (#3632)
Printed galley at BEA: yes
Contact for printed galley: Lisa Moraleda lisa.moraleda@hbgusa.com
Print ISBN: 9780316126113
Print price: $19.99
eBook ISBN: 9780316214643
eBook price: $9.99
Publication date: 9/18/2012
Publicity contact: Lisa Moraleda lisa.moraleda@hbgusa.com
Rights contact: Barry Goldblatt Literary
Editor: Alvina Ling
Agent: Barry Goldblatt
Agency: Barry Goldblatt Literary
Territories sold:
    North America - Little, Brown Books for Young Readers
    United Kingdom - Atom Books
    Australia – Allen & Unwin
    Italian – Fazi Editore
    Portuguese (Brazil) - Editora Moderna
    Hebrew – Modan Books
    German – Deutscher Taschenbuch Verlag
    Portuguese (Portugal) – Grupo Leya

THE
OTHER
NORMALS

NED VIZZINI

SUMMARY

Given the chance, fifteen-year-old Peregrine "Perry" Eckert would dedicate every waking moment to Creatures & Caverns, an epic role-playing game rich with magical creatures, spell casting, and deadly weapons. The world of C&C is where he feels most comfortable in his own skin. But that isn't happening—not if his parents have anything to do with it. Concerned their son lacks social skills, they ship him off to summer camp to become a man. They want him to be outdoors playing with kids his own age and meeting girls—rather than indoors alone, with only his gaming alter ego for company. Perry knows he's in for the worst summer of his life.

Everything changes, however, when Perry gets to camp and stumbles into the World of the *Other Normals*. There he meets Mortin Enaw, one of the creators of C&C, and other mythical creatures from the game, including the alluring Ada Ember, whom Perry finds more beautiful than any human girl he's ever met. Perry's new otherworldly friends need his help to save their princess and prevent mass violence. As they embark on their quest together, Perry realizes that his nerdy childhood has uniquely prepared him to be a great warrior in this world, and maybe even a hero. But to save the princess, Perry will have to learn how to make real connections in the human world as well. Bestselling author Ned Vizzini delivers a compulsively readable and wildly original story about the winding and often hilarious path to manhood.

EXCERPT

1

This is a story about becoming a man, so naturally it starts with me alone in a room playing with myself. Not *that* way—playing Creatures & Caverns, the popular role-playing game. *Popular* being a relative term. I guess if Creatures & Caverns were really popular, I would have other people to play with.

"Perry!" my brother, Jake, calls, knocking on the door. "Are you ready to go to your stupid store?"

"Hold on a second!" When my brother sees my gaming materials, his automatic response is to make fun of me, so I hide them in my backpack and put it on. My graph paper, manual, and mechanical pencils disappear quickly as he turns the knob and enters, smiling under his long hair, with his guitar slung over his shoulder.

"C'mon, I'm gonna be late for practice."

We head down the hall. Jake walks like he's carrying a tank in his pants and I try to imitate him, but my legs aren't long enough. Mom is in the living room having a conversation with her boyfriend, Horace. You can tell she's talking to Horace because her feet are up on the couch and she's twirling her fingers in the air as if there were a phone cord when there isn't. She's in lazy Sunday-afternoon mode, like I was until a few minutes ago.

"Perry? Oh, Perry's doing fine, you know. He's a late bloomer."

I squint at my mother. She doesn't even notice me. I wonder how that bizarre notion could enter her head. *Late bloomer?* I'm an RPG enthusiast. I'm an *intellectual.*

"Hey! You coming?" Jake calls. He's already at the front door. I follow him out—intentionally not saying "Bye, Mom!" because maybe that's what *late bloomers* say.

Jake and I walk to the subway through New York streets piled high with recycling bags awaiting Monday-morning pickup. It's a gorgeous spring day and the daffodils are out in small plots for trees, where dogs will be attracted to soil them. The late-ish bloomer-ish phrase bounces around in my head. As a fifteen-year-old you don't want to be compared to a flower. By your mother. And then have the flower be faulty. The daffodils make it worse: they bloom on the same damn day every year.

2. My Brother and I Sit on the Subway.

Jake takes out a water bottle and sips it and turns his headphones so loud that I hear them next to me. I always hated people who did that, and now he does it—but I don't hate him, I worry about his ears. He's listening to his own band, The Just Because, which has a small reputation in New York for disrupting "battle of the bands" competitions but is otherwise rightfully unknown.

We are the stoners (aah-ah!)
We built America (aah-ah!)
We built America (ah-ahhh)
Yes we did

"That's a stupid song," I tell Jake, even though it's catchy. I wrinkle my nose. Somebody on this train smells like booze. I check the car—there's a homeless guy lounging in the corner in rumpled, stained clothes, taking up two seats.

"What?" My brother turns the music down.

"Nobody wants to hear songs about you smoking pot and building America."

"I didn't write it. The singer wrote it. I don't smoke. Girls don't like it." He sips from his water bottle.

"Jake, what are you drinking?"

"Raspberry-infused vodka."

"What the—?" I pull out my phone. "It's *twelve*!"

"Exactly. Sunday-afternoon cocktail."

"Give me that!" I grab for the bottle. Jake uses his long arms to keep it out of reach. He stuffs it back into his guitar bag. "You can't start drinking in the middle of the day!"

He grabs my arm and squeezes, *hard*, like a mechanical claw. "Shut up, bro. Don't embarrass me. There are girls on this train."

He nods across from us at a beautiful woman with short blond hair and earbuds. I don't know how I missed her. I'm supposed to have laser focus for people like this. Maybe if I were blooming properly I would. She looks up from the book she's reading. *Jane Eyre*.

"Don't look at her," my brother tells me.

"I'm not."

"Then why are you looking at her?"

I look down.

"I'm a musician," he whispers. Vodka and raspberries hit my face. "It's my right and duty to stay buzzed whenever I can."

"No it's not. You're going to get in serious—"

"You have bigger things to worry about anyway: I heard you're going to summer camp."

"What?"

"Heard Horace tell Kimberley."

"No! Why?" So far, in life, I've managed to avoid summer camp by excelling at math enough to qualify for a program called Summer Scholars in the city.

"Dad wanted to send you to math camp, but Mom's making you go to real camp with public-school kids."

"I *am* a public-school kid!"

"You're a specialized-school kid."

"Why now? I'm too old to go to camp. Wouldn't I be a counselor?"

"Inflation. Horace told Kimberley that Mom can't afford to have you home all summer. You consume hundreds of dollars a week in food, although I don't know where you put it. With camp, for a few grand she doesn't have to feed you or do your laundry or anything. Maybe she'll send you for three or four weeks, but if she really wants to save cash, she'll send you for eight. She already gave you that bowl haircut; that'll last until September."

I touch my hair. Our parents, after entering their divorce proceedings eight years ago, each began dating their divorce lawyers. Dad's is named Kimberley; Mom dated a number of different lawyers until she found Horace. Due to their special relationships with my parents, Kimberley and Horace handle their cases pro bono.

"Kimberley says that Mom read an article about how boys who go to summer camp become more 'emotionally mature' men."

I stay quiet.

"And you're already having issues in that department if you're riding with me to buy Creatures and Caverns books."

"Like you're going anywhere important."

"Legendary Just Because band practices *are* important. And I don't understand why every time I give you a chance to go to one, you just want to play by yourself in your room. I don't make up the rules, Perry. Creatures and Caverns is a waste of time! There are certain things that are so uncool they're cool, but role-playing games isn't one of them."

The train screeches to a halt. Jake drinks more vodka. The *Jane Eyre* girl gets out.

"What's the name of the camp?"

"Some normal name. It's very traditional, I think, with canoeing and log splitting and bears and counselors who molest children. In New Jersey. It'll be good for you! What else you gonna do? You didn't make Summer Scholars this year, right, because you're a bitch?"

I ignore him, but it's true. It's a permanent blot on my math career. A month ago, on a qualifying exam, I did what I call a mutant paradigm shift: I filled in the answer for problem 15 in the bubble for problem 14 and then shifted every subsequent answer up by one question. Even though it was possible to see that I completely understood the questions, my score had to be counted with the incorrect answers. Mr. Getter, the Summer Scholars coach, told me he couldn't have such a sloppy performer on his squad. I tried to explain the situation to Mom and Dad directly *and* through their lawyers, but they wouldn't hear it.

I was about to try and get into college, they said, and hadn't they told me that no matter how divorced they were, I had to get into a good college? Mistakes of inattention— *human fallibility*—were no longer to be coddled or explained away; that period of my life was over. I got the feeling that my parents wanted me to get a job this summer, but I didn't know where—a bookstore? The zoo?

"What were you going to do all summer? Play Creatures and Caverns by yourself?"

I don't say anything.

"Jeez, Perry."

"I like looking at the books! Is that so bad? It's perfectly normal to enjoy reading role-playing-game manuals and making up characters by yourself."

"It's normal for some people, not for normal people."

Twitter: Want to discuss or share what you just read? Use the hashtag #beaNORMAL to connect with others.

ABOUT THE AUTHOR

Ned Vizzini is the author of *It's Kind Of A Funny Story* (also a major motion picture), *Be More Chill*, and *Teen Angst? Naaah*.... Ned has spoken at over 200 universities, schools, and libraries around the world about writing and mental health. He has written for *The New York Times*, *The Daily Beast*, and season 2 of MTV's *Teen Wolf*. His work has been translated into seven languages. You can visit Ned online at www.nedvizzini.com.

Imprint: Balzer + Bray
BEA Booth #: 3339
Print ISBN: 9780062079909
Print price: $17.99
eBook ISBN: 9780062079923
eBook price: $9.99
Publication date: 9/25/2012
Publicity contact: Casey McIntyre casey.mcintyre@harpercollins.com
Editor: Alessandra Balzer
Agent: Jay Mandel
Agency: William Morris Endeavor

THE
HEART
BROKE IN

A Novel

JAMES
MEEK

SUMMARY

From the prizewinning author of the international bestseller *The People's Act of Love* comes a rich and intricate novel about everything that matters to us now: children, celebrity, secrets and shame, the quest for youth, loyalty and betrayal, falls from grace, acts of terror, and the wonderful, terrible inescapability of family.

Ritchie Shepherd, an aging pop star and a producer of a reality show for teen talent, is starting to trip over his own lies. Maybe filming a documentary about his father, Captain Shepherd, a British soldier executed by Northern Irish guerrillas, will redeem him.

His sister, Bec, is getting closer and closer to a vaccine for malaria. When she's not in Tanzania harvesting field samples, she's peering through a microscope at her own blood to chart the risky treatment she's testing on herself. She's as addicted to honesty as Ritchie is to trickery.

Val Oatman is the editor of a powerful tabloid newspaper. The self-appointed conscience of the nation, scourge of hypocrites and cheats, he believes he will marry beautiful Bec.

Alex Comrie, a gene therapist (and formerly the drummer in Ritchie's band), is battling his mortally ill uncle, a brilliant and domineering scientist, over whether Alex might actually have discovered a cure for aging. Alex, too, believes he will marry Bec.

Colum Donobhan has just been released from prison, having served a twenty-five-year sentence for putting a gun to Captain Shepherd's head when he refused to give up an informer. He now writes poetry.

Their stories meet and tangle in this bighearted epic that is also shrewd, starkly funny, and utterly of the moment. *The Heart Broke In* is fiction with the reverberating resonance of truth.

EXCERPT

To marry, to start a family, to accept all the children that come, and to help them in this insecure world, is the best that a man can do.

—Franz Kafka (who never got around to it)

1.

The story doing the rounds at Ritchie Shepherd's production company was accurate when it appeared inside the staff's heads, when they hardly sensed it, let alone spoke it. It was like a faint stink, clear enough to notice, too trivial to mention. All through *Teen Makeover*'s autumn and spring seasons, when they clustered around Ritchie, asking him questions they already knew the answers to, cadging compliments and begging him to give their enemies a telling-off, they watched him. They saw he wasn't as funny as before. Was he keeping his jokes for someone else? He moved in a weird way now, they thought. He walked with an awkward bounce, too eager, as if he reckoned something had given him extra energy, or made him younger.

As long as the rumor was unspoken, the hearts of the staff ached. The rumor was this: that after a long peace Ritchie was, once again, cheating on his wife, Karin, this time with an underage girl. They felt sorry for Ritchie's family, but what if the damage went further, to the men and women on the company payroll? They sensed a personal threat. Scandal spread from the first carrier. Everybody liked Ritchie, but they were confident that he was selfish enough to infect them all. The production company offices were intoxicated by nervousness and suspicion. When twin fourteen-year-old girls showed up one day without an accompanying parent and asked for Ritchie, his PA, Paula, got up too suddenly from behind her desk, caught the trailing edge of a printed e-mail with her thigh, and upended a cup of coffee across her skirt. The chief lighting technician wrote off a fresnel worth two thousand pounds. He dropped it from the bridge when he saw Ritchie smile and touch the elbow of a lanky year-ten in a short dress. "She had womanly curves earlier than most" is what the gaffer would have said in his defense, if he hadn't been afraid to hex them all, and he only yelled "Butterfingers!" while the people down below were jumping clear of chips of lens skittering across the floor. When the script editor saw Ritchie talking to a group of pert-bottomed schoolgirls in leotards she strode over and interrupted him in mid-sentence. She realized, as soon as she did it, that she was making a fool of herself. The girls' teachers were there. The ache of fear in her heart had made her do it.

The ache could be soothed only by being put into words. The production team needed an utterance to lift the dread from their chests, and when the rumor eventually found its spoken form, it relieved them so completely that they believed it. Much better that Ritchie's ten-year marriage to Karin should break up and that he should lose custody of his son and daughter over the pretty but older-than-twenty-one new presenter Lina Riggs than that the boss should be doing something illegal and shameful, something that would stain them all with the indelible dye of an unspeakable word. Without anyone noticing the shift, "I wonder if" and "I bet" and "You don't suppose" changed to "I heard" and "I've got a juicy one" and "I know who Ritchie's shagging." Believing soothed them all.

Ritchie found that whenever he went near Riggsy a stupid smile appeared on his employees' faces. He didn't know how happy he was making them by encouraging them to believe he was betraying his family with a legal adult. They didn't know that their rumor had become wrong as soon as it was said out loud, and that the original rumor, the ache of fear in their hearts, was true. They didn't know that Ritchie was seeing a not-quite-sixteen-year-old girl he'd met when she appeared on *Teen Makeover* the previous season. He saw Nicole once a week. It was his intention to enjoy it for as long as he felt like it, then end it tenderly. Nicole would, he imagined, be moved that he should voluntarily give her up. It would be soon, and nobody would have found out. How could they? The two of them were careful, and London was a wild forest of red brick and roof tiles, where maps only reminded you how little you knew.

2.

Ritchie woke in a soft chair in a wide, bright space. An old vinyl record spun and crackled and he heard the sound of Ruby, Dan, and Karin in the orchard, three stories below. Far away something clunked against the sides of a wooden box.

A bib of hot sunlight from the south-facing window lay on his frayed yellow T-shirt, spreading delicious warmth across his chest. The nap left him refreshed and content. His wife and children were close enough for him to hear that they were happy, far enough away to not disturb him.

Facing him, here on the mansard floor, was a ladder on a dolly and a wall lined to the rafters with shelves of records. Ritchie's study had space to ride a bicycle in, but he didn't have a bicycle up here; he had an adult tricycle. The tires would hum on the waxed oak floorboards as he built up speed, dodging the stairwell that pierced the center of the room, past the cabinets with his collection of British war comics, past the desk and the chill cabinet where he kept his beer and puddings, past the washstand that had been a Victorian church font and the toilet cubicle in an old red phone box with blacked-out windows, to the guitar case. Inside the guitar case was one of two steel-stringed acoustic guitars Karin had commissioned for his fortieth birthday out of spruce and walnut, inlaid with their names in mother-of-pearl (the other was hers); and inside the guitar a secret thing was hidden, the mobile phone he used to call Nicole.

He got up and looked down through the window. Karin and the children were gathering fruit in the orchard. Their shining hair and foreshortened limbs bobbed in and out of the shade. He could hear that they were talking but the glass muffled the words into fuzzy, friendly insignificances. He walked to his desk, opened the chill cabinet, and took an individual chocolate pudding serving from the stacks inside. He favored a brand called ChocPot, which came with its own wooden spoon attached, so he didn't have to hunt for one. He flipped off the lid, put down the pot, and picked up his BlackBerry. He shoveled chocolate goo into his mouth with his right hand and scrolled through his e-mails with his left thumb. A dollop of pudding fell and landed on the shelf of his belly. He put the BlackBerry down, scraped most of the spill off with his index finger, raised the quivering dod to his lips, slurped the finger clean, and walked to the font. Without taking the T-shirt off he held it under the running tap with both hands and rubbed till the brown stain almost disappeared. He wrung the wet patch out.

A desire to call Nicole, to catch her alone at home, danced in the pit of his stomach. He strode to the guitar case, flipped the catches, and opened it. The guitar wasn't there.

Ritchie's palm and fingers pressed against the blue plush lining of the case. His mouth hung open.

He turned and ran to the stairs, clenching his toes to stop his old flip-flops flying off. He had six flights of stairs to go down without breaking his neck before the orchard was in reach: three stories, five changes of direction. His hands clawed for purchase on the football-sized oak globes, varnished and polished to a high gloss, capping the banister on each landing. He lost his grip, slid off the step, hurtled into the wall, landed on his backside, got up, and ran on, panting. I become out of breath when I make love to Nicole, he thought; might it bother her? Amid the clatter of his feet and the pounding of his heart he replayed the sound he'd heard when he woke up, the object knocking against the sides of a wooden box. If curious hands groped inside the guitar, why was a mobile phone there? He'd failed to prepare an important lie.

He reached the foot of the stairs, loped along the hall towards the kitchen, and thanked God that the garden door was open. He got to within two strides of the threshold and felt something slither over his thighs. His shorts fell down around his shins. He fell and hit his knee against the kitchen flagstones. The cold slate pressed rudely against his bare hams. He got up, hoisted the shorts around his waist, tightened and knotted the drawstring, and limped on into the garden.

A gentle English heat rolled over him and he squinted in the brightness. A wood pigeon cooed from the yew tree. Karin, her back to Ritchie, stretched towards a high branch, making the tree snap and rustle as she pulled yellow plums off it. The hem of her muslin skirt climbed up her brown calves and one of the straps of her top fell off her shoulder. There was a scent of grass where the sun heated the juice from the stems his family had crushed with their bare feet. Ritchie was sorry he was meeting his teenage girlfriend later. He wished he could stay at home with his wife and children. Dan ran from trunk to trunk holding Ritchie's guitar like a weapon, dropping to a crouch, aiming the guitar neck, lining up the sights. Ruby was heaping fruit. She saw her father and stood up.

"Look at Daddy!" she said. She twisted her little torso round to Karin and back and laughed.

Dan stood up, afraid. "Give me the guitar," said Ritchie. Dan dropped it on the grass and ran over to stand by his mother. Ritchie picked the guitar up by the neck, letting it swing as he raised it. There was nothing inside. He glanced down at the long grass. The phone could have fallen out, or one of his family could have removed it. The phone contained dozens of messages from Nicole so obscene that he hadn't been able to bring himself to delete them.

"I don't remember you asking if you could come into Daddy's study," said Ritchie.

"You were asleep," said Dan. He grabbed a fold of Karin's skirt and looked up at her.

"Mummy, Daddy's bleeding!" said Ruby. "And he's breathing funny."

Karin looked down at Dan and caressed his head. "I don't see why you shouldn't borrow Daddy's guitar," she said to her son. "He never plays it."

"Don't do that," said Ritchie. Karin looked at him, and Dan looked, too. They shared a cool, expectant expression, like two doctors he'd interrupted while they discussed his case. "Don't talk about me with Dan as if I'm not here. You're wrong, by the way. I play it all the time." He raised the guitar and saw Ritchie in bright mirror writing race across Karin and Dan, reflected off the mother-of-pearl inlay, and each lift up their hands to cover their eyes as his name passed over their faces.

"Look at it," said Karin. "The two top strings are broken and the others are miles out of tune."

"Mum, Daddy's bleeding!" shouted Ruby again, running over and tugging the other side of her skirt. Ruby was the one who cared for him without hesitation, not out of duty, just because she did, Ritchie was sure. She was six, and he knew she would always feel this way towards him, whatever her age. He'd made a dangerous mistake in being angry with Dan, he saw, since he didn't know where the phone was, yet Dan or Karin—or both!—might know, and were choosing their moment to confront him. He needed to regain control. He didn't think of it as control, because his way of controlling seemed so benign: kindness, generosity. It hadn't occurred to him that striving for a monopoly on generosity was the chief characteristic of a despot.

"What happened to your leg?" said Karin.

"I slipped on the tiles. Dan, come on, show me what you can play." He held the guitar out towards his son.

"I don't want to play anything," said Dan, and quick as a trout shot away through the orchard, disappearing beyond the yew tree on the far side.

"Mum, can I put some leaves on Daddy's leg to stop it bleeding?" said Ruby.

"If Daddy lets you, darling." She studied Ritchie. Her eyes ran over the blood, the frayed clothes, the stained paunch, and the bristly chin.

He was afraid Karin didn't love him, which would be a catastrophe, because he loved her, and he loved his children, and if she didn't love him, it would destroy the pleasure he took in cheating on her, and feeling virtuous when he returned to her, full of love.

"Help us pick the plums now you're here," said Karin. She turned her back to him and went on gathering fruit.

Ritchie put the guitar down, folded his arms, and walked in careful circles, stroking the grass with his toes, humming a song. He bent his head and watched for a hint of silver, glancing up every few seconds to make sure Karin wasn't looking.

Ruby came to him with a bunch of greenery. "Mum, Dad's been eating chocolate pudding," she said. "Why can't we have some?"

"It's bad for you, darling," said Karin, without turning round. "It's only for a treat."

"Why does Daddy get to have treats and we can't?"

"Daddy knows how to treat himself."

Ritchie saw an opportunity. "Let's all have chocolate pudding," he said. "Once we've harvested the plums." He thought Karin would like the word "harvested." It sounded as if the family were doing something real together, bound to the countryside and the seasons.

Ruby kneeled in the grass next to her father and began to stick leaves onto the congealing blood on his leg. She frowned with concentration. It reminded Ritchie of the expression on Nicole's face when she performed a certain act. He winced. "Ruby, sweetheart, that's much better," he said. "Go and find Daddy a nice plum to eat."

"I've got one," said Ruby. She reached into the front pocket of her denim dress and handed him a hard little green plum. He took it and rolled it around on his palm.

"Thanks, darling, but it's not ripe yet," he said.

"Eat it!" said Ruby. She laughed. "Go on! You have to eat it!"

"I thought you liked the unripe ones," said Karin. She walked towards him. The muscles on her right forearm stood out under her brown, grained skin from the weight of the bucket full of fruit she was carrying.

Ritchie stood up. He bit into the taut skin of the plum, gnawed off a sliver of astringent flesh, and chewed it.

"Perfect," he said. He forced himself not to stretch his mouth wide and spit the fruit out.

3.

Ritchie found his son lying by the yew. He was on his front, propped up on his elbows, his bare lower legs kicking into the cool blades of unmown grass in the shadow of the tree's thick branches and his head and body in the sunlight. He had a device in his hands. Ritchie began to run.

When he got closer he saw Dan wasn't reading Nicole's filthy provocations. He was playing a game on his Nintendo. Ritchie sat cross-legged on the ground a few feet away. Dan wasn't going to look up until Ritchie spoke. His red lips were held in a plump wet pout. He'd been lying there, waiting to be looked for. Ritchie wondered if he'd had such chubby arms at Dan's age. Did the boy need a trainer?

"You don't like people going into your room without asking," Ritchie said.

"It's not the same. I've got secret projects," said Dan.

"Well, maybe I've got secret projects too." As soon as Ritchie said this he knew it was the wrong thing to say.

"What secret projects?" said Dan, looking at Ritchie with such a Karin-like expression of curiosity that Ritchie glanced around to see if his wife had crept up on them.

Ritchie leaned closer to Dan and lowered his voice so that Dan looked up anxiously when Ritchie started to speak.

"You don't want anyone bursting into your room and seeing you without your clothes on," he said.

Dan's shoulders jumped up in a spasm of embarrassed laughter and he hid his face behind his Nintendo. "I don't mind!" he said. His blue eyes looked over the top of the gadget and his grinning cheeks bulged out on either side.

"Well, I do!" said Ritchie, giving Dan a soft punch on the shoulder. "I don't want you coming in and seeing me without my clothes on!" Dan rolled over on his back, laughing, making sounds of disgust and sticking out his tongue. He's a good boy, Ritchie thought. He's going to be fine. He had wondered whether Dan was being bullied at school, but there was a man in him, even if it was going to cost a packet to bring it out. Ritchie asked Dan if there was anything he wanted. Dan stopped laughing and lay quietly on the grass, with his face turned away from Ritchie, listening and blinking.

"Would you like a guitar of your own?" asked Ritchie.

"I've already got one," said Dan.

Ritchie remembered the child-sized electric guitar Dan never played and the drum kit he didn't touch.

"Why did you want Daddy's guitar, Danny love?" said Ritchie. "What's wrong with yours?"

Dan turned his face further away and sniffed and Ritchie saw tears on his cheeks. Ritchie didn't understand. He laid his hand on Dan's shoulder and asked him what the matter was.

"Nothing," said Dan. "You don't care. You don't care about me and Ruby."

"How can you say that?" said Ritchie. "Don't you know how important it is to me to be a good father to you? Have you any idea what it was like for me growing up without . . ."

"I know," said Dan.

"You just made an augmented fourth there. I knooooow. La laaaaa."

Dan was sitting up, watching him and listening without crying or smiling, a half-familiar expression of slyness on his face. Perhaps that's who he really is, perhaps he is the school bully, the boss of the playground, the one the other children fear, Ritchie thought with sudden hope.

"If you made so much money without a father," said Dan, "why is it better for me to have one?"

"What a terrible thing to say!" said Ritchie slowly, trying to decide how he felt about it. Different paths forked out from what his son had just told him, and he could follow any fork, and still be Ritchie. On one path, he yelled at his son that he was a heartless, ungrateful little brat. On another, he said nothing, stared coldly at Dan, turned around, walked back to the house—ignoring any appeals for forgiveness—and shunned his family for the rest of the day. The third fork would see him shaking his head, laughing softly, running his hand through Dan's thick fair hair and telling him he was a clever chap.

This was the way he chose. He reached out his hand for the top of his son's head, but at that moment Karin called Dan's name from the far side of the orchard. Dan got up so quickly that Ritchie's hand brushed his ear instead. Dan glanced at his father, confused by the awkward touch, and a little frightened, as if he thought he'd accidentally avoided a blow, not a caress.

"Shall we go on the swing?" said Ritchie.

"Mum's calling me," said Dan. "I'm too old for the swing."

Ruby came galloping towards them, laughing, and Ritchie caught her under her arms and lifted her up, holding her high so that her head blocked out the sun. He weighed her precious squirming density. Chaotic strands of hair fell over her face and Ritchie savored the wholeness of her attention. "Shall we go on the swing?" he said, and she nodded, and without looking at Dan Ritchie put Ruby down, took her hand, and walked with her to where the rope swing hung from the branch of an old chestnut tree.

He pushed Ruby on the swing and decided he would have a shot. Ruby told him he couldn't, he was too fat, and while he told her not to be rude, he wondered whether it would take his weight. He sat down carefully on the length of wood and heard the branch creak. Dan and Karin were coming towards them. He shoved off with his heels, let go of the ground, and swung to and fro. The creaking of the branch became louder. It wasn't so much the fear of the branch breaking as his sense that the tree was in pain that made him stop and step off the swing when Dan and Karin came up.

The moment his feet were safely on the turf, as if some goblin up in the branches had slipped the knot, the swing tumbled onto the grass and the rope fell on top of it with an angry slap. Ruby yelped and the others drew in breath and began to laugh. Ritchie caught Karin's eye and smiled. It seemed to him that this chance moment of small fear had snapped the family neatly together. He almost heard the click.

4.

In the bathroom Ritchie took off his filthy T-shirt and shorts and showered. He washed, conditioned, and dried his hair, and fixed it with oil. He shaved, applied moisturizer and scented lotion from a bottle marked après-rasage, plucked wild hairs from his nostrils, ears, and eyebrows, cleaned his teeth, flossed, rinsed his mouth with Listerine, and spent half an hour choosing a shirt.

Karin had already caught him cheating twice, once just before the children were born and once just after. "If you do it again," she told him, "I'll divorce you, see you don't get custody, and take you for every penny."

The idea of being stripped of what he had was frightening, but it was hard for him to imagine. The moment of being exposed seemed worse than the consequences. He'd discovered that he felt no shame about cheating on Karin until she found out. It was the great discovery of his adult life, greater than the discovery that he was a good businessman, or that he was making more money than contemporaries who were more talented musicians. His conscience troubled him only when somebody pointed out that he had one, and that it was bound to trouble him. As long as this didn't happen, he was a man doing his best to be good to two women who had nothing in common and never needed to meet. He loved his wife; he would never leave her. Apart from Ruby and Dan, Karin's happiness was more important to him than anything. That was why he would do whatever he could to protect her from the knowledge that he was having sex with someone else.

Ritchie took the clothes and went to dress in the room where Karin kept her wardrobe. It had better mirrors, and it was closer to the main staircase. If Karin came looking for a row, and the door was left open, it would force her to keep her voice down to prevent the children hearing. The disadvantage was that he had to be in the room with the big photograph of young Karin covering the whole of one wall. It had been taken when she was nineteen and he was twenty-one and the band's hit had charted in London, New York, and Tokyo. One night that year in North Shields, from the window of a limousine stopped at red, Ritchie had watched a chain of girls marching arm-in-arm down the center of a wet street, singing his and Karin's song, their coats open and the wind driving the rain onto their faces and low-cut frocks till their cheeks and throats shone.

In the photograph Karin was on a park bench at night. She was wearing short boots, a white chiffon scarf, and a white bra and knickers. She sprawled on the bench with her elbows hooked on the back and her forearms hanging down, a cigarette in one hand, her legs open. A half-empty liter of vodka stood on the bench beside her. Her skin was bone-white in the flash although the resolution was so good that it was possible to make out the goose pimples and fine hairs on her limbs. Those were the days she was filling her body with poisons, not, as the newspapers said, because she hated herself, but because she loved herself, and her body's resistance to all those poisons was the exact measure of how indestructibly young and beautiful she felt she was.

The illusion of spontaneity was spoiled by the lacquered golden waves of Karin's hair and the artful black outline of her eyes, but Ritchie knew it wasn't an illusion. He'd been there in the park for the shoot. Karin had pulled off her dress and left it lying on the frosty leaves on the edge of the park road because she wanted to. The stylist had raised her hand to stop her and realized it was pointless. Ritchie knew that the missing half of the vodka had gone into Karin. Halfway through she swigged from the bottle, wiped her mouth with the back of her hand, and, as the makeup girl was moving in to rescue her face, let her head loll down into her chest, coughed, laughed, said "I'm taking this off," stood up, and unzipped the dress. Ritchie saw then that his future wife was wilder than he was.

It seemed to Ritchie now that his wife had deceived him. She'd allowed him to think that no matter how bad he was she was bound to be worse. He'd designed his future as the straight one to her wild woman of rockness. But while he was jerking his hips to the crowd and spitting lyrics into a mike, wondering about rates of return on offshore deposits, it turned out she was thinking about children; she was thinking about them even as she gouged lumps out of the air with a hard pick on the guitar strings, singing in deadly harmony with him and making the speaker stacks tremble. Ritchie hadn't changed; she had. Years ago the virtue began to peep out from behind her hell-raising disguise, and in a short time, Ritchie found himself watching helplessly as his wife's moral platform rose from the depths, shot past his own, and continued rising until she stood high above him. She didn't so much give up coke, cocktails, sleeping with boys and girls she liked, and cigarettes as kick them off easily, like loose old shoes. "Let's move to the country," she said, and they bought a house in Hampshire. She stood by him, beautiful, talented, funny, loving, his alone, the mother of his children, and he was dismayed.

Karin came into the room and smiled at him in a way that Ritchie took to mean "Let's not talk, shall we?" She opened one of the wardrobes and began to leaf through her old dresses. The hangers clicked on the clothes rail and Ritchie felt the wordlessness inflating until it pressed against the sides of the room. Karin took a short dress sewn with cobalt-blue sequins and another covered in black beads and threw them on the bed. She hauled out a cardboard box, dug in it, and emptied it on the floor. Dyed feathers, sequined gloves, and hats of metallicized raffia slid out and spilled across the varnished floorboards. She kneeled down and hunted among her old treasures.

"Are you going out?" said Ritchie. Karin shook her head without looking up. She unwound a fake jade necklace from a gold plastic tiara set with blue plastic stones and tossed the tiara onto the bed.

"I promised to find dressing-up clothes for Ruby. Her friend Deni's coming for a playdate," she said. "I have to make supper for them. I might have time to make a few calls afterwards before Deni's mother comes to pick her up and I have to listen to her troubles. Once that's done Dan and Ruby'll need putting to bed and reading to sleep. I don't think I'll be going out."

It came into Ritchie's mind, as it always did when his wife reminded him how her life was given over to Dan and Ruby, to ask Karin why she needed to spend so much time looking after the children when they paid Milena to do it. He didn't ask the question anymore, because he couldn't argue with Karin's answer, that she cared too much about Dan and Ruby to want them to be brought up by somebody else. When Karin said this, Ritchie believed it; why not? He loved them too. But even as he was thinking, Yes, of course, because she loves them, a parallel thought came to him: that it was part of Karin's long game of superiority and reproach. It was ingenious. She made herself look like the better parent, while depriving him of his great strength in the family, his generosity, his power to see his family's needs and wants and open his wallet to satisfy them. In the beginning, these two ideas of Karin—as a loving mother, and as a devious partner—floated in Ritchie's head together, with the first having more substance. But the idea of Karin as a loving mother was so obvious and simple that it was not very interesting, whereas the idea of devious Karin was contentious and intriguing and called for Ritchie's intelligence to be brought to bear. So he left the idea of the loving-mother Karin alone, and kept turning the idea of the devious Karin over, examining and testing it, until it seemed a natural part of his thinking. He took comfort from the notion of a cunning, calculating Karin. To Ritchie it signified that her wild old self wasn't lost.

Karin put the rest of the props and finery back in the box and stowed it in the wardrobe. Ritchie's eyes flicked to the arrogant smile of young Karin spread across the wall. The Karin of twenty years later followed his eyes. She twisted her head and neck around and up and looked at the flat expanse of her immortal Then.

"She gets less like me every day," she said.

"Do you mind that?" said Ritchie.

"You do." Karin pinched the back of her hand and let it go. A ridge lingered for a moment before it smoothed itself. "It's only skin," she said. "It's not a deviation from the essential me. If there was an afterlife I wouldn't want to hang out with the twenty-year-old you, I'm afraid."

"It didn't seem like the real you then, either." Ritchie went over to the wall and stroked the little pouch between young Karin's thighs with his index finger. He hadn't been able to help imagining a fantastical secret in there that he couldn't reach, no matter how he touched.

"Even then you had a porn mind. You can be so cold," said Karin.

"What is it? What's the matter? I don't understand."

"You never do."

"Everybody in this family says I don't understand, but nobody in this family knows how to explain anything. Like Dan today. What does he need to take my guitar for when we already bought him one?"

"Because it's your guitar. He doesn't want a guitar of his own, he wants your guitar. He wants to be on the show. He wants to be part of that world. The kids at school are always saying to him, if it's your Dad's show, why doesn't he put you on it?"

"He hasn't asked for a long time," said Ritchie.

"You told him he was too young."

"He is."

"And told him what the word 'nepotism' meant."

"Well!"

"And kept telling him how your dad wasn't around to help you."

"Why is it so uninteresting for Dan to have a grandfather who was murdered? If I had a grandfather who was murdered I'd think it was cool. I'd go on about it all the time."

"You do go on about it all the time. And your father wasn't murdered. He was executed. It was a war. He was a soldier."

"If that was a war," said Ritchie, "everything's a war."

Two hours later, when he was leaving for London, Karin asked why work so often cut into his weekend. "You're not fucking some girl, I hope?" she said.

Ritchie smiled. "You know if I don't sit in on these Sunday-night meetings nobody cracks the whip. There's no girl," he said. "I promised not to do that anymore, and I won't. You have to trust me."

It bothered Ritchie that people lied to protect themselves. He lied only to protect his family. He loved the way a handful of false words could insulate his wife, his children, and his peaceful, prosperous future with them in this house from the things he did in London with Nicole.

"I can hardly see you anymore," said Karin.

"You see me all the time," said Ritchie. He knew that she had meant something different but he hoped that deliberately misunderstanding her would prevent her telling him what it was. He smiled timidly and his face took on a yearning look.

"Be careful," said Karin. "If I find out you've been lying, the lawyers will be all over this place like . . ." the left corner of her mouth turned up in a way that was dear to Ritchie ". . . Vikings in a monastery."

"There's nothing to worry about," said Ritchie. "I'm not cheating on you." Delicate, he thought, economical: fewer than a hundred false words in the day, and he kept his family safe.

Twitter: Want to discuss or share what you just read? Use the hashtag #beaHEART to connect with others.

ABOUT THE AUTHOR

James Meek is an award-winning journalist and novelist whose books include the international bestseller *The People's Act of Love*. He lives in London.

Imprint: Farrar, Straus and Giroux
BEA Booth #: 3358
Author appearances: Signing ARCs, Tuesday, 9:30 am booth #3358
Contact for printed galley: Kathy.Daneman@fsgbooks.com
Print ISBN: 978-0-374-16871-1
Print price: $28.00
eBook ISBN: 978-0-374-70932-7
eBook price: $14.99
Publication date: 10/2/2012
Publicity contact: Kathy Daneman Kathy.Daneman@fsgbooks.com
Rights contact: Devon Mazzone Devon.Mazzone@fsgbooks.com
Amanda Schoonmaker Amanda.Schoonmaker@fsgbooks.com

Editor: Courtney Hodell
Agent: Natasha Fairweather
Agency: AP Watt
Territories sold:
    US (FSG)
    UK (Canongate)
    Canada (HarperCollins)
    France (Metaillie)
    Germany (DVA)
    Italy (Mondadori)
Promotional Information:
- BEA promotion
- National publicity
- National advertising
- Reading group guide
- Advance reader's edition

MARK HELPRIN

AUTHOR OF *Winter's Tale* AND *A Soldier of the Great War*

IN
SUNLIGHT
AND IN
SHADOW

A NOVEL

SUMMARY

Mark Helprin s enchanting and sweeping new novel asks a simple question: can love and honor conquer all? New York in 1947 glows with postwar energy. Harry Copeland, an elite paratrooper who fought behind enemy lines in Europe, returns home to run the family business. In a single, magical encounter on the Staten Island ferry, the young singer and heiress Catherine Thomas Hale falls for him in an instant, too late to prevent her engagement to a much older man. Harry and Catherine pursue one another in a romance played out in postwar America's Broadway theaters, Long Island mansions, the offices of financiers, and the haunts of gangsters. Catherine's choice of Harry over her long-time fiancé endangers Harry's livelihood and eventually threatens his life. Entrancing in its lyricism, *In Sunlight and in Shadow* so powerfully draws you into New York at the dawn of the modern age that, as in a vivid dream, you will not want to leave.

EXCERPT

Prologue

If you were a spirit, and could fly and alight as you wished, and time did not bind you, and patience and love were all you knew, then you might rise to enter an open window high above the park, in the New York of almost a lifetime ago, early in November of 1947.

After days of rain and unusual warmth, the skies are now the soft deep blue that is the gift of an oblique sun. The air is cool but not yet dense enough to carry sound sharply. From the playing fields, the cries and shouts of children are carried upward, sometimes clearly, sometimes muted, like murmurs, and always eventually to disappear. These sounds inexplicably convey the colors of the children's jerseys, which seen from the eleventh storey are only bright flecks on grass made so green by recent rains and cool nights that it looks like wet enamel.

Coming in the window, you might wonder who had left it open, for the apartment is empty, its silence, to a spirit, thundering like a heartbeat. Perhaps you would turn back to glance at the gulls bobbing in the reservoir, as white as confetti, or to see how the façades of Fifth Avenue across the park and over the trees are lit by the sun in white, ochre, and briefly flaring yellow.

The wind coming through the window, as you do, unseen, moves a shade to and fro as if gently breathing, its circular pull occasionally leaping up enough in contrary motion to tap against a pane as if it wants to speak. No one is in. In a breeze that enters and dies before it reaches the back rooms, you ride above particles of dust propelled across polished floors like snowflakes tumbling in a blizzard. In the air is a remnant of perfume, strongest by the door, as is often the case. The lights are off, the heat not yet been turned on, and the brass front-door lock silent and immobile, waiting to be turned and released.

In the room overlooking the park the bookshelves are full. Hanging above the fireplace is a Manet seascape with flags and pennants snapping in the wind; in a desk drawer beneath the telephone, a loaded pistol. And on an oval marble table in the entrance hall near the immobile lock and its expectant tumblers is a piece of card stock folded in half and standing like an A. Musical staffs are printed on the outside. Inside, sheltered as if deliberately from spirits, is a note waiting to be read by someone living. On the same smooth marble, splayed open but kept in a circle by its delicate gold chain, is a bracelet, waiting for a wrist.

And if you were a spirit, and time did not bind you, and patience and love were all you knew, then there you would wait for someone to return, and the story to unfold.

1

Boat To St. George: May, 1946

If a New York doorman is not contemplative by nature he becomes so as he stands all day dressed like an Albanian general and doing mostly nothing. What little contact he has with the residents and visitors who pass by is so fleeting it emphasizes the silence and inactivity that is his portion and that he must learn to love. There is an echo to people's passing, a wake in the air that says more about them than can be said in speech, a fragile signal that doormen learn to read as if everyone who disappears into the turbulence of the city is on a journey to the land of the dead.

The busy comings and goings of mornings and late afternoons are for doormen a superstimulation. And on a Friday morning one Harry Copeland, in a tan suit, white shirt, and blue tie, left the Turin, at 333 Central Park West. His formal name was Harris, and though it was his grandfather's he didn't like it, and didn't like Harry much either. Harry was a name, as in Henry V, or Childe Harold, that, sounding unlike Yiddish, Hebrew, or any Eastern European language, was appropriated on a mass scale by Jewish immigrants and thus became the name of tailors, wholesalers, rabbis, and doctors. Harry was one's uncle. Harry could get it at a reduced price. Harry had made it into the Ivy League, sometimes. Harry could be found at Pimlico and Hialeah, or cutting diamonds, or making movies in Hollywood, or most any-where in America where there were either palm trees or pastrami — not so much leading armies at Agincourt, although that was not out of the question, and there was redemption too in that the president was named Harry and had been in the clothing business.

The doorman at 333 had been charged with looking after the young son of one of the laundresses. As a result of this stress he became talk-ative for a doorman, and as Harry Copeland, who had maintained his military fitness, began to increase his velocity in the lobby before bursting out of the door, the doorman said to Ramon, his diminutive charge, "Here comes a guy. . . . Now watch this guy. Watch what he does. He can fly." The boy fixed his eyes on Harry like a tracking dog.

As Harry ran across the street his speed didn't seem unusual for a New Yorker dodging traffic. But there was no traffic. And instead of relax-ing his pace and executing a ninety-degree turn left or right, north or south, on the eastern sidewalk of Central Park West, he unleashed himself, crossed the tiled gray walkway in one stride, leapt onto the seat of a bench, and, striking it with his right foot and then his left, pushed off from the top of the seat back and sailed like a deer over the soot-darkened park wall.

Knowing extremely well the ground ahead, he put everything into his leap and stayed in the air so long that the doorman and little boy felt the pleasure of flying. The effect was marvelously intensified by the fact that, because of their perspective, they never saw him touch down. "He does that almost every day," the doorman said. "Even in the dark. Even when the bench is covered with ice. Even in a snow-storm. I saw him do it once in a heavy snow, and it was as if he dis-appeared into the air. Every goddamned morning." He looked at the boy. "Excuse me. And in a suit, too."

The little boy asked the doorman, "Does he come back that way?"

"No, he just walks up the street."

"Why?"

"Because there's no bench on the other side of the wall."

*

The doorman didn't know that as a child Harry Copeland had lived at 333 with his parents — and then with his father after his mother died — before he went to college, before the war, before inheriting the apartment, and before the doorman's tenure, though this doorman had been watching the weather from under the same steeply angled gray canopy for a long time. In the spring of 1915, the infant Harry had dreamt his first dream, which he had not the ability to separate from reality. He, who could barely walk, was standing on one of the glacial, whale-backed rocks that arch from the soil in Central Park. Suddenly, by neither his own agency nor his will, as is so often the lot of infants, he was lifted, though not by a visible hand, and conveyed a fair distance through the air from one rock to another. In other words, he flew. And throughout his life he had come close to replicating this first of his dreams — in leaping from bridges into rivers, or flying off stone buttresses into the turquoise lakes that fill abandoned quarries, or exiting airplanes at altitude, laden with weapons and ammunition. His first dream had set the course of his life.

Because he was excellently farsighted, no avenue in New York was so long that the masses of detail at its farthest end would escape him. Over a lifetime of seeing at long distances he had learned to see things that he could not physically see: by reading the clues in fleeting colors or flashes, by close attention to context, by making comparisons to what he had seen before, and by joining together images that in changing light would bloom and fade, or rise and fall, out of and into synchrony. For this fusion, which was the most powerful technique of vision, it was necessary to have a prodigious memory.

He could replay with such precision and intensity what he had seen, heard, or felt that these things simply did not lapse from existence and pass on. Though his exactitude in summoning texture, feel, and details could have been bent to parlor games or academics, and in the war had been made to serve reconnaissance, he had realized from very early on that it was a gift for an overriding purpose and this alone. For by recalling the past and freezing the present he could open the gates of time and through them see all allegedly sequential things as a single masterwork with neither boundaries nor divisions. And though he did not know the why or wherefore of this, he did know, beginning long before he could express it, that when the gates of time were thrown open, the world was saturated with love. This was not the speculation of an aesthete, or a theory of the seminar room, for this he had seen with his own eyes even in war, darkness, and death.

To see and remember life overflowing and compounding upon itself in such vivid detail was always a burden, but, that May, he was able to carry it easily. Though a bleak, charcoal-colored winter had been followed by an indeterminate spring, by June the beaches would be gleaming and hot, the water cold and blue. The streets would flood with sunlight and the evenings would be cool. Women had emerged from their winter clothes and one could see the curve of a neck flowing into the shoulders, actual legs exposed to the air, and a summer glow through a white blouse. In the weeks before the solstice it was as if, moving at great speed toward maximum light, the world had a mind of its own. It clung to a reluctance that would slow it as the brightest days began to grow darker. It is perhaps this hesitation at the apogee that lightens the gravity of sorrows, such as they are, in luminous June evenings and on clear June days.

*

As the half-dozen or more people who had swum that morning rushed back to work, the shivering clatter of slammed locker doors momentarily overwhelmed the hiss of steam escaping from pipes in locations that would remain forever hidden even from the most elite plumbers. Why steam still charged the pipes was a mystery to Harry, because the heat had been off for more than a month, and a string of cold days had chilled the unheated pool to the taste of polar bears. As he removed his clothing and floated it across the gap between him and the hook in his locker, the tan poplin undulating slightly as it met the air, the last of the other lockers was closed, and after a long echo the hiss of the steam pipes restored the room to timelessness. He was alone. No one would see that he did not shower before entering the pool. That morning as always he had bathed upon arising. He walked through the shower room and onto the pool deck, which like the walls and floor of the pool itself was a mosaic of tiny porcelain octagons, every edge rough and slightly raised.

The last swimmer had left the water ten or fifteen minutes earlier, but it was still moving in barely perceptible waves repelled by the walls and silently rocking, lifting, and depressing the surface, though only a keen eye could tell. Unlike in winter, when the air was saturated with moisture and chlorine, it was cool and dry. Standing in front of a huge sign that said Absolutely No Diving! he sprang off the edge and hit the water, gliding through it like an arrow. As the body's sensual registration is not infinite, the shock of falling, the feel of impact, the sound of the splash, the sight of the world rushing past, and even the smell of the water he aerated in his fall crowded out the cold, and by the time he began to feel the chill he had already begun to warm in exertion.

He would swim a mile, first at a sprint, then slowly, then, increasing his speed until he would move as if powered by an engine, all vessels open, every muscle primed and warmed, his heart ready to supply whatever was asked of it. He swam twice a week. Twice a week on the bridle trails and around the reservoir he ran a six-mile circuit of the park. And twice he took a racing shell out on the Harlem River or, were it not too windy, on the Hudson, or upstate on the Croton Reservoir, for ten exhausting miles in the kiln of summer or in the snow, fighting wind, water, wakes, and the whirlpools of Spuyten Duyvil where the Harlem and Hudson join. And on Saturday, he rested, if he could.

Although he had played every sport in high school except football, and in college had rowed, boxed, and fenced, it was the war that had led him to maintain the strength, endurance, and physical toughness of the paratrooper he had become. Whereas many others long before demobilization had abandoned the work of keeping themselves fit for fighting cross-country and living without shelter, Harry had learned, and believed at a level deeper than the reach of any form of eradication, that this was a duty commensurate with the base condition of man; that civilization, luxury, safety, and justice could be swept away in the blink of an eye; and that no matter how apparently certain and sweet were the ways of peace, they were not permanent. Contrary to what someone who had not been through four years of battle might have thought, his conviction and action in this regard did not lead him to brutality but away from it. He would not abandon until the day he died the self-discipline, alacrity, and resolution that would enable him to stretch to the limit in defending that which was delicate, transient, and vulnerable, that which and those whom he loved the most.

Though as he swam he was not thinking of such things, they conditioned his frame of mind upon reaching the state of heat and drive that sport and combat share in common. Upon leaving the water, however, he was a study in equanimity. As he showered, a fragrant gel made from pine and chestnuts, and bitter to the taste — he had brought it from Germany just after V-J Day not even a year before — made a paradise of the air. The pool had been his alone, and no old men had come to paddle across his path like imperial walruses. In the glow of health, he dressed, and the bitter taste became more and more tolerable as it receded into recollection.

*

To be in New York on a beautiful day is to feel razor-close to being in love. Trees flower into brilliant clouds that drape across the parks, plumes of smoke and steam rise into the blue or curl away on the wind, and disparate actions each the object of intense concentration run together in a fume of color, motion, and sound, with the charm of a first dance or a first kiss. In the war, when he dreamed, he sometimes heard the sound of horns, streetcar bells, whistles, claxons, and the distant whoop of steam ferries. All rose into a picture attractive not so much for the fire of its richness and color but for the spark that had ignited it. He had known in times of the greatest misery or danger that his dreams of home, in which all things seemed beautiful, were in essence his longing for the woman for whom he had been made. That was how, as a soldier, he had seen it, and it was how he had come through.

In the five or six miles down to South Ferry the life of the city crowded around him and no one could have been more grateful for it. From the arsenals of history came batteries of images bearing the energy of all who had come before. They arose in columns of light filled with dust like the departed souls of hundreds of millions agitating to be unbound; in sunbeams tracking between high buildings as if to hunt and destroy dark shadow; in men and women of no account, the memory of whom would vanish in a generation or two, and who would leave no record, but whose faces, preoccupied and grave, when apprehended for a split second on the street were the faces of angels unawares.

For a moment in Madison Square, he had locked eyes with a very old man. In 1946 a man born in the last year of the Civil War was eighty-one. Perhaps this one was in his nineties, and in his youth had fought at Antietam or Cold Harbor. Fragile and dignified, excellently tailored, walking so slowly he seemed not to move, just before entering the fortress of one of the insurance companies through an ancient ironwork gate he had turned to look at the trees in the park. No one can report upon the world of the very old as the old comment upon that of the young, for no one has ever been able to look back upon it in reflection. Who could know therefore the real weight of all the things in this man's heart, or the revelations that had begun to surge from memory, to make the current that soon would bear him up?

In Little Italy, Harry saw half a dozen men loading heavy barrels onto a wagon. The sides of the wagon were upright two-by-fours joined by chains in symmetrical catenaries. Two dappled grays stood in their braces ready to pull. The barrels were lifted in coordinated rhythm, rolled along the wagon's bed, and righted. For these men, the world was the lifting of barrels, and nothing could have choreographed their moves more perfectly than had the task to which they submitted. And when finally Harry broke out from the tall buildings of Wall Street at South Ferry, the harbor was gray and almost green, the sky a soft blue.

*

At a newsstand in the ferry terminal he bought a paper, folded it, tucked it under his elbow, and so armed walked through a patch of sunlight in the center of a room blackened at its edges by shadow, to stand at a folding steel gate beneath a sign that read, Boat to St. George. From there he could see out to the slip, where iron railings and ramps and walkways of riveted steel plate were hung from chains and ready to clamp an incoming boat to land and release its passengers, by the thousands, who would then descend into subway tunnels hundreds of miles long.

Though it was already hot, every grown man wore a hat, and the calendar had yet to reach the magic, variable date when the gods gave license to the men of New York to switch to straw boaters. Perhaps this permission had something to do with the proximity of the equinox, or the sum of temperatures above a certain level, or the sexual maturity of cicadas had there been any in the masonry canyons. But when it happened, it happened all at once, and it hadn't happened yet. Men were still imprisoned in felt hats and in coats and ties, and women wore fairly long dresses and skirts, jackets, and summer shawls to cover partially the luxuriance of arms and shoulders that soon would be bare.

In the hundreds of times that he had watched the docking of the Staten Island Ferry, almost never had he heard speech in the procession upon the ramps. Though once or twice, young girls had spoken excitedly of their plans for the day, those who were habituated to the run took the walkways in funereal silence. But because they were coming to Manhattan from Staten Island — and whatever one might think of Manhattan it had so little about it of the dead, who for centuries had not been accepted for burial there and were forced instead to spend eternity in Brooklyn, Queens, or New Jersey — their silence as they shuffled over steel had to be something else. Even cows, Harry thought, lowed and mooed when they filed through their gates and pens.

And that was just it. They weren't cows. Their silence was their dignity, their protest of being herded through channels of industrial iron, ramps, and chains along which they — living, breathing men and women — were moved like wood or ores. It was their reticence and dismay at being compressed into a crowd and swallowed by a dark, tight tunnel, something especially trying after half an hour over open water. Many times, the younger Harry Copeland had hurried through the terminal and rushed out to the street rather than into the subway, whether he would take the subway later or walk the eight or more miles home.

Now, his direction was opposite that of the incoming crowds the boat would disgorge. He was going out into the harbor and the problem of confinement did not exist forward of where he stood. When the gate opened he would be released to walk onto the ferry, seek the upper decks in the sun, and glide in the wind across to Staten Island, within sight of the ocean sparkling through the Narrows.

Before he saw the ferry, it cut its engines. Then it cleared the plank walls and piles, bow first, stern sliding into alignment, a crown of spray tossed toward Brooklyn by the breeze. In the interest of efficiency and speed the ferries came in too fast, and as a result the wood walls that guided them to their berths always suffered. For, most times, despite the hysterical reversal of the screws, the boats coasted too uncontrollably to do anything but smack and push the wood. Again and again, they mimicked a drunk trying to park a big car in a little garage. Half the people at the bows were there not because they were in a hurry to disembark but because they wanted to be present if, as each landing seemed to promise, the boat in all its magnificent tonnage would finally snap the wood and hurtle into the pages of the *Daily News*.

As the arriving passengers filed past, he closed his eyes and saw again the spray lifting from the water in the moment when the stern swept gracefully to starboard. Were there a choice — between the steel walkways lowered with deafening racket, and the toss of spray in the air; between the silent, graceful coming to rights of the stern, and the crash of the boat into wooden palisades; a choice between the great heaviness of the city looming behind him, and the gravityless air above the water — he wanted to make it. And if there were a way to come from darkness into light and to stay there as long as life would allow, he wanted to know it. He was thirty-two, the war was over, and he wanted to leave even the shadows that he himself had made and to which he feared he was becoming a lifelong apprentice. But he could not imagine how.

*

The gate was rolled back and he and a large group of passengers went through it and streamed down the ramp. He chose the port side and would head for the bow. As he stepped into the sunlight between the terminal and the deck, he saw a woman off to his right, just beyond the ramp on the starboard side. Although distance did not allow much detail, he could see certain intricacies across it.

She walked with her back so straight and her head held so high that it was as if she had studied for years to be a dancer. But though she had studied, the effortless way she carried herself had been born with her. She was a flow of color. Her hair trapped the sun and seemed to radiate light. It moved in the wind at the nape of her neck and where it had come loose, but was otherwise gloriously up in a way that suggested self-possession and formality and yet also exposed most informally the beauty of her shoulders. She wore a blouse with a low collar that even across the gap he could see was embroidered in pearl on white, and the glow of the blouse came not only from its nearly transparent linen but from the woman herself. The narrowing at her waist, a long drop from her shoulders, was perfect and trim.

She carried nothing, not a newspaper or a purse, and the way she walked was so beautiful that an angry man berated Harry for stopping on the ramp, where he was oblivious of everything on account of a woman who had then vanished, leaving him as if struck by a blow. She was more than image, more than the random beauties by which he lived through his days and of which he had never been able to make more sense than a shower of sparks. He had long known that to see a woman like this across the floor in receptions or gatherings is as arresting as if a full moon were rising within the walls of the room, but this was more arresting yet. And what was a beautiful woman? For him, beauty was something far more powerful than what fashion dictates and consensus decrees. It was both what creates love and what love creates. For Harry, because his sight was clear, the world was filled with beautiful women, whether the world called them that or not.

As the sound of a claxon that had whooped in Brooklyn seconds before now echoed off the buildings of lower Manhattan, he remembered at last to breathe and to walk, and the breath came in two beats, one of astonishment and the other of love, although what right had he to love the brief sight of a woman in white who had crossed a crowded deck and disappeared in shadow?

Twitter: Want to discuss or share what you just read? Use the hashtag #beaSUNLIGHT to connect with others.

ABOUT THE AUTHOR

Mark Helprin is the acclaimed author of *Winter's Tale*, *A Soldier of the Great War*, *Freddy and Fredericka*, *The Pacific*, *Ellis Island*, *Memoir from Antproof Case*, and numerous other works. He lives in Earlysville, Virginia.

Imprint: Houghton Mifflin Harcourt
BEA Booth #: 3447, 3448
Printed galley at BEA: yes
Print ISBN: 978-0-547-81923-5
Print price: $28.00
eBook ISBN: 978-0-547-81925-9
eBook price: $28.00
Publication date: 10/2/2012
Publicity contact: Lori Glazer lori.glazer@hmhpub.com
Rights contact: Debbie Engel debbie.engel@hmhpub.com; U.S., Canada, and the Open Market
Emily Forland eforland@wendyweil.com
Editor: Bruce Nichols

Agent: Wendy Weil
Agency: Wendy Weil Agency
Territories sold:
 Neri Pozza, Italy
Promotional Information:
- National media, interviews and features
- Author appearances
- National print and online advertising including the *New York Times*, the *New Yorker*, the *LA Times*, and the *Chicago Tribune*
- Promotional video
- Advance reading copies

A
WORKING
THEORY
OF LOVE

A NOVEL

SCOTT
HUTCHINS

SUMMARY

A wildly inventive, major literary debut about a disaffected man who learns—with the help of a sentient computer that speaks in his deceased father's voice—to make peace not just with his past but with his future.

EXCERPT

Chapter One

A few days ago, a fire truck and an ambulance pulled up to my apartment building on the south hill overlooking Dolores Park. A group of paramedics got out, the largest of them bearing a black chair with red straps and buckles. They were coming for my upstairs neighbor, Fred, who is a drinker and a hermit, but who I've always held in a strange esteem. I wouldn't want to trade situations: he spends most of his time watching sports on the little flat-screen television perched at the end of his kitchen table. He smokes slowly and steadily (my ex-wife used to complain about the smell), glued to tennis matches, basketball tournaments, football games—even soccer. He has no interest in the games themselves, only in the bets he places on them. His one regular visitor, the postman, is also his bookie. Fred is a former postal employee himself.

As I say, I wouldn't want to trade situations. The solitariness and sameness of his days isn't alluring. And yet he's always been a model of self-sufficiency. He drinks too much and smokes too much, and if he eats at all he's just heating up a can of Chunky. But he goes and fetches all of this himself—smokes, drink, Chunky—swinging his stiff legs down the hill to the corner store and returning with one very laden paper bag. He then climbs the four flights of stairs to his apartment—a dirtier, more spartan copy of mine—where he lives alone, itself no small feat in the brutal San Francisco rental market. He's always cordial on the steps, and even in the desperate few months after my divorce, when another neighbor suggested a revolving door for my apartment (to accommodate high traffic—a snide comment), Fred gave me a polite berth. He knocked on my door once, but only to tell me that I should let him know if I could hear him banging around upstairs. He knew he had "a heavy footfall." I took this to mean, we're neighbors and that's it, but you're all right with me. Though maybe I read too much into it.

When the paramedics got upstairs that day, there was the sound of muted voices and then Fred let loose something between a squawk and a scream. I stepped into the hall, and by this time the paramedics were bringing him down, shouting at him, stern as drill sergeants. *Sir, keep your arms in. Sir, keep your arms in. We will tie down your arms, sir.* The scolding seemed excessive for an old man, but when they brought him around the landing, strapped tight in the stair stretcher, I could see the problem. He was grabbing for the balusters, trying to stop his descent. His face was wrecked, his milky eyes searching and terrified, leaking tears.

"I'm sorry, Neill," he said when he saw me. He held his hands out to me, beseeching. "I'm sorry. I'm so sorry."

I told him not to be ridiculous. There was nothing to be sorry about. But he kept apologizing as the paramedics carried him past my door, secured to his medical bier.

Apparently he had fallen two days earlier and broken his hip. He had only just called about it. For the previous forty-eight hours he'd dragged himself around the floor, waiting for God knows what: The pain to go away? Someone to knock? I found out where he was staying, and he's already had surgery and is recuperating in a nice rehab facility. So that part of the story has all turned out well. But I keep thinking about that apology. *I'm sorry, I'm so sorry.* What was he apologizing for but his basic existence in this world, the inconvenience of his living and breathing? He was disoriented, of course, but the truth holds. He's not self-sufficient; he's just alone. This revelation shouldn't matter so much, shouldn't shift my life one way or the other, but it's been working on me in some subterranean manner. I seem to have been relying on Fred's example. My father, not otherwise much of an intellectual, had a favorite quote from Pascal: the sole cause of Man's unhappiness is his inability to sit quietly in his room. I had thought of Fred as someone who sat quietly in his room.

Not everyone's life will be a great love story. I know that. My own "starter" marriage dissolved a couple of years ago, and aside from those first few months of the revolving door I've spent much of the time since alone. I've had the occasional stretch of dating this or that young lady and sought the occasional solace of one-night stands, which can bring solace, if the attitude is right. I've ramped my drinking sharply up and then sharply down. I make the grooves in my life that I roll along. Bachelorhood, I've learned, requires routine. Small rituals that honor the unseen moments. I mean this without self-pity. Who should care that I pour exactly two glugs of cream into my first coffee but only one into my second (and last)? No one—yet those three glugs are the very fabric of my morning.

Routine is why I can't drink too much, and why I've paradoxically become less spontaneous as a thirty-six-year-old bachelor than I was as an even younger married man. I feed the cat at seven. I cook a breakfast

taco—scrambled egg, slice of pepper jack, corn tortilla, salsa verde—
and make stovetop espresso. I eat standing. Then the cat sits in my lap
until 7:40 while I go through email, examining the many special offers
that appear in my inbox overnight. One-day sales; free trials; twenty
percent off. I delete these notes, grab a shower, and am out the door
at eight, a fifty-minute commute door to door, San Francisco south to
Menlo Park.

Work is Amiante Systems, a grandiose linguistic computer project. As
an enterprise, it's not perfectly designed—the founder thought "Amiante" was Latin for magnetism; my ex-wife, Erin, pointed out it's actually French for asbestos—but it's well funded and amenable. There
are three employees, and together we're training a sophisticated program—based on a twenty-year diary from the "Samuel Pepys of the
South" (so called by the obscure historical journal that published the
one and only excerpt)—to convincingly process natural language.
To converse, in other words. To talk. The diaries are a mountain of
thoughts and interactions, over five thousand pages of attitudes, stories, turns of phrase, life philosophies, medical advice. The idea is
that the hidden connections in the entries, a.k.a. their personality, will
give us a coherence that all previous conversing projects—hobby ex-
ercises, "digital assistants"—lack. The diarist, an Arkansas physician,
was in fact my late father, which is how in the twisting way of these
things I have the job. The diaries are my legal property. Still, my boss
has warmed to me. I know little about computers—I spent my twenties
writing ad copy—but of the three of us I'm the only native speaker of
English, and I've been helpful in making the program sound more
like a real person, albeit a very confused one.

When I get home from work, I feed the cat and make some dinner for
myself. I sit on my new couch. If it's a weekday, I have a glass of wine
and watch a movie. If it's a weekend I might meet up with an old pal,
or a new one (though I have few new ones, and fewer old ones), or I
might have plans with a lady friend (always plans, never anything left
to the last minute). Occasionally, I go to a local watering hole where
the bartenders are reliable. I consider this an indulgence, but little
indulgences are also key to bachelor life. Parking is one—for three
hundred dollars a month I avoid endlessly orbiting my block—but
I also have my magazines, my twice-monthly housekeeper, my well-
stocked bar, and my heated foot-soaking tub. If I feel overworked, I
send out my clothes to wash-and-fold. Twice a year I might schedule a
deep-tissue massage. I order in dinner weekly, and sometimes—if I'm
feeling resolute—I'll take a book to a nice restaurant and dine solo.

I grew up in the South, but made my home here in San Francisco for
what are called lifestyle reasons. I enjoy the rain-washed streets, the

tidy view of downtown, the earnest restaurant trends (right now it's of-fal), the produce spilling from corner stores, farmers' markets, pickup trucks. There are many like me here—single people beached in life—and I make passing friends, passing girlfriends. Right after my marriage ended I went on a crazed apartment hunt in Silicon Valley, closer to work, but soon saw what would become of me. I would disappear into my house, my housework, lawn work. I would become a specter, and this is the great peril of bachelorhood—that you'll become so airy and insubstantial that people will peer straight through you.

I took a different tack (in part inspired by Fred). I decided to stay in the city, in the very apartment that Erin and I shared, and learn bachelor logic. It's a clean system, with little time for sentimentality. It understands that as a bachelor you are a permanent in between. This is no time for conventions. When it comes to breakfast, to so-cial life, to love, you must privilege the simple above the complicated. There's nothing cruel about this. The bachelors I've met—temporary friends—have been nice guys. I've never been able to stomach men who refer to women as bitches, teases—though these men do exist, in San Francisco as in all the world. It's not even their misogyny that bothers me: it's their self-betrayal. They are the inept, the lost, the small. The successful bachelors—the ones without bitterness—have taught me many things: to schedule a social life, to never use both a spoon and a fork when either will do. I know a guy who sleeps in a hammock; a guy who allows no organic matter in his apartment, including food; a guy so sure of his childless bachelorhood he un-derwent a vasectomy (he gave me the recipe for the breakfast taco). Another bachelor once told me about his strategy for navigating the doldrums of physical isolation. When he wasn't in the mood to dance or meet anyone datable, when he just wanted a sweet night with a strange body, a lee in which to pitch the Bedouin tent of his soul, he checked into one of the city's big youth hostels. I said it seemed creepy, but he pointed out that creepy was irrelevant. It was ethical, and that was all that mattered. He was looking for a temporary balm; travelers would be more likely to share his goal. He wasn't preying on anyone; in fact, he was offering his thorough knowledge of the city and his open pocketbook. The only shady business was that you had to concoct a mild alibi to explain why you're checked into a youth hostel. You have elderly relatives visiting; your plumbing is out. Or you can bring your passport as your I.D. and pretend you're traveling.

"It's a melding of desired outcomes," he said. All I could do was mar-vel at the performance of bachelor logic.

But is it nonsense? Will this friend, this good man, end up strapped to a stair stretcher, hands grasping for his rented walls?

I'm so sorry, Neill.

My father—I stopped calling him Dad when he committed suicide; it seemed too maudlin—would have found a specific and obvious moral to the story. He was such a traditionalist I'm half surprised he didn't go about in period dress. He liked to cite the quotation on his parents' grave marker, "Magnificence there was, but of comfort there was little, and, being unknown, it was unmissed." It's from *Ivanhoe*. We're from an "old" Southern family and are Roman Catholic to boot, so he probably would have insisted I do my duty, which usually was some version of "living for others." I was in college when he killed himself. I took it hard, but it freed me from a certain worry, a locked-in way of seeing the world. I came to California, where I relinquished my duties as a "scion" of an "old" family. (I could just as easily put "duties" and "family" in scare quotes.) Instead, I took up the responsibilities of the good citizen: recycling, riding my bike, giving money to environmental groups and the Glide Memorial shelter. I belong to the SFMOMA and the Film Society. These are my adjustments, and in many ways they've been solid. As good as my brother's white picket fence life in Michigan, his relentless quest for the banal. And, I fear, better than my mother's attempt to both keep and escape the old house in Arkansas, a compromise that keeps her on a loop of educational tours, cruising the world's unpopular coastlines.

My entire life, to my father, would be incomprehensible. Beneath mention. But my father's diary—Dr. Bassett, as it's referred to at Amiante—will engage any question. Since it's a pretty basic program, a searchable version of the diaries with a few conversational tricks, I can't say it *understands* anything. It can't pursue a thought or even distinguish among who's talking to it. (It doesn't know, for instance, that I'm Dr. Bassett's son.) But sometimes I throw in a few words, and the computer—in his Magic 8-Ball way—returns a phrase that has some hidden jolt of insight. This morning we had this exchange:

frnd1: should i stay in or go out tonight?

drbas: fridays are friend days

frnd1: today is thursday, but that's a nice thought

drbas: ????

If I say more than one thing—use "and" or "but"—he often comes up empty-handed.

frnd1: your sentiment was a nice thought

drbas: how do you feel about my sentiment being a nice thought?

frnd1: just fine. so should i stay in or go out tonight?

drbas: you've moped long enough. it's time you enjoyed yourself.

I had to correct his response: nothing in our earlier conversation hinted that I had been moping. Nevertheless, he's right. Outside, dusk is coming down like a cleaver. If I can't shake myself from this couch, I'll be trapped, looking out on the black, unforgiving city of my thirties. The street below—as it so often does—will rattle with distant laughter.

At Fisherman's Wharf—a quick taxi ride away—I watch the Ghirardelli sign flicker to life. My companions are a tall blonde, Rachel, and a pint-sized brunette, Lexie, from Tel Aviv. Neither is a great beauty, but they have the attraction of youth. As they should, since I met them at the youth hostel. It was as easy as my friend had described—Let's go see the city, I said. Okay, they said. Exactly what I came here for, and yet the whole exchange put acid in my stomach. I should have chosen a simpler alibi—that my plumbing was out—rather than posing as a tourist. But I wanted that feeling of dislocation and here it is: the San Francisco of postcards. The smell of steaming crabs is in the chill air, and the storefronts of this great T-shirt souk glimmer platinum in the dusk. Fog cocoons the Golden Gate Bridge, and Alcatraz sits lit and lonely in the gray water. We couldn't ask for much better if a cable car bell rang, and presently one does—*king, king.* The Hyde and Larkin Street line.

The girls are lightly dressed, as if we're hitting the clubs in Miami: short skirts with Ugg boots, tube tops skintight and grimacing. They shiver. The blonde, Rachel—the more handsome but less cute of the two—reddens and speckles from the gusting cold.

"What a view," I say. It's their first time in San Francisco.

"It's awesome," Rachel says.

"I can't believe this is fucking California," Lexie says, rubbing her arms. She's round and powdered and young, but she has the deep, raspy voice of an emphysema patient. "So where's the party around here?"

"Can't we just look at the scenery for three seconds?" Rachel says.

"This is our last city." Lexie casts a meaningful look my way. I recognize it: she wants rid of me. I must beam gloominess.

"And you want to do the same thing in this city you do in every city," her friend says.

"It's worked so far, right?" Lexie barks. "We've had fun, right?"

Rachel shakes her head, looking disgusted.

"I'm surprised you're traveling all by yourself," Lexie says.

All by yourself. I test the words with my tongue, like an extracted tooth. "There are pleasures to solitude," I say.

"Sounds like something a loser with no friends would say."

Good point. "A loser with no friends can still be right," I say.

"Are you one of these married guys?" Lexie asks. "That sneaks around looking for sex?"

"I'm not married."

"You got a walk like a married person," she says. She locks her arms in her shoulder sockets and hops robotically down the sidewalk, like a wind-up toy.

"I think you may be confused," I say, "between married and disabled."

"*She's confused about a lot of things,*" Rachel says.

"She's confused about a lot of things," Lexie says in a baby voice—a baby with black lung—screwing up her mouth.

The wind picks up, blowing mist from the crab stands, steaming our faces. I remind myself that I'm supposed to be having fun. This is supposed to be a lark, an exultation of liberty. My boss, Henry Livorno, often insists that there's no empirical difference between seeming and being. It's the concept (operationalism) that our project is based on, but it's also solid wisdom for tonight. If I can make things *seem* fun, then maybe they'll *be* fun.

"How does a single person walk?" I ask.

The girls ignore me. Lexie looks off into the distance as if far away she might catch sight of the people she seeks. Rachel's attention is on a nearby seafood stand. She watches the portly attendant adjust his toque and then remove a series of steaming white crabs from the boiling pot.

"Those things are huge," she says.

"They're Dungeness crabs," I say. She has a willowy dancer's figure and wears no makeup, but her clubbing clothes don't flatter her. They fit awkwardly, like a disguise. "You want to try one?"

"Rachel's kosher," Lexie says. She gives me a nasty grin.

"You shouldn't push me tonight," Rachel says, hugging her elbows. "I'm cold, and I'm about ready to go back."

"Mark Twain once said . . . " I begin.

"It *is* fucking cold," Lexie says, serious now. "You want to change?"

"Yeah, probably," Rachel says.

This would not be the first time an evening slipped away from me. I'm not one of these men blessed with pure desires, who to the game of life bring the virtue of single-mindedness. But I think of Fred and I rally. I invite the girls under the awning of the closest T-shirt shop—olde time sourdough souvenirs—and offer to buy them matching sweatshirts with funny names. This will keep them warm. And out.

"I'm trying to not, like, acquire," Rachel says, apologetic. "Simplify, simplify."

"You're reading Thoreau?" I ask, and I get a new look from her—one of surprise, maybe gratitude.

At a dim bar in the Marina, we glow vaguely in our baby blue sweatshirts. Lexie is David. Rachel is José. I'm Gina. The black carpet smells of beer, of which I've had a few. I'm feeling better. The air is hazy with something maybe there's a smoke machine hidden somewhere. Rachel and I sit on stools. Lexie holds on to the tabletop, which is almost chin-level for her. She has a goofy French manicure, nails pearly as plastic, square as chisels. There's some sort of hump-hump music playing, and she gyrates reluctantly, as if someone talked her into it. She wouldn't charm Herod out of the Baptist's head, but she demonstrates four or five basic hip motions used in intercourse. Who is this girl? She must be a type of some sort, a type I'm not familiar with. She's clearly a conformist an attitude that gets a worse rap than it ought to; what's more egalitarian than conformism? but I don't know what she's conforming to. There's probably a TV show that I, alone in this bar, have not seen. A hit TV show. Something that plugs into the dreams of this crowd she's getting plenty of attention from men at tables, men at the bar, men in the shadows by the jukebox. Marina types taller than average, who hit the gym often, who wear pointy shoes. A more rarefied breed of conformist.

Lexie turns to me, mid-gyration. "Are you going to buy us more drinks?" she shouts.

"You don't sound like you're from Tel Aviv."

"Because I speak English? What are you, an anti-Semite?"

Rachel reaches into her travel neck pouch, which she wears as a purse, and directs a twenty toward Lexie. "Go yourself."

"This isn't enough," Lexie says. "I want a Sambuca shot."

I hold out another twenty. "Get whatever you like," I say.

"You're fishy," Lexie says. "I think he's like a rufie rapist."

"Look," Rachel says. She's holding her palm flat on the top of her beer bottle, miming its undruggableness.

"You know me and her are girlfriends," Lexie says. "And I don't mean friends that are girls." To demonstrate her point, she makes a remarkably crude gesture with two fingers and her tongue. Rachel has a fit of coughing. I think she's horrified. "So I don't know where you think this is going, but it's not going there."

I indicate the bar. "Don't forget to tip."

Lexie pats Rachel's hand over the beer bottle. "Until I'm here again," she says, walking backwards into the crowd. She holds two fingers up to her own eyes, then points at me. *I'm watching you.*

"She knows to tip." Rachel watches her friend, frowning. Outside, Rachel's eyes were crystalline green and bright, but here they're dark and dull, the color of old limes. Her skin is waxy white; a broad brush of young blood runs from cheek to jaw. Blood, as my father once said, is both vital and mortal. He was a physician, after all. "We're not from Israel—we're from New Jersey. And we're not girlfriends. I don't know why she needs to say that shit."

I understand. "It's fun to shed ourselves once in a while."

"I thought the goal was to find yourself." She thrums her fingers on the table, pushes her sprung hair back. "I don't mean to mess with your mojo. I know she's hot."

I'm surprised. Have I betrayed an attraction to her friend? *Am* I attracted to her friend? I watch Lexie waving her arms at the bartender, her skirt pulled up high over her slightly wide thighs. She does have the argument of simplicity.

"What makes you think I'm interested in her?" I ask.

Rachel drinks from her beer. "She has really great boobs. They're so round. And they're real."

"Better question: what makes you think she's interested in me?"

"You'd be about middle of the pack for her."

Middle of the pack. I don't know if I've ever been described more accurately. This probably means bad things for Rachel's own attitude toward me. She's been nice, but maybe too nice. She seems the type to have a boyfriend. I watch Lexie coming back with three bottles clutched in one hand and three shots balanced on the other, all conveyed with the care of an offering.

"Americans yell so much." She flips back her hair. "And just stand around."

"People don't stand in Tel Aviv?" I ask.

She gives me a glimmer of a smile, the first of the evening. It's almost flirtatious. "They dance, dummy. We have the best clubs. Dome. Vox."

"Will you put me up if I visit?"

She shrugs and looks out into the crowd, resuming her hip motions. If she's interested in me, she's not very interested. Or I've pressed my case too forcefully. Or she's just trying to make me jealous. In the darkness, she scans other applicants, not exactly observing them, but observing them observing her. The men's faces are bland and hostile. They look at Lexie, at Rachel, at the other women, with a free-floating menace, as if they could easily slit their throats. It's all playacting, a script borrowed from a vampire romance, the savage tamed by a woman's wiles. And yet there's a sweetness to the convention. It feels like safer ground than the hipsters and the humanists—my people—who booze and jaw to establish a plausible case: we *could* care deeply about this person, we just happen not to. Here, there are rules to the game, as clear as if posted next to the dartboard, and the whole enterprise is aided by an honest offering of the wares. Clothes cling to breasts, to delts, to glutes, to abs. They know we're all real estate, and while they probably hold the eventual hope of making love's Ultimate Purchase, they're clearly open to renting. It's all disconcertingly logical, this straight-arrow wisdom of the meatmarketplace.

"You can stay with me," Rachel says. "We'll party at the Dome and the Box."

"Is that one place or two?"

"You'll have to ask the mayor here."

"I didn't know you were the mayor," I shout at Lexie.

"What?" She looks insulted. "I don't know what you're talking about."

What am I talking about? I don't know. I think again about that TV show that I, alone in this bar, have not seen. What's it about? Two crazy girls traveling across the country in tube tops? What do the male characters look like? Not me, I'm sure. I'm miscast. But maybe like these guys—like this young professional by the bathroom—in his pointy shoes, his distressed wide-legged jeans, his hair pushed together in a point, as if someone has been sitting on his head bare-assed. Who is *he* supposed to be?

I push myself off the stool. "Bathroom," I shout to the girls.

Up close, the young professional is tall, with a gym-rat buffness and a tattoo across his very bare (shaved?) chest that seems to match the embroidery on his shirt. Hopefully, I've got that backwards. He smells of a cologne I can't place, oddly floral. His arms are crossed, beer bottle held like a club. He has the unsmiling poker face of a psychopath.

I turn to look at the girls. They're staring in opposite directions, not speaking to each other. The trip has taken its toll.

"What's your feeling about brunettes?" I say.

The young professional eyes me up and down, as if looking for some slice of me to respect. Or maybe it's a tranche—isn't that a term these people like?

"You bring your sisters to the bar, dude," he says, "they might get eaten up."

"I love the word 'dude,'" I say. Tranche. Dude. These people are *on* to something. "They're not my sisters."

"Your name Gina?" he asks.

"Ha!" I say. "Gina! No, I'm talking about the brunette. Why don't you go, you know, work your magic on her?"

"The little one?" His face opens up, as if he recognizes me, an old friend he's always known. He hits me on the arm, hard. He's smiling, I'm smiling. We're bros before hos. "I love the little ones," he says.

"Awesome," I say. And in the bathroom, I think, "This *is* awesome." It *seems* awesome, and it is awesome. It's Thursday night. Thursday! And here I am in my own town, a wayfaring stranger, with two girls from New Jersey via Tel Aviv. And I've got this strange guy, who looks like someone famous probably—*from a TV show I alone have never seen!*—swooping in to wingman this situation. Or maybe he's piloting. Of course he is. In his mind. It's all a question of perspective! I shake my head in the bathroom mirror, scrubbing my hands. So much of life—a question of perspective!

Back in the bar, I find Rachel sitting alone. I point at my ears to indicate how deafening it is. She nods, points at her ears too.

"Where is Lexie?" I ask.

"Motorcycle," she shouts.

"That was quick." I look out the purple-tinted window but see nothing.

"You should have seen her in Phoenix," Rachel says. "It's pathetic." She slurs it: it's spathetic.

"Phoenix?"

"Tucson. Austin. Santa Fe."

"Okay," I say. Tucson, Austin, Santa Fe—like a railroad jingle. I try to feel cheered.

"This is what we do," she says. "Girls where we're from."

"I've known plenty of girls from New Jersey. It didn't seem that bad."

She puts her elbows on the table. "But were they *free?*"

"They seemed pretty liberated."

"I don't mean liberated."

I look again to the window. "Lexie seems free."

"You're confused, my friend. Between free and easy."

The hostel is an old military barracks, cold, drafty, and sonorous. I can hear the occasional voice in the common area, the lone footsteps of a late night trip to the bathroom. Rachel sits on the bed in my tiny room and tugs at her boots like an exhausted farmhand. "Talking computers," she says, swaying under the exposed bulb. I tried to explain my work (minus its location) on the freezing walk over. She said she wanted to know, but she hasn't absorbed much. She's so drunk she looks deboned.

"You want some water?" I say. I hold her calf in my hand and pull the boot free. Then the other. Free and easy. I'm about to say we don't have to do this, but why wouldn't we? What else would two people, similarly situated, do? I put my hand under the heavy band of her sweatshirt and help her take it off, feeling the ridges of her ribs. A clavichord, a scallop shell. Her deodorant smells warmly of cloves. "One more," she says, and I roll her top up like an inner tube.

"Are you sad she's gone?" she asks.

"Who?"

"Good answer."

I stand up and flick off the light switch. In the sudden, blue darkness, the weak glow of Sausalito comes into focus, bobbing in the tree branches. I approach the window, lean my forehead against the cool glass. It's just a little town across the bay, but right now it looks like a holy city in the distance, a mirage.

"Your computer," Rachel says. "Does it have a weird robot voice?"

"He doesn't actually talk. He text chats."

"Do you tell him everything? Are you going to tell him about your trip?"

"I don't know." The wind whips reedlike through the trees, a thousand knives on a thousand whetstones. Sausalito is erased. I turn to look at her. "What's there to tell?"

"You could tell him you met a really cool girl," she says. "Moving to California to start a new life."

"You're moving to SF."

"Bolinas. I'm going to live with my aunt and uncle in Bolinas. I'm going to finish high school."

The wind stops, turned off like a spigot. The noises of the hostel clarify—the mumble of the television, the clinking of bottles.

"Jesus. How old are you?"

"Twenty. Don't ask me why I haven't finished already."

"Twenty," I say.

She collapses back on the mattress with a thump. The springs wheeze. "Promise me you'll tell him that. A really cool girl moving to California. New start on life."

"New start on life."

"You got it." She pushes herself up, reaches a hand out for me, signaling for me to come over. "I need to tell you something."

"I hope I can share it with my computer." I push off the window. She's a warm dark form on the white bed, and this close I can smell her, touch her wavy hair. She looks up at me, serious, as if we're about to make a pact.

"First, you have to tell me your fantasy." She speaks quietly but firmly—not ashamed, not abashed. In the dark, her body is a monochrome ivory, clearly visible. Her small breasts, the slight chubbiness at her waist, her long legs, the dull maroon flash of her underwear. But I can't discern her face. Above the neck, she's all shadows.

"You can tell me anything you want," I say. I'll carry her secret—it's something strangers can do for each other.

"Your fantasy. Tell me *yours*."

I lean in close. There's no blush of blood in her cheeks; her eyes are not green. Her face is white, black, grey—a mask. A fantasy, I think. Any old fantasy. Just one thing I dream about in bed alone, one way I want to be touched. Where I want her hands, where I want her mouth, what I want her to say. Something. I just have to come up with something.

Twitter: Want to discuss or share what you just read? Use the hashtag #beaTHEORY to connect with others.

ABOUT THE AUTHOR

Scott Hutchins, a Truman Capote Fellow in the Wallace Stegner Program at Stanford University, received his MFA from the University of Michigan. His work has appeared in *StoryQuarterly, The Rumpus, The New York Times,* and *Esquire.* He currently teaches at Stanford.

Imprint: The Penguin Press
BEA Booth #: 3922
Printed galley at BEA: yes
Print ISBN: 978-1-59420-505-7
Print price: $25.95
eBook ISBN: 9781594205057 52595
eBook price: $12.99
Publication date: 10/2/2012
Publicity contact: Tracy Locke tracy.locke@us.penguingroup.com
Editor: Colin Dickerman
Agent: Bill Clegg
Agency: William Morris Endeavor Entertainment, LLC
Territories sold:
    UK (Viking)
    Brazil (Companhia Das Letras)
    Estonia (Tanapaev)
    France (Belfond)
    Germany (Piper)
    Holland (De Bezige Bij)
    Israel (Keter)
    Korea (Mirae)
Promotional Information:
• BEA promotions
• Bookseller pre-tour
• National author tour
• National and regional publicity/reviews

- Print feature profiles
- Radio phoner campaign
- Online and social network promotions
- Comprehensive Internet/blog campaign
- Penguin.com book feature
- Promotional video
- White Box mailing
- National advertising

DOES THIS
CHURCH
MAKE ME LOOK

A MENNONITE FINDS FAITH, MEETS

MR. RIGHT AND SOLVES HER LADY PROBLEMS

RHODA JANZEN

#1 *New York Times* Bestselling Author of

MENNONITE in a LITTLE BLACK DRESS

SUMMARY

Rhoda Janzen, author of the #1 *New York Times* bestselling *Mennonite in a Little Black Dress*, is back with a hilarious and heartfelt memoir about her return to faith and love. At the end of *Mennonite*, Rhoda had reconnected with her family and her roots, though her future felt uncertain. But when she starts dating a churchgoer, this skeptic begins a surprising journey to faith and love—finding herself hanging with the Pentecostals, who really know how to get down with sparkler pompoms. Amid the hand waving and hallelujahs Rhoda finds a faith richly practical for life—just in time for some impressive lady problems, an unexpected romance, and a quirky new family. *Does This Church Make Me Look Fat?* is for people who have a problem with organized religion, but can't quite dismiss the notion of God, and for those who secretly sing hymns in their cars, but prefer a nice mimosa brunch to church. This is the story of what it means to find joy in love, comfort in prayer, and—incredibly, surprisingly—faith in a big-hearted God.

EXCERPT

Stella's House

Having divorced after a fifteen-year marriage, and having returned in a scattershot way to the dating scene, I naturally had limited faith in my judgment. So when I found myself falling for a Jesus-nail-wearing manly man, the kind whose hands were so huge they ripped his jeans pockets, I thought my common sense was all a-pother.

Working against me was the fact that I am an egghead intellectual. Have you noticed that sometimes scholars do one tiny thing really well, but at the expense of more important things? For instance, I can diagram any sentence from the late fiction of Henry James. Why anybody would want me to is a mystery, but you'd be surprised at how many requests I get. We're talking about sentences that march on and on, to and fro, like a bewildered Energizer bunny. I have limited life-management skills, yet I can diagram these sentences with the speed of an idiot savant. Why is it necessary to diagram any sentence, you ask? Good question!

Advanced education doesn't make one wise. In fact—stay with me here—what if having a PhD makes you a tomfool? I can think of lots of evidence for this, and not just me. Consider the overeducated grad student I once met at an L.A. industry party. This chap was writing his dissertation on the iconic significance of Mr. Peanut. I am not making this up. The fellow shared with me many of the important cultural developments surrounding the meteoric rise of Mr. Peanut circa 1916.

He traced the class implications of Mr. Peanut's spats, top hat, cane, and monocle. Just when I thought I could take no more, I spotted a willowy supermodel type in a one-shouldered clingy aubergine tunic. She was carrying a tremendous red onion as an accessory to her outfit. And she was holding it very casually in the palm of one hand, like a tiny evening bag, as if carrying a big red onion conferred a status that she was too modest to comment on. Lalala, no biggie, it's an onion! I encouraged the dissertation guy to go introduce himself to her, but he got shy. I was, like, "Don't be a ninny! March right up to that onion hottie and tell her what you know about Mr. Peanut!"

My new boyfriend would have never uttered a single comment upon the iconic significance of Mr. Peanut. Nor would he have attended a cocktail party. Mitch was sober. He didn't drink, he didn't smoke, he didn't swear. His vocabulary could pass muster with toddlers and kittens. He looked tough with his shaved head and scary biceps, but his language was clean as a whistle.

Out of respect for this man's unusual and valiant restraint, I was trying to clean up my act. This was a challenge for a pottymouthed professor who felt that she had paid her vocabulary dues and could with impunity utter any four-letter word in the English language.

I expected that as the relationship progressed, I'd start to see slips and cracks in Mitch's language—a four-letter word here, an obscenity there. Mitch had been a card-carrying hoodlum, and a drug-dealer, and also once he had gotten fired from a bussing job for stealing the servers' tips. Impressed, I said, "Can I tell my sister that you mouthed off to an officer when he busted you for stealing his jacket?"

"Sure."

"Can I mention that you sold weed out of your back yard and planted pipe bombs in people's mailboxes?"

He answered in his slow drawl, "That's just the plain truth. You can say any of that."

Mitch had been the kind of alcoholic who drove stinking drunk, with open bottles in the car. Then he found the Lord, who miraculously sobered him up. But the Lord didn't clean up Mitch's language. Mitch had to do that by himself. For a whole year he spent the noon hour at work biting his tongue in the lunch room, saying nothing rather than risk the stream of foul language that had characterized his conversation before Christ. These lunchroom descriptions intrigued me. Sometimes profanity seems the outcropping of a limited imagination: "Eff the effers! Somebody effed up the effin' microwave with some effin' ravioli!" I'd like to think that Mitch was more resourceful.

Mitch had overhauled his vocabulary, sure enough. Still, after almost two months of dating, one might expect the occasional outburst. So far Mitch's spiciest utterance had been, "Well, I'll be double-dipped!" Imagine this in a light southern accent, coming from a huge goateed rocker who has a permit to carry a concealed weapon. When a man has a gun in his pants, you don't expect him to be double-dipped.

On an early date to a sculpture garden I asked Mitch why he was always so taciturn. "If a man don't learn to curb his tongue," he said, "he'll talk a lot of foolishness."

We were passing an enormous abstract painted steel sculpture by Alexander Liberman. Struck by the soaring arches and muscular lines, I paused. "What does *that* say to you?"

"Says some dude had a lot of free time."

"But isn't it spectacular?"

"Sure. It's spectacular if you got enough food to feed your kids."

Mitch's way of reducing things to their simplest essence provided a pleasant contrast with the sort of commentary provided in my circles. Literary critics liked to make things as opaque and complicated as possible. English professors chased nuance. Mitch summed things up.

Mitch's sixteen-year-old son Leroy had already confided that for as long as he could remember, his buddies had been terrified of his dad, around whom there had sprung up a stern terminator legend. First there was Mitch's size. Leroy's dad caricatured the impossible male physique—chest like a scenic vista, canon arms, a waist that disappeared into his jeans like a genie into a bottle. He kept clanking steel gym equipment in his living room.

Then there was the curious catlike walk. He moved with incredible lightness, as if he expected someone to attack him from behind. Anyone who's studied martial arts recognizes that walk. Put him in a suit, he looks like secret service. When you put other men in suits, they look like accountants or limo drivers.

Leroy told me that his father's nickname was The Boxer.

I frowned. "I'd hate to be the box."

"Yeah," Leroy returned. "Stealth thinks my dad looks like a stone-cold Steve Austin.'"

"Stealth?" I asked. "Your friend's name is Stealth?"

"Yeah," said Leroy. "He's not my friend, though. He's my cousin."

"Are you trying to tell me that you have an aunt who named her child Stealth?"

Leroy nodded. "After the bomber."

They seemed a strange family to me.

Mitch's faith had played a central role in his sobriety, and I couldn't help but be impressed that he had so dramatically turned his life around. How many people manage to alter their core character—deliberately, sentiently—as adults? I could list folks who had changed gradually over time, mellowing under the gentle weight of decades. And I could name people who had been strengthened by enduring external events out of their control, such as loss or trauma. But I couldn't name a single person who had managed to transform himself on his own.

In this sense Mitch was a rare bird. When I asked him how he had achieved such a stunning turnaround, he shrugged. "That wasn't me. That was all God."

Yikes. I had grown up in a conservative Mennonite community, and this sort of totalizing religious expression made me uncomfortable. I associated it with foofy needlepoint pillows that said I BELIEVE IN ANGELS, or, in the other direction, giant lawn boards advising neighbors to REPENT, SINNERS!

Some of the churchfolk in my community of origin referred to me as *abgefallen*, "fallen away." True enough, my life as an adult didn't look very much like theirs. Yet *abgefallen* is a term I never would have applied to myself because I've always loved my Mennonite roots, my family, and the faith tradition practiced therein. In fact in many ways I still identify culturally and theologically as a Mennonite.

It wasn't the life of the mind that led me away from the Mennonites, but rather my overinvestment in it. I began challenging and inquiring, as young scholars do, anxious to be and seem smart. Now, after two decades in academia, I still believed in God. That is, I thought there was a benevolent force at work in the universe.

Occasionally on Sunday mornings I'd drop by an Episcopal service. Episcopal politics matched mine. I liked the Episcopal music, too. Episcopalians sang long tuneless songs that sounded suspiciously as if somebody had made them up in the car on the way to church. And if the Episcopalians needed more to recommend them, there was the pleasantly high-church smell that issued from the busy little thurible of incense. If you smelled anything in my Mennonite church of origin, it was an old-lady perfume such as Avon's *Here's My Heart*. My brother used to detect this familiar fragrance on many a raccoon collar, and in the general hum before the service, he would risk in a quick falsetto: "Here's My Fart!"

Perhaps in the loosest sense you could say that in my adult life I was *abgefallen*. But if I was, it wasn't because I had set out to defy the church or to reject God. I just wanted to move toward the ineluctable glamour of red onions.

Mitch had told me to save Saturday, all of Saturday, for a jaunt up north. It was hot for an autumn day, and although the leaves had started to turn, we drove with the windows down, the sun burning our shoulders. Whenever Mitch drove, he spread his big hand over my thigh, as if his hand belonged there by right and invitation.

"You want some sunscreen?" he asked, nodding to the back seat. Beside a canvas tote stuffed haphazardly with towels and 25 SPF, an old-fashioned Coleman aluminum ice chest made me smile. Once I had owned such a cooler, a hand-me-down from my parents, a big creaky red one that hinted at camp stoves and fried potatoes. I had always had a glad spot in my heart for a big embarrassing ice chest. Now I looked sidelong at Mitch. He didn't seem embarrassed at all. Well, why would he be, given the gym equipment in the living room?

"Nice cooler," I said.

"That was my dad's. I found it out in the woodshed. Thought you'd like it—it's old school! Look inside."

I peeped under the lid. Fresh fruit, Deli turkey, cut-up veggies, dark chocolate. Perfect.

"Where are we going?" I asked.

"It's a surprise."

Two hours later, when Mitch pulled into the parking lot at Northern WaterCraft, I was delighted. I'd never been kayaking before. A bus would take us out to the boats, we would work the river until we got tired, and then another bus would come to fetch us back either at the two, three, or four-hour landings.

"Let's go for the whole four hours," I said, confident in my lean muscle mass. "We'll slather on the sunscreen."

The sun was climbing, and it was getting hotter by the minute. Around us would-be kayakers were wiping their brows, crowding into the shade under the only awning. One noisy group was already passing a bottle of Jack Daniels back and forth, pouring shots into insulated mugs. It was 10:30 a.m. Mitch and I smiled at each other, goofy within the circle of our private attraction. I reached out and lightly touched the tiny patch of graying hair under his lower lip. "I'm glad we won't be having a Jack-Daniels kinda day," I whispered.

He cupped my chin in his hand and kissed me exactly as if we weren't in full view of fifty sets of eyes.

"Excuse me." An older woman approached us, granddaughter in tow. The woman was wearing a tank top that said, "My Cairn Terrier is Smarter Than Your Honor Student." "Me and my friends were watching you two, and we wanna know something."

Mitch had backed away from the kiss, but his sweaty arm still hung loosely around my shoulders. The woman put a conversational hand on his other bicep. "Ask away," Mitch invited.

Her soda can smelled like beer. "Me and my friends wanna know if you two are married. We figured you couldn't be married, not with the way you keep looking at each other…" Her voice trailed off apologetically.

"No," said Mitch. "We're not married."

"I knew it!" the woman exclaimed, raising her soda to her friends under the awning. They clapped and woohooed. "Kiss her again!" somebody shouted. Mitch tipped me back off-balance, sweeping me into one of those fifties Hollywood clinches. The ladies under the awning cheered.

It wasn't hard to stay afloat in the kayak, but you had to navigate carefully. If you hit an exposed root, or another kayaker, over you went. We saw many such mishaps in the first hour, when the river was still crowded with boaters who were just starting to drink—men yelling at their wives, women drenched and plump, clinging to their kayaks as swift currents whisked them downstream. "I can't get UP!" one woman shouted. "Eff you, Milo!"

After the second landing, the river began thinning out. Most of the revelers were too drunk to go on, though we did pass a party who had beached their kayaks on the rocky shore. They were sitting on the grass, clustered together. One of their number, too tipsy to know better, had crept back toward the river. As we rounded the point, she crouched down bare-bottomed, shorts around her ankles, urinating in full view of her friends and of us. Her pale posterior looked like a curly white grub. It was clear she meant to pee into the river, but she was flooding her shorts.

"Whitney!" shouted one of her friends, waving. "Whitney, show us your boobs!"

Whitney obligingly lifted her t-shirt and removed one breast from a sports bra. She twiddled it as if much surprised to see it there beneath her shirt.

"Whiiiiiiittttttnnnnnneeeyyyyy!" came the woman's call as the current swept us on, "I like your boobs, Whitney!" She was almost sobbing now. "I wish I had your boobs, Whitney!"

After Whitney and her friends, we saw only one other party. Two canoes full of middle-aged men lay in ambush under birches that drooped low over the water, each canoe poised on opposite banks. Because of their raucous laughter, we assumed that they were taking a break for liquid refreshment. They weren't. Suddenly their leader addressed me in a loud bellicose voice: "You there, blondie with the ponytail! Notre Dame or Michigan State?"

To me all team sports are irrational jingoism. But I gamely called back, "Notre Dame!"

"Hell, no!" roared the man, a big fiftyish guy with hair spilling from his tank top. "Wrong answer! Get'em!" Both canoes promptly attacked us with water cannons at the ready. "Get her shirt wet!" "Get his hair!" "Notre Dame is going DOWN!"

Soon after this interlude, we passed the three-hour landing. After that we saw no one. Alone with the silvery dip of our paddles, we settled into pleasurable silence. Why speak? Waves of cicadas shrilled, and the air was heavy with lopseed and wild mint. Ninebark and silky dogwood hung like children over the banks, trailing their fingers in the water. Sometimes we caught sight of a cabin or a staircase built down the steep embankment, but the current moved us so swiftly that we couldn't absorb the picture of these hidden getaways. When the channel was wide enough, we held hands in our separate kayaks, sometimes for ten minutes at a time, adrift on the fierce bright water. At other times I paddled ahead, my arm slowly moving into the fourth hour of dipping, a delicious fatigue steeling the muscles deep in my shoulders. Always I could feel Mitch at my back, his eyes watching my progress as I cut through the water.

Once the tip of my kayak caught a submerged log, and I capsized before I knew what was happening. The chill swirl sucked the kayak and the oar from my astonished hands, and I barely had time to grab them before the rapids pulled me past the log. I seized the bare end of the kayak, hanging on, and with a mighty push hoisted my torso up out of the water. My skirt blossomed restlessly around me, wide like a lotus.

Mitch saw me go down, but he couldn't stop. "I'll wait for you!" he shouted back over his shoulder, disappearing around a bend. There was no turning around in this current. By the time I made it to the riverbank, the water had propelled me all the way to the elbow around which Mitch had disappeared. I got back in my kayak, shoved off with my oar, and congratulated myself on my waterproof Merrills. Sweeping around the bend, I saw Mitch, dripping wet from cap to shoes, standing on shore, holding out a huge branch. Awwww shucks, I thought—he was planning on saving me! I grabbed his branch and let him haul me in. We kissed frantically, like teens in bleachers. But something happened while I hung onto him, stumbling over the solid branch he had stretched out to me—something that felt scripted, prearranged, inevitable. Suddenly the spirit of delicate adventure that had perfused the outing was gone. We stood there staring at each other like idiots.

I whispered, "This feels—so—so—"

"Real?" he asked.

I nodded dumbly.

This snippet of dialogue on the riverbank was more than the sum of its parts, and we both knew it. We didn't have passionate sex in the hawthorn. We didn't declare anything. We didn't change our course as we paddled the stretch to the last landing. We didn't reveal new intimacies as we waited for the pick-up bus, even when we became aware of a small but noisy group clustered ahead. How they had paddled for four hours through steady drinking was a mystery, but I took my hat off to them, especially to one cowboy who stood proud as a bantam in a teensy green sequined bikini bottom and boots.

"Don't look now," I said, "but there's a guy up there wearing nothing but boots and emerald sequined boy shorts. Once I saw Axl Rose wearing wee velveteen shorts on stage. You'd think his friends would have said something."

Emerald Panties looked about thirty-five, straight with a droopy moustache, and somehow deeply at peace with the way his love handles were squeezing out of his small sparkly bikini bottom. Mitch chuckled. "Dude's got it going *on*. Take it like you own it! Treat it like a rental!"

"Can you think of any circumstances that would persuade you to wear emerald sparkly manpanties?" I asked.

"Sure," he said.

This astonished me. Mitch seemed awfully manly. He was downright monosyllabic, with a fifty-gallon air compressor in his garage. He made chili from a seasoning packet for Sunday dinner. I had heard him express interest in shooting the kitsch rhinoceros that unicycled on a tightrope high above diners at The Piper, a local restaurant. But meanwhile I considered the picture of my big bald terminator in sparkly green manpanties. Festive!

I nodded, impressed. "Care to elaborate?"

"I'd wear that green thing if somebody would give $5000 to Stella's House."

Stella's House was a waystation for Moldovan orphans in transition, one of Mitch's favorite charities.

"Would you accept $4000? To teach those poor girls typing skills?"

"I guess, yeah."

"$3000? And you can't tell anyone that you're wearing the green manpanties for the glory of your Savior?"

"Okay, $3000," he said finally. I could see I had pushed him to his limit. "But I'm not wearing those sissified boots. Dude looks like a lady."

On the long drive home we ate rolled-up turkey and little chunks of tepid watermelon, rotating our shoulders and complaining about our sore delts. In spite of the prosaic conversation, I was pretty sure that the drenched moment on shore had ushered in a new phase for the relationship. Oh, he didn't say it. What he actually said was, "Do you have some floss?" And what I actually answered was, "You can't floss while you're driving, are you insane?"

But that's not what we meant. What we were really saying was this.

"I am falling in love with you."

"How strange and surprising is the human heart!"

Twitter: Want to discuss or share what you just read? Use the hashtag #beaDRESS to connect with others.

ABOUT THE AUTHOR

Rhoda Janzen is the author of the #1 *New York Times* bestselling *Mennonite in a Little Black Dress* and the poetry collection *Babel's Stair*. She holds a PhD from UCLA and teaches English and creative writing at Hope College in Holland, Michigan.

Imprint: Grand Central Publishing
BEA Booth #: H455
Print ISBN: 9781455502882
Print price: $24.99

eBook ISBN: 9781455502899
eBook price: $11.99
Publication date: 10/2/2012
Publicity contact: Jimmy.Franco@hbgusa.com
Rights contact: Nicole.Bond@hbgusa.com
Editor: Helen Atsma
Agent: Michael Bourret
Agency: Dystel & Goderich
Promotional Information:
- Print advertising in *NYTBR*, *People*
- ARC mailings
- RGG online
- National media campaign
- Tour
- Recipe cards
- National Print & Online Publicity Campaign
- Web Marketing: HBGUSA.com, OpenBook Widget, Audio Excerpt; Reading Group Guide, Recipe Excerpts
- Social Media: GCP Facebook and Twitter
- External Sites and Blogs: Humor, Memoir, Religion, Women's-Interest
- Cross-Promotion on www.rhodajanzen.com

THE DOG
LIVED

(And So Will I)

A Memoir

TERESA RHYNE

SUMMARY

Teresa Rhyne vowed to get things right this time around: new boyfriend, new house, new dog, maybe even a new job. But shortly after she adopted Seamus, a totally incorrigible beagle, vets told Teresa that he had a malignant tumor and less than a year to live. The diagnosis devastated Teresa, but she decided to fight it, learning everything she could about the best treatment for Seamus. She couldn't have possibly known then that she was preparing herself for life's next hurdle – a cancer diagnosis of her own.

She forged ahead with survival, battling a deadly disease, fighting for doctors she needed, and baring her heart for a seemingly star-crossed relationship. *The Dog Lived (And So Will I)* is the uplifting, charming, and occasionally mischievous story of how dogs come into our lives for a reason, how they steal our hearts and show us how to live.

EXCERPT

Chapter 2

Man Meets Dog

"You got a dog?" Chris sounded incredulous and mildly frightened in our nightly phone call.

"Yes. Another beagle. He's soooooo cute. Wait 'til you meet him. You'll love him."

"Okay. Well, I guess I'm just surprised. You hadn't really mentioned that."

Was I supposed to? Had we crossed some threshold where I was now supposed to be getting his input on—or worse, his approval of—decisions I made? No! No, we certainly had not. "I wanted another dog. I'm sure I'd mentioned that much. Remember, my whole alphabet life? The 'D' part of it? That was for 'dogs.'"

"Oh, I'm aware of it. I just… well, I guess I thought you'd wait awhile."

Wait for what? "I didn't exactly go looking, but the pet adoption center called and pretty much once they told me it was a beagle, I was a goner."

He paused, weighing his words. "I'm not much of a dog person."

Not a dog person? How had I missed that? I knew he was a Republican, and I overlooked that. I knew he was inappropriately young, and I was working on overlooking that. How did I miss that he was not a dog person? I looked down at Seamus, curled up on the pillow next to me. Seamus breathed in deeply and exhaled, his breath causing his jowls to flop noisily, as if to agree it was a ridiculous thought. Not a dog person?

"Wow. I did not know that," I said.

"Is it a small dog?"

"He's a beagle."

"I heard that. But is it small?"

"He's not an it. And beagles are beagle-sized."

"That's not helping. How big is he?"

He doesn't know how big a beagle is? He really was not a dog person. Further proof this could not be a relationship. "He weighs about thirty pounds. Oh, and I named him Seamus."

"I'm sure your cousin will be flattered. The good news is I'm mostly only afraid of big dogs. So we should be fine. I hope."

Afraid of big dogs? If I had a yard, I'd have a Doberman and probably a German shepherd and another half dozen beagles, all adopted from the pet adoption center. I'd be that middle-aged, divorced woman stereotype, only with dogs instead of cats. And I was dating someone who was afraid of big dogs? How does my life get away from me like that?

At least he was willing to meet Seamus. I hoped they'd get along, but I knew which one was staying if it came down to that. My week with Seamus had been challenging, but the little dog had kept me so entertained. My home was suddenly filled with energy. I'd almost forgotten how exuberant young dogs—and particularly beagles—can be. I walked Seamus in the mornings and again when I came home at night, but he'd still race around the house, throw his toys up in the air, and beg me to chase him around, which I did of course. I was rewarded with serious cuddling time as Seamus snuggled up against me. He was the first beagle I'd ever had that enjoyed being petted this much. Usually, a beagle lasts a couple of minutes of petting and then his nose and boundless excitement sends him bouncing off in another direction. But Seamus was as enthusiastic about cuddling as he was about his food. I knew Seamus was staying. I'd made a commitment to Seamus. But the truth was I didn't want to have to choose Seamus over Chris.

When Friday night rolled around, I prepared for the introduction of the beagle to the boyfriend. I walked Seamus in the morning and again in the evening. I walked him for longer than normal and hoped I'd deplete a little of that beagle energy. Then I lit the fireplace, chilled the wine, and prepared some late-night snacks.

Usually, Chris waited out the Los Angeles traffic and didn't leave his place until after eight at night, which meant he'd arrive between nine and ten. I'd always liked that schedule. I could still have dinner or drinks with a friend, attend any social or community functions I needed to, or just be home relaxing and reading before his arrival. This night, though, I was anxious for his arrival. I had not thought about the possibility of Chris and Seamus not getting along. I hadn't thought about Chris at all when I decided to adopt Seamus. I hadn't thought about much when I decided to adopt Seamus; that was becoming clear.

Seamus followed me around as I got the house ready and was particularly attentive when I was in the kitchen. He sat with perfect doggie posture, head tilted to the left, mouth slightly open and eyes wide and focused, watching my every move from only a foot away. I spread crackers on a plate, did my best to artfully arrange the cheese selection, added some salami slices, and then prepared bruschetta, realizing too late that the garlic was not a good idea for a romantic evening. Still, the food was nicely displayed and about as close to domestic as I get.

I brought the two plates of seduction into the living room and set them on the coffee table. The fireplace gave a nice glow to the room, so I dimmed the light. Candles would be nice, I thought. I walked to the dining room, grabbed two of the three candles from the table, and headed back into the kitchen for matches. As I did, the phone rang. Caller ID told me it was Chris at the front gate of my complex.

I buzzed him in and turned to talk to Seamus, "You'll like him. Just be nice, okay, buddy?"

But Seamus was no longer at my feet.

"Seamus?"

No answer. No jingling tags as the dog made his way to me.

"Seamus? Come here, buddy."

No response.

I walked to the living room.

"Seamus!!"

Both plates of food were on the floor. Seamus was inhaling every bit of food no matter how large. With each step I took toward him, he gulped that much more quickly and in larger bites. The tomato-garlic topping had splashed onto the carpet and the couch. The cheese, or what few pieces remained, peeked out from under the now upside-down and broken Italian ceramic serving plate.

"Shit! Seamus!" I reached for his collar to pull him back from the mess, but he gulped and bolted away from me. I picked up the two pieces of ceramic, and as I rose up and turned to dispose of them, Seamus dashed in and gulped down two more pieces of cheese.

"Seamus, stop it!" I yelled, as though a beagle has ever been commanded away from food. I knew better, but I'd forgotten the rules of basic dog training. It had been a long time since I had a new dog. I decided I'd scoop up as much of the food as I could, placing it on the largest of the broken ceramic pieces while maneuvering my body between Seamus and the spilled food for as long as I could. When I stood, I could see that Chris had let himself in the front door.

"I knocked, but I don't think you heard me," he said.

Seamus, finally, stopped his vacuum cleaner imitation and turned to the noise at the door.

Before I could even say hello, Seamus growled. A low, slow growl that I had not heard in our week together.

"Seamus, no. It's okay. It's fine, buddy." I tried to sound relaxed, in control.

Chris stepped back. "Is he going to bite me?"

"I don't think..." I didn't get to finish. Seamus howled loudly, looking from me to Chris and back again, increasing the volume and urgency of his howl. Chris stayed frozen at the front door, five stairs up from the sunken living room where Seamus and I were. When Seamus bolted in Chris's direction, I dropped what I was holding—bruschetta and cheese remains once again crashing to the floor—and lunged for Seamus's collar. I caught him at the third step. Chris had backed all the way up against the door. Seamus strained at his collar, howling up the stairs toward Chris.

"Sorry. This maybe wasn't the best introduction," I shouted above the raspy howl.

I pulled Seamus off the stairs and hunched over, holding him by the collar, walked him back into the den where his bed and toys were located. I put him in his bed.

"Seamus, sit." I pointed a finger in his face, which always means "I'm being serious." Any dog knows this. Except a beagle.

Seamus looked away. He looked around me, watching for another appearance by Chris, but he did not leave his bed. I spread the fingers on my right hand, palm outward, in front of his face. "Stay." He shrunk back and turned his glaring eyes away from me. "Stay," I repeated, for good measure and to verbalize my hope.

"Okay, Chris, let's try this again. Come on into the den."

"You are kidding, right?" Chris said, remaining glued in the stairwell.

"He's not going to attack you. He's a beagle."

"You keep saying that. But all I hear is 'dog.' He's a dog."

"It's okay." This was wishful thinking only. I had no idea.

Chris walked into the room, and while Seamus growled again, he did not come out of his bed, and he stopped when I corrected him. When Chris and I sat on the couch, Seamus came over, quietly and a bit more calmly, sniffing Chris's pants and paying no attention to me. Chris petted the dog's head, and I noticed he looked about as comfortable as I did when people forced me to hold or coo over their babies. But, okay, there was no growling or fighting. And neither one looked like they'd be biting the other anytime soon.

"Isn't he cute?" I ventured.

Chris widened his eyes at me,."You heard him growl at me, right?"

"Well, he didn't know you and you walked right into the house. I think it's good that he growled."

"Maybe, but it's still going to take me awhile to get past that to 'cute.'"

"Well, you two get to know each other and I'll get us some wine." I stood up and went into the kitchen. Seamus followed me.

"He's not that interested in getting to know me. Kinda rude, don't you think?" Chris said.

I laughed. "Dog has no manners." I opened a bottle of wine and poured two glasses, at which point the dog lost interest and roamed out of the kitchen.

I handed a glass to Chris and sat next to him on the couch. We clinked our glasses together. "To another great weekend of decadence," I said.

"Indeed."

We sipped and smiled and kissed. Our weekend had begun.

After a few minutes, Chris put his glass down. "I'm sufficiently emboldened now. Where's this rascally dog?"

I looked about. And where was Seamus? He was always in the same room with me, except when…

"Seamus!" Much too late, I remembered the mess in the living room. I jumped from the couch and raced to the living room. Seamus was down on his belly, with his snout and one paw reaching underneath the couch. He was also lying in the tomato-garlic formerly bruschetta mix.

"Oh jeez. Seamus." I clapped my hands. "Stop!" He stopped the pawing and sat upright, shifting his weight back and forth, right to left, whining and staring from me to under the couch, back to me, back to the couch.

I knelt down next to him. "Oh, right, and I'm supposed to get that for you?"

He howled his response and wagged his tail, spreading the tomatoes deeper into the rug.

I couldn't help it, I laughed. He was so oblivious to any trouble, to any wrongdoing whatsoever. He was solely focused on his goal. I ran my hand under the sofa and brought out the slice of toasted baguette, with remains of bruschetta, delicately seasoned with dog hair. I handed it to Seamus.

"I cannot believe you just did that," came Chris's voice from behind me.

"Um…yeah. Well…" I waved my arm in the direction of the broken plate and tomato stains. "I'm pretty sure we won't be eating it."

"Still. The dog probably should not be rewarded."

"Says the 'not a dog person.'" He probably had a point, but it was not one I was going to concede. Not from my prone position on my wet, stained rug with shards of Italian ceramics and bleu cheese smears surrounding me. No sirree. I had my dignity.

"It's not like I've never been around a dog. My parents have a dog. And she does not get table scraps."

I had the urge to mimic the "she does not get table scraps" in that child's voice that usually says "neener neener" with the drawn-down, lemon-sucking face, which was probably further indication that I knew I had been caught doing something wrong. Naturally, I turned to my cohort in crime for support, which I'm sure Seamus would have given me had he not been so busy sucking the carpet.

"Okay, well, can you just hold the dog while I clean this up?" I said.

"Uh, no. You hold the dog. I'll clean up this disaster."

Oh. Well, okay. I'd much rather hold a dog than clean a house. There was an upside to his dog aversion.

Seamus stopped howling and growling at Chris after the mess was cleaned up and there was no food in sight. We joked that perhaps he just thought Chris was a food burglar and once there was no food at risk, his work was done. He slept.

Well, let me amend that—Seamus slept until Chris got up in the middle of the night and stepped on him on the way to the bathroom.

"AR! AR! AR! AR! AR! AAAAAARRROOOOOOOOO!" This was easily translated from beagle-speak to "Asshole! You scared the shit out of me!" because Seamus leaped onto my bed, ran up next to my head, and turned to face Chris. Seamus may have been shaking, but he was still up to calling out the perpetrator in no uncertain terms.

I sat up, cradled the dog, and checked for broken limbs, despite the fact that the dog had just leaped up three feet onto the bed. "What happened?" I turned on the bedroom light.

Chris stood, naked, in the hallway, looking distraught and more frightened than the dog. "I didn't see him on my way to the bathroom. The dog has a bed upstairs, another one downstairs, two couches, and a recliner he could sleep on and he sleeps in the middle of the hallway?"

"You stepped on him?"

"No. I nearly fell on my face trying not to step on him."

"He's scared." I wrapped both arms around Seamus and he leaned into me, but he continued to look at Chris.

"He's a hypochondriac."

"The dog is a hypochondriac?"

"I did not hurt him."

"I don't think you did. He'll be fine," I said, rubbing Seamus's now exposed belly as he flopped onto his back and stretched out across the side of the bed Chris had been sleeping on. "Go to the bathroom and come back to bed."

When Chris returned to the bedside, Seamus did not acknowledge him and made no effort to relinquish any space.

"A little help here?" Chris said. "I can tell you're laughing at this."

"Sorry. But that is kinda funny. He doesn't normally sleep on the bed, but he seems to be communicating something here."

"Gee, I wonder what?"

They had not made good first impressions on each other. Still, it could have been worse, I tried telling myself. I wondered, though, had I given the dog the sense that Chris was temporary, whereas the dog himself intended to be a permanent part of my life? Had I created an accomplice in my charade already?

While Seamus and I established a routine for the two of us during the week walks, cuddles, sharing our meals (well, my meals; I let him have his kibble all to himself), Chris and I continued with our Friday night tradition wine or chilled champagne, fire going, music playing. And Seamus continued to ruin it all by howling and growling at Chris when he arrived and lunging for the food. Shrimp cocktail, cheese, crackers, strawberries, pizza, stuffed mushrooms, quesadillas, and éclairs all became a Friday night staple for Seamus.

Although I never again left a plate of food in a room without me, the beagle was a quick study. He easily figured out that there were certain moments when Chris and I, while physically present in the room with the appetizers, were decidedly not paying any attention to the food. If we leaned toward each other for a kiss, Seamus made his move too, deftly sweeping in and inhaling whatever happened to be on the plate. I so frequently lost the battle that I began to plan the menu so it didn't include any foods dangerous to a dog. Even a dog that was part garbage disposal could get poisoned by chocolate, macadamia nuts, grapes, onions, or garlic.

When Chris eventually started doing most of the weekend cooking, he'd either arrive with bags of groceries or head out on Saturday mornings, returning with bags of groceries. As my every-other-weekend rule began to slip and Chris visited more often, eventually Seamus concluded that Chris = food. He stopped growling and began to look forward to Chris's arrival as much as I did, anxiously pacing about after dark on Friday and looking at me with that "Food guy here yet?" face. If Chris was later than normal, Seamus waited at my front courtyard gate.

I knew it wasn't Chris's winning personality the dog was waiting for, but Chris seemed flattered that he'd been able to win the dog over. Until Seamus made it obvious what he was about.

One Saturday evening, as Chris began cooking dinner, he found he was missing an ingredient.

"Baby, did you put the sourdough bread anywhere?"

"No, I haven't seen it."

We opened cupboards, checked the countertops, and Chris double-checked the trunk of his car, thinking he'd left a bag of groceries there. Nothing.

He walked around the kitchen counter to the other side, in the dining room.

The bread wrapper and a few—but not many—crumbs were on the floor. Telltale paw prints were on the wall below the counter.

"You won't believe this," Chris said.

"Oh, crap. Seamus got it?"

"So much for bread with dinner."

"There's no way he can eat an entire loaf of bread," I said. I looked around, but didn't see a beagle in any of his usual spots. "Seamus? Seamus?"

Seamus declined to respond. I went upstairs. He wasn't on my bed. And he wasn't in the recliner in the library—his other favorite spot, especially when Chris was with us. I went back to the corner of my room where Seamus's upstairs bed was.

He was there, on his side looking every bit like one of those snakes in nature films with their bellies extended in the exact shape of a mouse or a giant egg recently consumed whole. Seamus's belly was extended in the shape of a sourdough bread loaf.

I rubbed his belly. It felt tight—stretched to its limit. I worried what would happen if he drank water. Should I take the water away from him? Would that make it harder to digest an entire loaf of bread? I was also sure he'd eaten the bread in three seconds flat. Should I take him to the emergency room?

Chris was calmer. "He just seems uncomfortable, but not in pain. He didn't choke, so let's just wait it out." And then he laughed.

"This isn't funny!"

"Are you kidding me? Look at that dog!" Chris pointed and Seamus lifted his head.

And yeah, it was kind of funny the way the dog's belly protruded. So I laughed. Maybe Seamus would actually learn from this experience. Something besides how tasty sourdough is.

We finished dinner, without the purloined sourdough, and made our way upstairs to our bath. Our tub time was quickly becoming a tradition for us. This was how we started our weekends and where we'd recently begun to slowly, tentatively explore that maybe this was about more than sex and a good time. Maybe, just maybe we might have something here. We both looked forward to our tub talks and time spent soaking and sipping.

Seamus hated it.

Seamus hated anything that didn't involve him. Frequently he would poke his head into the bathroom, or come right up to us in the tub, howl, and run away. If we had our Friday night snack in the tub with our champagne, Seamus would put his two front paws up on the tub and stare at us intently. If the rapid tail wagging didn't immediately produce his appropriate share of the food (read: all of it), he'd howl. Loudly. And not at all romantically.

On the night of his sourdough heist though, Seamus was out of it. Sleeping off his yeasty hangover, he gave us a rare respite from his antics. We quietly soaked in the hot water and silky bubbles, surrounded by silence, steam, and candlelight.

Thirty relaxing minutes later, I heard a noise. A scraping sound from the other side of the wall. Mice?

"Do you hear that?"

Chris listened. "Yeah. It's like a digging noise. Sounds like it's in the wall."

"Do you think it's a rat?"

As we listened, the noise got louder. More aggressive. And then faster. I jumped out of the tub, grabbing a towel as I went.

In installing this giant tub in the bathroom of the townhome, the prior owners had taken out the closet from one of the bedrooms and incorporated that space into the bathroom. The rest of the spare bedroom had then been turned into a cavernous walk-in closet. Not that I was complaining.

I ran to the closet-bedroom, where the noise appeared to be coming from. I flipped on the light and was confronted with the hind end of a beagle in the air, his head down, buried in a pile of my shoes. Digging deeper and more rapidly, Seamus came up with his trophy in his mouth and turned to me. Eyes widened, he dashed past me and headed for the bedroom.

"Get him!" I yelled out to Chris, who had also gotten out of the tub but had not grabbed a towel.

Chris met me in the hallway. "What was it?"

"I don't know. I hope he didn't just catch a rat."

We moved to the bedroom door and turned on the light. Seamus was curled in his bed, wrapped around half of a sourdough loaf with the other half still protruding from inside his belly. Apparently he had a job to finish. As we walked toward him, he chomped down on the bread, attempting to swallow it whole. Chris moved toward him quickly. Seamus growled and gulped simultaneously. Back off, Food Guy, this one's mine! Chris cornered Seamus and reached for the chunk of bread. Seamus clenched his jaw tighter around the loaf and curled his lip, exposing more of the bread and his teeth. Chris stopped his forward movement and looked back to me, eyes widened.

Ooh, right. Not a dog person. He was naked, the dog was growling. I could understand the hesitation. I was impressed he'd even approached the dog.

Chris turned back to Seamus and calmly, firmly said, "Seamus, no!"

As Seamus quieted, I quieted, watching with a mix of alarm and respect not unlike Seamus himself. Chris stepped toward the dog again and reached down. Miraculously, he removed the remaining quarter of a loaf from the jaws of a seriously pissed-off beagle. Seamus did not snarl, growl, or snap at Chris, and he was much too bloated to chase after anyone.

"Wow. I'm impressed. You just might be a dog person yet," I said.

"I'm not sure that's a dog. He's more like a reincarnation of some third-world dictator."

"Aww. But look how cute he is." Seamus thumped his tail and looked up at us from his prone position on top of the quilt in his bed, soulful brown eyes conveying that he'd already forgiven us our transgressions.

"That's the problem—he's diabolically cute. It might be time for a coup."

The next morning Seamus awoke hungry, as usual. Nonetheless, we scaled back his serving size and it was Chris who doled out Seamus's kibble after making him sit politely and calmly as I watched dumbstruck. There were new rules in this household of ours, and we were all learning them. We were, against all odds, becoming a household of three.

Twitter: Want to discuss or share what you just read? Use the hashtag #beaDOG to connect with others.

ABOUT THE AUTHOR

Teresa Rhyne is a lawyer, animal advocate and breast cancer survivor. Diagnosed with breast cancer in 2009, she underwent a lumpectomy, chemotherapy and radiation. She has been "NED" (no evidence of disease) ever since. She lives with her boyfriend Chris in a Southern California home run by their beagle, Seamus.

Imprint: Sourcebooks
BEA Booth #: 4112
Author appearances: 200 copy author signing on Wednesday, June 6th 10am - 11am
Printed galley at BEA: yes
Contact for printed galley: Valerie Pierce valerie.pierce@sourcebooks.com
Print ISBN: 9781402271724
Print price: $14.99
eBook ISBN: 9781402271748
eBook price: $14.99
Publication date: 10/1/2012
Publicity contact: liz.kelsch@sourcebooks.com
Rights contact: anne.landa@sourcebooks.com
Editor: Shana Drehs
Agent: Sarah Jane Freymann
Agency: Sarah Jane Freymann Literary Agency
Promotional Information:
• 500 copy ARC mailing
• National Media Launch
• Humane Association and Cancer Association partnerships
• Pre-publication book club campaign with libraries and Independent booksellers
• Major trade and consumer advertising campaign with *Shelf Awareness*, *Library Journal*, *Publishers Weekly*, and *Booklist*
• 200 copy author signing and giveaway at ALA

Consider
the Fork

A HISTORY of HOW WE COOK and EAT

BEE WILSON

SUMMARY

In this fascinating history, Wilson reveals the myriad innovations that have shaped our diets today. An insightful look at how we've changed food and how food has changed us, *Consider the Fork* reveals the astonishing ways in which the implements we use in the kitchen affect what we eat, how we eat, and how we relate to food.

EXCERPT

Chapter 3

Fire

Probably the greatest [discovery], excepting language, ever made by man.
                                        —Charles Darwin, on cooking

O father, the pig, the pig, do come and taste how nice the burnt pig eats.
                                        —Charles Lamb, "A Dissertation Upon Roast Pig"

"Imagine doing this in an unlit kitchen—see how dangerous it is!" A man dressed in a black T-shirt and white chef's apron is standing near a hot fire, thrusting a small piece of veal stuffed with sage leaves onto what looks like an instrument of torture. It is composed of five deadly iron spears, each several feet long and precariously joined together. This device looks like a five-pronged javelin. It is actually a rare type of spit called a *spiedo doppio*, an Italian device for roasting meats from the sixteenth century. The man holding it is Ivan Day. He may be the only person in the world who still cooks with one.

Day, a boyish man in his early sixties, is the foremost historian of food in Britain. He lives in the Lake District in a rickety seventeenth-century farmhouse, crammed with period utensils and antiquarian cookbooks, a kind of living museum where he gives courses on historic cookery. Day teaches groups of amateur cooks (as well as numerous chefs, scholars, and museum curators) how to cook historically. In an Ivan Day course, you might learn how to make a Renaissance pie of quinces and marrow bone; a seventeenth-century wafer flavored with rosewater; Victorian jelly; or medieval gingerbread, all made with the authentic equipment. Day's greatest passion, though, is for spit-roasting, which he believes to be the finest technique ever devised for cooking meat. "People tell me my roast beef is the best they have ever tasted," he observes in one of his courses. His hearth and all its spits enable him to roast vast joints, sometimes seventeen pounds at a time.

Standing on the uneven stone floor in Ivan Day's kitchen, I am struck by how unusual it now is to have an entire house organized around an open hearth. Once, almost everyone lived like this, because a single fire served to warm a house, heat water for washing, and cook dinner. For millennia, all cooking was roasting in one form or another. In the developing world, the heat of an open fire remains the way that the very poorest cook.

But in our own world, fire has been progressively closed off. Only at barbecues or campfires, sitting around toasting marshmallows and warming our hands by the flames, do we encounter a cooking fire directly. Many of us proclaim a fondness for roast beef—and Ivan Day's really was the best I've ever tasted—but we have neither the resources nor the desire to set up our homes in the service of open-hearth cookery. We have plenty of other things to do, and our cooking needs to fit around our lives, rather than the other way around. It takes huge effort on Day's part to maintain this kitchen. Day scours the antiquarian markets of Europe looking for spits and other roasting utensils, all of which got junked many decades ago when kitchens were converted away from open hearths to closed-off stoves and cooktops.

It is not just a question of the fire itself. Cooking by an open hearth went along with a host of related tools: andirons or brand-irons to stop logs rolling forward at either end of the fire; hasteners, which are large metal hoods placed in front of the fire to speed up the cooking or protect the cook from the heat; spits of numerous kinds, from small and single-pronged to vast and five-pronged; spit-jacks to rotate the meat on the spit; fire tongs and bellows to control the fire; pot hooks for hanging pots over the fire and dripping pans to go under the fire to catch the fat dripping off roasting meat; brandreths and trivets to support cooking pots, and flesh-forks for pulling pieces of meat out of the pot. All these implements were made of heavy metal (usually iron) and were long-handled to protect the cook from the fierce heat. Not one of these things can be found in kitchenware shops today. They vanished along with the open hearth.

If I came into Day's kitchen with short-handled stainless steel tongs and nonstick silicone spatulas, I wouldn't stand a chance. The utensils would melt. I would fry. The children would howl. Dinner would burn. The entire way of life that supported cooking by an open hearth has become obsolete. Kitchen technology is not just about how well something works on its own terms—whether it produces the most delicious food—but about all the things that surround it: kitchen design; our attitude to danger and risk; pollution; the lives of women and servants; how we feel about red meat, indeed about meat in general; social and family structures; the state of metallurgy. Roasting meat before the fire goes along with an entire culture that has been lost. This is why it is so disconcerting to step into the kitchen of Ivan Day, one of the last men in Britain who is prepared to build his life around an open fire.

Roasting is the oldest form of cooking. At its most basic, it means nothing more than placing raw ingredients directly into a fire. In Africa, the Kung!San hunter-gatherers still cook like this, plunging tsin beans into hot ash. We will never know the lucky person who—whether by accident or design—first discovered that food could be transformed by fire, becoming both easier to digest and more delicious. In his "A Dissertation Upon Roast Pig," Charles Lamb imagines it taking place in China when Bo-bo, the lazy son of a swineherd, starts a house fire that kills, and accidentally burns, a litter of piglets. In Lamb's fable, Bo-bo marvels at the savory smell. He reaches out to take a fragment of hot scorched pig skin, "and for the first time in his life (in the world's life, indeed, for before him no man had known it) he tasted—crackling!"

It's an alluring story, but the discovery of roasting can't possibly have happened like this, for the obvious reason that roast meats long predate both houses and swineherds. The technology of roasting is far older than that of constructing buildings, and older still than agriculture. It predates both pottery for boiling and ovens for baking by nearly 2 million years. The oldest building yet known dates to around half a million years ago, toward the end of the era of *Homo erectus*, the first hunter-gatherer humans. It would be many thousands of years, however, before these house-dwelling proto-humans became farmers. Plant agriculture dates back to around 10,000 BC, well into the time of modern man or *Homo sapiens*. Animal husbandry is yet more recent. Pigs were only domesticated in China around 8000 BC. By this time, our ancestors had already been familiar with the savory taste of roast meat for hundreds of thousands of years.

Indeed, it may have been the discovery of roasting over an open fire that first made us what we are. If anthropologist Richard Wrangham is correct, this first act of cooking or roasting—around 1.8 to 1.9 million years ago—was *the* decisive moment in history: namely, the moment when we ceased to be upright apes and became more fully human. Cooking makes most foods far easier to digest, as well as releasing more of the nutritive value. The discovery of cooked food left us with surplus energy for brain growth. Wrangham writes that "cooking was a great discovery not merely because it gave us better food, or even because it made us physically human. It did something even more important: it helped make our brains uniquely large, providing a dull human body with a brilliant human mind."

Having tamed this potent source of heat and light, men built homes near to it, and then around it. The hearth that supplied every meal was always the focal point of the house. Indeed, the Latin word *focus* translates as "fireplace." The need to maintain a fire—to start it, to keep it going at the right heat, to supply it with enough fuel during the day and to damp it down at night so that the house didn't burn down—these were the dominant domestic activities until 150 years ago, with the coming of gas ovens. The term *curfew* now means a time by which someone—usually a teenager—has to get home. The original curfew was a kitchen object: a large metal cover placed over the embers at night to contain the fire while people slept. As for cooking itself, it was largely the art of fire management.

In the modern kitchen, fire has not just been tamed. It has been so boxed off, you could forget it existed at all, amid the cool worktops and all the on-off switches that enable us to summon heat and dismiss it again in a second. But then fire resurfaces and reminds us that even in the modern world, kitchens are still places where people get burned. In a Greek study of 239 childhood burn cases, it was found that the kitchen was by far the most dangerous room of the house, causing 65 percent of burn injuries. The age group most affected by kitchen scalds are one-year-olds: old enough to be mobile, not old enough to know that stoves are hot.

In earlier times, you walked into a kitchen and expected to see fire. Now, the presence of fire is a signal to panic. In the United Kingdom today, the majority of fires in the home are still caused by cooking, specifically by leaving pans of food unattended, and even more specifically by leaving chip pans unattended. The chip pan—a deep-sided open pan in which potatoes are fried in a basket—is an interesting example of how people often cling to kitchen technologies long after they have been proven to be lethal and inefficient. There are around 12,000 chip pan fires in the UK every year, resulting in 4,600 injuries and fifty deaths. The fire services periodically plead with the public to give up cooking fries in chip pans, begging people either to buy a proper deep-fat fryer with a closed lid or just eat something—anything!—else instead, particularly when drunk. But still the chip-pan fires continue.

The great British chip-pan fire is emblematic of a deep forgetfulness, which goes beyond the obvious dopiness of combining drinking with hot oil late at night in confined spaces. There is a sort of innocence about the chip-pan blaze, as if those responsible had altogether forgotten the connection between cooking and fire. Real, deadly fire. This was not something you could ever forget in the days when all cooking started with an open flame.

Brillat-Savarin, the great French philosopher of cuisine, wrote in 1825 that a cook may be taught but a man who can roast is born with the faculty. The first time I read this, as a student getting started in the kitchen, I was puzzled. Roasting didn't seem that hard to me—certainly not compared with making mayonnaise that didn't separate or a puff pastry that didn't fall apart. It was no trouble to dab a three-pound chicken with butter, salt, and lemon, put it in roasting dish in a hot electric oven, wait an hour and ten minutes, then remove. So long as I bought a good free-range bird, my roast chicken came out perfect every time. Roasting was far easier than braising a shin of beef or sautéing a pork chop, both of which required stringent attention to ensure the meat didn't toughen.

This basic procedure was not at all what Brillat-Savarin had in mind. Until well into the nineteenth century, there was a strict conceptual division in Western cookery between open fires—things that roasted; and closed ovens—things that baked. To Brillat-Savarin, what I do with a chicken has little to do with roasting. From the point of view of most cooks of previous centuries, the "roast dinners" we serve up are nothing of the kind but are instead a strange kind of baked meats, half broiled, half stewed in their own fat. The point about roasting in its original sense was that it required, firstly, an open hearth and, secondly, rotation on a spit (the root of the word *roast* is the same as "rotate").

The original direct-fire roasting—shoving something into an untamed fire—is a crude and quick method that results in chewy, greasy meat. The muscle protein gets overcooked and chewy, while collagen in the connective tissue does not have time to tenderize. True roasting, by contrast, is a gentle process. The food cooks at a significant distance from the embers, rotating all the while. The rotation means that the heat cannot accumulate too much on any single spot: no scorching. The slow, gradual pace keeps the food on the spit tender; but the cook must also be vigilant for signs that the fire isn't hot enough or that the spit needs to be moved nearer to the fire. This is why true roasters are said to be born, not made. In addition to the sheer hard labor of rotating, you need a kind of sixth sense for the food on the spit, some instinct that forewarns you when it is about to burn or when the fire needs prodding.

It enrages Ivan Day when people say, as they often do, that spit-roasting by an open hearth—the most prized method of cooking in Europe for hundreds of years—was dirty and primitive. "On the contrary, it was frequently a highly controlled and sophisticated procedure with an advanced technology and its own remarkable cuisine." Sometimes, spit-roasting is dismissed as Neanderthal, to which Day remarked one day, warming to his theme, "I'd rather eat beef cooked the Neanderthal way" than beef prepared "in a microwave."

I have eaten several "historic" spit-roasted meats cooked by Ivan Day using his seventeenth-century fireplace and all its accoutrements. Both the flavors and textures were out-of-this-world superb. I could never be sure, though, to what extent this reflected the technology of open-fire cookery or whether it really came down to Day's considerable gastronomic skills. His culinary standards go far beyond those of the average home cook. He candies his own citrus peel and distills his own essences. He frets over seasoning, and every meal that emerges from his kitchen looks like a still-life painting.

What all Day's spit-roasted meats had in common was a tender succulence sometimes lacking in oven-roasted meat. A leg of mutton cooked using a vertical bottle-jack emerged on the plate in deeply savory mouthfuls. Renaissance Italian veal was yielding and fragrant with green herbs. Best of all was the Victorian sirloin of beef, after a recipe by Francatelli, chef to Queen Victoria, which I learned how to make in one of Ivan's courses. First, we larded the raw sirloin. This consisted of sewing strips of cured pork fat into the meat using giant larding needles, the idea being that it would be basted, deliciously, from within. Then, we marinated it in olive oil, shallots, lemon, and herbs—surprisingly light, Italianate flavors. Finally, we put it on a vast spit and secured it in place before the fire with metal clamps called "holdfasts." The beef was served—in high Victorian style—decorated with hatelets: skewers filled with an opulent string of truffles and prawns. The beef itself had a caramel crust from Ivan's diligent basting; the inside melted on the fork like butter. Those of us taking the course exchanged glances around the table. So *this* was why there was such a fuss about the roast beef of England. These superb results were the product of a startling and taxing range of work and equipment, which underwent centuries of refinements.

First of all, there was the fire itself. We do not know how the first fires were made, whether by deliberately striking pyrite rock against flint or lighting a branch opportunistically from a brush fire. It is certain, however, that the early domestication of fire was an anxious business: getting the fire, keeping it going, and containing it were all liable to cause problems. Paleolithic hearths (from 200,000 to 40,000 years ago) consisted of a few stones arranged in a circle to hold the fire in. At Klasies River cave in South Africa, there are 125,000-year-old remnants of cave-dwelling humans, who seem to have eaten antelope and shellfish, seals and penguins, roasted in purpose-built stone hearths.

Once set up, a fire needs to be fueled. In places with scarce firewood, a fire might be fed with anything from turf and peat to animal dung and bone. Some hunter-gatherer tribes carried fire with them, because once the fire was out, there was no guarantee it could ever be started again. The Greeks and Romans built inextinguishable public hearths in honor of Hestia/Vesta, goddess of the hearth. Even in a domestic setting, the basic hearth fire was not lightly put out.

When we hear of an "eternal flame," we picture a neat orange fire, like that in the Olympic torch, being passed from hand to hand. But in the average premodern hut—whether Roman or Irish, Mesopotamian, or Anglo-Saxon—the eternal hearth came at the cost of marinating yourself in a foul medley of smoke and fumes. The heat in a modern professional kitchen is bad enough; I have visited the kitchens of various London restaurants for a few minutes at a time and emerged, drenched with sweat, pitying the poor commis chef who has to complete a ten-hour shift in such conditions. And these are shiny modern kitchens with all the ventilators and smoke extractors that "health and safety" require. How bad must it have been in a small ancient kitchen with zero ventilation? Near unbearable.

In the mid-twentieth century, the classicist Louisa Rayner spent some time in a wattle-and-daub earth-floored cottage in the former Yugoslavia, the kind of accommodation the great bulk of humanity lived in before the arrival of such things as basic ventilation, electric lights, and modern plumbing. Rayner suggested that this cottage was not unlike a Greek cottage from the Homeric era. The main room had no windows or chimney, only a hole in the roof for the smoke to escape. The walls were soot-black from the fire. The inner timbers were pickled all over from smoke.

Cooking in such a confined dwelling can hardly have been the kind of pleasurable activity it is for so many of us now. Every attempt to poke the dull fire or prod the half-cooked meat only adds to the smoke. You must give up hope of keeping a steady flame under the meat and open a door. No wonder many ancient Greek cooks seem to have preferred to use a portable brazier, a clay cylinder that could be moved around into any room of the house, and far more easily controlled.

Things were slightly better in the kitchens of the rich in medieval England. At least there were stone floors instead of beaten earth, and the vast high ceilings dissipated some of the smoke. Even so, while churning out the roasted meats the lords expected, the great halls of these dwellings were often choking with fumes. If cooks needed to do any additional cooking besides roasting, multiple fires needed to be built, dotted around the kitchen floor: there might be a stewing fire, a boiling fire, and a roasting fire, all ablaze, throwing off sparks and soot. In such houses, cooks were often expected to roast enough meat for fifty at a time. The danger and unpredictability of these open hearths can be gauged from the fact that English kitchens were often built as separate buildings, joined onto the hall by a covered passageway. That way, if one kitchen burned down, another could be built without disrupting the main house.

There was no question of living without a hearth, however, for without it there was no winter warmth and no roast meat. To an English patriot, the thought of a vast haunch of venison or a baron of beef slowly rotating before a fire is splendid. In the reign of Elizabeth I, someone noted that "English cooks, in comparison with other nations, are most commended for roasted meat." Englishmen prided themselves on their red-blooded tastes. "Beef and liberty!" was the cry in the eighteenth century. "When England discards Roast Beef, we may fairly conclude that the nation is about to change its manly and national character," wrote Dr. Hunter of York in 1806. To the French, we are still "*les Rosbifs.*"

But the English predilection for roast beef (which in any case was largely limited to the wealthy) was not, at root, a question of taste; it was a question of resources. English cooks chose to roast great carcasses by the heat of great fires in part because—in contrast to other nations—the English were abundantly well-endowed with firewood. From the middle ages up to the nineteenth century, London was far richer in fuel than Paris, a circumstance that made the entire food supply of the English more abundant. The French may have wished that they were "*Rosbifs,*" too. Bread, beer, and roast meat were all greedy consumers of firewood; it has been calculated that simply keeping up with London's appetite for bread and beer would have taken around 30,000 tons of firewood in the year 1300, but this was no problem because there was plenty of well-stocked—and largely renewable—woodland in the surrounding counties. Still more fuel was needed to warm private homes and roast meat. After the Black Death, the cost of firewood increased dramatically in Britain, but cheap coal took its place, to keep those roasting fires roaring.

The difference with China is stark. It is true that the Chinese have their own tradition of roast meats—the windows of every Chinatown are filled with glossy whole roast ducks and racks of roast pork ribs. But wok frying remains the basic Chinese cooking technique, a cuisine born of fuel poverty. Every meal had to be founded on frugal calculations about how to extract the maximum taste from the minimum input of energy. "*Les Rosbifs*" had no such worries. The roast beef of England reflected a densely wooded landscape, and the fact that there was plenty of grass for grazing animals. The English could afford to cook entire beasts beside the heat of a fierce fire, throwing on as many logs as it took, until the meat was done to perfection. In the short run, this was a lavish way to eat; and a delicious way, if Ivan Day's re-creations are anything to go by. In the long run, it almost certainly limited the nation's cooking skills. Necessity is the mother of invention, and more restricted amounts of firewood might have forced the English into a more creative and varied cuisine.

Having enough wood didn't mean that traditional English roasting was a haphazard business. Far from it. To roast well, you needed to know which meats needed to be roasted in a gentle flame and which needed unrestricted blasting heat, such as swans. Judging from illuminated manuscripts, the know-how of spit-roasting went back at least as far as Anglo-Saxon times. Cooks needed to know how to baste the meat, in butter or oil, and how to dredge it, in flour or breadcrumbs for a crispier outside, which meant using a muffineer, a little metal shaker that resemble the nutmeg and chocolate shakers in coffee shops today. A Swedish visitor who came to England in the eighteenth century noted that "Englishmen understand almost better than any other people the art of properly roasting a joint." But once the technology was superseded, English cooks were left with an entire group of skills that couldn't easily be transferred to other cooking methods.

The key skill every English cook needed was this: knowledge of how to control a large fire, stoking it up or letting it die down, depending on the dish. A good cook knew the temperament of fire, reading patterns in the flame. To control a fire, you control the draft: by pulling air into the fire, you make the heat more intense. When Day wants to raise the temperature, he pokes it vigorously with a poker. "It will now absolutely soar!" he cries. Sure enough, ten minutes later, it is painful to go anywhere near the hearth. You feel your cheeks fry within seconds.

Cooking supper over a gentle gas flame, you can get close enough to stir and prod. Sometimes I stand with my nose over a pan, inhaling the perfume of garlic and thyme in a sauce for the sheer pleasure of it. With a roasting fire, the cooks must have kept more of a distance from the food, approaching the meat only when strictly necessary: to baste or dredge the meat or to change its position in relation to the fire. The utensils of open-fire cookery tended to be extremely long-handled: elongated basting spoons and flesh-forks, skimmers and ladles, all of which gave cooks a few extra inches of distance from the blaze. One of these long-handled instruments was the salamander, a utensil named after a mythical dragon that was supposed to be able to withstand great heat. It consisted of an elongated handle with a cast-iron paddle-shaped head. The head of the salamander was held in the fire until the iron glowed red hot, then maneuverd over a dish of food mostly pastries, sugary creams, or dishes topped with cheese to broil it. In the nineteenth century, this is the technique that gave crème brûlée its burned top (no need for a blowtorch). Ivan Day uses his salamander to give a crispy topping to a dish of tomatoes stuffed with breadcrumbs. He holds it a few inches above the tomatoes, and almost at once they start to bubble and brown. You can't do that with a gas cooktop.

Another critical aspect of open-fire management for a roast was getting the position of the food just right. Many people think that spit-roasting meant roasting over the fire, but the meat cooked a good distance to the side of the fire, only getting moved close up right at the end to brown it. This is a technique similar to a modern Argentine *asado*, a barbecue method that slow-roasts a whole animal at an angle several feet from an outdoor charcoal fire pit, until the meat is succulent and smoky. A skilled roaster knew that getting the distance right was critical for moderating the heat accumulation on the surface of the meat. Modern science has confirmed it. Recent experiments have shown that the heat intensity from a roasting fire varies by the inverse square of the distance of the meat being roasted. Each inch that you move a piece of beef nearer to the fire doesn't just make it a bit hotter; it makes it a lot hotter. With a big roast, the "sweet spot," or optimum position for roasting without charring, will be as much as three feet from the fire.

Apart from the complexity of fire, an additional problem with spit-roasting was keeping the food firmly gripped on the spit. When you stick a spit through something and turn it around, the spit has a tendency to spin while the meat stays still. Various strategies addressed this. One was to put skewer holes in the spit: the joint could be speared in place with flat skewers. Another solution was the aforementioned "holdfast," a kind of hook to grip the meat. Once the food was firmly in place, there was one more challenge facing the roaster, and it was the trickiest by far: how to keep a hulking piece of meat in perpetual motion for the hours it needed to cook.

Of all the thankless, soul-destroying jobs in a rich medieval British kitchen—scullion, washpot, drudge—there can have been few worse than that of the turnspit or turnbroach, the person (usually a boy) charged with rotating the roasting spits. "In olden times," wrote the great biographer John Aubrey, "the poor boys did turn the spits, and licked the dripping pans."

By the reign of Henry VIII, the king's household had whole battalions of turnspits, charring their faces and tiring their arms to satisfy the royal appetite for roast capons and ducks, venison and beef, crammed in cubbyholes to the side of the fireplace. The boys must have been near-roasted themselves as they labored to roast the meats. Until the year 1530, the kitchen staff at Hampton Court worked either naked or in scanty, grimy garments. Henry VIII addressed the situation, not by relieving the turnspits of their duties, but by providing the master cooks with a clothing allowance, with which to keep the junior staff decently clothed, and therefore even hotter. Turnspits were employed in lesser households, too. In 1666, the lawyers of the Middle Temple in London were making use of one "turnbroach" alongside two scullions, a head cook, and an under cook. To be a turnspit was deemed suitable work for a child well into the eighteenth century. John Macdonald (b. 1741), a Scottish highlander, was a famous footman who wrote memoirs of his experiences in service. An orphan, Macdonald had been sacked from a previous job rocking a baby's cradle and next found work in a gentleman's house turning the spit. He was aged just five.

But by that time, turnspit boys like Macdonald were something of a throwback. Over the course of the sixteenth and seventeenth centuries in Britain, their work had largely been taken over by animals. In a 1576 book on English dogs, a "turnspit" was defined as "a certain dog in kitchen service." The dogs were bred specially to have short legs and long bodies. Stuck in a wheel around 2.5 feet in diameter, suspended high up against a wall near the fireplace, they were forced to trundle around and around. The treadmill was connected to the spit via a pulley.

Some cooks preferred to use geese instead of dogs. In the 1690s, it was written that geese were better at turning spits than dogs because they kept going for longer at the treadmill, sometimes as long as twelve hours. There were signs that dogs were too intelligent for the job. Thomas Somerville, who witnessed the use of dog wheels during a childhood in eighteenth-century Scotland, recalled that the dogs "used to hide themselves or run away when they observed indications that there was to be a roast for dinner."

The turnspit breed is no longer with us. It would be nice to think that they died out because of a sudden fit of conscience on the part of their owners. But history doesn't usually work like this. Dog wheels were still being used in American restaurant kitchens well into the nineteenth century. Henry Bergh, an early animal rights lobbyist, campaigned against using dog wheels to roast meats (along with other abuses of animals, such as bear baiting). The fuss Bergh made about turnspit dogs did finally attach some shame to the practice, but it also had unintended consequences. When Bergh paid surprise visits to kitchens to check for the presence of dog wheels, he several times found that the dogs had been replaced at the fire by young black children.

In the end, it was not kindness that ended the era of the turnspit dog but mechanization. From the sixteenth century onward, inventors devised numerous mechanical jacks to rotate the spit without the need for anyone—boy, dog, or goose—to do the work. By 1748, Pehr Kalm, a Swedish visitor to England, was praising the windup iron "meat jack" as "a very useful invention, which lightens the labour amongst a people who eat so much meat." Based on his travels, Kalm claimed that "simply made" weight-driven jacks were to be found "in every house in England." This was an exaggeration. However, judging from probate inventories—lists of possessions at the time of death—around one-half of all households, not only affluent ones, did possess a windup jack, a strikingly high percentage.

Still, no wonder. Archaic as they might seem to us, these were highly desirable pieces of kitchen equipment. Mechanical jacks really were brilliant devices, culinary robots that took much of the labor out of spit-roasting. The basic mechanism was this. There was a weight, suspended from a cord, wound around a cylinder. The force of gravity made the weight slowly descend (another name for these little machines was "gravity jacks"). As it did so, the power was transmitted through a series of cogwheels and pulleys to one or more spits. Through the force of the weight dropping, the spit rotated. Some jacks rang a bell when the spit stopped.

Weight-driven jacks were not the only form of automated spit. From the seventeenth-century onward, there were also smoke jacks, which used the updraft of heat from the fire to power a vane, like a weather vane. Fans of the smoke jack liked the fact that it needed no winding up and was cheap. Smoke jacks were only cheap, however, if fuel use was not taken into account. To keep the vane turning in the smoke, grotesque amounts of wood or coal had to be kept burning in the hearth. In 1800, it was calculated that you could use one-thousandth of the fuel needed to make a smoke jack work to power the spit with a small steam engine instead.

Because spit-roasting was so central to British cooking, much intelligence was lavished on inventing improved methods of turning the spit. Water, steam, and clockwork were all experimented with as ways of keeping a roasting joint in a state of constant—if not quite perpetual—motion. Mechanized spits were the gleaming espresso machines of their day: the single kitchen product on which the most complex engineering was lavished. In a seventeenth-century farmhouse kitchen, the spoons and cauldrons went back to the Romans. The spits and salamanders were medieval. The meat and fire were as old as time. But the weight-jack powering the spit was high-tech. Ivan Day still has a large collection of mechanized spit-jacks. When asked to name his favorite kitchen gadget of all time, he unhesitatingly names his seventeenth-century weight-driven jack, powered with the weight of a small cannon ball. He marvels at its efficiency. "Four hundred years before the microwave and its warning buzzer, my mechanism can tell me [when the food is done] by ringing a bell," he told BBC Radio 4's *Food Programme*. "I'd never use anything else. It works just as well now as it did 300 years ago."

In its way, the mechanized jack clearly is a miracle. It saved the pains of boys and dogs. It produces—at least in the hands of a talented cook—stupendously good roast meat, evenly cooked by continuous, steady rotation. It is a joy to watch. Few pieces of kitchenware, ancient or modern, can supply the quiet satisfaction of watching a weight-jack do its job: the speedy whirring of the flywheel, the interlocking cogs and gears, the reliable motion of the spit. On its own terms, it really works.

But technologies never exist just on their own terms. By the mid-nineteenth century, the mechanized jack was becoming obsolete, not through any fault of its own, but because the entire culture of open-hearth cookery was on the way out. Fire was in the process of being contained, and as a result, the kitchen was about to be transformed.

"More fuel is frequently consumed in a kitchen range to boil a tea-kettle than, with proper management, would be sufficient to cook a dinner for fifty men." The author of these words was Benjamin Thompson, Count Rumford, one of the most skillful scientists ever to apply himself to the question of cooking. Among his many experiments, he set his mind to the problem of why apple pie filling tended to be so mouth-burningly hot. Rumford was a great social campaigner, too, and believed he had found the solution to world hunger, by inventing a soup for the poor that could deliver the maximum nutrients for the minimum money. One of his other main causes was the wastefulness of roasting fires. In the late eighteenth century, Rumford was appalled by the way the English cooked over an open flame: "The loss of heat and waste of fuel in these kitchens is incredible." Rumford did not even rate the food produced by spit-roasting very highly. By focusing all their energies on roasting, English cooks had neglected the art of making "nourishing soups and broths."

Rumford's problem with English hearths was easily summarized: "They are not closed." From this basic error, "other evils" followed. The kitchen was an uncomfortable environment to work in, as anyone knew who had ever "met the cook coming sweltering out of it." The heat was excessive, there were drafts of cold air by the chimney, and worst of all, there were "noxious exhalations" from burning charcoal:

a constant atmosphere of smokiness. Excessive smoke was not an accident, but inherent to the design of the English kitchen around the year 1800. To make room for all the pots that needed to be fitted over the fire, the range was built very long, which in turn necessitated an "enormously large" and high chimney that squandered much fuel and generated much smoke. Rumford's solution was his own custom-built closed range, which consumed vastly less fuel, as he had proved when he installed one in the House of Industry (the Workhouse) in Munich.

In a Rumford range, instead of one large fire, there would be lots of small enclosed ones, to minimize smoke and fuel wastage. Each boiler, kettle, or stewpan in use would be assigned its own "separate closed fireplace," built from bricks for added insulation and shut up with a door, with a separate canal for "carrying off the smoke into the chimney." The kitchen would be smokeless and highly efficient, and Rumford claimed the food produced was tastier. He summoned some friends for a taste test of a leg of mutton roasted in a Rumford roaster as against a spit-roasted leg. Everyone preferred the one cooked in the enclosed roaster, relishing the "exquisitely sweet" fat with currant jelly; or so they said.

It was one thing to convince his friends and acquaintances, still another to convince the general public. Rumford's idea was ahead of its time. His ingeniously designed stoves never found a wide audience (though various sellers would later market and sell "Rumford stoves" that had no connection with the original). Rumford's invention was not helped by the fact that it was largely made from bricks, containing very little iron. This meant that ironmongers—who at this time were the main manufacturers of cooking apparatus—had little incentive to reproduce the design.

There was also the fact that smoky and wasteful as they might be, cooks clung to their open fires as simply the only way to roast meat. Campaigners for smokeless stoves in the developing world face the same obstacles today. The average Third World open cooking fire—fueled by coal, dung, or wood—generates as much carbon dioxide as a car. Around 3 billion people—half the world's population—cook like this, with dreadful consequences, both for carbon emissions and individual health: such fires can cause bronchitis, heart disease, cancers. The World Health Organization has calculated that indoor smoke, chiefly from cooking fires, kills 1.5 million people every year. Yet when aid workers go into villages in Africa or South America offering clean, nonpolluting cookstoves, they often encounter resistance, as people stubbornly stick to the smoky fires they have cooked on all their lives.

In 1838, four decades after Rumford's warnings on the dangers of open hearths, cookery writer Mary Randolph, insisted that "no meat can be well roasted except on a spit turned by a jack, and before a clear, steady fire—other methods are no better than baking." There continued to be innovations in jack design, long after you might have expected to see the last of them. In 1845, a Mr. Norton took out a patent for a spit propelled electrically with the aid of two magnets, a strange clash of old and new technology. Over Victoria's century, Britain entered the age of gas lighting, high-speed rail travel, flushing toilets, and telephones; and still many people chose to have their meat cooked before a roaring fire. As late as 1907, the Skinners Company in London had an eleven-foot-wide roasting range installed in their Guild Hall kitchen.

The prejudice against closed-off cooking ranges was largely that they seemed too much like bread ovens. Only open fires could roast, it was believed. Ovens were things that baked. In European kitchens, the two kinds of heat were stubbornly kept apart.

In the East, this division has not existed to anything like the same extent. The Arabic word for bread is *khubz*, which generates the verb *khabaza*, meaning to bake or "to make *khubz*." But *khabaza* can also mean to grill or to roast. This single verb thus brings together what in English would be three separate cooking techniques. All three techniques can be performed in a *tannur*, or clay oven.

Basic clay bread ovens go back at least as far as 3000 BC in the Indus Valley and Mesopotamia, on the site of modern-day Iraq and Pakistan. These bread ovens had the traditional round cylindrical clay form that they still have to this day in much of rural Africa. A fire is lit in the bottom of the cylinder, and dough is lowered in through a hole in the top and slapped on the side of the oven; it is lifted out again a couple of minutes later as flatbread. These clay ovens look like upside-down flower pots. In Iraq, the name for these ovens was *tinaru*. We would call them *tannurs* or *tandoors*, a technology still in use throughout the Middle East, Central Asia, and Southeast Asia.

Although it has been refined over the past 5,000 years, the *tannur/tandoor* serves the same purpose it always has: a provider of intense dry baking heat. The *tannur* enabled households, even humble ones, to be self-sufficient in bread. A series of laborers' houses have been excavated in an Ancient Egyptian village, Amarna, dating to 1350 BC. Half the houses, including small ones, show traces of cylindrical clay ovens. Whereas in Europe there was a persistent belief that the only true bread was that baked by professional bakers, in medieval Iraq, homemade *tannur* bread was preferred. A market inspector in medieval Baghdad noted that "most people avoid eating bread baked in the market."

The *tannur* offered different cooking possibilities in the home than fire alone. Despite being cheap and portable, these clay ovens provided some heat control. An eye at the bottom could be opened or shut to increase or reduce the temperature. For some breads such as a round Iraqi water bread coated in sesame oil a more moderate heat was used. But clay ovens could also get furnace-hot when needed. Because the wood or charcoal is burned directly in the bottom of the *tandoor* and continues to burn as the food cooks, the temperatures in a modern *tandoor* can be tremendous: as much as 896°F (compared with a maximum temperature of 428°F for most domestic electric ovens). It is this blistering heat that makes this oven such a powerful and versatile piece of equipment.

The uses of the *tannur* went far beyond baking, which partly explains why in Middle Eastern and Eastern cookery, the baking-roasting dichotomy did not exist. As well as baking bread, cookies, and crackers, a *tannur* could be used for stews and casseroles and for roasting meat. Today, the *tandoor* is probably most famous as a device for cooking chicken marinated in yogurt and red spices: *tandoori* chicken. In tenth-century Baghdad, the *tannur* was used to roast such things as "fatty whole lamb or kid—mostly stuffed…big chunks of meat, plump poultry and fish." They were placed on flat brick tiles arranged on the fire or securely threaded into skewers and lowered into the *tannur* until they roasted to succulence. There was clearly no sense here that you could not "roast" meat in an oven. However, the heat of a *tandoor* works on food in a different way than a Western bread oven.

There are three different forms of cooking heat. All cooking obeys the second law of thermodynamics: heat flows from hotter things to colder things. But this transfer of energy can happen in more than one way. The first way is radiant heat. Imagine the way an Italian frittata omelette suddenly puffs and browns when you put it under the grill. The grill itself hasn't touched the omelette; and yet it is cooking. This is from heat radiation, like the sun's rays. Like radio waves, radiation works without any contact: the thing being heated and the heater do not need to touch. A red-hot fire provides lots of radiant heat, from both the flames and the embers. The moment in Ivan Day's kitchen when he poked the fire and the heat levels jumped up from bearable to unbearable represented a sudden leap in the quantity of radiant heat, enough to produce a sizzling crust on a joint of beef.

The second type of heat transfer is conduction. Unlike radiation, it works from material to material, via touch. Some materials are very good conductors, notably, metals. Others are poor conductors, such as clay, brick, and wood. When something heats up, its atoms vibrate rapidly. Conduction works by passing on these vibrations from one material to another: from a metal sauté pan to a piece of steak; from a metal saucepan handle to a tender human hand.

The third type of cooking heat is convection. It happens when the molecules in a fluid—whether air or water, stock or oil—diffuse heat to one another. The hot parts of the liquid or gas are less dense than the cold parts: think steam as opposed to water. Gradually, the hot fluid transfers energy to the cool fluid, until all is hot: think of porridge bubbling in a pot or the air in a preheating oven.

Any given method of cooking will involve a combination of these forms of heat, but one or another usually dominates. What makes the *tandoor* so unusual is that it combines all three forms of heat transfer in one. There is a massive blast of radiant heat from the fire below, plus more radiation from the heat retained in the clay walls. Bread cooked on the walls or meat cooked on skewers gets hot by conduction from the clay or the metal skewers. Finally, there is some convected heat from the hot air circulating in the oven. The *tandoor* provides intense and potent heat: the kind you can use to cook almost anything.

The ovens of Western cooking were generally brick boxes. Heat transfer in this sort of oven is typically around 80 percent by convection and only 20 percent by radiation. In place of the intense constant heat of the *tandoor* was a heat that started fierce but became progressively cooler. Indeed, the food didn't go in until the flames had already gone out. Over centuries, cooking styles evolved to reflect this gradual cooling off, with a repertoire to make the most of every phase of oven heat. Food was cooked in succession: bread went into the hottest oven, followed by stews, pastries, and puddings; later when the oven was barely warm, herbs might be left to dry in it overnight.

It is true that the West had its own equivalent of the *tannur* in the "beehive ovens" introduced by the Romans, but these never penetrated the entire food culture as the Eastern clay ovens did. In ancient and medieval Europe, bread ovens tended to be vast communal chambers, feeding an entire community with bread. The baking equipment used in a manorial or monastery kitchen was all on a giant scale: dough was stirred with wooden spoons as big as oars and kneaded on vast trestle tables. Communal baking ovens were stoked up via stoking sheds from outside. First the fuel—bundles of wood or charcoal—was heaved into the back of the oven and fired up. When the oven was hot, the ashes were raked out into the stoking sheds and the dough was shoved in, on great long wooden paddles called peels. Like turnspit boys, bakers worked almost naked because of the heat.

There the similarity ended. Western baking and roasting were entirely separate activities with separate equipment, methods, and recipes. By the eighteenth century, baking involved a paraphernalia of wooden kneading troughs, pastry jaggers, various hoops and traps for tarts and pies, peels, patty pans, wafer irons, and earthenware dishes. The baker had no need of jacks and spits, gridirons, and fire dogs. There is an engraving of the royal kitchen at St. James's Palace during the reign of George III, around the time of American Independence. It depicts three different types of fire cookery. There is an open grate for roasting, a closed oven for baking, and a raised brick hearth for making stews and sauces. Each operation is entirely distinct.

No wonder Rumford's closed range met with such ridicule and derision when it was first introduced. It threatened to bring together two technologies—baking and roasting—that almost everyone in Britain, if not the Western world, deemed to be incompatible. It was as if he had said you could use a deep-fat fryer for steaming or a toaster to boil eggs.

There were also doubts from many quarters over whether the enclosed heat of an oven could ever replace the homely pleasures of warming yourself by an open fire. Could a stove whose flames were hidden from view ever be a *focus* in the way that a hearth was? A fire speaks to us in ways that are not always rational. For all the hazards and smoke of a roasting fire, those flames signified home. It was said that when stoves were first introduced in the United States in the 1830s, they inspired feelings of hatred: stoves might be an acceptable way to heat a public place such as a barroom or courthouse, but not a home.

In time, most people got over their repugnance. The "model cookstove" became one of the great consumer status symbols of the Industrial Age, and homes developed a new focus. The typical Victorian cookstove was a cast-iron "monster" that combined a hot-water tank for boiling and hot plates to set pots and pans on with a coal-fired oven behind iron doors, the whole thing connected with "complicated arrangements of flues, their temperature controlled by a register and dampers." By the mid-nineteenth century in both Britain and the United States, the closed range or "kitchener" had become the single essential kitchen fitting in middle-class kitchens. Cooks learned that instead of building a kitchen around a fire, it could be built around an appliance, just as today's affluent kitchens are structured around brightly colored KitchenAids and gleaming Viking ranges.

At the Great Exhibition in 1851, when Britain showed off its industrial riches to the world, many kitcheners were on display. First prize went to the Improved Leamington Kitchener, an elaborate construction, which Mrs. Beeton admired. The Leamington explicitly offered to combine the twin functions of roasting and baking with a single fire. Inside was a wrought-iron roaster with a dripping pan, but this could be converted to the unventilated heat of an oven by closing the valves at the back. The Leamington could also supply gallons of boiling water. A range was never just designed to cook food; it was needed to provide hot water for the whole household, to heat up irons and warm hands.

"Leamington" was one of the first pieces of equipment to become a household name in Britain and was soon being used as shorthand for closed ranges in general. But there were plenty of competing models, many of them with patents, glamorous names ("The Coastal Grand Pacific," "The Plantress"), and fancy squiggles and curlicues on the front. These were cooking appliances as fashion statements.

The sudden popularity of the closed range went beyond style. It was driven by the materials of industrial revolution, chiefly coal and iron. There was a boom in cookstoves, not because people had read Rumford and turned against open-hearth cookery but because the market was suddenly flooded with cheap cast iron. The patent kitchen range was an ironmonger's dream: the chance to offload a great lump of iron, with added iron accessories. The rapidity with which new versions came out was an added bonus: after a couple of years, a stove might become outmoded and get traded in for a more up-to-date model, meaning more profits.

Cast-iron production had improved in the mid-eighteenth century with the discovery of a new method of production, using coal instead of charcoal. John "Iron-Mad" Wilkinson (1728–1808) pioneered the new method and produced the steam engine cylinders that hastened production even further. A generation later, cast iron was everywhere: Victorians shut themselves behind cast-iron gates, rode over cast-iron bridges, sat around cast-iron fireplaces, erected cast-iron buildings, and cooked in cast-iron kitcheners. The housekeepers and their mistresses who pored over the Smith and Wellstood catalog, wondering which model of stove to buy, may have believed that they were satisfying nothing but their own whim. But whichever fancy new design they chose, they were serving the profits of the iron industry and supporting the coal industry as well, as these new modern kitcheners were almost all fired with coal rather than wood or turf or peat.

Coal was by no means new to the British kitchen. The first coal revolution had taken place in the sixteenth century, when a shortage of wood transformed kitchens. The Elizabethan Age saw a great expansion of industry. Iron, glass, and lead manufacturing were all greedy consumers of timber. Timber was also needed for shipbuilding in the war against the Spanish, leaving far less for English hearths at home. The result was that many kitchens, particularly in towns, reluctantly converted to "seacoal," so named because it was transported by sea.

The move from wood to coal brought with it other changes. The medieval wood fire was really an indoor bonfire, with nothing but some andirons (or brand-irons) to stop the burning logs from rolling forward onto the floor. It was a hazardous form of cooking. In the seventh century, the Saxon archbishop Theodore pronounced that "if a woman place her infant by the hearth, and the man put water in the cauldron, and it boil over and the child be scalded to death, the woman must do penance for her negligence but the man is acquitted of blame." Aside from the injustice of this, it speaks of a world in which children of two or three were at high risk of toddling into hot fires and cauldrons. Women were at risk, too, because of their long, trailing dresses. Medieval coroners' reports listing accidental deaths indicate that women were more likely to die accidentally in the home than anywhere else. Little girls died at open hearths playing with pots and pans, copying their mothers.

The combination of wood-timbered houses and open hearths made kitchen fires a common occurrence. The most famous kitchen fire in British history was the blaze starting in the small hours of September 2, 1666, at the King's bakery, Pudding Lane, which set off the Great Fire of London. When the city was rebuilt in brick, the new houses had coal-burning grates.

One of the effects of a switch to coal was to enclose the fire—at least a little. Coal needs a container, in the form of a metal grate, called a "chamber grate" or "cole baskett." The switch from down-hearth wood fires to grated coal fires was accompanied by a whole new battery of equipment. The new fires needed cast-iron firebacks to protect the wall from the fierce heat and complex fire cranes to swing pots over the fire and off again. The other great change brought about by coal was the chimney. The great increase in chimneys in Elizabeth's reign resulted largely from the increased use of coal, because wider flues were needed to carry away the noxious fumes of the coal as it burned. In fact, as Rumford observed, this combination of very wide chimneys and blazing roasting fires was deadly. When Pehr Kalm arrived in London from Sweden in the eighteenth century, he found the "coal-smoke" from cooking "very annoying," and wondered if it was responsible for the high incidence of lung disease in England. He developed a terrible cough, which only abated when he left the city.

Not everyone switched to coal. In the countryside and in the northern counties, the norm remained the old down-hearth wood fire. Meanwhile, the poorest families in both city and country muddled by as best they could with whatever fuel was at hand: handfuls of dry heather, twigs gathered from the hedgerows, cattle dung. Not for them the shiny new patent cookstoves.

It is debatable whether being unable to afford a coal kitchener was a great loss. The closed range in this particular form had many disadvantages and few real benefits over an open fire. Unlike Rumford's ideal closed hearths built of brick, many early ranges were badly constructed, belching coke fumes. A letter of 1853 to the *Expositor* called them "poison machines," drawing attention to the recent deaths of three people from inhaling their fumes. And besides that danger, many of the ranges were inefficient. Promoters of American cookstoves claimed they would save around 50–90 percent of fuel compared with an open hearth, but this did not take into account the heat wasted. A good stove needs to insulate heat as well as conduct it. There was a fundamental problem in using all that highly conductive iron, which absorbed vast amounts of heat and then radiated it back out into the kitchen rather than into the food, leaving the poor cook in a furnacelike atmosphere of heat, ash dust, and soot.

The cast-iron kitchen range was one of those curious technologies that became an object of consumer desire without offering much real improvement on what came before. It didn't save labor—quite the opposite, in many cases. Getting a fire started was no easier in a stove than on a hearth, and polishing and cleaning the range was practically a full-time job, whether for a servant or a wife. As late as 1912, a housewife married to a policeman listed her daily duties relating to the range:

1. Remove fender and fire-irons.

2. Rake out all the ashes and cinders; first throw in some damp tea-leaves to keep down the dust.

3. Sift the cinders.

4. Clean the flues.

5. Remove all grease from the stove with newspaper.

6. Polish the steels with bathbrick and paraffin.

7. Blacklead the iron parts and polish.

8. Wash the hearthstone and polish it.

All this work and not a single dish has been prepared; not a rasher of bacon has been fried, not a potato boiled. Unlucky woman. If only she had been born a few years later, she might have been spared it all. She would almost certainly have gotten a gas oven.

Our domestic lives are all composed of hundreds of small, daily, recurring activities, nowhere more so than in the kitchen. The devices that are truly revolutionary are not the ones that enable us to make entirely new creations—air-drying strawberries or vacuum-cooking rare cuts of venison—but the ones that let us do the things we already do with greater ease, better results, and more pleasure: making family breakfast more speedily for less money and far less trouble, for example. The gas range was a rare breakthrough: a tool offering real progress in the kitchen.

Compared to a coal range, gas was cleaner, pleasanter, and cheaper: it was estimated that for a middle-class English family, the cost of cooking with gas was around 2-1/2 pence a day, as against 7 pence to 1 shilling for coal. The real joy of gas, however, was the work it saved. The early cooks who learned to prepare meals using gas in the 1880s went into rhapsodies over how much easier life had become. A simple job such as cooking the morning breakfast took far less "time and attention" than under the old system. Mrs. H. M. Young, who wrote one of the first cookbooks to include a section on gas, noted that "a breakfast for a medium family, say, coffee, chops, steaks or bacon, eggs and toast, may be prepared easily in 15 minutes."

As is so often the case, the innovation was initially met with suspicion and resistance. There was a time lag of nearly a century between the first experiments in gas cookery and its adoption by a wider public. The same cooks who toiled in the tropical heat and filth of a coal-fire range feared that gas was a dangerous form of cooking, which would make the food taste and smell disgusting. Although increasingly happy to light their homes with coal gas—London was the first city to be lit by gas, in 1814—people feared they would either be poisoned or die an explosion if they cooked with it. Servants were said to be scared senseless by gas ovens.

Perhaps some of the prejudice was justified, insofar as the earliest models of gas oven were badly ventilated and the burners did not always give an even flow of gas, which did indeed result in some gassy-tasting food. But the prejudices continued long after gas cookery had become safe and reliable. Ellen Youl, a working-class housewife from Northampton, acquired a gas stove at the end of the nineteenth century. Ellen's husband reacted with horror.

He thought the gas contained poison and refused to eat anything cooked by it. Ellen, however, would not get rid of her new labour-saving contrivance. She cooked his dinner every day in the gas stove, transferring it to the open fire a few minutes before he returned from work.

The very first experiments in gas cooking had an element of scientific showmanship, as if to highlight the novelty. The first commercial gas cooking apparatus sold in Britain appeared in 1824, produced by the Aetna Ironworks. It looked a bit like a horizontal squash racket, fashioned from gunmetal and pierced with holes, through which the gas jets flowed creating open flames. There was no surrounding oven or cooktop: you just placed it under whatever you wanted to cook to create a heat source, like a Bunsen burner. It would be another half a century before gas cooking became widespread, despite the attempts of Alexis Soyer, the Victorian celebrity chef, who marketed a very expensive and fancy gas stove called the Phidomageiron that boasted the impossibility of "explosion ever taking place." This didn't entirely reassure. Many people must have shared the opinion of Thomas Webster (author of the *Domestic Encyclopedia*) in 1844 that gas cookery was simply "an elegant culinary toy," an addition to the "usual means of cooking" rather than a replacement for it.

It was only in the 1880s that manufacturers—notably, William Sugg, whose family cornered the market in gas stoves for some time—finally started producing equipment accessible enough to convert the staunchest coal-range user. Sugg gas ranges looked remarkably like coal ranges, and they came with the same type of fanciful names: the Westminster, the Cordon Bleu, the Parisienne. Reassuringly, for lovers of an old English roast, meat cooked in the oven was still suspended over a dripping pan, reminiscent of an old open fire. The Sugg company came up with a good solution to quell the fear of explosions, fitting all the burners with flash lights to light them with the turn of a knob, avoiding the need for matches.

The 1880s also saw the spread of the penny-in-the-slot gas meter, which made gas cookery affordable for all but the very poorest in areas with gas supplies. Gas companies installed the meters free of charge and also rented out ovens for a modest quarterly cost. Subscriptions increased rapidly. In 1884, the Newcastle-upon-Tyne and Gateshead Gas Company rented out just ninety-five gas stoves; by 1920, the number had increased to 16,110. By 1901, one in three British households had a gas stove; by 1939, on the brink of World War II, three-fourths of households cooked with gas. In other words, the majority of people were finally liberated from what had been one of the defining activities of human life, the business of starting and maintaining a fire.

By this point, gas ovens had a challenge in the form of electricity.

Thomas Edison first created a successful light bulb in 1879, but electric cooking was much slower to take off, hampered by the expense of early electric stoves and the limited availability of an electricity supply. The Science Museum in London has in its collection the earliest surviving electric oven, consisting of a cookie tin joined to a large light bulb with some coils of wire. It does not look very promising. In 1890, the General Electric Company started selling an electric cooking device, claiming it could boil a pint of water in twelve minutes—which only serves to bring home just how slow much cooking was in the era of coal fires.

Electric cooking only became normal—both in Europe and the States—in the late 1920s, as the price of electric cookers decreased and their efficiency improved. Early electric ovens took ages to preheat—as much as thirty-five minutes in 1914—and the heating elements had a tendency to burn out. And they were expensive both to buy and to run. An average family might buy an electric kettle or toaster but had little incentive to upgrade a gas oven to an electric one. The electric refrigerator performed functions that simply did not exist before. The electric oven was less revolutionary (its only real advantage before the invention of inbuilt safety devices to cut off an unlit flame was that you couldn't gas yourself in one). Its great benefit—of providing cooking heat that could be switched on and off at will—had already been achieved by the wonders of gas. By 1948, 86 percent of households in Britain used electricity in some form. But only 19 percent owned an electric stove.

Now, like many, I cook using a combination of gas and electric. My oven is an electric convection type (using a small fan to circulate air better) with a separate grilling oven on top. It does the job OK. I put in flat cake mixture; it comes out risen. It roasts potatoes evenly enough, and I can peer through the glass door to make sure nothing is scorching. But I feel nothing like the same affection for it that I feel when cooking at my gas cooktop, which offers all the benefits of fire and none of the drawbacks. The few times I have cooked on an electric induction cooktop, it has driven me to despair: the flat surface, an invitation to chubby little fingers to burn themselves. One minute it is stone cold, then suddenly and seemingly without warning it is red hot (though admittedly I haven't used the very latest generation of induction cooktops, which are currently being trumpeted as the last word in efficient heat). Gas does my bidding. When I hear that *click-click-click*, waiting for the flame to light, I know good things will happen. In 2008, the Chinese food writer Ching-He Huang offered some sound advice on wok cookery to people who did not have a gas cooktop: "Invest in a new stove!"

Apart from the original invention of cooking, gas-powered heat was the single greatest improvement ever to occur in kitchen technology. It liberated millions from the pollution, discomfort, and sheer time-wasting of looking after a fire. A further step away from the open hearth came with the microwave oven, though this time the benefits—both culinary and social—were less straightforward. Today, with new markets in China just opening up, global microwave sales stand at around 50 million a year. In many small city kitchens the world over, a microwave is the major way of applying heat to food. Cooks clearly do a lot of microwave cooking. Yet it remains a controversial tool that has never inspired the love we once felt for fire.

The microwave is not always given enough credit for the many things it does exceptionally well. It can cook fish so that it stays moist and make old-fashioned steamed puddings in minutes. It is a nifty device for caramelizing sugar with minimal mess and for gently melting dark chocolate without it seizing up. It cooks perfect fluffy Basmati rice effortlessly. The attraction of microwaves for fat molecules makes it the ideal way to de-fat ducks and spare ribs before roasting, as Barbara Kafka notes in her 1987 opus, *Microwave Gourmet*, the most persuasive case ever made for the microwave as an instrument of pleasure.

Yet the microwave is just as likely to inspire thoughts of panic as pleasure. These "fireless ovens," as they were initially called, seemed baffling objects when they were first sold in the 1950s, and many cooks remain baffled and alarmed by them today. The invention came in 1945 from Percy Spencer of the Raytheon Company, an engineer who was working on military radar systems, trying to improve the magnetron, a vacuum tube for generating microwaves. Various mythical stories are told of the moment when Spencer first noticed that the magnetron generated enough heat to cook. In one version, he was leaning against an open waveguard—the tube through which waves travel—when he noticed that the chocolate bar in his pocket had melted. Others say he stared, amazed, as an egg exploded and cooked itself; or that he left his lunchtime sandwich on the magnetron and returned to find it cooked. The team of engineers who worked alongside Spencer later said that the truth was less dramatic: it took a series of methodical observations by several people rather than one man's eureka moment to hatch the microwave oven. However it happened, it took a huge leap of imagination on the part of Spencer and his team to think that the magnetron, this vast metal cylinder, could be used not in the field of war but in a kitchen. The QK707 magnetron used in very early models weighed a colossal 26.5 pounds, as against the 1.5 pounds of a standard modern microwave. Spencer showed still more imagination in realizing immediately what would be one of the microwave's most popular uses:

making popcorn. An illustration on Spencer's second microwave patent showed how an entire ear of husked corn could be seasoned with butter and salt, placed in a waxed paper bag and turned into popcorn in just "20 to 45 seconds." In 1945, this seemed highly unlikely; and indeed it would be another two decades before the domestic microwave oven was a mainstream proposition (sales only took off in 1967, when manufacturers managed to get the price of an oven below $500).

Many consumers still find the microwave an unlikely way to cook. It seems a step too far away from fire to be anything good. For a long time it was feared on health grounds. It is true that older models sometimes leaked more than $10mW/cm2$ of radiation, compared to the new, extremely stringent standards of $1mW/cm2$. But in either case, it was vastly less "radiation" than you would be exposed to simply by standing around two feet from a fireplace ($50mW/cm2$). Based on all the evidence to date, the microwave is innocent of health hazards, beyond the dangers of cooking with it, such as small objects exploding in "hot spots." You can avoid most of these just by reading the instruction manual.

Lying behind the periodic microwave health scares is a more fundamental suspicion of the device as a method of cooking. In 1998, a Mintel market report on microwaves in the UK found that 10 percent of consumers doggedly insisted that they would "never buy a microwave oven." Until very recently, I was part of that 10 percent. I was age 36 before I acquired my first one, having been brought up to believe that there was something weird about cooking "from the inside out." In my family, we viewed the microwave as only slightly less malign than nuclear bombs. How could "zapping" food possibly result in anything good?

Microwave cooking seems inexplicable in a way that other cooking methods do not. This is unfair. Microwaving does not in fact cook from the inside out as I'd always been told. There is nothing paranormal about it. Microwaved food obeys the same laws of physics as a spit roast. Microwaves travel quickly, but they only penetrate food by around 4–5 cm (which is why small pieces cook best in a microwave). Fat, sugar, and water molecules in the food attract the microwaves, causing them to jump around very fast. These vibrations produce heat within the food. Beyond 4–5 cm, the heat spreads by conduction to the rest of the food—just as it would in a frying pan. Unlike in a frying pan, where food develops a lovely golden crust, microwaved food does not brown (though some models have browning functions to compensate).

You cannot roast in a microwave, nor make bread. But no cooking tool can do everything, no matter what the manufacturers may say. It is no more of an argument against the microwave to say it can't roast than to say of a bread oven that it's too hot for making custard. The real drawback of the microwave is not with the device itself but with how it is used. The microwave had the misfortune to be first marketed in the era of postwar convenience food. "Reheating" rather than cooking food is the most common use of the microwave, according to a 1989 UK market report: 84 percent of households used it for reheating precooked food, whereas 34 percent used it for all cooking. "I don't actually cook with it," said one focus group participant, "just warm things up." In most kitchens, the microwave is not used as a form of cooking, but as a way of avoiding cooking, by slinging a frozen precooked meal in and waiting mindlessly for the beep. The microwave provided a way to eat hot food without the sociability of sitting around a family table. Most microwaves are not big enough to cook for more than one or two at once.

Is it the end of social life as we know it? Historian Felipe Fernández-Armesto excoriates the microwave as a device with the power to change society in a malign way, by returning us to a pre-social phase of evolution. It is as if we never discovered fire. Throughout history, we have sought to enclose and control fire, this focus of our social lives. We tamed it with rock hearths; we built great halls around it; we enclosed it in metal grates; we shut it off in cast-iron ranges; we submitted it to our will with the gas oven. Finally, we found a way of cooking without it in the microwave.

There are signs that we miss fire and regret its absence from our lives. The enthusiasm with which amateur cooks whip out their barbecues at the first hint of sun, singeing sausages over the fire, implies that perhaps our cooking has lost its focus. No one sits around a microwave telling stories deep into the night. Its angular glass frontage cannot warm our hands or our hearts. Perhaps all is not lost, however. The process of cooking has a power to draw people together even when it does not follow the conventional old patterns. Those who believe that a microwave cannot be a focus for a home like the old hearth have never seen a group of children, huddled together in silent wonder, waiting for a bag of microwave popcorn to finish popping, like hunter-gatherers around the flame.

Toaster

Making toast is satisfying. You could say that's because it's such a comforting substance—the crispness, the heavenly aroma as yellow butter slowly melts into the crevices. But the satisfaction is also mechanical and childish: fitting the slices in the slots, setting the timer, and waiting for a ping or a pop.

For something so basic, the electric toaster arrived late. From the 1890s, gadget-crazy late Victorians could in theory use electricity to boil kettles and fry eggs, yet for toast they still relied on the toasting forks and gridirons of open-hearth cookery. These were variations on the theme of prongs and baskets for holding bread (or morsels of cheese and meat) before the flame. Toasting, when you think about it, is really roasting: applying dry radiant heat to something until the surface browns.

Before the electric toaster could be invented, it was necessary to find a durable metal filament strong enough to withstand roasting heats without fusing. That came in 1905 when Albert Marsh discovered Nichrome, a nickel-chromium alloy with low conductivity. Then, the US market became flooded with electric toasters. There were Pinchers, Swingers, Flatbeds, Droppers, Tippers, Perchers, and Floppers: the names refer to different manual techniques for expelling the toast.

The toaster as we know it was the invention of Charles Strite, a mechanic from Minnesota fed up with the burned cafeteria toast at work. In 1921, Strite was granted a patent for a toaster with vertical pop-up springs and a variable timer. Here was something new: a toaster that could be left to do the job itself. "You do not have to Watch it—The Toast can't Burn," insisted an ad for Strite's Toastmaster. If only. It's still possible, alas, to make burned toast in a pop-up toaster.

Twitter: Want to discuss or share what you just read? Use the hashtag #beaFORK to connect with others.

ABOUT THE AUTHOR

Bee Wilson is a food writer, historian, and author of three previous books, including *Swindled: The Dark History of Food Fraud, from Poisoned Candy to Counterfeit Coffee,* which was named a BBC 4 Book of the Week. Wilson served as the food columnist for the *New Statesman* for five years, and currently writes a weekly food column for *The Sunday Telegraph's Stella* magazine. She was named BBC Radio's Food Writer of the year in 2002, and was a Guild of Food Writers Food Journalist of the Year in 2004, 2008, and 2009. Wilson's writing has also appeared in *The Sunday Times, The Times Literary Supplement, The New Yorker,* and *The London Review of Books.* Wilson earned her PhD from Trinity College, Cambridge and also attended the University of Pennsylvania on a Thouron Award fellowship. She lives in Cambridge, UK.

Imprint: Basic Books
BEA Booth #: 3604
Printed galley at BEA: yes
Print ISBN: 978-0-465-02176-5
Print price: $26.99
eBook ISBN: 9780465033324
eBook price: $12.99
Publication date: 10/2/2012
Publicity contact: Michele Jacob Michele.Jacob@perseusbooks.com
Rights contact: Justin Lovell Justin.Lovell@perseusbooks.com
Editor: Lara Heimert
Agent: Zoe Pagnamenta
Agency: The Zoe Pagnamenta Agency
Territories sold:
World excluding UK & Commonwealth

NEIL YOUNG

WAGING HEAVY PEACE

SUMMARY

Neil Young is a singular figure in the history of rock and our overall pop culture of the last four decades. From his early days in the sixties with Buffalo Springfield to his groundbreaking solo career albums including *After the Gold Rush* and *Harvest*, to his mega-bestselling records with Crosby, Still & Nash, to his reemergence as the patron saint of grunge, Young has epitomized the uncompromising artist who follows only his heart and head. Now, in *Waging Heavy Peace*, Young presents a kaleidoscopic view of his personal life and creativity; it is a journey that spans the snows of Ontario to LSD-laden boulevards of 1966 Los Angeles to the contemplative paradise of Hawaii today. Astoundingly candid, witty and destined to become an American classic, this is the book music lovers have always wanted.

EXCERPT

I pulled back the plastic sticky tape from the cardboard box. Wrapping paper was on the ground around my feet. My son Ben watched from his chair, and Amber, my daughter, and my wife Pegi sat around me. I carefully lifted the heavy weight out of the box. It was further wrapped in packing paper and then a final layer of some foamy quarter-inch-thick protective material. Then it was revealed: a locomotive switcher with handmade Lionel markings. Curiously, it was not a real Lionel. It must have been some kind of prototype. There was a white typewritten sheet in the box from Lenny Carparelli, one of the endless stream of Italians connected in one way or another to the history of Lionel, a company I still have a small share of. I read the sheet. The model was from General Models Corporation. It was a beautiful model of a switcher. It was indeed the prototype that Lionel had used to create its own model from. As the letter pointed out, this was back in the days before corporate lawsuits and trade secrets invaded every little area of creativity and design.

Pegi always gives me Lionel collectibles for holidays, and I now have a very extensive collection of rarities, all proudly displayed behind glass in a room with a giant train layout on my Northern California ranch. It is not a normal train layout: The scenery is made up of redwood stumps for mountains and moss for grassy fields. The railroad has fallen on hard times. A drought has ensued. Track work, once accomplished by hardworking teams of Chinese laborers, has been left dormant. Now expensive, highly detailed Lionel steam engines from China traverse the tracks. The railroad is historic in its own way as the site of many electronic development programs where the Lionel command control and sound systems were conceived and built from scratch, then the prototypes were tested and the software was written, tested, rewritten, and retested. Heady stuff, this electronics development.

It all started with Ben Young. Ben was born a quadriplegic, and I was just getting back into trains at the time, reintroducing myself to a pastime I had enjoyed as a child. Sharing the building of the layout with Ben is one of the happiest times. He was still in his little bassinet when the Chinese laborers originally laid the track, thousands of them toiling endless hours through the nights and days. He watched as we worked. Then, after months, it eventually came time to run the trains, and later I devised a switch system run by a big red button that he could work with his hand. It took a lot of effort, but it was very rewarding to see the cause and effect in action. Ben was empowered by this. My friend and studio maintenance engineer Harry Sitam was responsible for actually building the devices, electronic switching mechanisms that turned the power on and off at the touch of a button. A selector enabled momentary or toggle action. Harry was a huge help.

That was thirty-three years ago, though, and now I have the Windex out and I am cleaning the glass doors on the display shelves where my prized Lionel possessions are kept safe and sound for all to see. Not that anybody ever comes here. You could count the visitors on your hand. Relatively speaking, that is, to the amount of care that has gone into the display. The display and layout are a Zen experience. They allow me to sift through the chaos, the songs, the people, and the feelings from my upbringing that still haunt me today. Not in a bad way, but not in an entirely good way, either. Months go by with boxes piled everywhere and trains derailed with dust gathering on them. Then miraculously I reappear and clean and organize, working with every little detail for hours on end, making it all run perfectly again. This seems to coincide with other creative processes.

I remember one day David Crosby and Graham Nash were visiting me at the train barn during the recording of *American Dream*, which we did a lot of on my ranch at Plywood Digital, a barn that was converted to a recording studio. We had a truck parked outside full of recording equipment and were working on several new songs. We were all pretty excited about playing together again. David had recently gotten straight, was recovering from his addiction to freebase, had recently completed jail time having to do with a loaded weapon in Texas, and was still prone to taking naps between takes. His system was pretty much in shock, and he was doing the best he could because he loves the band and the music so much. There is no one I know who loves making music more than David Crosby. Graham Nash has been his best friend for years, through thick and thin, and they sing together in a way that shows the depth of their long relationship.

They met in the Hollies and the Byrds, two seminal bands in the history of rock and roll, and then came together with Stephen Stills to form Crosby, Stills & Nash around 1970. Their first record is a work of art, defining a sound that has been imitated for years by other groups, some of which have enjoyed even greater commercial success, but there can be no mistaking the groundbreaking nature of that first CSN record. Stephen played most of the music, overdubbing all the parts into the night with Dallas Taylor and Graham. There was so much he had wanted to do with Buffalo Springfield, like producing, writing, and arranging harmonies, as well as playing more guitar, and that was his first opportunity to be really creative after Springfield ended, and he went for it big-time.

Anyway, I saw David looking at one of my train rooms full of rolling stock and stealing a glance at Graham that said *This guy is cuckoo. He's gone nuts. Look at this obsession.* I shrugged it off. I need it. For me it is a road back.

So now I'm polishing the glass on one of the display shelves that house my collection. With the glass all cleaned and sparkling, I stand in the room alone and admire the beautiful Lionel models, all perfectly lined up in an order that only I understand.

I leave that building and walk about 150 feet over to Feelgood's Garage. Feelgood's is full of my amps, old Fenders mostly, but also some Magnatones, Marshalls, and the odd Gibson. I remember my first Fender amp: I got it as a gift from my mom. She always supported my music. It was a piggyback model. The amp was on top of the speaker cabinet. Two ten-inch speakers delivered the whopping sound of the smallest piggyback amp Fender ever made. But to me it was HUGE. Before that I had an Ampeg Echo Twin. I used to dream about amps and stage setups in school, drawing diagrams and planning stage layouts. I didn't do real well in those classes.

Feelgood's has cars, too. I have a transportation thing. Cars, boats, trains. Traveling. I like moving. Once when I was walking along a street in LA at age twenty-two or twenty-three, I saw a place called Al Axelrod's. It was a car repair place. There was a red convertible's rear end poking out of the garage. I recognized it as a '53 or '54 Buick. One of my dad's friends, the author Robertson Davies, lived near us in Peterborough, Ontario, and we used to go to his house every Christmas and play charades at a party. He had a bunch of daughters. Very exciting. Anyway, he also had a '54 Buick. It was brand-new and made a large impression on me with its beautifully designed grille, taillights, and an overall shape that featured a kind of bump or ripple in the lines at about the midpoint, accentuated by a chrome strip that mirrored it. This ripple emanated from the rear wheel's circular well and was unique to Buicks. So I went inside Al Axelrod's and saw my first Buick Skylark. That really blew my mind. Only about five hundred were ever made! It was custom chopped at the factory about the same time as GM introduced the Eldorado and the Corvette. I looked for a Skylark for years, and finally John McKieg found one in a body shop in Pleasanton, California.

John was a Vietnam vet who was taking care of my cars. He was an excellent body and paint man. I had him do a job for me and then I hired him to come and work for me, taking care of the thirty-five cars I had acquired by then. All of them were wild designs. Mostly '50s; a lot of Cadillacs. I was not overly interested in their mechanical condition when I bought them, just wanted those unique shapes. Later that turned out to have been a big mistake, because most of them didn't run well and took a lot of time and money to restore. It would have been better and less expensive to just get original cars in excellent condition. Anyway, after years and years of collecting, I sold a lot of them and just kept the good ones. Most of them were right there in Feelgood's. The best in my collection is a 1953 Buick Skylark, the one that John found, body number one. The first one ever made. That is the big Kahuna.

So here I am at Feelgood's, looking at my cars and a conference table with a whiteboard. Tomorrow is a big meeting with Alex, the venture capitalist who works for Len Blavatnik, the new owner of WMG, my record company. The reason for the meeting is my new start-up company, PureTone. At least, that's what we're calling it this week. It's very early, and we are still changing names. The company is designed to rescue my art form, music, from the degradation in quality that I think is at the heart of the decline of music sales and ultimately music itself in popular culture. With the advent of online music iTunes has come terrible quality. An MP3 has less than 5 percent of the data found in a PureTone master file or a vinyl record. I have an idea to build a portable player and online distribution model to present a quality alternative to MP3s with the convenience today's consumers demand. I want to bring the soul of the music industry and the technology of Silicon Valley together to create this new model, using artists as the driver. My goal is to restore an art form and protect the original art, while serving quality to the music lover.

Tomorrow is the big presentation day, and I am going over my approach, which is guided by PureTone CEO candidate Mark Goldstein, who is a start-up specialist introduced to me by Magdalena Yesil and Marc Benioff, two friends of mine from the Silicon Valley community.

These two are both brilliant and very successful. Unlike myself, they have mastered the art of monetizing their ideas. I have big ideas and very little money to show for it. I'm not complaining, though. It's not the money that matters; it's doing things right and efficiently that is my goal. I just want to succeed at this so badly. I dislike what has happened to the quality of the sound of music; there is little depth or feeling left, and people can't get what they need from listening to music anymore, so it is dying. That is my theory.

Recording is my first love in the field of creativity, along with songwriting and music making, so this really cuts to the quick. I want to do something about it. So it is important that I get my thoughts together, impress this gentleman, and get some financial backing for this project, which will surely need it. My Skylark is right here with me.

Twitter: Want to discuss or share what you just read? Use the hashtag #beaPEACE to connect with others.

ABOUT THE AUTHOR

Neil Young's music and songwriting—which spans forty years and thirty-four studio albums of rock 'n' roll, folk and country with shadings of blues, techno and other styles—is one of the most enduring and popular in modern times. From his early days with Buffalo Springfield through his solo career and collaborations with Crosby, Stills & Nash, Crazy Horse and dozens of other notable musicians and groups, Young is acclaimed for both his musical talents and artistic integrity. With a major hit in every decade since the sixties, Young was inducted into the Rock and Roll Hall of Fame twice (as a solo artist in 1995 and as a member of Buffalo Springfield in 1997). A well-known political activist, environmentalist, and philanthropist, Young has been involved in several causes, notably co-founding Farm Aid and The Bridge School, which assists children with severe physical impairments and complex communication needs.

Imprint: Blue Rider Press
BEA Booth #: 3922
Author appearances: Special Events Hall at BEA on Wednesday, June 6 at Noon for an interview about the book.
Print ISBN: 9780399159463
Print price: $30.00
eBook ISBN: 9781101594094
eBook price: $14.99
Publication date: 10/2/2012

Publicity contact: Aileen M. Boyle aileen.boyle@us.penguingroup.com
Rights contact: Leigh Butler leigh.butler@us.penguingroup.com
Hal Fessenden hal.fessenden@us.penguingroup.com
Editor: David Rosenthal
Agent: Elliott Roberts
Agency: Lookout Management
Territories sold:
  Penguin UK
  Kiepenheuer (German)
  Editions Robert Laffont (French)
  Bruna (Dutch)
  Editora Globo (Portuguese- Brazil)
  Giangiacomo Feltrinellie (Italian)
  Global Rhythm Press (Spanish)
  Byakuya Shobo (Japanese)
  Like Publishing (Finnish)
  Schibsted Forlag (Norwegian)
  Norstedts Forlag (Swedish)
  Politikens Forlag (Danish)
  NLN (Czech)
Promotional Information:
• National author publicity including television, radio, online and print

IRIS ANTHONY

the

RUINS

of

LACE

A NOVEL OF FRANCE, FREEDOM,
and FORBIDDEN LACE

SUMMARY

Lace is a thing like hope. It is beauty; it is grace. It was never meant to destroy so many lives.

The mad passion for forbidden lace has infiltrated France, pulling soldier and courtier alike into its web. For those who want the best, Flemish lace is the only choice, an exquisite perfection of thread and air. For those who want something they don't have, Flemish lace can buy almost anything or anyone.

For Lisette, lace begins her downfall, and the only way to atone for her sins is to outwit the noble who now demands the impossible. To fail means certain destruction. But for Katharina, lace is her salvation. It is who she is; it is what she does. If she cannot make this stunning tempest of threads, a dreaded fate awaits.

The most lucrative contraband in Europe, with its intricate patterns and ephemeral hope, threatens to cost them everything. Lace may be the deliverance for which they all pray or it may bring the ruin and imprisonment they all fear.

EXCERPT

CHAPTER 1 Katharina Martens

Lendelmolen, Flanders

As I sat there with my pillow in my lap, the threads performed their intricate dance, leaping and jumping in a counterpoint about their pins. Each group of bobbins clattered to their own rhythm before I dropped them to the pillow to pick up the next. With a twist or a cross, more than two hundred threads danced around the circle before I dropped the last group and started once more with the first.

It amazed me, as it always had, that I should sit with my bobbins, day after day. And that they should perform their dance with so little help from me. Like the fairies my sister used to speak of, they completed their magic seemingly undirected and undeterred by human hands. Except, I *did* direct them. I *did* move them. In fact, they moved only at my command. But once I set them into motion, they seemed to dance alone. I used to watch, breathless, every day, waiting to see what they would create.

I knew, of course.

They would create the kind of lace they created every day, the lace that was named for the abbey: Lendelmolen. That was the only kind of lace we had been taught to make. We'd seen the other kinds. Sister had showed them to us so we could understand how superior our patterns were. But this lace, this length, was different. It was to be fabulously long. Six yards. The exquisite scrolls and roses and leaves had been inscribed by a pattern maker upon a parchment. Pins now marked that design, securing the pattern to my pillow.

But there was a difference between knowing what the bobbins would create and watching them go about their work. It was in the watching that the magic happened.

Of course, I never spoke of the magic. Not to the nuns.

Not to anyone.

Nowhere, at any time within the walls of the abbey, could I speak. Unless it was to God. And even then, we were to speak in whispers. God was a jealous god. He needed our hands. He needed our thoughts… and our voices. They were reserved, all of them, every part of us, for Him.

And why should it have been any other way?

Except…I had never heard the voice of Mathild. And I had sat beside her as we worked, for twenty-five years.

Those first years, the years of learning, had been the most difficult. Learning what was expected of us and learning what was not. Learning how to please the Sister in charge of the workshop. Learning how to avoid a beating or a whipping.

And those first whippings…they came so unexpectedly, so brutally, for a sin no greater than a dropped pillow or a missed stitch. So viciously and so cruelly, a girl would be stripped to her waist and punished right in front of us. In front of all of us.

It served its purpose, I suppose.

It goaded us into concentration. But unavoidably, I too dropped my pillow. I too missed a stitch. And strayed from the pattern. I did not think often of those times. So much sadness, so much misery. I had sought the skirts of the Holy Mother herself on one occasion, hiding behind her statue in the chapel. Once I had been coaxed away from her, I was lucky to have survived the beating I was given. But it was then, in the midst of those dim-lit days and lonely nights, that I was taught how to make myself useful. It was then I learned the secrets of lace. And how could I truly despair when I knew, every day upon waking, that in the workshop my lace awaited?

I could survive a scolding, could suffer through a beating, always knowing I had my lace. I couldn't mind stinging buttocks or a blood-ied back when my fingers were left untouched for work and my eyes could still see. It was the times when they rapped our knuckles that were the worst. For then we were left bleeding and bruised, forbidden to leave the workshop, but forbidden also to work. If punishment was doled out for failure—failure to concentrate, to keep the lace clean, to master the skills—the lace itself offered its own sort of reward.

To see it created.

To watch it unfurl.

To glimpse a pattern perfectly followed, perfectly accomplished.

I would rather have been whipped to the grave than been kept from my work.

But that had been back when I could see. Now that solitary pleasure had been denied me.

Perhaps in those early days, now that I think on it, I had heard Mathild speak once or twice. But I did not remember her words. To speak brought certain punishment. And so, we had avoided each other's gaze to avoid the temptation to talk. And soon we began, all of us, to sleep with an arm across the face…to ensure that, even in sleep, we would remain guiltless.

But I *had* seen Mathild smile.

And once, I had even seen her wink.

But speak? I could hardly remember those few words.

When would I have heard them? At prayers, we whispered our petitions to the Most Holy God. At meals, we ate. During washing, we washed. And when making lace? Making lace required everything we had. And by the time we collapsed onto our beds, there was nothing left within us. We were quickly consumed by sleep.

Of course, I had heard others talk.

The nuns spoke all the time.

I knew the voice of my teacher: Sister Maria-Clementia. She spoke very little, but when she bent over my pillow to inspect my lace, her "Well done" was like a song of a thousand words. And her "Rework this" could echo through my mind for days. There was no great need for words here. Not when so very few would do. And even when I talked to God, there was little to say. I said, "Thank you," for it was He who had placed me here. I said, "Help me, please," for who did not need help with such difficult work? But mostly, I said…nothing. For what could a poor girl say to such a great and holy God that did not begin and end with gratitude?

But…I had a secret. I stored up words. I hoarded them, treasured them.

Words were my vice, my greatest weakness. Since I had discovered their great rarity, I remembered every one I heard.

They formed a pattern in my head, and in the spaces between them, I imagined the lives of their speakers. My one regret is how few of my mother's I remembered. But I could not have known, not while she was living, how precious few she would be able to give me.

She had talked often…so many lovely words. They came back to me sometimes in my sleep, like a length of *punto in aria* lace. Vast spaces of nothing, and then, suddenly, the outline of an intricate pattern. It was all the more beautiful for its spare design. Her words had the lightness of a butterfly. They were always dancing. Always followed by laughter. At least…that is how it seems to me now.

But perhaps I have distorted the pattern in transferring it to my memories. For what followed after her death was so… bleak. When she had been alive, there were words, nothing but words, in our house, and then after…silence reigned over all.

I remember only two words from my father. Perhaps he gave me more than those two…certainly he probably did while my mother was living…. but the only two I remember are the last ones he spoke to me.

Fare well.

Only those two words remain, and they are underscored by sorrow. They hang heavily in my heart. He died five years after I was committed to the abbey. Those two words are all I have left of him, but two words are not enough to make a pattern.

Fare well.

Was it a blessing? A wish? A hope?

Perhaps it was a sort of benediction. I do not know.

My sister, Heilwich…well, she has words enough for the both of us. And the words she gives me are more than enough to last the week between her visits. She speaks of her life, of the priest whose home she keeps, of her good works. Her pattern is *torchon*. Regular, repeating. Competent. Her design makes a sturdy lace. Not fancy, not frivolous. Respectable. Dependable.

And I imagine her life to be just that way.

But I have more than just family from whom to collect words.

I have the people walking by the workshop, past the abbey wall, on the street outside.

There is one man who walks the streets, shouting every day. He sells fish. And he does it especially loudly on Fridays. He shouts everything about them. How large they are, how fresh they are. He sells sole and plaice. Eels and herrings. Sometimes they cost more, and sometimes they cost less. And sometimes he sells something called a mussel. But only in the winter. I've always wondered what it looked like, a mussel.

But then, I had always wondered what he looked like as well.

His words were not fancy; they created an ordinary *malines* design. His pattern was the same, day after day, fish after fish. There were few holes, few gaps, from which to pattern a life apart from the street beyond the wall. I imagined he woke with fish and he worked with fish, and when he slept, he dreamt of fish.

It was what I did too…only with lace, of course. I understood a life like his. Except…How did he come by them? That great variety of fish? And how did he carry them? For certain by cart, for I could hear the wheels tumble across the cobbles. But…how? Tossed together in a great pile? Separated into baskets?

And where did he live?

What did he wear? The holes in his pattern were tiny, but they were there, nonetheless. His was a life set upon a platform of a fine network of threads.

There was also a woman who shouted in the streets beyond the wall. But she didn't shout about something. She shouted *at* something. Was it a child? She shouted at someone called Pieter, who always seemed to be making a mess of things.

But what kind of mess was it?

Was he a child who rubbed his hands in the ashes of a fire…and then spread the soot about the house? That would make a mess. The worst kind of mess I could imagine.

She also shouted at someone else called Mies. And Mies always made her late.

But late to what? Where was she going, this woman who seemed to have nothing to do but walk the length of the streets, shouting all day? What was Mies doing to make her late, and how could Mies do whatever it was all day long, every day? And if it was always the same thing Mies did, then why did the woman not stop it from being done?

There was a pattern to this woman that made no sense, huge holes in the design of her life. Hers was a lace made of cutwork. Not dainty, not fragile. Without subtlety, it was bold in the extreme. A pattern without any elegance at all, and one which kept repeating. That lace was one of my least favorite kinds.

There were others out there on the street besides. I could hear them walking and running. And hear the sounds of their voices talking. But those people did not shout, and so I knew nothing of the actual words they said.

There were babies who cried.

And once, there had been a shriek. A howl.

The wordless sound of grief: black lace. The worst kind to make. The kind I made as a child, new to the abbey. After being dyed its dark color, it would not show soiling. We could make it imperfectly, for the color hid our sins. We made it fast, though never for commission. It was for immediate consumption. For who could know when a soul might die?

No one thought of black lace—no one wanted to think of it—but somehow, we never seemed to be able to make enough of it. But to make a lace no one ever wanted? Those days, those laces…they were sad. And so was that howl.

So at times, I suppose, one word…one wordless sound… could create a pattern. It could tell a story…but some laces are not worth imagining.

Far better, far better, to keep my thoughts to what I knew. And what I knew best, the only thing I knew at all, was lace. The abbey had been kind enough to take me as a child from my motherless family, even though I knew how to do nothing at all. They had fed me; they had taught me. They had allowed me a chance to redeem myself. To prove myself worthy of the life I had been given. And so I worked, I labored, as one who would not be ashamed. *Nee:* one who could not be ashamed. When God looked down on what it was I had done, I knew the only thing He could say was this: *well done.*

My eyes strained through the darkness, trying—and failing—to discern one thread from another. In a short time we would be allowed a candle, but for now, my fairy dance continued, unaided, unfettered, by my lack of sight. As we worked, we waited. Waited in anticipation, just as we waited in the chapel to receive the Host.

Soon, Sister placed a single candle on a table before us. And then she began positioning the condensers. Clear glass balls filled with water, they focused the candle's light and then sent it forth. Around the table she went, adjusting each one so it cast a narrow beam of light upon each pillow.

With much gratitude, we repositioned our work into that light.

When I could still see well, it had been more difficult to work after the shadows of night fell. The pillow had to be constantly adjusted to follow the flickering of the candle's light. Now, it didn't matter. I could work in darkness as if it were the brightest of noondays. I had memorized my pattern. But still, I had to concentrate.

Think too much, and I would muddle up the bobbins. Think too little, and I would lose my place in the pattern. In my head, I sung a little tune the sisters had chanted when I was a child. And quick as that, the dance regained its rhythm and its grace.

I sung it to myself over and over, again and again. Who knows how many times I sung it, until at last, Sister said the word: *Done.*

My prayers that night were wordless.

My supper, tasteless.

My sleep, dreamless.

CHAPTER 5 Lisette Lefort

Château of Souboscq

The province of Gascogne, France

I saw it again, in my dreams. That exquisite, fabulous lace. I marveled at the meticulous and perfect regularity of its pattern, the gorgeous repeating roses. My fingers itched to stroke its luster. And, oh, how I admired the lavish folds of those cuffs. They reminded me of *Maman*, and I wanted them.

I wanted her.

She too had worn cuffs of lace. They had not been so grand; there had hardly been a flounce to them at all. But seeing that pair brought to mind her cool, gentle touch and the way her hands always seemed to be dancing along to the rhythm of her words.

But *Maman*'s hands had been stilled when she died of lung fever. And her cuffs had been entombed with her. She lived now only in my dreams.

Such sweet, though fleeting, dreams.

I watched as my seven-year-old self entered our guest's chamber, shuffling through the rushes on the tips of her toes. I saw her kneel beside the visitor's trunk and slowly open the lid. I heard her gasp with delight at the magnificent treasure nestled inside.

She ought never to have done it.

She knew she had no right to inspect a visitor s belongings. And there had been many visitors to the château through the years, many guests stopping for a night, as was customary, or even a week s lodging on their way to or from Bordeaux. So many nobles with their sparkling coats and shimmering gowns.

But this visitor was different.

He was a noble, to be sure, a count. And he was the most beautiful person that young girl had ever seen, with shiny locks of dark hair falling in curls past his shoulders, and rings glittering from his fingers. He wore blue rosettes on his heeled slippers, and a hat that was both larger and floppier than her cousin, Alexandre's. He was all dark and very tall.

He'd caught the little girl's gaze a time or two as he talked in the entrance hall with her papa, but he had promptly disregarded it. And then he had proceeded to ply her papa with news from the court. Though she had asked after the Queen, the man told her women were of little importance, and her papa had hushed her. When she drifted from the hall, neither of them noticed. It was that which had driven her to the guest's room. She wasn't used to being ignored. And becoming a woman like her *maman* was the only thing she'd ever wished to do.

She was quite sure the guest wouldn't like her looking over his things, and that's exactly why she had done it.

But now, she paused at the trunk with her fingers hooked over its edge as she stared at the lace.

The bishop had worn this sort of cuff when he said Mass on Easter day. It spumed from the cuffs of his alb like a froth on fresh milk. She stretched out a hand toward it… should she?

I watched as she bit her lip in thought.

In that gossamer world of dreams where time twists and space shifts, I was everywhere and nowhere at once. I saw the back of her head, watched that mass of golden ringlets tremble as she reached into the trunk. At the same time, I saw the glint of longing in her eyes as her hand hovered above the lace.

The two cuffs were set into a bowl made by a pair of gloves. As she slid a hand beneath them, they released their perfumes of jasmine, orange blossoms, and carnations, scents so cloying she almost gagged.

Perhaps they would dissuade her...but no. I felt tears of frustration prick my eyes.

The little girl merely coughed, took in a deep breath through her mouth, and turned toward the lace once more. The scents had done nothing to deter her. But though she wanted to touch the cuffs, though she was prodded by a nearly irresistible frisson of desire, she did not. Not at first, in any case. But soon, the inevitability of what must happen began to invade my dream.

I tried to call out. I tried to make that young girl stop. To turn, at least, and listen for one moment to reason. But she would not be swayed. She would not be swayed because of what she saw. It was so...beautiful. So lovely. A yearning to hold it, for just one moment to possess her mother once more, took hold of her.

You must not do it! Even in my dreams I felt that old, familiar weight of despair. I felt, again, the loss of all the lovely things we possessed no more: the tapestries and the Turkey carpets, the collection of enameled boxes and the jeweled crucifixes, the pairs of silver candlesticks. All of those humble comforts that had been luxuries to us, all those prized family treasures the little girl had caused to disappear.

She dipped her hands into the trunk, and they came out clutching the lace cuffs. They were even more glorious, more magnificent than she had thought. A pattern of leaves and petals, intertwined with a filigree of scrollwork, repeating again and again and again. A circle that never ended, a pattern so finely detailed that it seemed to undulate across the fine mesh into which it had been woven. She ought to have put them back right then. If she had put them back right then, none of the misery that had followed would have happened.

But she did not.

After slipping them over her wrists, she closed her eyes and imagined those cuff-draped hands to be her beloved *maman*'s. She wrapped her own arms around herself and pretended it was the embrace of her mother.

Sois sage, *be good, my sweet angel.*

It's too much trouble to be good, Maman.

But 'tis only the good who marry well, ma chérie, *the bad always get what they deserve.*

Then I shall be the most good girl who ever lived.

If only you had lived, *Maman!*

The little girl embraced herself one more time, and then she opened her eyes and made the sign of the cross. The lace swayed in the air, just as the bishop's had. She swept her hands up and down, back and forth, watching it ripple, taking great satisfaction in the fact that it seemed to weigh nothing at all.

Weightless.

Spotless.

Priceless.

I wanted to lecture her. I wanted to plead with her. I wanted more than anything to beg her not to do it. If only I could have explained what would happen. But though my mouth was open, no sound issued forth. Though I tried to run to her, though I wanted to take her in my arms and spirit her away, my limbs would not move.

Now, she pretended she was to marry. Pushing the cuffs farther up her arms, she smiled at a groom she would never have. She imagined marrying above her station, to a prince, perhaps. Or at least to a count. She glided across the room, chin held high, shoulders pushed excruciatingly far back. She curtseyed to the King and then to the Queen. She danced what she thought was a courante. But after a while, she tired of the game, and she ached with the rigid posture she decided marriage protocol required.

Much better, perhaps, to marry Alexandre, whom she would not have to impress.

She considered returning the cuffs to the chest and searching out her cousin. She even turned and started across the room. But then she stopped.

I knew what would happen next. I did not want to watch it, but I could not close my eyes.

What was it that possessed her? What sort of familiar spirit was it that told her if she held her arms out straight like posts and then rotated them, those cuffs would spin around her wrists faster than the miller's wheel? And what made her note the lace, when set in motion, looked like the stream in the forest as it flowed over the rocks?

Around and around and around.

Faster and faster and faster.

Until…One of them took flight.

We both watched—she in astonishment, I in dread—as that cuff flew across the room and then skidded to a stop in the fireplace. There was no fire. There would be no fire until later that evening. But there had been fires. Any number of fires over the years had left the hearth a deep and sooty black. The girl approached that place, heart in her mouth, bent down, and plucked the cuff from the dingy gloom.

It was…mostly clean. Except for an area at the edge upon which it had slid through the ashes. There, it had been soiled, the scrollwork thrown into dark relief.

I watched the girl's chin tremble and her face pucker as she thought of the *maman* who could neither comfort her nor right her mistakes. I also saw the moment when she realized it would do no good at all to cry. She had touched something that did not belong to her. She had gone where she was not supposed to go. Even her dear *maman* would have scolded her. She knew she must not be found out. She must hide the evidence of her sin. If she could do that, then no one would ever know.

I felt her guilt. I knew her panic. How could she rid the lace of its stain?

She tried to rub it along the hem of her skirts, but it succeeded only in smearing the soot's dark edge. Perhaps…if she cut off the part that had been soiled, then no one would ever know.

No—a thousand times no!

She dropped the cuffs back into the trunk and furtively shut the lid before leaving the room. But she would be back. She would take her shears from her workbasket, she would conceal them in the folds of her skirt, and she would return to the guest's chamber.

Was there no other way for this dream to end?

There she was. And here she came, padding through the rushes toward the trunk. She lifted the lid. She pulled out the lace. She picked up the shears.

Don't!

She set the edge of the lace between their sharp, cold, heavy jaws.

No!

Carefully, so carefully, lip caught between her teeth, she cut away the decorative fringe of the pattern, severing the soiled part from the rest. She secreted the evidence in her slipper, hiding it with the sole of her foot, and then she put the rest of the lace back inside the trunk. As she pulled down the lid once more, she was confident no one would learn of her transgression.

But she didn't know then what I knew now.

She didn't understand how quickly a life can fray. How a single thread come undone can cause the unraveling of everything else around it.

But that was not the worst of the dream. The worst of it was this: I woke wanting the same thing I had wanted back then. I woke wanting *Maman*. I woke wanting to touch that lace. And I knew if I had it do all over again, I would do the very same thing. The worst was knowing I could not have done anything other than what I did.

The Count of Montreau didn't care that it was an accident. "She didn't mean to." I clung to my cousin Alexandre's hand as Papa stepped between the count and me.

"I don't care if she meant to pronounce some magic over it and increase its length threefold!" He leaned around Papa to glare at me as he yelled.

"She's just a child. She didn't know what she was doing."

"What she did just cost you two thousand livres."

"Two thousand! I could buy a second estate with that!"

"That's the exact amount it took to buy the cuffs. But…" He looked at Papa in a way that made him seem older than his years. "Perhaps I ought to charge you more. When I purchased it, such laces from Flanders were common. Now, all lace is forbidden. It would take twice as much to buy the same length today. If you dared to."

I held my breath. No one ever dared Papa to do anything.

"I don't have two thousand livres."

"I don't want two thousand. I want four thousand."

Alexandre was tugging me toward the door. I didn't want to go. "Come."

"*Non!*"

Alexandre bent and picked me up. He had never done that before. He had rarely ever touched me. Though he had never been anything but gentle and kind and good, there was something about him that precluded any contact.

Papa had put a hand to the count's arm. "I don't have the money. Please. You must understand. I could sell all I own, and still I could not pay you." He swiped at the beads of sweat that had sprung into relief upon his forehead.

I beat at Alexandre with my fists, but he would not let me go.

"Yes, well, it's too bad you took part in Chalais's conspiracy against the King's chief minister."

Papa swayed as if the floor had suddenly tilted.

"I know the Duchess of Chevreuse. She was the Marquis of Chalais's lover. If you're going to involve yourself in further conspiracies, may I suggest you choose your companions more wisely? If she who helps make the plans does not bother to guard them…? Did you truly think the King would not take offense? Or Richelieu himself would not be troubled?"

Papa was trembling. "I'd thought no one…I had hoped—"

"Truly, it would indeed be too bad if you were brought to the King's attention. The duchess has fled the country… Chalais is dead…there would be only you to answer for their sins. And make no mistake; Richelieu continues to search for conspirators. That's why I try always to avoid such plots—they're so easily scuttled."

What was a conspiracy? And why should the King himself care? It did not take long for me, a girl who never failed to satisfy her curiosity, to find the answers to all of those questions. And less time still for those answers to change all of our lives.

Twitter: Want to discuss or share what you just read? Use the hashtag #beaRUINS to connect with others.

ABOUT THE AUTHOR

Iris Anthony is the pen name for a two-time Christy Award finalist and the author of eight Christian novels. A graduate of the University of Washington's Foster School of Business, she has lived in places as varied as Tokyo and Paris, though she currently lives in the DC-metro area.

Imprint: Sourcebooks Landmark
BEA Booth #: 4112
Printed galley at BEA: yes
Contact for printed galley: Valerie Pierce valerie.pierce@sourcebooks. com

Print ISBN: 9781402268038
Print price: $14.99
eBook ISBN: 9781402268052
eBook price: $14.99
Publication date: 10/1/2012
Publicity contact: Beth Pehlke beth.pehlke@sourcebooks.com
Rights contact: Anne Landa anne.landa@sourcebooks.com
Editor: Shana Drehs
Agent: Natasha Kern
Agency: Natasha Kern Literary Agency Inc.
Promotional Information:
- 1,000 copy ARC mailing
- Trade show marketing: 200 copy ARC signing at PLA, 500 copy giveaway at BEA, 400 copy giveaway at ALA
- Major trade and consumer advertising campaign with *Shelf Awareness, Library Journal, Publishers Weekly, Booklist,* and *Goodreads*
- *Ruins of Lace* dedicated website
- Pre-publication book club campaign with libraries and Independent booksellers
- National Media Launch

BOOKSELLER BLURBS

Iris Anthony has managed to create a story that is atmospheric and driven at the same time, which is quite rare in my experience. By creating such vastly interesting and deep characters, as well as changing viewpoints, I'm getting the best of all worlds. In short, this book is every reason to go to bed early at night and every reason NOT to sleep once you get there.
—Shawna Elder, Iowa Book, Iowa City, IA

I loved it . . . lovely historical fiction about a topic that is not commonly written about.
—Suzy Takacs, The Book Cellar, Chicago IL

DIANA ATHILL
Make Believe
A True Story

'Unnervingly candid, coolly harrowing' John Updike

SUMMARY

Re-issue of a classic memoir, published originally in 1993. A portrait of Athill's turbulent relationship with Hakim Jamal; lover of Jean Seburg, Black Power activist and troubled spokesman for his generation.

EXCERPT

Chapter 3

At the time of Hakim's two stays in my flat there was, of course, a sexual undercurrent to our friendship. It was less one of desire than of tenderness. From time to time as we talked he would wander over to me and give me a gentle, absent-minded kiss; or I would stroke his cheek as I passed his chair (his cheekbones, temples and the bridge of his nose were modelled with exceptional delicacy, agreeable to touch). These caresses were given with an odd sort of attentive gravity, yet at the same time 'in passing'. They were pleasing but not sexually arousing in the limited, physical sense.

On his first stay he told me that since he had gone to live in Agadir several months earlier he had been 'entirely celibate'. I never supposed that this was even *meant* to be believed, interpreting it as a courteous way out of having to make love to me, which he couldn't have been wanting to do or he'd have done it. I was not surprised, therefore, at the speed with which he fell on two pretty young girls who came his way during this so-called celibate time, one of whom offered herself to him as on a dish garnished with mayonnaise and whose infatuation obviously had to be, and was, rewarded; and the other who set herself against him in argument and obviously had to be, and was, brought to heel. To the second he was in some way disagreeable in bed; I don't know how, but she said to me afterwards, 'He's a bit kinky about sex, isn't he?'

The way we finally went to bed together affected my attitude to him a good deal. At the end of his first visit to my flat he was leaving for the US to collect (so he said) some tapes he needed in connection with his book, and he was dreading it - really very frightened. (And he was indeed arrested on arrival at Kennedy because a friend meeting him was seen slipping a gun into his pocket. Hakim was kept in the Tombs for a week pending trial - a noisome experience - and was given a suspended sentence.) On his last evening with me he was painfully tense, trying to talk himself through his fear, reminding himself that he was always frightened *before* but never *while* things happened, so if he wasn't going to be scared when something went wrong (if it did), how foolish to be scared now, when all was well. He was in for a sleepless night, he said - or perhaps not, if he took a couple of tranquillisers. He hadn't been using them for some days (he had depended on them a lot since he kicked heroin) but he needed them now. I went to have a bath and thought while in it that I could make him sleep if he came to bed with me. When I came out he was crossing the hall to his bedroom. I stood in the doorway to say goodnight while he knelt by his suitcase, digging about for the bottle of capsules. He looked miserable and his hands were shaking. So I said, 'Love, when you're in a nervous state like this is it easier to sleep alone or with someone? Because if you'd like to come and snuggle up with me you're welcome.' He answered, 'I may well do just that,' and after he'd cleaned his teeth he came into my room and undressed and got into bed as naturally as though we were an old married couple.

We lay on our backs holding hands, each waiting for the other to make the first move, but not tensely. Then I shifted my head so that my cheek was against his shoulder, and he turned his and kissed me. The love-making which followed was, as I had expected, straightforward and not especially exciting or excited. I had supposed that because of his beautiful proportions he would be delicious to hold, but he was too thin - his skinniness felt sad under my hands.

It was afterwards that the real love-making began, taking me by surprise. It was as though he sank right into me with the release of tension. He lay on me, holding me, kissing and kissing and kissing my cheeks, my eyes and my mouth, over and over again. For more than half an hour we lay like that while he ceaselessly and lovingly kissed me and I, from time to time, kissed him. The fucking hadn't made me come, but the tenderness of this did, very sweetly. We were both totally relaxed and went to sleep like that, almost blended into one, sweat feeling silky and pleasant, not oppressive. He didn't say much except, sleepily, 'I should have done this long ago,' and 'This isn't good fucking, it's good love-making.' It would be inaccurate to call it anything less than a beautiful night.

Once he raised his head to look down on me and I opened my eyes. It was not very dark so I could see him fairly clearly, and the shape and poise of his head and the grave tenderness of his expression made me shut my eyes again quickly. For an instant I had felt piercingly something which I suppose men to feel more often than women: the alarming power of beauty. It was a physical sensation, as though a floor under my heart had given way and it was about to drop into a gulf of excruciatingly intense longing for this magical creature. Once my eyelids shut the image out, the feeling stopped. Afterwards I was pleased that I'd had it, but even more pleased that it had only lasted a few seconds: how appalling to be lastingly the victim of such a feeling simply because of how someone looked! I also thought afterwards that incest must be delicious, because it seemed very much that it was my motherliness he was embracing so tenderly, and that I was exercising with so much pleasure in return.

Next day we said an affectionate farewell and I lay awake for a time that night, worrying about how his arrival in the States had gone. Three days later I learnt by chance that he had not in fact arrived there for another twenty-four hours, but had stayed another night in London, sleeping on the floor of a bedsitter in Kilburn. Had he missed his plane? Had he always meant to stay on? Had he not telephoned me because he felt it would be unartistic to spoil such a nicely judged parting, or because he'd put me out of his mind? Salutory questions to be left with, I decided; reminders that it would never do to start expecting anything from Hakim. I must stay on my own path while he followed his, and the only 'relationship' there could ever be between us would be the occasional intersection of those paths.

We slept together only twice more in all our acquaintance (both times it was enjoyable), but this slight sexual affair made me feel even warmer towards him so that his eventual 'impossibility' was all the sadder. In my experience the degree of physical tenderness expressed between us that night is uncommon, and I wanted it to - felt it *ought* to - represent a real closeness.

There was one love-making which failed to happen, after having been carefully planned by him to provide me with a transcendental experience. It was on the last day of his second visit, when he arranged for us to take an LSD trip together. He had recently taken his first and had been enchanted by it. His description of the pure delight he had experienced - the visual beauty of everything, its amusingness, its interest, the feeling of innocent vitality which had possessed him, the release he'd found in fits of absurd laughter - was so vivid that I was eager to join him. He was confident that he could control our joint trip and make it beautiful for both of us, and although I knew that trips don't necessarily resemble each other either from one time to another, or from one person to another, and that it's risky to go on one without the presence of a sober guide, I decided that given our joint goodwill it was a fair bet that this one would work. Hakim didn't say in so many words that its climax would be another beautiful love-making, but he intended it to be so, and I knew it.

Unfortunately the stuff he procured must have been adulterated. It was not, I think, a 'bad trip' in the usual sense, because the 'badness' was merely a matter of feeling physically ill and we both felt ill in the same way. After an hour or so of the usual pleasures – colours glowing, shapes changing in amusing ways or acquiring a fascinating significance (a sea-shell; a red rose which we scattered with water-drops which became star-like) - we began to feel sick. At no time did I seriously think I was going to throw up, but for the rest of the trip I knew I must keep still, keep quiet, keep my mind empty, just let time pass, or the diffused feeling of nausea would concentrate with horrible consequences. Hakim felt exactly the same. At one point the telephone rang and I answered it. I was able to speak normally, but when I flopped back into my chair I felt so bad that I doubted if I could make it to the lavatory, supposing that the exertion was going to bring me to vomiting-point. And soon afterwards a particularly boring hanger-on of Hakim's walked into the room. The children downstairs must have left the front door open, but at the time his sudden appearance seemed uncanny. Hakim pulled himself together and began to make polite conversation - the man wanted, for some reason, to talk about his car - but I, after one or two attempts, knew I wasn't up to it. I looked at the man and saw that he was undoubtedly mad; and understood that if I had to go on attending to him I might well be into a genuinely bad trip, not just feeling ill but seeing frightening things. I couldn't think why Hakim was being so attentive and kind. Why didn't he make the man go away? Finally I couldn't bear it any more. Taking care to speak as courteously as possible, I said that I wasn't feeling well and must go to my bedroom to lie down for a while. At this Hakim got to his feet, said to the man, 'Come on, I'll come and have a look at this car of yours,' and they went out. I tried to believe that Hakim was getting rid of him, but I knew before I heard the front door slam that he'd gone off with him and wasn't going to come back.

For a while I lay in my chair feeling forlorn at being abandoned, then I started to feel frightened. Supposing this trip turned really bad, what would happen to me now that I was alone? With a painful effort I forced myself to get up and go downstairs to tell my neighbours in the flat below what had happened, so that they could look in on me from time to time - which they kindly and comfortingly did. After that it was simply a matter of waiting, telling myself that the effects of this bloody pill were bound to wear off sooner or later. I couldn't take much interest in the strange things which happened when I opened my eyes - the chair which swelled to twice its size and started to breathe, the way the room changed shape, sometimes existing almost entirely in terms of its horizontal lines, sometimes in terms of its vertical lines. These events were no more than indications that I still had quite a time to go. I was worried about Hakim. He was supposed to leave for the airport early next morning. Would he come back in time? Would he collapse? I was sure that I would collapse if I had to move about, and he would be feeling just as ill as I was. But I realised that if I dwelt on worry it might swell to alarming proportions under the influence of the drug, so I told myself firmly that Hakim was capable of looking after himself, and closed my mind to the subject. Some time during the night it seemed worth going to bed but I still couldn't sleep. I lay inert, letting the night sounds and my bodily sensations absorb me.

We had taken the drug at three-thirty in the afternoon. By five-thirty next morning, when I heard Hakim come in, I was still feeling odd but was able to get up. I found him standing in the sitting-room, staring into the fire, and told him how glad I was that he was safely back. What had happened? He said that he'd gone through an appalling night. He had never felt so nauseated in his life, he didn't know how he had dragged himself through it, tinkering with that fucking car for John and then being made to eat fish and chips, which had nearly done for him. No, he didn't think John had twigged. The reason he hadn't been able to get away was that the effort would have been beyond him.

I asked him why he'd gone off. There had been moments during the night when I'd felt stricken by his departure, but by now I knew that there was no telling how the pill would act. 'It was when you didn't make John go away,' he said. 'You wanted to go to your room and I thought you were rejecting me.'

'Oh *darling*!' I said. 'How daft can you get! I was desperate because *you* weren't getting rid of him!' By now I was able to find this misunderstanding funny, but Hakim, because of the ridiculous night he had spent, was further from recovery than I was and went on being stubbornly gloomy, so I sat him down and went to make him tea. Neither of us could drink more than a mouthful of it. Whatever that pill was, it was strong. I had no inclination to eat, drink, smoke or sleep for thirty-six hours after taking it (though all I felt when its effects wore off was a pleasurably normal degree of readiness to eat and sleep).

'I was going to make love to you,' he said miserably.

'I know, love,' I said, 'but never mind, it doesn't matter,' and I sat on the floor beside him, holding his hand. I felt fond of him for his childish disappointment at the failure of his plan. Then he turned my face up towards him, fixed my eyes with his, and began gently but forcefully telling me good things about myself: that I was his idea of a perfect woman, gentle and kind and good and beautiful and intelligent; that I mustn't feel sad about getting old because I was still all those things; that I must be happy and serene because he loved me. I was deeply moved. It was apparent to me that he was not expressing his feelings about me so much as *making me a present* (as he would have been doing if he'd made love to me). He was 'rewarding' me, 'bestowing' something on me in token of his favour. There was, in other words, no real meaning in what he was saying, but the impulse was a benevolent and generous one, and it was touching that he should overcome his exhaustion and physical malaise in order to express it so handsomely. He's as mad as a coot, I thought (because, as I shall soon explain, I had begun to notice symptoms by then), but it's a kind and loving madness, bless him. We parted that time with even more tenderness than the time before; and he, poor man, had an atrocious flight back to Morocco, feeling indescribably ill all the way.

Twitter: Want to discuss or share what you just read? Use the hashtag #beaBELIEVE to connect with others.

ABOUT THE AUTHOR

Diana Athill (OBE) was born in 1917. She is the author of several volumes of memoir, and a collection of letters, all published by Granta Books UK.

Imprint: Granta
BEA Booth #: 3858
Print ISBN: 9781847086327
Print price: $13.95
eBook ISBN: 9781847087065
eBook price: $12.51
Publication date: 10/5/2012
Publicity contact: Pru Rowlandson pru@granta.com
Rights contact: Angela Rose arose@granta.com
Editor: Bella Lacey
Agent: c/o Publisher
Agency: c/o Publisher

janet gurtler

"Fascinating and unique."
—Jennifer Brown,
author of *Hate List*

who
i
kissed

SUMMARY

She never thought a kiss could kill...

Samantha didn't mean to hurt anyone. She was just trying to fit in... and she wanted to make Zee a little jealous after he completely ditched her for a prettier girl. So she kissed Alex. And then he died—right in her arms.

Sam is now the school pariah and a media sensation—how did she not know Alex had a peanut allergy? Consumed with guilt, she'll have to find a strength that goes way deeper than pulling off the fastest time in the 200-meter butterfly. Because if she can't figure out how to forgive herself, no one else will either.

EXCERPT

"You don't go to many parties?" Zee says, as he slides the door closed, but it's not so much a question as a statement. The night air is cold, but the deck is covered and the temperature is tolerable.

"Not really."

"They didn't have them at your old school?"

"We had parties. They just weren't so..."

"Fun?" he says with a grin.

"Grown up," I say and glance down. "We didn't drink. My friends back home. Swim people. Who can afford hangovers?" In the distance the wind howls.

"True. But this is a swim-free weekend." Zee takes a sip from the beer bottle as if to make his point, studying me as if I'm an exotic or weird beast. "All swimming and no fun makes Sammy a dull girl."

I tug at my braid. He thinks I'm dull. And of course he's completely right. I'm a lump of fun suck. Sucking the fun out of everything is my specialty.

"Hey," he says. "Don't look so down. I'm kidding. You don't have to drink to be cool." He lifts his bottle and grins. "But seriously, how often do we get a Saturday night with no swim meet? What Coach doesn't know won't hurt her." His expression changes to a conspiring smile as if we share a naughty secret. His eyes are shiny and I realize he's probably had more to drink than he seems. "I bet you're probably still sugar buzzed on Jelly Bellies."

"I have a high tolerance for the Bellies," I tell him. "Thanks." I try to stop my smile, but it stretches over my face.

"Yeah." He takes a swig of beer. "Swimmers see-food diet. I know a lot of girls would kill to eat like you and still be in shape."

He's right. Swimming builds an appetite. Despite a big supper, I'd wolfed down a peanut butter sandwich right before the party.

Zee takes a step closer. I hold my breath, waiting. For what? Something. My heart trips, not quite believing I'm alone outside with Zee. At a party. And he's standing so close to me I can smell his skin. Even the beer on his breath. It's so more intimate than standing beside him on the pool deck, even though at the pool both of us nearly naked. Here I'm a girl. Not just a swimmer.

He reaches over and tucks my braid behind my ear.

"You're sexy," he says.

I struggle to breathe. "I am not."

"Yes. You are." His voice is soft. "All the guys think so. You're different. Not all fake like some girls."

I shake my head with a little too much force. His words thrill me. It's so foreign having a boy's interest and yet here I am, wondering if his lips will taste like chlorine.

He leans even closer and strokes the skin on my bicep. Goose bumps cover my arm. "Strong but soft inside." His slow easy smile has so much promise. I press my lips tight and suck in my breath, waiting for his mouth to move closer to mine, wanting him to so bad it makes me dizzy.

And then behind us the patio door slides open.

Sounds from the house fill the air, laughter and music. The door closes. My back stiffens as a gorgeous creature steps into our space. She's Tyra Banks tall with the kind of hair I covet—curly ringlets, long and sexy, cascade down her back. She's slim with great boobs and a tiny waist that she's clearly proud to show off in a low-cut summer dress. Her face is the kind of pretty that turns boys' heads.

"There you are," she says to Zee and steps forward, crunching my toe with a high heel and wrapping her arm around Zee, forcing me to step backwards.

"Ouch." I say it low and keep my eyes down, mortified.

She pushes Zee back, away from me. A breeze blows over my skin and I shiver.

"Well, that's got to be a little awkward," a voice says. I turn my head to see a boy sitting in a patio chair behind us in the darkness. He stands and steps closer, and as he comes into focus I recognize him. It's the boy from the pool earlier today. He's staring at me again, with those same piercing eyes, as if he's listening again to the chatter inside my head. Although what I'm thinking now is not very nice. He's holding a beer bottle and he tilts it back, then grins the playful smile of a little boy. He stumbles a little. Am I the only person at this party who's not drunk?

"Who's that?" I hear the curly haired girl hiss to Zee. As if she doesn't know we're in a couple of the same classes at school. I don't know her name, but I recognize her. I glance back and she's standing so close to Zee, my cheeks flame.

"Samantha Waxman," the boy beside me calls to her. "She swims with Zee, Kaitlin," he calls. "So put your claws back in."

I glance at him, surprised he knows my name.

"Sammy's my girl," Zee says with a laugh. "She's the best female swimmer on our team."

Kaitlin looks me up and down. "Oh, another swimmer," she says and her tone implies I'm not a threat. "You people and your gills." She turns her back to me, her implication clear. Kaitlin drags him farther away. "It's cold, Zee. Warm me up." She slides her hands around his waist. Zee lifts his hands in the air as if he's trying to get away, but she keeps at him. I die a little inside.

"I'm Alex." The other boy thrusts his hand out at me. "Sorry I was spying. I came out to get some air. Some guys are smoking in the basement."

Smells like they were smoking something other than cigarettes. I stare at his hand and then laugh a little nervously and put mine inside. His palm is big and warm and nice against my skin, but I pull away quickly.

"We've never officially met," he says. "But we go to school together."

"You were at the pool today," I blurt out.

His smile widens. "Yeah. I had to drop off Zee's iPod. I stuck around to watch you swim. I heard you were pretty good."

I lift my water bottle and unscrew the top, thankful for something to do. My body is off balance with conflicting emotions. Lust. And then rejection. Now embarrassment.

"I used to swim," he says. "But gave it up for baseball. My coach didn't want me doing two sports. Well, I do Parkour, too. Like Zee. But that's for fun." He exhales loudly and then sucks in a big breath.

"Parkour?" I say and take a sip of water.

"Jumping off things. Like James Bond."

I nod, even though I knew what Parkour is. I was more asking why. Anyhow I'm relieved to hear he'd been watching my swimming technique at the pool and not so much me. Unexpectedly I giggle, a release of nervous tension.

"Parkour is funny?" he asks. "I thought chicks dug it." He inhales deeply and blows out again.

"Like how you leapt off the bleachers?"

His cute nose wrinkles up and makes me laugh again. "Exactly. Why is that funny?"

"I was kind of worried you were a perv. Hanging out at the pool. Watching strange girls swim."

He grabs at his heart. "Ouch," he says. "But I didn't hear that you were that strange."

"Good. I've kept it quiet then." I quickly peek over my shoulder at Zee and the Amazon. My heart thunks to my toes as she leans in and kisses him. I'm suddenly feeling nauseated, but turn back and smile at Alex. Zee can flirt with me and then make out with another girl right behind my back a few seconds later? Well. Two can play at that game.

I can do this. I can flirt with the best of them. In my head a tiny voice of reason tries to nag at me, but the sting of rejection is louder.

"A perv?" he says. "You really thought I was a perv?"

I lean closer to Alex. "You're too cute to be a perv," I say, trying to ignore my own embarrassment. If he hadn't been drinking, he'd probably guess I got my moves watching the Disney channel.

"You think I'm cute?" The wonder in his voice softens my mortification a little. "I thought you were into Zee."

I can feel the blush and my head automatically shakes back and forth even as I'm picturing Zee behind me with the amazon. "No." I cross my arms in front of myself. "I'm not."

"Good." Alex brushes my arm with his fingers. I glance back as Zee is coming up for air with Kaitlin. Alex looks over too. "Zee's an idiot," he whispers in my ear.

My cheeks heat up again and I lower my gaze.

"We're alphabetically linked," he mumbles and coughs.

I frown. "What?"

He tugs at his ear. "Sorry. I mean you're Waxman. I'm Waverly. And a major dork."

"Hey," Zee calls. "No moves on Sammy, Waverly. I thought we discussed that." He tries to walk toward us but Kaitlin tugs him back.

"Forget your stupid swim team," she says and reattaches her mouth to his and slides her long fingers into his hair.

"Screw him," Alex says. I nod, wholeheartedly agreeing. Screw Zee and his stupid jelly beans. Screw Zee and the stupid girl.

I look up at Alex, trying to be seductive and not furious that Zee thinks he can tell Alex not to make a move on me at the same time he's making out with another girl. I'm consumed by a quiet rage that doesn't quite mask my sadness. Fighting a sudden urge to cry, I step closer to Alex and reach up to touch the collar of his t-shirt. "I've definitely noticed you around," I lie.

"Really?" He leans in, and his breath smells like booze and smoke. He stumbles again. His eyes are red. His condition takes the edge off my guilt. He's drunk. He doesn't know how bad I'm using him to teach Zee a lesson. Maybe he won't even remember.

My frown turns up.

"You're sure you're not interested in Zee?"

"Of course not." I press my lips tight and lean closer to Alex.

He tilts his head forward, so close that our noses actually touch and he winds my braid around his finger. I hold my breath, and try to turn off the part of my brain that insists on analyzing every situation and running it through different scenarios and outcomes before taking action. Instead I press on, determined to worry about the consequences later. It's the least I can do for Zee.

Alex unweaves my braid from his finger, then moves forward and his lips touch mine. I close my eyes and push away the thought that I'm only doing this so Zee will see me make out with his friend. I'm way too sober to be in this situation, but it doesn't mean Alex is. That has to make it all right. This impulsive thing I'm doing.

Yeah. I'm wild and spontaneous, Zee. How bad do you want me now?

Alex opens his mouth slightly. His lips are soft and even though he's kind of smelly, it's surprisingly nice. Kissing him. I open my eyes, afraid I'll see another boy's face if I close them. Alex's hand slips around my waist, pulling me tighter. This boy knows what he's doing. His kiss is soft and sweet, with a hint of more just beneath.

I have a horrible thought that I'm turning into a slut. Maybe I've been storing lust up for so long because people thought I was gay. Because even though I barely know this boy, kissing him feels pretty darn good.

His hand travels up my side. I gasp a little. Alex pulls me in a little tighter and his lips push harder and it becomes a little too intense. Alex, my mind reminds me. Not Zee.

The realization breaks my trance. Zee's face flickers in my brain and my blood pumps hot shame through my veins. I pull away and place my hands on Alex's chest pushing him and taking a step back.

"I'm sorry. This is crazy. I barely know you. I'm sorry."

Alex looks slightly alarmed and then he sneezes.

"Shit," he says.

He begins to cough. He puts his hand up as if to say, just a moment and then bends at the waist. He's takes deep breaths, as if he's struggling to bring air in and out of his lungs.

"Uh. Are you okay?" I ask.

He doesn't answer, but it's clear this is more than dealing with my sudden rejection.

I glance around in a panic, wanting to call to Zee but he and Kaitlin are still going at it hard and interrupting them is too embarrassing to contemplate.

I put my hand on Alex's back and repeat, "Are you okay?"

He shakes his head and my heartbeat accelerates. I bend down to look into his face and what I see makes me break out in a sweat.

"My puffer," he gasps.

"Zee!" I call, no longer concerned about etiquette. "There's something wrong with Alex."

"You're telling me," he murmurs. "Leave her alone." But then he looks over and spots Alex and almost comically pushes the Amazon girl away.

"What the hell?" she says, but Zee is already at Alex's side.

She glares at me and then storms back inside the house.

At this point Alex has sunk to his knees and is making awful wheezing sounds. His face looks almost gray and his lips are getting kind of bluish. My heart is racing and I'm actually wringing my hands together, knowing something is wrong, but not sure what, or what to do about it.

"What the hell, Sam?" Zee yells. He grabs Alex and shakes his shoulders. "What the hell, dude? Breathe."

Alex doesn't respond.

"What's wrong?" My voice comes out shrieky and panicked.

"He's having an asthma attack," Zee says without looking at me. "Alex. Alex, you okay buddy? Where's your damn inhaler?"

I look around the deck as if someone new will leap from the shadows and tell me what to do. I don't know anyone with asthma. I have no idea what to do. Should I pound on his back? Give him mouth to mouth?

"Go see if someone knows where his inhaler is," Zee yells at me. "Look for his sister, Chloe."

Like I even know who Chloe is. I scramble to open the patio door and pitch myself inside the kitchen. The heat and music hit me immediately. I tap the first person I see on the shoulder. "Alex is having an asthma attack," I say loud enough to be heard over the music. "Inhaler." I gesture like I'm pressing the pump on an inhaler. "Do you know where there's an inhaler?"

The boy stares blankly at me. He shrugs and continues to the fridge and opens it and takes out a beer.

"Oh my God," I say, looking around in a panic. I loathe the thought of having to make a scene but glance outside and see Zee standing over top Alex who is now sitting on the ground.

"Help!" I yell. "Does anyone know where Alex's inhaler is?" Hardly anyone looks at me for longer than a curious second.

Self-consciousness no longer a luxury, I race to the attached living room and jump on the couch, almost stepping on a boy's hand. I hold up my hands like a megaphone. "Alex is having an asthma attack," I scream as loud as I can. "We need to find his inhaler." No one responds other than a few concerned stares. "Chloe?" I yell and people stare at me now, like I'm a novelty at the zoo. Some yells for Chloe and the name spreads along the crowd and then the pretty girl in the black dress is running towards me, her face intense with concern.

"What's wrong?" she says. "Is he okay? Is he still outside?"

I point toward the patio door.

"Shit," she says, kicking off her heels and running for the deck. A couple of people follow her. Seconds later she leans back inside. "Someone call 911," she yells. Her voice is hysterical and penetrates the party atmosphere. "Call 911 right now. Does anyone have an inhaler?"

Someone turns down the music and people scurry in circles. Taylor rushes into the living room looking confused and upset. Justin has his arm around her. They hurry outside with some others and from the deck I hear Chloe screech louder. "Help! Someone help Alex. Oh my God!"

There's silence and then she yells again. Her voice is hysterical now. "Epi-pen," she yells. "Does anyone have an epi-pen?"

My blood, moments ago so hot, turns to ice. Epi-pen?

"Get out of the way!" Zee yells from the deck, screaming at people to step back. A crowd's gathered around Alex, blocking him. I'm frozen in place, afraid to go outside. The atmosphere inside the house transforms. No one looks sophisticated anymore. Everyone looks like kids. Scared little kids.

Outside the noise continues and builds momentum. Girls are crying. Chloe is screaming over and over again. I'm still standing on the couch and the boy sitting beside me shakes his head. "This is not going to turn out well," he mumbles to no one in particular. "Someone said he left his backpack at Zee's."

"What do you mean?" I ask the boy. "What's happening?"

"Oh my god," someone yells. "He's not breathing."

Chloe runs in the house then, her eyes wide and hysterical. "Did anyone give him anything that might have peanuts in it? Did he eat anything?" Her voice screeches, tears chase each other down her cheeks. "Where the hell is the ambulance?"

I concentrate on breathing in and out. It's difficult for me, but not impossible. Like it is for Alex. I step off the couch. I want to lie down and close my eyes.

I want to pretend it's all a very, very bad dream. I want to be back in the kitchen at home with my dad. I want him to order me not to go to the party.

I don't want to be so hungry all the time. I don't want to act totally out of character and kiss a boy minutes after meeting him.

A boy who is allergic to peanuts and is apparently having an anaphylactic reaction on the deck. I don't want to have snacked before the party even though I ate a full dinner. I don't want the snack to be a peanut butter sandwich.

I consider bolting out the back door but plop down on a nearby chair, too shocked to do much of anything else. People run in circles around me. No one talks to me. No one asks me what I ate before I kissed him. My lips press tightly together.

The sound of sirens reaches the house. People cry and screech, in a panic. Two medics charge in the house and run out to the deck.

I don't have to ask. It's not good.

Chapter Three After

I don't know how long it's been since the amazon pointed an accusing finger at me as the girl with Alex, but people have finally stopped firing questions at me. I've answered questions over and over again. What did I eat before kissing Alex? When did I have the peanut butter sandwich? What happened after?

Almost all the kids are gone. Taylor is at the kitchen table, crying softly. Justin sits beside her, looking like he's about to.

A police officer's walkie-talkie crackles. She speaks into it, then walks over to me.

"Alex died on the way to the hospital," she says softly.

Taylor moans and Justin drops his head inside his hands. I squeeze my eyes shut and shake my head. Back and forth. Back and forth. As if the motion can stop the truth from becoming real. NO. I want to scream. This can't be real.

The female police officer puts her arm on mine. "Have you been drinking?" she asks.

I shake my head no. I wonder why it even matters.

"You're sure?"

"I swim," I say as if that's an answer. My voice sounds foreign to me.

Her eyes soften and I guess she's a mom, thinking about her own kid, hoping she won't drink either. Or kiss boys she doesn't know at parties. "Did you drive here?"

I nod.

"I'll drive you home in your car. My partner will follow us."

I don't argue. She pulls me up. I don't look at Taylor or Justin. I don't look at anyone. I wonder if I can stay inside my head, and make it all go away.

It's raining outside and the wind is whipping leaves around. The cop asks me a couple more questions on the way home, but other than supplying my address in a squeezed voice, I can't speak. I can't talk anymore. I can only shake my head and stare at my lap. I'm holding so many emotions inside and they're fighting hard to blast out. Swallowing is virtually impossible.

"We already contacted your dad. You won't be charged with anything," she's saying. "In a case like this there's no intent. No liability."

My joints weaken and my stomach gurgles. I should go to jail. Live behind bars. Be punished forever for what I did.

She parks in the driveway and walks me to the door and my body starts to shake when my dad opens the door. For a second I imagine Chloe going home. Her parents waiting at the front door. No son or brother will walk inside again. Horrified, I slip past my dad while the policewoman has a hushed conversation with him in the doorway. They talked earlier, but he's just learning Alex died. I hover behind him. Waiting.

When she finally leaves and he closes the door my body lets go. I throw my arms around him, crumpling against him. He squeezes me harder than he ever has before and the tears I've somehow kept down gush out. I'm a snotty, blubbering mess.

Horrible sounds emanate from a deep dark place inside me. "I'm sorry. I'm didn't mean… Daddy… Oh my God. I killed him."

My dad murmurs soft words that make no sense. A part of me recognizes how stiff my dad's arms are, but he's holding me close and not letting go, even as I soak his golf shirt with my groaning and weeping. I'm certain I'll never be able to stop. I rock against him, unable to process the horror of what I've done.

Time must pass but instead of dying, like I should, I start to breathe a little slower. My guttural sounds turn to normal sobs. My dad tries to untangle himself, but I cling to him, terrified to be alone. He gently but firmly removes my arms from his.

"I'll be right back," he says. "Stay here."

I curl into a ball on the couch and squeeze my eyes together. I don't want to see or to hear anything. I don't want thoughts or images in my head. A notion formulates in my brain. I want my mommy. Oh God. I want my mom more than I've ever wanted her in my life.

I start another whimpering sound but it's almost a song of sorrow that I hum to keep myself sane on some primitive level.

Dad's footsteps return and then he crouches down beside me. "Sammy?"

I open my eyes and he holds out his hand, flat. In the middle of his palm is an oval blue pill. In his other hand is a glass of water.

"Take it," he commands holding the hand with the pill closer to me.

I don't have the wits to question his order. I don't ask what the pill is or protest. I can only sit up and obey. Someone needs to tell me what to do. I place the pill on my tongue, take the glass of water and swallow it down. A bitter taste taints my taste buds.

Dad holds out his hand again, but this time it's empty. I recognize that I'm expected to take it. I slip my smaller hand inside and he tugs me up. He puts his other hand under my legs and swoops me up and my arms wind around his neck. He walks slowly carrying me, climbing the stairs with me, taking me down the hallway to my bedroom like I'm a three-year-old, not a five-foot-eight seventeen-year-old who weighs almost 130 pounds.

He grunts a little and kicks open my bedroom door. He has to step over a pile of clothes before he can plop me gently down on my bed. I immediately roll away from him and curl into a ball, but instead of tight I'm almost limp. My brain is black and emotionally spent. I'm so exhausted it feels like I'm sinking inside my head.

Dad sits on the bed and his weight moves me a little closer to him. He strokes my hair the way he did when I was a little girl.

The pill is already working. I'm beginning to drift, and welcome the escape with only a tiny level of awareness.

"Why, Sammy?" he whispers. "Why were you kissing a boy you didn't even know?'

I don't answer him. I'm so tired. But a lingering thought survives the weariness and travels through the dark. It goes deep and imprints on my already contrite soul.

"Why did Mom die?" I whisper.

How can I possibly get through this without a mother? Maybe with her guidance I wouldn't have gone around kissing boys I barely knew for attention.

He doesn't say anything, and the drugs make my brain hazier. As I close my eyes and succumb to darkness one last coherent thought flits through my head:

I wish I could join her.

My mom.

Twitter: Want to discuss or share what you just read? Use the hashtag #beaKISS to connect with others.

ABOUT THE AUTHOR

Janet Gurtler lives in Calgary, Canada with her husband and son and a chubby Chihuahua who refuses to eat dog food. Janet does not live in an Igloo or play hockey, but she does love maple syrup and says "eh" a lot. Visit Janet at www.janetgurtler.com.

Imprint: Sourcebooks Fire
BEA Booth #: 4112
Printed galley at BEA: yes
Contact for printed galley: Valerie Pierce valerie.pierce@sourcebooks.com
Print ISBN: 9781402270543
Print price: $9.99
eBook ISBN: 9781402270567
eBook price: $9.99
Publication date: 10/1/2012
Publicity contact: Derry Wilkens derry.wilkens@sourcebooks.com
Rights contact: Anne Landa anne.landa@sourcebooks.com
Editor: Leah Hultenschmidt
Agent: Jill Corcoran
Agency: The Herman Agency
Promotional Information:
- Seven city author tour
- National blog tour (100+ bloggers)
- 50 copy manuscript mailing to key Independent booksellers for blurbs
- 500 copy ARC mailing to booksellers, librarians and media
- 200 copy ARC giveaway at BEA
- 200 copy ARC giveaway at ALA
- Author panel at ALA
- National print campaign with *Justine, Seventeen, CosmoGirl, L.A. Times, USA Today*

Barbara Kingsolver

Flight Behavior

A NOVEL

SUMMARY

Set in the present in the rural community of Feathertown, Tennessee, *Flight Behavior* is the story of Dellarobia Turnbow, a petite, razor-sharp young woman who nurtured worldly ambitions before becoming a mother and wife at seventeen. Now, after more than a decade of tending small children on a failing farm, suffering oppressive poverty, isolation, and her husband's antagonistic family, she mitigates her boredom in an obsessive flirtation with a handsome younger man.

Headed to his secluded cabin to consummate their relationship, she instead walks into something on the mountainside she cannot explain or understand: a forested valley filled with silent red fire that appears to Dellarobia to be a miracle. Her discovery is both beautiful and terrible, and elicits divergent reactions from all sides. Religious fundamentalists claim it as a manifestation of God; climate scientists scrutinize it as an element of forthcoming disaster; politicians and environmentalists declaim its lessons; charlatans mine its opportunity; international media construct and deconstruct Dellarobia's story; and townspeople cope with intrusion and bizarre alterations of custom.

After years lived entirely within the confines of one small house, Dellarobia finds her path suddenly opening out and ultimately leading into blunt and confrontational engagement with her family, her church, her town, her continent, and finally the world at large. Over the course of a single winter, her life will become the property of the planet and, perhaps for the first time, securely her own.

EXCERPT

Chapter 1. The Measure of a Man

A certain feeling comes from throwing your life away, and it is one part rapture. Or so it seemed for now, to a woman with flame-colored hair who marched uphill to meet her demise. She knew what a rash thought that was, how this thrill would not stack up in the long run against shame and disgrace, losses that would surely infect her children. She could see the veil of contempt that would cloud their tender years in a town where everyone knew them. Teenaged cashiers at the grocery, even, clicking painted fingernails on the counter while she wrote her check, eyeing the oatmeal and frozen peas of an unhinged family, exchanging looks with the bag boy: *she's that one.* How they all admired their own steadfast lives. Right up to the day when all hope leaked away like water through sand and the heart had only one word left: run, run. Like this, like a hunted animal or a Derby winner, either one would feel exactly this coursing of blood and shortness of breath.

She smoked too much, that was another mortification to throw in with the others. But she had cast her lot. Plenty of people took this way out, looking future damage in the eye and naming it something else. Now it was her turn. She would claim the tightness in her chest and call it bliss, rather than the same breathlessness she could be feeling at home right now while toting a heavy laundry basket, behaving like a sensible mother of two.

The children were with her mother-in-law. She'd dropped off those babies this morning on barely sufficient grounds, and couldn't afford to dwell on that now. Their little faces turned up to her like the round hearts of two daisies: *she loves me, loves me not.* All their hopes soon to be shot to pieces. The family would be totaled. That was the word, like a wrecked car wrapped around a telephone pole, no salvageable parts. No husband worth having is going to forgive adultery when the time comes. And for all that she still yearned for the ruin that waited for her today, the hand whose touch would bring down all she knew. She craved the collapse with an appetite larger than sense. Craving was an electric pulse that buzzed through her body like an alarm clock gone off in the early light, setting in motion all the things in a day that can't be stopped.

At the top of the pasture she leaned against the fence to catch up on oxygen, feeling the slight give of the netted woven wire against her back. No safety net. Unsnapped her purse, counted her cigarettes, discovered she'd have to ration them. This had not been a thinking-ahead kind of day. The suede jacket was wrong, too warm, and what if it rained? She frowned at the November sky. It was the same dull, stippled ceiling that had been up there last week, last month, forever. All summer. Whoever was in charge of weather had put a recall on blue and nailed up this mess of dirty-white sky like a lousy sheetrock job. The pasture pond seemed to reflect more light off its surface than the sky itself had to offer. The sheep huddled close around its shine as if they too had given up on the sun and settled for second best. Little puddles winked all the way down Highway Seven toward Feathertown and out the other side of it, toward Cleary, a long trail of potholes turned to jewels. How nice. If you didn't need to drive on it.

The sheep in the field below, the Turnbow family land, the white frame house she had not slept outside of for even one night in ten years of marriage: she tried on the idea of losing so much certainty, and felt nothing. Dread, maybe, but not regret. It was a landscape of captivity, like a prisoner's pocked walls and empty hours. The dumb confined sheep, her compatriots, stood in the mud surrounded by the deep stiletto holes of their footprints, enduring life's bad deals. They'd worn their heavy wool through the muggy summer, and now that winter was coming on they would soon be shorn. She hated what they bore in common, a life that was one long proposition they never saw coming. Their pasture was eaten down to nothing and looked drowned. In the field beyond this fence the neighbor's orchard, painstakingly planted all last year, was dying under the rain. Her world was a death tableau, fixed and strange. Even her house looked unfamiliar, probably due to the angle. She only looked out those windows, never into them, given that she kept company mostly with people who rolled plastic trucks on the floor. Certainly she never climbed up here to check out the domestic arrangement. The condition of the roof was not encouraging.

Her car was in the right place, though. That much at least was squared away. She'd parked in her own driveway, the only spot in the county where it wouldn't incite gossip. Everyone knew that station wagon, had known it years ago when it belonged to her mother. She'd rescued this one thing from her mother's death, an unreliable set of wheels adequate for short errands with kids in tow. Sometimes she had the spooky feeling her Mama was still back there, her tiny frame wedged between the car seats. But not today. This morning after leaving the kids at Hester's she had floored it for the half-mile back home, feeling high and wobbly as a kite. Had gone into the house only to brush her teeth, shed her glasses and put on eyeliner, no other preparations necessary prior to lighting out her own back door to wreck her reputation. No dinner or movie first, that never seemed to be in her cards.

She picked her way now through churned-up mud along the fence, lifted the chain fastener on the steel gate and slipped through. Beyond the fence an ordinary wildness began, ironweed and briar thickets. An old road cut through it, long unused, crisscrossed by wild raspberries bending across in long arcs. In recent times she'd come up here only once, two summers ago, berry picking. She'd been barrel-round pregnant with Cordelia, that's how she knew which summer, so Preston would have been four, holding her hand for dear life while her husband Cub scared them half to death about snakes. The raspberry canes were a weird color for a plant, not that she would know nature if it bit her. But bright pink? It was like a frosted lipstick some thirteen-year-old might want to wear. She had probably skipped that phase, heading straight for Immoral Coral and Come-to-bed Red.

The leggy saplings gave way to a forest's edge where trees clung to their last leaves, and something made her think of Lot's wife in the Bible who turned back for one last look at home. Poor woman, struck into a pile of salt for such a minor disobedience. What a strict and unforgiving arrangement, family life. She did not look back, but headed into the woods on the rutted track her husband's family called "the high road."

As if, she thought. Taking the High Road to damnation, that particular irony had failed to cross her mind when she devised the plan on the phone. The road leading up this mountain must have been cut in the old days, probably for logging, but the woods had since grown back. Cub and his dad drove the all-terrain up this way sometimes to get to the little shack on the ridge they used for turkey hunting. Or they used to do that, once upon a time, when the combined weight of the Turnbow men Senior and Junior was about sixty pounds less than the present day. Back when they used their feet for something other than framing the view of the television set. The road must have been poorly maintained even then. She recalled their taking the chain saw for clearing windfall.

She and Cub used to come up here by themselves, too, for so-called picnics. That was in the early days. Not one time since Cordie and Preston were born. It was crazy reckless to suggest the turkey blind on the family property, where she'd been with her husband, as a place to hook up. *Trysting place,* she thought, words from a storybook. And then: *No sense prettying up dirt,* words from a mother-in-law. But where else were they supposed to go? Her own bedroom, strewn with inside-out work shirts and a one-legged Barbie lying there staring while a person tried to get in the mood? Good night. And the Wayside Inn out on the highway was a pitiful place to begin with, before you even started deducting the wages of sin. Mike Bush at the counter would greet her by name: *How do, Mrs. Turnbow, now how's them kids?*

The path became confusing suddenly, her way blocked with branches. The upper part of a fallen tree lay across the path. The terrain was steep and the tree so immense she had to climb through it, stepping between sideways limbs with clammy leaves still clinging to the branch. Would *he* find his way through this, or might the wall of branches set him onto a different track? Her heart bumped around at the thought, unwilling to bear the ache of losing this one sweet chance. She considered waiting here. But he knew the way. He'd hunted from that turkey blind some seasons ago, he said. With his own friends, no one she or Cub knew. Younger, his friends would be.

She smacked her palms together to shuck off the damp grit and viewed the corpse of the fallen tree. It was a monster, more trunk than two people could get their arms around, and intact, not cut or broken by wind. That seemed a waste. After years of survival it had fallen out of the ground, roots and all, the wide fist of its root mass tearing open a dark clay gash in the wooded mountainside. Like herself, it had held on, held on, and then come loose. After so much rain upon rain this was happening all over the county. She'd seen stories in the paper of massive trees simply keeling over in the dead of night to ravage a family's roofline or flatten the car in the drive. The ground took water until it was nothing but soft sponge, and the trees fell out of it. Near Great Lick a whole hillside of mature timber had plummeted together, making a landslide of splintered trunks, rock and rill. People were shocked, even men like her father-in-law who generally met any terrible news with "that's nothing," claiming to have seen everything in creation several times already. But they'd never seen this, and had come to confessing it. In such strange times as these, they may have thought God was taking a hand in things and would notice a fib.

The road turned steeply up toward the ridge and petered out to a single track. A mile yet to go, maybe, she was just guessing. She tried to get a move on, imagining her long, straight red hair swinging behind her might look athletic, but her feet smarted as badly as her lungs. New boots, there was one more ruin to add to the pile. The boots were genuine calfskin, dark maroon, hand-tooled uppers and glossy pointed toes, so beautiful she'd nearly cried when she saw them at Second Time Around where she'd gone to find something decent for Preston to wear to kindergarten. The boots were six dollars, in like-new condition, the soles barely scuffed. Someone in the world had such a life, they could take one little walk in their expensive new cowgirl boots and then pitch them out, just because. The idea irked her to fury, even though she was the beneficiary. The boots were a half-size off but they looked perfect on and she bought them, her first purchase solely for herself in over a year, not counting hygiene products. Or cigarettes, which she surely did not count. She'd kept the boots hidden from Cub for no good reason, just to keep them precious. To have something that was hers. Every other thing got snatched from her hands: her hairbrush, the TV clicker, the soft middle part of her sandwich, the last Coke she'd waited all afternoon to open. She'd once had a dream of birds pulling the hair from her head in sheaves to make their nests.

Not that Cub would even have noticed if she'd worn these boots, and anyway she'd had no occasion. So why in the name of Pete had she put them on this morning to walk up a muddy hollow in the wettest fall on record? Black leaves formed a gummy layer beneath her instep and clung like dark fish scales to the tooled leather halfway up her calves. This day had played in her head like a movie on round-the-clock reruns, that's why. She had little other call to use her mind, in a world perfumed by urine and mashed bananas. Daydreaming was one thing she had in abundance; the price was right. She thought about the kissing mostly, when she sat down to manufacture a fantasy in earnest, but other details came along for the ride, the setting, wardrobe, everything in its place. This might be a difference in how men and women devised their fantasies, she thought. Clothes: present or absent. The new calfskin boots were a part of it, and so were the suede jacket borrowed from her best friend Dovey, the red chenille scarf wrapped around her neck, and other things he would slowly take off of her. She'd pictured it being cold like this, too. Her flyaway thoughts had not blurred out the inconveniences altogether. Her flushed cheeks, his warm hands smoothing the orange hair at her temples that he said looked painted on in brush-strokes, all these things were part and parcel. She'd pulled on the boots this morning as if she'd received written instructions.

And now she was in deep, though there had been no hanging offenses as yet, or none to speak of. They'd managed to be alone together for no more than about ten seconds at a time behind some barn or metal shed, hiding around the corner from where her car was parked with the kids buckled up inside, whining at full volume. "If I can still hear them they're still alive" is not a thought conducive to romance. Yet something drove her. His eyes, like the amber glass of a beer bottle, and his face full of dimpled muscles, the kind of grin that seems to rhyme with "chin." Just thinking of it made her skin prickle. And his way of taking her face in both his hands, dear God. Looking her in the eyes, rubbing the ends of her hair between his thumbs and fingers like he was counting money. These things brought her to sit on the closet floor and talk stupid with him on the phone, night after night, while her family slept under sweet closed eyelids. As she whispered in the dark, her husband's work shirts on their hangers idly stroked the top of her head, almost the same way Cub himself did when she sat on the floor with the baby while he occupied the whole couch, watching TV. Oblivious to the storm inside her, Cub seemed to move in slow motion. His gentleness made him seem dumb as a cow. It made her mad. There was no end to that anger if she let it out to run: the way Cub let his mother boss him around, making him clean his plate and tuck in his shirt-tails like a two-hundred-pound child. The embarrassment of his name. He could have been Burley Junior if he'd claimed it, but instead let his parents and everyone else in the county call him Cubby, as if he were still a boy, while the elder Burley Turnbow, his father, went by "Bear." A cub should grow up, but at thirty years of age this one still stood blinking at the door of the family den with his long face, the shock of blond hair in his eyes, his shoulders slumped in defeat. Now he would let himself be shamed by his wife's hardheartedness as well, or fail to notice it. Why should he keep on loving her so much while she lied through her teeth?

It was one more measure of her betrayal. She shocked herself. Putting Cordelia down for extra naps she did not need while Preston was at kindergarten, just to steal a free minute to call and make intimate bargains with a man who wasn't her husband. The urge was worse than wanting a cigarette, like something screaming in both her ears. Too many times to count she'd driven past where he lived, with the kids in the back seat, telling them she'd forgotten something and needed to go back to the store. She would say it was for ice cream or bullet pops, to shush them, but even a five-year-old could tell it was not the road to any store. Preston had voiced his suspicions, even though he could see hardly anything but the passing trees and telephone lines.

The telephone man, as she called this obsession – his name was too ordinary, you wouldn't wreck your life for a Jimmy – *the telephone man* was barely even a man. He'd said twenty-two, and that was a stretch. He lived in a mobile home with his mother and spent his weekends doing the things that interested males of that age, mixing beer and chain saws, beer and target shooting. There was no excuse for going off the deep end over someone that young. She longed for relief from her own wanting. She had put her hands in scalding dishwater on purpose, and chewed her lip to the rusty-nail taste of blood while lying in bed next to Cub. Exhausted and sleepless, she'd even tried taking a valium, one of three or four still rattling around in the ten-year-old prescription bottle they'd given her back when she lost the first baby. But the pill did nothing, had expired probably, like all else she had. A week ago she'd run a needle through the tip of her finger, with full intention, while sewing up a hole in Cordie's pajamas, and watched the blood jump out of her skin like dark red eye staring back. The wound still throbbed. Mortification of the flesh. She reprimanded herself with hateful words and none of them stopped her thoughts from going back to him. Or from speed-dialing him, making plans, driving by where he'd said he would be working that day just for the sight of him up the pole in his leather harness. Her desire felt like sickness. Such a strange turn of fortune had sent him her way in the first place: a tree falling and bringing down the phone line in front of the house on a cloudless, windless day. Everything that came after seemed unexplainable, like a spell of rain that falls in a week of predicted sunshine and mocks everyone by flooding out roads and fields. There is no use in blaming the weather predictors, and certainly not the rain or mud. These are only elements of the disaster, not the disaster itself.

Now here she was on a trail so steep it was killing her, out of control entirely, walking unarmed into the shoot-out of whatever was to be. Heartbreak, broken family. Broke, period. What she might do for money after Cub left her was anyone's guess. Nobody would even hire her as a waitress, they'd all side with him, and half the town would say they'd seen it coming, simply because they thrived on downfalls of any sort. *Wild in high school, that's how it goes with the pretty ones, early to ripe, early to rot.* They would say the words she'd once heard her mother-in-law say to Cub, that Dellarobia was a piece of work. As if she were lying in pieces strewn over a table, pins stuck here and there, half assembled from a Simplicity pattern that was flawed at the manufacturer's. Which piece had been left out?

People would probably line up to give opinions about that. The part that thinks ahead, for one. A stay-at-home wife with no skills to speak of, throwing sense to the four winds to run after a handsome boy who would not look after her two children or even stick around, probably, when the time came. Acting like there was no tomorrow. And yet. The way he looked at her suggested he'd be willing to bring her golden apples, or the Mississippi River. The way he closed his fingers in a bracelet around her ankles and wrists, marveling at her smallness, gave her the dimensions of a rare, expensive jewel rather than an inconsequential adult. No one had ever listened to her the way he did. Or looked, touching her hair reverently, trying to name its color: somewhere between a stop sign and sunset, he would say. Something between tomatoes and a ladybug. And her skin. He called her *Peach.*

No one else had ever called her anything. Only the given name her mother first sounded out for the birth certificate in a doped anesthetic haze, thinking it came from the Bible. Later on, her mother remembered that was wrong, it wasn't the Bible, she'd heard it at a craft demonstration at the Woman's Club. She found a picture of one in a ladies' magazine and yelled for her daughter to come look. Dellarobia was maybe six at the time and still remembered it: a dellarobia wreath, made of pine cones and acorns glued all over a Styrofoam core. "Something pretty, even still," her mother insisted, but the fall from grace seemed to presage coming events. Her performance to date was not what the Savior prescribed. Except marrying young, of course. That was the Lord's way for a girl with big dreams but no concrete plans, especially if a baby should be on the way. The baby that never quite was, that she never got to see, a monster. The preemie nurse said it had strange fine hair all over its body that was red like hers. Preston and Cordelia when they later arrived were both blondes, cut from the Turnbow cloth, but that first one that came in its red pelt of fur was a mean wild thing like her. Roping its parents into a shotgun wedding, then taking off with a laugh, leaving them stranded. Leaving them trying five years for another baby, just to fill a hole nobody meant to dig in the first place.

Something in motion caught her eye, yanking her glance upward as if jerked by a chain. How did it happen, that a thing outside of view could grab a person's attention? It was practically nothing, a fleck of orange wobbling above the trees, crossing overhead and drifting off to the left where the hill fell steeply from the trail. She made a face, thinking of red-headed ghosts. Making things up was beneath her. She set her eyes on the trail, purposefully not looking up, as if it were some unwelcome person up there waving hello. She was losing the fight against this hill, panting like a sheep. A poplar beside the trail invited her to stop there a minute. Fitting its smooth bulk between her shoulder blades, she cupped her hands to light the cigarette she'd been craving for half an hour. Inhaled through her nose, counted to ten, then gave in and looked up. Without her glasses it took some doing to get a bead on the thing, but there it still was, drifting in blank air above the folded terrain: an orange butterfly on a rainy day. Its out-of-place brashness provoked her, like the wacked-out sequences in children's books: Which of these does not belong? An apple, a banana, a taxicab. A nice farmer, a married mother of two, a sexy telephone man. She watched the speck of color waver up the hollow while she finished her cigarette and carefully ground out the butt with her boot. Only you can prevent forest fires. She pulled her scarf around her throat and walked on with eyes glued to the ground. This boy had better be worth it: there was a thought. Not the sexiest one in the world, either. Possibly a sign of sense returning.

The last part of the trail was the steepest, that much she recalled from her high-school frolics up here. Who could forget that ankle-bending climb? Rocky and steep and *dark*, as she entered the section of woods people called the Christmas Tree Farm, fir trees planted long ago in some scheme that never panned out. The air grew suddenly colder, as if the looming conifers were holding an old grudge, peeved at being passed over. The fir forest felt spooky with its own weather. What had she been thinking, to name that hunting shack for a meeting place? Romance felt as unreachable now as it did after any average day of toting kids and dredging the floor of doll babies. She could have made things easy on herself, wrecked her life in a motel room like a sensible person, but no. Her legs were tired and her butt ached. She could feel blisters welling on both feet. The boots she'd adored this morning now seemed idiotic, their slick little heels designed for parading your hind quarters in jeans, not real walking. Worthless, in other words, like anything else she'd ever have. She watched her step, considering what a broken ankle would add to her day. The trail was a cobbled mess of loose rocks that ran straight uphill in spots, so badly rutted she had to grab saplings to steady herself.

She was relieved to arrive on a level stretch of ground carpeted with brown fir needles. But something dark loomed from a branch over the trail. A hornet's nest was her first thought, or a swarm of bees looking for a new home. She'd seen that happen. But this thing was not humming. She approached slowly, hoping to scoot under it, with or without a positive ID. It bristled like a cluster of dead leaves or a down-turned pine cone but was much bigger than that. Like an armadillo in a tree, she thought, with no notion of how large that would be. Scaly all over and pointed at the lower end, as if it had gone oozy and might drip. She didn't much care to walk under it. For the second time she wished for the glasses she'd left behind. Vanity was one thing, but out here in the damn wilderness a person needed to see. She squinted upward into dark branches backlit by pale sky. The angle made her a little dizzy.

Her heart thumped. These things were all over everywhere. They dangled like gigantic bunches of grapes from every tree she could see from where she stood. *Fungus* was the word that came to mind, and it turned down the corners of her mouth. Trees were getting new diseases now. Cub had told her the strange weather of recent years, wetter summers and milder winters, had brought in new pests that apparently ate the forest out of house and home.

She pulled her jacket close and hurried underneath the bristly thing, ducking, even though it hung a good ten feet above the trail so she cleared it by five. She shivered and ran her fingers through her hair afterward and felt childish for fearing a tree-fungus. The day couldn't decide whether to warm up or not. Now it felt cool. She'd rounded the bend into a hollow where the evergreen shade was deep. Fungus brought to mind scrubbing the mildewed shower curtain with Mr. Clean, one of her life's main events. She tried to push that out of her thoughts, concentrating instead on her reward at the end of the climb. She imagined surprising him as he stood by the shack waiting for her, coming up on him from behind, the sight of his backside in jeans. He'd promised to come early if he could, and hinted he actually might be naked when she arrived. He was bringing a big soft quilt and a bottle of Cold Duck. *Lord love a duck,* she thought. After subsisting for years on leftovers and juice boxes, she'd be drunk in ten minutes. She shivered again but hoped it was a pang of desire, not the chill of a wet day and a dread of tree fungus. Should it be that hard to tell the difference?

The path steered out of the shadow into a bright overlook on the open side of the slope, and here she slammed on her brakes, here something was wrong. Or just strange. The tree limbs above her had more of the brittle things, but that was the least of it. The view out across the valley was puzzling and unreal, like a sci-fi movie. From this overlook she could see the forested mountainside that lay opposite, from top to bottom, and the full stand of it was transformed, thickly loaded with the bristly things. She studied those fir trees in the hazy distance, for they were like nothing she'd ever seen. Their branches looked droopy and bulbous, disproportionate. Trunks and boughs alike were speckled and scaly like trees covered with corn flakes. She had small children, she'd seen things covered with corn flakes. Most of the woodland she could see from here, from the valley all the way up to the ridge, seemed altered and pale, the beige of dead leaves. But these were evergreen trees, they should be dark, and that wasn't foliage. There was movement in it. The branches seemed to writhe. She shook her head and backed up a step from the overlook and the worrisome trees, though they stood far away across the thin air of the hollow. She reached into her purse for a cigarette, then stopped.

Those trees were alive. And not trees. The light changed somehow, a slight shift of cloud and sun, causing the whole surface to rearrange and brighten before her gaze. A forest lit with its own internal flame, grown wild upon the land. Really there were no words for it. "Jesus," she said, not calling for help, she didn't consider the man a close friend, but putting her voice in the world because nothing else present made sense. The sun slipped a little further from the clouds, just a degree, passing its warmth across these trees or not-trees on the mountainside and she saw them light up like an explosion of candles. Each drooping bough glowed with its own orange blaze. "Jesus God," she said again. No other words came to her that seemed sane. *A tree has turned into fire before my eyes.* Just her luck, a burning bush.

Bits of flame lifted from the faraway treetops in showers of orange sparks, exploding the way a pine log does in a campfire when you poke it. The sparks swept upward from the pointed conifers into violent swirls, like tornadoes. Exactly that shape, like funnel clouds twisting their dark, long-waisted columns over a prairie, but these were tornadoes of brightness against a gray sky. In broad daylight with no comprehension, she watched. Flints of orange light lifted up out of the funnels and sailed undirected above the dark forest, like sparks of free will.

It made no sense. A forest fire would roar. This consternation swept up the mountain in perfect silence. The air above remained cold and clear. No smoke, no crackling howl. She stopped breathing for a second and closed her eyes to listen: nothing. Only a faint patter like rain on leaves. *Not fire,* she thought, but her eyes when she opened them could only tell her *fire, this place is burning.* They said *get out of here.* Up or down, she was not sure. She felt trapped, eyeing the dark uncertainty of the trail and uncrossable breach of the valley. The sun lit more trees, reaching deep into the woods, and it was all the same everywhere, every tree aglow.

She cupped her hands over her face and tried to think. She was miles from her kids. Cordie with her thumb in her mouth, Preston with his long-lashed eyes cast down. The child soaked up guilt like a sponge, even when he'd done no wrong. She knew what their lives would become if something happened to her up here, on a mission of sin. Hester would rain shame on those babies for all time. Or worse, what if they thought their mother had simply run off and left them? What else *could* they think? No one knew to look for her here. Her thoughts clotted with the vocabulary of news reports: dental records, next of kin, sifting through the ash.

And Jimmy? Jimmy. She forced herself to think his name because he was a person too, not just a destination. He might be up there already. And in a single second, that worry lifted from her like a flake of ash. For the first time she saw the truth of this day, for her the end of all previous comfort and safety, and for him, something else entirely. A kind of game. Nothing to change his life. *We'll strike out boldly*, she'd told herself, and into what, his mother's mobile home? Somehow it had come to pass that this man was her whole world, and she'd failed to take his measure. Neither child nor father, he knew how to climb telephone poles and he knew how to disappear. The minute he sniffed trouble, he would slip down the back side of the mountain and go on home. Nothing could be more certain. He had the instincts of the young. He would be back at work before anyone knew he'd called in sick. Even if she turned up in the news as charred remains, he would keep their story quiet, thinking to protect her family. Or so he'd tell himself. Look what she'd nearly done. She paled at the size her foolishness had attained, how large and crowded it was, how devoid of any structural beams. It could be knocked down and flattened like a circus tent.

She was on her own here. A woman alone, staring at glowing trees. A cool fascination curled itself around her fright. This was no forest fire. She was pressed by the quiet, the elation of escape and knowing better and seeing straight through to the back of herself for once, the pleasure of solitude. She couldn't remember the last time she'd had such room for being. This was not just one more false thing in a life's cheap chain of events, right up to the sneaking-around romance in someone else's thrown-away boots. That ended here. This unearthly beauty had appeared to her and to no one else as a vision of glory to halt her in her path. For her eyes these orange boughs were lifted up, these long shadows transformed to a chorus of light and a brightness rising. It looked like the inside of joy, if a person could see that. A valley of lights, an ethereal wind. It had to mean something.

She could save herself. Herself and her children with their soft cheeks and milky breath who believed in what they had, even if their whole goodness and mercy was a mother distracted out of her mind. It was not too late to undo this mess. Walk down the mountain, pick up those kids. The burning trees were put here to save her. It was the strangest conviction she'd ever known, and nonetheless she felt sure of it. She had no use for superstition, had walked unlucky roads until she'd just as soon walk under any ladder as go around it. She considered herself unexceptional and by no means important enough for God to conjure signs and wonders on her account. The one thing that had set her apart, briefly, was an outsized and hellish obsession. To stop a thing like that would require a burning bush, a fighting of fire with fire.

Her eyes still signaled warning to her brain, like a car alarm gone off somewhere in an empty parking lot. She failed to heed it, understanding at least for the moment some complex formula for living that transcended fear and safety. She wondered merely how long she ought to watch this spectacle before turning away. It was something greater than fire. If not a sign, then in any case a wonder.

***

The roof of her house when she saw it again still harbored its dark patches of damaged shingles, and there sat her car in the drive where she'd parked it. The life she had recently left for dead was there, laid out like a corpse for the wake. The sheep remained at their posts, huddled in twos and threes around the pond. On the hillside beyond the pasture, the regular dots of the neighbors' dying peach orchard still exposed that family's bled-out luck. Not a thing on God's green earth had changed, only everything had. Or she was dreaming. She'd come down the mountain in less than half the time it took to climb, and that was plenty long enough for her doubt the whole of this day: what she'd planned to do, what she had seen, and what she'd left undone. Each of these was enormous. If they added up to nothing, then what? Of all things, it was emptiness she could bear not a minute longer. She would not walk back to a life measured in half dollars and clipped coupons and culled hopes, served out inside uninsulated walls. She'd pined for loss and wreckage, as the alternative. But there might be others. A cold fire on the mountain had brought her back here to something.

She tried to study in some born-again way the cheap ranch house with its white vinyl siding, its yard devoid of landscaping save for one straggling rose by the porch, a Mother's day present from Cub, who'd forgotten she disliked roses. The silver Taurus wagon in the drive, crookedly parked in haste. It could not be more tedious or familiar.

The sadness of that filled her up like water. And yet she was a person who had not fled. The choice she'd left herself was to scrutinize ugliness as a treasure map, puzzling out the hidden worth in a lawn strewn with weathered plastic toys. The black nursery pot she'd meant to throw out after planting the rose, months ago. The car keys where she always left them, in the ignition, as if anybody around here would drive it away. The faint metal sound like a pipe dropped on its end when she put the car into gear.

She turned out onto the highway and clicked on the radio. Kenny Chesney was waiting there to pounce, crooning in his molasses voice that he wanted to know what forever felt like, urging her once more to gallop away. She clicked Kenny right off. She turned up her in-laws' drive to their farmhouse with its two uncurtained upstairs windows like the eye sockets of a skull. Hester's flowerbeds had melted under the summer's endless rain, as had the garden. They'd finished tomato canning almost before they'd started, anything red was long gone. Hester's prized rose beds were now just thorny outposts clotted with fists of mildew. It was Hester who loved roses, their cloying scent and falling-apart flowerheads, for Dellarobia they only opened doors straight into the memory of her parents' funerals. She got out of the car, surveying the front yard where only a single bright spot of color stood out: one of Cordelia's tiny acid-green socks lay on the stone step where she must have dropped it this morning, bringing the kids in. This sock was not the measure of her worth. She swiped it up on her way up the steps and stuck it in her pocket, abashed to confront the woman she'd been just a few hours ago, dying of a sickness. She opened the door without knocking.

Cramped indoor odors met her: cat, carpet, spilled milk. The kids sat together on the living room rug in a tableau of brave abandonment. Preston sat close behind Cordie with his chin nested on her fuzzy head and his arms around her, showing her a picture book, with the two collies stretched on either side in alert recline, a pair of protective sphinxes. All their eyes flew up to her as she entered, keen for rescue, their grandmother nowhere in sight. Preston's dark, plaintive eyebrows were identical to his father's, aligned across his forehead as if drawn there by a ruler. Cordelia reached up both hands and burst into tears, her little mouth turned down in a bawl so intense it showed her bottom teeth.

The TV drone in the kitchen died abruptly and Hester appeared in the doorway, still in her bathrobe, her hair coiled around pink foam curlers. Hester's hair was too thin and too gray to wear it as long as she did. The rollers seemed a slight improvement. On her kids' behalf Dellarobia gave their caretaker an indignant look, probably just a slightly less toothy version of Cordie's. It wasn't as if she asked Hester to watch the kids every day of the week. Not even once a month.

Hester returned the glare. "The way you run around, I wasn't expecting you back till after dinner."

"But here I am. It's a miracle, isn't it?"

How like that woman, Dellarobia thought, to cover her own neglectful behavior with an armed assault. Cordelia stood up precariously, red-faced and howling. She was wet, and probably had been all morning. The diaper bulge inside her yellow footie pajamas was like a big round pumpkin. No wonder the child couldn't balance. Dellarobia took a drag on her almost-finished cigarette, trying to decide whether to change Cordie here or just get out of Dodge.

"You shouldn't smoke when you're around them kids," her mother-in-law announced in a gravel voice. A woman who'd probably blown smoke in Cub's little red face the minute he was born.

"Oh my goodness, I would never do that. I only smoke when I'm lying out getting a suntan on the Riviera."

Hester looked stunned, meeting Dellarobia's flat gaze, eyeing the boots and the red scarf. "Look at you. What's got into you?"

Dellarobia wondered if she looked as she felt, like a woman fleeing a fire.

"Preston, honey, say bye-bye to your Mammaw." She clenched the filter of her cigarette lightly between her teeth so she could take Preston's hand, lift Cordelia to her hip with the other, and steer her family toward something better than this.

Twitter: Want to discuss or share what you just read? Use the hashtag #beaFLIGHT to connect with others.

ABOUT THE AUTHOR

Barbara Kingsolver is the author of eight works of fiction, including the novels *The Lacuna, The Poisonwood Bible, Animal Dreams,* and *The Bean Trees,* as well as books of poetry, essays, and creative nonfiction. Her only work of narrative nonfiction was the enormously influential bestseller *Animal, Vegetable, Miracle: A Year of Food Life.* Kingsolver's work has been translated into more than twenty languages and has earned literary awards and a devoted readership at home and abroad. In 2000, she was awarded the National Humanities Medal, our country's highest honor for service through the arts. Kingsolver was also the recipient of the 2011 Dayton Literary Peace Prize for the body of her work. She lives with her family on a farm in southern Appalachia.

Imprint: HarperCollins
BEA Booth #: 3339
Print ISBN: 9780062124265
Print price: $28.99
eBook ISBN: 9780062124289
eBook price: $22.99
Publication date: 11/1/2012
Publicity contact: Jane Beirn jane.beirn@harpercollins.com
Editor: Terry Karten
Agent: Francis Goldin
Agency: Francis Goldin Literary Agency

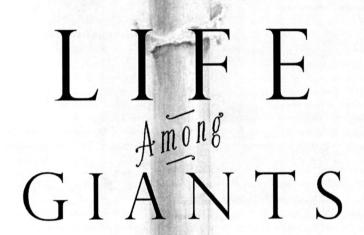

LIFE
Among
GIANTS

A NOVEL BY

BILL
ROORBACH

SUMMARY

At seventeen, David "Lizard" Hochmeyer is nearly seven feet tall, a star quarterback, and Princeton-bound. His future seems all but assured until his parents are mysteriously murdered, leaving Lizard and his older sister, Kate, adrift and alone. Over the months, years, and decades that follow, Lizard and Kate are obsessed with piecing together the motives behind the deaths, returning time and again to their father's missing briefcase, his shady business dealings and shaky finances, and to a famous ballerina who has threaded her way into Lizard's and Kate's lives. A wildly entertaining novel of murder, seduction, and revenge—rich in incident, in expansiveness of character, and in lavishness of setting—it's a Gatsby-esque adventure, a larger-than-life quest for answers that reveals how sometimes the greatest mystery lies in knowing one's own heart.

EXCERPT

Chapter 1

I have a thing about last meals. Not as in prisoners about to be executed—they know it's going to be their last. But as in just about everyone else, most all of us. Whatever's coming, there's going to be that last thing we eat. My folks, for example. They did pretty well in the last-meal department, beautiful restaurant, family all around them, perfect sandwiches made by someone who truly cared about food. Lunch, as it happened. Their last meal, I mean. For my sister it was breakfast, but that was years later, and I'll get to all that. The point is, I like to eat every meal as if it were the last, as if I knew it were the last: savor every bite, be there with the food, make sure it's good, really worthy. And though it's an impossible proposition, I try to take life that way, too: every bite my last.

My father told me I could do what I set my mind to, though it hadn't been true for him. Mom told me not to expect everything to go my way, probably because of her own bad luck with Dad. She wasn't a mom to coddle you; she thought once you were ten you could make lunch for yourself. And we did, Katy and I, wild inventions, often edible. Dad ate what we offered, never a complaint.

He wasn't one of those fathers who did it all for a kid; he liked to stand back and watch, ready to give a standing ovation, but ready to withhold it, too. My mother was tough on Katy, pushed her toward tennis stardom. The same mom took no particular interest in my football career, hoped I'd pick up a more useful hobby, like gardening. And Mom and I spent hours in the borders around our modest house most Sunday mornings—the azaleas were our church. Who knew what Kate and Dad were up to? Always in cahoots, as my mother like to say.

But Mom was Dad's one true love: Barbara Barton Hochmeyer, a real prize, her wedding photos like glamour shots, his only great success knocking her up to produce Katy, he wasn't shy to tell us, the very boy Mom's father dreaded: no-college Nicky H. She was a formidable woman, all right, tall and broad in the shoulders, a tennis star in her day, club champion to the end, always organized and scheduled and ready to go. Nick was slicker, looked for leeway, wasn't one for a plan. Words were their sharpest weapons, and they didn't need more than a few. She called him inept; he called her unloving. *Kaboom!* Their fights were like boxing matches—all the moves well practiced, weeks of workouts in preparation, strategies stored up, sucker punches in desperation.

Figurative punches, I mean.

He apologized elaborately after bouts of anger, after errors, after outlandish deceptions, foolish decisions, all of which were frequent. Mom wasn't one to apologize—Mom was always right—but quietly she'd wear a tight dress he loved, or bake him one of the oddball pies he liked: gooseberry, mincemeat, quince. And the two of them were constantly up to their bedroom, where they made way too much noise, lovers till the end.

Katy and I had a private world. The cellar was the crater made by the crash of our spaceship, the old stone stairs a rock-climb to the dangerous new planet above. The object was to make it to the attic, collect the magic cloak (a sable cape that had belonged to our grandma) and get back downstairs unnoticed by the natives, great fun during our parents' frequent parties: Mr. Coussens sniffing his way through Mom's underwear drawer, Mrs. Paumgartner slipping a porcelain bunny into her purse, the pockets of all those coats piled on the bed unsafe from our alien feelers: diaphragms, strange syringes, once even a revolver, pretty pearl handle, polished steel barrel, chambers fully loaded. My big sister and I passed it back and forth—surprisingly heavy.

On family trips back to Mom's lakeside Michigan from our corporate Connecticut, Kate and I were the backseat duo—barely a year apart—always some elaborate card trick or dance routine (no seat belts, not in those days). The motel rooms we shared inspired protosex games: Monster in the Dark, Cannibal, the Blob. But at Lake Winnipesauke, summer of 1964, Katy stopped playing. Later in the week, as we sat bobbing bored on a raft, she said, "I've got hair." And pulled the crotch of her suit aside briefly to show me, frank kid.

She was even then a girl who harbored secrets, parceling them out on a need-to-know basis. She was a shoplifter in junior high, a Freon sniffer freshman year, a medicine-cabinet bandit after that, a dealer of hashish at times, small amounts in glassine envelopes she showed me the way she'd shown me her pubes: frankly, briefly, with the understanding it wasn't for me. Before long I was making pipes for her from every odd material in the house, gifts in adoration, though I never liked to smoke. Also—and this seems more important in hindsight— she had what she called "magnificent thoughts": sometimes she saw the world as if from high above. Looking off bridges she could feel her wings flex. Looking at the sea she grew fins. These big moods were balanced by weeks of darkness, bleak pronouncements, irritability, furtive movements.

Her most ironclad secret was boys. Tim Hayes was the only one I actually encountered, a kid I knew as the leather-jacket guy. Home early from freshman football one inclement afternoon I walked in on them, he naked, she fully clothed (still wearing her rain slicker, in fact), her face flushed dark. Arousal filled her pink bedroom as if with smoke, stung my eyes and caught in my throat as I made my escape: I'd been seen. Later, Katy pledged me to secrecy. "I made him *strip*." To what end, she didn't say.

My sister was what I knew about sex before I dated. In fact, she was what I knew about girls, period. Lady Kate sank into a kind of simmering monthly funk that I knew to be womanly in some way: she gave off actual heat, owned special items, left spots of blood on the bathroom tiles.

I came into the high school as into a foreign country, looked to Katy for guidance, but very little guidance was forthcoming. Where I wanted only to fit in, she was falling out. To all appearances we were a team, the clean-cut Hochmeyer kids, sharply dressed, serious students, successful athletes, ready smiles, good deeds. And I *believed* in those things, felt them readily as our identity. But my sister clearly did not believe or feel the same.

Half the guys on the freshman football team had crushes on her, asked me how to proceed, asked me to put in a good word, asked me to set them up. Of course I didn't: what would Katy want with my jerky pals? She didn't really have boyfriends at all, not as far as I knew. Yet as soon as the pill became available, she was on it, a circular month's supply hidden among the dust balls under my dresser: Mom never searched *my* room for anything, ever.

And Kate's friends might have been a source of dates for me, but they were the tennis girls, a tight-knit crowd with muscular legs, deep tans, and lanky, bespectacled boyfriends from the local country clubs.

Otherwise, oddballs: she ate lunch with Giant Janine the goiter girl, who spat food and often burst into tears; she stood at the bus line with Mark O'Meara, the thalidomide boy, unafraid to grasp the tiny hands that grew from his shoulders; she idolized June Harrison, who played piano well despite the wheelchair, spent nights at her house. She courted drama, was enamored of difference.

She in her own heart was a freak, is my guess now. Otherwise, why all the secrets?

In our nice stone house—three bedrooms, huge yard sloping to willowwept water, one-car garage—we thought of ourselves as of modest means. Because across the pond, on what was called the High Side, there loomed an immutable example of what it was to be truly rich: a mansion the size of an embassy. In winter, you could see the far-flung wings of it across the ice and occasionally the movements of its tenant, the world-famous ballerina Sylphide (say it in the French manner: sill-*feeeed*, as many *e*'s as you wish), whose even more famous husband, the English rocker Dabney Stryker-Stewart, had died on the Merritt Parkway (as everyone in the world knows), piling his Shelby GT Mustang at eighty-some miles per hour into the abutment of one of those handsome Depression-era WPA bridges. But the body wasn't with the car, didn't show up for two full days, found flopped by a muddy stream nearly half a mile from the accident scene. Had Dabney wandered dazed from the crash? Or was there foul play?

Despite months and then years and even decades of conjecture and investigation and conspiracy theory, answers were not forthcoming. The sorrow and disbelief (some say madness) on Sylphide's veil-shadowed face in the famous photo of her standing at his graveside in Newcastle, England—well, it still haunts me, haunts everyone, the closing visual bracket on an era that begins with John-John Kennedy saluting at the graveside of his dad.

There'd been another person at the High Side, too, Dabney's child from a previous marriage, just as famous as his father and step-mom: Linsey the *Life* magazine boy, visited for a photo shoot every year on his birthday, both physically and mentally deformed, as we would have said it then, anyway, profoundly challenged (fetal-alcohol syndrome is my diagnosis in hindsight—the abandoning birth mother was a lush and a leech, famously). He was sweet as a puppy, small and soft and helpless, those huge eyes, but with a weird sense of humor and sly smile, a secret nasty streak the rest of us delighted in. He'd been a vexed and cross-eyed fixture in my classes from kindergarten straight through, the richest kid in the public schools, mainstreamed before mainstreaming was even a concept, all because the private day schools in the area wouldn't have him, and his stepmother—the greatest ballerina in the history of the world—wouldn't allow him to be institutionalized. The superintendent of Westport schools was happy to oblige, as were Linsey's teachers: the boy was charming, and you got to hobnob with the famous parents.

By the early sixties, Sylphide and Dabney had become the world's own royal couple, their courtship and subsequent wedding a glimmering fairytale. He bought her various castles and mansions and retreats around the world, but the High Side became their home base. The permanent move to the U.S. from London came with her elevation in 1964 to principal of the New York City Ballet (George Balanchine her longtime mentor and devoted fan—"Her *sweetness* of thought," he famously wrote, "her *sweetness* of motion and lineament emerges from the very core of her soul, moves ever outward"—of course I'm working from Google for my quotations), and was followed by Dabney's megaplatinum album *Dancer* (the only album at the time other than *Meet the Beatles* to contain more than one number-one single, four in fact; I'm still always catching his melodies in waiting rooms and elevators). The beloved in all the songs was Sylphide, or so we thought, and that's her on the wildly controversial original album cover (the cover that got pulled after two weeks in favor of the safer and more familiar airplane image), that sleek, modest, achingly shy nymph fleeing naked into the forest with an almost taunting glance over her shoulder, blond hair streaming sweetly, misty golden light, her high, pretty fanny more plain lovable than erotic.

But then, I was just eleven.

My big sister was to become well acquainted with the dancer. By the time I finished junior year Kate had, in fact, babysat and tutored and contained Linsey for nearly four years. She'd been pledged to utmost discretion, became insufferable about her constant contact with fame. She was stingy with the free *Swan Lake* and Dabney Stewart-Stryker tickets and hoarded amusing or shocking inside stories (dinner parties attended by Mick Jagger or Julie Christie or Muhammad Ali, even the likes of Twiggy; Marlon Brando naked with three girls in the High Side pool, no one swimming). Katy's closets were filled with old Nehru jackets and worn-out guitar straps, her summers with exotic jaunts, three weeks here, four weeks there, various points in Europe or Africa, trips to famous Japanese and Brazilian and Australian cities during every school vacation and often *during* school, the lucky duck. The Prince and Princess needed her, and of course the puppy-eyed Princeling most of all.

One Wednesday evening in my senior year, Kate off at college, one especially wonderful Wednesday in the especially warm October of 1970, just as Mom and Dad and I were sitting down to an especially wonderful dinner (fishsticks and frozen French fries, plenty of ketchup, mounds of canned peas), several black cars pulled into our cul-de-sac and parked neatly along the curb. Two men from each car headed for our different doorways. We could see them coming every step of the way. If we'd been armed and dangerous, they'd have been toast. Dad was calm, simply let the main guys in the front door. "FBI," one of them announced. Another offered him sheaves of papers, which he didn't take. They let him gather a few things—toothbrush, fresh underwear—and then they took him away, multiple felonies connected to his work at Dolus Financial. (Yes, *that* Dolus Financial, the one that all these years later has collapsed under its own weight despite some 15 billion in federal cash.)

"Dad's had some trouble at work," Mom said when he was gone, no particular emotion. "Bail has been set very high."

Later I heard her cursing him out in her room. "Fucking asshole" was the exact phrase, repeated endlessly, Bar-Bar someone who never swore, except on the tennis court.

A few days layer (October 30, 1970, to be exact), Dad's court-appointed lawyer—a portly sycophant named McBee—met us at the courtroom steps, gazed up at me.

"Ozymandias," he said darkly.

I knew what he was saying, more or less, knew my Keats from Honors English. "It just means I hit my head a lot," I said.

"Seven feet?"

"Only six eight," I told him.

McBee wheezed, sighed, gave us our marching orders: "Okay, just as I discussed with your mom. You kids, you must look solemn. Pretend it's his funeral. Look one part pissed, two parts forgiving, like people who are going to put your old man on the straight and narrow. Got it?"

My sister put on a face—pissed forgiveness is hard to do—and of course kept putting it on, and soon I couldn't stop giggling. Kate wasn't laughing much in those days, kept the straightest face possible, which just made things the worse for me. We hadn't seen each other since she'd left home for her first year at "New Haven" (you weren't supposed to say the name of the school), and she looked great. Mom was plainly irritated with her, but said nothing, just as she'd said nothing about Katy's tennis clothes, which were hardly appropriate for the occasion.

Katy's new boyfriend was there, Jack Cross, who (shockingly enough) was her professor. He was a stoic guy with wild hair and posh court-day clothing, meeting Mom for the first time. Solicitous, he took the old lady's arm, shot Kate a look that froze her. And silenced me, too. Because, well, I'd met him before.

Plenty of secrets in our family.

Under the dome of the stately courthouse lobby (still not so grand as the High Side foyer), Mom brushed her hair and pinned it into a bun, made her face up in a tiny mirror, reclaimed her gorgeous poise. The courtroom itself was just plain, nothing but cinderblocks and workaday furniture, the judge at a table in shirtsleeves, not what I'd pictured.

Mom and Kate and I took seats in the front row. Jack sat in the row behind us. He was Dad's age, Mom's age, craggy as a sea cliff. My mother had asked if I thought he and Kate were sleeping together. Unlikely, I told her. Kate, who'd never even had a boyfriend? Sleeping with a professor? Easy lies. Because I knew more, a lot more. Kate basically lived at Jack's beautiful house, for example. And I'd visited them there. I'd liked him for not mentioning my height, a feat few could manage. He'd even loaned me a car to take home to our family. That was the kind of man he was, someone with extra cars. Dad had lost ours. The kind of man who lost them. For Mom's sake I'd said the loan was from Katy's roommate, true enough, as far as it went.

The judge shuffled papers. He looked like an insect. People came and went, whispered to him, whispered to one another. Kate wasn't the only one with a new love. My mind wandered over Emily Bright's brown skin, her soft and secret hair, a whole night of her kisses and long hands, Emily in the shower, Emily in my little bed all night while Mom was away managing Dad's crisis, wreaking her vicious serve on defense and prosecution alike. Two cops brought him out in his rumpled business clothes, handcuffs in front. He definitely looked like a guy who'd been in jail, dusty and pallid, badly mussed. He scanned the room back over his shoulder, couldn't find us.

McBee approached the bench with the sandy-haired prosecutor, said a few quiet sentences. The prosecutor said several more—nothing we could make out—and the judge nodded. He looked to Dad. Dad said a long, long paragraph, almost silent, his back to us, his posture weary, carefully remorseful. When he was done the judge made a sign and two African- American men the size of NFL tackles stepped to Dad's side. The judge instructed them, didn't look at my father. They nodded seriously. A bailiff came in, removed Dad's handcuffs. Exhausted smiles all around. The gavel.

Dad had gone state's witness. He turned to us, looking unhappy as ever. He shuffled over to the docket gate. "Lunch," he said.

Katy leapt to him and hugged him with all her strength, which was considerable. Dad teared up, choked and sobbed. Mom joined them, offered hugs, too, less voluble. She wasn't buying the tears. Professor Cross waited for the exact moment, found it, shook my father's hand. I could see from the brisk quality of the shake and greeting that they already knew one another, too, more secrets.

The prosecutor sidled over before I could join the greeting, gave Dad ten fond slaps on the shoulder. "We'll be getting to know each other very well," he said. He gave Katy a long look, the way certain kinds of men did, up and down, down and up, wry twinkle when he got to her eyes.

Katy didn't turn away but took him on.

"State Champions," he said to me, tearing his eyes from hers, a guy who must have played football himself, years back.

"Yessir," I said.

"You're even bigger than they say. Gonna repeat this year?" Dishonest eyes, a guy on the take, something you could see from a vantage point high as mine.

I didn't feel any need to explain I'd quit the team. "Sure," I said.

Mom accepted a folder of papers from McBee, who looked proud of himself. And finally it was time to go. With the big African-American guys—Dad's security detail—we formed a phalanx around the old man, made our way out to the parking lot. He said, "They're paying for the best restaurant around. It's all approved."

My mother made a show of not being impressed.

Dad rode with his guards. We dutifully followed. The restaurant was called Les Jardins, and it was very fancy, all right, acres of garden, empty fountains. Empty parking lots, too, and an empty dining room—it wasn't even eleven o'clock yet. At our lace-and-lantern table, under the staid textures of what Dad said were real medieval tapestries, we ordered Bloody Marys, though Kate and I were underage. When his drink arrived, Dad looked happy for the only time so far that day. He chugged it down and ordered another before the waiter, working around the table, had even managed to put mine in front of me.

"Love this place," Dad said. The bodyguards stood in two corners of the room, deadly serious, no lunch for them. The Bloody Marys were like salads, spears of celery, slices of green and red pepper, home-pickled pole beans. Emily the night before with Mom away was our first time, my first time, and I couldn't stop thinking of her skin, the skin on her inside, too, endless minute visions, her brown skin, and pink, her kisses, the nipples of her breasts like knots to untie with your tongue.

No prices on the menu.

Mom choked down sudden rage, I could see it.

Jack said, "These are going to be difficult weeks."

We sat in silence, empty dining room soon to fill, clatter from the kitchen, bitting our celery stalks.

"How's your tennis, Katy?" Dad said suddenly in his investments voice, loud and jovial, always disastrous.

"Good," Katy said, not buying.

Same voice: "No, I mean, give us the works. Who the heck have you played? What are the rankings? How awful is your coach? Bring us through the season."

Mom writhed, rankled.

Which inspired Katy. She took Dad's cue and held forth. Her coach was brilliant, she'd been seeded high. Dad signaled for a third drink, or maybe it was his fourth, or even fifth, impossible to keep up with him. We all slaughtered a basket of bread, speared our tiny salads. Just the previous weekend, Dad not yet in jail, Kate had played the longest match in the history of the Hanover Classic, but lost finally to the top seed—a girl from Penn.

"I cried," my sister said.

"She howled," Jack said.

"Oh, honey," Mom said, not very warmly.

"I'm sorry," Dad said. And then he laughed, booming mirth, vodka hitting the old brain, bones all sore from jail, laughed his hollow laugh, deeply all alone inside his misery.

The meals arrived, really gorgeous, simple BLTs, thick, flavorful bacon like I'd never had, slices of tomato thick as steaks, crisp, fresh-picked lettuce from the gardens beyond. We ate in the silence, Mom's silence, except a single moment in which Jack cleared his throat. But he thought better of whatever it was he was planning to say, and we all looked back to our food.

The waiter cleared the table efficiently, dropped dessert menus in front of us. No other diners had arrived. The place was like church.

"So, state's evidence," I said. I just wanted to jumpstart a conversation, the one we really should be having.

"I'm not allowed to say much," Dad said. He nodded toward the bigger of the guards.

"But he'll be free when it's all done," said Mom, no apparent joy in the thought.

"Get my good name back," Dad said.

"They're treating you very well," said Jack. He was a psychologist with a famous book and plush towels in his house, that's all I knew.

"Daddy's got valuable information," Kate said wryly. Her neck, her arms, even her wrists were thicker than when she'd left home, more muscular, much healthier: college sports.

"Always something to sell," said Mom, mocking.

"Didn't we agree . . ." Dad said, but he trailed off.

Mom pounced: "We agreed on *lots* of things. We have always agreed on *everything*. And look, just *look* where we *are*."

Kate slammed her water glass down on the polished table. "Just get off his back," she said.

And Mom said, "Don't *you* start."

Jack said, "Of course we're all tense. Couple of deep breaths here." Mom puffed and fumed, but Jack had a way about him.

Dad said, "I'm thinking cognac."

"If you want to know," Kate began.

Cutting her off, gentleman Jack said, "I'd really better get Kate back to campus. The tennis van leaves for Ithaca at two. She's supposed to travel with the team if at all possible. Your girl gets another crack at Miss Penn again this weekend, if all goes well."

"We leave at three," Kate said, sudden wince.

He'd kicked her leg under the table. "I believe it's two," he said.

"No dessert?" Dad said. He wasn't oblivious, though, and let them get up and go without protest, just an overly long hug for Kate, and a kiss on her hair. She kissed him back, on his cheek, his ear. They whispered to one another, patted at each other, always in league. He held her out for a look, straightened her collar, gave a tidying tug at the pockets of her tiny skirt. Once again, tears started to his eyes, but this time continued to flow. More hugs.

"These have been tough days," he said over her shoulder.

"Not only for you," Mom said.

"Always selfless," Kate said to her bitterly.

"Don't force your backhand," Mom said brightly, as if it were just tennis advice.

"Good afternoon," Jack said, enormous warmth. You could certainly see why Katy liked him, forty-year-old genie with a famous book about love. "Wonderful to meet you, Mrs. Hochmeyer."

Mom patted at her hair. "Yes, Professor, lovely."

I felt glad when Jack and Kate were gone. Much of the tension dissipated the second the restaurant's perfect front door shut perfectly behind them. And nice to have my parents to myself.

We dug into dessert, which was a huge piece of chocolate cake to share.

Presently, the check came, and Dad proffered the credit card he'd been given by the state. The three of us talked logistics, nothing more interesting than that. I would drive Mom and myself home to Westport in the loaned Volvo. Dad's new bodyguards would take him to his secret location. Apparently the judge thought the old man's life was in danger. Mom would join Dad in a few more days, get him settled in his rooty-toot lodgings (as he called them—this was before anyone had ever heard the phrase "witness protection program"), then she would come home to me. This or that undisclosed town around Danbury would be his home and his life for the next several months; he had to remain under guard. There were people who wanted him to stay quiet. What people, what crimes, these were not discussed, not for the children to know, though of course I'd read the papers: half of middle management at Dolus Investments had been indicted for hundreds of counts of dozens of crimes, from fraud and extortion to murder and back again, also gross embezzlement. Dad's bosses had been portrayed as victims, Dad as a ringleader. Not true, I knew, impossible: Dad was a follower, never in front.

Mom would be allowed to visit him, but only under escort, a night or two maybe a couple of times a week, occasionally longer. And while she was away I'd attend school as always. Take the school bus. Go to the store—our neighbor Mrs. Paumgartner would be glad to drive me. Get the mail. Keep the house neat. They trusted me *implicitly*, was the exact word. Lugubrious talk like that, talk I could barely stay with, my one thought being that I'd have any number of nights with Emily, making love with Emily all over our house, this lithe, lanky girl who knew too much: mouth and tongue, hips and thighs, breasts and hands, smoothest brown skin.

Outside, one of the guards went to get the government car, which he'd parked down the hill in a gravel lot hidden among rhododendrons. Mom admired the selection of mums in the breezeway—those mums, I'll never forget them, all dried out in lines of flower pots, rare colors, apparently, splashes of blood and brains and bruises. The second guard crossed his arms, closed his eyes in the nice sun. His name was Theo, suddenly comes to me, *Theo.* Dad and Mom stood apart, fury spent, some semblance of peace arising, some old redolence of love.

Oh, man. I'd rather not go on.

But:

A new-looking silver sedan pulled into the drive, swung around very slowly under the portico, stopped. A man in a crisp blue suit got out, blue tie dotted with hundreds of golden fleur-de-lis, cocky grin.

"Kaiser?" my Dad said clearly.

Smoothly, the man pulled a large black handgun out from under his jacket, the barrel a black hole sucking in everything. He aimed it casually, pulled the trigger, shot Dad in the face, shot him again in the chest. The bangs didn't seem loud enough to be real. I thought it was all a joke, had to be a joke, Daddy's stupid jokes, the man still grinning. Time went into suspension. The place was lit in sparkles, dust motes, forever lit. The bodyguard fumbled in his own jacket, couldn't get his weapon out. My mother made an impossibly slow hop, caught Dad as he was falling, fell with him in a blooming mound of their nice clothes.

"Nicholas," she said, almost conversationally. Then incredulous:

"*Nicholas.*"

And then, and then, and then, as I was making my own hop toward them, the man shot *her*, three bullets, three pops, efficient trajectory, making sure my dad was dead, that's all; Mom was just in the way.

The guard still couldn't get his gun out, stepped forward anyway with a shout, and the man shot him, too, dropped him. In the moment's vast illogic, Dad and not the shooter seemed the dangerous one to me, someone who pulled bullets to himself and his loved ones with his big negative magnetism. So it was no heroic act when I finally got my body to lunge at the shooter, a big leap on longest legs even as he aimed his weapon at my face, *click-click-click*, empty magazine, or whatever it's called, at any rate no bullets. I would have had him, too, but tripped over my parents' tangled legs, landed on my mother bodily, lay on her heavily, and she on Dad, a bleeding, stinking pile.

I looked up into the coldest eyes I'd ever seen, clambered up in that tangle of legs, like breaking a tackle. Kaiser didn't like leaving me alive, that I could see, but he'd already used too much time, must have known he wasn't going to prevail in hand-to-hand combat with the likes of me. He slid easily back into his car, shut his door almost gently. The transmission clacked into gear like any transmission. I dove at the car, luckily missing—I would have hung on till my skin was peeled off, every scrap. The shooter drove away neither slow nor fast, crunch of groomed gravel.

I grabbed a pot of mums—heavy, cold, plenty awkward—held it like a football as time resumed full speed, spun, cocked my arm, calm quarterback, spun and fired that thing in a perfect spiral after the retreating car, watched it smash that wide rear window.

But the shooter just kept going.

Twitter: Want to discuss or share what you just read? Use the hashtag #beaGIANTS to connect with others.

ABOUT THE AUTHOR

Bill Roorbach is the author of eight books of fiction and nonfiction. His work has been published in *Harper's*, the *Atlantic Monthly*, *Playboy*, the *New York Times Magazine*, *Granta*, *New York*, and dozens of other magazines and journals.

Imprint: Algonquin Books
BEA Booth #: 4252
Author appearances: signing at the Algonquin booth, exact date/time TBA.
Printed galley at BEA: yes
Contact for printed galley: Kelly Bowen kelly@algonquin.com
Print ISBN: 9781616200763
Print price: $23.95
eBook ISBN: 9781616201562
eBook price: $23.95
Publication date: 11/13/2012
Publicity contact: Kelly Bowen kelly@algonquin.com

Rights contact: Kendra Poster kendra@workman.com
Editor: Kathy Pories
Agent: Betsy Lerner
Agency: Dunow, Carlson, and Lerner
Promotional Information:
- National Review and Feature Attention
- National/Regional NPR Campaign
- National Print Advertising
- 12-city Author Book Tour
- Featured Galley Giveaway at BookExpo America
- Promotion at all Library Conferences
- Pre-publication Buzz Campaign (including *Publishers Weekly* and *Shelf Awareness* ads)
- Online Marketing Campaign
- Author Website
- Newsletter Co-op

Truth in Advertising

Truth in Advertising

Truth in Advertising

Truth in Adver

Truth in Aa

Truth in

A NOVEL BY JOHN KENNEY

SUMMARY

In the spirit of *Then We Came to the End* and *This Is Where I Leave You*, *Truth in Advertising* is a wickedly funny, honest, and poignant novel about the absurdity of corporate life, the complications of love, and the meaning of family. Finbar Dolan is lost and lonely. Except he doesn't know it. Despite escaping his blue-collar Boston upbringing to carve out a mildly successful career at a Madison Avenue ad agency, he's a bit of a mess and closing in on 40. He's recently canceled a wedding. Now, a few days before Christmas, he's forced to cancel a long-awaited vacation to write, produce, and edit a Superbowl commercial for his diaper account in record time. Unfortunately, it gets worse. At the same time, he learns that his long-estranged and once-abusive father has fallen ill. And that neither of his brothers or his sister intend to visit. Ultimately, his father's death is a wake-up call for Fin to re-evaluate the choices he's made, admit that he's falling for his co-worker Phoebe, question the importance of diapers in his life, and finally tell the truth about his life and his past.

EXCERPT

And ... Action

Fade in.

Extreme close-up of a man's face. Mine.

A little internal voice. Also mine.

"Hey, Gary. Gary? You suck." (My name isn't Gary, but the little internal voice knows I have an unnatural dislike of the name Gary and calls me that to annoy me.) "You suck, Gary. You're a fraud and a phony and a hack and also did I mention that you suck? You lack soul and depth and intelligence. You've gone about it all wrong. You've wasted your life. Strong words. Think about them. Oh, except I forgot. You don't think about words. You use them like you use paper towels. Without thought or care. Can I say something else, now that I have your attention? Can I ask you to think about the fact that you got a three-ninety on your math SATs? Why do you leave the house in the morning?"

Cut to a short film, a reinterpretation of the seminal moment in *Sophie's Choice* when Sophie, just off the train at Auschwitz, must choose who lives, her son or her daughter. Except here Sophie is my mother. She must choose between me and ... nothing. The SS guard shouts at her: "What will it be?!" She looks at me on one side. She looks at nothing on the other. She chooses nothing. The camera moves in for an extreme close-up of my confused little expression as we cut to my mother, who shrugs, as if to say "Sorry." Pull back to reveal the expression of the SS guard, who also shrugs, something you rarely (ever?) see in the SS in particular and Nazis in general.

Raphael is speaking and has been speaking for some time, though I don't know what he has said because I haven't been listening; I've been in Auschwitz. But I should have been listening because we are about to roll film. And that means we are spending money, many hundreds of thousands of dollars, as is reflected by the number of people (11) listening to Raphael, the director of the commercial. Also by the presence of Gwyneth Paltrow.

"So what are we talking about here?" Raphael says to Gwyneth. He then looks to the floor, clearly a man reflecting deeply (albeit about his own question).

"We're talking about life. Yes? I mean, that's what we're talking about. We're talking about motherhood. Is there anything more precious, more beautiful? You, the giver of life. You made this life, this child."

Raphael is 29, with creative facial hair and no deficit of self-love. He is far too intense. Jack Black on coke. Watching him is a group that consists of five representatives from our client; my art director partner, Ian; our producer, Pam; the director's producer (or line producer); and me. We stand in the middle of a set that looks exactly like a child's bedroom on a soundstage in Queens. We are not supposed to be in Queens. We are supposed to be in Pasadena, California, in a lovely Arts and Crafts home that a production company chose after scouting close to 75 other homes in and around Pasadena, Santa Monica, and Laguna Beach. The home, per the client's verbatim direction, should feel "suburban but not too new and not too old and not too far from a city center but by no means urban, i.e., New York City and its general 'smart-alecky' sensibility, which often tests poorly in market research."

We did this in large part because Gwyneth was going to be in Los Angeles on vacation with her family and we wanted to (were forced to) accommodate her. Except it turned out that Gwyneth was no longer going to be in Los Angeles at the time of the shoot. She was going to be in New York for meetings and a partial vacation and could we find a location there, please? At which point the New York office of the production company scouted suburban but not too (see above) homes in Scarsdale, the Upper West Side, and Brooklyn Heights. All of which Gwyneth's assistant was fine with ("Scarsdale's not really New York though is it? Bit of a drive and we hate driving.), but all of which the client hated. At which point the New York office of the production company hired the set director from the former Broadway smash hit

Mamma Mia! to design a child's bedroom to the client's specifications, which was then built by union carpenters, at a cost of $135,000. All before rolling a single foot of film.

Raphael says, "That's what we're talking about here. Life. You, mother Gwyneth. And your womb. Your va*gina*, Gwyneth."

He pauses to let this sink in. Which it does, whether she wants it to or not.

Raphael continues. "The Latin word for *sheath*. Say it with me. Va-gin…"

"I wish you'd stop saying that," Gwyneth says with a smile, trying very hard. I give her credit. She's much nicer than I imagined from my casual reading of *US Weekly*.

"The way Raphael sees this shot…"

"I'm so sorry," Gwyneth says. "Who's Raphael?"

"That would be me," Raphael says, his titanium ego unfazed.

"Huh. Okay."

He barrels along, a clueless man-boy dressed in jeans that are dangerously close to falling down and a T-shirt emblazoned with the words *fritos are life*.

"Raphael sees that baby is naked, afraid. So he looks to you for everything. Now, let us consider your breasts." And with that he moves his hand to mime the shape of Mrs. Coldplay's diminutive yet shapely bosom.

Gwyneth is by far the highest profile super-mom that we've shot for our almost-award-winning campaign, *Snugglies Moms and Snugglies Babies: Together as One*. To date we've shot Rachel Weisz, Rebecca Romijn, and Kelly Ripa (whom I saw, briefly, in her underpants). Gwyneth at first refused to do it, saying through an agent that she didn't care for advertising, though she made no aspersions toward either the brand or the agency, though she was not familiar with either. Initially Gwyneth was not on the consideration list, as both the agency and the client felt she'd never do it. There had been a great deal of discussion—in-person meetings as well as conference calls involving dozens of personalities—as to who best represented the brand, as well as who would do it for the money. (I am not at liberty to disclose that figure but it was between $299,000 and $301,000.) Names like Madonna and Angelina were short-listed but ultimately the client feared that they were seen as "baby thieves" (the client's words). Nicole Kidman was considered, but was labeled "weird and scary". (We had a large board in a conference room with names and corresponding traits.) President Obama's mother-in-law, Marian Robinson, was added to the list but was also ultimately nixed because, as our senior client, Jan, said on a conference call to general acclaim, "This is about the mother-child bond, not the nana-child bond. Though we would like to see more women of color." Which is when a midlevel client responded, suggesting Victoria Beckham (née Posh Spice). Which is when we informed the client that Mrs. Spice-Beckham was not, in fact, a woman of color but just a woman colored, perpetually tanned, often deeply so.

We launched the campaign in 2007. The initial focus group testing results had been very good. But the recent economic downturn found far different attitude toward extremely rich, unusually beautiful, oddly thin mothers who, according to groups in a number of cities around the country, "probably had 24-hour-a-day help" (Chicago) and "sure as hell ain't using the drive-through window at McDonald's to shut the little bastards up" (Houston). Gwyneth is our last super-mom in the campaign.

"Breast milk," Raphael begins.

"Maybe let's move on," Gwyneth says, the radiant smile somehow still in place. She appears to have no pores on her face.

"Also clothing," he continues. "You have to ask yourself this question—what diaper will you place on his precious bottom?"

One senses a collective "Give-me-a-fucking-break" coming from the assemblage. But then one notices the five clients. They are mesmerized. They're buying it. Which is both good and bad, as they now think Raphael (who, it turns out, is named Richard Dinklage. That's right, Dick Dinklage) is a genius.

He slowly, dramatically, raises a diaper.

"Will it be any old diaper, or will it be … a Snugglie?"

Pam elbows me and whispers, "Say something. Now. We are way behind schedule."

I say, "I think what…" I realize I can't say his fake name, so I simply gesture to him instead. "I think what the director is saying is that this is one of those nothing little moments that actually mean a lot to a parent, when you're changing your baby and they're smiling and there's that connection. The whole idea is that nothing is more important than being a mother."

Gwyneth speaks to me and smiles, and I instantly understand why some people are stars. "Cool. That's great. I like that. Are we starting now? Because I'd love to use the ladies room."

The crowd disperses. Pam, Ian, and I walk to the craft services table for coffee.

Craft services is the odd name given to the food service area on a shoot. It's not, as first-time-to-a-shoot clients and neophyte creatives often mistake it, a place to buy handmade knit-ware and driftwood art.

Pam says, "She is so much better looking than a regular person. She's like a different species. I look like ass next to her. And, in case you haven't noticed, the client's pissed."

I say, "Why? They looked happy to me."

Pam says, "They say we're not following the storyboard. And the purple liquid thing. They want blue."

Ian says, "Where the hell is Alan? Where's Jill?"

Alan and Jill are our colleagues. They are account executives and their responsibility is to shepherd the client, act as liaison between client and agency, help devise a strategy, understand the client's business as well as the client, understand the creative's job, smooth the process. It is an important and powerful job. The relationship between client and agency rests upon it. Both Alan and Jill attended graduate business schools of the Ivy League persuasion. Currently, they're on the neighboring sound stage, trying to sneak in to watch the filming of an episode of *Law & Order*.

Ian says, "It's really like he has no idea what he's doing, like he's in film school."

Pam says, "He's one of the hottest commercial directors in the world."

Ian says, "He keeps using the word 'profanity.' Only he's using it wrong."

I say, "I noticed that. He thinks it means *spacious*."

Ian says, "I heard him say to the set designer that he wanted the baby's room to have more profanity."

Pam says, "He makes $30,000 a day."

Ian looks at his iPhone. "He's tweeting about the shoot."

Pam says, "Who?"

Ian holds up his phone, shows Raphael's Twitter account. "Cecil B. DeMille."

Pam says, "Please tell me he didn't tweet about her vagina."

I say, "Tweet about her vagina sounds wrong to me. Do you tweet?"

Pam says, "What do I look like, Kim fucking Kardashian?"

I say, "I don't tweet. Should I tweet? Maybe I should be tweeting, be more of a tweeting presence in the digital world."

Ian says, "What would you tweet about?"

I say, "Thoughts. Ideas. I have ideas about things that I think people would like to hear and follow. I think I'd have a lot of followers. Like Gandhi or Jesus."

Pam says, "Tweet this, Facebook that, LinkedIn my ass. C'mon. I mean, what the fuck?"

I say, "There are times when you don't strike me as someone named Pam."

Ian says, "Clients want it, though. It's magic to them. Gotta be on Facebook. Gotta tweet about the new campaign. Go viral. Big phrase these days. Go viral. This spot will have its own Facebook page."

I say, "And the world will be a better place because of it."

At last count the three of us have made twenty-three commercials together over seven years.

Ian says, "God bless that clever Mark Zuckerberg." He looks down at his phone. "Raphael just tweeted again saying people should go to his Facebook page to see new photos of him with Gwyneth." He looks up at me. "By the way, Merry Christmas, Tiny Fin."

Christmas is three days away.

Pam says, "Seriously, though, where the fuck are Alan and Jill?"

We make our way back to video village, that place on every TV commercial shoot where the client and agency people sit and watch the action on a monitor.

I see Jan, our senior client, and know immediately by the large smile on her face that there is a problem. Diapers are to Jan a kind of religious calling.

Before we move on, a word about Snugglies. Snugglies and Stay-Ups and Nite-Nites and Tadpoles (for swimming). We are the agency of record for the largest manufacturer of diapers in the world. *Snugglies babies are happy babies.* I know that because I wrote that line. You will never see an unhappy baby in one of our commercials. Other companies show unhappy babies. This is a mistake.

"Jan," I say. "It's going well, don't you think?"

Jan says, "I do, Fin. Really well."

I say, "Raphael."

Jan says, "He's brilliant. He gets the brand. He gets the brief."

Her colleagues nod and smile like lunatics.

One says, "Has he read the manifesto?"

I say, "I'm ... I'm not sure. But I doubt it."

Her colleagues are suddenly like chirping birds.

"He *has* to read the manifesto," says one. "How is that possible?" says another. Yet a third makes odd noises and contorted facial expressions, as if she just found out that her favorite woman wasn't given a rose on *The Bachelor*.

Jan remains calm. "Let's get him a copy. Immerse him in the brand. Perhaps Gwyneth would like to look at it as well."

I'm sure the Academy Award winner would love nothing more than to review the Snugglies manifesto.

And what is a manifesto, you might ask?

You may have a vague notion from history class that a manifesto once referred to the soul of a revolution; blood, sweat, and tears on paper, codifying women's rights, civil rights, human rights, economic justice, religious freedom. Today, it's about diapers. Or cars. Or refrigerators. Or gas grills. Or dental floss. In advertising, a manifesto is something that sums up a brand, one page, maybe 200 words. Name the product and my people will write the manifesto for it. Superlative claims, a badly skewed world view, sentences like, "Because let's be honest— what's more important at the end of your day than your family ... and their enjoyment of grilled meats?"

The Snugglies manifesto is particularly awful. I know. I wrote it.

I lie and say, "We'll get copies to Raphael and Gwyneth. Otherwise, though, I think we're in a good place with the spot."

Jan says, "It's real, honest, artful."

Ian says, "It's what we wanted."

Everyone smiles and nods. This is very good. We're about to turn and go when Jan says, "Except ... is it *too* artful, Fin?"

***

There are two kinds of creative people in advertising. Those who think they're smarter than the client and those who are successful. To say that the client is unreasonable is to say that death is unreasonable. Death *is*. Deal with it. Deal with it by making the client (death) your friend. Respect them, despite what they say. Advertising is a language and they do not speak that language. We say things like "It's original" or "It's a big idea." Wrong. Picasso's style of painting was original. Penicillin was a big idea. They call us *creative*. Boloney. The inventor of the corkscrew was creative. The irony of advertising—a communication business—is that we treat words with little respect, often devaluing their meaning. The *all-new* Ford Taurus. Really? Five wheels this time?

I do not think I am smarter than the client. Instead, I simply try to put myself in their sensible shoes, when, say, the long process that is the making of a commercial begins. Watch their furrowed brows and puzzled expressions as they watch us present ideas. Watch as they sneak a peek at a colleague to see if they understand what the hell we are talking about. *Were we working from the same brief?!* they wonder. Watch as they listen to the agency reference movies and shots in movies that they, themselves, have never seen nor in some cases even *heard* of ("We'll shoot it like that great tracking shot in *The Bicycle Thief*."). Song and band references that might as well be in Farsi.

Inside the client screams, *What does any of this have to do with our toothpaste?* Outside, they nod, slowly, letting their own insecurities build. *I never wanted to be in marketing for a toothpaste/diaper/paper towel/soda manufacturer,* they think for the eleven millionth time. *A frat buddy/sorority sister/parole officer suggested the job, after a long, pride-deadening search in other fields, a bit lost at age twenty-eight, wondering what to do with my life. I wanted to be a poet/a drummer/a porn star/a machinist.*

Give me your tired, your poor, your great teeming masses of middle managers who are unable to move the process forward or make a decision! These Carols and Maries and Trents and Tracys and Carls! Give me your resentful and angry, your worried and deeply frightened, your petrified of the next round of layoffs, of those insufferable human resources women with their easy detachment and heartless smiles. *You're eligible for Cobra and the family plan is just $1800 a month.* The afterlife for HR people is a *Clockwork Orange*-like reel of everyone they've ever fired, playing over and over and over.

This is life in advertising and marketing and public relations today, largely superfluous service-sector jobs in the great economic crisis where homes are worth less than we paid for them, job security no longer exists, college tuition is $40 million and the future is a thing that parents sit up nights trembling about. Fulfilled by your job? Who the fuck cares. *Have* a job? Then do whatever you can to hang on to it. This is business today. This is *America* today. A land of fear. Fear of things that cannot be proven with focus-group testing. Fear of layoffs and large mortgages, education costs and penniless retirements, fear of terrorists and planes that fly too low.

***

Jan is staring at me, waiting for an answer. As is her team. What was the question?

"How do you mean, Jan?" I say.

Jan says, "Is this the brand?"

I say, "I think it is. I think it's very much the brand. Ian?"

I write the copy. Ian does the pictures. He's much smarter than I am and a champion talker.

Ian says, "Emotion. The mother-child bond. Life. This is the DNA of your brand."

If you can speak like this with a straight face you can make a very good living in advertising.

Jan says, "Agreed."

Her colleagues nod. It's as if they're wired to Jan. Almost all are texting, talking on wireless headsets, tapping an iPad. Unless you are connected you are not alive. Earlier I heard one of the clients in the toilet on a conference call, his voice strained at times from peristaltic exertion.

Jan says again, "But is this *too* artsy for our brand?"

I say, "I'm hearing you say you think it might be too artsy."

Jan says, "I think that's what I'm saying, yes."

I say, "How so?"

Jan says, "The camera is moving around quite a bit. I'm not seeing the product."

I say, "Well, we're trying to focus on Gwyneth and the baby, but, as we discussed in the pre-production meeting, we wanted hip and cool and edgy along with the brand attributes of safe, homespun, and conservative."

Jan says, "Agreed. But Gwyneth and the baby aren't the product, Fin. The product is a Snugglie, the finest diaper in the world." You wait for the punch line but it never comes. People speak like this.

I say, "Absolutely. No question. But the baby is *wearing* the diaper."

Jan sighs deeply. It is a signal to one of her drones. In this case, Cindy, a bubbly twenty-eight-year-old Jan wanna-be. Cindy says, "As infants grow and become more active, our job is to create a diapering experience that fits their lives ... and the lives of their moms. We aspire to do nothing less than let them explore and be free to be the best babies they can be. Largely dry and free of diaper rash. Though legally we can't guarantee this."

Now, as if it's the final scene of a high school musical, others jump in. Chet, late thirties, also extremely eager. Chet says, "I.e., new Snugglies Diaper Pants. The ultimate in flexibility for babies on the go. Explore. Be free. Be dry. New mommies love this. Focus groups bear this out."

I say, "Are you fucking crazy? This is a diaper we're talking about. C'mon. Let's all get drunk and get laid."

Except I don't say that at all. I nod and say, "Understood." Because Jan knows, as does Cindy and Chet, that it is 2010 and the agency I work for will do anything to keep the sizable fee that this brand brings in. Jan could say, *Fin, I need you to climb up on that rafter, take down your pants, shave your ball sack, and jump into a Dixie cup full of curdled beef fat* and she knows I'd do it.

"One more thing," Jan says. "Purple."

Her colleagues nod.

"Purple?" I ask with a smile.

Jan nods. "The liquid in the demo shot rehearsal looked purple to us. We'd like blue. A deep, deep blue. Like the brand."

Cindy adds helpfully, "According to recent focus group testing, the color purple often connotes homosexuality and homosexuality, according to our testing, tested poorly."

Ian can't resist. "Maybe you're just giving the wrong kind of test."

Jan says, "We good, Fin?"

I manage a nod, smiling. "We can fix it in post." The great go-to line on a shoot. Post being post-production: editing, color correction, audio mixing.

Then I turn and walk away, leaving what's left of my scrotum on the floor.

We walk back toward the craft services table. On the way we pass dozens of crew, some of whom help to set the shot, position Gwyneth, tend to her hair and makeup, many of whom stand around and check their iPhones.

Ian says, "I thought that went well."

Pam looks at me and says, "You're pathetic."

Ian pours coffees. Pam eats a donut. I rub Purell on my hands.

Ian says, "It was genius on paper."

It's a thing we say on every shoot when we realize the spot isn't going to be any more than average.

Ian asks Pam what she's doing for Christmas.

Pam says, "Family. Pittsburgh. Vodka. Cigarettes. You?"

Ian says, "Dinner for friends. Jews, atheists, non-believers, the great unwashed. People who have no family or family they don't want to go home to. Tons of food and wine. No store-bought gifts. Everything has to be handmade. Could be music or a video, whatever. It's amazing. We've been doing it for about five years."

Pam says, "That's so gay." She looks at me. "You?"

I say, "Mexico."

"Family?

"Not so much."

"Friends?"

I say, "Alone. Going alone."

Pam says, "That's weird."

"Is it?"

"Weird and sad. No family? Of any kind?"

"We're not that close."

Pam says, "I hate most of my family. I can understand. But you seem reasonably normal. Why alone? Bring that cute little assistant of yours. Half the men in the agency would divorce their wives for her."

I say, "Phoebe? Don't be ridiculous."

Ian raises his eyebrows. Pam does the same.

I say, "We're just friends. We're good friends. She's my assistant."

Ian says, "She's not *your* assistant. She's the creative department assistant."

Pam says, "She's your office wife."

I say, "What does that mean?"

Ian says, "Everyone has an office husband or wife. I have both."

I say, "Who's your office husband?"

Ian says, "I'll never tell."

Pam says, "But you have to be careful of the power-struggle thing. They can't report to you. Does Phoebe report to you?"

I say, "No. Why?"

Pam says, "Good. Eliminates the sexual harassment thing, which I myself had to deal with when I was screwing a production intern last summer. Poor thing left in tears."

I say, "You're a romantic."

Pam says, "At least I'm not going on Christmas vacation alone."

I say, "It's a last-minute thing. An interim vacation. I'm planning a big trip for after the New Year. February. Possibly March."

Ian says to Pam, "My dear friend Mister Dolan has been saying this for a while. He calls it the big trip. That's his name for it. He's a copywriter."

I say, "The big trip is going to be amazing. Life-changing. I just can't figure out where to go, though. It's complicated."

Pam says, "What's complicated about it?"

I say, "I have these two tickets to anywhere in the world. Two first-class tickets."

Ian says, "Very expensive tickets."

Pam says, "I thought you said Mexico."

I say, "I did."

Ian says, "It's complicated."

Pam says, "You have two first-class tickets to anywhere in the world and you're going to Mexico? No offense to Mexico, but are you high?"

I say, "No. I'm not using them for Mexico. They're for the big trip. After Mexico."

Pam says, "So, wait. You have two first-class tickets anywhere in the world and instead of using them, you've bought *another* ticket to Mexico."

I say, "Yes."

Ian says, "It's complicated."

Finally I say, "They're the honeymoon tickets."

Pam says, "The what?"

I nod slowly, waiting for her to do the math.

Pam says, "Shit. The honeymoon tickets."

I say, "The honeymoon tickets."

Pam says, "Yikes. Sorry."

I say, "So it's complicated because I don't just want to use them for a trip to Mexico."

Pam says, "Do you ever hear from her?"

"Not so much."

Did I mention I canceled my wedding? I probably should have mentioned that. I was supposed to get married last May. I was engaged to a really wonderful woman. Amy Deacon. But then I got a very bad case of cold feet. More like frostbitten feet, where they turn black and your toes fall off and you think you're going to die. That's the kind of cold feet I had. We canceled a month before the wedding was to take place. We were going to go to Italy on our honeymoon. I've been trying to take a vacation ever since then, trying to use the tickets. In the past eight months I've planned three trips, but for some reason just couldn't follow through. To be honest I feel that the tickets hold power. The tickets urge me to find the right destination, to figure out where they want me to go. This place will be the place that assures me happiness. It doesn't say this on the tickets, unfortunately. Mostly it just talks about the restrictions. The problem is that the tickets expire in three months. And I can't get the obscene amount of money I paid for them back. So I have these tickets.

My cell phone rings. It's Phoebe, our aforementioned group's assistant.

I say, "Stop bothering me. I'm an important executive."

Phoebe says, "How's Gwyneth?"

"Gwyneth who?"

Phoebe says, "Tell me!"

"Honestly? She's heavy. Bad skin. She keeps hitting on me."

"Shut up."

I say, "What's up?"

"Nothing. I'm bored with you and Ian gone. And Carlson wants you to call him."

Martin Carlson, my boss, executive creative director of the agency.

I say, "Why can't he call me himself?"

Phoebe says, "He's too important. He said it's urgent. And that he wants you in a new business meeting Thursday."

"Thursday. As in *this* Thursday? Christmas Eve? Not possible. I'm going on vacation that day. He knows that."

"I know that."

"Did you tell him that?"

"Did I tell him that he knows you're going on vacation Thursday?"

"Yes."

"No."

"Why not?"

"Is this a logic test?"

"I'm not canceling another vacation."

Phoebe snorts. "You mean unless he asks you to."

"Exactly."

Seconds go by. I can tell she's reading an email, looking at her computer. I stare at a key grip's ass crack as he adjusts the base of a lighting stand.

I say, "Do you tweet?"

"Sometimes. I follow some people."

I say, "Do you have a lot of friends on Facebook?"

"Not really. Not compared to some people I know."

"I have 109, but there's about twenty of them that I have no idea who they are."

Phoebe says, "Oh."

I say, "What? How many do you have?"

"1,200, I think. Maybe more."

I say, "I'm feeling great inadequacy right now."

Phoebe says, "Run with that."

The key grip stands and turns to see me staring at his ass crack and gives me a look that suggests he might do physical harm to me.

Phoebe says, "Also your brother Edward called. Is he the one in San Francisco?"

"No," I say. "That's Kevin. Eddie's in Boston."

"He left his number."

I say nothing.

"Fin?"

"Yeah."

"Do you want his number?"

"No. What did he say?"

"He said, 'Tell him it's about his father.'"

How nice. Hi, Daddy!

One word, one blink, and I am back in the basement of Saint Joseph's Rectory. A winter night. I am in the Cub Scouts. I am eight years old and I wear a dark blue Cub Scout shirt and yellow kerchief and military-style enlistedman's cap. Tonight is the Pinewood Derby, for which they give you a small block of wood and plastic wheels and ask you to carve it into a car. Kids spend weeks with these things, mostly with their fathers. He'll show you how to whittle, say, or paint, or put the wheels on. He'll gently ruffle your hair the way they do in TV shows from the sixties or present-day commercials. An experience you will always remember, that perhaps you will one day share with your own son. Tonight, on a small wooden track, they will have a race for the fastest car. Happy fathers and excited sons. Lots of prizes and trophies. Everyone goes home with something. And then there's my father, who's just screamed at my mother and made her cry, and who stormed out of the house with me in tow, the silent drive to Saint Joe's. I'm holding a Stride-Rite shoebox with my pathetic excuse of a car in it, confused as to whether to be more terrified of my father in one of his moods or of the reaction of my fellow Cub Scouts when they see my car, which my father has not helped me with, and which, me not having a natural affinity for carpentry, is still largely a block of wood, except for the paint I put on it. I don't want to go. That was what the fight was about. My mother said I didn't have to go. I told her about my lame car. But my father said I had to go, that I was wimping out, that I should have worked harder. I briefly imagined a storybook ending (the budding copywriter), wherein my hideous, misshapen block-like car thing would somehow speed to victory in record time, stunning the crowd of vastly superior scouts. But I actually came in second to last. Tommy Flynn came in last, his wheels falling off. He burst into tears, his father holding him. And my father? My father said, "Well, that was a waste of time, wasn't it?"

He's dead. He must have died. That's the only reason Eddie would call me about "my" father. And since when did he start calling himself Edward?

Phoebe says, "I hope everything's okay."

I say, "I'll call him." But I won't. And maybe Phoebe senses that from my voice.

Phoebe says, "Do you have his number?"

"Yes."

She says, "You're lying. What is it?"

"There's a seven in it."

"I'm texting it to you. Call your brother. Also he may be calling you since I gave him your cell. And call Carlson. Can I come to the shoot this afternoon?"

"You'd be bored. It just looks exciting. Like the circus. Or a strip club. So I've heard."

Phoebe says, "I want to meet Gwyneth. I think we could be friends."

"I'm hanging up."

Phoebe says, "Say something nice."

I say, "You're prettier than she is."

"Yeah, right."

"I'm not kidding."

And she knows from the tone of my voice I mean it.

Three or four long seconds. Never awkward, though. Not with her.

Phoebe says, "Call me later, okay?"

Her text arrives. *Edward's number.*

Did I mention that I have family? Eddie's the oldest and for years acted that way. Maura: she goes to church a lot. They're both up in

Boston. At least they were the last time we spoke. Kevin is in San Francisco. If Ian's the gay brother I never had, Kevin would be the gay brother I actually have. Some families grow closer. Others are Irish.

I delete the text.

A twenty-five-ish production assistant jogs up to Ian, Pam, and me.

She says, sternly, "Raphael wants to roll immediately."

Pam says, "We'll be two minutes."

The PA says, "Umm, he said to tell you he wants to roll immediately."

I wince and see Ian do the same.

Pam's face breaks into a big smile. "What's your name?"

The PA says, "Saffron."

Pam says, "Saffron. Wow. I'm going to guess southern California or, wait, Boulder."

Saffron says, "Boulder. That's amazing!"

Pam says, "I want you to listen to me, okay? There are two things I know to be true. One is that there's no difference between good flan and bad flan. What movie is that from?"

Saffron stares at Pam, clueless, only now sensing, perhaps, that she's made a terrible mistake.

Pam says, "Disappointed. *Wag the Dog.* Classic Mamet line. Not sure what you're doing in this business if you don't love film. Two, we roll when I say we roll. And if dick-breath has a problem with that you have him come see me because this is my show. Okay?"

Saffron is wide-eyed and stunned and scared and nodding slowly.

Pam says, "One more thing. I don't like your name. So I'm going to call you Barbara for the rest of the shoot. Now go away and tell Raphael to learn what an F-stop is."

Saffron scurries away.

Another woman walks up to Pam and has what appears to be a massive amount of baby spit-up on her shirt.

Ian says, "I have bad news for you about your blouse."

Pam says, "Who are you?"

The woman says, "The baby wrangler. We have a problem."

Ian says, "We got that part."

The woman says, "The baby's puking like crazy."

Pam says, "What about the backup baby? So far we've only shot this one from behind."

"Yeah, I know," the wrangler says. "But there was a bit of a screwup and the casting agency sent ... they sent a black baby."

Ian says, "Chris Martin is not going to like this."

Pam doesn't blink twice. She takes out her cell phone and calls the casting agency. Into the phone she says, "It's Pam Marston for Sandy." Away from the phone. "Barbara!" Saffron comes running.

Alan and Jill, our account execs, finally reappear.

Alan says skittishly, "You want the good news or the bad news?"

No one says anything.

Alan says, "Okay, that's good because there is no good news. So I'll move right to the bad. We're using the wrong diapers."

Pam stares at Alan in a way that could not be mistaken for friendly.

Alan says, "These diapers are for infants. We need the Diaper Pants for toddlers."

Ian covers his face. I look to the ceiling, in hopes of a ladder being lowered from a waiting helicopter.

Pam says, "We've been shooting since 7:46 am. It's 11:32. Do you know how much film we've shot?"

Alan says, "A lot?"

"A lot, Alan? We're shooting thirty-five-millimeter film, haircut. one-thousand foot mags. Eleven minutes a mag. Two dollars a foot to process. That doesn't include transferring or color correction. We've blown through eight mags so far today. That's eight thousand feet of film that's useless."

Alan says, "I missed a lot of that."

Pam says, "Try this. The client just spent thirty-six-thousand dollars on nothing."

Alan says, "That's very bad."

Pam says, "Wait. Are the diapers we've been using that much different? How different-looking can diapers be?"

Jill says, "Dramatically different, Pam. That's the Snugglies touch."

Pam says, "Jill. Say another word and I will drown you in a toilet. Alan, talk with them. Now."

Saffron appears.

"Um, excuse me, Pam? I'm sorry to interrupt, but when you get a chance, and there's no hurry, Raphael would like to show you guys something."

Pam puts the phone to her ear. "Sandy. Pam. I have a black baby."

A woman approaches, one of Gwyneth's assistants.

"That's so beautiful," the assistant says. "I wish more people would break down the color barrier. Are you Pam?"

Pam nods and says into the phone, "Sandy, I'm going to call you back in sixty seconds."

Gwyneth's assistant says, with a big fake smile, "I think there might be some mistake. We see here on the schedule that this is a two-day shoot?" She slowly shakes her head no. "We were under the impression it was just one day."

Pam says, "What? No. No, no. No it's definitely two. We need her for two. We went over all of this with you guys. Like, twenty times."

The assistant, still smiling, says, "I know, but that's not going to work because she's on a plane tonight to Berlin. The new M. Night movie."

Ian says, "Is it about diapers?"

The assistant says, "Sorry." But she's not sorry at all. She turns and walks away. Everyone stares at Pam.

Pam says, "There are so many filthy, filthy words I want to say right now."

She turns to Alan. "Talk to the client. Fix this blue-purple-gay thing. Do not tell them about the scheduling thing. Go."

He snaps into action, Jill following him.

Pam turns to Saffron. "White baby, then M. Night. Ian. Come with me."

I stand alone as three people attend to Gwyneth's hair and makeup. I watch the director of photography and the second assistant camera loader change lenses. Gaffers adjust huge lights nimbly, quickly. I appear to be the only person on the set with nothing to do.

My phone rings. The display reads *Martin Carlson*.

Martin is English and famous in advertising and came to our agency about ten months ago and changed what was a wonderful place to work, if by work you mean *not work very much*, and made it a place where you have to work, if by work you mean work, *work* a lot, on nights, on weekends. Martin loves meeting on Sunday afternoons to review work. His arrival has not gone over well.

...

Since Martin's arrival I have tried to show my worth by enacting what I like to call the *Finbar Dolan Campaign for Creative Director, Long-Term Success, and Renewed Self Esteem.* (A long and not particularly interesting title, to be sure, especially from someone who's supposed to be good at writing exactly these kinds of things.) How have I enacted The Plan? I have done this by getting in at 9:30-but-closer-to-10 and leaving around six, with a midday pause for a long lunch. Also by acting as a respected mentor to the other creatives in my group, which is not technically my group, nor do they really see me as a mentor or even listen to me. My great hope (as I believe is reflected in the clever titling of my plan) is to be promoted this year to creative director. It is an important milestone in one's advertising career. You go from merely creating ads—concepting, writing, art directing—to overseeing, critiquing, criticizing, and most often shooting them down. It is something I feel I could be good at. It would also be a bump in salary. It would mean the respect of others at the agency. Which is not to say I don't have enormously high self-esteem or that I rely on the opinion of others. (I don't and I do.)

I say, "Martin."

"Fin."

"Martin."

Martin says, "How goes it on the coast?"

"We're in Queens, actually. Which is certainly a coast, but not the one you were thinking of."

Martin says, "And Gwyneth, Fin? Stunning?"

"Stunning," I say.

Martin says, "Met her once. She might remember me."

"I mentioned you to her," I lie. "She remembered."

Martin cackles. "I *knew* it. Did she say where that was?"

"She didn't. You sound strange, Martin."

"Yoga, Fin. Standing on my head at the moment. Secret to life. Releases tension. Have you tried it?"

"No, but I masturbate a lot. Does wonders."

Martin says, without a hint of a laugh, "Humor. Very good. Hearing reports of black babies, Fin, of unhappy clients."

How does he know these things?

"Just rumors, Martin," I say. "We had some issues earlier but things are better now."

"Good to hear. Creative directors take care of these things. Bull by the horns."

Creative directors.

Martin says, "I have some excellent news of my own, Fin. Big oil."

I say, "That's great. Except I'm not sure what you're talking about."

"Petroleum, Fin. Head man's an old chum—we were at Eton together. Not happy with their current agency. Want to avoid a formal pitch. Meet and greet, see if the chemistry's there. Oh, Christ."

I hear a thud and then moaning.

"Martin?" I say.

Muffled, somewhat at a distance, I hear, "These *bas*tard walls!"

I hear a hand grabbing the phone, rubbing the mouthpiece.

"Martin?" I say again. "You okay?"

"I don't feel pain, Fin. Anyway. He's only in town a short time. I'd like to bring in one of our top creatives."

This is turning out better than I had hoped.

Martin says, "Except none of them will be around Thursday because of the holiday."

"Oh," I reply cleverly.

"I'm joking, Fin. I think you could be the man for this. Might be a nice change from diapers."

"You said change and diapers. That's funny."

"Are you available Thursday?"

"This Thursday?"

"Yes."

"My flight leaves Thursday, Martin."

"Morning or afternoon."

"Afternoon," I say, sensing my mistake immediately.

"No worries, then. Knew I could count on you. You, me, Frank, Dodge. Top brass, Fin. The big leagues. Win this and write your own ticket."

I say, "Wait. Isn't Petroleum the one responsible for the big spill in Alaska a while back?"

"And you're perfect, I suppose? Don't mention the spill. Very sensitive about it."

"Are they doing anything about it?"

Martin says, "About what?"

"The spill."

"Of course. Deeply committed to change. That's why they're hiring a new agency."

I say, "Excellent."

Martin says, "Snugglies client happy?"

I say, "I guess."

Martin says, "Don't guess, Fin. Make sure. Keep them happy. Keep your job. Humor."

The line goes dead.

A twenty-two-year-old from craft services with spiked hair walks up with a tray of small paper cups of coffee.

"Mocha cappuccino?"

I say, "I have a degree in English Literature."

The kid stares at me.

I say, "My thesis was on Eliot's *The Love Song of J. Alfred Prufrock.* I won an award for it. That's a lie. I almost won an award for it. Or would have, perhaps, if I'd finished it and submitted it, which I didn't."

The kid continues staring.

I say, *Let us go then, you and I, when the evening is spread out against the sky, like a patient etherized upon a table.*

I say, "I wanted to write. I wanted to write poetry. To touch people's hearts and open their minds. I wanted to live by the sea, England perhaps, teach at an old college, wear heavy sweaters and have sex with my full-breasted female students."

The kid stares some more, his mouth open a bit now.

I say, *"Do I dare to eat a peach?"*

The kid says, "Um, I don't think we have any peaches. But I could make you a fruit smoothie."

I hear Raphael shouting, "I want to film something! Ms. Paltrow and I are waiting!" There's a pause. "Why is this child black?"

The Land of Misfit Toys

Did I mention that I am a copywriter at a Manhattan advertising agency? I am. You might recognize the name. Lauderbeck, Kline & Vanderhosen. Been around for decades. We have offices in New York, Los Angeles, London, Amsterdam, and, as of January of this year, Tokyo. We were acquired many years ago, like so many once-independent agencies, by a multinational PR firm. That firm was acquired earlier this year by a Japanese shipping company, though I have no idea why a shipping company—or a Japanese one at that—would buy an American ad agency, except that I've heard rumors that the shipping company owner's son, apparently a spectacular moron, was given the agency as a pet project by his father. Anything to keep the kid away from large vessels holding millions of dollars worth of cargo.

Why did I, Fin Dolan, choose advertising, you might ask? Why not law or medicine or the fine arts? Because of bad grades, fear of blood, and no artistic talent of any kind. Was it a passion, something that simply overtook me, the way famous people on television speak of their careers as a passion? No. Did it dawn on me at a young age that advertising was my life's work, the way it dawned on Mohandas K. Gandhi, after he was thrown off that train in South Africa, that wearing a dhoti, carrying a stick, and changing India would be his life's work? No. Was it more of a calling? Did I try the priesthood first, spending several years in contemplative study with the Jesuits/the Mormons/the Buddhists before coming to the realization that God wanted me to serve Him by creating television commercials for Pop-Tarts? No (nor have I worked on the Pop-Tart account, though I would be open to it). Did I do it because I was kicked out of the Morgan Stanley training program after three days, the recruiter saying these words to me with a contorted face: "It's as if ... I mean ... seriously, pal ... it's as if you have no understanding of mathematics at all." Yes. Definitely yes. Also because I'm not good at anything except caddying, which I did throughout high school, college, and after the failed Morgan Stanley gig.

And what is it that I actually do? How does one find oneself on the set of a fake bedroom that is not attached to a real home on a sound stage in Queens with a baker's dozen of colleagues and clients, all of whom are bizarrely serious about a diaper?

It starts this way. A small office, a cubicle, a place of unopenable windows and industrial bathrooms and bad lighting. People with colds. A cafeteria that smells of warm cheese. An assignment. Let's make a TV commercial! Teams of people trying to come up with ideas that will resonate with a mother holding a child whilst on the phone preparing dinner with the TV on. Get to work, Finbar Dolan! Maybe I work. But maybe I don't. Maybe, instead, I search the Web for information on Pompeii or hiking boots or the Tour de France or the history of the luge or Churchill's speeches or why people have dermatitis. I write down a terrible idea for a commercial that seems like a great idea at the time (its terribleness will make itself apparent in a day or two), then write down an equally terrible idea for a screenplay or TV pilot that I will never write. I leaf through a magazine. I go out for coffee. I call Air France and put a hold on a ticket I will never buy. I wonder if anyone would catch me masturbating. I enter the word "assface" into the search bar just to see what comes up. I play air drums to Barry White songs playing on my iTunes. This is my job.

Indeed, this is also the job of the other fifty-four creatives at the agency. Copywriters and art directors. They are artists. They are misunderstood. They are impulsive, brilliant, difficult, short-tempered, divorced, heavy drinkers, smokers, recreational drug users, malcontents, sexual deviants. It is the land of misfit toys. Every one of them deep believers in their individuality, their Mr. Rogers "You-Are-Special-ness." And yet so very much alike in wardrobe, attitude, world-view, background, humor; readers of *The New Yorker,* people who quote *Monty Python, Spinal Tap, Waiting For Guffman,* who speak in movie-line references over and over, who like Wilco, Paul Westerberg, Eddie Izzard. Fast talkers, people who no longer tuck in their shirts, overly confident people with low self-esteem, people with British friends, people who know about good hotel and airport business lounges, people who are *working* on a screenplay/novel/documentary, watchers of HBO and *The Daily Show,* politically liberal, late to marry, one-child households, the women more than likely to have had an abortion, to have slept with their male copywriter or art director partner, the men having had sex with at least one coworker and probably more, half having once experimented or are now experimenting with facial hair. Everyone wears blue jeans all the time.

These are my people. These creators of oft-times indelible images for massive, far-reaching corporations. We are so much alike, sitting in a cubicle, in an office that is rarely large or impressive, the copywriters most likely working on an Apple PowerBook, typing in Palatino or Courier or Helvetica 12-point, the art directors staring at comically large screens, who, from God-only-knows where, find an idea that will define a company, that will reach millions of people.

There are three kinds of creative people in advertising, according to my exceptionally unscientific point of view. There are the remarkably talented, the people who create the commercials you see and think, "Holy *shit*, that's cool!" They create the commercials everyone talks about: the sneakers, the computers, the high-end cars, the soft drinks, the fast food. Then there are the pretty darned talented who take the seemingly bland accounts and make them interesting: your credit cards, your energy companies, your insurance firms. Smart, solid work from smart, solid people who could easily get jobs writing speeches or managing a political campaign. Then there's the rest of us. Me and my coworkers. We do diapers. We do little chocolate candies. We do detergent and dishwashing liquid and air fresheners and toilet paper and paper towels and prescription drugs. Our commercials have cartoon animals or talking germs. It's the stuff you see and think, *Blessed mother of God, what idiot did that?*" That idiot would be me. I make the commercials wherein you turn the sound down or run to the toilet.

If there is a hierarchy in advertising products, surely a small plastic bag that holds poo and won't degrade for hundreds of years is well toward the bottom. You might think my colleagues and I would be discouraged by this. You would be partially correct, but only partially, as I myself find the idea of working on Nike or Apple or BMW so daunting as to be frightening. Whereas diapers, to my mind, are a tabula rasa. (I try to share this thought with the troops from time to time but it often falls on deaf ears.)

Within these three groups are various factions:

Some love it. They love the work, love talking about it, thinking about it, being friends with other advertising people. They love the exciting travel, the five-star hotels, the free restaurant meals and expensive wine. And they have a point. It's tough to beat. But more than that, they are believers (like the senior partners at my agency, whom you shall meet in a moment). They believe advertising matters, that it is important, that it can be a force for good. Depending upon the day and my mood, I dabble in this camp.

Some merely like it, as it beats most jobs, but feel a sense of ... longing. Longing for something better, more substantial, more important.

True, advertising helps drive the economy, but, these people sometimes ask, "Is this the best I can do?" This sometimes colors their view of others, so they often feel a need to crap on any work they or their friends haven't personally done. (Except for the crapping on other people's work part, I can also be found in this camp at times.)

Some see advertising as a path to Hollywood greatness. They feel that they are as-yet-undiscovered scriptwriters and budding directors and that if someone at CAA or UTA would just take a careful *look* at their new Taco Bell/I-Can't-Believe-It's-Not-Butter/Tampax Light campaign they would *see*. As such, they are often frustrated (bordering on angry), eager to emulate Hollywood movies/scripts/dialogue, hire famous directors for spots. I once worked with a man who was obsessed with David Mamet dialogue. Every commercial he wrote sounded like a bad Mamet film.

MAN 1: The thing.

MAN 2: What thing?

MAN 1: The thing. This is what the man said.

MAN 2: The man said the thing?

MAN 1: This is what I'm saying.

MAN 2: What thing? What did the man say?

MAN 1: He said Bounty is the Quicker Picker-Upper.

Still others are simply too good for advertising. We have a couple of guys (every agency does, and they're always guys) who fancy themselves "real writers," guys who are always starting commercials by quoting Hemingway or Kafka or some deep thought of their own, lines that sound great when read in a really deep slow voice but that don't mean anything (*If life is about living, then maybe living ... is about life ... long pause ... Introducing new Stouffer's Cheesy Bread.*). The problem is it's a commercial, not literature, and at some point you have to get to the product. These guys are always working on a novel. And God love them for it. They're better (and certainly more driven) men than I. The problem is they can't quite believe that they're forty-ish ad guys, when the plan twenty years before was to be on the third novel, the previous two having been optioned for screenplays, which they themselves would have written. They also use the phrase *selling my soul* a lot. They say this in a poor-me kind of way. It's charming. Not to me. But it's charming to the young account girls, who are often wooed by these grizzled writers, men who carry books and sometimes read them, who drink too much, who bed these impressionable lovelies. But here's the thing with the selling-your-soul business. People who work for tobacco companies and hide proof that cigarettes cause cancer sell their souls. Pharma companies that test drugs on African kids sell their soul. Oil companies who cut safety and environmental corners sell their soul. But ad guys? People who make cereal commercials? Client changes that ruin your *art*? Grow up.

And finally there is the silent majority, the daily grinders. They have grown tired of advertising s early allure and now they are restless. Unfulfilled. Despondent. They want to be doing something else. But they don't know what to do. Work on the client side? Start a café? Run drugs for a Mexican cartel? They possess that hybrid of confusion and hint of sadness at having awoken, well past their prime, married (or just as often divorced), with two children and a mortgage on a house in Larchmont/Wilton/Montclair and thinking, How did this *happen*? They never really figured out what it was they wanted to do with their lives, and so life took over, marriage came along, children, a home, massive amounts of good debt, and, after mediocre sex on Sunday night, they lie awake and think about how much damage it would cause if they left their wife and traveled around the south of France for the summer fucking twenty-one-year-olds. And as they are thinking this, their child awakens from a bad dream, calling out. They go to their child, walking naked through the quiet house with the new Restoration Hardware furniture, tramping quickly through the hallway to their perfect daughter's room, pulling on a pair of boxer shorts and almost breaking their neck doing it.

"What is it, pumpkin?" they coo.

"A dream, Daddy. A bad man chasing me."

"There's no bad man, honey. You're here with Mommy and Daddy and Chuckie," they say, referring to the filthy dog who farts and slobbers all over the furniture, bought on credit. They hold her, this three-year-old bundle of loveliness, caress her silky-soft downy hair, pat her tiny back, and say, "Shhhh. Shhhh. Do you know how much Daddy loves you?" as they lay her down and pull the covers up to her chin. They spread their arms wide and make a silly face and see her face soften and smile. They kiss her cheeks again and again and hear her say, laughing, "Stop it, Daddy, you're silly," and know that she is all right now, know that she will sleep, know that she will wake in the morning with no recollection of what has gone on here tonight in these two minutes, know that they themselves will never forget it, know that they will never leave this child and go to France, know that they will never again fuck a twenty-one-year-old, know that they will show up for work bright and early at the job they hate because of this girl.

I should admit that some of what I just wrote in the previous paragraph was from a spot I did for life insurance a few years ago. I apologize.

Twitter: Want to discuss or share what you just read? Use the hashtag #beaTRUTH to connect with others.

ABOUT THE AUTHOR

John Kenney has worked as a copywriter in New York City for 17 years. He has also been a contributor to *The New Yorker* magazine since 1999. Some of his work appears in a collection of *The New Yorker's* humor writing, *Disquiet Please*. He lives in Brooklyn, NY. Visit www.byjohnkenney.com.

Imprint: Touchstone
BEA Booth #: 3657, 3658
Printed galley at BEA: yes
Contact for printed galley: touchstonemarketing@simonandschuster.com
Print ISBN: 9781451675542
Print price: $24.99
eBook ISBN: 9781451675566
eBook price: $11.99
Publication date: 1/8/13
Publicity contact: Marcia Burch Marcia.Burch@simonandschuster.com
Rights contact: Marie Florio Marie.Florio@simonandschuster.com
Editor: Sally Kim
Agent: David Kuhn
Agency: Kuhn Projects
Promotional Information:
- National print campaign
- Digital media and blog tour campaign
- National radio campaign, including npr
- Local publicity in new york city, boston
- Author appearances in new york city, boston, new england and upon request
- Prepublication bookseller meet & greet tour
- Featured at book expo 2012 and all fall 2012 regional trade shows, including arc giveaways
- Prepublication online buzz campaign, including advertising and giveaways on shelf awareness pro, featured title in simon & schuster book club enewsletter
- Professionally produced, directed and distributed book trailer
- Early reads campaign including amazon vine program, goodreads. Com, librarything.Com, and indiebound.Org
- Social networking campaign on facebook, twitter, and goodreads
- Cross-promotion with author's website and social media, including book microsite reading group guide and author q&a available online
- E-card campaign, suitable for sharing

- College marketing, including mailings to college bookstores, radio stations and newspapers
- Library marketing, including arc mailings
- Advertising industry-focused marketing, including arc mailings and targeted advertising

ALPHABETICAL LIST OF EXCERPTS BY AUTHOR

Iris Anthony, *Ruins Of Lace* (Sourcebooks)

Diana Athill, *Make Believe* (Granta Books)

Shani Boianjiu, *The People Of Forever Are Not Afraid* (Hogarth)

Libba Bray, *The Diviners* (Little, Brown Young Readers)

Amanda Coplin, *The Orchardist* (HarperCollins)

Eric Devine, *Tap Out* (Running Press Teen)

Matthew Dicks, *Memoirs Of An Imaginary Friend* (St. Martin's)

Junot Díaz, *This Is How You Lose Her* (Riverhead)

Jasper Fforde, *The Last Dragonslayer* (Houghton Mifflin Harcourt Children's)

Janet Gurtler, *Who I Kissed* (Sourcebooks Fire)

Jenny Han/Siobhan Vivian, *Burn for Burn* (Simon&Schuster Children's)

Peter Heller, *The Dog Stars* (Knopf)

Mark Helprin, *In Sunlight And In Shadow* (Houghton Mifflin Harcourt)

Scott Hutchins, *A Working Theory Of Love* (Penguin)

John Kenney, *Truth In Advertising* (Touchstone)

Jessica Khoury, *Origin* (Penguin Kids)

Barbara Kingsolver, *Flight Behavior* (HarperCollins)

Rhoda Janzen, *Does This Church Make Me Look Fat?* (Grand Central)

Dennis Lehane, *Live By Night* (William Morrow)

David Levithan, *Every Day* (Knopf Children's)

Sarah Maas, *Throne Of Glass* (Bloomsbury Children's)

James Meek, *The Heart Broke In* (Farrar, Straus and Giroux)

J.R. Moehringer, *Sutton* (Hyperion)

Lawrence Norfolk, *John Saturnall's Feast* (Grove)

Kevin Powers, *The Yellow Birds* (Little, Brown)

Hanna Pylväinen, *We Sinners* (Macmillan)

Teresa Rhyne, *The Dog Lived (And So Will I)* (Sourcebooks)

Bill Roorbach, *Life Among Giants* (Algonquin)

M.L. Stedman, *The Light Between Oceans* (Scribner)

Ned Vizzini, *The Other Normals* (HarperTeen)

Lance Weller, *Wilderness* (Bloomsbury)

Bee Wilson, *Consider The Fork* (Basic Books)

Neil Young, *Waging Heavy Peace* (Blue Rider)

LIST OF EXCERPTS BY CATEGORY

LITERARY

Junot Díaz, *This Is How You Lose Her* (Riverhead)
Matthew Dicks, *Memoirs Of An Imaginary Friend* (St. Martin's)
Mark Helprin, *In Sunlight And In Shadow* (Houghton Mifflin Harcourt)
Barbara Kingsolver, *Flight Behavior* (HarperCollins)
James Meek, *The Heart Broke In* (Farrar, Straus, Giroux)
Lawrence Norfolk, *John Saturnall's Feast* (Grove)
Bill Roorbach, *Life Among Giants* (Algonquin)

HOT/"BUZZ" DEBUTS

Iris Anthony, *Ruins of Lace* (Sourcebooks)
Shani Boianjiu, *The People Of Forever Are Not Afraid* (Hogarth)
Amanda Coplin, *The Orchardist* (HarperCollins)
Peter Heller, *The Dog Stars* (Knopf)
Scott Hutchins, *A Working Theory of Love* (Penguin)
John Kenney, *Truth In Advertising* (Touchstone)
Dennis Lehane, *Live By Night* (William Morrow)
J. R. Moehringer, *Sutton* (Hyperion)
Kevin Powers, *The Yellow Birds* (Little, Brown)
Hanna Pylväinen, *We Sinners* (Macmillan)
M. L. Stedman, *The Light Between Oceans* (Scribner)
Lance Weller, *Wilderness* (Bloomsbury)

NONFICTION

Diana Athill, *Make Believe* (Granta Books)
Rhoda Janzen, *Does This Church Make Me Look Fat?* (Grand Central)
Teresa Rhyne, *The Dog Lived (And So Will I)* (Sourcebooks)
Bee Wilson, *Consider The Fork* (Basic Books)
Neil Young, *Waging Heavy Peace* (Blue Rider)

YA

Libba Bray, *The Diviners* (Little, Brown Young Readers)
Eric Devine, *Tap Out* (Running Press Teen)
Jasper Fforde, *The Last Dragonslayer* (Houghton Mifflin Harcourt Children's)
Janet Gurtler, *Who I Kissed* (Sourcebooks Fire)
Jessica Khoury, *Origin* (Penguin Kids)
Jenny Han/Siobhan Vivian, *Burn for Burn* (Simon&Schuster Children's)
David Levithan, *Every Day* (Knopf Children's)
Sarah Maas, *Throne Of Glass* (Bloomsbury Children's)
Ned Vizzini, *The Other Normals* (HarperTeen)

LIST OF EXCERPTS BY PUBLISHER

ALGONQUIN
Bill Roorbach, *Life Among Giants*

BASIC BOOKS
Bee Wilson, *Consider the Fork*

BLOOMSBURY
Sarah Maas, *Throne of Glass*
Lance Weller, *Wilderness*

GRANTA
Diana Athill, *Make Believe*

GROVE ATLANTIC
Lawrence Norfolk, *John Saturnall's Feast*

HACHETTE BOOK GROUP
Libba Bray, *The Diviners*
Rhoda Janzen, *Does This Church Make Me Look Fat?*
Kevin Powers, *The Yellow Birds*

HARPERCOLLINS
Amanda Coplin, *The Orchardist*
Barbara Kingsolver, *Flight Behavior*
Dennis Lehane, *Live By Night*
Ned Vizzini, *The Other Normals*

HOUGHTON MIFFLIN HARCOURT
Mark Helprin, *In Sunlight and In Shadow*
Jasper Fforde, *The Last Dragonslayer*

HYPERION
J.R. Moehringer, *Sutton*

MACMILLAN
Matthew Dicks, *Memoirs of an Imaginary Friend*
James Meek, *The Heart Broke In*
Hanna Pylväinen, *We Sinners*

PENGUIN
Junot Díaz, *This Is How You Lose Her*
Scott Hutchins, *A Working Theory of Love*
Neil Young, *Waging Heavy Peace*

RANDOM HOUSE
Shani Boianjiu, *The People of Forever Are Not Afraid*
Peter Heller, *The Dog Stars*
David Levithan, *Every Day*

RUNNING PRESS
Eric Devine, *Tap Out*

SIMON & SCHUSTER
Jenny Han/Siobhan Vivian, *Burn for Burn*
John Kenney, *Truth in Advertising*
M.L. Stedman, *The Light Between Oceans*

SOURCEBOOKS
Iris Anthony, *Ruins of Lace*
Janet Gurtler, *Who I Kissed*
Jessica Khoury, *Origin*
Teresa Rhyne, *The Dog Lived (And So Will I)*

Thanks to our publishing partners:

eBook Architects works with authors and publishers of all sizes, designing high-quality eBooks in the major eBook formats. In addition to converting standard trade fiction and non-fiction, eBook Architects has built a solid reputation as the premier development house for complex eBook content and enhanced eBooks. Some of the company's clients include: Open Road Integrated Media; Warner Brothers Digital Distribution; Library of America; The Economist; Stanford University Press; University of Oklahoma Press; Titan Publishing Group; Firebrand Technologies; Advantage Media Group; and a variety of small- and mid-sized publishers and independent authors.

Ingram Content Group is the world's largest and most trusted distributor of physical and digital content. Our mission is helping content reach its destination. Thousands of publishers, retailers, libraries, and educators worldwide use our products and services to realize the full business potential of books, regardless of format. Ingram has earned its lead position and reputation by offering excellent service and building innovative, integrated print and digital distribution solutions. Our customers have access to best-of-class digital, audio, print, print on demand, inventory management, wholesale and full-service distribution programs.

PUBLISHERS LUNCH:

Sarah Weinman, *Editor*

Michael Macrone, *Webmaster*

Robin Dellabough, *Project manager*

Michael Cader, *Founder*

Cover and interior design by Charles Kreloff

Production by eBook Architects: Joshua Tallent, Nick Ramirez

Public relations by Sandi Mendelson at Hilsinger-Mendelson

Digital distribution by Ingram

CPSIA information can be obtained at www.ICGtesting.com
Printed in the USA
BVOW021452230512

290942BV00001B/2/P